Also by John Updike

POEMS

The Carpentered Hen (1958) · *Telephone Poles* (1963) · *Midpoint* (1969) · *Tossing and Turning* (1977) · *Facing Nature* (1985) · *Collected Poems 1953–1993* (1993) · *Americana* (2001)

NOVELS

The Poorhouse Fair (1959) · *Rabbit, Run* (1960) · *The Centaur* (1963) · *Of the Farm* (1965) · *Couples* (1968) · *Rabbit Redux* (1971) · *A Month of Sundays* (1975) · *Marry Me* (1976) · *The Coup* (1978) · *Rabbit Is Rich* (1981) · *The Witches of Eastwick* (1984) · *Roger's Version* (1986) · *S.* (1988) · *Rabbit at Rest* (1990) · *Memories of the Ford Administration* (1992) · *Brazil* (1994) · *In the Beauty of the Lilies* (1996) · *Toward the End of Time* (1997) · *Gertrude and Claudius* (2000) · *Seek My Face* (2002)

SHORT STORIES

The Same Door (1959) · *Pigeon Feathers* (1962) · *Olinger Stories* (a selection, 1964) · *The Music School* (1966) · *Bech: A Book* (1970) · *Museums and Women* (1972) · *Problems and Other Stories* (1979) · *Too Far to Go* (a selection, 1979) · *Bech Is Back* (1982) · *Trust Me* (1987) · *The Afterlife* (1994) · *Bech at Bay* (1998) · *Licks of Love* (2000) · *The Complete Henry Bech* (2001)

ESSAYS AND CRITICISM

Assorted Prose (1965) · *Picked-Up Pieces* (1975) · *Hugging the Shore* (1983) · *Just Looking* (1989) · *Odd Jobs* (1991) · *Golf Dreams: Writings on Golf* (1996) · *More Matter* (1999)

PLAY

Buchanan Dying (1974)

MEMOIR

Self-Consciousness (1989)

CHILDREN'S BOOKS

The Magic Flute (1962) · *The Ring* (1964) · *A Child's Calendar* (1965) · *Bottom's Dream* (1969) · *A Helpful Alphabet of Friendly Objects* (1996)

THE EARLY STORIES

1953 — 1975

John Updike

THE EARLY STORIES
1953–1975

Alfred A. Knopf   New York

2003

Copyright © 2003 by John Updike

All rights reserved under International and Pan-American Copyright Conventions. Published in the United States by Alfred A. Knopf, a division of Random House, Inc., New York, and simultaneously in Canada by Random House of Canada Limited, Toronto. Distributed by Random House, Inc., New York.
www.aaknopf.com

The quotations from St. Augustine's *Confessions* in "Believers" and "Augustine's Concubine" are as translated by Edward B. Pusey; in "Believers," the quotation from the Venerable Bede is from *The Old English Version of Bede's Ecclesiastical History of the English People*, ed. T. Miller.

Knopf, Borzoi Books, and the colophon are registered trademarks of
Random House, Inc.

Eighty of these stories were first published in *The New Yorker*. The other twenty-three appeared in the following magazines thus:

The Atlantic Monthly: "Augustine's Concubine," "Nakedness." *Audience:* "Minutes of the Last Meeting," "When Everyone Was Pregnant." *Big Table:* "Archangel." *Esquire:* "The Slump," "The Tarbox Police." *Harper's Magazine:* "Believers," "Eros Rampant," "Sublimating," "Your Lover Just Called." *New World Writing:* "The Sea's Green Sameness." *Oui:* "Transaction." *Playboy:* "Gesturing," "I Am Dying, Egypt, Dying," "Killing," "Nevada." *The Saturday Evening Post:* "Eclipse," "The Lucid Eye in Silver Town." *The Transatlantic Review:* "The Crow in the Woods," "During the Jurassic," "The Invention of the Horse Collar," "Under the Microscope."

Library of Congress Cataloging-in-Publication Data
Updike, John.
[Short stories. Selections]
The early stories, 1953–1975 / John Updike.— 1st ed.
p. cm.
ISBN 1-4000-4072-8
1. United States—Social life and customs—20th century—Fiction. I. Title.
PS3571.P4A6 2003
813'.54—dc21   2002044824

Manufactured in the United States of America
First Edition

Contents

MARRIED LIFE

FAMILY LIFE

THE TWO ISEULTS

TARBOX TALES

FAR OUT

THE SINGLE LIFE

Foreword

THIS IS a collection. A selection, surely, is best left to others, when the writer is no longer alive to obstruct the process. Any story that makes it from the initial hurried scribbles into the haven of print possesses, in this writer's eyes, a certain valor, and my instinct, even forty years later, is not to ditch it but to polish and mount it anew. However, I did omit two stories, "Intercession" and "The Pro," which were already safely reprinted in *Golf Dreams* (1996), and two more, "One of My Generation" and "God Speaks," which, both of them first-person reminiscences based on college memories, trembled insecurely on the edge of topical humor, and felt dated.

These grudging omissions left one hundred and three stories, composed between 1953 and 1975. The oldest is "Ace in the Hole," submitted toward the end of 1953 by a married Harvard senior to Albert Guerard's creative-writing course. Guerard, the very model of a cigarette-addicted Gallic intellectual, who nonetheless faithfully attended the Crimson's home basketball games, liked the story—he said it frightened him, an existential compliment—and suggested I send it to *The New Yorker*, which turned it down. The next year, though, after "Friends from Philadelphia" and some poems had been accepted by the magazine in my first post-collegiate summer, I resubmitted the story and it was accepted. With modifications to the coarse exchange with which it begins, it was run in April of 1955, toward the back of the magazine; such was the reading public's appetite for fiction then that "casuals" (a curious in-house term lumping fiction and humor) appeared in "the back of the book" as well as up front. The story is entangled, in my memory of those heady days of the dawning literary life, with the sudden looming, in the lobby of the Algonquin, of J. D. Salinger, a glowingly handsome tall presence not yet notoriously reclusive; he shook my hand before we were taken in to lunch with our respective editors, William Shawn and Katharine White. He said, or somebody later said he said, that he had noticed and liked "Ace in the Hole." His own stories, encountered in another writing course (taught by Kenneth Kempton), had been revelations to me of how the form, terse and tough in the Thirties and Forties, could accommodate a more expansive post-war sense of American reality; the bottle of wine that ends "Friends from Philadelphia" owes something to the Easter chick found in the bottom of the wastebasket at the end of "Just Before the War with the Eskimos." But my main debt, which may not be evident, was to Hemingway; it was he who showed us all how much tension and complexity unalloyed dialogue can convey, and how much poetry lurks in the simplest nouns and predicates. Other eye-openers for me were Franz Kafka and John O'Hara, Mary McCarthy and John Cheever, Donald Barthelme and Vladimir Nabokov, James Joyce and James Thurber and Anton Chekhov.

The year 1975 seemed an apt cut-off; it was the one and only full year of my life when I lived alone. My marriage, of twenty-two years, to a barefoot, Unitarian, brunette Radcliffe graduate was ending, but all of these stories carry its provenance. Perhaps I could have made a go of the literary business without my first wife's faith, forbearance, sensitivity, and good sense, but I cannot imagine how. We had lived, from 1957 on, in Ipswich, a large, heterogenous, and rather out-of-the-way town north of Boston, and my principal means of support, for a family that by 1960 included four children under six, was selling short stories to *The New Yorker*. I had in those years the happy sensation that I was mailing dispatches from a territory that would be terra incognita without me. The old Puritan town was rich in characters and oral history. Though my creativity and spiritual state underwent some doldrums, the local life and the stimulation of living with growing children, with their bright-eyed grasp of the new, never left me quite empty of things to say. A small-town boy, I had craved small-town space. New York, in my twenty months of residence, had felt full of other writers and of cultural hassle, and the word game overrun with agents and wisenheimers. The real America seemed to me "out there," too homogenous and electrified by now to pose much threat of the provinciality that people used to come to New York to escape. Out there was where I belonged, immersed in the ordinary, which careful explication would reveal to be extraordinary. These notions propelled the crucial flight of my life, the flight from the Manhattan—the Silver Town, as one of my young heroes pictures it—that I had always hoped to live in. There also were practical attractions: free parking for my car, public education for my children, a beach to tan my skin on, a church to attend without seeming too strange.

I arrived in New England with a Pennsylvania upbringing to write out of my system. The first section of these early stories, "Olinger Stories," appeared as a Vintage paperback in 1964. It has been long out of print, though a few professors who used to assign it have complained. Its eleven stories constitute, it may be, a green and slender whole—the not unfriendly critic Richard Locke once wrote of their "hothouse atmosphere"—but the idea of assembling my early stories (half of them out of print) presented, to me, no temptation stronger than the one of seeing *Olinger Stories* back together. Their arrangement, which is in order of the heroes' ages, has been slightly changed: "Flight" and "A Sense of Shelter" both feature a high-school senior, but the one of "Flight" seemed on reconsideration older, further along in his development. All the stories draw from the same autobiographical well—the only child, the small town, the grandparental home, the move in adolescence to a farm—but no attempt is made at an overall consistency. As I wrote in the original introduction,

> I have let the inconsistencies stand in these stories. Each started from scratch. Grand Avenue here is the Alton Pike there. In "Pigeon Feathers" the grandfather is dead, in "Flight" the grandmother. In fact, both of my mother's parents lived until I was an adult. In fact, my family moved eleven miles away from the town when I was thirteen; in "Friends from Philadelphia" the distance is one mile, in "The Happiest I've Been" it has grown to four. This strange distance, this less than total remove from my milieu, is for all I know the crucial detachment of my life. . . . The hero is always returning, from hundreds of miles finally.

And, intoxicated by the wine of self-exegesis, I went on:

> It surprised me, in making this arrangement, to realize that the boy who wrestles with H. G. Wells and murders pigeons is younger than the one who tells Thelma Lutz she shouldn't pluck her eyebrows. But we age unevenly, more slowly in society than in our own skulls. Among these eleven brothers, some are twins. John Nordholm and David Kern, having taken their turn as actors, reappear as narrators. And optically bothered Clyde Behn seems to me a late refraction of that child Ben who flees the carnival with "tinted globes confusing his eyelashes."

Of the sections that follow, two, "Out in the World" and "Tarbox Tales," take their titles from a Penguin collection, *Forty Stories*, selected by me and published in 1987. Their contents, however, have shifted and expanded, and the remaining five sections are newly invented, to give some friendly order—as in my five non-fiction collections—to so large a number of items. As the writer-editor shuffles his stories back and forth, he begins to see all sorts of graceful and meaningful transitions and sub-surface currents: each set seems to have a purling flow that amounts to a story of its own, a story in turn part of a larger tale, the lived life evoked by these fragments chipped from experience and rounded by imagination into impersonal artifacts. The reader, however, does not have access to the writer's core of personal memory, and is furthermore free to read the stories in any order he chooses. Each is designed to stand on its own, though perhaps the stories concerning Joan and Richard Maple, scattered herein though collected in a Fawcett paperback called (after a television script) *Too Far to Go* (1979) and in a Penguin edition titled (by me) *Your Lover Just Called*, do gain from being grouped. My other sequential protagonist, the writer Henry Bech, is represented only by his first manifestation, when I didn't know he was to star in an ongoing saga, now bound in *The Complete Henry Bech* (Everyman's).

The index dates the titles by the time of composition rather than of publication. Introducing *Forty Stories*, I wrote, "Social contexts change; it is perhaps useful to know that 'The Hillies' was written in 1969, and 'A Gift from the City' in 1957." And that "Ethiopia" was written when Haile Selassie was still in power and "Transaction" when "transactional analysis" was the hottest psychological fad. Rereading everything in 2002, I was startled by the peaceful hopes attached to Iraq in "His Finest Hour," amazed by the absurdly low prices of things in Fifties and Sixties dollars, and annoyed by the recurrence of the now suspect word "Negro." But I did not change it to "black"; fiction is entitled to the language of its time. And verbal correctness in this arena is so particularly volatile that "black," which is inaccurate, may some day be suspect in turn. "Negro" at least is an anthropological term, unlike the phrase "of color," which reminds me that in my childhood the word "darkie" was, in the mouths of middle-aged ladies, the ultimate in polite verbal discrimination. As to the word "fairies," used twice in "The Stare" to refer to gay men, I doubt that it was ever not offensive to those designated, but it was much used, with its tinge of contempt, by heterosexuals of both genders, and after pondering, pencil in hand, for some pained minutes, I let it remain, as natural to the consciousness of the straight, distraught male who is my protagonist. After all, *The New Yorker*'s fastidious editors let it slip by, into the issue of April 3, 1965. In general, I reread these stories without looking for trouble, but where an opportunity to help my younger self leaped out at me, I took it, deleting an adjective here, adding a clarifying phrase there. To have done less would have been a forced abdication of artistic conscience and habit. In prose there is always room for improvement, well short of a Jamesian overhaul into an overweening later manner.

My first editor at *The New Yorker* was Katharine White, who had done so much to shape the infant magazine only three decades before. After accepting four stories of mine and sending back a greater number, she, with her husband, came to visit the young Updikes and their baby girl in Oxford, and offered me a job at the magazine. Of the year or two when we shared the premises—before she followed E. B. White to Maine, giving up the high position of fiction editor—I remember her technique of going over proofs with me side by side at her desk, which made me fuzzy-headed and pliant, and how she once wrinkled her nose when asking me if I knew why my writing, in the instance before us, wasn't very good. She had made her way in Harold Ross's otherwise all-boy staff and could be brusque, though there was no mistaking her warm heart and high hopes for the magazine. My next editor, until 1976, was never brusque; William Maxwell brought to his editorial functions a patient tact and gentle veracity that offered a life-lesson as much as a lesson in writing. My fiction editor since has been Katharine White's son, Roger Angell, whose continued vitality and sharpness into his eighties gives me, at the outset of my seventies, hope for the future. All three, not to mention the unsung copyeditors and fact checkers, contributed many improving touches to these stories and on occasion inspired large revisions, though my theory in general is that if a short story doesn't pour smooth from the start, it never will. Though it was more than once alleged, in the years 1953–75, that *The New Yorker* promoted a gray sameness in its fiction, it permitted me much experimentation, from the long essayistic conglomerations capping the Olinger stories to the risky and risqué monologues of "Wife-Wooing" and "Lifeguard." The editors published so much fiction they could run the impulsive brief opus as well as the major effort, and as William Shawn settled into his long reign he revealed a swashbuckling streak of avant-gardism, a taste for Barthelme and Borges that woke up even the staidest in his stable to new possibilities.

Some of the more far-out stories are unduly precious to me, but readers of *Museums and Women* will not find here the illustrations of pond life, Jurassic life, horse-harness technology, or the baluchitherium that adorned the relevant pages; after a long, would-be cartoonist's flirtation with graphic elements, I have decided that pictures don't mix with text. Text, left to its own devices, enjoys a life that floats free of any specific setting or format or pictographic attachments. Only a few Greek letters and a lone bar of music (in "Son") have posed a challenge to the hard-working keyboarders of the volume at hand.

The technology reflected in these stories harks back to a time when automatic shifts were an automotive novelty and outdoor privies were still features of the rural landscape, and it stops well short of the advent of personal computers and ubiquitous cell phones. My generation, once called Silent, was, in a considerable fraction of its white majority, a fortunate one—"too young to be warriors, too old to be rebels," as it is put in the story "I Will Not Let Thee Go, Except Thou Bless Me." Born in the early Depression, at a nadir of the national birthrate, we included many only children given, by penny-pinching parents, piano lessons and a confining sense of shelter. We acquired in hard times a habit of work and came to adulthood in times when work paid off; we experienced when young the patriotic cohesion of World War II without having to fight the war. We were repressed enough to be pleased by the relaxation of the old sexual morality, without suffering much of the surfeit, anomie, and venereal disease of younger generations. We were simple and hopeful enough to launch into idealistic careers and early marriages, and pragmatic enough to adjust, with an American shrug, to the ebb of old certainties. Yet, though spared many of the material deprivations and religious terrors that had dogged our parents, and awash in a disproportionate share of the world's resources, we continued prey to what Freud called "normal human unhappiness."

But when has happiness ever been the subject of fiction? The pursuit of it is just that—a pursuit. Death and its adjutants tax each transaction. What is possessed is devalued by what is coveted. Discontent, conflict, waste, sorrow, fear—these are the worthy, inevitable subjects. Yet our hearts expect happiness, as an underlying norm, "the fountain-light of all our day" in Wordsworth's words. Rereading, I found no lack of joy in these stories, though it arrives by the moment and not by the month, and no lack of affection and goodwill among characters caught in the human plight, the plight of limitation and mortality. Art hopes to sidestep mortality with feats of attention, of harmony, of illuminating connection, while enjoying, it might be said, at best a slower kind of mortality: paper yellows, language becomes old-fashioned, revelatory human news passes into general social wisdom. I could not but think, during this retrospective labor, of all those *New Yorker*s, a heedless broad Mississippi of print, in which my contributions among so many others appeared; they serviced a readership, a certain demographic episode, now passed into history—

all those birch-shaded Connecticut mailboxes receiving, week after week, William Shawn's notion of entertainment and instruction. What would have happened to me if William Shawn had not liked my work? Those first checks, in modest hundreds, added up and paid for my first automobile. Without *The New Yorker*, I would have had to walk. I would have existed, no doubt, in some sort, but not the bulk of these stories.

They were written on a manual typewriter and, beginning in the early Sixties, in a one-room office I rented in Ipswich, between a lawyer and a beautician, above a cozy corner restaurant. Around noon the smell of food would start to rise through the floor, but I tried to hold out another hour before I tumbled downstairs, dizzy with cigarettes, to order a sandwich. After I gave up cigarettes, I smoked nickel cigarillos to allay my nervousness at the majesty of my calling and the intricacy of my craft; the empty boxes, with their comforting image of another writer, Robert Burns, piled up. Not only were the boxes useful for storing little things like foreign coins and cufflinks, but the caustic aura of cigars discouraged visitors. I felt that I was packaging something as delicately pervasive as smoke, one box after another, in that room, where my only duty was to describe reality as it had come to me—to give the mundane its beautiful due.

OLINGER STORIES

You'll Never Know, Dear,
How Much I Love You

CARNIVAL! In the vacant lot behind the old ice plant! Trucks have been unloading all afternoon; the WhirloGig has been unfolded like a giant umbrella, they assembled the baby Ferris wheel with an Erector Set. Twice the trucks got stuck in the mud. Straw has been strewn everywhere. They put up a stage and strung lights. Now, now, gather your pennies; supper is over and an hour of light is left in the long summer day. See, Sammy Hunnenhauser is running; Gloria Gring and her gang have been there all afternoon, they never go home, oh hurry, let me go; how awful it is to have parents that are poor, and slow, and sad!

Fifty cents. The most Ben could beg. A nickel for every year of his life. It feels like plenty. Over the roof of crazy Mrs. Moffert's house, the Ferris wheel tints the air with pink, and the rim of this pink mixes in his excitement with the great notched rim of the coin sweating in his hand. This house, then this house, and past the ice plant, and he will be there. Already the rest of the world is there, he is the last, hurrying, hurrying, the balloon is about to take off, the Ferris wheel is lifting; only he will be left behind, on empty darkening streets.

Then there, what to buy? There are not so many people here. Grownups carrying babies mosey glassily on the straw walks. All the booth people, not really gypsies, stare at him, and beckon weakly. It hurts him to ignore the man with the three old softballs, and the old cripple at the merry-go-round, and the fat lady with her plaster Marys, and the skeleton suspended behind a fountain of popcorn. He feels his walking past them as pain. He wishes there were more people here; he feels a fool. All of this machinery assembled to extract from him his pathetic fifty cents. He watches at a distance a thickset man in earnestly rolled-up shirtsleeves twirl a great tinselled wheel with a rubber tongue that patters slower and slower on a circle of nails until it stops between two, and the number there wins. Only a sailor and two boys in yellow silk high-school athletic jackets play. None win. The thick tattooed arm below the rolled-up shirt-sleeve carefully sweeps their nickels from a long board divided and numbered as if for hopscotch. The high-school boys, with sideburns and spotty whiskers on their bright-pink jaws, put down nickels again leadenly, and this time the man spinning the wheel shouts when it stops, seems more joyful than they, and reaches into his deep apron pocket and pours before them, without counting, a perfect little slipping stack of nickels. Their gums showing as if at a dirty joke, the two boys turn—the shimmer on their backs darts and shifts in cool z's—and walk away, while the man is shouting, "Hey, uh winneh. Hey, uh winneh, evvybody wins." His board is bare, and as his mouth continues to form the loud words his eyes lock Ben into a stare of heartbreaking brown blankness that seems to elucidate with paralyzing clarity Ben's state: his dungarees, his fifty cents, his ten years, his position in space, and above the particulars the immense tinted pity, the waste, of being at one little place instead of everywhere, at any time. Then the man looks away, and twirls the wheel for his own amusement.

The fifty-cent piece feels huge to Ben's fingers, a wide oppressive rigidity that must be broken, shattered into twinkling fragments, to merge in the tinsel and splinters of strewn straw. He buys, at the first stand he strikes, a cone of cotton candy, and receives, with the furry pink pasty uncoiling thing, a quarter, a dime, and a nickel: three coins, tripling his wealth.

Now people multiply, crowd in from the houses of the town, which stand beyond the lot on all sides in black forbidding silhouettes like the teeth of a saw. The lights go on; the faces of the houses flee. There is nothing in the lot but light, and at its core, on the stage, three girls wearing white cowboy hats and white spangled skirts and white boots appear, and a man also in white and bearing a white guitar strung with gold. The legs around Ben crush him toward the stage; the smell of mud mingles with the bright sight there. One of the girls coughs into the microphone and twists its neck, so a sharp whine pierces from the loudspeakers and cuts a great crescent through the crowd, leaving silence as harvest. The girls sing, toe-tapping gingerly: "The other *night*, dear, as I lay *sleep*ing, I dreamt I *held* you in my *arms*." The spangles on their swishing skirts spring prickles like tears in Ben's eyes. The three voices sob, catch, twang, distend his heart like a rubber band at the highest pitch of their plaint. "—I was mis*take*n, and I *hung* my *head*, a-and *cried*." And then the unbearable rising sugar of the chorus that makes his scalp so tight he fears his head will burst from sweet fullness.

The girls go on to sing other songs, less good, and then they give way to a thin old man in suspenders and huge pants he keeps snapping and looking down and whooping into. He tells horrible jokes that make the nice fat ladies standing around Ben—nice fat factory and dust-mop women that made him feel protected—shake with laughter. He fears their quaking, feels threatened from beneath, as if there is a treacherous stratum under this mud and straw. He wanders away, to let the words of "You Are My Sunshine" revolve in his head. "Please don't *take* my *sun*-shine *away*." Only the money in his pocket weighs him; get rid of it, and he will sail away like a dandelion seed.

He goes to the booth where the wheel is turning, and puts his nickel on the board in a square marked 7, and loses it.

He puts the dime there, and it too is taken away.

Squeezed, almost hidden, between the crusty trousered haunches of two adults, he puts down his quarter, as they do, on the inner edge, to be changed. The tattooed man comes along, picking up the quarters and pouring, with his wonderfully automatic fingers, the little slipping stacks of five nickels; Ben holds his breath, and to his horror feels his low face catch in the corner of the man's absent-minded eyes. The thick solemn body snags in its smooth progress, and Ben's five nickels are raggedly spaced. Between the second and third there is a gap. A blush cakes Ben's cheeks; his gray-knuckled fingers, as they push out a nickel, are trembling sideways at each other. But the man goes back, and spins the wheel, and Ben loses three nickels one after another. The twittering wheel is a moon-faced god; but Ben feels humanity clouding the space between him and it, which should be unobstructed. When the tattooed arm—a blue fish, an anchor, the queer word PEACE—comes to sweep in his nickels, he feels the stippled skin breathing thought, and lowers his head against the expected fall of words. Nothing is said, the man moves on, returns to the wheel; but Ben feels puzzled pressure radiating from him, and the pointed eyes of a man in a suit with chalk stripes who has come to stand at the far side of the stand intersect this expanding circle, and Ben, hurry-ing to pour his money down a narrowing crack, puts down his last two nickels, still on 7.

The rubber tongue leaps into pattering and as the wheel whirls the tat-tooed man leans backward to hear the one in chalk stripes talk; this one's tongue patters silently but a tiny motion of his smooth hand, simultane-ous with a sideways stab of his eyes, is toward Ben.

The rubber tongue slows, flops, stops at 7—no, 8. He lost, and can leave. The floor of his stomach lifts queerly. "Hey, kid." The man with terrible spoiled arms comes over. Ben feels that no matter how fast he would run those arms would stretch and snare him.

"Huh?"

"How old are you, kid?"

"Ten."

"Whatsamatta with ya, ya daddy rich?"

A titter moves stiffly among the immense adult heads all around. Ben understands the familiar role, that he has undergone a hundred times with teachers and older boys, of being a comic prop. He understands everything, and wants to explain that he knows his eyes are moist and his cheeks red but that it's because of joy, freedom, not because of losing. But this would be too many words; even the one-word answer "No" sticks to the roof of his mouth and comes loose with a faint tearing noise.

"Here." With his exciting expert touch, the tattooed man flicks Ben's two coins back across the painted number. Then he digs into his pocket. He comes up with the usual little stack of five, drops four, but holds the fifth delicately between the tips of two fingers and a thumb, hesitates so that Ben can reread PEACE in blue above his wrist, and then flips the fifth nickel up into his palm and thence down with a plunge into his dirty sagging apron pouch.

"Now move away from the board, kid, move away. Don't come back."

Ben fumbles the coins into his hands and pushes away, his eyes screwed to the sharp edge of painted wood, and he shoulders blindly backward through the legs. Yet all the time, in the midst of the heat and water welling up from springs all over his body, he is figuring, and calculates he's been gypped. Forty: he had the quarter and dime and nickel, and they gave him back only six nickels: thirty. The injustice. They pretend he's too little to lose and then keep a dime. The waste. The lost dime seems a tiny hole through which everything in existence is draining. As he moves away, his wet knees jarring, trying to hide forever from every sailor and fat woman and high-schooler who witnessed his disgrace, the six nickels make a knobbed weight bumping his thigh through his pocket. The spangles, the splinters of straw and strings of light, the sawtooth peaks of houses showing behind the heads of grown-ups moving above the scent of grassy mud are hung like the needles of a Christmas tree with the transparent, tinted globes confusing his eyelashes.

Thus the world, like a jaded coquette, spurns our attempts to give ourselves to her wholly.

The Alligators

JOAN EDISON came to their half of the fifth grade from Maryland in March. She had a thin face with something of a grownup's tired expression and long black eyelashes like a doll's. Everybody hated her. That month Miss Fritz was reading to them during homeroom about a girl, Emmy, who was badly spoiled and always telling her parents lies about her twin sister, Annie; nobody could believe, it was too amazing, how exactly when they were despising Emmy most Joan should come into the school with her show-off clothes and her hair left hanging down the back of her fuzzy sweater instead of being cut or braided and her having the crust to actually argue with teachers. "Well, I'm sorry," she told Miss Fritz, not even rising from her seat, "but I *don't* see what the point is of homework. In Baltimore we never had any, and the *little* kids there knew what's in these books."

Charlie, who in a way enjoyed homework, was ready to join in the angry moan of the others. Little hurt lines had leaped up between Miss Fritz's eyebrows and he felt sorry for her, remembering how when, that September, John Eberly had half on purpose spilled purple Sho-Card paint on the newly sandpapered floor she had hidden her face in her arms on the desk and cried. She was afraid of the school board. "You're not in Baltimore now, Joan," Miss Fritz said. "You are in Olinger, Pennsylvania."

The children, Charlie among them, laughed, and Joan, blushing a soft brown color and raising her voice excitedly against the current of hatred, got in deeper by trying to explain, "Like there, instead of just *reading* about plants in a book, we'd one day all bring in a flower we'd *picked* and cut it open and look at it in a *microscope*." Because of her saying this, shadows, of broad leaves and wild slashed foreign flowers, darkened and complicated the idea they had of her.

Miss Fritz puckered her orange lips into fine wrinkles, then smiled. "In the upper levels you will be allowed to do that in this school. All things come in time, Joan, to patient little girls." When Joan started to argue *this*, Miss Fritz lifted one finger and said with that extra weight adults always have, held back in reserve, "No. No more, young lady, or you'll be in *serious* trouble with me." It gave the class courage to see that Miss Fritz didn't like her either.

After that, Joan couldn't open her mouth in class without there being a great groan. Outdoors on the macadam playground, at recess or fire drill or waiting in the morning for the buzzer, hardly anybody talked to her except to say "Stuck-up" or "Emmy" or, worst, "Whore, whore, from Balti-more." Boys were always yanking open the bow at the back of her fancy dresses and flipping little spitballs into the curls of her hanging hair. Once John Eberly even cut a section of her hair off with a yellow plastic scissors stolen from art class. This was the one time Charlie saw Joan cry actual tears. He was as bad as the others: worse, because what the others did because they felt like it, he did out of a plan, to make himself more popular. In the first and second grade he had been liked pretty well, but somewhere since then he had been dropped. There was a gang, boys and girls both, that met Saturdays—you heard them talk about it on Mondays—in Stuart Morrison's garage, and took hikes and played touch football together, and in winter sledded on Hill Street, and in spring bicycled all over Olinger and did together what else he couldn't imagine. Charlie had known the chief members since before kindergarten. But after school there seemed nothing for him to do but go home promptly and do his homework and fiddle with his Central American stamps and go to Tarzan movies alone, and on weekends nothing but beat monotonously at marbles or Monopoly or chess Darryl Johns or Marvin Auerbach, who he wouldn't have bothered at all with if they hadn't lived right in the neighborhood, they being at least a year younger and not bright for their age either. Charlie thought the gang might notice him and take him in if he backed up their policies without being asked.

In science, which 5A had in Miss Brobst's room across the hall, he sat one seat ahead of Joan and annoyed her all he could, in spite of a feeling that, both being disliked, they had something to share. One fact he discovered was, she wasn't that bright. Her marks on quizzes were always lower than his. He told her, "Cutting up all those flowers didn't do you much good. Or maybe in Baltimore they taught you everything so long ago you've forgotten it in your old age."

Charlie drew; on his tablet, where she could easily see over his shoulder, he once in a while drew a picture titled "Joan the Dope": the profile of a girl with a lean nose and sad mincemouth, the lashes of her lowered eye as black as the pencil could make them, and the hair falling, in ridiculous hooks, row after row, down through the sea-blue cross-lines clear off the bottom edge of the tablet.

March turned into spring. One of the signals was, on the high-school grounds, before the cinder track was weeded and when the softball field was still four inches of mud, Happy Lasker came with the elaborate airplane model he had wasted the winter making. It had the American star on the wingtips and a pilot painted inside the cockpit and a miniature motor that burned real gas. The buzzing, off and on all Saturday morning, collected smaller kids from Second Street down to Lynoak. Then it was always the same: Happy shoved the plane into the air, where it climbed and made a razzing noise a minute, then nose-dived and crashed and usually burned in the grass or mud. Happy's father was rich.

In the weeks since she had come, Joan's clothes had slowly grown simpler, to go with the other girls', and one day she came to school with most of her hair cut off, and the rest brushed flat around her head and brought into a little tail behind. The laughter at her was more than she had ever heard. "Ooh. Baldy-paldy!" some idiot girl had exclaimed when Joan came into the cloakroom, and the stupid words went sliding around class all morning. "Baldy-paldy from Baltimore. Why is old Baldy-paldy red in the face?" John Eberly kept making the motion of a scissors with his fingers and its juicy ticking sound with his tongue. Miss Fritz rapped her knuckles on the windowsill until she was rubbing the ache with the other hand, and finally she sent two boys to Mr. Lengel's office, delighting Charlie an enormous secret amount.

His own reaction to the haircut had been quiet: to want to draw her, changed. He had kept the other drawings folded in his desk, and one of his instincts was toward complete sets of things, Batman comics and A's and Costa Rican stamps. Halfway across the room from him, Joan held very still, afraid, it seemed, to move even a hand, her face a shamed pink. The haircut had brought out her forehead and exposed her neck and made her chin pointier and her eyes larger. Charlie felt thankful once again for having been born a boy, and having no sharp shocks, like losing your curls or starting to bleed, to make growing painful. How much girls suffer had been one of the first thoughts he had ever had.

His caricature of her was wonderful, the work of a genius. He showed it to Stuart Morrison behind him; it was too good for him to appreciate, his dull egg eyes just flickered over it. Charlie traced it onto another piece of tablet paper, making her head completely bald. This drawing Stuart grabbed, and it was passed clear around the room.

That night he had the dream. He must have dreamed it while lying there asleep in the morning light, for it was fresh in his head when he woke. They had been in a jungle. Joan, dressed in a torn sarong, was swimming in a clear river among alligators. Somehow, as if from a tree, he was looking down, and there was a calmness in the way the slim girl and the green alligators moved, in and out, perfectly visible under the window-skin of the water. Joan's face sometimes showed the horror she was undergoing and sometimes looked numb. Her hair trailed behind and fanned when her face came toward the surface. He shouted silently with grief. Then he had rescued her; without a sense of having dipped his arms in water, he was carrying her in two arms, himself in a bathing suit, and his feet firmly fixed to the knobby back of an alligator which skimmed upstream, through the shadows of high trees and white flowers and hanging vines, like a surfboard in a movie short. They seemed to be heading toward a wooden bridge arching over the stream. He wondered how he would duck it, and the river and the jungle gave way to his bed and his room, but through the change persisted, like a pedalled note on a piano, the sweetness and pride he had felt in saving and carrying the girl.

He loved Joan Edison. The morning was rainy, and under the umbrella his mother made him take this new knowledge, repeated again and again to himself, gathered like a bell of smoke. Love had no taste, but sharpened his sense of smell so that his oilcloth coat, his rubber boots, the red-tipped bushes hanging over the low walls holding back lawns all along Grand Street, even the dirt and moss in the cracks of the pavement each gave off clear odors. He would have laughed, if a wooden weight had not been placed high in his chest, near where his throat joined. He could not imagine himself laughing soon. It seemed he had reached one of those situations his Sunday-school teacher, poor Miss West with her little mustache, had been trying to prepare him for. He prayed, *Give me Joan.* With the wet weather a solemn flatness had fallen over everything; an orange bus turning at the Bend and four birds on a telephone wire seemed to have the same importance. Yet he felt firmer and lighter and felt things as edges he must whip around and channels he must rush down. If he carried her off, did rescue her from the others' cruelty, he would have defied the gang and made a new one, his own. Just Joan and he at first, then others escaping from meanness and dumbness, until his gang was stronger and Stuart Morrison's garage was empty every Saturday. Charlie would be a king, with his own touch-football game. Everyone would come and plead with him for mercy.

His first step was to tell all those in the cloakroom he loved Joan Edison now. They cared less than he had expected, considering how she was hated. He had more or less expected to have to fight with his fists. Hardly anybody gathered to hear the dream he had pictured himself telling everybody. Anyway, that morning it would go around the class that he had said he loved her, and though this was what he wanted, to in a way open a space between him and Joan, it felt funny nevertheless, and he stuttered when Miss Fritz had him go to the blackboard to explain something.

At lunch, he deliberately hid in the variety store until he saw her walk by. The homely girl with her he knew turned off at the next street. He waited a minute and then came out and began running to overtake Joan in the block between the street where the other girl turned down and the street where he turned up. It had stopped raining, and his rolled-up umbrella felt like a commando's bayonet. Coming up behind her, he said, "Bang. Bang."

She turned, and under her gaze, knowing she knew he loved her, he felt his face go hot and he stared down. "Why, Charlie," her voice said with her Maryland slowness, "what are you doing on this side of the street?" Carl the town cop stood in front of the elementary school to get them on the side of Grand Street where they belonged. Now Charlie would have to cross the avenue again, by himself, at the Bend, a dangerous five-spoked intersection.

"Nothing," he said, and used up the one sentence he had prepared ahead: "I like your hair the new way."

"Thank you," she said, and stopped. In Baltimore she must have had manners lessons. Her eyes looked at his, and his vision jumped back from the rims of her lower lids as if from a brink. Yet in the space she occupied there was a great fullness that lent him height, as if he were standing by a window giving on the first morning after a snow.

"But, then, I didn't mind it the old way either."

"Yes?"

A peculiar reply. Another peculiar thing was the tan beneath her skin; he had noticed before, though not so closely, how when she colored it came up a gentle dull brown more than red. Also, she wore something perfumed.

He asked, "How do you like Olinger?"

"Oh, I think it's nice."

"Nice? I guess. I guess maybe. Nice Olinger. I wouldn't know, because I've never been anywhere else."

She luckily took this as a joke and laughed. Rather than risk saying something unfunny, he began to balance the umbrella by its point on one finger and, when this went well, walked backwards, shifting the balanced umbrella, its hook black against the patchy blue sky, from one palm to the other, back and forth. At the corner where they parted he got carried away and in imitating a suave sophisticated gent leaning on a cane bent the handle hopelessly. Her amazement was worth twice the price of his mother's probable scolding.

He planned to walk Joan again, and farther, after school. All through lunch he kept calculating. His father and he would repaint his bike. At the next haircut he would have his hair parted on the other side to get away from his cowlick. He would change himself totally; everyone would wonder what had happened to him. He would learn to swim, and take her to the dam.

In the afternoon the momentum of the dream wore off somewhat. Now that he kept his eyes always on her, he noticed, with a qualm of his stomach, that in passing in the afternoon from Miss Brobst's to Miss Fritz's room Joan was not alone, but chattered with others. In class, too, she whispered. So it was with more shame—such shame that he didn't believe he could ever face even his parents again—than surprise that from behind the dark pane of the variety store he saw her walk by in the company of the gang, she and Stuart Morrison throwing back their teeth and screaming and he imitating something and poor moronic John Eberly tagging behind like a thick tail. Charlie watched them walk out of sight behind a tall hedge; relief was as yet a tiny fraction of his reversed world. It came to him that what he had taken for cruelty had been love, that far from hating her everybody had loved her from the beginning, and that even the stupidest knew it weeks before he did. That she was the queen of the class and might as well not exist, for all the good he would get out of it.

Pigeon Feathers

WHEN THEY MOVED TO FIRETOWN, things were upset, displaced, re-arranged. A red cane-back sofa that had been the chief piece in the living room at Olinger was here banished, too big for the narrow country parlor, to the barn, and shrouded under a tarpaulin. Never again would David lie on its length all afternoon eating raisins and reading mystery novels and science fiction and P. G. Wodehouse. The blue wing chair that had stood for years in the ghostly, immaculate guest bedroom, gazing through the windows curtained with dotted swiss toward the telephone wires and horse-chestnut trees and opposite houses, was here established importantly in front of the smutty little fireplace that supplied, in those first cold April days, their only heat. As a child, David had been afraid of the guest bedroom—it was there that he, lying sick with the measles, had seen a black rod the size of a yardstick jog along at a slight slant beside the edge of the bed and vanish when he screamed—and it was disquieting to have one of the elements of its haunted atmosphere basking by the fire, in the center of the family, growing sooty with use. The books that at home had gathered dust in the case beside the piano were here hastily stacked, all out of order, in the shelves that the carpenters had built along one wall below the deep-silled windows. David, at thirteen, had been more moved than a mover; like the furniture, he had to find a new place, and on the Saturday of the second week he tried to work off some of his disorientation by arranging the books.

It was a collection obscurely depressing to him, mostly books his mother had acquired when she was young: college anthologies of Greek plays and Romantic poetry, Will Durant's *The Story of Philosophy*, a soft-leather set of Shakespeare with string bookmarks sewed to the bindings, *Green Mansions* boxed and illustrated with woodcuts, *I, the Tiger*, by Manuel Komroff, novels by names like Galsworthy and Ellen Glasgow and Irvin S. Cobb and Sinclair Lewis and "Elizabeth." The odor of faded taste made him feel the ominous gap between himself and his parents, the insulting gulf of time that existed before he was born. Suddenly he was tempted to dip into this time. From the heaps of books piled around him on the worn old floorboards, he picked up Volume II of a four-volume set of *The Outline of History*, by H. G. Wells. Once David had read *The Time Machine;* this gave him a small grip on the author. The book's red binding had faded to orange-pink on the spine. When he lifted the cover, there was a sweetish, moldy smell, and his mother's maiden name written in unfamiliar handwriting on the flyleaf—an upright, bold, yet careful signature, bearing a faint relation to the quick scrunched backslant that flowed with marvellous consistency across her shopping lists and budget accounts and Christmas cards to college friends from this same, vaguely menacing long ago.

He leafed through, pausing at drawings, done in an old-fashioned stippled style, of bas-reliefs, masks, Romans without pupils in their eyes, articles of ancient costume, fragments of pottery found in unearthed homes. He knew it would be interesting in a magazine, sandwiched between ads and jokes, but in this undiluted form history was somehow sour. The print was determinedly legible, and smug, like a lesson book. As he bent over the pages, yellow at the edges, they seemed rectangles of dusty glass through which he looked down into unreal and irrelevant worlds. He could see things sluggishly move, and an unpleasant fullness came into his throat. His mother and grandmother fussed in the kitchen; the puppy, which they had just acquired, as a watchdog in the country, was cowering, with a sporadic panicked scrabble of claws, under the dining table that in their old home had been reserved for special days but that here was used for every meal.

Then, before he could halt his eyes, David slipped into Wells's account of Jesus. He had been an obscure political agitator, a kind of hobo, in a minor colony of the Roman Empire. By an accident impossible to reconstruct, he (the small *h* horrified David) survived his own crucifixion and presumably died a few weeks later. A religion was founded on the freakish incident. The credulous imagination of the times retrospectively assigned miracles and supernatural pretensions to Jesus; a myth grew, and then a church, whose theology at most points was in direct contradiction of the simple, rather communistic teachings of the Galilean.

It was as if a stone that for months and even years had been gathering weight in the web of David's nerves snapped them and plunged through the page and a hundred layers of paper underneath. These fantastic falsehoods—plainly untrue: churches stood everywhere, the entire nation was founded "under God"—did not at first frighten him; it was the fact that they had been permitted to exist in an actual human brain. This was the initial impact—that at a definite spot in time and space a brain black with the denial of Christ's divinity had been suffered to exist. The universe had not spat out this ball of tar but allowed it to continue in its blasphemy, to grow old, win honors, wear a hat, write books that, if true, collapsed everything into a jumble of horror. The world outside the deep-silled windows—a rutted lawn, a whitewashed barn, a walnut tree frothy with fresh green—seemed a haven from which David was forever sealed off. Hot washrags seemed pressed against his cheeks.

He read the account again. He tried to supply out of his ignorance objections that would defeat the complacent march of these black words, and found none. Survivals and misunderstandings more farfetched were reported daily in the papers. But none of them caused churches to be built in every town. He tried to work backwards through the churches, from their brave high fronts through their shabby, ill-attended interiors back into the events at Jerusalem, and felt himself surrounded by shifting gray shadows, centuries of history, where he knew nothing. The thread dissolved in his hands. Had Christ ever come to him, David Kern, and said, "Here. Feel the wound in My side"? No; but prayers had been answered. What prayers? He had prayed that Rudy Mohn, whom he had purposely tripped so he cracked his head on their radiator, not die, and he had not died. But for all the blood, it was just a cut; Rudy came back the same day, wearing a bandage and repeating the same teasing words. He could never have died. Again, David had prayed for two separate war-effort posters he had sent away for to arrive tomorrow, and though they did not, they did arrive, some days later, together, popping through the clacking letter slot like a rebuke from God's mouth: *I answer your prayers in My way, in My time*. After that, he had made his prayers less definite, less susceptible of being twisted into a scolding. But what a tiny, ridiculous coincidence this was, after all, to throw into battle against H. G. Wells's engines of knowledge! Indeed, it proved the enemy's point: hope bases vast premises on foolish accidents, and reads a word where in fact only a scribble exists.

His father came home. Though Saturday was a free day for him, he had been working. He taught school in Olinger and spent his free days performing, with a kind of panic, needless errands. A city boy by birth, he was frightened of the farm and seized any excuse to get away. The farm had been David's mother's birthplace; it had been her idea to buy it back. With a determination unparalleled in her life, she had gained that end, and moved them all here—her son, her husband, her mother. Granmom, in her prime, had worked these fields alongside her husband, but now she dabbled around the kitchen, her hands waggling with Parkinson's disease. She was always in the way. Strange, out in the country, amid eighty acres, they were crowded together. His father expressed his feelings of discomfort by conducting with Mother an endless argument about organic farming. All through dusk, all through supper, it rattled on.

"Elsie, I *know*, I know from my education, the earth is nothing but chemicals. It's the only damn thing I got out of four years of college, so don't tell me it's not true."

"George, if you'd just walk out on the farm you'd know it's not true. The land has a *soul*."

"Soil, has, no, soul," he said, enunciating stiffly, as if to a very stupid class. To David he said, "You can't argue with a femme. Your mother's a real femme. That's why I married her, and now I'm suffering for it."

"*This* soil has no soul," she said, "because it's been killed with superphosphate. It's been burned bare by Boyer's tenant farmers." Boyer was the rich man they had bought the farm from. "It used to have a soul, didn't it, Mother? When you and Pop farmed it?"

"Ach, yes; I guess." Granmom was trying to bring a forkful of food to her mouth with her less severely afflicted hand. In her attempt she brought the other hand up from her lap. The crippled fingers, dull red in the orange light of the kerosene lamp in the center of the table, were welded by disease into one knobbed hook.

"Only human indi-vidu-als have souls," his father went on, in the same mincing, lifeless voice. "Because the Bible tells us so." Done eating, he crossed his legs and dug into his ear with a match; to get at the thing inside his head he tucked in his chin, and his voice came out low-pitched at David. "When God made your mother, He made a real femme."

"George, don't you read the papers? Don't you know that between the chemical fertilizers and the bug sprays we'll all be dead in ten years? Heart attacks are killing every man in the country over forty-five."

He sighed wearily; the yellow skin of his eyelids wrinkled as he hurt himself with the match. "There's no connection," he stated, spacing his words with pained patience, "between the heart and chemical fertilizers. It's alcohol that's doing it. Alcohol and milk. There is too much cholesterol in the tissues of the American heart. Don't tell me about chemistry, Elsie; I majored in the damn stuff for four years."

"Yes, and I majored in philosophy and I'm not a penny wiser. Mother, put your waggler *away!*" The old woman started, and the food dropped from her fork. For some reason, the sight of her bad hand at the table cruelly irritated her daughter. Granmom's eyes widened behind her cock-eyed spectacles. Circles of silver as fine as thread, the frames clung to the red notches they had carved over the years into her little white beak. In the orange flicker of the kerosene lamp, her dazed misery seemed infernal. David's mother began, without noise, to cry. His father did not seem to have eyes at all, just jaundiced sockets of wrinkled skin. The steam of food clouded the scene, which was grim but familiar and distracted David from the formless dread that worked, sticky and sore, within him, like a too-large wound trying to heal.

He had to go to the bathroom. He took a flashlight down through the wet grass to the outhouse. For once, his fear of spiders there felt trivial. He set the flashlight, burning, beside him, and an insect alighted on its lens, a tiny insect, a mosquito or flea, made so fine that the weak light projected its X-ray onto the wall boards: the faint rim of its wings, the blurred strokes, magnified, of its long hinged legs, the dark cone at the heart of its anatomy. The tremor must be its heart beating.

Without warning, David was visited by an exact vision of death: a long hole in the ground, no wider than your body, down which you are drawn while the white faces above recede. You try to reach them but your arms are pinned. Shovels pour dirt into your face. There you will be forever, in an upright position, blind and silent, and in time no one will remember you, and you will never be called by any angel. As strata of rock shift, your fingers elongate, and your teeth are distended sideways in a great under-ground grimace indistinguishable from a strip of chalk. And the earth tumbles on, and the sun expires, and unaltering darkness reigns where once there were stars.

Sweat broke out on his back. His mind seemed to rebound off a solid-ness. Such extinction was not another threat, a graver sort of danger, a kind of pain; it was qualitatively different. It was not even a conception that could be voluntarily pictured; it entered him from outside. His protesting nerves swarmed on its surface like lichen on a meteor. The skin of his chest was soaked with the effort of rejection. At the same time that the fear was dense and internal, it was dense and all around him; a tide of clay had swept up to the stars; space was crushed into a mass. When he stood up, automatically hunching his shoulders to keep his head away from the spiderwebs, it was with a numb sense of being cramped between two huge, rigid masses. That he had even this small freedom to move surprised him. In the narrow shelter of that rank shack, adjusting his pants, he felt—his first spark of comfort—too small to be crushed.

But in the open, as the beam of the flashlight skidded with frightened quickness across the remote surfaces of the barn and the grape arbor and the giant pine that stood by the path to the woods, the terror descended. He raced up through the clinging grass pursued, not by one of the wild animals the woods might hold, or one of the goblins his superstitious grandmother had communicated to his childhood, but by spectres out of science fiction, where gigantic cinder moons fill half the turquoise sky. As David ran, a gray planet rolled inches behind his neck. If he looked back, he would be buried. And in the momentum of his terror, hideous possibilities—the dilation of the sun, the triumph of the insects, the crabs on the shore in *The Time Machine*—wheeled out of the vacuum of make-believe and added their weight to his impending oblivion.

He wrenched the door open; the lamps within the house flared. The wicks burning here and there seemed to mirror one another. His mother was washing the dishes in a little pan of heated pump-water; Granmom hovered near her elbow. In the living room—the downstairs of the little square house was two long rooms—his father sat in front of the black fireplace restlessly folding and unfolding a newspaper as he sustained his half of the argument. "Nitrogen, phosphorus, potash: these are the three replaceable constituents of the soil. One crop of corn carries away hundreds of pounds of"—he dropped the paper into his lap and ticked them off on three fingers—"nitrogen, phosphorus, potash."

"Boyer didn't grow corn."

"*Any* crop, Elsie. The human animal—"

"You're killing the *earth*worms, George!"

"The human animal, after thousands and *thou*sands of years, learned methods whereby the chemical balance of the soil may be maintained. Don't carry me back to the Dark Ages."

"When we moved to Olinger the ground in the garden was like slate. Just one summer of my cousin's chicken dung and the earthworms came back."

"I'm sure the Dark Ages were a fine place to the poor devils born in them, but I don't want to go there. They give me the creeps." Daddy stared into the cold pit of the fireplace and clung to the rolled newspaper in his lap as if it alone were keeping him from slipping backwards and down, down.

Mother came into the doorway brandishing a fistful of wet forks. "And thanks to your DDT there soon won't be a bee left in the country. When I was a girl here you could eat a peach without washing it."

"It's primitive, Elsie. It's Dark Age stuff."

"Oh, what do *you* know about the Dark Ages?"

"I know I don't want to go back to them."

David took from the shelf, where he had placed it this afternoon, the great unabridged Webster's Dictionary that his grandfather had owned. He turned the big thin pages, floppy as cloth, to the entry he wanted, and read

> **soul** . . . 1. An entity conceived as the essence, substance, animating princi-
> ple, or actuating cause of life, or of the individual life, esp. of life manifested
> in psychical activities; the vehicle of individual existence, separate in nature
> from the body and usually held to be separable in existence.

The definition went on, into Greek and Egyptian conceptions, but David stopped short on the treacherous edge of antiquity. He needed to read no further. The careful overlapping words shingled a temporary shelter for him. "Usually held to be separable in existence"—what could be fairer, more judicious, surer?

His father was saying, "The modern farmer can't go around sweeping up after his cows. The poor devil has thousands and *thou*sands of acres on his hands. Your modern farmer uses a scientifically arrived-at mixture, like five-ten-five, or six-twelve-six, or *three*-twelve-six, and spreads it on with this wonderful modern machinery which of course we can't afford. Your modern farmer can't *afford* medieval methods."

Mother was quiet in the kitchen; her silence radiated waves of anger.

"No, now, Elsie: don't play the femme with me. Let's discuss this calmly like two rational twentieth-century people. Your organic-farming nuts aren't attacking five-ten-five; they're attacking the chemical-fertilizer crooks. The monster firms."

A cup clinked in the kitchen. Mother's anger touched David's face; his cheeks burned guiltily. Just by staying in the living room he associated himself with his father. She appeared in the doorway with red hands and tears in her eyes, and said to the two of them, "I knew you didn't want to come here but I didn't know you'd torment me like this. You talked Pop into his grave and now you'll kill me. Go ahead, George, more power to you; at least I'll be buried in good ground." She tried to turn and met an obstacle and screamed, "Mother, stop hanging on my *back!* Why don't you go to *bed?*"

"Let's all go to bed," David's father said, rising from the blue wing chair and slapping his thigh with a newspaper. "This reminds me of death." It was a phrase of his that David had heard so often he never considered its sense.

Upstairs, he seemed to be lifted above his fears. The sheets on his bed were clean. Granmom had ironed them with a pair of flatirons saved from the Olinger attic; she plucked them hot off the stove alternately, with a wooden handle called a goose. It was a wonder, to see how she managed. In the next room, his parents grunted peaceably; they seemed to take their quarrels less seriously than he did. They made comfortable scratching noises as they carried a little lamp back and forth. Their door was open a crack, so he saw the light shift and swing. Surely there would be, in the last five minutes, in the last second, a crack of light, showing the door from the dark room to another, full of light. Thinking of it this vividly frightened him. His own dying, in a specific bed in a specific room, specific walls mottled with a particular wallpaper, the dry whistle of his breathing, the murmuring doctors, the dutiful relatives going in and out, but for him no way out but down, into that hole. *Never walk again, never touch a doorknob again.* A whisper, and his parents' light was blown out. David prayed to be reassured. Though the experiment frightened him, he lifted his hands high into the darkness above his face and begged Christ to touch them. Not hard or long: the faintest, quickest grip would be final for a lifetime. His hands waited in the air, itself a substance, which seemed to move through his fingers; or was it the pressure of his pulse? He returned his hands to beneath the covers, uncertain if they had been touched or not. For would not Christ's touch *be* infinitely gentle?

Through all the eddies of its aftermath, David clung to this thought about his revelation of extinction: that there, in the outhouse, he had struck a solid something qualitatively different, a base terror dense enough to support any height of construction. All he needed was a little help; a word, a gesture, a nod of certainty, and he would be sealed in, safe. The reassurance from the dictionary had melted in the night. Today was Sunday, a hot fair day. Across a mile of clear air the church bells called, *Celebrate, celebrate.* Only Daddy went. He put on a coat over his rolled-up shirtsleeves and got into the little old black Plymouth parked by the barn and went off, with the same pained hurried grimness of all his actions. His churning wheels, as he shifted too hastily into second, raised plumes of red dust on the dirt road. Mother walked to the far field, to see what bushes needed cutting. David, though he usually preferred to stay in the house, went with her. The puppy followed at a distance, whining as it picked its way through the stubble but floundering off timidly if one of them went back to pick it up and carry it. When they reached the crest of the far field, his mother asked, "David, what's troubling you?"

"Nothing. Why?"

She looked at him sharply. The greening woods crosshatched the space beyond her half-gray hair. Then she showed him her profile, and gestured toward the house, which they had left a half-mile behind them. "See how it sits in the land? They don't know how to build with the land any more. Pop always said the foundations were set with the compass. We must get a compass and see. It's supposed to face due south; but south feels a little more *that* way to me." From the side, as she said these things, she seemed handsome and young. The smooth sweep of her hair over her ear had a calm that made her feel foreign to him. He had never regarded his parents as consolers of his troubles; from the beginning they had seemed to have more troubles than he. Their frailty had flattered him into an illusion of strength; so now on this high clear ridge he jealously guarded the menace all around them, blowing like an invisible breeze— the possibility of all this wide scenery's sinking into everlasting darkness. The strange fact that, though she came to look at the brush, she carried no clippers, for she had a fixed prejudice against working on Sundays, was the only comfort he allowed her to offer.

As they walked back, the puppy whimpering after them, the rising dust behind a distant line of trees announced that Daddy was speeding home from church. When they reached the house he was there. He had brought back the Sunday paper and the vehement remark, "Dobson's too intelligent for these farmers. They just sit there with their mouths open and don't hear a thing the poor devil's saying."

"What makes you think farmers are unintelligent? This country was made by farmers. George Washington was a farmer."

"They are, Elsie. They are unintelligent. George Washington's dead. In this day and age only the misfits stay on the farm. The lame, the halt, the blind. The morons with one arm. Human garbage. They remind me of death, sitting there with their mouths open."

"My *father* was a farmer."

"He was a frustrated man, Elsie. He never knew what hit him. The poor devil meant so well, and he never knew which end was up. Your mother'll bear me out. Isn't that right, Mom? Pop never knew what hit him?"

"Ach, I guess not," the old woman quavered, and the ambiguity for the moment silenced both sides.

David hid in the funny papers and sports section until one-thirty. At two, the catechetical class met at the Firetown church. He had transferred from the catechetical class of the Lutheran church in Olinger, a humiliating comedown. In Olinger they met on Wednesday nights, spiffy and spruce, in a very social atmosphere. Afterwards, blessed by the brick-faced minister on whose lips the word "Christ" had a pugnacious juiciness, the more daring of them went with their Bibles to a luncheonette and gossiped and smoked. Here in Firetown, the girls were dull white cows and the boys narrow-faced brown goats in old men's suits, herded on Sunday afternoons into a threadbare church basement that smelled of stale hay. Because his father had taken the car on one of his endless errands to Olinger, David walked, grateful for the open air, the lonely dirt road, and the silence. The catechetical class embarrassed him, but today he placed hope in it, as the source of the nod, the gesture, that was all he needed.

Reverend Dobson was a delicate young man with great dark eyes and small white shapely hands that flickered like protesting doves when he preached; he seemed a bit misplaced in the Lutheran ministry. This was his first call. It was a split parish; he served another rural church twelve miles away. His iridescent-green Ford, new six months ago, was spattered to the windows with red mud and rattled from bouncing on the rude back roads, where he frequently got lost, to the malicious satisfaction of some parishioners. But David's mother liked him, and, more pertinent to his success, the Haiers, the sleek family of feed merchants and tractor salesmen who dominated the Firetown church, liked him. David liked him, and felt liked in turn; sometimes in class, after some special stupidity, Dobson directed toward him out of those wide black eyes a mild look of disbelief, a look that, though flattering, was also delicately disquieting.

Catechetical instruction consisted of reading aloud from a work booklet answers to problems prepared during the week, problems like, "I am the _____, the _____, and the _____, saith the Lord." Then there was a question period in which no one ever asked any questions. Today's theme was the last third of the Apostles' Creed. When the time came for questions, David blushed and asked, "About the Resurrection of the Body—are we conscious between the time when we die and the Day of Judgment?"

Dobson blinked, and his fine small mouth pursed, suggesting that David was making difficult things more difficult. The faces of the other students went blank, as if an indiscretion had been committed.

"No, I suppose not," Reverend Dobson said.

"Well, where is our soul, then, in this gap?"

The sense grew, in the class, of a naughtiness occurring. Dobson's shy eyes watered, as if he were straining to keep up the formality of attention, and one of the girls, the fattest, simpered toward her twin, who was a little less fat. Their chairs were arranged in a rough circle. The current running around the circle panicked David. Did everybody know something he didn't know?

"I suppose you could say our souls are asleep," Dobson said.

"And then they wake up, and there is the earth like it always is, and all the people who have ever lived? Where will Heaven be?"

Anita Haier giggled. Dobson gazed at David intently, but with an awkward, puzzled flicker of forgiveness, as if there existed a secret between them that David was violating. But David knew of no secret. All he wanted was to hear Dobson repeat the words he said every Sunday morning. This he would not do. As if these words were unworthy of the conversational voice.

"David, you might think of Heaven this way: as the way in which the goodness Abraham Lincoln did lives after him."

"But is Lincoln conscious of it living on?" He blushed no longer with embarrassment but in anger; he had walked here in good faith and was being made a fool.

"Is he conscious now? I would have to say no. But I don't think it matters." His voice had a coward's firmness; he was hostile now.

"You don't."

"Not in the eyes of God, no." The unction, the stunning impudence, of this reply sprang tears of outrage in David's eyes. He bowed them to his work book, where short words like Duty, Love, Obey, Honor were stacked in the form of a cross.

"Were there any other questions, David?" Dobson asked, more softly. The others were rustling, collecting their books.

"No." David made his voice firm, though he could not look up at the man.

"Did I answer your question fully enough?"

"Yes."

In the minister's silence the shame that should have been his crept over David: the burden and fever of being a fraud were placed upon *him*, who was innocent, and it seemed, he knew, a confession of this guilt that on the way out he was unable to face Dobson's stirred gaze, though he felt it probing the side of his head.

Anita Haier's father gave him a ride down the highway as far as the dirt road. David said he wanted to walk the rest, and figured that his offer was accepted because Mr. Haier did not want to dirty his dark new Oldsmobile with dust. This was all right; everything was all right, as long as it was clear. His indignation at being betrayed, at seeing Christianity betrayed, had hardened him. The road reflected his hardness. Pink stones thrust up through its packed surface. The April sun beat down from the center of the afternoon half of the sky; already it had some of summer's heat. Already the fringes of weeds at the edges of the road were bedraggled with dust. From the reviving grass and scruff of the fields that he walked between, insects were sending up a monotonous, automatic chant. In the distance a tiny figure in his father's coat was walking along the edge of the woods. His mother. He wondered what joy she found in such walks; to him the brown stretches of slowly rising and falling land expressed only a huge exhaustion.

Flushed with fresh air and happiness, she returned from her walk earlier than he had expected, and surprised him at his grandfather's Bible. It was a stumpy black book, the boards worn thin where the old man's fingers had held them; the spine hung by one weak hinge of fabric. David had been looking for the passage where Jesus says to the good thief on the cross, "Today shalt thou be with Me in paradise." He had never tried reading the Bible for himself before. What was so embarrassing about being caught at it was that he detested the apparatus of piety. Fusty churches, creaking hymns, ugly Sunday-school teachers and their stupid leaflets—he hated everything about them but the promise they held out, a promise that in the most perverse way, as if the homeliest crone in the kingdom were given the prince's hand, made every good and real thing, ball games and jokes and big-breasted girls, possible. He couldn't explain this to his mother. There was no time. Her solicitude was upon him.

"David, what are you doing?"

"Nothing."

"What are you doing at your grandfather's Bible?"

"Trying to read it. This is supposed to be a Christian country, isn't it?"

She sat down beside him on the green sofa, which used to be in the sun parlor at Olinger, under the fancy mirror. A little smile still lingered on her face from the walk. "David, I wish you'd talk to me."

"What about?"

"About whatever it is that's troubling you. Your father and I have both noticed it."

"I asked Reverend Dobson about Heaven and he said it was like Abraham Lincoln's goodness living after him."

He waited for the shock to strike her. "Yes?" she said, expecting more.

"That's all."

"And why didn't you like it?"

"Well—don't you see? It amounts to saying there isn't any Heaven at all."

"I don't see that it amounts to that. What do you want Heaven to be?"

"Well, I don't know. I want it to be *something*. I thought he'd tell me what it was. I thought that was his job." He was becoming angry, sensing her surprise. She had assumed that Heaven had faded from his head years ago. She had imagined that he had already entered, in the secrecy of silence, the conspiracy that he now knew to be all around him.

"David," she asked gently, "don't you ever want to rest?"

"No. Not forever."

"David, you're so young. When you get older, you'll feel differently."

"Grandpa didn't. Look how tattered this book is."

"I never understood your grandfather."

"Well, I don't understand ministers who say it's like Lincoln's goodness going on and on. Suppose you're not Lincoln?"

"I think Reverend Dobson made a mistake. You must try to forgive him."

"It's not a *question* of his making a mistake! It's a question of dying and never moving or seeing or hearing anything ever again."

"But"—in exasperation—"darling, it's so *greedy* of you to want more. When God has given us this wonderful April day, and given us this farm, and you have your whole life ahead of you—"

"You think, then, that there is a God?"

"Of course I do"—with deep relief, that smoothed her features into a reposeful oval. He had risen in his unease; he was afraid she would reach out and touch him.

"He made everything? You feel that?"

"Yes."

"Then who made Him?"

"Why, Man. Man." The happiness of this answer lit up her face radiantly, until she saw his gesture of disgust. She was so simple, so illogical; such a femme.

"Well, that amounts to saying He doesn't exist."

Her hand reached for his wrist but he backed away. "David, it's a mystery. A miracle. It's a miracle more beautiful than any Reverend Dobson could have told you about. You don't say houses don't exist because Man made them."

"No. God has to be different."

"But, David, you have the *evidence*. Look out the window at the sun; at the fields."

"Mother, good grief. Don't you see"—he rasped away the roughness in his throat—"if when we die there's nothing, all your sun and fields and whatnot are all, ah, *horror?* It's just an ocean of horror."

"But, David, it's not. It's so clearly not that." And she made an urgent, opening gesture with her hands that expressed a willingness to receive his helplessness; all her grace and maternal nurturing were gathered into a passive intensity that intensely repelled him. He would not be wooed away from the truth. *I am the Way, the Truth . . .*

"No," he told her. "Just let me alone."

He found his tennis ball behind the piano and went outside to throw it against the side of the house. There was a patch high up where the brown stucco laid over the sandstone masonry was crumbling away; he kept trying with the tennis ball to chip more pieces off. It was difficult, aiming up; the ball kept falling short.

Superimposed upon his deep ache was a smaller but more immediate worry—that he had hurt his mother. He heard his father's car rattling on the straightaway, and went into the house, to make peace before he arrived. To his relief, she was not giving off the stifling damp heat of her anger, but instead was cool, decisive, maternal. She handed him an old green book, her college text of Plato.

"I want you to read the Parable of the Cave," she said.

"All right," he said, though he knew it would do no good. Some story by a dead Greek just vague enough to please her. "Don't worry about it, Mother."

"I *am* worried. Honestly, David, I'm sure there will be something for us. As you get older, these things seem to matter a great deal less."

"That may be. It's a dismal thought, though."

His father bumped at the door. The locks and jambs stuck here. But before Granmom could totter to the latch and let him in, he had knocked it open. He had been in Olinger dithering with track-meet tickets. Although Mother usually kept her talks with David a secret between them, she called instantly, "George, David is worried about death!"

Daddy came to the doorway of the living room, his shirt pocket bristling with pencils, holding in one hand a pint box of melting ice cream and in the other the knife with which he was about to divide it into four sections, their Sunday treat. "Is the kid worried about death? Don't give it a thought, David. I'll be lucky if I live till tomorrow, and I'm not worried. If they'd taken a buckshot gun and shot me in the cradle I'd be better off. The *world*'d be better off. Hell, I think death is a wonderful thing. I look forward to it. Get the garbage out of the way. If I had the man here who invented death, I'd pin a medal on him."

"Hush, George. You'll frighten the child worse than he is."

This was not true; he never frightened David. There was no harm in his father, no harm at all. Indeed, in the man's lively self-disgust the boy felt a kind of ally. A distant ally. He saw his position with a certain strategic coldness. Nowhere in the world of other people would he find the hint, the nod, he needed to begin to build his fortress against death. They none of them believed. He was alone. In that deep hole.

In the months that followed, his position changed little. School was some comfort. All those sexy, perfumed people, wisecracking, chewing gum, all of them doomed to die, and none of them noticing. In their company David felt that they would carry him along into the bright, cheap paradise reserved for them. In any crowd, the fear ebbed a little; he had reasoned that somewhere in the world there must exist a few people who believed what was necessary, and the larger the crowd, the greater the chance that he was near such a soul, within calling distance, if only he was not too ignorant, too ill-equipped, to spot him. The sight of clergymen cheered him; whatever they themselves thought, their collars were still a sign that somewhere, at some time, someone had recognized that we cannot, *cannot*, submit to death. The sermon topics posted outside churches, the flip, hurried pieties of disc jockeys, the cartoons in magazines showing angels or devils—on such scraps he kept alive the possibility of hope.

For the rest, he tried to drown his hopelessness in clatter and jostle. The pinball machine at the luncheonette was a merciful distraction; as he bent over its buzzing, flashing board of flippers and cushions, the weight and constriction in his chest lightened and loosened. He was grateful for all the time his father wasted in Olinger. Every delay postponed the moment when they must ride together down the dirt road into the heart of the dark farmland, where the only light was the kerosene lamp waiting on the dining-room table, a light that drowned their food in shadow and made it sinister.

He lost his appetite for reading. He was afraid of being ambushed again. In mystery novels people died like dolls being discarded; in science fiction immensities of space and time conspired to annihilate the human beings; and even in P. G. Wodehouse there was a threat, a bland mockery that acquired bite in the comic figures of futile clergymen. All gaiety seemed minced out on the skin of a void. All quiet hours seemed invitations to dread.

Even on weekends, he and his father contrived to escape the farm; and when, some Saturdays, they did stay home, it was to do something destructive—tear down an old henhouse or set huge brush fires that threatened, while Mother shouted and flapped her arms, to spread to the woods. Whenever his father worked, it was with rapt violence; when he chopped kindling, fragments of the old henhouse boards flew like shrapnel and the ax-head was always within a quarter of an inch of flying off the handle. He was exhilarating to watch, sweating and swearing and sucking bits of saliva back into his mouth.

School stopped. His father took the car in the opposite direction, to a highway construction job where he had been hired for the summer as a timekeeper, and David was stranded in the middle of acres of heat and greenery and blowing pollen and the strange, mechanical humming that lay invisibly in the weeds and alfalfa and dry orchard grass.

For his fourteenth birthday his parents gave him, with jokes about him being a hillbilly now, a Remington .22. It was somewhat like a pinball machine to take it out to the old kiln in the woods where they dumped their trash, and set up tin cans on the kiln's sandstone shoulder and shoot them off one by one. He'd take the puppy, who had grown long legs and a rich coat of reddish fur—he was part chow. Copper hated the gun but loved the boy enough to accompany him. When the flat, acrid crack rang out, he would race in terrified circles that would tighten and tighten until they brought him, shivering, against David's legs. Depending upon his mood, David would shoot again or drop to his knees and comfort the dog. Giving this comfort returned some comfort to him. The dog's ears, laid flat against his skull in fear, were folded so intricately, so—he groped for the concept—*surely*. Where the dull-studded collar made the fur stand up, each hair showed a root of soft white under the length, black-tipped, of the metal color that had lent the dog its name. In his agitation Copper panted through nostrils that were elegant slits, like two healed cuts, or like the keyholes of a dainty lock of black, grained wood. His whole whorling, knotted, jointed body was a wealth of such embellishments. And in the smell of the dog's hair David seemed to descend through many finely differentiated layers of earth: mulch, soil, sand, clay, and the glittering mineral base.

But when he returned to the house, and saw the books arranged on the low shelves, fear dully returned. The four adamant volumes of Wells like four thin bricks, the green Plato that had puzzled him with its dialogue form and hard-to-picture shadow show, the dead Galsworthy and "Elizabeth," Grandpa's mammoth dictionary, Grandpa's old Bible, the limp-covered Bible that he himself had received on becoming confirmed a member of the Firetown Lutheran Church—at the sight of these, the memory of his fear reawakened and came around him. He had grown stiff and stupid in its embrace. His parents tried to think of ways to entertain him.

"David, I have a job for you to do," his mother said one evening at the table.

"What?"

"If you're going to take that tone perhaps we'd better not talk."

"What tone? I didn't take any tone."

"Your grandmother thinks there are too many pigeons in the barn."

"Why?" David turned to look at his grandmother, but she sat there staring at the burning lamp with her usual expression of bewilderment. Her irises were pale discs of crazed crystal.

Mother shouted, "Mom, he wants to know why!"

Granmom made a jerky, irritable motion with her bad hand, as if generating the force for utterance, and said, "They foul the furniture."

"That's right," Mother said. "She's afraid for that old Olinger furniture that we'll never use. David, she's been after me for a month about those poor pigeons. She wants you to shoot them."

"I don't want to kill anything especially," David said.

Daddy said, "The kid's like you are, Elsie. He's too good for this world. Kill or be killed, that's my motto."

His mother said loudly, "Mother, he doesn't want to do it."

"Not?" The old lady's eyes distended as if in alarm, and her claw descended slowly to her lap.

"Oh, I'll do it, I'll do it tomorrow," David snapped, and a pleasant crisp taste entered his mouth with the decision.

"And I had thought, when Boyer's men made the hay, it would be better if the barn doesn't look like a rookery," his mother added needlessly.

A barn, in day, is a small night. The splinters of light between the dry shingles pierce the high roof like stars, and the rafters and crossbeams and built-in ladders seem, until your eyes adjust, as mysterious as the branches of a haunted forest. David entered silently, the gun in one hand.

Copper whined desperately at the door, too frightened to come in with the gun yet unwilling to leave the boy. David stealthily turned, said "Go away," shut the door on the dog, and slipped the bolt across. It was a door within a door; the double door for wagons and tractors was as high and wide as the face of a house.

The smell of old straw scratched his sinuses. The red sofa, half hidden under its white-splotched tarpaulin, seemed assimilated into this smell, sunk in it, buried. The mouths of empty bins gaped like caves. Rusty oddments of farming—coils of baling wire, some spare tines for a harrow, a handleless shovel—hung on nails driven here and there in the thick wood. He stood stock-still a minute; it took a while to separate the cooing of the pigeons from the rustling in his ears. When he had focused on the cooing, it flooded the vast interior with its throaty, bubbling outpour: there seemed no other sound. They were up behind the beams. What light there was leaked through the shingles and the dirty glass windows at the far end and the small round holes, about as big as basketballs, high on the opposite stone side walls, under the ridge of the roof.

A pigeon appeared in one of these holes, on the side toward the house. It flew in, with a battering of wings, from the outside, and waited there, silhouetted against its pinched bit of sky, preening and cooing in a throbbing, thrilled, tentative way. David tiptoed four steps to the side, rested his gun against the lowest rung of a ladder pegged between two upright beams, and lowered the gunsight into the bird's tiny, jauntily cocked head. The slap of the report seemed to come off the stone wall behind him, and the pigeon did not fall. Neither did it fly. Instead it stuck in the round hole, pirouetting rapidly and nodding its head as if in frantic agreement. David shot the bolt back and forth and had aimed again before the spent cartridge had stopped jingling on the boards by his feet. He eased the tip of the sight a little lower, into the bird's breast, and took care to squeeze the trigger with perfect evenness. The slow contraction of his hand abruptly sprang the bullet; for a half-second there was doubt, and then the pigeon fell like a handful of rags, skimming down the barn wall into the layer of straw that coated the floor of the mow on this side.

Now others shook loose from the rafters, and whirled in the dim air with a great blurred hurtle of feathers and noise. They would go for the hole; he fixed his sight on the little moon of blue, and when a pigeon came to it, shot him as he was walking the twenty inches of stone that would have carried him into the open air. This pigeon lay down in that tunnel of stone, unable to fall either one way or the other, although he was alive enough to lift one wing and cloud the light. The wing would sink back, and he would suddenly lift it again, the feathers flaring. His body blocked that exit. David raced to the other side of the barn's main aisle, where a similar ladder was symmetrically placed, and rested his gun on the same rung. Three birds came together to this hole; he got one, and two got through. The rest resettled in the rafters.

There was a shallow triangular space behind the crossbeams support- ing the roof. It was here they roosted and hid. But either the space was too small, or they were curious, for now that his eyes were at home in the dusty gloom David could see little dabs of gray popping in and out. The cooing was shriller now; its apprehensive tremolo made the whole vol- ume of air seem liquid. He noticed one little smudge of a head that was especially persistent in peeking out; he marked the place, and fixed his gun on it, and when the head appeared again, had his finger tightened in advance on the trigger. A parcel of fluff slipped off the beam and fell the barn's height onto a canvas covering some Olinger furniture, and where its head had peeked out there was a fresh prick of light in the shingles.

Standing in the center of the floor, fully master now, disdaining to steady the barrel with anything but his arm, he killed two more that way. Out of the shadowy ragged infinity of the vast barn roof these impudent things dared to thrust their heads, presumed to dirty its starred silence with their filthy timorous life, and he cut them off, tucked them back neatly into the silence. He felt like a creator; these little smudges and flickers that he was clever to see and even cleverer to hit in the dim recesses of the rafters—out of each of them he was making a full bird. A tiny peek, probe, dab of life, when he hit it blossomed into a dead enemy, falling with good, final weight.

The imperfection of the second pigeon he had shot, who was still lift- ing his wing now and then up in the round hole, nagged him. He put a new clip into the stock. Hugging the gun against his body, he climbed the ladder. The barrel sight scratched his ear; he had a sharp, garish vision, like a color slide, of shooting himself and being found tumbled on the barn floor among his prey. He locked his arm around the top rung—a fragile, gnawed rod braced between uprights—and shot into the bird's body from a flat angle. The wing folded, but the impact did not, as he had hoped, push the bird out of the hole. He fired again, and again, and still the little body, lighter than air when alive, was too heavy to budge from its high grave. From up here he could see green trees and a brown corner of the house through the hole. Clammy with the cobwebs that gathered between the rungs, he pumped a full clip of eight bullets into the stubborn shadow, with no success. He climbed down, and was struck by the silence in the barn. The remaining pigeons must have escaped out the other hole. That was all right; he was tired of it.

He stepped with his rifle into the light. His mother was coming to meet him, and it tickled him to see her shy away from the carelessly held gun. "You took a chip out of the house," she said. "What were those last shots about?"

"One of them died up in that little round hole and I was trying to shoot it down."

"Copper's hiding behind the piano and won't come out. I had to leave him."

"Well, don't blame me. *I* didn't want to shoot the poor devils."

"Don't smirk. You look like your father. How many did you get?"

"Six."

She went into the barn, and he followed. She listened to the silence. Her hair was scraggly, perhaps from tussling with the dog. "I don't suppose the others will be back," she said wearily. "Indeed, I don't know why I let Mother talk me into it. Their cooing was such a comforting noise." She began to gather up the dead pigeons. Though he didn't want to touch them, David went into the mow and picked up by its tepid, horny, coral-colored feet the first bird he had killed. Its wings unfolded disconcertingly, as if the creature had been held together by threads that now were slit. It did not weigh much. He retrieved the one on the other side of the barn; his mother got the three in the middle and led the way across the road to the little south-facing slope of land that went down toward the foundations of the vanished tobacco shed. The ground was too steep to plant and mow; wild strawberries grew in the tangled grass. She put her burden down and said, "We'll have to bury them. The dog will go wild."

He put his two down on her three; the slick feathers let the bodies slide liquidly on one another. David asked, "Shall I get you the shovel?"

"Get it for yourself; *you* bury them. They're your kill. And be sure to make the hole deep enough so Copper won't dig them up." While he went to the tool shed for the shovel, she went into the house. Unlike his usual mother, she did not look up, either at the orchard to the right of her or at the meadow on her left, but instead held her head rigidly, tilted a little, as if listening to the ground.

He dug the hole, in a spot where there were no strawberry plants, before he studied the pigeons. He had never seen a bird this close before.

The feathers were more wonderful than dog's hair, for each filament was shaped within the shape of the feather, and the feathers in turn were trimmed to fit a pattern that flowed without error across the bird's body. He lost himself in the geometrical tides as the feathers now broadened and stiffened to make an edge for flight, now softened and constricted to cup warmth around the mute flesh. And across the surface of the infinitely adjusted yet somehow effortless mechanics of the feathers played idle designs of color, no two alike, designs executed, it seemed, in a controlled rapture, with a joy that hung level in the air above and behind him. Yet these birds bred in the millions and were exterminated as pests. Into the fragrant open earth he dropped one broadly banded in slate shades of blue, and on top of it another, mottled all over in rhythms of lilac and gray. The next was almost wholly white, but for a salmon glaze at its throat. As he fitted the last two, still pliant, on the top, and stood up, crusty coverings were lifted from him, and with a feminine, slipping sensation along his nerves that seemed to give the air hands, he was robed in this certainty: that the God who had lavished such craft upon these worthless birds would not destroy His whole Creation by refusing to let David live forever.

Friends from Philadelphia

IN THE MOMENT before the door was opened to him, he glimpsed her thigh below the half-drawn shade. Thelma was home, then. She was wearing the Camp Winniwoho T-shirt and her quite short shorts.

"Why, my goodness: Janny!" she cried. She always pronounced his name, John, to rhyme with "Ann." Earlier that summer, she had visited New York City, and tried to talk the way she thought they talked there. "What on earth ever brings you to me at this odd hour?"

"Hello, Thel," he said. "I hope—I guess this is a pretty bad time." She had been plucking her eyebrows again. He wished she wouldn't do that.

Thelma extended her arm and touched her fingers to the base of John's neck. It wasn't a fond gesture, just a hostesslike one. "Now, Janny. You know that I—my mother and I—are always happy to be seeing you. Mother, who do you ever guess is here at this odd hour?"

"Don't keep John Nordholm standing there," Mrs. Lutz said. Thelma's mother was settled in the deep-red settee watching television and smoking. A coffee cup being used as an ashtray lay in her lap, and her dress was hitched so that her knees showed.

"Hello, Mrs. Lutz," John said, trying not to look at her broad, pale knees. "I really hate to bother you at this odd hour."

"I don't see anything odd about it." She took a deep-throated drag on her cigarette and exhaled through her nostrils, the way men do. "Some of the other kids were here earlier this afternoon."

"I would have come in if anybody had told me."

Thelma said, "Oh, Janny! Stop trying to make a martyr of yourself. Keep in touch, they say, if you want to keep up."

He felt his face grow hot and knew he was blushing, which made him blush all the more. Mrs. Lutz shook a wrinkled pack of Herbert Tareytons at him. "Smoke?" she said.

"I guess not, thanks a lot."

"You've stopped? It's a bad habit. I wish I had stopped at your age. I'm not sure I'd even *begun* at your age."

"No, it's just that I have to go home soon, and my mother would smell the smoke on my breath. She can smell it even through chewing gum."

"Why must you go home soon?" Thelma asked.

Mrs. Lutz sniffled. "I have sinus. I can't even smell the flowers in the garden or the food on the table any more. Let the kids smoke if they want, if it makes them feel better. I don't care. My Thelma, she can smoke right in her own home, her own living room, if she wants to. But she doesn't seem to have the taste for it. I'm just as glad, to tell the truth."

John hated interrupting, but it was close to five-thirty. "I have a problem," he said.

"A problem—how gruesome," Thelma said. "And here I thought, Mother, I was being favored with a social call."

"Don't talk like that," Mrs. Lutz said.

"It's sort of complex," John began.

"Talk like what, Mother? Talk like what?"

"Then let me turn this off," Mrs. Lutz said, snapping the right knob on the television set.

"Oh, Mother, and I was listening to it!" Thelma toppled into a chair, her legs flashing. When she pouted, John thought, she was delicious.

Mrs. Lutz had set herself to give sympathy. Her lap was broadened and her hands were laid palm upward in it.

"It's not much of a problem," John assured her. "But we're having some people to dinner from Philadelphia." He turned to Thelma and added, "If anything is going on tonight, I can't get out."

"Life is just too, too full of disappointments," Thelma said.

"Look, is there?"

"Too, too full," Thelma said.

Mrs. Lutz made fluttery motions out of her lap. "These Philadelphia people."

John said, "Maybe I shouldn't bother you about this." He waited, but she just looked more and more patient, so he went on. "My mother wants to give them wine, and my father isn't home from school yet. He might not get home before the liquor store closes. It's at six, isn't it? My mother's busy cleaning the house, so I walked in."

"She made you walk the whole mile? Poor thing, can't you drive?" Mrs. Lutz asked.

"*Sure* I can drive. But I'm not sixteen yet."

"You look a lot taller than fifteen."

John looked at Thelma to see how she took that one, but Thelma was pretending to read a rented novel wrapped in cellophane.

"I walked all the way to the liquor store," John told Mrs. Lutz, "but they wouldn't give me anything without written permission. It was a new man."

"Your sorrow has rent me in twain," Thelma said, as if she was reading it from the book.

"Pay no attention, John," Mrs. Lutz said. "Frank will be home any second. Why not wait until he comes and let him run down with you for a bottle?"

"That sounds wonderful. Thanks an awful lot, really."

Mrs. Lutz's hand descended upon the television knob. Some smiling man was playing the piano. John didn't know who he was; there wasn't any television at his house. They watched in silence until Mr. Lutz thumped on the porch outside. The empty milk bottles tinkled, as if they had been nudged. "Now, don't be surprised if he has a bit of a load on," Mrs. Lutz said.

Actually, he didn't act at all drunk. He was like a happy husband in the movies. He called Thelma his little pookie-pie and kissed her on the forehead; then he called his wife his big pookie-pie and kissed her on the mouth. Then he solemnly shook John's hand and told him how very, very happy he was to see him here and asked after his parents. "Is that goon still on television?" he said finally.

"Daddy, please pay attention to somebody else," Thelma said, turning off the television set. "Janny wants to talk to you."

"And *I* want to talk to *Johnny*," Thelma's father said. He spread his arms suddenly, clenching and unclenching his fists. He was a big man, with shaved gray hair above his ears, which were small and flat to his head. John couldn't think of the word to begin.

Mrs. Lutz explained the errand. When she was through, Mr. Lutz said, "People from Philadelphia. I bet their name isn't William L. Trexler, is it?"

"No. I forget their name, but it's not that. The man is an engineer. The woman went to college with my mother."

"Oh. College people. Then we must get them something very, very nice, I should say."

"Daddy," Thelma said. "*Please.* The store will close."

"Tessie, you hear John. People from college. People with diplomas. And it is very nearly closing time, and who isn't on their way?" He took

John's shoulder in one hand and Thelma's arm in the other and hustled them through the door. "We'll be back in one minute, Mamma," he said.

"Drive carefully," Mrs. Lutz said from the shadowed porch.

Mr. Lutz drove a huge blue Buick. "I never went to college," he said, "yet I buy a new car whenever I want." His tone wasn't nasty, but soft and full of wonder.

"Oh, Daddy, not *this* again," Thelma said, shaking her head at John, so he could understand what all she had to go through. When she looks like that, John thought, I could bite her lip until it bleeds.

"Ever driven this kind of car, John?" Mr. Lutz asked.

"No. The only thing I can drive is my parents' Plymouth, and that not very well."

"What year car is it?"

"I don't know exactly." John knew perfectly well it was a 1940 model, bought second-hand after the war. "It has a gear shift. This is automatic, isn't it?"

"Automatic shift, fluid transmission, directional lights, the works," Mr. Lutz said. "Now, isn't it funny, John? Here is your father, an educated man, with an old Plymouth, yet at the same time I, who never read more than ten, twenty books in my life . . . It doesn't seem as if there's justice." He slapped the fender, bent over to get into the car, straightened up abruptly, and said, "Do you want to drive it?"

Thelma said, "Daddy's asking you something."

"I don't know how," John said.

"It's very easy to learn, very easy. You just slide in there—come on, it's getting late." John got in on the driver's side. He peered out of the windshield. It was a wider car than the Plymouth; the hood looked wide as a boat.

Mr. Lutz asked him to grip the little lever behind the steering wheel. "You pull it toward you like *that*, that's it, and fit it into one of these notches. 'P' stands for 'park'—for when you're not going anywhere. 'N,' that's 'neutral,' like on the car you have, I hardly ever use it, 'D' means 'drive'—just put it in there and the car does all the work for you. You are using that one ninety-nine per cent of the time. 'L' is 'low,' for very steep hills, going up or down. And 'R' stands for—what?"

"Reverse," John said.

"Very, very good. Tessie, he's a smart boy. He'll never own a new car. And when you put them all together, you can remember their order by the sentence 'Paint No Dimes Light Red.' I thought that up when I was teaching my oldest girl how to drive."

"Paint No Dimes Light Red," John said.

"Excellent. Now, let's go." He reached over and put the car key in the ignition lock, his other keys dangling.

A bubble was developing in John's stomach. "What gear do you want it in to start?" he asked Mr. Lutz.

Mr. Lutz must not have heard him, because all he said was "Let's go" again, and he drummed on the dashboard with his fingertips. They were thick, square, furry fingers.

Thelma leaned up from the back seat. Her cheek almost touched John's ear. She whispered, "Put it at 'D.' "

He did, then he looked for the starter. "How does he start it?" he asked Thelma.

"I never watch him," she said. "There was a button in the last car, but I don't see it in this one."

"Push on the pedal," Mr. Lutz sang, staring straight ahead and smiling, "and away we go. And ah, ah, *waay* we go."

"Just step on the gas," Thelma suggested. John pushed down firmly, to keep his leg from trembling. The motor roared and the car bounded away from the curb. Within a block, though, he could manage the car pretty well.

"It rides like a boat on smooth water," he told his two passengers. The simile pleased him.

Mr. Lutz squinted ahead. "Like a what?"

"Like a boat."

"Don't go so fast," Thelma said.

"The motor's so quiet," John explained. "Like a sleeping cat."

Without warning, a truck pulled out of Pearl Street. Mr. Lutz, trying to brake, stamped his foot on the empty floor in front of him. John could hardly keep from laughing. "I see him," he said, easing his speed so that the truck had just enough room to make its turn. "Those trucks think they own the road," he said. He let one hand slide away from the steering wheel. One-handed, he whipped around a bus. "What'll she do on the open road?"

"That's a good question, John," Mr. Lutz said. "And I don't know the answer. Ninety, maybe."

"The speedometer goes up to a hundred and ten." Another pause— nobody seemed to be talking. John said, "Hell. A baby could drive one of these."

"For instance, you," Thelma said. That meant she had noticed how well he was driving.

There were a lot of cars at the liquor store, so John had to double-park the big Buick. "That's close enough, close enough," Mr. Lutz said. "Don't get any closer, whoa!" He was out of the car before John could bring it to a complete stop. "You and Tessie wait here," he said. "I'll go in for the liquor."

"Mr. Lutz. Say, Mr. Lutz," John called.

"Daddy!" Thelma shouted.

Mr. Lutz returned. "What is it, boys and girls?" His tone, John noticed, was becoming reedy. He was probably getting hungry.

"Here's the money they gave me." John pulled two wadded dollars from the change pocket of his dungarees. "My mother said to get something inexpensive but nice."

"Inexpensive but nice?" Mr. Lutz repeated.

"She said something about California sherry."

"What did she say about it? To get it? Or not to?"

"I guess to get it."

"You guess." Mr. Lutz shoved himself away from the car and walked backward toward the store as he talked. "You and Tessie wait in the car. Don't go off somewhere. I'll be only one minute."

John leaned back in his seat and gracefully rested one hand at the top of the steering wheel. "I like your father."

"You don't know how he acts to Mother," Thelma said.

John studied the clean line under his wrist and thumb. He flexed his wrist and watched the neat little muscles move in his forearm. "You know what I need?" he said. "A wristwatch."

"Oh, Jan," Thelma said. "Stop admiring your own hand. It's really disgusting."

A ghost of a smile flickered over his lips, but he let his strong, nervous fingers remain as they were. "I'd sell my soul for a drag right now."

"Daddy keeps a pack in the glove compartment," Thelma said. "I'd get them if my fingernails weren't so long."

"*I'll* get it open," John said. He did. They fished one cigarette out of the old pack of Old Golds they found and took alternate puffs. "Ah," John said, "that first drag of the day, clawing and scraping its way down your throat."

"Be on the lookout for Daddy. They hate my smoking."

"Thelma."

"Yes?" She stared deep into his eyes, her face half hidden in shadow.

"Don't pluck your eyebrows."

"I think it looks nice."

"It's like calling me 'Jan.' " There was a silence, not awkward.

"Get rid of the rette, Jan. Daddy just passed the window."

Being in the liquor store had put Mr. Lutz in a soberer mood. "Here you be, John," he said, in a businesslike way. He handed John a tall, velvet-red bottle. "Better let me drive. You drive like a veteran, but I know the short cuts."

"I can walk from your house, Mr. Lutz," John said, knowing Mr. Lutz wouldn't make him walk. "Thanks an awful lot for all you've done."

"I'll drive you up. People from Philadelphia can't be kept waiting. We can't make this young man walk a mile, now can we, Tessie?" Nobody knew what to say to this last remark, so they kept quiet all the way, although several things were bothering John.

When the car stopped in front of his house, a country house but close to the road, he forced himself to ask, "Say, Mr. Lutz. I wonder if there was any change?"

"What? Oh. Goodness. I nearly forgot. You'll have your daddy thinking I'm a crook." He reached into his pocket and without looking handed John a dollar, a quarter, and a penny.

"This seems like a lot," John said. The wine must be cheap. Maybe he should have let his mother call his father at school to pick it up, like she had wanted to.

"It's your change," Mr. Lutz said.

"Well, thanks an awful lot."

"Goodbye, now, my friend," Mr. Lutz said.

"So long." John slammed the door. "Goodbye, Thelma. Don't forget what I told you." He winked.

The car pulled out, and John walked up the path. "Don't forget what I told you," he repeated to himself, winking. The bottle was cool and heavy in his hands. He glanced at the label; it read *Château Mouton-Rothschild 1937*.

A Sense of Shelter

SNOW FELL against the high school all day, wet big-flaked snow that did not accumulate well. Sharpening two pencils, William looked down on a parking lot that was a blackboard in reverse; car tires had cut smooth arcs of black into the white, and wherever a school bus had backed around, it had left an autocratic signature of two *V*'s. The snow, though at moments it whirled opaquely, could not quite bleach these scars away. The temperature must be exactly freezing. The window was open a crack, and a canted pane of glass lifted outdoor air into his face, coating the cedar-wood scent of pencil shavings with the transparent odor of the wet windowsill. With each revolution of the handle his knuckles came within a fraction of an inch of the tilted glass, and the faint chill this proximity breathed on them sharpened William's already acute sense of shelter.

The sky behind the shreds of snow was stone-colored. The murk inside the high classroom gave the air a solidity that limited the overhead radiance to its own vessels: six globes of dull incandescence floated on the top of a thin sea. The feeling the gloom gave him was not gloomy but joyous; he felt they were all sealed in, safe; the colors of cloth were dyed deeper, the sound of whispers was made more distinct, the smells of tablet paper and wet shoes and varnish and face powder pierced him with a sharp sense of possession. These were his classmates sealed in, his, the stupid as well as the clever, the plain as well as the lovely, his enemies as well as his friends, his. He felt like a king and seemed to move to his seat between the bowed heads of subjects that loved him less than he loved them. His seat was sanctioned by tradition; for twelve years he had sat at the rear of classrooms, William Young, flanked by Marsha Wyckoff and Andy Zimmerman. Once there had been two Zimmermans, but one went to work in his father's greenhouse, and in some classes—Latin and trig— there were none, and William sat at the edge of the class as if on the lip of a cliff, and Marsha Wyckoff became Marvin Wolf or Sandra Wade. It was always a desk, though; its surface altered from hour to hour but from the blue-stained ink well his mind could extract, like a chain of magicians' handkerchiefs, memories from the first grade on.

As a senior he was a kind of king, and as a teacher's pet another kind, a puppet king, who gathered in appointive posts and even, when the vote split between two football heroes, some elective ones. He was not popular, he had never had a girl, his intense friends of childhood had drifted off into teams and gangs, and in large groups—when the whole school, for instance, went in the fall to the beautiful, dung-and-cotton-candy-smelling county fair—he was always an odd man, without a seat on the bus home. But exclusion is itself a form of inclusion. He even had a nickname: Mip, because he stuttered. Taunts no longer much frightened him; he had come late into his physical inheritance, but this summer it had arrived, and he at last stood equal with his large, boisterous parents, and had to unbutton his shirt cuffs to get his wrists through them, and discovered he could pick up a basketball with one hand. So, his long legs blocking two aisles, he felt regal even in size and, almost trembling with happiness under the high globes of light beyond whose lunar glow invisible snowflakes were drowning on the gravel roof of his castle, he could believe that the long delay of unpopularity had been merely a consolidation, that he was at last strong enough to make his move. Today he would tell Mary Landis he loved her.

He had loved her ever since, a fat-faced tomboy with freckles and green eyes, she deftly stole his rubber-lined schoolbag on the walk back from second grade along Jewett Street and outran him—simply had better legs. The superior speed a boy was supposed to have failed to come; his kidneys burned with panic. In front of the grocery store next to her home she stopped and turned. She was willing to have him catch up. This humiliation on top of the rest was too much to bear. Tears broke in his throat; he spun around and ran home and threw himself on the floor of the front parlor, where his grandfather, feet twiddling, perused the newspaper and soliloquized all morning. In time the letter slot rustled, and the doorbell rang, and Mary gave his mother the schoolbag and the two of them politely exchanged whispers. Their voices had been to him, lying there on the carpet with his head wrapped in his arms, indistinguishable. Mother had always liked Mary. From when she had been a tiny girl dancing along the hedge on the end of an older sister's arm, Mother had liked her. Out of all the children that flocked, similar as pigeons, through the neighborhood, Mother's heart had reached out as if with claws and fastened on Mary. He never took the schoolbag to school again, he refused to touch it. He supposed it was still in the attic, still faintly smelling of its rubber lining.

Fixed high on the plaster like a wren clinging to a barn wall, the buzzer sounded the two-minute signal. In the middle of the classroom Mary Landis stood up, a Monitor badge pinned to her belly. Her broad red belt was buckled with a brass bow and arrow. She wore a lavender sweater with the sleeves pushed up to expose her forearms, a delicately cheap effect. Wild stories were told about her; perhaps it was merely his knowledge of these that put the hardness in her face. Her eyes seemed braced for squinting and their green was frosted. Her freckles had faded. William thought she laughed less this year; now that she was in the Secretarial Course and he in the College Preparatory, he saw her in only one class a day, this one, English. She stood a second, eclipsed at the thighs by Jack Stephens' zebra-striped shoulders, and looked back at the class with a stiff, worn glance, as if she had seen the same faces too many times before. Her habit of perfect posture emphasized the angularity she had grown into. There was a nervous edge, a boxiness in her bones, that must have been waiting all along under the childish fat. Her eye sockets were deeply indented, and her chin had a prim set that seemed in the murky air tremulous and defiant. Her skirt was cut square and straight. Below the waist she was lean; the legs that had outrun him were still athletic; she starred at hockey and cheerleading. Above, she was ample: stacked. She turned and in switching up the aisle encountered a boy's leg thrown into her path. She coolly looked down until it withdrew. She was used to such attentions. Her pronged chest poised, Mary proceeded out the door, and someone she saw in the hall made her smile, a wide smile full of warmth and short white teeth, and love scooped at William's heart. He *would* tell her.

In another minute, the second bell rasped. Shuffling through the perfumed crowds to his next class, he crooned to himself, in the slow, overenunciated manner of the Negro vocalist who had brought the song back this year:

> "Lah-vender blue, dilly dilly,
> Lavendih gree-heen;
> *Eef* I were king, dilly dilly,
> You would be queen."

.   .   .

The song gave him an exultant sliding sensation that intertwined with the pleasures of his day. He knew all the answers, he had done all the work, the teachers called upon him only to rebuke the ignorance of the others. In trig and soc. sci. both it was this way. In gym, the fourth hour of the morning, he, who was always picked near the last, startled his side by excelling at volleyball, leaping like a madman, shouting like a bully. The ball felt light as a feather against his big bones. His hair in wet quills from the shower, he walked in the icy air to Luke's Luncheonette, where he ate three twenty-cent hamburgers in a booth with three juniors. There was Barry Kruppman, a tall, hyperthyroid-eyed boy who came on the school bus from the country town of Bowsville and who was an amateur hypnotist; he told the tale of a Portland, Oregon, businessman who under hypnosis had been taken back through sixteen reincarnations to the condition of an Egyptian concubine in the household of a high priest of Isis. There was Barry's friend Lionel Griffin, a pudgy simp whose blond hair puffed out above his ears in two slick waxed wings. He was rumored to be a fairy, and in fact did seem most excited by the transvestite aspect of the soul's transmigration. And there was Lionel's female sidekick Virginia, a drab little mystery who chain-smoked English Ovals and never said anything. She had sallow skin and smudged eyes and Lionel kept jabbing her and shrieking, making William wince. He would rather have sat with members of his own class, who filled the other booths, but he would have had to force himself on them. These juniors welcomed his company. He asked, "Wuh-well, was he ever a c-c-c-cockroach, like Archy?"

Kruppman's face grew serious; his furry lids dropped down over the bulge of his eyes, and when they drew back, his pupils were as small and hard as BBs. "That's the really interesting thing. There was this gap, see, between his being a knight under Charlemagne and then a sailor on a ship putting out from Macedonia—that's where Yugoslavia is now—in the time of Nero; there was this gap, when the only thing the guy would do was walk around the office snarling and growling, see, like this." Kruppman worked his blotched ferret face up into a snarl and Griffin shrieked. "He tried to bite one of the assistants and they think that for six hundred years"—the uncanny, unhealthy seriousness of his whisper hushed Griffin momentarily—"for six hundred years he just was a series of wolves. Probably in the German forests. You see, when he was in Macedonia"—his whisper barely audible—"he murdered a woman."

Griffin squealed in ecstasy and cried, "Oh, Kruppman! Kruppman, how you do go on!" and jabbed Virginia in the arm so hard an English

Oval jumped from her hand and bobbled across the Formica table. William gazed over their heads in pain.

The crowd at the soda counter had thinned so that when the door to the outside opened he saw Mary come in and hesitate there for a second where the smoke inside and the snow outside swirled together. The mixture made a kind of—Kruppman's ridiculous story had put the phrase in his head—wolf-weather, and she was just a gray shadow caught in it alone. She bought a pack of cigarettes from Luke and went out again, a kerchief around her head, the pneumatic thing above the door hissing behind her. For a long time she had been at the center of whatever gang was the one: in the second grade the one that walked home up Jewett Street together, and in the sixth grade the one that went bicycling as far away as the quarry and the Rentschler estate and played touch football Saturday afternoons, and in the ninth grade the one that went roller-skating at Candlebridge Park with the tenth-grade boys, and in the eleventh grade the one that held parties lasting past midnight and that on Sundays drove in caravans as far as Philadelphia and back. And all the while there had been a succession of boyfriends, first Jack Stephens and Fritz March in their class and then boys a grade ahead and then Barrel Lord, who was a senior when they were sophomores and whose name was in the newspapers all football season, and then, this last summer, someone out of the school altogether, a man she met while working as a waitress in Alton. So this year her weekends were taken up, and the party gang carried on as if she had never existed, and nobody saw her much except in school and when she stopped by in Luke's to buy a pack of cigarettes. Her silhouette against the big window had looked wan, her head hooded, her face nibbled by light, her fingers fiddling on the veined counter with her coins. He yearned to reach out, to comfort her, but he was wedged deep in the shrill booths, between the jingling of the pinball machine and the twanging of the jukebox. The impulse left him with a disagreeable feeling. He had adored her too long to have his investment diminished by pity.

The two hours of the school afternoon held Latin and a study hall. In study hall, while the five people at the table with him played tic-tac-toe and sucked cough drops and yawned, he did all his homework for the next day. He prepared thirty lines of Vergil, Aeneas in the Underworld. The study hall was a huge low room in the basement of the building; its coziness crept into Tartarus. On the other side of the custard-colored wall the circular saw in the woodworking shop whined and gasped and then whined again; it bit off pieces of wood with a rising, somehow terrorized inflection—bzzzzzup! He solved ten problems in trigonometry. His mind cut neatly through their knots and separated them, neat stiff squares of answer, one by one from the long plank of problems that connected plane geometry with solid. Lastly, as the snow drifted down on a slant into the cement pits outside the steel-muntinned windows, he read a short story by Edgar Allan Poe. He closed the book softly on its pleasing final shudder. He gazed at the red, wet, menthol-scented inner membrane of Judy Whipple's yawn, rimmed with flaking pink lipstick, and yielded his conscience to the snug sense of his work done, of the snow falling, of the warm minutes that walked through their shelter so slowly. The perforated acoustic tiling above his head seemed the lining of a tube that would go all the way: high school merging into college, college into graduate school, graduate school into teaching at a college—section man, assistant, associate, *full* professor, possessor of a dozen languages and a thousand books, a man brilliant in his forties, wise in his fifties, renowned in his sixties, revered in his seventies, and then retired, serenely waiting until the time came for the last transition from silence to silence, and he would die, like Tennyson, with a copy of *Cymbeline* beside him on the moon-drenched bed.

After school he had to go to Room 101 and cut a sports cartoon into a stencil for the school paper. He liked the high school best when it was nearly empty. Then the janitors went down the halls sowing seeds of red wax and making an immaculate harvest with broad brooms, gathering all the fluff and hairpins and wrappers and powder that the animals had dropped that day. The basketball team thumped in the hollow gymnasium; the cheerleaders rehearsed behind drawn curtains on the stage. In Room 101 two empty-headed typists with stripes bleached into their hair banged away between giggles and mistakes. At her desk Mrs. Gregory, the faculty sponsor, wearily passed her pencil through misspelled news copy on tablet paper. William took the shadow box from the top of the filing cabinet and the styluses and little square plastic shading screens from their drawer and the stencil from the closet where the typed stencils hung, like fragile scarves, on hooks. "B-BALLERS BOW, 57–42," was the headline. He drew a tall b-baller bowing to a stumpy pagan idol, labelled "W" for victorious Weiserton High, and traced the drawing in the soft blue wax with the fine loop stylus. His careful breath grazed his knuckles. His eyebrows frowned while his heart bobbed happily on the giddy prattle of the typists. The shadow box was simply a black frame holding a pane of glass and lifted at one end by two legs so that the lightbulb, fitted in a metal tray, could slide underneath. As he worked, his eyes smarting, he mixed himself up with the lightbulb, felt himself burning under a slanting roof upon which a huge hand scratched. The glass grew hot; the danger in the job was pulling the softened wax with your damp hand, distorting or tearing the typed letters. Sometimes the center of an *o* stuck to your skin like a bit of blue confetti. But he was expert and cautious. He returned the things to their places feeling airily tall, heightened by Mrs. Gregory's appreciation, which she expressed by keeping her back turned, in effect stating that other staff members were undependable but William did not need to be watched.

In the hall outside Room 101 only the shouts of a basketball scrimmage reverberated; the chant of the cheerleaders had been silenced. Though he had done everything, he felt reluctant to leave. Neither of his parents— both worked—would be home yet, and this building was equally his home. He knew all its nooks. On the second floor of the annex, beyond the art room, there was a strange, narrow boys' lavatory that no one ever seemed to use. It was here one time that Barry Kruppman tried to hypnotize him and cure his stuttering. Kruppman's voice purred and his irises turned tiny in the bulging whites and for a moment William felt himself lean backward involuntarily, but he was distracted by the bits of bloodshot vein in the corners of those popping eyes. The folly of giving up his will to this weirdo occurred to him; he refused to let go and go under, and perhaps therefore his stuttering had continued.

The frosted window at the end of the long little room cast a watery light on the green floor and made the porcelain urinals shine like slices of moon. William washed his hands with exaggerated care, enjoying the lavish amount of powdered soap provided for him in this civic castle. He studied his face in the mirror, making infinitesimal adjustments to attain the absolutely most flattering angle, and then put his hands below his throat to get their strong, long-fingered beauty into the picture. As he walked toward the door he sang, closing his eyes and gasping as if he were a real Negro whose entire career depended upon the recording:

> "Who—told me so, dilly dilly,
> Who told me soho?
> *Aii* told myself, dilly dilly,
> I told me so."

When he emerged into the hall it was not empty: one girl walked down its varnished perspective toward him, Mary Landis, a scarf on her head and books in her arms. Her locker was up here, on the second floor of the annex. His own was in the annex basement. A ticking sensation that existed neither in the medium of sound nor of light crowded against his throat. She flipped the scarf back from her hair and in a conversational voice that carried well down the clean planes of the hall said, "Hi, Billy." The name came from way back, when they were both children, and made him feel small but brave.

"Hi. How are you?"

"Fine." Her smile broadened out from the *F* of this word.

What was so funny? Was she really, as it seemed, pleased to see him? "Du-did you just get through cheer-cheer-cheerleading?"

"Yes. Thank God. *Oh*, she's so awful. She makes us do the same stupid locomotives for every cheer; I told her, no wonder nobody cheers any more."

"This is M-M-Miss Potter?" He blushed, feeling that he made an ugly face in getting past the *M*. When he got caught in the middle of a sentence the constriction was somehow worse. He admired the way words poured up her throat, distinct and petulant.

"Yes, Potbottom Potter," she said, "she's just aching for a man and takes it out on us. I wish she would get one. Honestly, Billy, I have half a mind to quit. I'll be so glad when June comes, I'll never set foot in this idiotic building again."

Her lips, pale with the lipstick worn off, crinkled bitterly. Foreshortened from the height of his eyes, her face looked cross as a cat's. It a little shocked him that poor Miss Potter and this kind, warm school stirred her to what he had to take as actual anger; this grittiness in her was the first abrasive texture he had struck today. Couldn't she see around teachers, into their fatigue, their poverty, their fear? It had been so long since he had spoken to her, he wasn't sure how coarse she had become. "Don't quit," he brought out of his mouth at last. "It'd be n-n-n-nuh—it'd be nothing without you."

He pushed open the door at the end of the hall for her and as she passed under his arm she looked up and said, "Why, aren't you sweet?"

The stairwell, all asphalt and iron, smelled of galoshes. It felt more secret than the hall, more specially theirs; there was something magical in the rapid multiplication of planes and angles as they descended that lifted the spell on his tongue, so that words came as quickly as his feet pattered on the steps.

"No, I mean it," he said, "you're really a beautiful cheerleader. But then you're beautiful period."

"I've skinny legs."

"Who told you that?"

"Somebody."

"Well, *he* wasn't very sweet."

"No."

"Why do you hate this poor old school?"

"Now, Billy. You know you don't care about this junky place any more than I do."

"I love it. It breaks my heart to hear you say you want to get out, because then I'll never see you again."

"You don't care, do you?"

"Why, sure I care; you *know*"—their feet stopped; they had reached bottom, the first-floor landing, two brass-barred doors and a grimy radiator— "I've always li-loved you."

"You don't mean that."

"I do too. It's ridiculous but there it is. I wanted to tell you today and now I have."

He expected her to laugh and go out the door, but instead she showed an unforeseeable willingness to discuss this awkward matter. He should have realized before this that women enjoy being talked to. "It's a very silly thing to say," she asserted tentatively.

"I don't see why," he said, fairly bold now that he couldn't seem more ridiculous, and yet picking his words with a certain strategic care. "It's not *that* silly to love somebody, I mean what the hell. Probably what's silly is not to do anything about it for umpteen years, but, then, I never had an opportunity, I thought."

He set his books down on the radiator and she set hers down beside his. "What kind of opportunity were you waiting for?"

"Well, see, that's it; I didn't know." He wished, in a way, she would go out the door. But she had propped herself against the wall and plainly awaited more conversation. "Yuh-you were such a queen and I was such a nothing and I just didn't really want to presume." It wasn't very interesting; it puzzled him that she seemed to be interested. Her face had grown quite stern, her mouth small and thoughtful, and he made a gesture with his hands intended to release her from the bother of thinking about it. After all, it was just a disposition of his heart, nothing permanent or expensive; perhaps it was just his mother's idea anyway. Half in impatience to close the account, he asked, "Will you marry me?"

"You don't want to marry me," she said. "You're going to go on and be somebody."

He blushed in pleasure; is this how she saw him, is this how they all saw him; as nothing now, but in time somebody? Had his hopes always been obvious? He dissembled, saying, "No, I'm not. But anyway, you're great now. You're so pretty, Mary."

"Oh, Billy," she said, "if you were me for just one day you'd hate it."

She said this rather blankly, watching his eyes; he wished her voice had shown more misery. In his world of closed surfaces a panel, carelessly pushed, had opened, and he hung in this openness paralyzed, unable to think what to say. Nothing he could think of quite fit the abruptly immense context. The radiator cleared its throat. Its heat made, in the intimate volume just this side of the doors on whose windows the snow beat limply, a provocative snugness. He supposed he should try to kiss her, and stepped forward, his hands lifting toward her shoulders. Mary sidestepped between him and the radiator and put the scarf back on. She lifted the cloth like a broad plaid halo above her head and then wrapped it around her chin and knotted it so she looked, in her red galoshes and bulky coat, like a peasant woman in a movie about Europe. With her hair swathed, her face seemed pale and chunky, and when she recradled the books in her arms her back bent humbly. "It's too hot in here," she said. "I've got to wait for some-body." The disconnectedness of the two statements seemed natural in the fragmented atmosphere his stops and starts had produced. She bucked the brass bar with her shoulder and the door slammed open; he followed her into the weather.

"For the person who thinks your legs are too skinny?"

"Could be, Mip." As she looked up at him a snowflake caught on the lashes of one eye. She jerkily rubbed that cheek on the shoulder of her coat and stamped a foot, splashing slush. Cold water gathered on the back of his thin shirt. He put his hands in his pockets and pressed his arms against his sides to keep from shivering.

"Thuh-then you wo-won't marry me?" His instinct told him the only way back was by going forward, ridiculously.

"We don't know each other," she said.

"My God," he said. "Why not? I've known you since kindergarten."

"What do you know about me?"

This awful seriousness of hers; he must dissolve it. "That you're not a virgin." But instead of making her laugh this made her face go dead and turned it away. Like beginning to kiss her, it was a mistake. In part, he felt grateful for his mistakes; they were like loyal friends who are nevertheless embarrassing. "What do you know about *me?*" he asked, setting himself up for a finishing insult but dreading it. He hated the stiff feel of his smile between his cheeks; he glimpsed, as if the snow were a mirror, how hate-ful he looked.

"That you're basically very nice."

Her reply blinded him to his physical discomfort, set him burning with regret. "Listen," he said, "I did love you. Let's at least get that straight."

"You never loved anybody, Billy," she said. "You don't know what it is."

"O.K.," he said. "Pardon me."

"You're excused."

"You better wait in the school," he told her. "He's-eez-eez going to be a long time."

She didn't answer and walked a little distance, along the slack cable that divided the parking lot from the softball field. One bicycle, rusted as if it had been there for years, leaned in the rack, its fenders supporting crescents of white.

The warmth inside the door felt heavy. William picked up his books and ran his pencil across the black ribs of the radiator before going down the stairs to his locker in the annex basement. The shadows were thick at the foot of the steps; suddenly it felt late, he must hurry and get home. He was seized by the irrational fear that the school authorities were going to lock him in. The cloistered odors of paper, sweat, and, from the wood-shop at the far end of the basement hall, sawdust no longer flattered him; the tall green double lockers appeared to study him critically through the three air slits near their tops. When he opened his locker, and put his books on his shelf, below Marvin Wolf's, and removed his coat from his hook, his self seemed to crawl into the long dark space thus made vacant, the humiliated, ugly, educable self. In answer to a flick of his large hand the steel door weightlessly floated shut, and through the length of his body he felt so clean and free he smiled. Between now and the happy future predicted for him he had nothing, almost literally nothing, to do.

Flight

AT THE AGE OF SEVENTEEN I was poorly dressed and funny-looking, and went around thinking about myself in the third person. "Allen Dow strode down the street and home." "Allen Dow smiled a thin sardonic smile." Consciousness of a special destiny made me both arrogant and shy. Years before, when I was eleven or twelve, just on the brink of ceasing to be a little boy, my mother and I, one Sunday afternoon — my father was busy, or asleep — hiked up to the top of Shale Hill, a child's mountain that formed one side of the valley that held our town. There the town lay under us, Olinger, perhaps a thousand homes, the best and biggest of them climbing Shale Hill toward us, and beyond them the blocks of brick houses, one- and two-family, the homes of my friends, sloping down to the pale thread of the Alton Pike, which strung together the high school, the tennis courts, the movie theatre, the town's few stores and gasoline stations, the elementary school, the Lutheran church. On the other side lay more homes, including our own, a tiny white patch placed just where the land began to rise toward the opposite mountain, Cedar Top. There were rims and rims of hills beyond Cedar Top, and, looking south, we could see the pike dissolving in other towns and turning out of sight amid the patches of green and brown farmland, and it seemed the entire county was lying exposed under a thin veil of haze. I was old enough to feel uneasy at standing there alone with my mother, beside a wind-stunted spruce tree, on a long spine of shale. Suddenly she dug her fingers into the hair on my head and announced, "There we all are, and there we'll all be forever." She hesitated before the word "forever," and hesitated again before adding, "Except you, Allen. You're going to fly." A few birds were hung far out over the valley, at the level of our eyes, and in her impulsive way she had just plucked the image from them, but it felt like the clue I had been waiting all my childhood for. My most secret self had been made to respond, and I was intensely embarrassed, and irritably ducked my head out from under her melodramatic hand.

She was impulsive and romantic and inconsistent. I was never able to develop this spurt of reassurance into a steady theme between us. That she continued to treat me like an ordinary child seemed a betrayal of the vision she had made me share. I was captive to a hope she had tossed off and forgotten. My shy attempts to justify irregularities in my conduct—reading late at night or not coming back from school on time—by appealing to the image of flight were received with a startled blank look, as if I were talking nonsense. It seemed outrageously unjust. Yes, but, I wanted to say, yes, but it's *your* nonsense. And of course it was just this that made my appeal ineffective: her knowing that I had not made it mine, that I cynically intended to exploit both the privileges of being extraordinary and the pleasures of being ordinary. She feared my wish to be ordinary; once she did respond to my protest that I was learning to fly, by crying with red-faced ferocity, "You'll never learn, you'll stick and die in the dirt just like I'm doing. Why should you be better than your mother?"

She had been born ten miles to the south, on a farm she and her mother had loved. Her mother, a small fierce woman who looked more like an Arab than a German, worked in the fields with the men, and drove the wagon to market ten miles away every Friday. When still a tiny girl, my mother rode with her, and my impression of those rides is of fear—the little girl's fear of the gross and beery men who grabbed and hugged her, her fear of the wagon's breaking, of the produce's not selling, of her father's condition when at nightfall they returned. Friday was his holiday, and he drank. His drinking is impossible for me to picture, for I never knew him except as an enduring, didactic, almost Biblical old man, whose one passion was reading the newspapers and whose one hatred was of the Republican Party. There was something public about him; now that he is dead I keep seeing bits of him attached to famous politicians—his watch chain and his plump, square stomach in old films of Theodore Roosevelt, his high-top shoes and the tilt of his head in a photograph of Alfalfa Bill Murry. Alfalfa Bill is turning his head to talk, and holds his hat by the crown, pinching it between two fingers and a thumb, a gentle and courtly grip that reminded me so keenly of my grandfather that I tore the picture out of *Life* and put it in a drawer.

Laboring in the soil had never been congenial to my grandfather, though with his wife's help he prospered by it. Then, in an era when success was hard to avoid, he began to invest in stocks. In 1922 he bought our large white home in the town—its fashionable section had not yet shifted to the Shale Hill side of the valley—and settled in to reap his dividends. He believed to his death that women were foolish, and the broken hearts of his two must have seemed specially so. The dignity of finance for the indignity of farming must have struck him as an eminently advantageous exchange. It strikes me that way, too, and how to reconcile my idea of those fear-ridden wagon rides with the grief that my mother insists she and her mother felt at being taken from the farm? Perhaps prolonged fear is a ground of love. Or perhaps, and likelier, the equation is long and complex, and the few factors I know—the middle-aged woman's mannish pride of land, the adolescent girl's pleasure in riding horses across the fields, their common feeling of rejection in Olinger—are enclosed in brackets and heightened by coefficients that I cannot see. Or perhaps it is not love of land but its absence that needs explaining, in my grandfather's fastidiousness and pride. He believed that as a boy he had been overworked, and bore his father a grudge that my mother could never understand. Her grandfather to her was a saintly slender giant, over six feet tall when this was a prodigy, who knew the names of everything, like Adam in Eden. In his old age he was blind. When he came out of the house, the dogs rushed forward to lick his hands. When he lay dying, he requested a Gravenstein apple from the tree on the far edge of the meadow, and his son brought him a Krauser from the orchard near the house. The old man refused it, and my grandfather made a second trip, but in my mother's eyes the outrage had been committed, an insult without provocation. What had his father done to him? The only specific complaint I ever heard my grandfather make was that, when he was a boy and had to fetch water for the men in the fields, his father would tell him sarcastically, "Pick up your feet; they'll come down themselves." How incongruous! As if each generation of parents commits atrocities against their children which by God's decree remain invisible to the rest of the world.

I remember my grandmother as a little dark-eyed woman who talked seldom and was always trying to feed me, and then as a hook-nosed profile pink against the lemon cushions of the casket. She died when I was seven. All the rest I know about her is that she was the baby of twelve children, that while she was alive she made our yard one of the most beautiful in town, and that I am supposed to resemble her brother Pete.

My mother was precocious; she was fourteen when they moved, and for three years had been attending the county normal school. She graduated from Lake College, near Philadelphia, when she was only twenty, a tall handsome girl with a self-deprecatory smile, to judge from one of the curling photographs kept in a shoebox that I was always opening as a child, as if it might contain the clue to the quarrels in my house. My mother stands at the end of our brick walk, beside the elaborately trimmed end of our privet hedge—in shape a thick square column mounted by a rough ball of leaf. The ragged arc of a lilac bush in flower cuts into the right edge of the photograph, and behind my mother I can see a vacant lot where there has been a house ever since I can remember. She poses with a kind of country grace in a long light-colored coat, un-buttoned to expose her beads and a short yet somehow demure flapper dress. Her hands are in her coat pockets, a beret sits on one side of her bangs, and there is a swank about her that seemed incongruous to me, examining this picture on the stained carpet of an ill-lit old house in the closing years of the Thirties and in the dark of the warring Forties. The costume and the girl in it look so up-to-date, so formidable. It was my grandfather's pleasure, in his prosperity, to give her a generous clothes allowance. My father, the penniless younger son of a New Jersey Presby-terian minister, had worked his way through Lake College by waiting on tables, and still speaks with mild resentment of the beautiful clothes that Lillian Baer wore. This aspect of my mother caused me some pain in high school; she was a fabric snob, and insisted on buying my slacks and sport shirts at the best store in Alton, and since we had little money, she bought me few, when of course what I needed was what my classmates had—a wide variety of cheap clothes.

At the time the photograph was taken, my mother wanted to go to New York. What she would have done there, or exactly what she wanted to do, I don't know; but her father forbade her. "Forbid" is a husk of a word today, but at that time, in that old-fashioned province, in the mouth of an "indulgent father," it apparently was still vital, for the force of that forbidding continued to be felt in the house for years, and when I was a child, as one of my mother's endless harangues to my grandfather climbed toward its weeping peak, I could feel it around and above me, like a large root encountered by an earthworm.

Perhaps in a reaction of anger my mother married my father, Victor Dow, who at least took her as far away as Wilmington, where he had made a beginning with an engineering firm. But the Depression hit, my father was laid off, and the couple came to the white brick house in Olinger, where my grandfather sat reading the newspapers that traced his stocks' decline into worthlessness. I was born. My grandmother went around as a cleaning lady, and grew things in our quarter-acre yard to sell. We kept chickens, and there was a large plot of asparagus. After she had died, in a frightened way I used to seek her in the asparagus patch. By midsummer it would be a forest of dainty green trees, some as tall as I was, and in their frothy touch a spirit seemed to speak, and in the soft thick net of their intermingling branches a promise seemed to be caught, as well as a menace. The asparagus trees were frightening; in the center of the patch, far from the house and the alley, I would fall under a spell, and become tiny, and wander among the great smooth green trunks expecting to find a little house with a smoking chimney, and in it my grandmother. She herself had believed in ghosts, which made her own ghost potent. Even now, sitting alone in my own house, I hear a board creak in the kitchen and look up fearing she will come through the doorway. And at night, just before I fall asleep, her voice calls my name in a penetrating whisper, or calls, *"Pete."*

My mother went to work in an Alton department store, selling curtain fabric for fourteen dollars a week. During the daytime of my first year of life it was my father who took care of me. He has said since, flattering me as he always does, that it was having me on his hands that kept him from going insane. It may have been this that has made my affection for him so inarticulate, as if I were still a wordless infant looking up into the mothering blur of his male face. And that same shared year helps account, perhaps, for his gentleness with me, for his willingness to praise, as if everything I do has something sad and crippled about it. He feels sorry for me; my birth coincided with the birth of a national misery—only recently has he stopped calling me by the nickname "Young America." Around my first birthday he acquired a position teaching arithmetic and algebra in the Olinger high school, and though he was too kind and humorous to quell discipline problems, he endured his job day by day and year by year and eventually came to occupy a place in this alien town, so that I believe there are now one or two dozen ex-students, men and women nearing middle age, who carry around with them some piece of encouragement my father gave them, or remember some sentence of his that helped shape them. Certainly there are many who remember the antics with which he burlesqued his discomfort in the classroom. He kept a confiscated cap pistol in his desk, and upon getting an especially stupid answer, he would take it out and, wearing a preoccupied, regretful expression, shoot himself in the head.

My grandfather was the last to go to work. It was humbling work. He was hired by the borough crew, men who went around the streets shovelling stones and spreading tar. Bulky and ominous in their overalls, wreathed in steam, and associated with dramatic and portentous equipment, these men had grandeur in the eyes of a child, and it puzzled me, as I walked to and from elementary school, that my grandfather refused to wave to me or confess his presence in any way. Curiously strong for a fastidious man, he kept at it well into his seventies, when his sight failed. It was my task then to read his beloved newspapers to him as he sat in his chair by the bay window, twiddling his high-top shoes in the sunshine. I teased him, reading too fast, then maddeningly slow, skipping from column to column to create one long chaotic story; I read him the sports page, which did not interest him, and mumbled the editorials. Only the speed of his feet's twiddling betrayed vexation. When I'd stop, he would plead mildly in his rather beautiful, old-fashioned, elocutionary voice, "Now just the obituaries, Allen. Just the names, to see if anyone I know is there." I imagined, as I rudely barked at him the list of names that might contain the name of a friend, that I was avenging my mother; I believed that she hated him, and for her sake I tried to hate him also. From her incessant resurrection of mysterious grievances buried far back in the sunless earth of the time before I was born, I had been able to deduce only that he was an evil man, who had ruined her life, that fair creature in the beret. I did not understand. She fought with him not because she wanted to fight but because *she could not bear to leave him alone.*

Sometimes, glancing up from the sheet of print where our armies swarmed in retreat like harried insects, I would catch the old man's head in the act of lifting slightly to receive the warm sunshine on his face, a dry frail face ennobled by its thick crown of combed corn-silk hair. It would dawn on me then that his sins as a father were likely no worse than any father's. But my mother's genius was to give the people closest to her mythic immensity. I was the phoenix. My father and grandmother were legendary invader-saints, she springing out of some narrow vein of Arab blood in the German race and he crossing over from the Protestant wastes of New Jersey, both of them serving and enslaving their mates with their prodigious powers of endurance and labor. For my mother felt that she and her father alike had been destroyed by marriage, been made captive by people better yet less than they. It was true, my father had loved Mom Baer, and her death made him seem more of an alien than ever. He, and her ghost, stood to one side, in the shadows but separate from the house's dark core, the inheritance of frustration and missed opportunities that had descended from my grandfather to my mother to me, and that I, with a few beats of my grown wings, was destined to reverse and redeem.

At the age of seventeen, in the fall of my senior year, I went with three girls to debate at a high school over a hundred miles away. They were, all three, bright girls, A students; they were disfigured by A's as if by acne. Yet even so it excited me to be mounting a train with them early on a Friday morning, at an hour when our schoolmates miles away were slumping into the seats of their first class. Sunshine spread broad bars of dust down the length of the half-empty car, and through the windows Pennsylvania unfurled a brown scroll scribbled with industry. Black pipes raced beside the tracks for miles. At rhythmic intervals one of them looped upward, like the Greek letter Ω. "Why does it do that?" I asked. "Is it sick?"

"Condensation?" Judith Potteiger suggested in her shy, transparent voice. She loved science.

"No," I said. "It's in pain. It's writhing! It's going to grab the train! Look out!" I ducked, honestly a little scared. All the girls laughed.

Judith and Catharine Miller were in my class, and expected me to be amusing; the third girl, a plump small junior named Molly Bingaman, had not known what to expect. It was her fresh audience I was playing to. She was the best dressed of the three, and the most poised; this made me suspect that she was the least bright. She had been substituted at the last moment for a sick member of the debating team; I knew her just by seeing her in the halls and in assembly. From a distance she seemed dumpy and prematurely adult, with a trace of a double chin. But up close she was gently fragrant, and against the weary purple cloth of the train seats her skin seemed luminous. She had beautiful skin, heartbreaking skin a pencil dot would have marred, and large blue eyes equally clear. She and I sat side by side, facing the two senior girls, who more and more took on the wan slyness of matchmakers. It was they who had made the seating arrangements.

We debated in the afternoon, and won. Yes, the German Federal Republic *should* be freed of all Allied control. The school, a posh castle on the edge of a miserable coal city, was the site of a statewide cycle of debates that was to continue into Saturday. There was a dance Friday night in the gym. I danced with Molly mostly, though to my annoyance she got in with a set of Harrisburg boys while I conscientiously pushed Judith and Catharine around the floor. We were stiff dancers, the three of us; only Molly made me seem good, floating backward from my feet fearlessly as her cheek rumpled my moist shirt. The gym was hung with orange and black crepe paper in honor of Halloween, and the pennants of all the competing schools were fastened to the walls, and a twelve-piece band pumped away blissfully on the year's sad tunes—"Heartaches," "Near You," "That's My Desire." A great cloud of balloons gathered in the steel girders was released. There was pink punch, and a local girl sang.

Judith and Catharine decided to leave before the dance was over, and I made Molly come too, though she was in a literal sweat of pleasure; her perfect skin in the oval above her neckline was flushed and glazed. I realized, with a little shock of possessiveness and pity, that she was unused to attention back home, in competition with the gorgeous Olinger ignorant.

We walked together to the house where the four of us had been boarded, a large frame house owned by an old couple and standing with lonely dignity in a semi-slum. Judith and Catharine turned up the walk, but Molly and I, with a diffident decision that I believe came from her initiative, continued, "to walk around the block." We walked miles, stopping off after midnight at a trolley-car-shaped diner. I got a hamburger, and she impressed me by ordering coffee. We walked back to the house and let ourselves in with the key we had been given; but instead of going upstairs to our rooms we sat downstairs in the dark living room and talked softly for more hours.

What did we say? I talked about myself. It is hard to hear, much less remember, what we ourselves say, just as it might be hard for a movie projector, given life, to see the shadows its eye of light is casting. A transcript, could I produce it, of my monologue through the wide turning point of that night, with all its word-by-word conceit, would distort the picture: this living room miles from home, the street light piercing the chinks in the curtains and erecting on the wallpaper rods of light the size of yardsticks, our hosts and companions asleep upstairs, the incessant sigh of my voice, coffee-primed Molly on the floor beside my chair, her stockinged legs stretched out on the rug; and this odd sense in the room, a tasteless and odorless aura as of a pool of water widening.

I remember one exchange. I must have been describing the steep waves of fearing death that had come over me ever since early childhood, about one every three years, and I ended by supposing that it would take great courage to be an atheist. "But I bet you'll become one," Molly said. "Just to show yourself that you're brave enough." I was flattered. Within a few years, while I still remembered many of her words, I realized how touchingly gauche our assumption was that an atheist is a lonely rebel; for mobs of men are united in atheism, and oblivion—the dense leadlike sea that would occasionally sweep over me—is to them a weight as negligible as the faint pressure of their wallets in their hip pockets. This grotesque and tender misestimate of the world flares in my memory of our conversation like one of the innumerable matches we struck.

The room filled with smoke. Too weary to sit, I lay down on the floor beside her, and stroked her silver arm in silence, yet still was too timid to act on the wide and negative aura that I did not understand was of compliance. On the upstairs landing, as I went to turn into my room, Molly came forward purposefully and kissed me. With clumsy force I entered the negative space that had been waiting. Her lipstick smeared in little unflattering flecks into the skin around her mouth; it was as if I had been given a face to eat, and the presence of bone—skull under skin, teeth behind lips—impeded me. We stood for a long time under the burning hall light, until my neck began to ache from bowing. My legs were trembling when we finally parted and sneaked into our rooms. In bed I thought, "Allen Dow tossed restlessly," and realized it was the first time that day I had thought of myself in the third person.

On Saturday morning, we lost our debate. I was sleepy and verbose and haughty, and some of the students in the audience began to boo whenever I opened my mouth. The principal came up on the stage and made a scolding speech, which finished me and my cause, untrammelled Germany. On the train back, Catharine and Judith arranged the seating so that they sat behind Molly and me, and spied on only the tops of our heads. For the first time, on that ride home, I felt what it was to bury a humiliation in the body of a woman. Nothing but the friction of my face against hers drowned out the echo of those boos. When we kissed, a red shadow would well under my lids and eclipse the hostile hooting faces of the debate audience, and when our lips parted, the bright inner sea would ebb, and there the faces would be again, more intense than ever. With a shudder of shame I'd hide my face on her shoulder, and in the warm darkness there, while a frill of her prissy collar gently scratched my nose, I felt united with Hitler and all the villains, traitors, madmen, and failures who had managed to keep, up to the moment of capture or death, a woman with them. This had puzzled me. In high school females were proud and remote; in the newspapers they were fantastic monsters of submission. And now Molly administered reassurance to me with small motions and bodily adjustments that had about them a strange flavor of the practical.

Our parents met us at the station. I was startled at how tired my mother looked. There were deep blue dents on either side of her nose, and her hair seemed somehow dissociated from her head, as if it were a ragged, half-gray wig she had put on carelessly. She had become in middle age a heavy woman, and her weight, which she usually carried upright, like a kind of wealth, had slumped away from her ownership and seemed, in the sullen light of the railway platform, to weigh on the world. I asked, "How's Grandpa?" He had taken to bed several months before, with pains in his chest.

"He still sings," she said, rather sharply. For entertainment in his increasing blindness my grandfather had long ago begun to sing, and his shapely old voice would pour forth hymns, forgotten comic ballads, and camp-meeting songs at any hour. His memory seemed to improve the longer he lived.

My mother's irritability was more manifest in the private cavity of the car; her heavy silence oppressed me. "You look so tired, Mother," I said, trying to take the offensive.

"That's nothing to how you look," she answered. "What happened up there? You stoop like an old married man."

"Nothing happened," I lied. My cheeks were parched, as if her high steady anger had the power of giving sunburn.

"I remember that Bingaman girl's mother when we first moved to town. She was the smuggest little snip north of the pike. They're real old Olinger stock, you know. They have no use for hillbillies."

My father tried to change the subject. "Well, you won one debate, Allen, and that's more than I would have done. I don't see how you do it."

"Why, he gets it from you, Victor. I've never won a debate with you."

"He gets it from Pop Baer. If that man had gone into politics, Lillian, all the misery of his life would have been avoided."

"Dad was never a debater. He was a bully. Don't go with little women, Allen. It puts you too close to the ground."

"I'm not *going* with *any*body, Mother. Really, you're so fanciful."

"Why, when she stepped off the train, from the way her chins bounced I thought she had eaten a canary. And then making my poor son, all skin and bones, carry her bag. When she walked by me I honestly was afraid she'd spit in my eye."

"I had to carry somebody's bag. I'm sure she doesn't know who you are." Though it was true I had talked a good deal about my family the night before.

My mother turned away from me. "You see, Victor—he defends her. When I was his age that girl's mother gave me a cut I'm still bleeding from, and my own son attacks me on behalf of her fat little daughter. I wonder if her mother put her up to catching him."

"Molly's a nice girl," my father interceded. "She never gave me any trouble in class, like some of those smug bastards." But he was curiously listless, for so Christian a man, in pronouncing this endorsement.

I discovered that nobody wanted me to go with Molly Bingaman. My friends—for on the strength of being funny I did have some friends, classmates whose love affairs went on over my head but whom I could accompany, as clown, on communal outings—never talked with me about Molly, and when I brought her to their parties gave the impression of ignoring her, so that I stopped taking her. Teachers at school would smile an odd tight smile when they saw us leaning by her locker or hanging around in the stairways. The eleventh-grade English instructor— one of my "boosters" on the faculty, a man who was always trying to "challenge" me, to "exploit" my "potential"—took me aside and told me how dense she was. She just couldn't grasp the logical principles of restrictive and non-restrictive clauses. He confided her parsing mistakes to me as if they betrayed—as indeed in a way they did—limits that her graceful social manner concealed. Even the Fabers, an ultra-Republican couple who ran a luncheonette near the high school, showed pleasure whenever Molly and I broke up, and persistently treated my attachment as being a witty piece of play, like my pretense with Mr. Faber of being a Communist. The entire town seemed ensnarled in my mother's myth, that escape was my proper fate. It was as if I were a sport that the ghostly elders of Olinger had segregated from the rest of the livestock and agreed to donate in time to the air; this fitted with the ambiguous sensation I had always had in the town, of being simultaneously flattered and rejected.

Molly's parents disapproved because in their eyes my family was déclassé. It was so persistently hammered into me that I was too good for Molly that I scarcely considered the proposition that, by another scale, she was too good for me. Further, Molly herself shielded me. Only once, exasperated by some tedious, condescending confession of mine, did she state that her mother didn't like me. "Why not?" I asked, genuinely surprised. I admired Mrs. Bingaman—she was beautifully preserved—and I always felt jolly in her house, with its white woodwork and matching furniture and vases of iris posing before polished mirrors.

"Oh, I don't know. She thinks you're flippant."

"But that's not true. Nobody takes himself more seriously than I do."

While Molly protected me from the Bingaman side of the ugliness, I conveyed the Dow side more or less directly to her. It infuriated me that nobody allowed me to be proud of her. I kept, in effect, asking her, Why was she stupid in English? Why didn't she get along with my friends? Why did she look so dumpy and smug?—this last despite the fact that she often, especially in intimate moments, looked beautiful to me. I was especially angry with her because this affair had brought out an ignoble, hysterical, brutal aspect of my mother that I might never have had to see otherwise. I had hoped to keep things secret from her, but even if her intuition had not been relentless, my father, at school, knew everything. Sometimes, indeed, my mother said that she didn't care if I went with Molly; it was my father who was upset. Like a frantic dog tied by one leg, she snapped in any direction, mouthing ridiculous fancies—such as that Mrs. Bingaman had pushed Molly on me just to keep me from going to college and giving the Dows something to be proud of—that would make us both suddenly start laughing. Laughter in that house that winter had a guilty sound. My grandfather was dying, and lay upstairs singing and coughing and weeping as the mood came to him, and we were too poor to hire a nurse, and too kind and cowardly to send him to a "home." It was still his house, after all. Any noise he made seemed to slash my mother's heart, and she was unable to sleep upstairs near him, and waited the nights out on the sofa downstairs. In her desperate state she would say unforgivable things to me even while the tears streamed down her face. I've never seen so many tears as I saw that winter.

Every time I saw my mother cry, it seemed I had to make Molly cry. I developed a skill at it; it came naturally to an only child who had been surrounded all his life by unhappy adults. Even in the heart of intimacy, half naked each of us, I would say something to keep her at a distance. We never made love in the final, coital sense. My reason was a mixture of idealism and superstition; I felt that if I took her virginity she would be mine forever. I depended overmuch on a technicality; she gave herself to me anyway, and I took her anyway, and have her still, for the longer I travel in a direction I could not have travelled with her the more clearly she seems the one person who loved me without advantage. I was a homely, comically ambitious poor boy, and I even refused to tell her I loved her, to pronounce the word "love"—an icy piece of pedantry that shocks me now that I have almost forgotten the pressured context in which it seemed wise.

In addition to my grandfather's illness, and my mother's grief, and my waiting to hear if I had won a scholarship to the one college that seemed good enough for me, I was burdened with managing too many petty affairs of my graduating class. I was in charge of yearbook write-ups, art editor of the school paper, chairman of the Class Gift Committee, director of the Senior Assembly, and teachers' workhorse. Frightened by my father's tales of nervous breakdowns he had seen, I kept listening for the sounds of my brain snapping, and the image of that gray, infinitely interconnected mass seemed to extend outward, to become my whole world, one dense organic dungeon, and I felt I had to get out; if I could just get out of this, into June, it would be blue sky, and I would be all right for life.

One Friday night in spring, after trying for over an hour to write thirty-five affectionate words for the yearbook about a null girl in the Secretarial Course I had never spoken a word to, I heard my grandfather begin coughing upstairs with a sound like dry membrane tearing, and I panicked. I called up the stairs, "Mother! I must go out."

"It's nine o'clock."

"I know, but I have to. I'm going crazy."

Without waiting to hear her answer or to find a coat, I left the house and backed our old car out of the garage. The weekend before, I had broken up with Molly again. All week I hadn't spoken to her, though I had seen her once in Faber's, with a boy in her class, averting her face while I, hanging by the side of the pinball machine, made rude wisecracks in her direction. I didn't dare go up to her door and knock so late at night; I just parked across the street and watched the lit windows of her house. Through their living-room window I could see one of Mrs. Bingaman's vases of hothouse iris standing on a white mantel, and my open car window admitted the spring air, which delicately smelled of wet ashes. Molly was probably out on a date with that moron in her class. But then the Bingamans' door opened, and her figure appeared in the rectangle of light. Her back was toward me, a coat was on her arm, and her mother seemed to be shouting. Molly closed the door and ran down off the porch and across the street and quickly got into the car, her eyes downcast. *She came.* When I have finally forgotten everything else—her powdery fragrance, her lucid cool skin, the way her lower lip was like a curved pillow of two cloths, the dusty red outer and wet pink inner—I'll still be grieved by this about Molly, that she came to me.

After I returned her to her house—she told me not to worry, her mother enjoyed shouting—I went to the all-night diner just beyond the Olinger town line and ate three hamburgers, ordering them one at a time, and drank two glasses of milk. It was after one o'clock when I got home, but my mother was still awake. She lay on the sofa in the dark, with the radio sitting on the floor murmuring Dixieland piped up from New Orleans by way of Philadelphia. Radio music was a steady feature of her insomniac life; not only did it help drown out the noise of her father upstairs but she seemed to enjoy it in itself. She would resist my father's pleas to come to bed by saying that the New Orleans program was not over yet. The radio was an old Philco we had always had; I had once drawn a fish on the orange disc of its celluloid dial, which had looked to my eyes like a fishbowl.

Her loneliness caught at me; I went into the living room and sat on a chair with my back to the window. For a long time she looked at me tensely out of the darkness. "Well," she said at last, "how was little hotpants?" The vulgarity this affair had brought out in her language appalled me.

"I made her cry," I told her.

"Why do you torment the girl?"

"To please you."

"It doesn't please me."

"Well, then, stop nagging me."

"I'll stop nagging you if you'll solemnly tell me you're willing to marry her."

I said nothing to this, and after waiting she went on in a different voice, "Isn't it funny, that you should show this weakness?"

"Weakness is a funny way to put it when it's the only thing that gives me strength."

"Does it really, Allen? Well. It may be. I forget, you were born here."

Upstairs, close to our heads, my grandfather, in a voice frail but still melodious, began to sing: "There is a happy land, far, far away, where saints in glory stand, bright, bright as day." We listened, and his voice broke into coughing, a terrible rending cough growing in fury, struggling to escape, and loud with fear he called my mother's name. She didn't stir. His voice grew enormous, a bully's voice, as he repeated, "Lillian! Lillian!" and I saw my mother's shape quiver with the force coming down the stairs into her; she was like a dam; and then the power, as my grandfather fell momentarily silent, flowed toward me in the darkness, and I felt intensely angry, and hated that black mass of suffering, even while I realized, with a rapid, light calculation, that I was too weak to withstand it.

In a dry tone of certainty and dislike—how hard my heart had become!—I told her, "All right. You'll win this one, Mother; but it'll be the last one you'll win."

My pang of fright, following this unprecedentedly cold insolence, blot-

ted my senses; the chair ceased to be felt under me, and the walls and furniture of the room fell away—there was only the dim orange glow of the
radio dial down below. In a husky voice that seemed to come across a
great distance my mother said, with typical melodrama, "Goodbye,
Allen."

The Happiest I've Been

NEIL HOVEY came for me wearing a good suit. He parked his father's gray Chrysler on the dirt ramp by our barn and got out and stood by the open car door in a double-breasted tan gabardine suit, his hands in his pockets and his hair combed with water, squinting up at a lightning rod an old hurricane had knocked crooked.

We were driving to Chicago, so I had dressed in worn-out slacks and an outgrown corduroy shirt. But Neil was the friend I had always been most relaxed with, so I wasn't very disturbed. My parents and I walked out from the house, across the low stretch of lawn that was mostly mud after the thaw that had come on Christmas Day, and my grandmother, though I had kissed her goodbye inside the house, came out onto the porch, stooped and rather angry-looking, her head haloed by wild old woman's white hair and the hand more severely afflicted by Parkinson's disease waggling at her breast in a worried way. It was growing dark and my grandfather had gone to bed. "Nev-er trust the man who wears the red necktie and parts his hair in the middle," had been his final advice to me.

We had expected Neil since midafternoon. Nineteen, almost twenty, I was a college sophomore home on vacation; that fall I had met in a fine-arts course a girl I had fallen in love with, and she had invited me to the New Year's party her parents always gave and to stay at her house a few nights. She lived in Chicago and so did Neil now, though he had gone to our high school. His father did something—sell steel was my impression, a huge man opening a briefcase and saying, "The I-beams are very good this year"—that required him to be always on the move, so that at about thirteen Neil had been boarded with Mrs. Hovey's parents, the Lancasters. They had lived in Olinger since the town was incorporated. Indeed, old Jesse Lancaster, whose sick larynx whistled when he breathed to us boys his shocking and uproarious thoughts on the girls that walked past his porch all day long, had twice been burgess. Neil's father meanwhile got a stationary job, but he let Neil stay to graduate; after the night he graduated, Neil drove throughout the next day to join his parents. From Chicago to this part of Pennsylvania was seventeen hours. In the twenty months he had been gone Neil had come east fairly often; he loved driving and Olinger was the one thing he had that was close to a childhood home. In Chicago he was working in a garage and getting his overlapping teeth straightened by the Army so they could draft him. Korea was on. He had to go back, and I wanted to go, so it was a happy arrangement. "You're all dressed up," I accused him immediately.

"I've been saying goodbye." The knot of his necktie was loose and the corners of his mouth were rubbed with pink. Years later my mother recalled how that evening his breath to her stank so strongly of beer she was frightened to let me go with him. "*Your* grandfather always thought *his* grandfather was a very dubious character," she said then.

My father and Neil put my suitcases into the trunk; they contained all the clothes I had brought home, for the girl and I were going to go back to college on the train together, and I would not see my home again until spring.

"Well, goodbye, boys," my mother said. "I think you're both very brave." In regard to me she meant the girl as much as the roads.

"Don't you worry, Mrs. Nordholm," Neil told her quickly. "He'll be safer than in his bed. I bet he sleeps from here to Indiana." He looked at me with an irritating imitation of her own fond gaze. When they shook hands goodbye it was with an equality established on the base of my helplessness. His being so slick startled me, but, then, you can have a friend for years and never see how he operates with adults.

I embraced my mother and over her shoulder tried to take, with the camera of my head, a snapshot I could keep of the house, the woods behind it and the sunset behind them, the bench beneath the walnut tree where my grandfather cut apples into skinless bits and fed them to himself, and the ruts in the soft lawn the bakery truck had made that morning.

We started down the half-mile of dirt road to the highway that, one way, went through Olinger to the city of Alton and, the other way, led through farmland to the Turnpike. It was luxurious after the stress of farewell to two-finger a cigarette out of the pack in my shirt pocket. My family knew I smoked but I didn't do it in front of them; we were all too sensitive to bear the awkwardness. I lit mine and held the match for Neil.

It was a relaxed friendship. We were about the same height and had the same degree of athletic incompetence and the same curious lack of whatever it was that aroused loyalty and compliance in beautiful girls. But it seemed to me the most important thing—about both our friendship and our failures to become, for all the love we felt for women, actual lovers—was that he and I lived with grandparents. This improved both our backward and forward vistas; we knew about the bedside commodes and midnight coughing fits that awaited most men, and we had a sense of childhoods before 1900, when the farmer ruled the land and America faced west. We had gained a dimension that made us gentle and humorous among peers but diffident at dances and hesitant in cars. Girls hate boys' doubts: they amount to insults. Gentleness is for married women to appreciate. (This is my thinking then.) A girl who has received out of nowhere a gift worth all Africa's ivory and Asia's gold wants more than just a good guy to bestow it on.

Coming onto the highway, Neil turned right toward Olinger instead of left toward the Turnpike. My reaction was to twist and assure myself through the rear window that, though a pink triangle of sandstone stared through the bare treetops, nobody at my house could possibly see.

When he was again in third gear, Neil asked, "Are you in a hurry?"

"No. Not especially."

"Schuman's having his New Year's party two days early so we can go. I thought we'd go for a couple hours and miss the Friday-night stuff on the Pike." His mouth moved and closed carefully over the dull, silver, painful braces.

"Sure," I said. "I don't care." In everything that followed there was this sensation of my being picked up and carried.

It was four miles from the farm to Olinger; we entered by Buchanan Road, driving past the tall white brick house I had lived in until I was thirteen. My grandfather had bought it before I was born and his stocks became bad, which had happened in the same year. The new owners had strung colored bulbs all along the front-door frame and the edges of the porch roof. Downtown the cardboard Santa Claus still nodded in the drugstore window but the loudspeaker on the undertaker's lawn had stopped broadcasting carols. It was quite dark now, so the arches of red and green lights above Grand Avenue seemed miracles of lift; in daylight you saw the bulbs were just hung from a straight cable by cords of different lengths. Larry Schuman lived on the other side of town, the newer side. Lights ran all the way up the front edges of his house and across the rain gutter. The next-door neighbor had a plywood reindeer-and-sleigh floodlit on his front lawn and a snowman of papier-mâché leaning tipsily (his eyes were *x*'s) against the corner of his house. No real snow had fallen yet that winter. The air this evening, though, hinted that harder weather was coming.

The Schumans' living room felt warm. In one corner a blue spruce drenched with tinsel reached to the ceiling; around its pot surged a drift of wrapping paper and ribbon and boxes, a few still containing presents, gloves and diaries and other small properties that hadn't yet been absorbed into the mainstream of affluence. The ornamental balls were big as baseballs and all either crimson or indigo; the tree was so well dressed I felt self-conscious in the same room with it, without a coat or tie and wearing an old green shirt too short in the sleeves. Everyone else was dressed for a party. Then Mr. Schuman stamped in comfortingly, crushing us all into one underneath his welcome, Neil and me and the three other boys who had showed up so far. He was dressed to go out on the town, in a camel topcoat and silvery silk muffler, smoking a cigar with the band still on. You could see in Mr. Schuman where Larry got the red hair and white eyelashes and the self-confidence, but what in the son was smirking and pushy was in the father shrewd and masterful. What the one used to make you nervous the other used to put you at ease. While Mr. was jollying us, Zoe Loessner, a new interest of Larry's and the only other girl at the party so far, was talking nicely to Mrs., nodding with her entire neck and fingering her Kresge pearls and blowing cigarette smoke through a corner of her mouth, to keep it away from the middle-aged woman's face. Each time Zoe spat out a plume, the shelf of honey hair overhanging her temple bobbed. Mrs. Schuman beamed serenely above her mink coat and rhinestone pocketbook. It was odd to see her dressed in the trappings of the prosperity that usually supported her good nature invisibly, like a firm mattress under a bright homely quilt. Everybody loved her. She was a prime product of the county, a Pennsylvania Dutch woman with sons, who loved feeding her sons and who imagined that the entire world, like her life, was going well. I never saw her not smile, except at her husband. At last she moved him into the outdoors. He turned at the threshold and did a trick with his knees and called in to us, "Be good, and if you can't be good, be careful."

With them out of the way, the next item was getting liquor. It was a familiar business. Did anybody have a forged driver's license? If not, who would dare to forge theirs? Larry could provide India ink. Then again, Larry's older brother Dale might be home and would go if it didn't take too much time. However, on weekends he often went straight from work to his fiancée's apartment and stayed until Sunday. If worse came to worst, Larry knew an illegal place in Alton, but they really soaked you. The problem was solved strangely. More people were arriving all the time and one of them, Cookie Behn, who had been held back one year and hence was deposited in our grade, announced that last November he had become in honest fact twenty-one. I at least gave Cookie my share of the money feeling a little queasy, sin had become so handy.

The party was the party I had been going to all my life, beginning with Ann Mahlon's first Halloween party, which I attended as a hot, lumbering, breathless, and blind Donald Duck. My mother had made the costume, and the eyes kept slipping, and were farther apart than my eyes, so that even when the clouds of gauze parted it was to reveal the frustrating depthless world seen with one eye. Ann, who because her mother loved her so much as a child had remained somewhat childish, and I and another boy and girl who were not involved in any romantic crisis went down into the Schumans' basement to play circular Ping-Pong. Armed with paddles, we stood each at a side of the table and when the ball was stroked ran around it counterclockwise, slapping the ball and screaming. To run better, the girls took off their heels and ruined their stockings on the cement floor. Their faces and arms and shoulder sections became flushed, and when a girl lunged forward toward the net the stiff neckline of her semi-formal dress dropped away and the white arcs of her brassiere could be glimpsed cupping fat, and when she reached high her shaved armpit gleamed like a bit of chicken skin. An earring of Ann's flew off and the two connected rhinestones skidded to lie near the wall, among the Schumans' power mower and badminton poles and empty bronze motor-oil cans twice punctured by triangles. All these images were immediately lost in the whirl of our running; we were dizzy before we stopped. Ann leaned on me getting back into her shoes.

When we pushed it open the door leading down into the cellar banged against the newel post of the carpeted stairs going to the second floor; a third of the way up these, a couple sat discussing. The girl, Jacky Iselin, cried without emotion—the tears and nothing else, like water flowing over wood. Some people were in the kitchen mixing drinks and making noise. In the living room others danced to records: 78s then, stiff discs stacked in a ponderous leaning cylinder on the spindle of the Schumans' console. Every three minutes with a click and a crash another dropped and the mood abruptly changed. One moment it would be "Stay as Sweet as You Are": Clarence Lang with the absolute expression of an idiot standing and rocking monotonously with June Kaufmann's boneless sad brown hand trapped in his and their faces, staring in the same direction, pasted together like the facets of an idol. The music stopped; when they parted, a big squarish dark patch stained the cheek of each. Then, the next moment, it would be Goodman's "Loch Lomond" or "Cherokee," and nobody but Margaret Lento wanted to jitterbug. She was a former interest of Larry's who was attending the party anyway; she lived outside of Olinger and had come with another girl. Mad, she danced by herself, swinging her head recklessly and snapping her backside; a corner of her skirt flipped a Christmas ball onto the rug, where it shattered into a dozen convex reflectors. Female shoes were scattered in pairs about the room. Some were flats, resting under the sofa shyly toed in; others were high heels lying cockeyed, the spike of one thrust into its mate.

Sitting alone and ignored in a great armchair, I experienced within a warm keen dishevelment, as if there were real tears in my eyes. Had things been less unchanged they would have seemed less tragic. But the girls who had stepped out of these shoes were with few exceptions the ones who had attended my life's party. The alterations were so small: a haircut, an engagement ring, a franker plumpness. While they wheeled above me I sometimes caught from their faces an unfamiliar glint, off of a hardness I did not remember, as if beneath their skins these girls were growing more dense. The brutality added to the features of the boys I knew seemed a more willed effect, more desired and so less grievous. Considering that there was a war on, surprisingly many were present, 4-F or at college or simply waiting to be called. Shortly before midnight the door rattled and there, under the porchlight, looking forlorn and chilled in their brief athletic jackets, stood three members of the class ahead of ours who in the old days always tried to crash Schuman's parties. At Olinger High they had been sports stars, and they still stood with that well-coördinated looseness, a look of dangling from strings. The three of them had enrolled together at Melanchthon, a small Lutheran college on the edge of Alton, and in this season played on the Melanchthon basketball team. That is, two did; the third hadn't been good enough. Schuman, out of cowardice more than mercy, let them in, and they hid without hesitation in the basement, and didn't bother us, having brought their own bottle.

There was one novel awkwardness. Darryl Bechtel had married Emmy Johnson and the couple came. Darryl had worked in his father's greenhouse and was considered dull; it was Emmy that we knew. At first no one danced with her, and Darryl didn't know how, but then Schuman, perhaps as host, dared. Others followed, but Schuman had her in his arms most often, and at midnight, when we were pretending the new year began, he kissed her; a wave of kissing swept the room now, and everyone struggled to kiss Emmy. Even I did. There was something about her being married that made it extraordinary. Her cheeks in flame, she kept glancing around for rescue, but Darryl, embarrassed to see his wife dance, had gone into old man Schuman's den, where Neil sat brooding, sunk in mysterious sorrow.

When the kissing subsided and Darryl emerged, I went in to see Neil. He was holding his face in his hands and tapping his foot to a record playing on Mr. Schuman's private phonograph: Krupa's "Dark Eyes." The arrangement was droning and circular and Neil had kept the record going for hours. He loved saxophones; I guess all of us children of that Depression vintage did. I asked him, "Do you think the traffic on the Turnpike has died down by now?"

He lifted down the tall glass on the cabinet beside him and took a convincing swallow. His face from the side seemed lean and somewhat blue. "Maybe," he said, staring at the ice cubes submerged in the ochre liquid. "The girl in Chicago's expecting you?"

"Well, yeah, but we can call and let her know, once *we* know."

"You think she'll spoil?"

"How do you mean?"

"I mean, won't you be seeing her all the time after we get there? Aren't you going to marry her?"

"I have no idea. I might."

"Well, then: you'll have the rest of Kingdom Come to see her." He looked directly at me, and it was plain in the blur of his eyes that he was sick-drunk. "The trouble with you guys that have all the luck," he said slowly, "is that you don't give a fuck about us that don't have any." Such an assault coming from Neil surprised me, as had his blarney with my mother hours before. In trying to evade his wounded stare, I discovered there was another person in the room: a girl sitting with her shoes on, reading *Holiday*. Though she held the magazine in front of her face I knew from her clothes and her unfamiliar legs that she was the friend Margaret Lento had brought. Margaret didn't come from Olinger but from Riverside, a section of Alton, not a suburb. She had met Larry Schuman at a summer job in a restaurant and for the rest of high school they had more or less gone together. Since then, though, it had dawned on Mr. and Mrs. Schuman that even in a democracy class distinctions exist, probably welcome news to Larry. In the cruellest and most stretched-out way he could manage he had been breaking off with her throughout the year now nearly ended. I had been surprised to find her at this party. Obviously she had felt shaky about attending and had brought the friend as the only kind of protection she could afford. The other girl was acting just like a guard hired for the night.

There being no answer to Neil, I went into the living room, where Margaret, insanely drunk, was throwing herself around as if wanting to break a bone. Somewhat in time to the music she would run a few steps, then snap her body like a whip, her chin striking her chest and her hands flying backward, fingers fanned, as her shoulders pitched forward. In her state, her body was childishly plastic; unharmed, she would bounce back from this jolt and begin to clap and kick and hum. Schuman stayed away from her. Margaret was small, not more than 5′2″, with the smallness ripeness comes to early. She had bleached a section of her black hair platinum, cropped her head all over, and trained the stubble into short curls like those on antique statues of boys. Her face seemed quite coarse from the front, so her profile was classical unexpectedly. She might have been Portia. When she was not putting on her savage pointless dance she was in the bathroom being sick. The pity and the vulgarity of her exhibition made everyone who was sober uncomfortable; our common guilt in witnessing this girl's rites brought us so close together in that room that it seemed never, not in all time, could we be parted. I myself was perfectly sober. I had the impression then that people only drank to stop being unhappy, and I nearly always felt at least fairly happy.

Luckily, Margaret was in a sick phase around one o'clock, when the elder Schumans came home. They looked in at us briefly. It was a pleasant joke to see in their smiles that, however corrupt and unwinking we felt, to them we looked young and sleepy: Larry's friends. Things quieted after they went up the stairs. In half an hour people began coming out of the kitchen balancing cups of coffee. By two o'clock four girls stood in aprons at Mrs. Schuman's sink, and others were padding back and forth carrying glasses and ashtrays. Another blameless racket pierced the clatter in the kitchen. Out on the cold grass the three Melanchthon athletes had set up the badminton net and in the faint glow given off by the house were playing. The bird, ascending and descending through uneven bars of light, glimmered like a firefly.

Now that the party was dying, Neil's apathy seemed deliberately exasperating, even vindictive. For at least another hour he persisted in hearing "Dark Eyes" over and over again, holding his head and tapping his foot. The entire scene in the den had developed a fixity that was uncanny;

the girl remained in the chair and read magazines, *Holiday* and *Esquire*, one after another. In the meantime, cars came and went and raced their motors out front. Larry Schuman had taken Ann Mahlon off and didn't come back; that left Zoe Loessner to be driven home by Mr. and Mrs. Bechtel. The athletes had carried the neighbor's artificial snowman into the center of the street and disappeared. Somehow in the shuffle of arrangements at the end Neil had contracted to drive Margaret and the other girl home. Margaret was convalescing in the downstairs bathroom. I unlocked a little glass bookcase ornamenting a desk in the dark dining room and removed a volume of Thackeray's Works. It turned out to be Volume II of *Henry Esmond*. I began it, rather than break another book out of the set, which had been squeezed in there so long the bindings had sort of interpenetrated.

Henry was going off to war again when Neil finally appeared in the archway and said, "O.K., Norseman. Let's go to Chicago." "Norseman" was a variant of my name he used only when feeling special affection.

We turned off all the lamps and left the hall bulb burning against Larry's return. Margaret Lento seemed chastened. Neil gave her his arm and led her into the back seat of his father's stately car; I stood aside to let the other girl get in with her, but Neil indicated that I should sit in the back. I supposed he realized this left only the mute den-girl to go up front with him. She sat well over on her side, was all I noticed. Neil backed into the street and with unusual care steered past the snowman. Our headlights made vivid the fact that the snowman's back was a hollow right-angled gash; he had been built up against the corner of a house.

From Olinger, Riverside was diagonally across Alton. The city was sleeping as we drove through it. Most of the stoplights were blinking green. Among cities Alton had a bad reputation; its graft and gambling and easy juries and bawdy houses were supposedly notorious throughout the Middle Atlantic states. But to me it always presented an innocent face: row after row of houses built of a local dusty-red brick the shade of flowerpots, each house fortified with a tiny, awninged, balustraded porch, and nothing but the wealth of movie houses and beer signs along its main street to suggest that its citizens loved pleasure more than the run of mankind. Indeed, as we moved at moderate speed down these hushed streets bordered with parked cars, a limestone church bulking at every corner and the sodium streetlamps keeping watch from above, Alton seemed less the ultimate center of an urban region than itself a suburb of some vast mythical metropolis, like Pandemonium or Paradise. I was conscious of evergreen wreaths on door after door and of stained-glass fanlights in which each house number was embedded. I was also conscious that every block was one block farther from the Turnpike.

Riverside, fitted into the bends of the Schuylkill, was not so regularly laid out. Margaret's house was one of a short row, composition-shingled, which we approached from the rear, down a short cement alley speckled with drains. The porches were a few inches higher than the alley. Margaret asked us if we wanted to come in for a cup of coffee, since we were going to Chicago; Neil accepted by getting out of the car and slamming his door. The noise filled the alley, alarming me. I wondered at the easy social life that evidently existed among my friends at three-thirty in the morning. Margaret did, however, lead us in stealthily, and she turned on only the kitchen switch. The kitchen was divided from the living room by a large sofa, which faced into a littered gloom wherein distant light from beyond the alley spilled over the windowsill and across the spines of a radiator. In one corner the glass of a television set showed; the screen would seem absurdly small now, but then it seemed disproportionately elegant. The shabbiness everywhere would not have struck me so definitely if I hadn't just come from Schuman's place. Neil and the other girl sat on the sofa; Margaret held a match to a gas burner and, as the blue flame licked an old kettle, doled instant coffee into four flowered cups.

Some man who had once lived in this house had built by the kitchen's one window a breakfast nook, nothing more than a booth, a table between two high-backed benches. I sat in it and read all the words I could see: "Salt," "Pepper," "Have Some Lumps," "December," "Mohn's Milk Inc.—A Very Merry Christmas and Joyous New Year—Mohn's Milk Is *Safe* Milk—'Mommy, Make It Mohn's!,' " "matches," "*HOTPOINT,*" "p r e s s," "Magee Stove Federal & Furnace Corp.," "God Is In This House," "Ave Maria Gratia Plena," "Shredded Wheat Benefits Exciting New Pattern Kungsholm." After serving the two on the sofa, Margaret came to me with coffee and sat down opposite me in the booth. Fatigue had raised two blue welts beneath her eyes.

"Well," I asked her, "did you have a good time?"

She smiled and glanced down and made the small sound "Ch," vestigal of "Jesus." With absent-minded delicacy she stirred her coffee, lifting and replacing the spoon without a ripple.

"Rather odd at the end," I said, "not even the host there."

"He took Ann Mahlon home."

"I know." I was surprised that she knew, having been sick in the bathroom for that hour.

"You sound jealous," she added.

"Who does? I do? I don't."

"You like her, John, don't you?" Her using my first name and the quality of her question did not, although except for a few parties we had hardly met, seem forward, considering the hour and that she had brought me coffee. There is very little further to go with a girl who has brought you coffee.

"Oh, I like everybody," I told her, "and the longer I've known them the more I like them, because the more they're me. The only people I like better are ones I've just met. Now, Ann Mahlon I've known since kindergarten. Every day her mother used to bring her to the edge of the schoolyard for months after all the other mothers had stopped." I wanted to cut a figure in Margaret's eyes, but they were too dark. Stoically she had gotten on top of her weariness, but it was growing bigger under her.

"Did you like her then?"

"I felt sorry for her being embarrassed by her mother."

She asked me, "What was Larry like when he was little?"

"Oh, bright. Kind of mean."

"Was he mean?"

"I'd say so. Yes. In some grade or other he and I began to play chess together. I always won until secretly he took lessons from a man his parents knew and read strategy books."

Margaret laughed, genuinely pleased. "Then did he win?"

"Once. After that I really tried, and after *that* he decided chess was kid stuff. Besides, I was used up. He'd have these runs on people where you'd be down at his house every afternoon, then in a couple months he'd get a new pet and that'd be that."

"He's funny," she said. "He has a kind of cold mind. He decides on what he wants, then he does what he has to do, you know, and nothing anybody says can change him."

"He does tend to get what he wants," I admitted guardedly, realizing that to her this meant her. Poor bruised little girl, in her mind he was all the time cleaving with rare cunning through his parents' objections straight to her.

My coffee was nearly gone, so I glanced toward the sofa in the other room. Neil and the girl had sunk out of sight behind its back. Before this it had honestly not occurred to me that they had a relationship, but now that I saw, it seemed plausible and, at this time of night, good news, though it meant we would not be going to Chicago yet.

So I talked to Margaret about Larry, and she responded, showing really quite an acute sense of him. To me, considering so seriously the person-

ality of a childhood friend, as if overnight he had become a factor in the
world, seemed absurd; I couldn't deeply believe that even in her world he
mattered much. Larry Schuman, in little more than a year, had become
nothing to me. The important thing, rather than the subject, was the
conversation itself—the quick agreements, the slow nods, the weave
of different memories; it was like one of those Panama baskets shaped
underwater around a worthless stone.

She offered me more coffee. When she returned with it, she sat down,
not opposite, but beside me, lifting me to such a pitch of gratitude and
affection the only way I could think to express it was by *not* kissing her, as
if a kiss were another piece of abuse women suffered. She said, "Cold.
Cheap bastard turns the thermostat down to sixty," meaning her father.
She drew my arm around her shoulders and folded my hand around her
bare forearm, to warm it. The back of my thumb fitted against the curve
of one breast. Her head went into the hollow where my arm and chest
joined; she was terribly small, measured against your own body. Perhaps
she weighed a hundred pounds. Her lids lowered and I kissed her two
lush eyebrows and then the spaces of skin between the rough curls, some
black and some bleached, that fringed her forehead. Other than this I
tried to keep as still as a bed would be. It *had* grown cold. A shiver starting on the side away from her would twitch my shoulders when I tried to
repress it; she would frown and unconsciously draw my arm tighter. No
one had switched the kitchen light off. On Margaret's foreshortened
upper lip there seemed to be two pencil marks; the length of wrist my
badly fitting sleeve exposed looked pale and naked against the spiralling
down of the smaller arm held beneath it.

Outside, on the street the house faced, there was no motion. Only once
did a car go by: around five o'clock, with twin mufflers, the radio on and
a boy yelling. Neil and the girl murmured together incessantly; some of
what they said I could overhear.

"No. Which?" she asked.

"I don't care."

"Wouldn't you want a boy?"

"I'd be happy whatever I got."

"I know, but which would you *rather* have? Don't men want boys?"

"I don't care. You."

Somewhat later, Mohn's truck passed on the other side of the street.
The milkman, well bundled, sat behind headlights in a warm orange volume the size of a phone booth, steering one-handed and smoking a cigar
that he set on the edge of the dashboard when, his wire carrier vibrant, he

ran out of the truck with bottles. His passing led Neil to decide the time had come. Margaret woke up frightened of her father; we hissed our farewells and thanks to her quickly. Neil dropped the other girl off at her house, a few blocks away; he knew where it was. Sometime during that night I must have seen this girl's face, but I have no memory of it. She is always behind a magazine or in the dark or with her back turned. Neil married her years later, I know, but after we arrived in Chicago I never saw him again either.

A pre-dawn light touched the clouds above the black slate roofs as, with a few other cars, we drove through Alton. The moon-sized clock of a beer billboard said ten after six. Olinger was deathly still. The air brightened as we moved along the highway; the glowing wall of my home hung above the woods as we rounded the long curve by the Mennonite dairy. With a .22 I could have had a pane of my parents' bedroom window, and they were dreaming I was in Indiana. My grandfather would be up, stamping around in the kitchen for my grandmother to make him break-fast, or outside, walking to see if any ice had formed on the brook. For an instant I genuinely feared he might hail me from the peak of the barn roof. Then trees interceded and we were safe in a landscape where no one cared about us.

At the entrance to the Turnpike Neil did a strange thing: he stopped the car and had me take the wheel. He had never trusted me to drive his father's car before, as if my not knowing all about crankshafts and carburetors the way he did handicapped my competence to steer. But now he was quite complacent. He hunched in his gabardine suit under an old mackinaw and leaned his head against the metal of the window frame and soon was asleep. We crossed the Susquehanna on a long smooth bridge below Harrisburg, then began climbing toward the Alleghenies. In the mountains there was snow, a dry dusting like sand, that waved back and forth on the road surface. Farther along there had been a fresh fall that night, about two inches, and the plows had not yet cleared all the lanes. I was passing a Sunoco truck on a high curve when without warning the scraped section gave out and I realized I might skid into the fence if not over the edge. The radio was singing "Carpets of clover, I'll lay right at your feet," and the speedometer said eighty. Nothing happened; the Chrysler stayed firm in the snow and Neil slept through the danger, his face turned skyward and his breath struggling in his nose. It was the first time I heard a contemporary of mine snore.

When we came into tunnel country the flicker and hollow amplification stirred Neil awake. He sat up, the mackinaw dropping to his lap, and lit a cigarette. A second after the scratch of his match occurred the moment of which each following moment was a slight diminution, as we made the long irregular descent toward Pittsburgh. There were many reasons for my feeling so happy. We were on our way. I had seen a dawn. This far, Neil could appreciate, I had brought us safely. Ahead, a girl waited who, if I asked, would marry me, but first there was a vast trip: many hours and towns interceded between me and that encounter. There was the quality of the ten a.m. sunlight as it existed in the air ahead of the windshield, filtered by the thin overcast, blessing irresponsibility—you felt you could slice forever through such a cool pure element—and springing, by implying how high these hills had become, a widespreading pride: Pennsylvania, your state—as if you had made your life. And there was knowing that twice since midnight a person had trusted me enough to fall asleep beside me.

The Persistence of Desire

PENNYPACKER'S OFFICE still smelled of linoleum, a clean, sad scent that seemed to lift from the checkerboard floor in squares of alternating intensity; this pattern had given Clyde as a boy a funny nervous feeling of intersection, and now he stood crisscrossed by a double sense of himself, his present identity extending down from Massachusetts to meet his disconsolate youth in Pennsylvania, projected upward from a distance of years. The enlarged, tinted photograph of a lake in the Canadian wilderness still covered one whole wall, and the walnut-stained chairs and benches continued their vague impersonation of the Shaker manner. The one new thing, set squarely on an orange end table, was a compact black clock constructed like a speedometer; it showed in arabic numerals the present minute—1:28—and coiled invisibly in its works the two infinities of past and future. Clyde was early; the waiting room was empty. He sat down on a chair opposite the clock. Already it was 1:29, and while he watched, the digits slipped again: another drop into the brimming void. He glanced around for the comfort of a clock with a face and gracious, gradual hands. A stopped grandfather matched the other imitation antiques. He opened a magazine and immediately read, "Science reveals that the cells of the normal human body are replaced *in toto* every seven years."

The top half of a Dutch door at the other end of the room opened, and, framed in the square, Pennypacker's secretary turned the bright disc of her face toward him. "Mr. Behn?" she asked in a chiming voice. "Dr. Pennypacker will be back from lunch in a minute." She vanished backward into the maze of little rooms where Pennypacker, an eye, ear, nose, and throat man, had arranged his fabulous equipment. Through the bay window Clyde could see traffic, gayer in color than he remembered, hustle down Grand Avenue. On the sidewalk, haltered girls identical in all but name with girls he had known strolled past in twos and threes. Small-town perennials, they moved rather mournfully under their burdens of bloom. In the opposite direction packs of the opposite sex carried baseball mitts.

Clyde became so lonely watching his old street that when, with a sucking exclamation, the door from the vestibule opened, he looked up gratefully, certain that the person, this being his home town, would be a friend. When he saw who it was, although every cell in his body had been replaced since he had last seen her, his hands jerked in his lap and blood bounded against his skin.

"Clyde Behn," she pronounced, with a matronly and patronizing yet frightened finality, as if he were a child and these words the moral of a story.

"Janet." He awkwardly rose from his chair and crouched, not so much in courtesy as to relieve the pressure on his heart.

"Whatever brings you back to these parts?" She was taking the pose that she was just anyone who once knew him.

He slumped back. "I'm always coming back. It's just you've never been here."

"Well, I've"—she seated herself on an orange bench and crossed her plump legs cockily—"been in Germany with my husband."

"He was in the Air Force."

"Yes." It startled her a little that he knew.

"And he's out now?" Clyde had never met him, but, having now seen Janet again, he felt he knew him well—a slight, literal fellow, to judge from the shallowness of the marks he had left on her. He would wear eyebrow-style glasses, be a griper, have some not-quite-negotiable talent, like playing the clarinet or drawing political cartoons, and now be starting up a drab avenue of business. Selling insurance, most likely. Poor Janet, Clyde felt; except for the interval of himself—his splendid, perishable self—she would never see the light. Yet she had retained her beautiful calm, an unsleeping tranquillity marked by that pretty little lavender puffiness below the eyes. And either she had grown slimmer or he had grown more tolerant of fat. Her thick ankles and the general *obstinacy* of her flesh used to goad him into being cruel.

"Yes." Her voice indicated that she had withdrawn; perhaps some ugliness of their last parting had recurred to her.

"I was 4-F." He was ashamed of this, and his confessing it, though she seemed unaware of the change, turned their talk inward. "A peacetime slacker," he went on, "what could be more ignoble?"

She was quiet a while, then asked, "How many children do you have?"

"Two. Age three and one. A girl and a boy; very symmetrical. Do you"—he blushed lightly, and brushed at his forehead to hide it—"have any?"

"No, we thought it wouldn't be fair, until we were more fixed."

Now the quiet moment was his to hold; she had matched him failing for failing. She recrossed her legs, and in a quaint strained way smiled.

"I'm trying to remember," he admitted, "the last time we saw each other. I can't remember how we broke up."

"I can't either," she said. "It happened so often."

Clyde wondered if with that sarcasm she intended to fetch his eyes to the brink of tears. Probably not; premeditation had never been much of a weapon for her, though she had tried to learn it from him.

He moved across the linoleum to sit on the bench beside her. "I can't tell you," he said, "how much, of all the people in this town, you were the one I wanted to see." It was foolish, but he had prepared it to say, in case he ever saw her again.

"Why?" This was more like her: blunt, pucker-lipped curiosity. He had forgotten it.

"Well, hell. Any number of reasons. I wanted to say something."

"What?"

"Well, that if I hurt you it was stupidity, because I was young. I've often wondered since if I did, because it seems now that you were the only person outside my family who ever, actually, *liked* me."

"Did I?"

"If you think by doing nothing but asking monosyllabic questions you're making an effect, you're wrong."

She averted her face, leaving, in a sense, only her body—the pale, columnar breadth of arm, the freckled crescent of shoulder muscle under the cotton strap of her summer dress—with him. "You're the one who's making effects." It was such a wan, senseless thing to say to defend herself; Clyde, virtually paralyzed by so heavy an injection of love, touched her arm icily.

With a quickness that suggested she had foreseen this, she got up and went to the table by the bay window, where rows of overlapping magazines were laid. She bowed her head to their titles, the nape of her neck in shadow beneath a half-collapsed bun. She had always had trouble keeping her hair pinned.

Clyde was blushing intensely. "Is your husband working around here?"

"He's looking for work." That she kept her back turned while saying this gave him hope.

. . .

"Mr. Behn?" The petite secretary-nurse, switching like a pendulum, led him back through the sanctums and motioned for him to sit in a high hinged chair padded with black leather. Pennypacker's equipment had always made him nervous; tons of it were marshalled through the rooms. A complex tree of tubes and lenses leaned over his left shoulder, and by his right elbow a porcelain basin was cupped expectantly. An eye chart crisply stated gibberish. In time Pennypacker himself appeared: a tall, stooped man with mottled cheekbones and an air of suppressed anger.

"Now what's the trouble, Clyde?"

"It's nothing; I mean it's very little," Clyde began, laughing inappropriately. During his adolescence he had developed a joking familiarity with his dentist and his regular doctor, but he had never become cozy with Pennypacker, who remained, what he had seemed at first, an aloof administrator of expensive humiliations. He had made Clyde wear glasses when he was in the third grade. Later, he annually cleaned, with a shrill push of hot water, wax from Clyde's ears, and once had thrust two copper straws up Clyde's nostrils in a futile attempt to purge his sinuses. Clyde always felt unworthy of Pennypacker—felt himself to be a dirty conduit balking the smooth onward flow of the doctor's reputation and apparatus. He blushed to mention his latest trivial stoppage. "It's just that for over two months I've had this eyelid that twitters and it makes it difficult to think."

Pennypacker drew little circles with a pencil-sized flashlight in front of Clyde's right eye.

"It's the left lid," Clyde said, without daring to turn his head. "I went to a doctor up where I live, and he said it was like a rattle in the fender and there was nothing to do. He said it would go away, but it didn't and didn't, so I had my mother make an appointment for when I came down here to visit."

Pennypacker moved to the left eye and drew even closer. The distance between the doctor's eyes and the corners of his mouth was very long; the emotional impression of his face close up was like that of those first photographs taken from rockets, in which the earth's curvature was made apparent. "How do you like being in your home territory?" Pennypacker asked.

"Fine."

"Seem a little strange to you?"

The question itself seemed strange. "A little."

"Mm. That's interesting."

"About the eye, there were two things I thought," Clyde said. "One was, I got some glasses made in Massachusetts by a man nobody else ever went to, and I thought his prescription might be faulty. His equipment seemed so ancient and kind of full of cobwebs—like a Dürer print." He never could decide how cultured Pennypacker was; the Canadian lake argued against it, but he was county-famous in his trade, in a county where doctors were as high as the intellectual scale went.

The flashlight, a tepid sun girdled by a grid of optical circles behind which Pennypacker's face loomed dim and colorless, came right to the skin of Clyde's eye, and the vague face lurched forward angrily, and Clyde, blind in a world of light, feared that Pennypacker was inspecting the floor of his soul. Paralyzed by panic, he breathed, "The other was that something might be in it. At night it feels as if there's a tiny speck deep in under the lid."

Pennypacker reared back and insolently raked the light back and forth across Clyde's face. "How long have you had this flaky stuff on your lids?"

The insult startled Clyde. "Is there any?"

"How long have you had it?"

"Some mornings I notice little grains like salt that I thought were what I used to call sleepy-dust—"

"This isn't sleepy-dust," the doctor said. He repeated, "This isn't sleepy-dust." Clyde started to smile at what he took to be kidding of his babyish vocabulary, but Pennypacker cut him short with "Cases of this can lead to loss of the eyelashes."

"Really?" Clyde was vain of his lashes, which in his boyhood had been exceptionally long, giving his face the alert and tender look of a girl's. "Do you think it's the reason for the tic?" He imagined his face with the lids bald and the lashes lying scattered on his cheeks like insect legs. "What can I do?"

"Are you using your eyes a great deal?"

"Some. No more than I ever did."

Pennypacker's hands, blue after Clyde's dazzlement, lifted an intensely brown bottle from a drawer. "It may be bacteria, it may be allergy; when you leave I'll give you something that should knock it out either way. Do you follow me? Now, Clyde"—his voice became murmurous and consolatory as he placed a cupped hand, rigid as an electrode, on the top of Clyde's head—"I'm going to put some drops in your eyes so we can check the prescription of the glasses you bought in Massachusetts."

Clyde didn't remember that the drops stung so; he gasped outright and wept while Pennypacker held the lids apart with his fingers and worked them gently open and shut, as if he were playing with snapdragons. Penny-packer set preposterously small, circular dark-brown glasses on Clyde's face and in exchange took away the stylish horn-rims Clyde had kept in his pocket. It was Pennypacker's method to fill his little rooms with wait-ing patients and wander from one to another like a dungeon-keeper.

Clyde heard, far off, the secretary's voice tinkle, and, amplified by the hollow hall, Pennypacker's rumble in welcome and Janet's respond. The one word "headaches," petulantly emphasized, stood up in her answer. Then a door was shut. Silence.

Clyde admired how matter-of-fact she had sounded. He had always admired this competence in her, her authority in the world peripheral to the world of love, in which she was so docile. He remembered how she could face up to waitresses and teachers and how she would bluff her mother when this vigilant woman unexpectedly entered the screened porch where they were supposed to be playing cribbage. Potted elephant plants sat in the corners of the porch like faithful dwarfs; robins had built a nest in the lilac outside, inches from the screen. It had been taken as an omen, a blessing, when, one evening, their being on the glider no longer distressed the robins.

The wallpaper he saw through the open door seemed as distinct as ever. Unlike, say, the effects of Novocain, the dilation of pupils is impal-pable. He held his fingernails close to his nose and was unable to distin-guish the cuticles. He touched the sides of his nose, where tears had left trails. He looked at his fingers again, and they seemed fuzzier. He couldn't see his fingerprint whorls. The threads of his shirt had melted into an elusive liquid surface.

A door opened and closed, and another patient was ushered into a con-sulting room and imprisoned by Pennypacker. Janet's footsteps had not mingled with the others. Without ever quite sacrificing his reputation for good behavior, Clyde in high school had become fairly bold in heckling teachers he considered stupid or unjust. He got out of his chair, looked down the hall to where a white splinter of secretary showed, and quickly walked past a closed door to one ajar. His blood told him, *This one.*

Janet was sitting in a chair as upright as the one he had left, a two-pronged comb in her mouth, her back arched, and her arms up, bundling her hair. As he slipped around the door, she plucked the comb from between her teeth and laughed at him. He saw in a little rimless mirror cocked above her head his own head, grimacing with stealth and gro-tesquely costumed in glasses like two chocolate coins, and appreciated her laughter, though it didn't fit with what he had prepared to say. He said it anyway: "Janet, are you happy?"

She rose with a practical face and walked past him and clicked the door shut. As she stood facing it, listening for a reaction from outside, he gathered her hair in his hand and lifted it from the nape of her neck, which he had expected to find in shadow but which was instead, to his distended eyes, bright as a candle. He clumsily put his lips to it.

"Don't you love your wife?" she asked.

"Incredibly much," he murmured into the fine neck-down.

She moved off, leaving him leaning awkwardly, and in front of the mirror smoothed her hair away from her ears. She sat down again, crossing her wrists in her lap.

"I just got told my eyelashes are going to fall out," Clyde said.

"Your pretty lashes," she said somberly.

"Why do you hate me?"

"Shh. I don't hate you now."

"But you did once."

"No, I did *not* once. Clyde, what *is* this bother? What are you after?"

"Son of a bitch, so I'm a bother. I knew it. You've just forgotten, all the time I've been remembering; you're so *damn* dense. I come in here a bundle of pain to tell you I'm sorry and I want you to be happy, and all I get is the back of your neck." Affected by what had happened to his eyes, his tongue had loosened, pouring out impressions; with culminating incoherence he dropped to his knees beside her chair, wondering if the thump would bring Pennypacker. "I must see you again," he blurted.

"Shh."

"I come back here and the only person who was ever pleasant to me I discover I maltreated so much she hates me."

"Clyde," she said, "you didn't maltreat me. You were a sweet boy to me."

Straightening up on his knees, he fumbled his fingers around the hem of the neck of her dress and pulled it out and looked down into the blurred cavity between her breasts. He had a remembrance of her freckles going down from her shoulders into her bathing suit. His glasses hit her cheek.

She stabbed the back of his hand with the points of her comb and he got to his feet, rearing high into a new, less sorrowful atmosphere. "When?" he asked, short of breath.

"No," she said.

"What's your married name?"

"Clyde, I thought you were successful. I thought you had beautiful children. Aren't you happy?"

"I am, I am; but"—the rest was so purely inspired its utterance only grazed his lips—"happiness isn't everything."

Footsteps ticked down the hall, toward their door, past it. Fear emptied his chest, yet with an excellent imitation of his old high-school flippancy he blew her a kiss, waited, opened the door, and whirled through it. His hand had left the knob when the secretary, emerging from the room where he should have been, confronted him in the linoleum-smelling hall. "Where could I get a drink of water?" he asked plaintively, assuming the hunch and whine of a blind beggar. In truth, he had, without knowing it, become thirsty.

"Once a year I pass through your territory," Pennypacker intoned as he slipped a growing weight of lenses into the apparatus on Clyde's nose. He had returned to Clyde more relaxed and chatty, now that all his little rooms were full. Clyde had tried to figure out from the pattern of noise if Janet had been dismissed. He believed she had. The thought made his eyelid throb. He didn't even know her married name. "Down the Turnpike," Pennypacker droned on, while his face flickered in and out of focus, "up the New Jersey Pike, over the George Washington Bridge, up the Merritt, then up Route 7 all the way to Lake Champlain. To hunt the big bass. There's an experience for you."

"I notice you have a new clock in your waiting room."

"That's a Christmas present from the Alton Optical Company. Can you read that line?"

"H, L, F, Y, T, something that's either an S or an E—"

"K," Pennypacker said without looking. The poor devil, he had all those letters memorized, all that gibberish—abruptly, Clyde wanted to love him. The oculist altered one lens. "Is it better this way? . . . Or this way?"

At the end of the examination, Pennypacker said, "Though the man's equipment was dusty, he gave you a good prescription. In your right eye the axis of astigmatism has rotated several degrees, which is corrected in the lenses. If you have been experiencing a sense of strain, part of the reason, Clyde, is that these heavy tortoiseshell frames are slipping down on your nose and giving you a prismatic effect. For a firm fit you should have metal frames, with adjustable nose pads."

"They leave such ugly dents on the sides of your nose."

"You should have them. Your bridge, you see"—he tapped his own—"is recessed. It takes a regular face to support unarticulated frames. Do you wear your glasses all the time?"

"For the movies and reading. When I got them in the third grade you told me that was all I needed them for."

"You should wear them all the time."

"Really? Even just for walking around?"

"All the time, yes. You have middle-aged eyes."

Pennypacker gave him a little plastic squeeze bottle of drops. "That is for the fungus on your lids."

"Fungus? There's a brutal thought. Well, will it cure the tic?"

Pennypacker impatiently snapped, "The tic is caused by muscular fatigue."

Thus Clyde was dismissed into a tainted world where things evaded his focus. He went down the hall in his sunglasses and was told by the secretary that he would receive a bill. The waiting room was full now, mostly with downcast old men and myopic children gnawing at their mothers. From out of this crowd a ripe young woman arose and came against his chest, and Clyde, included in the close aroma her hair and skin gave off, felt weak and broad and grand, like a declining rose. Janet tucked a folded note into the pocket of his shirt and said conversationally, "He's waiting outside in the car."

The neutral, ominous "he" opened wide a conspiracy Clyde instantly entered. He stayed behind a minute, to give her time to get away. Ringed by the judging eyes of the young and old, he felt like an actor snug behind the blinding protection of the footlights; he squinted prolongedly at the speedometer-clock, which, like a letter delivered on the stage, in fact was blank. Then, smiling ironically toward both sides, he left the waiting room, coming into Pennypacker's entrance hall, a cubicle equipped with a stucco umbrella stand and a red rubber mat saying, in letters so large he could read them, WALK IN.

He had not expected to be unable to read her note. He held it at arm's length and slowly brought it toward his face, wiggling it in the light from outdoors. Though he did this several times, it didn't yield even the simplest word, just wet blue specks. Under the specks, however, in their intensity and disposition, he believed he could make out the handwriting—slanted, open, unoriginal—familiar to him from other notes received long ago. This glimpse, through the skin of the paper, of Janet's old self quickened and sweetened his desire more than touching her had. He tucked the note back into his shirt pocket and its stiffness there made a shield for his heart. In this armor he stepped into the familiar street. The maples, macadam, shadows, houses, cars were to his violated eyes as brilliant as a scene remembered; he became a child again in this town, where life was a distant adventure, a rumor, an always imminent joy.

The Blessed Man of Boston, My Grandmother's Thimble, and Fanning Island

I SAW HIM only for a moment, and that was years ago. Boston had been beaten by the White Sox. It was a night game, and when it was over, as the crowd, including myself and my friends, pushed with that suppressed Occidental panic up the aisles toward the exit ramps, he, like the heavy pebble of gold that is not washed from the pan, was revealed, sitting alone, immobile and smiling, among the green seats. He was an old Chinese man, solidly fat, like a Chevrolet dealer, and he wore faded black trousers and a white shirt whose sleeves were rolled up. He sat with one arm up on the back of the seat beside him and smiled out toward the field, where the ground crew was unfurling the tarp across the foreshortened clay diamond and the outfield under the arc lights looked as brilliant and flat as a pool-table felt. And it flashed upon me, as I glimpsed this man sitting alone and unperturbed among the drained seats, that here was the happy man, the man of unceasing and effortless blessing. I thought then to write a novel, an immense book, about him, recounting his every move, his every meal, every play, pitch, and hesitation of every ball game he attended, the number of every house he passed as he walked Boston's three-decker slums, the exact position and shape of every cracked and flaking spot on the doorways, the precise sheen and rust of every floriate and convoluted fancy of ironwork that drifted by his legs, the chalk marks, the bricks (purple-tinted, ochre-smeared, red), the constellations of lint and stain in his tiny bachelor's room (green walls, painted pipes coughing with steam, telephone wiring stapled along the baseboard), the never precisely duplicated curl of the smoke off his rice, the strokes of sound composing the hatchings of noise at his back, every stifled cry, every sizzle of a defective neon-sign connection, every distant plane and train, every roller-skate scratch, everything: all set sequentially down with the bald simplicity of a litany, thousands upon thousands of pages, ecstatically uneventful, divinely and defiantly dull.

But we would-be novelists have a reach as shallow as our skins. We walk through volumes of the unexpressed and like snails leave behind a faint thread excreted out of ourselves. From the dew of the few flakes that melt on our faces we cannot reconstruct the snowstorm.

The other night I stumbled downstairs in the dark and kicked my wife's sewing basket from the halfway landing. Needles, spools, buttons, and patches scattered. In gathering the things up, I came upon my grandmother's thimble. For a second I did not know what it was; a stemless chalice of silver weighing a fraction of an ounce had come into my fingers. Then I knew, and the valves of time parted, and after an interval of years my grandmother was upon me again, and it seemed incumbent upon me, necessary and holy, to tell how once there had been a woman who now was no more, how she had been born and lived in a world that had ceased to exist, though its mementos were all about us; how her thimble had been fashioned as if in a magical grotto in the black mountain of time, by workmen dwarfed by remoteness, in a vanished workshop now no larger than the thimble itself and like it soon doomed, as if by geological pressures, to be crushed out of shape. O Lord, bless these poor paragraphs, that would do in their vile ignorance Your work of resurrection.

The thimble was her wedding present to me and my wife. I was her only grandchild. At the time I was married, she was in her late seventies, crippled and enfeebled. She had fought a long battle with Parkinson's disease; in my earliest memories of her she is touched with it. Her fingers and back are bent; there is a tremble about her as she moves through the dark, odd-shaped rooms of our house in the town where I was born. Crouched in the hall outside my grandparents' room—which I never entered—I can hear her voice, in a whispering mutter that pierces the wall with little snapping stabs, irritably answer a question that my grandfather had asked inaudibly. It is strange: out of their room, he speaks louder. When she bends over me, I smell a mixture of must, something like cough medicine, and old cloth permeated with dried sunlight. In my childhood she was strong, endowed with possessions and resources. By the time I married, she had become so weak only her piercing will carried her up and down the stairs of the little country house to which we had moved—the very house where she had lived as a bride. She spoke with great difficulty; she would hang impaled in the middle of a sentence, at a loss for the word, her watery eyes and wild white hair transfixed. She had no possessions. Except for her clothes and her bed, the elegant silver thimble—a gift from her father, inscribed with her maiden initials—was her last property, and she gave it to us.

In those days each departure from her I thought was the last. When I left to be married, I did not expect to see her alive again. But when, at the end of the summer, my wife and I returned, it was my grandfather, and not she, who had died. He had died minutes before we arrived. His body lay on the floor of their bedroom, his mouth a small black triangle in a face withered beyond recognition. The room was dimly lit by the warm glow of a kerosene lamp. I was afraid of his body; it surprised me that she did not seem to be. I was afraid that his body would move. I called "Grandpa" in an experimental whisper and flinched in fear of an answer.

My grandmother sat on the edge of the bed, dazed, smiling slightly to greet me. She was confused, like a craftsman who looks up after a long period of concentration. The sanest of old men, my grandfather had on his last day lost his mind. He had bellowed; she had struggled to restrain him. He thought the bed was on fire and sprang from it; she clung to him, and in their fall to the floor he died. But not quite. My mother rushed up the stairs and cried, "What are you doing?"

"Why, we're on the floor," her father told her with level sarcasm, and his heart stopped.

My father met our headlights on the lawn; he was panting. "Jesus," he said to me, "you've come at a funny time; we think Pop's died." My parents-in-law were with us; my wife's father, a surgeon, an intimate of death, went upstairs to the body. He came down, smiling, and said that there was no pulse, though the wrist was still warm. Then, when I went upstairs, I saw my grandmother smiling in much the same abstracted, considerate way as he.

She sat, worn and cleansed by her struggle, on the edge of the bed with two hollows. She was a little woman informed by a disproportionate strength. Carrying her husband through his death had been her last great effort. From that moment on, her will tried to arrange itself for defeat, and its power of resistance became an inconvenience to her. I hugged her quickly, afraid too of her body, which had so lately embraced the one on the floor. My mother, behind me, asked her if she wanted to come downstairs with the others. My grandmother refused, saying, "A little while yet," and making a tremulous impatient motion of explanation or dismissal.

She knew, perhaps, what I was shocked to discover when, descending the steps with trembling knees, and tingling all over as if from a bath, I went downstairs: that we have no gestures adequate to answer the imperious gestures of nature. Among deaf mountains human life pursues a comic low road. The sherry that my mother had purchased toward our arrival was served; the wait for the undertaker became overlaid with a subdued version of the party she had meant to have. My father-in-law with a chilling professional finesse carved the cold ham; my mother, tautly calm, as if at the center of contradictory tensions, made one or two of her witticisms; my father's telephone conversation with our Lutheran minister was as bewildered and bewildering as his conversations with this young man always were. Without knowing what I had expected instead, I was amazed; the chatter seemed to become unbearably loud and I blurted, thinking of my grandmother listening above our heads, "Why can't you let the old man rest?" My mother looked at me in startled reproval, and I felt again the security of being her clever but inexperienced boy; there were things I didn't understand.

The minister came with a drawn white face that cracked in relief at finding laughter in the house. At church softball he had broken his ankle sliding into second base, and limped still. His prayers seemed to chip pieces from our hearts and float them away. The undertaker's men, droll wooden figures like the hangmen of old, came and trundled the body out the door. Thus, as if through a series of pressure locks, we were rescued from the presence of death.

My grandmother did not attend the funeral. She was wise, for the Masons made it ridiculous with their occult presumption. My grandmother, whose love of activity had been intense, stayed inside the house, and more and more in bed. When my wife and I went away again—I had a year of college left—I said goodbye to her in my heart. But when we returned at Christmas, she was alive, and she was alive in June, though by now completely bedridden.

Blindly her will gave battle. My grandfather had been a vigorous booster of exercise as the key to longevity. Obeying, perhaps, an echo of her husband's voice, my grandmother would ask to be lifted by her hands into a sitting position, and then lowered, and lifted again, until the person doing it for her lost patience and in exasperation quit. She liked company, though almost all power of speech had forsaken her. "Up. Up," that fierce and plaintive request, was all I could understand. We knew that the disease touched only her tongue; that in that wordless, glaring head the same alert and appetitive mind lived. But a mind shorn of agency ceases to exist in our world, and we would speak together in her room as if it were empty. Certain now that this was my last time with her—my wife and I were going to England for a year—I spent some summer afternoons in my grandmother's room. I knew she could hear, but we had never spoken much to each other, so I would read or write in silence. I remember sitting in the rocking chair at the foot of the bed, near the spot where my grandfather's body had lain that night in warm lamplight, and writing, while the sun streamed in through the geraniums on the window-sill, a piece of light verse about what I imagined the sea voyage I was soon to take would be like.

> That line is the horizon line.
> The blue above it is divine.
> The blue below it is marine.
> Sometimes the blue below is green.

Reading this stanza now, I see, as if over the edge of the paper, my grandmother's nostrils. Her head was sunk foreshortened in the pillow. Decrepitude pressed unevenly on her body, twisted it out of symmetry; one nostril was squeezed into teardrop-shape, and the other was a round black hole through which she seized the air. The whole delicate frame of her existence seemed suspended from this final hungry aperture, the size of a dime, through which her life was sustained.

In England I hesitated to tear open each letter from home, for fear it would contain the news of her death. But, as if preserved in the unreality of those days that passed without weight on an island whose afternoon was our morning and whose morning was our night, she survived, and was there when we returned. We had had a baby girl. We put the child, too young to creep, on my grandmother's bed beside the hump of her legs, so that for an interval four generations were gathered in one room, and without moving her head my grandmother could see her entire progeny: my mother, myself, and my daughter. Later, at the old woman's funeral, my child, by then alert to things around her, smiled and from my arms stretched her hand toward the drained and painted body in the casket, perhaps in some faint way familiar.

My grandmother had died, finally, when I was far away, in Boston. I was at a party; it was a Saturday night. I went to the phone with a cigarette in my hand and Cointreau on my breath; my mother, her voice miniature with distance, began the conversation with the two words, "Grammy went." They had found her dead in the morning and had not been able to reach me until now. It was, of course, a blessing; my mother's health had been nearly broken by nursing her own mother. Now we were all released. I returned to the party and told my news, which was received respectfully; it was a small party, of old friends. But the party spirit cannot be suppressed a whole evening, and when it revived I suppose I joined it.

I vowed, groping for some fitness, for the commensurate gesture, to go to a Lutheran church the next morning. But when Sunday morning came, I slept late, and the vow seemed a troublesome whim. I did not go.

I did not go. This refusal seems to be a face at that party and I am about to quarrel with it, but other memories come and touch my elbow and lead me away.

When we were all still alive, the five of us in that kerosene-lit house, on Friday and Saturday nights, at an hour when in the spring and summer there was still abundant light in the air, I would set out in my father's car for town, where my friends lived. I had, by moving ten miles away, at last acquired friends: an illustration of that strange law whereby, like Orpheus leading Eurydice, we achieve our desire by turning our back on it. I had even gained a girl, so that the vibrations were as sexual as social that made me jangle with anticipation as I clowned in front of the mirror in our kitchen, shaving from a basin of stove-heated water, combing my hair with a dripping comb, adjusting my reflection in the mirror until I had achieved just that electric angle from which my face seemed beautiful and everlastingly, by the very volumes of air and sky and grass that lay mutely banked about our home, beloved. My grandmother would hover near me, watching fearfully, as she had when I was a child, afraid that I would fall from a tree. Delirious, humming, I would swoop and lift her, lift her like a child, crooking one arm under her knees and cupping the other behind her back. Exultant in my height, my strength, I would lift that frail brittle body weighing perhaps a hundred pounds and twirl with it in my arms while the rest of the family watched with startled smiles of alarm. Had I stumbled, or dropped her, I might have broken her back, but my joy always proved a secure cradle. And whatever irony was in the impulse, whatever implicit contrast between this ancient husk, scarcely female, and the pliant, warm girl I would embrace before the evening was done, direct delight flooded away: I was carrying her who had carried me, I was giving my past a dance, I had lifted the anxious caretaker of my childhood from the floor, I was bringing her with my boldness to the edge of danger, from which she had always sought to guard me.

There is a photograph of my grandmother and me at the side of the first house. There is snow on the ground. The brick walk has been cleared. I am in a snowsuit, and its bulk makes my walking doubly clumsy. We are both of us dark against the snow and the white brick wall of the house. I am unsteady; my grandmother's black shape bends over me with a predatory solicitude, holding one of my hands in a hand that has already become, under the metamorphosis of her disease, a little clawlike. She was worried that I would fall, that I would not eat enough, that the bigger boys of the neighborhood would harm me, that a cold would strangle me; and her fears were not foolish. There *was* danger in that kind house. Tigers of temper lurked beneath the furniture, and shadows of despair followed my father to the door and flattened themselves against the windows as he walked down the shaded street alone.

I remember watching my mother iron in the dining room. Suddenly her hand jumps to her jaw; her face goes white; shock unfocuses her eyes. Her teeth had given her a twinge that started tears flowing down her cheeks as she resumed ironing. I must have cried out, for she smiled at my face. I told her she must go to the dentist, and returned to my coloring book. The comforting aroma of heated cloth folded over the glimpsed spark of pain. Now around that cold spark, isolated in memory, the air of that house crystallizes: our neglected teeth, our poor and starchy diet, our worn floors, our musty and haunted halls. I sit on the carpet—which under the dining table had retained its fresh nap and seemed to me jungle-grass—and my mother stands at the ironing board, and around us, like hieroglyphs haloing the rigid figures of a tomb mural, are the simple shapes of the other three: my grandfather a pyramid sitting rereading the newspaper in the dwindling light of the front parlor, my father a forked stick striding somewhere in the town, my grandmother, above us in her room or behind us in the kitchen, a crescent bent into some chore. As long as her body permitted, she worked.

The night we moved, my mother and I came through the wet black grass around the edge of the sandstone farmhouse and saw, framed in the doorway, close to us yet far away, like a woman in a Vermeer, my grandmother reaching up with a trembling match to touch the wick of a lamp on the high kitchen mantel. My mother's voice, in recalling that moment to me years later, broke as she added, "She was always doing things like that." Like lighting a lamp. Always lighting a lamp.

And through that "always" I fall into the volume of time that preceded my birth, where my grandmother is a figure of history made deceptively tangible by her persistence into my days. She was the youngest of a dozen children, all of whom, remarkably in that mortal era, lived to maturity. She was the baby, her father's favorite and her brothers' darling. Toward the end of her life, when hallucinations began to walk through the walls of her room and stand silently in the corners, her brothers, all of whom she had long outlived, became again vivid to her. I became one of them; she would ask for me with Pete's name. He was her youngest brother,

her own favorite. His brown photograph, mounted on stiff cardboard stamped with gold scrolls, had been set up on the table beside her bed. He displayed a hook nose and the dandified hauteur of a rural buck braced to have his picture taken. Like the eyes of an icon, his snapping black eyes—alone in the photograph unfaded—overlooked her deathbed.

I believe her first language was Pennsylvania German. As some parents speak secrets in French in front of the children, my grandparents used this dialect on my mother. Only two words have descended to me— *ferhuttled* and *dopich*, respectively meaning "confused" and "lethargic." They were frequent words with my grandmother; it is the way other people must have looked to her. Shaped like a sickle, her life whipped through grasses of confusion and lethargy that in a summer month grew up again as tall as before.

As with the blessed man of Boston, I should here provide a catalogue of her existence: her marriage to a man ten years older, the torment of her one childbirth, the eddies of fortune that contained her constant labor. The fields, the hired men, the horses, the stones of the barn and the fireplace, the three-mile inns on the road to market. The birth of my mother: the lamplight, the simmering water, the buggy clattering for the tipsy doctor, fear like a transparent paste on the ceiling, the hours of pain piled higher and higher—my grandmother was a little woman, and the baby was large. Her size at the outset my mother felt as an insult ineradicably delivered to the woman who bore her, the first of a thousand painful failures to do the normal thing. But to me, from my remote perspective, in which fable, memory, and blood blend, the point of the story is the survival. Both survived the ordeal. And in the end all my impressions of my grandmother's life turn on the point of her survival.

When we returned to the farm where my mother had been born, my grandmother insisted on fetching the water from the spring. In spite of all our warnings, she would sneak off with the bucket and on her unsteady legs tote it back up the slope of grass, brimful, strangely little of it spilled. One summer day my mother and I were standing at the side of the house. The air was vibrating with the noises of nature, the pressing tremolo of insects and birds. Suddenly my mother's face, as if from a twinge of her teeth, went rapt and white: "Listen!" Before I could listen she ran down the lawn toward the spring, I following, and there we found my grandmother doubled up over the water, hanging, by the pressure of one shoulder, to the sandstone wall that cupped the spring on three sides. The weight of the bucket had pulled her forward; she had thrown herself sideways and, unable to move, had held herself from drowning by sheer adhesion of will until her faint, birdlike whimper for help flew to the attuned ears of her child. Death had to take her while she slept.

She never to my knowledge went outside the boundaries of Pennsylvania. She never saw a movie; I never saw her read. She lived in our nation as a fish lives in the deep sea. One night, when she thought—wrongly— that she was dying, I heard her ask, "Will I be a little debil?" I had never before heard her curiosity range so far. When presented with disagreeable information, she would look stunned, then with a glimmer of a smile say slowly, "Ach, I guess not," wishing the obstacle away as easily as a child.

Of course, I came upon her late, with a child's unknowing way of seeing. No doubt the innocence of my vision of her is my own innocence, her ignorance mine. I am told that in her day she was sophisticated and formidable. She liked fine clothes, good food, nice things. She was one of the first women in the region to drive a car. This automobile, an Overland, spinning down the orange dirt roads of rural valleys now filled with ranch houses and Philadelphia commuters, recedes into a landscape and a woman whom I must imagine, a woman who is not my grandmother at all.

The initials were K.Z.K. Picking up that thimble, with its crown of stipples like a miniature honeycomb, and its decorative rim of five-petalled flowers tapped into the silver, I felt at my back that night a steep wave about to break over the world and bury us and all our trinkets of survival fathoms down. For I feel that the world is ending, that the mounting mass of people will soon make a blackness in which the glint of this silver will be obliterated; it is this imminent catastrophe that makes it imperative for me to cry now, in the last second when the cry will have meaning, that once there was a woman whom one of the continents in one of its terrains caused to exist. That the land which cast her up was harsher, more sparsely exploited, more fertile than it is now. That she was unique; that she came toward the end of the time when uniqueness was possible. Already identical faces throng the street. She was projected onto my own days by her willed survival; I lived with her and she loved me and I did not understand her, I did not care to. She is gone now because we deserted her; the thimble seems a keepsake pressed into my hand by a forsaken woman as in the company of others I launched out from an island into a wilderness.

Such simplicities bring me to the third of my unwritten stories. It is a simple story, a story of life stripped of the progenitive illusion, perfected out of history: the slam of a door in an empty house. "Let us imagine,"

Pascal invites us, "a number of men in chains, and all condemned to death. . . ."

Fanning Island is an isolated Pacific island near the equator. It now supports a relay station for the transoceanic telegraph. When Captain Fanning discovered it, it was uninhabited, but bore signs of habitation: a rectangular foundation of coral blocks, a basalt adze, some bone fish-hooks, a few raised graves containing drilled porpoise teeth and human bones. All these things were old.

Understand that the Polynesian islands were populated accidentally, as seed in nature is sown. On the wide waste of ocean many canoes and praus were blown astray; short planned voyages were hazardous and extended navigation was impossible. Some drifted to other populated islands, and thorns there swallowed them. Some starved on the barren expanse of the Pacific; some fell southward into Antarctic ice. Some washed up on atolls with only the rats in the canoes still alive. A few—a very few; Nature with her mountain of time plays a spendthrift game— survived to reach an uninhabited but inhabitable island. When the company of survivors included fertile women, population took place. The souls shed by one nation became the seeds of another. No return was possible. The stars are a far weaker guide than armchair theorists believe. Accident, here as elsewhere, is the generating agency beneath the seemingly achieved surface of things.

What must have happened is this. A company of men in a large canoe, sailing among the Marquesas, were blown away. Eventually they were cast up on Fanning Island. They built a house, fished, and lived. No women were among them, so their numbers could only diminish. The youngest among them may have lived for fifty years. The bones of this man whom no one remained to bury moldered away and vanished. No sign of disaster is found to explain the disappearance of the men. None is needed.

Qu'on s'imagine un nombre d'hommes dans les chaînes, et tous condamnés à la mort, dont les uns étant chaque jour égorgés à la vue des autres, ceux qui restent voient leur propre condition dans celle de leurs semblables, et, se regardant les uns et les autres avec douleur et sans espérance, attendent à leur tour. C'est l'image de la condition des hommes.

—We came from Hiva Oa, and carried pigs and messages for Nuku Hiva, below the horizon. My father was chief. The taboo was strong, and we carried no women in the prau. The wind dropped, and returned from another quarter. The sea grew too smooth, and lustrous like the inside of a coconut; the southern sky merged with the sea. In the storm there were lost many pigs and an old man who had seen Nuku Hiva as a boy. When the sky cleared, it was night, and the stars were scrambled. At dawn the horizon all around us was unbroken; we strained to see when the great waves lifted us high. We sang to the sun, and slept in the shade of the bodies of the wakeful. The storm had torn away the hut. The cowards infected us. But the singing gave me comfort, and my father's presence sheltered me. He was the tallest and bravest, yet was among those first to yield up life. We devoured his body; his strength passed into me, though I was young. I long felt the island approaching. It gave the men hope and gaiety to touch me. The island first seemed a cloud; but Marheyo saw birds. Our sails were gone, and we paddled with hands that had lost shape. Our skin shredded in the water. Our throats had become stuck; we were silent. Two days and a night it took us to reach the island; at the second dawn its arms were reaching for us. We saw green bush and coconut palms above the rock. Before our strengths were fully revived, Karnoonoo and I fought. Though he had been a man feared in the village, I won, and killed him, grieving. We took thought to shelter. We built a house of stone, carving the soft rock, like ash, with our axes. We harvested fruit and fish, and learned to make tapa from the strange bark. We buried our dead. We carved a god from a log of the prau. We made women of one other. I was the youngest; I gave myself to those men whom I desired, the best-natured. It was not always the old who died. Demons of apathy seized Mehivi, the clown, and Kory-Kory, who had tended the god. The horizon seemed always about to speak to us; for what had we been brought here? We lived, and though we saw the others turn cold, and the jaws sink, and the body turn stiff and light like a child's canoe, those who remained were not sure that they would die. We buried them with the amulets we brought from the village. Now I am the last. I buried Marheyo, the three-fingered, a season ago, and at night he speaks to me.

This is the outline; but it would be the days, the evocation of the days . . . the green days. The tasks, the grass, the weather, the shades of sea and air. Just as a piece of turf torn from a meadow becomes a *gloria* when drawn by Dürer. Details. Details are the giant's fingers. He seizes the stick and strips the bark and shows, burning beneath, the moist white wood of joy. For I thought that this story, fully told, would become without my willing it a happy story, a story full of joy; had my powers been greater, we would know. As it is, you, like me, must take it on faith.

Packed Dirt, Churchgoing, a Dying Cat, a Traded Car

DIFFERENT THINGS move us. I, David Kern, am always affected—reassured, nostalgically pleased, even, as a member of my animal species, made proud—by the sight of bare earth that has been smoothed and packed firm by the passage of human feet. Such spots abound in small towns: the furtive break in the playground fence dignified into a thoroughfare, the trough of dust underneath each swing, the blurred path worn across a wedge of grass, the anonymous little mound or embankment polished by play and strewn with pebbles like the confetti aftermath of a wedding. Such unconsciously humanized intervals of clay, too humble and common even to have a name, remind me of my childhood, when one communes with dirt down among the legs, as it were, of presiding presences. The earth is our playmate then, and the call to supper has a piercing eschatological ring.

The corner where I now live was recently widened so that the cars going back and forth to the summer colony on the Point would not be troubled to slow down. My neighbor's house was sold to the town and wrecked and picked clean by salvagers and finally burned in a great bonfire of old notched beams and splintered clapboards that leaped tree-high throughout one whole winter day's cold drizzle. Then bulldozers, huge and yellow and loud, appeared on the street and began to gnaw, it seemed, at the corner of our house. My third child, a boy not yet two, came running from the window in tearful panic. After I tried to soothe him with an explanation, he followed me through the house sobbing and wailing " 'Sheen! 'Sheen!" while the machines made our rooms shake with the curses of their labor. They mashed my neighbor's foundation stones into the earth and trimmed the levelled lot just as my grandmother used to trim the excess dough from the edge of the pieplate. They brought the curve of the road right to the corner of my property, and the beaten path that does for a sidewalk in front of my home was sheared diagonally by a foot-high cliff.

Last night I was coming back from across the street, fresh from an impromptu civic lamentation with a neighbor at how unsightly, now that the snow was melted, the awkward-shaped vacant lot the bulldozers had left looked, with its high raw embankment gouged by rivulets and littered with old chimney bricks. And soon, we concluded, now that spring was here, it would be bristling with weeds. Crossing from this conversation, I noticed that where my path had been lopped the cliff no longer existed; feet—children's feet, mostly, for mostly children walk in our town—had worn the sharpness away and molded a little ramp by which ascent was easier.

This small modification, this modest work of human erosion, seemed precious to me not only because it recalled, in the slope and set of the dirt, a part of the path that long ago had led down from my parents' back yard to the high-school softball field. It seemed precious because it had been achieved accidentally, and had about it that repose of grace which is beyond willing. We in America have from the beginning been cleaving and baring the earth, attacking, reforming the immensity of nature we were given. We have explored, on behalf of all mankind, this paradox: the more matter is outwardly mastered, the more it overwhelms us in our hearts. Evidence—gaping right-of-ways, acres mercilessly scraped, bleeding mountains of muddy fill—surrounds us of a war that is incapable of ceasing, and it is good to know that now there are enough of us to exert a counter-force. If craters were to appear in our landscape tomorrow, the next day there would be usable paths threading down the blasted sides. As our sense of God's forested legacy to us dwindles, there grows, in these worn, rubbed, and patted patches, a sense of human legacy—like those feet of statues of saints which have lost their toes to centuries of kisses. One thinks of John Dewey's definition of God as the union of the actual and the ideal.

There was a time when I wondered why more people did not go to church. Taken purely as a human recreation, what could be more delightful, more unexpected than to enter a venerable and lavishly scaled building kept warm and clean for use one or two hours a week and to sit and stand in unison and sing and recite creeds and petitions that are like paths worn smooth in the raw terrain of our hearts? To listen, or not listen, as a poorly paid but resplendently robed man strives to console us with scraps of ancient epistles and halting accounts, hopelessly compromised by words, of those intimations of divine joy that are like pain in that, their instant gone, the mind cannot remember or believe them; to witness the windows donated by departed patrons and the altar flowers arranged by withdrawn hands and the whole considered spectacle lustrous beneath its patina of long use; to pay, for all this, no more than we are moved to give—surely in all democracy there is nothing like it. Indeed, it is the most available democratic experience. We vote less than once a year. Only in church and at the polls are we actually given our supposed value, the soul-unit of one, with its noumenal arithmetic of equality: one equals one equals one.

My preaching corrupts the words and corrupts me. Belief builds itself unconsciously and in consciousness is spent. Throughout my childhood I felt nothing in church but boredom and an oppressive futility. For reasons my father never explained, he was a dutiful churchman; my mother, who could use her senses, who had read Santayana and Wells, stayed home Sunday mornings, and I was all on her side, on the side of phenomena, in those years, though I went, with the other children, to Sunday school. It was not until we moved from the town and joined a country church that I, an adolescent of fifteen, my head a hotbed of girls and literature, felt a pleasant emotion in church. During Lent—that dull season, those forty gray days during which the earth prepares the resurrection that the church calendar seizes upon as conveniently emblematic—I ushered with my father at the Wednesday-night services. We would arrive in our old car—I think it was the '38 Chevrolet then—on those raw March nights and it pleasantly surprised me to find the building warm, the stoked furnace already humming its devotions in the basement. The nave was dimly lit, the congregation small, the sermon short, and the wind howled a nihilistic counterpoint beyond the black windows blotted with garbled apostles; the empty pews, making the minister seem remote and small and emblematic, intensified our sensation of huddling. There was a strong sepia flavor of early Christianity: a minority flock furtively gathered within a dying, sobbing empire. From the rear, the broad back and baked neck of the occasional dutiful son loomed bullishly above the black straw hats of the mischievous-looking old ladies, gnarled by farmwork, who sat in their rows like withered apples on the shelves of a sweet-smelling cellar. My father would cross and uncross and recross his legs and stare at his thoughts, which seemed distant. It was pleasant to sit beside him in the rear pew. He was not much of a man for sitting still. When my parents and I went to the movies, he insisted on having the aisle seat, supposedly to give his legs room. After about twenty minutes he would leap up and spend the rest of the show walking around in the back of the theatre drinking water and talking to the manager while my mother and I, abandoned, consoled ourselves with the flickering giants of make-believe. He had nothing of the passive in him; a church always became, for him, something he helped run. It was pleasant, and even exciting, when the moment for action came, to walk by his side up the aisle, the thump of our feet the only sound in the church, and to take the wooden, felt-floored plates from a shy blur of white robes and to administer the submission of alms. Coins and envelopes sought to cover the felt. I condescended, stooping gallantly into each pew. The congregation seemed the Others, reaching, with quarters glittering in their fingers, toward mysteries in which I was snugly involved. Even to usher at a church mixes us with the angels, and is a dangerous thing.

The churches of Greenwich Village had this second-century quality. In Manhattan, Christianity is so feeble its future seems before it. One walks to church past clattering cafeterias and glowering news vendors in winter weather that is always a shade of Lent, on pavements spangled with last night's vomit. The expectantly hushed shelter of the church is like one of those spots worn bare by a softball game in a weed-filled vacant lot. The presence of the city beats like wind at the glowing windows. One hastens home afterward, head down, hurrying to assume the disguise—sweaters and khaki pants—of a non-churchgoer. I tried not to go, but it was not in me not to go. I never attended the same church two Sundays in succession, for fear I would become known and be expected. To be known by face and name and financial weight robs us of our unitary soul, enrolls us against those Others. Devil's work. We are the others. It is of the essence to be a stranger in church.

On the island the very color of my skin made me strange. This island had been abandoned to the descendants of its slaves. Their church was on a hill; it has since been demolished, I have learned from letters, by a hurricane. To reach it one climbed a steep path made treacherous by the loose rubble of coral rock, jagged gray clinkers that bore no visible relation to the pastel branches that could be plucked, still pliant, from the shallows by Maid's Beach. Dull-colored goats were tethered along the path; their forelegs were tangled in their ropes so tightly that whenever they nodded the bush anchoring them nodded in answer. For windows the church possessed tall arched apertures filled not with stained glass but with air and outward vision; one could see the goats stirring the low foliage and the brightly dressed little girls who had escaped the service playing on the packed dirt around the church. The service was fatiguingly long. There were exhaustive petitionary prayers (for the Queen, the Prime Minister, Parliament) and many eight-versed hymns sung with a penetrating, lingering joy and accompanied by a hand-pumped organ. The organ breathed in and out, loud and soft, and the congregation, largely female, followed its ebb and flow at a brief but noticeable distance; their lips moved behind the singing, so I seemed immersed in an imperfectly synchronized movie. Musical stress, the West Indian accent, and elision worked upon the words a triple distortion. "Lait eth's waadsa *cull* raio-ind . . ." Vainly seeking my place in the hymn—for without a visual key I was lost—I felt lifted within a warm, soughing milk, an aspiring chant as patient as the nodding of the goats.

Throughout the service, restless deacons slipped in and out of the windows. Bored myself—for we grow sated even with consolation—I discovered that without moving from my pew I too could escape through those tall portals built to admit the breeze. I rested my eyes on earth's wide circle round. From this height the horizon of the sea was lifted halfway up the sky. The Caribbean seemed a steeply tilted blue plane to which the few fishing boats in the bay below had been attached like magnetized toys. God made the world, Aquinas says, in play.

Matter has its radiance and its darkness; it lifts and it buries. Things compete; a life demands a life. On another English island, in Oxford—it is a strange fact about Americans, that we tend to receive our supernatural mail on foreign soil—I helped a cat die. The incident had the signature: decisive but illegible. For years I did not tell my wife about it, for fear it would frighten her. Some hours before, I had left her at the hospital in the early stages of labor. Wearing a sterilized gown and mask, I had visited her in a white-tiled room along whose walls gleaming gutters stood ready to drain torrents of blood. Her face, scrubbed and polished, was fervent like a child's, and she seemed, lying there swathed in white, ready for nothing so much as a graduation ceremony. She would break off talking, and listen as if to the distant voice of a schoolmistress, and her face would grow rapt, and when the contraction had passed she would sigh and say, "That was a good one," and chatter some more to me of how I would feed myself alone and to whom I would send telegrams.

Shooed from the room, stripped of my mask, I tried to wait, and was told, the comical useless husband of American cartoons, to run on home; it would be "a time." I went outside and took a bus home. It was the last day of March. I had been born in March, and had looked forward to welcoming my child to the month; but she was late. We lived on Iffley Road, and around midnight, for some reason—I think to mail a letter, but what letter could have been that important?—I was out walking a few blocks from our flat. The night was cold enough for gloves. The sensations of turning into a father (or, rather, the lack of sensations: the failure of sympathetic pain, the anesthetized dread, the postponement of pride) made the street seem insubstantial. There was not that swishing company of headlights that along an American road throws us into repeated relief. The brick homes, save for an occasional introverted glow in an upstairs window, were dark in their vehement English privacy behind the thatchy hedges and spiked walls. The streetlamps—wintry, reserved—drained color from everything. Myself a shadow, I noticed another in the center of the road. A puddle of black, as I watched, it curled on itself; its ends lifted from the macadam and seemed to stretch in a yawn. Then it became inert again. I was horrified; the shape was about the size of a baby. When it curled the second time, I went to it, my footsteps the only sound in the street.

It was a cat that had been struck by a car. Struck but not quite killed: a testament to the modest speed and sensible size of English automobiles. By the impersonal witness of the lamps burning in the trees I couldn't be sure what color its fur was—it seemed orange-yellow, tabbied with stripes of dark ginger. The cat was plump and wore a collar. Someone had loved it. Blackness from one ear obscured one side of its head and when I touched here it was like a cup. For the third time, the cat stretched, the tips of its hind feet quivering luxuriously in that way cats have. With a great spastic effort it flipped over onto its other side, but made no cry. The only sound between us was my crooning as I carried it to the side of the street and laid it behind the nearest hedge.

A sallow upstairs light in this home was glowing. I wondered if the cat was theirs. Was it their love invested in my hands? Were they watching as I pushed, crouching, with my burden through their hedge? I wondered if I would be taken for a trespasser; as an American, I was nervous of English taboos. In my own country it was a not uncommon insult to kill a cat and throw the body into an enemy's yard, and I was afraid that this might be taken that way. I thought of writing a note to explain everything, but I had no paper and pen. I explained to the cat, how I was taking her (I felt the cat was female) out of the street so no more cars would hit her, how I would put her here in the nice safe dirt behind the hedge, where she could rest and get well. I did not believe she would get well; I think she was dead already. Her weight had felt dead in my hands and when I laid her down she did not stretch or twitch again.

Back in my flat, I discovered that one glove was smeared with blood. Most of the palm and three of the fingers were dyed wine-brown. I hadn't realized there was so much blood. I took off my gloves and carefully wrote a note, explaining that I had found this cat in the middle of the street, still alive, and that I had put it behind this hedge to be safe. If, as I thought, the cat was dead, I hoped that the finders would bury it. After some deliberation, I signed my name and address. I walked back and tucked the note under the cat's body, which seemed at home behind the hedge; it suffered my intrusion a trifle stiffly. It suggested I was making too much fuss, and seemed to say to me, *Run on home.*

Back in my flat once more, I felt abruptly tired, though my heart was pounding. I went to bed and set the alarm for three and read a book. I remember the title, it was Chesterton's *The Everlasting Man.* I turned off the light and prayed for my wife and, though I did not believe myself capable of it, fell asleep. The alarm at three came crashing into some innocent walk of a dream and my frail head felt like a hollow cup. I dressed and went out to the public phone booth a block away and called the hospital. A chirping voice, after some rummaging in the records, told me that several hours ago, in the first hour of April (in the United States it was still March), a perfect female infant had been born. To me.

The next morning, after all the telegrams had been managed, I went back to the hedge, and the cat and my note were gone. Though I had left my address, I never received a letter.

When we returned from England, we bought a car. We had ordered it through my parents from folders they had sent us, and though its shade of blue was more naïve, more like a robin's egg, than we had expected, this '55 Ford proved an excellent buy. Whether being shuffled from side to side of West Eighty-fifth Street every morning or being rammed in second gear up a washed-out mountain road in Vermont, it never complained. In New York hot tar from a roof-patching job rained onto its innocent paint, and in Vermont its muffler was racked and rent on a shelf of rock, and in Massachusetts it wallowed, its hot clutch stinking, up from more than one grave of snow. Not only sand and candy wrappers accumulate in a car's interior, but heroisms and instants of communion. Americans make love in their cars, and listen to ball games, and plot their wooing of the dollar: small wonder the landscape is sacrificed to these dreaming vehicles of unitary personhood.

In the beginning, my wife and I would lovingly lave with soap and warm water the unflecked skin of the hood as if it were the thorax of a broad blue baby, and toward the end we let the gallant old heap rust where it would. Its eggshell finish grew grizzled with the stains of dropped maple seeds. Its doors balked at closing; its windows refused to roll down. But I somehow never believed we would ever trade it in, though the little girl born across the ocean in the ominous turning of April, now a vocal and status-conscious democrat of nearly six, applied more and more pressure. The deal was consummated while my soul had its face turned, and Detroit contracted to devour her offspring. But before the new car arrived, there was a month's grace, and in this grace I enjoyed a final fling with my car, my first, my only—for all the others will be substitutes. It happened this way:

Dancing at a party with a woman not my wife, I took the opportunity to turn her hand in mine and kiss her palm. For some time her thighs had been slithering against mine, and, between dances, she developed a nervous clumsy trick of lurching against me, on tiptoe, and rubbing her breasts against my forearm, which was braced across my chest as I held a cigarette. My first thought was that I might burn her; my second, that Nature in her gruff maternal way had arranged one of her opportunities—as my mother, when I was a child, would unpredictably determine to give me a birthday or Halloween party. Obediently I bowed my head and kissed my friend's moist palm. As it withdrew from the advance, her fingertips caressed my chin in the absent-minded manner of one fingering the muzzle of an importunate dog. The exchange transposed us into a higher key; I could hardly hear my own voice, and our dancing lost all connection with the music, and my hand explored her spine from a great aerial distance. Her back seemed mysteriously taut and hard; the body of a strange woman retains more of its mineral content, not yet being transmuted into memory. In a sheltered corner of the room we stopped dancing altogether and talked, and what I distinctly remember is how her hands, beneath the steady and opaque appraisal of her eyes, in agitation blindly sought mine and seized and softly gripped, with infantile instinct, my thumbs. Just my thumbs she held, and as we talked she moved them this way and that as if she were steering me. When I closed my eyes, the red darkness inside my lids was vibrant, and when I rejoined my wife, and held her to dance, she asked, "Why are you panting?"

After we got home, and surveyed our four children, and in bed read a few pages made unbearably brilliant by the afterglow of gin, and turned out the light, she surprised me by not turning her back. Alcohol, with its loosening effect, touches women more deeply than men in this respect; or perhaps, like a matched pair of tuning forks, I had set her vibrating. Irritated by whatever illicit stimulations, we took it out on each other.

To my regret, I survived the natural bliss of satiety—when each muscle is like a petal snugly curved within the corolla—and was projected onto the seething, azoic territory of insomnia. That feathery anxious embrace of my erect thumbs tormented me in twenty postures. My stomach turned in love of that woman; I feared I would be physically sick and lay on my back gingerly and tried to soothe myself with the caress of headlights as they evolved from bright slits on the wall into parabolically accelerating fans on the ceiling and then vanished: this phenomenon, with its intimations of a life beyond me, had comforted wakeful nights in my earliest childhood. It was small comfort now. In Sunday school long ago I had been struck by the passage in which Jesus says that to lust after a woman in thought is the same as committing adultery. I found myself helplessly containing the conviction that wishes, not deeds, are judged. To crave a sin was to commit it; to touch the brink was to be on the floor of the chasm. The universe that so easily permitted me to commit adultery became, by logical steps each one of which went more steeply down than the one above it, a universe that would easily permit me to die. The depths of cosmic space, the maddening distension of time, history's forgotten slaughters, the child smothered in the dumped icebox, the recent breakdown of the molecular life-spiral, the proven physiological roots of the mind, the presence in our midst of idiots, Eichmanns, animals, and bacteria—all this evidence piled on, and I seemed already eternally forgotten. The dark vibrating air of my bedroom felt like the dust of my grave; the dust went up and up and I prayed upward into it, prayed, prayed for a sign, any glimmer at all, any microscopic loophole or chink in the chain of evidence, and saw none. I remembered a movie that had frightened me as a child; in it Jimmy Cagney, moaning and struggling, is dragged on rubber legs down the long corridor to the electric chair. I was that condemned man. My brain in its calcium vault shouted about injustice, thundered accusations into the lustreless and tranquil homogeneity of the air. Each second that my protest went unanswered justified it more certainly: the God who permitted me this fear was unworthy of existence. Each instant that my terror was extended amplified God's non-existence, so, as the graph of certain equations fluctuates more and more widely as it moves along the lateral coördinate, or as the magnetic motive-power in atom-smashers accelerates itself, I was caught in a vortex whose unbearably shrill pitch moved me at last to drop my weight on my wife's body and beg, "Wake up, Elaine. I'm so frightened."

I told her of the centuries coming when our names would be forgotten, of the millennia when our nation would be a myth and our continent an ocean, of the aeons when our earth would have vanished and the stars themselves be diffused into a uniform and irreversible cold. As, an hour before, I had transferred my lust to her, so now I tried to pass my fear into her. It seemed to offend her sense of good taste that I was jealous of future aeons and frantic because I couldn't live through them; she asked me if I had never been so sick I gave up caring whether I lived or died. This contemptible answer—animal stoicism—acquired a curious reinforcement: eventually, just as I had during the birth of my first child, I fell asleep. In my dreams, I was back in high school, with people I hadn't seen for years.

The next day, a Saturday, was my birthday. It passed like any day except that underneath the camouflage of furniture and voices and habitual actions I felt death like a wide army advancing. The newspaper told of nothing but atrocities. My children, wounded and appalled in their competition, came to me to be comforted and I was dismayed to see myself, a gutted shell, appearing to them as the embodiment and pledge of a safe universe. Friends visited, and for the first time truly in my life I realized that each face is suppressing knowledge of an immense catastrophe; our faces are dams that wrinkle under the strain.

Around six the telephone rang. It was my mother calling from Pennsylvania. I assumed she had called because of my birthday, so I chattered humorously about the discomforts of growing old for a minute before she could tell me, her voice growing faint, the news. My father was in the hospital. He had been walking around with chest pains for two weeks and suffered shortness of breath at night. She had finally coaxed him into a doctor's office; the doctor had taken a cardiogram and driven him straight to the hospital. He was a seriously sick man.

Instantly I was relieved. All day death had been advancing under cover and now it had struck, declared its position. My father had engaged the enemy and it would be defeated.

I was restored to crisp health in the play-world of action. That night we had a few friends in for my birthday party, and the next day I took the two older children to Sunday school and went myself to church. The faintly violet lozenge-panes of the tall white windows glowed and dimmed fitfully. It was a spottily overcast day, spitting a little snow. While

I was at church my wife had cooked a lamb dinner. As I drank the coffee it became clear that I must drive to Pennsylvania. My mother and I had agreed I would fly down and visit him in a few days; I would have to see about renting a car at the Philadelphia end. This was potentially awkward because, self-employed, I had no credit card. The awkwardness suddenly seemed easy to surmount. I would drive. The car would be traded in a few days; it had just been greased; I had a vision of escaping our foul New England spring by driving south. In half an hour my bag was packed. *Run on home.*

Along Route 128 I picked up a young sailor who rode with me all the way to New York and, for two hours through Connecticut, drove my car. I trusted him. He had the full body, the frank and fleshy blue-eyed face of the docile Titans—guileless, competent, mildly earnest—that we have fattened, an ocean removed from the slimming Latin passions and Nordic anxieties of Europe, on our unprecedented abundance of milk and honey, vitamins and protein. He was incongruously—and somehow reassuringly—tanned. He had got the tan in Key West, where he had spent twenty-four hours, hitching the rides to and from on Navy jets. He had spent the twenty-four hours sleeping on the beach and selecting souvenirs to send back to his parents and girlfriend. His parents lived in Salem, his girlfriend in Peabody. He wanted to marry her, but his parents had old-fashioned ideas, they thought he was too young. And a lot of these guys in the service say, Don't get married, don't ever get married. But she was a nice girl, not so pretty or anything, but really nice: he really wouldn't mind marrying her.

I asked him how old he was. He was twenty-two, and was being trained as an airplane mechanic. He wanted at the end of his hitch to come back to Salem and live. He figured an airplane mechanic could find some sort of job. I told him, with a paternal firmness that amazed my ears, to marry her; absolutely; his parents would get used to it. The thing about parents, I told him, was that secretly, no matter what you did, they liked you anyway. I told him I had married at the age of twenty-one and had never been sorry.

He asked me, "What do you do? Teach?"

This impressed me. My grandfather had been a teacher, and my father was a teacher, and from my childhood up it had been assumed by people that I in turn would become a teacher.

"No," I said. "I'm a writer."

He seemed less offended than puzzled. "What do you write?"

"Oh—whatever comes into my head."

"What's the point?"

"I don't know," I told him. "I wish I did. Maybe there are several points."

We talked less freely after that. At his request I left him off in wet twilight at a Texaco station near the entrance of the New Jersey Turnpike. He hoped to get a ride from there all the way to Washington. Other sailors were clustered out of the rain in the doorways of the station. They hailed him as if they had been waiting for him, and as he went to them he became, from the back, just one more sailor, anonymous, at sea. He did not turn and wave goodbye. I felt I had frightened him, which I regretted, because he had driven for me very well and I wanted him to marry his girl. In the dark I drove down the pike alone. In the first years of my car, when we lived in Manhattan, it would creep up to seventy-five on this wide black stretch without our noticing; now the needle found its natural level at sixty. The windshield wipers beat, and the wonderland lights of the Newark refineries were swollen and broken like bubbles by the raindrops on the side windows. For a dozen seconds a cross of blinking stars was suspended in the upper part of the windshield: an airplane above me was coming in to land.

I did not eat until I was on Pennsylvania soil. The Howard Johnsons in Pennsylvania are cleaner, less crowded, more homelike in their furnishings. The decorative plants seem to be honestly growing, and the waitresses have just a day ago removed the Mennonite cap from their hair, which is still pulled into a smooth bun flattering to their pallid, sly faces. They served me with that swift grace that comes in a region where food is still one of the pleasures. The familiar and subtle irony of their smiles wakened in me that old sense, of Pennsylvania knowingness—of knowing, that is, that the truth is good. They were the innkeeper's daughters, God had given us crops, and my wagon was hitched outside.

When I returned to the car, the music on the radio had changed color. The ersatz hiccup and gravel of Atlantic Seaboard hillbilly had turned, inland, backwards into something younger. As I passed the Valley Forge intersection the radio played a Benny Goodman quintet that used to make my scalp freeze. The speedometer went up to seventy without effort.

I left the toll road for our local highway and, slowing to turn into our dirt road, I was nearly rammed from behind by a pair of headlights that had been pushing, Pennsylvania style, six feet behind me. I parked beside my father's car in front of the barn. My mother came unseen into the yard, and, two voices calling in the opaque drizzle, while the dogs yapped deliriously in their pen, we debated whether I should move my car farther off the road. "Out of harm's way," my grandfather would have said. Complaining, I obeyed her. My mother turned as I carried my suitcase down the path of sandstone steppingstones, and led me to the back door as if I would not know the way. So it was not until we were inside the house that I could kiss her in greeting. She poured us two glasses of wine. Wine had a ceremonial significance in our family; we drank it seldom. My mother seemed cheerful, even silly, and it took an hour for the willed good cheer to ebb away. She turned her head and looked delicately at the rug, and the side of her neck reddened as she told me, "Daddy says he's lost all his faith."

"Oh, my." Since I had also lost mine, I could find nothing else to say. I remembered, in the silence, a conversation I had had with my father during a vacation from college. With the habitual simplicity of his eagerness to know, he had asked me, "Have you ever had any doubts of the existence of a Divine Being?"

"Sure," I had answered.

"I never have," he said. "It's beyond my ability to imagine it. The divinity of Jesus, yes; but the existence of a Divine Being, never." He stated this not as an attempt to influence me, but as a moderately curious fact he had that moment discovered about himself.

"He never was much one for faith," my mother added, hurt by my failure to speak. "He was strictly a works man."

I slept badly; I missed my wife's body, that weight of memory, beside me. I was enough of a father to feel lost out of my nest of little rustling souls. I kept looking out of the windows. The three red lights of the chimneys of the plant that had been built some miles away, to mine low-grade iron ore, seemed to be advancing over our neighbor's ridged field toward our farm. My mother had mistaken me for a stoic like my father and had not put enough blankets on the bed. I found an old overcoat of his and arranged it over me; its collar scratched my chin. I tipped into sleep and awoke. The morning was sharply sunny; sheep hustled, heads toppling, through the gauzy blue sky. It was authentic spring in Pennsylvania. Some of the grass in the lawn had already grown shiny and lank. A yellow crocus had popped up beside the BEWARE OF THE DOG sign my father had had an art student at the high school make for him.

I insisted we drive to Alton in my car, and then was sorry, for it seemed to insult their own. Just a few months ago my father had traded in on yet one more second-hand car: now he owned a '53 Dodge. But while growing up I had been ambushed by so many mishaps in my father's cars that I insisted we take the car I could trust. Or perhaps it was that I did not wish to take my father's place behind the wheel of his car. My father's place was between me and Heaven; I was afraid of being placed adjacent to that far sky. First we visited his doctor. Our old doctor, a man who believed that people simply "wore out" and nothing could be done about it, had several years ago himself worn out and died. The new doctor's office, in the center of the city, was furnished with a certain raw sophistication. Rippling music leaked from the walls, which were hung with semi-professional oils. He himself was a wiry and firm-tongued young man not much older than myself but venerable with competence and witnessed pain. Such are the brisk shepherds who hop us over the final stile. He brought down from the top of a filing cabinet a plaster model of the human heart. "Your own heart," he told me, "is nice and thin like this; but your dad's heart is enlarged. We believe the obstruction is here, in one of these little vessels on the outside, luckily for your dad."

Outside, in the streets of Alton, my own heart felt enlarged. A white sun warmed the neat façades of painted brick; chimneys red like peony shoots thrust through budding treetops. Having grown accustomed to the cramped, improvised cities of New England, I was impressed, like a tourist, by Alton's straight broad streets and handsome institutions. While my mother went off to buy my daughter a birthday present—April was nearly upon us—I returned a book she had borrowed from the Alton Public Library. I had forgotten the deep aroma of that place, mixed of dust and cleaning fluid and binder's glue and pastry baking in the bakery next door. Revisiting the shelf of P. G. Wodehouse that I had once read straight through, I took down *Mulliner Nights* and looked in the back for the stamped date, in '47 or '48, that would be me. I never thought to look for the section of the shelves where my own few books would be placed. They were not me. They were my children, touchy and self-willed.

In driving to the hospital on Alton's outskirts, we passed the museum grounds, where every tree and flower-bed wore a name-tag and black swans drifted through flotillas of crumbled bread. As a child I had believed literally that bread cast upon the waters came back doubled. Within the museum there were mummies with lips snarling back from their teeth in astonishment; a tiny gilt chair for a baby pharaoh; an elephant tusk carved into hundreds of tiny Chinamen and pagodas and squat leafy trees; miniature Eskimo villages that you lit up with a switch and peeped into like an Easter egg; cases of arrowheads; rooms of stuffed birds; and, upstairs, dower chests decorated with hearts and unicorns and tulips by the pious "plain people," and iridescent glassware from the kilns of Baron von Steigel, and slashing paintings of Pennsylvania woodland by the Shearer brothers, and bronze statuettes of wrestling Indians that stirred my first erotic dreams, and, in the round skylit room at the head of the marble stairs, a black-rimmed pool in whose center a naked green girl held to her pursed lips a shell whose transparent contents forever spilled from the other side, filling this whole vast upstairs—from whose Palladian windows the swans in their bready pond could be seen trailing fan-shaped wakes—with the trickle and splatter of falling water. The world then seemed to me an intricate wonder displayed for my delight with no price asked. Visible above the trees across the pond were rose glints of the hospital, an orderly multitude of tall brick rectangles set among levelled and well-tended grounds, an ideal city of the ill.

I had forgotten how grand the Alton hospital was. I had not seen its stately entrance, approached down a grassy mall, since, at the age of eight, I had left the hospital unburdened of my tonsils. Then, too, it had been spring, and the mall was bright with the first flush of green, and my mother was with me. I recalled it to her, and she said, "I felt so guilty. You were so sick."

"Really? I remember it as so pleasant." They had put a cup of pink rubber over my nose and there had been a thunderous flood of the smell of cotton candy and I opened my eyes and my mother was reading a magazine beside my bed.

"You were such a hopeful good boy," my mother said, and I did not look at her face for fear of seeing her crying.

I wondered aloud if a certain girl in my high-school class was still a nurse here.

"Oh, dear," my mother said. "Here I thought you came all this way to see your poor old father and all you care about is seeing—" And she used the girl's maiden name, though the girl had been married as long as I had.

Within the hospital, she surprised me by knowing the way. Usually, wherever we went, it was my father or I who knew the way. As I followed her through the linoleum maze, my mother's shoulders seemed already to have received the responsible shawl of widowhood. Like the halls of a palace, the hospital corridors were lined with petitioners, waiting for a verdict. Negro girls electrically dramatic in their starched white uniforms folded bales of cotton sheets; gray men pushed wrung mops. We went past an exit sign, down a stairway, into a realm where gaunt convalescents in bathrobes shuffled in and out of doorways. I saw my father diagonally through a doorway before we entered his room. He was sitting up in bed, supported sultanlike by a wealth of pillows and clad in red-striped pajamas.

I had never seen him in pajamas before; a great man for the shortest distance between two points, he slept in his underclothes. But, having been at last captured in pajamas, like a big-hearted lion he did not try to minimize his subdual, but lay fully exposed, without a sheet covering even his feet. Bare, they looked pale, thin-skinned, and oddly unused.

Except for a sullen lymphatic glow under his cheeks, his face was totally familiar. I had been afraid that his loss of faith would show, like the altered shape of his mouth after he had had all his teeth pulled. With grins we exchanged the shy handshake that my going off to college had forced upon us. I sat on the windowsill by his bed, my mother took the chair at the foot of the bed, and my father's roommate, a fortyish man flat on his back with a ruptured disc, sighed and blew smoke toward the ceiling and tried, I suppose, not to hear us. Our conversation, though things were radically changed, followed old patterns. Quite quickly the talk shifted from him to me. "I don't know how you do it, David," he said. "I couldn't do what you're doing if you paid me a million dollars a day." Embarrassed and flattered, as usual, I tried to shush him, and he disobediently turned to his roommate and called loudly, "I don't know where the kid gets his ideas. Not from his old man, I know that. I never gave the poor kid an idea in my life."

"Sure you did," I said softly, trying to take pressure off the man with the hurting back. "You taught me two things. One, always butter bread toward the edges because enough gets in the middle anyway; and, two, no matter what happens to you, it'll be a new experience."

To my dismay, this seemed to make him melancholy. "That's right, David," he said. "No matter what happens to you, it'll be a new experience. The only thing that worries me is that *she*"—he pointed at my mother—"will crack up the car. I don't want anything to happen to your mother."

"The car, you mean," my mother said, and to me she added, "It's a sin, the way he worships that car."

My father didn't deny it. "Jesus, I love that car," he said. "It's the first car I've ever owned that didn't go bad on me. Remember all those heaps we used to ride back and forth in?"

The old Chevy was always getting dirt in the fuel pump and refusing to start. Once, going down Firetown Hill, the left front wheel had broken off the axle; my father wrestled with the steering wheel while the tires screamed and the white posts of the guard fence floated toward my eyes. When the car slid sideways to a stop just short of the embankment, my father's face was stunned and the corners of his mouth dribbled saliva. I was surprised; it had not occurred to me to be frightened. The '36 Buick had drunk oil, a quart every fifty miles, and liked to have flat tires after midnight, when I would be sailing home with a scrubbed brain and the smell of lipstick in my nose. Once, when we had both gone into town and I had dropped him off and taken the car, I had absent-mindedly driven home alone. I came in the door and my mother said, "Why, where's your father?"

My stomach sank. "My Lord," I said, "I forgot I had him!"

As, smiling, I took in breath and prepared to dip with him into reminiscence of these adventures, my father, staring stonily into the air above his pale and motionless toes, said, "I love this place. There are a lot of wonderful gentlemen in here. The only thing that worries me is that Mother will crack up the car."

My mother was leaning forward pink-faced in the chair at the foot of the bed, trying to smile. He glanced at her and said to me, "It's a funny feeling. The night before we went to see the doctor, I woke up and couldn't get my breath and realized I wasn't ready to die. I had always thought I would be. It's a funny feeling."

"Luckily for your dad," "all his faith," "wonderful gentlemen": these phrases were borne in on me, and my tongue seemed pressed flat on the floor of its grave. The pajama stripes under my eyes stirred and streamed, real blood. I wanted to speak, to say how I still needed him and to beg him not to leave me, but there were no words, no form of words available in our tradition. A pillar of smoke poured upward from the sighing man in the other bed.

Into this pit hesitantly walked a plain, painfully clean girl with a pad and pencil. She had yellow hair, thick lips, and, behind pink-rimmed glasses, large eyes that looked as if they had been corrected from being crossed. They flicked across our faces and focused straight ahead in that tunnel-vision gaze of those who know perfectly well they are figures of fun; the Jehovah's Witnesses who come to the door wear that guarded expression. She approached the bed where my father lay barefoot and, suppressing a stammer, explained that she was from Lutheran Home Missions and that they kept accounts of all hospitalized Lutherans and notified the appropriate pastors to make visitations. Perhaps she had measured my father for a rebuff. Perhaps her eyes, more practiced in this respect than mine, spotted the external signs of loss of faith that I couldn't see. At any rate my father was a Lutheran by adoption; he had been born and raised a Presbyterian and still looked like one.

"That's *aw*fully nice of you," he told the girl. "I don't see how you people do it on the little money we give you."

Puzzled, she dimpled and moved ahead with her routine. "Your church is—?"

He told her, pronouncing every syllable meticulously and consulting my mother and me as to whether the word "Evangelical" figured in the official title.

"That would make your pastor Reverend—"

"Yeah. He'll be in, don't worry about it. Wild horses couldn't keep him away. Nothing he likes better than to get out of the sticks and drive into Alton. I didn't mean to confuse you a minute ago; what I meant was, just last week in church council we were talking about you people. We couldn't figure out how you do anything on the little money we give you. After we've got done feeding the furnace and converting the benighted Hindu there isn't anything left over for you people that are trying to help the poor devils in our own back yard."

The grinning girl was lost in this onslaught of praise and clung to the shreds of her routine. "In the meantime," she recited, "here is a pamphlet you might like to read."

My father took it from her with a swooping gesture so expansive I got down from the windowsill to restrain him physically, if necessary. That he must lie still was my one lever, my one certainty about his situation. "That's awfully nice of you," he told the girl. "I don't know where the hell you get the money to print these things."

"We hope your stay in the hospital is pleasant and would like to wish you a speedy recovery to full health."

"Thank you; I know you're sincere when you say it. As I was telling my son David here, if I can do what the doctors tell me I'll be all right. First time in my life I've ever tried to do what anybody ever told me to do. The kid was just telling me, 'No matter what happens to you, Pop, it'll be a new experience.' "

"Now, if you will excuse me, I have other calls to pay."

"Of course. You go right ahead, sick Lutherans are a dime a dozen. You're a wonderful woman to be doing what you're doing."

And she left the room transformed into just that. As a star shines in our Heaven though it has vanished from the universe, so my father continued to shed faith upon others. For the remainder of my visit with him his simple presence so reassured me, filled me with such a buoyant humor, that my mother surprised me, when we had left the hospital, by remarking that we had tired him.

"I hadn't noticed," I said.

"And it worries me," she went on, "the way he talks about the movies all the time. You know he never liked them." When I had offered to stay another night so I could visit him again, he had said, "No, instead of that why don't you take your mother tomorrow to the movies?" Rather than do that, I said, I would drive home. It took him a moment, it seemed, to realize that by my home I meant a far place, where I had a wife and children, dental appointments and work obligations. Though at the time I was impatient to have his consent to leave, it has since occurred to me that during that instant when his face was blank he was swallowing the realization that he could die and my life would go on. Having swallowed, he told me how good I had been to come all this way to see him. He told me I was a good son and a good father; he clasped my hand. I felt I would ascend straight north from his touch.

I drove my mother back to her farm and got my bag and said goodbye on the lawn. The little sandstone house was pink in the declining sunlight; the lawn was a tinkling clutter of shy rivulets. Standing beside the BEWARE OF THE DOG sign with its companion of a crocus, she smiled and said, "This is like when you were born. Your father drove through a snowstorm all the way from Wheeling in our old Model A." He had been working with the telephone company then; the story of his all-night ride was the oldest narrative in which I was a character.

Darkness did not fall until New Jersey. The hour of countryside I saw from the Pennsylvania Turnpike looked enchanted—the branches of the trees underpainted with budding russet, the meadows nubbled like new carpets, the bronze sun slanting on Valley Forge and Levittown alike. I do not know what it is that is so welcome to me in the Pennsylvania landscape, but it is the same quality—perhaps of reposing in the certainty that the truth is good—that exists in Pennsylvania faces. It seemed to me for this sunset hour that the world is our bride, given to us to love, and the terror and joy of the marriage is that we bring to it a nature not our bride's.

There was no sailor to help me drive the nine hours back. New Jersey began in twilight and ended in darkness, and Manhattan made its gossamer splash at show-time hour, eight o'clock. The rest of the trip was more and more steeply uphill. The Merritt Parkway seemed meaninglessly coquettish, the light-controlled stretch below Hartford maddeningly obstinate, and the hour above that frighteningly empty. Distance grew thicker and thicker; the intricate and effortful mechanics of the engine, the stellar infinity of explosive sparks needed to drive it, passed into my body, and wearied me. Repeatedly I stopped for coffee and the hallucinatory comfort of human faces, and after every stop my waiting car, companion and haven and willing steed, responded to my pressure. It began to seem a miracle that the car could gather speed from my numb foot; the very music on the radio seemed a drag on our effort, and I turned it off, obliterating earthly time. We climbed through a space fretted by scattered brilliance and bathed in a monotonous wind. I had been driving forever; houses, furniture, churches, women were all things I had innocently dreamed. And through those aeons my car, beginning as a mechanical assembly of molecules, evolved into something soft and organic and consciously brave. I lost first heart, then head, and finally any sense of my body. In the last hour of the trip I ceased to care or feel or in any real sense see, but the car, though its soul the driver had died, maintained steady forward motion, and completed the journey safely. Above my back yard the stars were frozen in place, and the shapes of my neighbors' houses wore the wonder that children induce by whirling.

Any day now we will trade it in; we are just waiting for the phone to ring. I know how it will be. My father traded in many cars. It happens so cleanly, before you expect it. He would drive off in the old car up the dirt road exactly as usual, and when he returned the car would be new to us, and the old was gone, gone, utterly dissolved back into the mineral world from which it was conjured, dismissed without a blessing, a kiss, a testament, or any ceremony of farewell. We in America need ceremonies, is I suppose, sailor, the point of what I have written.

In Football Season

DO YOU REMEMBER a fragrance girls acquire in autumn? As you walk beside them after school, they tighten their arms about their books and bend their heads forward to give a more flattering attention to your words, and in the little intimate area thus formed, carved into the clear air by an implicit crescent, there is a complex fragrance woven of tobacco, powder, lipstick, rinsed hair, and that perhaps imaginary and certainly elusive scent that wool, whether in the lapels of a jacket or the nap of a sweater, seems to yield when the cloudless fall sky like the blue bell of a vacuum lifts toward itself the glad exhalations of all things. This fragrance, so faint and flirtatious on those afternoon walks through the dry leaves, would be banked a thousandfold on the dark slope of the stadium when, Friday nights, we played football in the city.

"We"—we the school. A suburban school, we rented for some of our home games the stadium of a college in the city of Alton three miles away. My father, a teacher, was active in the Olinger High athletic department, and I, waiting for him beside half-open doors of varnished wood and frosted glass, overheard arguments and felt the wind of the worries that accompanied this bold and at that time unprecedented decision. Later, many of the other county high schools followed our lead; for the decision was vindicated. The stadium each Friday night when we played was filled. Not only students and parents came but spectators unconnected with either school, and the money left over when the stadium rent was paid supported our entire athletic program. I remember the smell of the grass crushed by footsteps behind the end zones. The smell was more vivid than that of a meadow, and in the blue electric glare the green vibrated as if excited, like a child, by being allowed up late. I remember my father taking tickets at the far corner of the wall, wedged into a tiny wooden booth that made him seem somewhat magical, like a troll. And of course I remember the way we, the students, with all of our jealousies and antipathies and deformities, would be—beauty and boob, sexpot and grind—crushed together like flowers pressed to yield to the black sky a concentrated homage, an incense, of cosmetics, cigarette smoke, warmed wool, hot dogs, and the tang, both animal and metallic, of clean hair. In a hoarse olfactory shout, these odors ascended. A dense haze gathered along the ceiling of brightness at the upper limit of the arc lights, whose glare blotted out the stars and made the sky seem romantically void and intimately near, like the death that now and then stooped and plucked one of us out of a crumpled automobile. If we went to the back row and stood on the bench there, we could look over the stone lip of the stadium down into the houses of the city, and feel the cold November air like the black presence of the ocean beyond the rail of a ship; and when we left after the game and from the hushed residential streets of this part of the city saw behind us a great vessel steaming with light, the arches of the colonnades blazing like portholes, the stadium seemed a great ship sinking and we the survivors of a celebrated disaster.

To keep our courage up, we sang songs, usually the same song, the one whose primal verse runs,

> Oh, you can't get to Heaven
> *(Oh, you can't get to Heaven)*
> In a rocking chair
> *(In a rocking chair)*,
> 'Cause the Lord don't want
> *('Cause the Lord don't want)*
> No lazy people there!
> *(No lazy people there!)*

And then repeated, double time. It was a song for eternity; when we ran out of verses, I would make them up:

> Oh, you can't get to Heaven
> *(Oh, you can't get to Heaven)*
> In Smokey's Ford
> *(In Smokey's Ford)*
> 'Cause the cylin*ders*
> *('Cause the cylin*ders)*
> Have to be rebored.
> *(Have to be rebored.)*

Down through the nice residential section, on through the not-so-nice and the shopping district, past dark churches where stained-glass windows, facing inward, warned us with left-handed blessings, down Warren

Avenue to the Running Horse Bridge, and across the bridge we walked, then two miles up the Alton Pike to Olinger, following the trolley tracks. My invention would become reckless:

> Oh, you can't get to Heaven
> *(Oh, you can't get to Heaven)*
> In a motel bed
> *(In a motel bed)*
> 'Cause the sky is blue
> *('Cause the sky is blue)*
> And the sheets are red.
> *(And the sheets are red.)*

Few of us had a license to drive, and fewer still had visited a motel. We were at that innocent age, on the borderline of sixteen, when damnation seems a delicious promise. There was Mary Louise Hornberger, who was tall and held herself with such upright and defiant poise that she was Mother in both our class plays, and Alma Bidding, with her hook nose and her smug smile caricatured in cerise lipstick, and Joanne Hardt, whose father was a typesetter, and Marilyn Wenrich, who had a gray front tooth and in study hall liked to have the small of her back scratched, and Nanette Seifert, with her button nose and black wet eyes and peach-down cheeks framed in the white fur frilling the blue hood of her parka. And there were boys—Henny Gring, Leo Horst, Hawley Peters, Jack Lillijedahl, myself. Sometimes these, sometimes less or more. Once there was Billy Trupp on crutches. Billy played football and, though only a sophomore, had made the varsity that year, until he broke his ankle. He was dull and dogged and liked Alma, and she with her painted smile led him on lovingly. We offered for his sake to take the trolley, but he had already refused a car ride back to Olinger and obstinately walked with us, loping his heavy body along on the crutches, his lifted foot a boulder of plaster. His heroism infected us all; we taunted the cold stars with song, one mile, two miles, three miles. How slowly we went! With what a luxurious sense of waste did we abuse this stretch of time! For as children we had lived in a tight world of ticking clocks and punctual bells, where every minute was an admonition to thrift and where tardiness, to a child running late down a street with his panicked stomach burning, seemed the most mysterious and awful of sins. Now, turning the corner into adulthood, we found time to be instead a black immensity endlessly supplied, like the wind.

We would arrive in Olinger after the drugstores, which had kept open for the first waves of people returning from the game, were shut. Except for the streetlights, the town was dark; it was betranced, like a town in a fable. We scattered, each escorting a girl to her door; and there, perhaps, for a moment, you bowed your face into that silent crescent of fragrance, and tasted it, and let it bite into you indelibly. The other day, in a town far from Olinger, I passed on the sidewalk two girls utterly unknown to me and half my age, and sensed, very faintly, that flavor from far off carried in their bent arms like a bouquet. And, continuing to walk, I felt myself sink into a chasm deeper than the one inverted above us on those Friday nights during football season.

After seeing the girl home, I would stride through the hushed streets, where the rustling leaves seemed torn scraps scattered in the wake of the game, and go to Mr. Lloyd Stephens' house. There, looking in the little square window of his front storm door, I could see down a dark hall into the lit kitchen where Mr. Stephens and my father and Mr. Jesse Honneger were counting money around a worn porcelain table. Stephens, a local contractor, was the school-board treasurer, and Honneger, who taught social science, was chairman of the high-school athletic department. They were still counting; the silver stacks slipped and glinted among their fingers, and the gold of beer stood in cylinders beside their hairy wrists. Their sleeves were rolled up. Smoke, like a fourth presence, wings spread, hung over their heads. They were still counting, so it was all right. I was not late. We lived ten miles away, and I could not go home until my father was ready. Some nights it took until midnight. I would knock and pull open the storm door and push open the real door and it would be warm in the contractor's hall. I would accept a glass of ginger ale and sit in the kitchen with the men until they were done. It was late, very late, but I was not blamed; it was permitted. Silently counting and expertly tamping the coins into little cylindrical wrappers of colored paper, the men ordered and consecrated this realm of night into which my days had never extended before. The hour or more behind me, which I had spent so wastefully, in walking when a trolley would have been swifter, and so wickedly, in blasphemy and lust, was past and forgiven me; it had been necessary; it was permitted.

Now I peek into windows and open doors and do not find that air of permission. It has fled the world. Girls walk by me carrying their invisible bouquets from fields still steeped in grace, and I look up in the manner of one who follows with his eyes the passage of a hearse, and remembers what pierces him.

OUT IN THE WORLD

The Lucid Eye in Silver Town

THE FIRST TIME I visited New York City, I was thirteen and went with my father. I went to meet my Uncle Quin and to buy a book about Vermeer. The Vermeer book was my idea, and my mother's; meeting Uncle Quin was my father's. A generation ago, my uncle had vanished in the direction of Chicago and become, apparently, rich; in the last week he had come east on business and I had graduated from the eighth grade with high marks. My father claimed that I and his brother were the smartest people he had ever met—"go-getters," he called us, with perhaps more irony than at the time I gave him credit for—and in his visionary way he suddenly, irresistibly felt that now was the time for us to meet. New York in those days was seven dollars away; we measured everything, distance and time, in money then. World War II was over, but we were still living in the Depression. My father and I set off with the return tickets and a five-dollar bill in his pocket. The five dollars was for the book.

My mother, on the railway platform, suddenly exclaimed, "I *hate* the Augusts." This surprised me, because we were all Augusts—I was an August, my father was an August, Uncle Quincy was an August, and she, I had thought, was an August.

My father gazed serenely over her head and said, "You have every reason to. I wouldn't blame you if you took a gun and shot us all. Except for Quin and your son. They're the only ones of us ever had any get up and git." Nothing was more infuriating about my father than his way of agreeing.

Uncle Quin didn't meet us at Pennsylvania Station. If my father was disappointed, he didn't reveal it to me. It was after one o'clock and all we had for lunch were two candy bars. By walking what seemed to me a very long way on pavements only a little broader than those of my home town, and not so clean, we reached the hotel, which sprouted somehow from the caramel-colored tunnels under Grand Central Station. The lobby smelled of perfume. After the clerk had phoned Quincy August that a man who said he was his brother was at the desk, an elevator took us to the twentieth floor. Inside the room sat three men, each in a gray or blue suit with freshly pressed pants and garters peeping from under the cuffs when they crossed their legs. The men were not quite interchangeable. One had a caterpillar-shaped mustache, one had tangled blond eyebrows like my father's, and the third had a drink in his hand—the others had drinks, too, but were not gripping them so tightly.

"Gentlemen, I'd like you to meet my brother Marty and his young son," Uncle Quin said.

"The kid's name is Jay," my father added, shaking hands with each of the two men, staring them in the eye. I imitated my father, and the mustached man, not expecting my firm handshake and stare, said, "Why, hello there, Jay!"

"Marty, would you and the boy like to freshen up? The facilities are through the door and to the left."

"Thank you, Quin. I believe we will. Excuse me, gentlemen."

"Certainly."

"Certainly."

My father and I went into the bedroom of the suite. The furniture was square and new and all the same shade of maroon. On the bed was an opened suitcase, also new. The clean, expensive smells of leather and lotion were beautiful to me. Uncle Quin's underwear looked silk and was full of fleurs-de-lis. When I was through in the lavatory, I made for the living room, to rejoin Uncle Quin and his friends.

"Hold it," my father said. "Let's wait in here."

"Won't that look rude?"

"No. It's what Quin wants."

"Now, Daddy, don't be ridiculous. He'll think we've died in here."

"No, he won't, not my brother. He's working some deal. He doesn't want to be bothered. I know how my brother works; he got us in here so we'd stay in here."

"*Really*, Pop. You're such a schemer." But I did not want to go in there without him. I looked around the room for something to read. There was nothing, not even a newspaper, except a shiny little pamphlet about the hotel itself. I wondered when we would get a chance to look for the Vermeer book, and what the men in the next room were talking about. I wondered why Uncle Quin was so short, when my father was so tall. By leaning out of the window, I could see taxicabs maneuvering like windup toys.

My father came and stood beside me. "Don't lean out too far."

I edged out inches farther and took a big bite of the high cold air spiced by the distant street noises. "Look at the green cab cut in front of the yellow," I said. "Should they be making U-turns on that street?"

"In New York it's O.K. Survival of the fittest is the only law here."

"Isn't that the Chrysler Building?"

"Yes, isn't it graceful, though? It always reminds me of the queen of the chessboard."

"What's the one beside it?"

"I don't know. Some big gravestone. The one deep in back, from this window, is the Woolworth Building. For years it was the tallest building in the world."

As, side by side at the window, we talked, I was surprised that my father could answer so many of my questions. As a young man, before I was born, he had travelled, looking for work; this was not *his* first trip to New York. Excited by my new respect, I longed to say something to remold that calm, beaten face.

"Do you really think he meant for us to stay out here?" I asked.

"Quin is a go-getter," he said, gazing over my head. "I admire him. Anything he wanted, from little on up, he went after it. Slam. Bang. His thinking is miles ahead of mine—just like your mother's. You can feel them pull out ahead of you." He moved his hands, palms down, like two taxis, the left quickly pulling ahead of the right. "You're the same way."

"Sure, sure." My impatience was not merely embarrassment at being praised; I was irritated that he considered Uncle Quin as smart as myself. At that point in my life I was sure that only stupid people took an interest in money.

When Uncle Quin finally entered the bedroom, he said, "Martin, I hoped you and the boy would come out and join us."

"Hell, I didn't want to butt in. You and those men were talking business."

"Lucas and Roebuck and I? Now, Marty, it was nothing that my own brother couldn't hear. Just a minor matter of adjustment. Both those men are fine men. Very important in their own fields. I'm disappointed that you couldn't see more of them. Believe me, I hadn't meant for you to hide in here. Now, what kind of drink would you like?"

"I don't care. I drink very little any more."

"Scotch-and-water, Marty?"

"Swell."

"And the boy? What about some ginger ale, young man? Or would you like milk?"

"The ginger ale," I said.

"There was a day, you know, when your father could drink any two men under the table."

As I remember it, a waiter brought the drinks to the room, and while we were drinking them I asked if we were going to spend all afternoon in this room. Uncle Quin didn't seem to hear, but five minutes later he suggested that the boy might like to take a look around the city—Gotham, he called it, Baghdad-on-the-Subway. My father said that that would be a once-in-a-lifetime treat for the kid. He always called me "the kid" when I was sick or had lost at something or was angry—when he felt sorry for me, in short. The three of us went down in the elevator and took a taxi ride down Broadway, or up Broadway—I wasn't sure. "This is what they call the Great White Way," Uncle Quin said several times. Once he apologized, "In daytime it's just another street." The trip didn't seem so much designed for sightseeing as for getting Uncle Quin to the Pickernut Club, a little restaurant set in a block of similar canopied places. I remember we stepped down into it and it was dark inside. A piano was playing "There's a Small Hotel."

"He shouldn't do that," Uncle Quin said. Then he waved to the man behind the piano. "How are you, Freddie? How are the kids?"

"Fine, Mr. August, fine," Freddie said, bobbing his head and smiling and not missing a note.

"That's Quin's song," my father said to me as we wriggled our way into a slippery curved seat at a round table.

I didn't say anything, but Uncle Quin, overhearing some disapproval in my silence, said, "Freddie's a first-rate man. He has a boy going to Colgate this autumn."

I asked, "Is that really your song?"

Uncle Quin grinned and put his warm broad hand on my shoulder; I hated, at that age, being touched. "I let them think it is," he said, oddly purring. "To me, songs are like young girls. They're all pretty."

A waiter in a red coat scurried up. "Mr. August! Back from the West? How are you, Mr. August?"

"Getting by, Jerome, getting by. Jerome, I'd like you to meet my kid brother, Martin."

"How do you do, Mr. Martin. Are you paying New York a visit? Or do you live here?"

My father quickly shook hands with Jerome, somewhat to Jerome's surprise. "I'm just up for the afternoon, thank you. I live in a hick town in Pennsylvania you never heard of."

"I see, sir. A quick visit."

"This is the first time in six years that I've had a chance to see my brother."

"Yes, we've seen very little of him these past years. He's a man we can never see too much of, isn't that right?"

Uncle Quin interrupted. "This is my nephew Jay."

"How do you like the big city, Jay?"

"Fine." I didn't duplicate my father's mistake of offering to shake hands.

"Why, Jerome," Uncle Quin said, "my brother and I would like to have a Scotch-on-the-rocks. The boy would like a ginger ale."

"No, wait," I said. "What kinds of ice cream do you have?"

"Vanilla and chocolate, sir."

I hesitated. I could scarcely believe it, when the cheap drugstore at home had fifteen flavors.

"I'm afraid it's not a very big selection," Jerome said.

"I guess vanilla."

"Yes, sir. One plate of vanilla."

When my ice cream came it was a golf ball in a flat silver dish; it kept spinning away as I dug at it with my spoon. Uncle Quin watched me and asked, "Is there anything especially Jay would like to do?"

"The kid'd like to get into a bookstore," my father said.

"A bookstore. What sort of book, Jay?"

I said, "I'd like to look for a good book of Vermeer."

"Vermeer," Uncle Quin pronounced slowly, relishing the *r*'s, pretending to give the matter thought. "Dutch school."

"He's Dutch, yes."

"For my own money, Jay, the French are the people to beat. We have four Degas ballet dancers in our living room in Chicago, and I could sit and look at one of them for hours. I think it's wonderful, the feeling for balance the man had."

"Yeah, but don't Degas's paintings always remind you of colored drawings? For actually *looking* at things in terms of paint, for the lucid eye, I think Vermeer makes Degas look sick."

Uncle Quin said nothing, and my father, after an anxious glance across the table, said, "That's the way he and his mother talk all the time. It's all beyond me. I can't understand a thing they say."

"Your mother is encouraging you to be a painter, is she, Jay?" Uncle Quin's smile was very wide, and his cheeks were pushed out as if each held a candy.

"Sure, I suppose she is."

"Your mother is a very wonderful woman, Jay," Uncle Quin said.

It was such an embarrassing remark, and so much depended upon your definition of "wonderful," that I dug at my ice cream, and my father asked Uncle Quin about his own wife, Edna. When we left, Uncle Quin signed the check with his name and the name of some company. It was close to five o'clock.

My uncle didn't know much about the location of bookstores in New York—his last twenty years had been spent in Chicago—but he thought that if we went to Forty-second Street and Sixth Avenue we should find something. The cab driver let us out beside a park that acted as kind of a back yard for the Public Library. It looked so inviting, so agreeably dusty, with the pigeons and the men nodding on the benches and the office girls in their taut summer dresses, that, without thinking, I led the two men into it. Shimmering buildings arrowed upward and glinted through the treetops. This was New York, I told myself: the silver town. Towers of ambition rose, crystalline, within me. "If you stand here," my father said, "you can see the Empire State." I went and stood beneath my father's arm and followed with my eyes the direction of it. Something sharp and hard fell into my right eye. I ducked my head and blinked; it was painful.

"What's the trouble?" Uncle Quin's voice asked.

My father said, "The poor kid's got something into his eye. He has the worst luck that way of anybody I ever knew."

The thing seemed to have life. It bit. "Ow," I said, angry enough to cry.

"If we can get him out of the wind," my father's voice said, "maybe I can see it."

"No, now, Marty, use your head. Never fool with the eyes or ears. The hotel is within two blocks. Can you walk two blocks, Jay?"

"I'm blind, not lame," I snapped.

"He has a ready wit," Uncle Quin said.

Between the two men, shielding my eye with a hand, I walked to the hotel. From time to time, one of them would take my other hand, or put one of theirs on my shoulder, but I would walk faster, and the hands would drop away. I hoped our entrance into the hotel lobby would not be too conspicuous; I took my hand from my eye and walked erect, defying the impulse to stoop. Except for the one lid being shut and possibly my face being red, I imagined I looked passably suave. However, my guardians lost no time betraying me. Not only did they walk at my heels, as if I might topple any instant, but my father told one old bum sitting in the lobby, "Poor kid got something in his eye," and Uncle Quin, passing the desk, called, "Send up a doctor to Twenty-eleven."

"You shouldn't have done that, Quin," my father said in the elevator. "I can get it out, now that he's out of the wind. This is happening all the time. The kid's eyes are too far front in his head."

"Never fool with the eyes, Martin. They are your most precious tool in life."

"It'll work out," I said, though I didn't believe it would. It felt like a steel chip, deeply embedded.

Up in the room, Uncle Quin made me lie down on the bed. My father, a handkerchief wadded in his hand so that one corner stuck out, approached me, but it hurt so much to open the eye that I repulsed him. "Don't torment me," I said, twisting my face away. "What good does it do? The doctor'll be up."

Regretfully my father put the handkerchief back into his pocket.

The doctor was a soft-handed man with little to say to anybody; he wasn't pretending to be the family doctor. He rolled my lower eyelid on a thin stick, jabbed with a Q-tip, and showed me, on the end of the Q-tip, an eyelash. My own eyelash. He dropped three drops of yellow fluid into the eye to remove any chance of infection. The fluid stung, and I shut my eyes, leaning back into the pillow, glad it was over. When I opened them, my father was passing a bill into the doctor's hand. The doctor thanked him, winked at me, and left. Uncle Quin came out of the bathroom.

"Well, young man, how are you feeling now?" he asked.

"Fine."

"It was just an eyelash," my father said.

"*Just* an eyelash! Well, I know how an eyelash can feel like a razor blade in there. But, now that the young invalid is recovered, we can think of dinner."

"No, I really appreciate your kindness, Quin, but we must be getting back to the sticks. I have an eight-o'clock meeting I should be at."

"I'm extremely sorry to hear that. What sort of meeting, Marty?"

"A church council."

"So you're still doing church work. Well, God bless you for it."

"Grace wanted me to ask you if you couldn't possibly come over some day. We'll put you up overnight. It would be a real treat for her to see you again."

Uncle Quin reached up and put his arm around his younger brother's shoulders. "Martin, I'd like that better than anything in the world. But I am solid with appointments, and I must head west this Thursday. They don't let me have a minute's repose. Nothing would please my heart better than to share a quiet day with you and Grace in your home. Please give her my love, and tell her what a wonderful boy she is raising. The two of you are raising."

My father promised, "I'll do that." And, after a little more fuss, we left.

"The child better?" the old man in the lobby called to us on the way out.

"It was just an eyelash, thank you, sir," my father said.

When we got outside, I wondered if there were any bookstores still open.

"We have no money."

"None at all?"

"The doctor charged five dollars. That's how much it costs in New York to get something in your eye."

"I didn't do it on purpose. Do you think I pulled out the eyelash and stuck it in there myself? *I* didn't tell you to call the doctor."

"I know that."

"Couldn't we just go into a bookstore and look a minute?"

"We haven't time, Jay."

But when we reached Pennsylvania Station, it was over thirty minutes until the next train left. As we sat on a bench, my father smiled reminiscently. "Boy, he's smart, isn't he? His thinking is sixty light-years ahead of mine."

"Who? Whose thinking?"

"My brother. Notice the way he hid in the bathroom until the doctor was gone? That's how to make money. The rich man collects dollar bills like the stamp collector collects stamps. I knew he'd do it. I knew it when he told the clerk to send up a doctor that I'd have to pay for it."

"Well, why *should* he pay for it? *You* were the person to pay for it."

"That's right. Why should he?" My father settled back, his eyes forward, his hands crossed and limp in his lap. The skin beneath his chin was loose; his temples seemed concave. The liquor was probably disagreeing with him. "That's why he's where he is now, and that's why I am where I am."

The seed of my anger was a desire to recall him to himself, to scold him out of being old and tired. "Well, why'd you bring along only five dollars? You might have known something would happen."

"You're right, Jay. I should have brought more."

"Look. Right over there is an open bookstore. Now if you had brought *ten* dollars—"

"Is it open? I don't think so. They just left the lights in the window on."

"What if it isn't? What does it matter to us? Anyway, what kind of art book can you get for five dollars? Color plates cost money. How much do you think a decent book of Vermeer costs? It'd be cheap at fifteen dollars, even second-hand, with the pages all crummy and full of spilled coffee." I kept on, shrilly flailing the passive and infuriating figure of my father, until we left the city. Once we were on the homeward train, my tantrum ended; it had been a kind of ritual, for both of us, and he had endured my screams complacently, nodding assent, like a midwife assisting at the birth of family pride. Years passed before I needed to go to New York again.

The Kid's Whistling

THINGS WERE NEARLY PERFECT: Christmas was three weeks away, Roy worked late every evening and was doubling his salary in overtime, and tonight rain was falling. Rain was Roy's favorite weather, and he never felt more at rest, more at home, than when working nights in his hot little room on the third floor of Herlihy's—the department store stretching dark and empty under him, the radio murmuring, maybe the rain tapping on the black skylight, the engines shuttling back and forth in the Fourth Street freight yards, half a mile away.

The one trouble was the kid's whistling. For ten months a year Roy had the Display Department to himself. If the orders for counter cards piled up, Shipping lent him a boy to help out. But at the beginning of November, Simmons, the store manager, hired a high-school kid to come in weekday evenings and on Saturdays. This year's helper was called Jack, and he whistled. He whistled all the time.

At the hand press, Jack was printing counter cards and rendering "Summertime." He seemed to feel the tune needed a cool, restrained treatment, for which Roy was grateful; he was all set to begin the Toy Department sign and wanted things to go well. Though the customary sans-serif or bold roman would have done, he planned to try Old English capitals. It was for his own satisfaction; no one would appreciate the extra effort, least of all Simmons. On a plywood board, ½″ × 1½″ × 11′, primed with off-white, Roy ruled the guidelines and pencilled the letters lightly, mostly to get the spacing. He lit a cigarette, puffed it a moment, not inhaling, then set it on the edge of the workbench. His drawing board was hinged to the second of four shelves; in working position, the board rested upon and overhung the rim of the waist-high bench at an angle of thirty degrees. When not in use, the board was supposed to hook into a loop screw attached to the top shelf, but the screw had worked out of the soft pine, and the board always hung down. This way, the lowest shelf was half concealed, and had become a cave of empty paint jars, forgotten memos, petrified brushes, scraps of Masonite. On the second shelf, in rainbow order, the jars of poster paints sat. The third shelf held jars of nails, boxes of tacks and staples, two staplers (one broken), colored inks (dried up), penholders in a coffee mug, pen points in a cigar box, brushes in a beer mug, three hammers, two steel rods intended to brace the arms of mannequins, and a hand-jigsaw frame without a blade; these things were not as well ordered as the poster paints. The tall space between the fourth shelf and the ceiling contained a blackened chaos of obsolete displays—silhouettes of Indians, firecrackers, reindeer, clouds, dollar signs. Shelves in ascending degrees of muddle also covered the wall on Roy's left. To his right, at some distance, were the kid and the hand press and the door out. Behind him were the power tools, some timber, and the mannequin closet, built into the dimmest corner of the room. Though Roy had a long-legged stool, he stood at his drawing board. He chose a No. 9 wedge brush and a jar of Sky Blue poster paint. He glanced into the lettering book, open to "Old English." He made certain the shaker of Silverdust was within reach.

Then, with no more hesitation, Roy dipped the brush and touched it to the board. The great crescent of the T went on without a tremor. The broad curve capping it had just the proper jaunty hint of a left-to-right downslant. With a No. 2 brush he added the hairlines. He quickly sprinkled Silverdust over the moist letter, blew the loose stuff away, and stepped back, pleased.

In his head Roy slammed a door shut on Jack's insistent version of "Lady Be Good." He shook his brush clean in a jar of water and executed the O in Deep Yellow. He was not sure that the yellow would stand out enough against the white, but it did, especially after the Silverdust was added.

Jack switched to "After You've Gone," doing it loud, tapping a foot. It got so trumpety that, in the middle of putting the hairline on the Y, Roy, afraid his hand might shake, turned and stared burningly at Jack's spine. It made no impression. Jack was tall, about six inches taller than Roy, and thin. His neck, no thicker than an arm, led into a muff of uncut hair. Clapping two pieces of wooden type on the table, the kid leaned back and let fly four enormous, jubilant notes.

"Hey, Jack," Roy called.

The boy turned. "Beg pardon?" He looked startled, exposed. He wasn't one of these mean kids, actually.

"How about a Coke?"

"Sure. If you're having one."

Roy didn't want a soft drink; he wanted quiet. But he had worked him-self into a position where there was nothing to do but go out into the dark hall, dig two dimes from his pocket, insert them in the machine, wait for the cold wet bottles to bump down, and take them back to the Display Department. When he gave Jack one, the boy offered him a nickel and five pennies. "Keep it," Roy told him. "Buy yourself a saxophone."

Jack's pleasant, ignorant face showed that the hint had been too subtle for him. "Want some peanuts?" he said, gesturing toward an ink-smudged can labelled PLANTERS.

The cold weight of the bottle in Roy's fingers made salted nuts seem appropriate. He took a good handful, then, noticing the can was nearly empty, dropped some back into it. As he fed them to himself, one by one, the kid watched him, apparently expecting conversation. Roy pointed with a loosely clenched hand at the sheaf of orders on the spindle. "Good night's work there."

"I can't get all them out tonight."

Roy knew this was so, but if he agreed, it might encourage the kid to loaf. He returned to his sign without another word. He polished off the fine lines of the *Y* and, in one slow, satisfying movement of his arm, did the tail. On with the Silverdust.

Washing both brushes, opening the jar labelled "Crimson," Roy was conscious of his hands. They were square and smooth, with dandified nails, and completely clean, yet not so white that they could not take a flattering tan from the contrast with the clean cuffs. The cuffs, folded back exactly twice and starched to about the stiffness of thin cardboard, pressed lightly on the flats of his forearms and gave him an agreeable packaged feeling. It was just as well he hadn't bawled the kid out. Roy knew it was only the boy's kind of peace, standing over there whistling, playing with type, his crusty apron snug around him, his can of salted peanuts and his pack of Philip Morris beside him on the table, God knows what going on in his brain. The kid smoked steadily. Once, when Roy asked Jack if he didn't smoke too much, Jack had said no, this was the only place he ever smoked, which was exactly the point, but Roy let it drop. It wasn't as if he was the kid's father.

Roy started the *L*. Jack started "If I Could Be with You One Hour Tonight," in an irritating, loose, whoopsy way, trying to be Coleman Hawkins or some bop shade. In exasperation, Roy switched on the radio he kept on the shelf. It was an old Motorola; its tubes were all but shot. Even on full, it wasn't loud enough for Jack to hear above his own noise. He kept on whistling, like he was a bird and this was some treetop.

Roy finished up the *L.* Suddenly Jack went quiet. Roy, hoping the kid wasn't offended, turned off the radio. In the silence, he heard the sounds that had really made the kid stop: the elevator door clanging shut and then high heels clicking.

More than a minute seemed to pass before the Display Department door opened. When it did, there was Maureen, wearing a transparent raincoat, moisture beaded all over it and in her clipped red hair. There was something aggressive about that soaked hair. She frowned in the bright fluorescent light. "It's dark out there," she said. "I got lost."

"The switch is right by the elevator," was all Roy could think of to say.

She walked past the printing machine, with the kid at it, and came to stand by Roy. She looked at the sign.

" 'Todl?' " she read.

" 'Toyl.' That's a *Y.*"

"But it's closed at the top. It looks like a *D* with a wiggly tail."

"This is Gothic lettering."

"Well, I don't want to argue. It's probably just me."

"How come you're down here? What's up?"

"The rain made me restless."

"You walked all the way? Who let you into the store?"

"It's only six blocks. I don't mind walking in the rain. I like it." Maureen's head was tilted and her hands were busy at an earring. "The watchman let me in. He said, 'I'll take you right on up, Mrs. Mays. He'll be glad to see you. He'll be real lonely and happy to see you.' "

"Orley let you in?"

"I didn't ask his name." She took a cigarette from Roy's pack.

"Better take off your raincoat," Roy said. "You don't want to catch cold."

She shrugged it off, draped it over the electric jigsaw, and stood, her legs spread as far as her narrow skirt allowed, smoking and studying the stuff in the top rack. Roy drew down the Orange and began painting the *A.*

"Orange next to red," she said. "Ooey."

"Hih," he grunted, not hard enough to jiggle his hand.

"What's in these boxes?"

"Boxes?" Roy was concentrating and barely heard what she said.

"*These* boxes."

He lifted the brush and looked around to see what she was pointing at. "Tinsel."

"Tinsel! Why, you have two, four, six, *six* huge crates of it here! What do you *do* with it all? Sleep in it? Do you feed it to cows?"

"You get a reduction for quantity."

She kicked one of the crates thoughtfully and moved on, inspecting. The last time Maureen had come into Herlihy's was over three months ago, to pick him up for dinner and a movie. She hadn't been in this mood then. "Why don't you clean this mess out?" she called in a resonant, boxed-in voice from the closet where the mannequins were stored.

"Be careful. Those things cost." Roy pointed up the big sweeping serif on the *A*.

She came back into the room. "What are these for?"

He doused the drying letter with Silverdust before turning to see what she meant. "They're pine boughs."

"I know *that*. I mean what are you going to *do* with them?"

"What do you mean, what am I going to do with them? Put them in the window, make wreaths. This is Christmas, for Chrissake."

He turned his back on her and stared at his sign. She came over and stood beside him. He began the *N*. As he completed the downstroke, his elbow touched her side, she was standing that close.

"When are you coming home?" she asked softly, for the first time acting like there was a third person in the room.

"What time is it now?"

"A little after nine."

"I don't see how I can get away before eleven. I have to finish this sign."

"It's almost done now."

"I have to finish the sign; then I thought the kid and I would hang it. And then there are other things to do. It piles up. I'll try to make it by eleven—"

"Roy, *really*."

"I'll try to make it by eleven, but I can't guarantee it. I'm *sorry*, honey, but Simmons is on my neck all the time. What the hell: I'm getting time and a half."

She was silent while he put the serifs on the *N*. "So I suppose there's no point in my waiting around here," she said at last.

The *N* looked fine. In fact, the entire sign was more than passable. He was rather proud of himself, that he hadn't let her showing up rattle him.

"I'll see you around eleven," Maureen said. "I'll keep awake if I can." She was putting on her raincoat.

"Here, let me walk you out."

"Oh, no." She lifted a long pale sarcastic palm. "Don't let *me* disturb you. Time and a half, you know. I can flounder out on my own."

Roy decided, seeing the mood she was in, that it would be better to let her make whatever point she thought she was making.

By way of patching things up, he watched her leave. He could tell from the cocky, hollow-backed way she walked toward the door that she knew his eyes were on her. Instead of passing by Jack's bench, she paused and said, "Hello. What keeps *you* up so late?"

Jack rolled his eyes toward the racks of freshly printed signs—*$1.50 ea. $2.98 per pair*; Pre-Xmas Panic Sale; *100% Silk MEN'S TIES*; *Mixed Unmentionables from 89¢*. "Printing these."

"All those on this little thing?" Maureen touched the press. "Inky!"

She showed Jack the first and second fingers of her hand; each was tipped with a crimson spot the size of a confetti bit. The kid poked around helplessly for a clean rag. The best he could do was offer her a corner of his apron. "Thank you so *much*," she said, wiping her fingers slowly, thoroughly. At the door, she smiled and said "Ta-ta, all," to a point in the room midway between her husband and the boy.

Roy chose to paint the last letter, *D*, in Sky Blue again, the same as the initial *T*. It would give the thing unity. As he formed the letter, first with the No. 9 brush, then with the No. 2, he was aware of something out of place, something askew, in his room, and with a section of his mind he tried to locate the trouble. This was a mistake. When the letter was covered with Silverdust, Roy stepped back and saw that he had botched it. The *D* was too plump, slightly out of scale and too close to the *N*. It was nothing Simmons or anybody would notice—who looked at signs, anyway?—but Roy knew it had been ruined, and now knew why. The kid had stopped whistling.

Ace in the Hole

THE MOMENT his car touched the boulevard heading home, Ace flicked on the radio. He needed the radio, especially today. In the seconds before the tubes warmed up, he said aloud, doing it just to hear a human voice, "Jesus. She'll pop her lid." His voice, though familiar, irked him; it sounded thin and scratchy, as if the bones in his head were picking up static. In a deeper register Ace added, "She'll murder me." Then the radio came on, warm and strong, so he stopped worrying. The Five Kings were doing "Blueberry Hill"; to hear them made Ace feel so sure inside that from the pack pinched between the car roof and the sun shield he plucked a cigarette, hung it on his lower lip, snapped a match across the rusty place on the dash, held the flame in the instinctive spot near the tip of his nose, dragged, and blew out the match, all in time to the music. He rolled down the window and snapped the match so it spun end over end into the gutter. "Two points," he said, and cocked the cigarette toward the roof of the car, sucked powerfully, and exhaled two plumes through his nostrils. He was beginning to feel like himself, Ace Anderson, for the first time that whole day. Not a good day, so far. He beat time on the accelerator. The car jerked crazily. "On Blueberry Hill," he sang, "my heart stood still. The wind in the willow tree"—he braked for a red light—"played love's suh-*weet* melodee—"

"Go, Dad, bust your lungs!" a kid's voice blared. The kid was riding in a '52 Pontiac that had pulled up beside Ace at the light. The profile of the driver, another kid, was dark over his shoulder.

Ace looked over at him and smiled slowly, just letting one side of his mouth lift a little. "Why don't you just shove it?" he asked, good-naturedly. It was only a couple of years since he had been their age.

But the kid, who looked Italian, lifted his thick upper lip and spat out the window. The spit gleamed on the asphalt like a half-dollar.

"Now isn't that pretty?" Ace said, keeping one eye on the light. "You miserable wop. You are *mis*erable." While the kid was trying to think of some smart comeback, the light changed. Ace dug out so hard he smelled burned rubber. In his rearview mirror he saw the Pontiac lurch forward a few yards, then stop dead, right in the middle of the intersection.

The idea of them stalling their fat tin Pontiac kept him in a good humor all the way home. He decided to stop at his mother's place and pick up the baby, instead of waiting for Evey to do it. His mother must have seen him drive up. She came out on the porch holding a plastic spoon and smelling of cake.

"You're out early," she told him.

"Goldman fired me," Ace told her.

"Good for you," his mother said. "I always said he never treated you right." She brought a cigarette out of her apron pocket and tucked it deep into one corner of her mouth, the way she did when something pleased her.

Ace lighted it for her. "Goldman was O.K. personally," he said. "He just wanted too much for his money. That kind does. I didn't mind working the Saturdays, but until eleven, twelve Friday nights was too much. Everybody has a right to some leisure."

"Well, I don't dare think what Evey will say, but I, for one, thank dear God you had the brains to get out of it. I always said that job had no future to it—no future of any kind, Freddy."

"I guess," Ace admitted. "But I wanted to keep at it, for the family's sake."

"Now, I know I shouldn't be saying this, but any time Evey—this is just between us—any time Evey thinks she can do better, there's room for you *and* Bonnie right in your father's house." She pinched her lips together. He could almost hear the old lady think, *There, I've said it.*

"Look, Mom, Evey tries awfully hard, and anyway you know she can't work that way. Not that *that*—I mean, she's a realist, too. . . ." He let the rest of the thought fade as he watched a kid across the street dribbling a basketball around a telephone pole that had a backboard and net nailed on it.

"Evey's a wonderful girl of her own kind. But I've always said, and your father agrees, Roman Catholics ought to marry among themselves. Now, I know I've said it before, but when they get out in the greater world—"

"*No*, Mom."

She frowned, smoothed herself, and said, "Your name was in the paper today."

Ace chose to let that go by. He kept watching the kid with the basket-ball. It was funny how, though the whole point was to get the ball up into the air, kids grabbed it by the sides and squeezed. Kids just didn't think. Push it up, *up*.

"Did you hear?" his mother asked.

"Sure, but so what?" Ace said. His mother's lower lip was coming at him, so he changed the subject. "I guess I'll take Bonnie."

His mother went into the house and brought back his daughter, wrapped in a blue blanket. The baby looked dopey. "She fussed all day," his mother complained. "I said to your father, 'Bonnie is a dear little girl, but without a doubt she's her mother's daughter.' You were the best-natured boy."

"Well, I *had* everything," Ace said with impatience. His mother blinked and didn't argue. He nicely dropped his cigarette into a brown flowerpot on the edge of the porch and took his daughter into his arms. She was getting heavier, solid. When he reached the end of the cement walk, his mother was still on the porch, waving to him. He was so close he could see the fat around her elbow jiggle, and he only lived a half-block up the street, yet here she was, waving to him as if he was going to Japan.

At the door of his car, it seemed stupid to him to drive the measly half-block home. "Never ride where you can walk," Coach Behn used to tell his boys. Ace left the ignition keys in his pocket and ran along the pavement with Bonnie laughing and bouncing at his chest. He slammed the door of his landlady's house open and shut, pounded up the two flights of stairs, and was panting so hard when he reached the door of his apartment that it took him a couple of seconds to fit the key into the lock.

The run must have tuned Bonnie up. As soon as he lowered her into the crib, she began to shout and wave her arms. He didn't want to play with her. He tossed some blocks and a rattle into the crib and walked into the bathroom, where he turned on the hot water and began to comb his hair. Holding the comb under the faucet before every stroke, he combed his hair forward. It was so long, one strand curled under his nose and touched his lips. He whipped the whole mass back with a single pull. He tucked in the tufts around his ears, and ran the comb straight back on both sides of his head. With his fingers he felt for the little ridge at the back where the two sides met. It was there, as it should have been. Finally, he mussed the hair in front enough for one little lock to droop over his forehead, like Alan Ladd. It made the temple seem lower than it was.

Every day, his hairline looked higher. He had observed all around him how blond men seem to go bald first. He remembered reading somewhere, though, that baldness shows virility.

On his way to the kitchen he flipped the left-hand knob of the television. Bonnie was always quieter with the set on. Ace didn't see how she could understand much of it, but it seemed to mean something to her. He found a can of beer in the refrigerator behind some brownish lettuce and those hot dogs Evey never got around to cooking. She'd be home any time. The clock said five-twelve. She'd pop her lid.

Ace didn't see what he could do but try and reason with her. "Evey," he'd say, "you ought to thank God I got out of it. It had no future to it at all." He hoped she wouldn't get too mad, because when she was mad he wondered if he should have married her, and doubting that made him feel crowded. It was bad enough, his mother always crowding him. He punched the two triangles in the top of the beer can, the little triangle first, and then the big one, the one he drank from. He hoped Evey wouldn't say anything that couldn't be forgotten. What women didn't seem to realize was that there were things you knew but shouldn't say.

He felt sorry he had called the kid in the car a wop.

Ace balanced the beer on a corner where two rails of the crib met and looked under the chairs for the morning paper. He had trouble finding his name, because it was at the bottom of a column on an inside sports page, in a small article about the county basketball statistics:

"Dusty" Tremwick, Grosvenor Park's sure-fingered center, copped the individual scoring honors with a season's grand (and we do mean grand) total of 376 points. This is within eighteen points of the all-time record of 394 racked up in the 1949–1950 season by Olinger High's Fred Anderson.

Ace angrily sailed the paper into an armchair. Now it was Fred Anderson; it used to be Ace. He hated being called Fred, especially in print, but, then, the sportswriters were all office boys anyway, Coach Behn used to say.

"Do not just ask for shoe polish," a man on television said, "but ask for *Emu Shoe Gloss*, the *only* polish that absolutely *guarantees* to make your shoes look shinier than new!" Ace turned the sound off, so that the man moved his mouth like a fish blowing bubbles. Right away, Bonnie howled. Ace turned it back on, loud enough to drown her out, and went into the kitchen, without knowing what he wanted there. He wasn't hungry; his stomach was tight. It used to be like that when he walked to the gymnasium alone in the dark before a game and could see the people from town, kids and parents, crowding in at the lighted doors. But once he was inside, the locker room would be bright and hot, and the other guys would be there, laughing and towel-slapping, and the tight feeling would leave. Now there were whole days when it didn't leave.

A key scratched at the door lock. Ace decided to stay in the kitchen. Let *her* find *him*. Her heels clicked on the floor for a step or two; then the television set went off. Bonnie began to cry. "Shut up, honey," Evey said. There was a silence.

"I'm home," Ace called.

"No kidding. I thought Bonnie got the beer by herself."

Ace laughed. She was in a sarcastic mood, thinking she was Lauren Bacall. That was all right, just so she kept funny. Still smiling, Ace eased into the living room and got hit with, "What are *you* smirking about? Another question: What's the idea running up the street with Bonnie like she was some football?"

"You saw that?"

"Your mother told me."

"You saw her?"

"Of course I saw her. I stopped by to pick up Bonnie. What the hell do you think—I read her tiny mind?"

"Take it easy," Ace said, wondering if Mom had told her about Goldman.

"Take it easy? Don't coach *me*. Another question: Why's the car out in front of her place? You give the car to her?"

"Look, I parked it there to pick up Bonnie, and I thought I'd leave it there."

"Why?"

"What do you mean, why? I just did. I just thought I'd get the exercise. It's not that far, you know."

"No, I don't know. If you'd been on your feet all day a block would look like one hell of a long way."

"O.K. I'm sorry."

She hung up her coat and stepped out of her shoes and walked around the room picking up things. She stuck the newspaper in the wastebasket.

Ace said, "My name was in the paper today."

"They spell it right?" She shoved the paper deep into the basket with her stocking foot. There was no doubt; she knew about Goldman.

"They called me Fred."

"Isn't that your name? What *is* your name anyway? Hero J. Great?"

There wasn't any answer, so Ace didn't try any. He sat down on the sofa, lighted a cigarette, and waited.

Evey picked up Bonnie. "Poor thing stinks. What does your mother do, scrub out the toilet with her?"

"Can't you take it easy? I know you're tired."

"You should. I'm always tired."

Evey and Bonnie went into the bathroom; when they came out, Bonnie was clean and Evey was calm. Evey sat down in an easy chair beside Ace and rested her stocking feet on his knees. "Hit me," she said, twiddling her fingers for the cigarette.

The baby crawled up to her chair and tried to stand, to see what he was giving her. Leaning over close to Bonnie's nose, Evey grinned, smoke leaking through her teeth, and said, "Only for grownups, honey."

"Eve," Ace began, "there was no future in that job. Working all Saturday, and then Friday nights on top of it."

"I know. Your mother told *me* all that, too. What I want from you is what happened."

She was going to take it like a sport, then. He tried to remember how it *did* happen. "It wasn't my fault," he said. "Goldman told me to back this '51 Chevy into the line that faces Church Street. He just bought it from an old guy this morning who said it only had thirteen thousand on it. So in I jump and start her up. There was a knock in the engine like a machine gun. I almost told Goldman he'd bought a squirrel, but you know I cut that smart stuff out ever since Larry Pallotta laid me off."

"You told me that story. What happens in this one?"

"Look, Eve. I *am* telling ya. Do you want me to go out to a movie or something?"

"Suit yourself."

"So I jump in the Chevy and snap it back in line, and there was a kind of scrape and thump. I get out and look and Goldman's running over, his arms going like *this*"—Ace whirled his own arms and laughed—"and here was the whole back fender of a '49 Merc mashed in. Just looked like somebody took a planer and shaved off the bulge, you know, there at the back." He tried to show her with his hands. "The Chevy, though, didn't have a dent. It even gained some paint. But *Goldman*, to *hear* him— Boy, they can rave when their pocketbook's hit. He said—" Ace laughed again. "Never mind."

Evey said, "You're proud of yourself."

"No, listen. I'm not happy about it. But there wasn't a thing I could *do*.

It wasn't my driving at all. I looked over on the other side, and there was just two or three inches between the Chevy and a Buick. *Nobody* could have gotten into that hole. Even if it had hair on it." He thought this was pretty good.

She didn't. "You could have looked."

"There just wasn't the *space*. Goldman said stick it in; I stuck it in."

"But you could have looked and moved the other cars to make more room."

"I guess that would have been the smart thing."

"I guess, too. Now what?"

"What do you mean?"

"I mean now what? Are you going to give up? Go back to the Army? Your mother? Be a basketball pro? What?"

"You know I'm not tall enough. Anybody under six-six they don't want."

"Is that so? Six-six? Well, please listen to this, Mr. Six-Foot-Five-and-a-Half: I'm fed up. I'm ready as Christ to let you run." She stabbed her cigarette into an ashtray on the arm of the chair so hard the ashtray spun to the floor, spilling its contents. Evey flushed and shut up.

What Ace hated most in their arguments was these silences after Evey had said something so ugly she wanted to take it back. "Better ask the priest first," he murmured.

She sat right up, snatching her stocking feet off his knees. "If there's one thing I don't want to hear about from you it's priests. You let the priests to me. You don't know a damn thing about it. Not a damn thing."

"Hey, look at Bonnie," he said, trying to make his tone easy.

Evey didn't hear him. "If you think," she went on, "if for one rotten moment you think, Mr. Fred, that the be-all and end-all of my life is you and your hot-shot stunts—"

"Look, Mother," Ace pleaded, pointing at Bonnie. The baby had picked up the copper ashtray and put it on her head for a hat.

Evey glanced down angrily. "Cute," she said. "Cute as her daddy."

The ashtray slid from Bonnie's head and she groped after it.

"Yeah, but watch," Ace said. "Watch her hands. They're sure."

"You're nuts," Evey said.

"No, honest. Bonnie's great. She's a natural. Get the rattle for her. Never mind, I'll get it." In two steps, Ace was at Bonnie's crib, picking the rattle out of the mess of blocks and plastic rings and beanbags. He extended the rattle toward his daughter, shaking it delicately. Made wary by this burst of attention, Bonnie reached with both hands; like two separate animals they approached from opposite sides and touched the smooth rattle simultaneously. A smile worked up on her face. Ace tugged weakly. She held on, and then tugged back. "She's a natural," Ace said, "and it won't do her any good because she's a girl. Baby, we got to have a boy."

"I'm not your baby," Evey said, closing her eyes.

Saying "Baby" over and over again, Ace backed up to the radio, neglected on a shelf behind the television. Without turning around, he manipulated the volume knob. In the moment before the tubes warmed up, Evey had time to say, "Wise up, Fred. What shall we do?"

The radio came in on something slow and tinkly: dinner music. Ace picked Bonnie up and set her in the crib. "Shall we dance?" he asked his wife, bowing.

"We need to talk."

"Baby. It's the cocktail hour."

"This is getting us no place," she said, rising from her chair, though.

"Fred Junior. I can see him now," he said, seeing nothing.

"We will have no Juniors."

In her crib, Bonnie whimpered at the sight of her mother being seized. Ace fitted his hand into the natural place on Evey's back and she shuffled stiffly into his lead. When, with a sudden injection of saxophones, the tempo quickened, he spun her out carefully, keeping the beat with his shoulders. Her hair brushed his lips as she minced in, then swung away, to the end of his arm; he could feel her toes dig into the carpet. He flipped his own hair back from his eyes. The music ate through his skin and mixed with the nerves and small veins; he seemed to be great again, and all the other kids were around them, in a ring, clapping time.

Tomorrow and Tomorrow and So Forth

WHIRLING, TALKING, 11D began to enter Room 109. From the quality of their excitement Mark Prosser guessed it would rain. He had been teaching high school for three years, yet his students still impressed him; they were such sensitive animals. They reacted so infallibly to merely barometric pressure.

In the doorway, Brute Young paused while little Barry Snyder giggled at his elbow. Barry's stagy laugh rose and fell, dipping down toward some vile secret that had to be tasted and retasted, then soaring artificially to proclaim that he, little Barry, shared such a secret with the school's full-back. Being Brute's stooge was precious to Barry. The fullback paid no attention to him; he twisted his neck to stare at something not yet coming through the door. He yielded reluctantly to the procession pressing him forward.

Right under Prosser's eyes, like a murder suddenly appearing in an annalistic frieze of kings and queens, someone stabbed a girl in the back with a pencil; she ignored the assault saucily. Another hand yanked out Geoffrey Langer's shirt-tail. Geoffrey, a bright student, was uncertain whether to laugh it off or defend himself with anger, and made a weak, half-turning gesture of compromise, wearing an expression of distant arrogance that Prosser recognized as having been his own in moments of schoolyard fear. All along the line, in the glitter of key chains and the acute angles of turned-back shirt cuffs, an electricity was expressed which simple weather couldn't generate.

Mark wondered if today Gloria Andrews would wear that sweater, an ember-pink angora, with very short sleeves. The virtual sleevelessness was the disturbing factor: the exposure of those two serene arms to the air, white as thighs against the delicate wool.

His guess was correct. A vivid pink patch flashed through the jiggle of arms and shoulders as the final knot of youngsters entered the room.

"Take your seats," Mr. Prosser said. "Come on. Let's go."

Most obeyed, but Peter Forry, who had been at the center of the group around Gloria, still lingered in the doorway with her, finishing some story, apparently determined to make her laugh or gasp. When she did gasp, he tossed his head with satisfaction. His apricot-colored hair bounced. Red-haired boys are all alike, Mark thought, with their white eyelashes and wise-guy faces, their mouths always twisted with an unearned self-confidence. Bluffers, the bunch of them.

When Gloria, moving in a considered, stately way, had taken her seat, and Peter had swerved into his, Mr. Prosser said, "Peter Forry."

"Yes?" Peter rose, scrabbling through his book for the assigned pages.

"Kindly tell the class the exact meaning of the words 'Tomorrow, and tomorrow, and tomorrow, / Creeps in this petty pace from day to day.' "

Peter glanced down at the high-school edition of *Macbeth* lying open on his desk. One of the duller girls tittered expectantly from the back of the room. Peter was popular with the girls; girls that age had minds like moths.

"Peter. With your book shut. We have all memorized this passage for today. Remember?" The girl in the back of the room squealed in delight. Gloria laid her own book face-open on her desk, where Peter could see it.

Peter shut his book with a bang and stared into Gloria's. "Why," he said at last, "I think it means pretty much what it says."

"Which is?"

"Why, that tomorrow is something we often think about. It creeps into our conversation all the time. We couldn't make any plans without thinking about tomorrow."

"I see. Then you would say that Macbeth is here referring to the, the date-book aspect of life?"

Geoffrey Langer laughed, no doubt to please Mr. Prosser. For a moment, Mark *was* pleased. But he shouldn't play for laughs at a student's expense. His paraphrase had made Peter's reading of the lines seem more ridiculous than it was. He began to retract. "I admit—"

But Peter was going on; redheads never know when to quit. "Macbeth means that if we quit worrying about tomorrow, and just lived for today, we could appreciate all the wonderful things that are going on under our noses."

Mark considered this a moment before he spoke. He would not be sarcastic. "Uh, without denying that there is truth in what you say, Peter, do you think it likely that Macbeth, in his situation, would be expressing such"—he couldn't help himself—"such sunny sentiments?"

Geoffrey laughed again. Peter's neck reddened; he studied the floor. Gloria glared at Mr. Prosser, the anger in her face clearly meant for him to see.

Mark hurried to undo his mistake. "Don't misunderstand me, please," he told Peter. "I don't have all the answers myself. But it seems to me the whole speech, down to 'Signifying nothing,' is saying that life is—well, a *fraud*. Nothing wonderful about it."

"Did Shakespeare really think that?" Geoffrey Langer asked, a nervous quickness pitching his voice high.

Mark read into Geoffrey's question his own adolescent premonitions of the terrible truth. The attempt he must make was plain. He turned his attention from Peter and looked through the window toward the steadying sky. The clouds were lowering, getting darker. "There is," Mr. Prosser slowly began, "much darkness in Shakespeare's work, and no play is darker than *Macbeth*. The atmosphere is poisonous, oppressive. One critic has said that in this play humanity suffocates." This was too fancy.

"In the middle of his career, Shakespeare wrote plays about men like Hamlet and Othello and Macbeth—men who aren't allowed by their society, or bad luck, or some minor flaw in themselves, to become the great men they might have been. Even Shakespeare's comedies of this period deal with a world gone sour. It is as if he had seen through the bright, bold surface of his earlier comedies and histories and had looked upon something terrible. It frightened him, just as some day it may frighten some of you." In his determination to find the right words, he had been staring at Gloria, without meaning to. Embarrassed, she nodded, and, realizing what had been happening, he nodded back.

He tried to make his remarks more diffident. "But then I think Shakespeare sensed a redeeming truth. His last plays are serene and symbolical, as if he had pierced through the ugly facts and reached a realm where the facts are again beautiful. In this way, Shakespeare's total work is a more complete image of life than that of any other writer, except perhaps for Dante, an Italian poet who wrote three centuries earlier." He had been taken far from the *Macbeth* soliloquy. Other teachers had been happy to tell him how the kids made a game of getting him talking. He looked toward Geoffrey. The boy was doodling on his tablet, indifferent. Mr. Prosser concluded, "The last play Shakespeare wrote is an extraordinary poem called *The Tempest*. Some of you may want to read it for your next book reports—the ones due May tenth. It's a short play."

. . .

The class had been taking a holiday. Barry Snyder was snicking BBs off the blackboard and glancing over at Brute Young to see if he noticed. "Once more, Barry," Mr. Prosser said, "and out you go." Barry blushed, and grinned to cover the blush, his eyeballs sliding toward Brute. The dull girl in the rear of the room was putting on lipstick. "Put that away, Alice," Mr. Prosser commanded. She giggled and obeyed. Sejak, the Polish boy who worked nights, was asleep at his desk, his cheek white with pressure against the varnished wood, his mouth sagging sidewise. Mr. Prosser had an impulse to let him sleep. But the impulse might not be true kindness, just the self-congratulatory, kindly pose in which he sometimes discovered himself. Besides, one breach of discipline encouraged others. He moved down the aisle and gently shook Sejak awake. Then he turned his attention to the mumble growing at the front of the room.

Peter Forry was whispering to Gloria, trying to make her laugh. The girl's face, though, was cool and solemn, as if a thought had been provoked in her head. Perhaps at least *she* had been listening to what Mr. Prosser had been saying. With a bracing sense of chivalrous intercession, Mark said, "Peter. I gather from this noise that you have something to add to your theories."

Peter responded courteously. "No, sir. I honestly don't understand the speech. Please, sir, what *does* it mean?"

This candid admission and odd request stunned the class. Every white, round face, eager, for once, to learn, turned toward Mark. He said, "I don't know. I was hoping *you* would tell *me*."

In college, when a professor made such a remark, it was with grand effect. The professor's humility, the necessity for creative interplay between teacher and student were dramatically impressed upon the group. But to 11D, ignorance in an instructor was as wrong as a hole in a roof. It was as if he had held thirty strings pulling thirty faces taut toward him and then had slashed the strings. Heads waggled, eyes dropped, voices buzzed. Some of the discipline problems, like Peter Forry, smirked signals to one another.

"Quiet!" Mr. Prosser shouted. "All of you. Poetry isn't arithmetic. There's no single right answer. I don't want to force my own impression on you, even if I *have* had much more experience with literature." He made this last clause very loud and distinct, and some of the weaker students seemed reassured. "I know none of *you* want that," he told them.

Whether or not they believed him, they subsided, somewhat. Mark judged he could safely assume his human-among-humans attitude again.

He perched on the edge of the desk and leaned forward beseechingly. "Now, honestly. Don't any of you have some personal feeling about the lines that you would like to share with the class and me?"

One hand, with a flowered handkerchief balled in it, unsteadily rose. "Go ahead, Teresa," Mr. Prosser said encouragingly. She was a timid, clumsy girl whose mother was a Seventh-Day Adventist.

"It makes me think of cloud shadows," Teresa said.

Geoffrey Langer laughed. "Don't be rude, Geoff," Mr. Prosser said sideways, softly, before throwing his voice forward: "Thank you, Teresa. I think that's an interesting and valid impression. Cloud movement has something in it of the slow, monotonous rhythm one feels in the line 'Tomorrow, and tomorrow, and tomorrow.' It's a very gray line, isn't it, class?" No one agreed or disagreed.

Beyond the windows actual clouds were moving rapidly, and erratic sections of sunlight slid around the room. Gloria's arm, crooked gracefully above her head, turned gold. "Gloria?" Mr. Prosser asked.

She looked up from something on her desk with a face of sullen radiance. "I think what Teresa said was very good," she said, glaring in the direction of Geoffrey Langer. Geoffrey snickered defiantly. "And I have a question. What does 'petty pace' mean?"

"It means the trivial day-to-day sort of life that, say, a bookkeeper or a bank clerk leads. Or a schoolteacher," he added, smiling.

She did not smile back. Thought wrinkles irritated her shining brow. "But Macbeth has been fighting wars, and killing kings, and being a king himself, and all," she pointed out.

"Yes, but it's just these acts Macbeth is condemning as 'nothing.' Can you see that?"

Gloria shook her head. "Another thing I worry about—isn't it silly for Macbeth to be talking to himself right in the middle of this war, with his wife just dead, and all?"

"I don't think so, Gloria. No matter how fast events happen, thought is faster."

His answer was weak; everyone knew it, even if Gloria hadn't mused, supposedly to herself, but in a voice the entire class could hear, "It seems so *stupid*."

Mark winced, pierced by the awful clarity with which his students saw him. Through their eyes, how queer he looked, with his soft hands, and his horn-rimmed glasses, and his hair never slicked down, all wrapped up in "literature," where, when things get rough, the king mumbles a poem nobody understands. The delight Mr. Prosser took in such crazy junk made not only his good sense but his masculinity a matter of doubt. It was gentle of them not to laugh him out of the room. He looked down and rubbed his fingertips together, trying to erase the chalk dust. The class noise sifted into unnatural quiet. "It's getting late," he said finally. "Let's start the recitations of the memorized passage. Bernard Amilson, you begin."

Bernard had trouble enunciating, and his rendition began, " 'T'mau 'n' t'mau 'n' t'mau.' " Mr. Prosser admired the extent to which the class tried to repress its amusement, and wrote "A" in his marking book opposite Bernard's name. He always gave Bernard A on recitations, despite the school nurse, who claimed there was nothing organically wrong with the boy's mouth.

It was the custom, cruel but traditional, to deliver recitations from the front of the room. Alice, when her turn came, was reduced to a helpless state by the first funny face Peter Forry made at her. Mark let her hang up there a good minute while her face ripened to cherry redness, and at last relented: "Very well, Alice—you may try again later."

Many of the youngsters knew the passage gratifyingly well, though there was a tendency to leave out the line "To the last syllable of recorded time" and to turn "struts and frets" into "frets and struts" or simply "struts and struts." Even Sejak, who couldn't have looked at the passage before he came to class, got through it as far as "And then is heard no more."

Geoffrey Langer showed off, as he always did, by interrupting his own recitation with bright questions. " 'Tomorrow, and tomorrow, and tomorrow,' " he said, " 'creeps in'—shouldn't that be '*creep* in,' Mr. Prosser?"

"It is 'creep*s*.' The trio is in effect singular. Go on." Mr. Prosser was tired of coddling Langer. If you let them, these smart students will run away with the class. "Without the footnotes."

" 'Creep*sss* in this petty pace from day to day, / To the last syllable of recorded time; / And all our yesterdays have lighted fools / The way to dusty death. Out, out—' "

"No, no!" Mr. Prosser jumped out of his chair. "This is poetry. Don't mushmouth it! Pause a little after 'fools.' " Geoffrey looked genuinely startled this time, and Mark himself did not quite understand his annoyance and, mentally turning to see what was behind him, seemed to glimpse in the humid undergrowth the two stern eyes of the indignant look Gloria had thrown Geoffrey. He glimpsed himself in the absurd position of acting as Gloria's champion in her inscrutable private war with this intelligent boy. He sighed apologetically. "Poetry is made up of *lines*," he began, turning to the class. Gloria was passing a note to Peter Forry.

The rudeness of it! To pass notes during a scolding that she herself had caused! Mark caged in his hand the girl's wrist—how small and frail it was!—and ripped the note from her fingers. He read it to himself, letting the class see he was reading it, though he despised such methods of discipline. The note went:

> Pete— I think you're *wrong* about Mr. Prosser. I think he's wonderful and I get a lot out of his class. He's heavenly with poetry. I think I love him. I really do *love* him. So there.

Mr. Prosser folded the note once and slipped it into his side coat pocket. "See me after class, Gloria," he said. Then, to Geoffrey, "Let's try it again. Begin at the beginning. Let the *words* talk, Geoffrey."

While the boy was reciting the passage, the buzzer sounded the end of the period. It was the last class of the day. The room quickly emptied, except for Gloria. The noise of lockers slamming open and books being thrown against metal and shouts drifted in:

"Who has a car?"

"Lend me a cig, pig."

"We can't have practice in this slop."

Mark hadn't noticed exactly when the rain started, but it was coming down hard now. He moved around the room with the window pole, closing windows and pulling down shades. Spray bounced in on his hands. He began to talk to Gloria in a crisp voice that, like his device of shutting the windows, was intended to protect them both from embarrassment.

"About note passing." She sat motionless at her desk in the front of the room, her short, brushed-up hair like a cool torch. From the way she sat, her naked arms folded at her breasts and her shoulders hunched, he felt she was chilly. "It is not only rude to scribble when a teacher is talking, it is stupid to put one's words down on paper, where they look much more foolish than they might have sounded if spoken." He leaned the window pole in its corner and walked toward his desk.

"And about love. 'Love' is one of those words that illustrate what happens to an old, overworked language. These days, with movie stars and crooners and preachers and psychiatrists all pronouncing the word, it's come to mean nothing but a vague fondness for something. In this sense, I love the rain, this blackboard, these desks, you. It means nothing, you see, whereas once the word signified a quite explicit thing—a desire to share all you own and are with someone else. It is time we coined a new word to mean that, and when you think up the word *you* want to use, I suggest that you be economical with it. Treat it as something you can spend only once—if not for your own sake, for the good of the language." He walked over to his own desk and dropped two pencils on it, as if to say, "That's all."

"I'm sorry," Gloria said.

Rather surprised, Mr. Prosser said, "Don't be."

"But you don't understand."

"Of course I don't. I probably never did. At your age, I was like Geoffrey Langer."

"I bet you weren't." The girl was almost crying; he was sure of that.

"Come on, Gloria. Run along. Forget it." She slowly cradled her books between her bare arm and her sweater, and left the room with that melancholy teen-age shuffle, so that her body above her hips seemed to float over the desks.

What was it, Mark asked himself, these young people were after? What did they want? *Glide*, he decided, the quality of *glide*. To slip along, always in rhythm, always cool, the little wheels humming under you, going nowhere special. If Heaven existed, that's the way it would be there. "He's heavenly with poetry." They loved the word. Heaven was in half their songs.

"Christ, he's humming." Strunk, the phys-ed teacher, had come into the room without Prosser's noticing. Gloria had left the door ajar.

"Ah," Mark said, "a fallen angel, full of grit."

"What the hell makes you so happy?"

"I'm not happy, I'm just serene. Now the day is over, et cetera."

"Say." Strunk came up an aisle with a disagreeably effeminate waddle, pregnant with gossip. "Did you hear about Murchison?"

"No." Mark mimicked Strunk's whisper.

"He got the pants kidded off him today."

"Oh dear."

Strunk started to laugh, as he often did before beginning a story. "You know what a goddamn ladies' man he thinks he is?"

"You bet," Mark said, although Strunk said that about every male member of the faculty.

"You have Gloria Andrews, don't you?"

"You bet."

"Well, this morning Murky intercepts a note she was writing, and the note says what a damn neat guy she thinks Murchison is and how she *loves* him!" Strunk waited for Mark to say something, and then, when he didn't, continued, "You could see he was tickled pink. But—get this—it turns out at lunch that the same damn thing happened to Fryeburg in history yesterday!" Strunk laughed and, still getting no response, gave Mark a little push—a schoolyard push. "The girl's too dumb to have thought it up herself. We all think it was Peter Forry's idea."

"Probably was," Mark agreed. Strunk followed him out to his locker, describing Murchison's expression when Fryeburg (in all innocence, mind you) told what had happened to him.

Mark turned the combination of his locker: 18, 24, 3. "Would you excuse me, Dave?" he said. "My wife may be out front waiting. She picks me up when it rains."

Strunk was too thick to catch Mark's anger. "Help yourself," he said. "I got to get over to the gym. Can't take the little darlings outside in the rain; their mommies'll write notes to Teacher." He clattered down the hall and wheeled at the far end, shouting, "Now, don't tell You-know-who! The ladies' man!"

Mr. Prosser took his coat from the locker and shrugged it on. He placed his hat upon his head. He fitted his rubbers over his shoes, pinching his fingers painfully, and lifted his umbrella off the hook. He thought of opening it right there in the vacant hall, as a kind of joke on himself, and decided not to. The girl had been almost crying; he was sure of that.

The Christian Roommates

ORSON ZIEGLER came straight to Harvard from the small South Dakota town where his father was the doctor. Orson, at eighteen, was half an inch under six feet tall, with a weight of 164 and an IQ of 155. His eczematous cheeks and vaguely irritated squint—as if his face had been for too long transected by the sight of a level horizon—masked a definite self-confidence. As the doctor's son, he had always mattered in the town. In his high school he had been class president, valedictorian, and captain of the football and baseball teams. (The captain of the basketball team had been Lester Spotted Elk, a full-blooded Chippewa with dirty fingernails and brilliant teeth, a smoker, a drinker, a discipline problem, and the only boy Orson ever had met who was better than he at anything that mattered.) Orson was the first native of his town to go to Harvard, and would probably be the last, at least until his son was of age. His future was firm in his mind: the pre-med course here, medical school either at Harvard, Penn, or Yale, and then back to South Dakota, where he had his wife already selected and claimed and primed to wait. Two nights before he left for Harvard, he had taken her virginity. She had cried, and he had felt foolish, having, somehow, failed. It had been his virginity, too. Orson was sane, sane enough to know that he had lots to learn, and to be, within limits, willing. Harvard processes thousands of such boys and restores them to the world with little apparent damage. Presumably because he was from west of the Mississippi and a Protestant Christian (Methodist), the authorities had given him as a freshman roommate a self-converted Episcopalian from Oregon.

When Orson arrived at Harvard on the morning of Registration Day, bleary and stiff from the series of airplane rides that had begun fourteen hours before, his roommate was already installed. "H. Palamountain" was floridly inscribed in the upper of the two name slots on the door of

Room 14. The bed by the window had been slept in, and the desk by the window was neatly loaded with books. Standing sleepless inside the door, inertly clinging to his two heavy suitcases, Orson was conscious of another presence in the room without being able to locate it; optically and mentally, he focused with a slight slowness.

The roommate was sitting on the floor, barefoot, before a small spinning wheel. He jumped up nimbly. Orson's first impression was of the wiry quickness that almost magically brought close to his face the thick-lipped, pop-eyed face of the other boy. He was a head shorter than Orson, and wore, above his bare feet, pegged sky-blue slacks, a lumberjack shirt whose throat was dashingly stuffed with a silk foulard, and a white cap such as Orson had seen before only in photographs of Pandit Nehru. Dropping a suitcase, Orson offered his hand. Instead of taking it, the roommate touched his palms together, bowed his head, and murmured something Orson didn't catch. Then he gracefully swept off the white cap, revealing a narrow crest of curly blond hair that stood up like a rooster's comb. "I am Henry Palamountain." His voice, clear and colorless in the way of West Coast voices, suggested a radio announcer. His handshake was metallically firm and seemed to have a pinch of malice in it. Like Orson, he wore glasses. The thick lenses emphasized the hyperthyroid bulge of his eyes and their fishy, searching expression.

"Orson Ziegler," Orson said.

"I know."

Orson felt a need to add something adequately solemn, standing as they were on the verge of a kind of marriage. "Well, Henry"—he lamely lowered the other suitcase to the floor—"I guess we'll be seeing a lot of each other."

"You may call me Hub," the roommate said. "Most people do. However, call me Henry if you insist. I don't wish to diminish your dreadful freedom. You may not wish to call me anything at all. Already I've made three hopeless enemies in the dormitory."

Every sentence in this smoothly enunciated speech bothered Orson, beginning with the first. He himself had never been given a nickname; it was the one honor his classmates had withheld from him. In his adolescence he had coined nicknames for himself—Orrie, Ziggy—and tried to insinuate them into popular usage, without success. And what was meant by "dreadful freedom"? It sounded sarcastic. And why might he not wish to call him anything at all? And how had the roommate had the time to make enemies? Orson asked irritably, "How long have you *been* here?"

"Eight days." Henry concluded every statement with a strange little pucker of his lips, a kind of satisfied silent click, as if to say, "And what do you think of *that?*"

Orson felt that he had been sized up as someone easy to startle. But he slid helplessly into the straight-man role that, like the second-best bed, had been reserved for him. "That *long?*"

"Yes. I was totally alone until the day before yesterday. You see, I hitchhiked."

"From *Oregon?*"

"Yes. And I wished to allow time enough for any contingency. In case I was robbed, I had sewed a fifty-dollar bill inside my shirt. As it turned out, I made smooth connections all the way. I had painted a large cardboard sign saying 'Harvard.' You should try it sometime. One meets some very interesting Harvard graduates."

"Didn't your parents worry?"

"Of course. My parents are divorced. My father was furious. He wanted me to fly. I told him to give the plane fare to the Indian Relief Fund. He never gives a penny to charity. And, of course, I'm old. I'm twenty."

"You've been in the Army?"

Henry lifted his hands and staggered back as if from a blow. He put the back of his hand to his brow, whimpered "Never," shuddered, straightened up smartly, and saluted. "In fact, the Portland draft board is after me right now." With a preening tug of his two agile hands—which did look, Orson realized, old: bony and veined and red-tipped, like a woman's— he broadened his foulard. "They refuse to recognize any conscientious objectors except Quakers and Mennonites. My bishop agrees with them. They offered me an out if I'd say I was willing to work in a hospital, but I explained that this released a man for combat duty and if it came to that I'd just as soon carry a gun. I'm an excellent shot. I mind killing only on principle."

The Korean War had begun that summer, and Orson, who had been nagged by a suspicion that his duty was to enlist, bristled at such blithe pacifism. He squinted and asked, "What *have* you been doing for two years, then?"

"Working in a plywood mill. As a gluer. The actual gluing is done by machines, but they become swamped in their own glue now and then. It's a kind of excessive introspection—you've read *Hamlet?*"

"Just *Macbeth* and *The Merchant of Venice.*"

"Yes. Anyway. They have to be cleaned with solvent. One wears long rubber gloves up to one's elbows. It's very soothing work. The inside of a gluer is an excellent place for revolving Greek quotations in your head. I memorized nearly the whole of the *Phaedo* that way." He gestured toward his desk, and Orson saw that many of the books were green Loeb editions of Plato and Aristotle, in Greek. Their spines were worn; they looked read and reread. For the first time, the thought of being at Harvard frightened him. Orson had been standing between his suitcases and now he moved to unpack. "Have you left me a bureau?"

"Of course. The better one." Henry jumped on the bed that had not been slept in and bounced up and down as if it were a trampoline. "And I've given you the bed with the better mattress," he said, still bouncing, "and the desk that doesn't have the glare from the window."

"Thanks," Orson said.

Henry was quick to notice his tone. "Would you rather have my bed? My desk?" He jumped from the bed and dashed to his desk and scooped a stack of books from it.

Orson had to touch him to stop him, and was startled by the tense muscularity of the arm he touched. "Don't be silly," he said. "They're exactly alike."

Henry replaced his books. "I don't want any bitterness," he said, "or immature squabbling. As the older man, it's my responsibility to yield. Here. I'll give you the shirt off my back." And he began to peel off his lumberjack shirt, leaving the foulard dramatically knotted around his naked throat. He wore no undershirt.

Having won from Orson a facial expression that Orson himself could not see, Henry smiled and rebuttoned the shirt. "Do you mind my name being in the upper slot on the door? I'll remove it. I apologize. I did it without realizing how sensitive you would be."

Perhaps it was all a kind of humor. Orson tried to make a joke. He pointed and asked, "Do I get a spinning wheel, too?"

"Oh, *that*." Henry hopped backward on one bare foot and became rather shy. "That's an experiment. I ordered it from Calcutta. I spin for a half hour a day, after yoga."

"You do yoga, too?"

"Just some of the elementary positions. My ankles can't take more than five minutes of the Lotus yet."

"And you say you have a bishop."

The roommate glanced up with a glint of fresh interest. "Say. You listen, don't you? Yes. I consider myself an Anglican Christian Platonist strongly influenced by Gandhi." He touched his palms before his chest, bowed, straightened, and giggled. "My bishop hates me," he said. "The one in Oregon, who wants me to be a soldier. I've introduced myself to the bishop here and I don't think he likes me, either. For that matter, I've antagonized my adviser. I told him I had no intention of fulfilling the science requirement."

"For God's sake, why *not?*"

"You don't really want to know."

Orson felt this rebuff as a small test of strength. "Not really," he agreed.

"I consider science a demonic illusion of human *hubris*. Its phantasmal nature is proved by its constant revision. I asked him, 'Why should I waste an entire fourth of my study time, time that could be spent with Plato, mastering a mass of hypotheses that will be obsolete by the time I graduate?' "

"My Lord, Henry," Orson exclaimed, indignantly defending the millions of lives saved by medical science, "you can't be serious!"

"Please. 'Hub.' I may be difficult for you, and I think it would help if you were to call me by my name. Now let's talk about you. Your father is a doctor, you received all A's in high school—I received rather mediocre grades myself—and you've come to Harvard because you believe it affords a cosmopolitan Eastern environment that will be valuable to you after spending your entire life in a small provincial town."

"Who the hell told you all this?" The recital of his application statement made Orson blush. He already felt older than the boy who had written it.

"University Hall," Henry said. "I went over and asked to see your folder. They didn't want to let me at first, but I explained that if they were going to give me a roommate, after I had specifically requested to live alone, I had a right to information about you, so I could minimize possible friction."

"And they *let* you?"

"Of course. People without convictions have no powers of resistance." His mouth made its little satisfied click, and Orson was goaded to ask, "Why did *you* come to Harvard?"

"Two reasons." He ticked them off on two fingers. "Raphael Demos and Werner Jaeger."

Orson did not know these names, but he suspected that "Friends of yours?" was a stupid question, once it was out of his mouth.

However, Henry nodded. "I've introduced myself to Demos. A charming old scholar, with a beautiful young wife."

"You mean you just went to his house and pushed yourself *in?*" Orson heard his own voice grow shrill; his voice, rather high and unstable, was one of the things about himself that he liked least.

Henry blinked, and looked unexpectedly vulnerable, so slender and bravely dressed, his ugly, yellowish, flat-nailed feet naked on the floor, which was uncarpeted and painted black. "That isn't how I would describe it. I went as a pilgrim. He seemed pleased to talk to me." He spoke carefully, and his mouth abstained from clicking.

That he could hurt his roommate's feelings—that this jaunty apparition had feelings—disconcerted Orson more deeply than any of the surprises he had been deliberately offered. As quickly as he had popped up, Henry dropped to the floor, as if through a trapdoor in the plane of conversation. He resumed spinning. The method apparently called for a thread to be wound around the big toe of a foot and to be kept taut by a kind of absent-minded pedal motion. While engaged in this, he seemed hermetically sealed inside one of the gluing machines that had incubated his philosophy. Unpacking, Orson was slowed and snagged by a complicated mood of discomfort. He tried to remember how his mother had arranged his bureau drawers at home—socks and underwear in one, shirts and handkerchiefs in another. Home seemed infinitely far from him, and he was dizzily conscious of a great depth of space beneath his feet, as if the blackness of the floor were the color of an abyss. The spinning wheel steadily chuckled. Orson's buzz of unease circled and settled on his roommate, who, it was clear, had thought earnestly about profound matters, matters that Orson, busy as he had been with the practical business of being a good student, had hardly considered. It was also clear that Henry had thought unintelligently. This unintelligence ("I received rather mediocre grades myself") was more of a menace than a comfort. Bent above the bureau drawers, Orson felt cramped in his mind, able neither to stand erect in wholehearted contempt nor to lie down in honest admiration. His mood was complicated by the repugnance his roommate's physical presence aroused in him. An almost morbidly clean boy, Orson was haunted by glue, and a tacky ambience resisted every motion of his unpacking.

The silence between the roommates continued until a great bell rang ponderously. The sound was near and yet far, like a heartbeat within the bosom of time, and it seemed to bring with it into the room the muffling foliation of the trees in the Yard, which to Orson's prairie-honed eyes had looked tropically tall and lush; the walls of the room vibrated with leaf shadows, and many minute presences—dust motes, traffic sounds, or angels of whom several could dance on the head of a pin—thronged the air and made it difficult to breathe. The stairways of the dormitory rumbled. Boys dressed in jackets and neckties crowded the doorway and entered the room, laughing and calling "Hub. Hey, Hub."

"Get up off the floor, Dad."

"Jesus, Hub, put your shoes on."

"Pee-*yew*."

"And take off that bandanna around your neck. Coat and tie required."

"And that nurse's cap."

"Consider the lilies, Hub. They toil not, neither do they spin, and yet I say unto you that Solomon in all his glory was not arrayed like one of these."

"Amen, brothers!"

"Fitch, you should be a preacher."

They were all strangers to Orson. Hub stood and smoothly performed introductions.

In a few days, Orson had sorted them out. That jostling conglomerate, so apparently secure and homogeneous, broke down, under habitual exposure, into double individuals: roommates. There were Silverstein and Koshland, Dawson and Kern, Young and Carter, Petersen and Fitch.

Silverstein and Koshland, who lived in the room overhead, were Jews from New York City. All Orson knew about non-Biblical Jews was that they were a sad race, full of music, shrewdness, and woe. But Silverstein and Koshland were always clowning, always wisecracking. They played bridge and poker and chess and Go and went to the movies in Boston and drank coffee in the luncheonettes around the Square. They came from the "gifted" high schools of the Bronx and Brooklyn respectively, and treated Cambridge as if it were another borough. Most of what the freshman year sought to teach them they seemed to know already. As winter approached, Koshland went out for basketball, and he and his teammates made the floor above bounce to the thump and rattle of scrimmages with a tennis ball and a wastebasket. One afternoon, a section of ceiling collapsed on Orson's bed.

Next door, in Room 12, Dawson and Kern wanted to be writers. Dawson was from Ohio and Kern from Pennsylvania. Dawson had a sulky, slouching bearing, a certain puppyish facial eagerness, and a terrible temper. He was a disciple of Sherwood Anderson and Ernest Hemingway and himself wrote in a stern, plain style. He had been raised as an atheist, and no one in the dormitory rubbed his temper the wrong way more often than Hub. Orson, feeling that he and Dawson came from opposite edges of that great psychological realm called the Midwest, liked him. He felt less at ease with Kern, who seemed Eastern and subtly vicious. A farm boy bent on urban sophistication, riddled with nervous ailments ranging from conjunctivitis to hemorrhoids, Kern smoked and talked incessantly. He and Dawson maintained between them a battery of running jokes. At night Orson could hear them on the other side of the wall keeping each other awake with improvised parodies and musical comedies based on their teachers, their courses, or their fellow-freshmen. One midnight, Orson distinctly heard Dawson sing, "My name is Orson Ziegler, I come from South Dakota." There was a pause, then Kern sang back, "I tend to be a niggler, and masturbate by quota."

Across the hall, in 15, lived Young and Carter, Negroes. Carter was from Detroit and very black, very clipped in speech, very well dressed, and apt to collapse, at the jab of a rightly angled joke, into a giggling fit that left his cheeks gleaming with tears; Kern was expert at breaking Carter up. Young was a lean, malt-pale colored boy from North Carolina, here on a national scholarship, out of his depth, homesick, and cold. Kern called him Brer Possum. He slept all day and at night sat on his bed playing the mouthpiece of a trumpet to himself. At first, he had played the full horn in the afternoon, flooding the dormitory and its green envelope of trees with golden, tremulous versions of languorous tunes like "Sentimental Journey" and "The Tennessee Waltz." It had been nice. But Young's sense of place—a habit of self-effacement that the shock of Harvard had intensified in him—soon cancelled these harmless performances. He took to hiding from the sun, and at night the furtive spitting sound from across the hall seemed to Orson, as he struggled into sleep, music drowning in shame. Carter always referred to his roommate as "Jonathan," mouthing the syllables fastidiously, as if he were pronouncing the name of a remote being he had just learned about, like La Rochefoucauld or Demosthenes.

Catty-corner up the hall, in unlucky 13, Petersen and Fitch kept a strange household. Both were tall, narrow-shouldered, and broad-bottomed; physiques aside, it was hard to see what they had in common, or why Harvard had put them together. Fitch, with dark staring eyes and the flat full cranium of Frankenstein's monster, was a child prodigy from Maine, choked with philosophy, wild with ideas, and pregnant with the seeds of the nervous breakdown he was to have, eventually, in April. Petersen was an amiable Swede with a transparent skin that revealed blue veins in his nose. For several summers he had worked as a reporter for the *Duluth Herald*. He had all the newsman's tricks: the side-of-the-mouth quip, the nip of whiskey, the hat on the back of the head, the habit of throwing still-burning cigarettes onto the floor. He did not seem quite to know why he was at Harvard, and in fact did not return at the end of the freshman year. But while these two drifted toward their respective rustications, they made a strangely well-suited couple. Each was strong where the other was helpless. Fitch was so uncoördinated and unorganized he could not even type; he would lie on his bed in pajamas, writhing and grimacing, and dictate a tangled humanities paper, twice the requested length and mostly about books that had not been assigned, while Petersen, typing with a hectic two-finger system, would obligingly turn this chaotic monologue into "copy." His patience verged on the maternal. In return, Fitch gave Petersen ideas out of the superabundance painfully cramming his big flat head. Petersen had absolutely no ideas; he could neither compare, contrast, nor criticize St. Augustine and Marcus Aurelius. Perhaps having seen, so young, so many corpses and fires and policemen and prostitutes had prematurely blighted his speculative faculty. At any rate, mothering Fitch gave him something practical to do, and Orson envied them.

He envied all the roommates, whatever the bond between them—geography, race, ambition, physical size—for between himself and Hub Palamountain he could see no link except forced cohabitation. Not that living with Hub was superficially unpleasant. Hub was tidy, industrious, and ostentatiously considerate. He rose at seven, prayed, did yoga, spun, and was off to breakfast, often not to be seen again until the end of the day. He went to sleep, generally, at eleven sharp. If there was noise in the dorm, he would insert rubber plugs in his ears, put a black mask over his eyes, and go to sleep anyway. During the day, he kept a rigorous round of appointments: he audited two courses in addition to taking four, he wrestled three times a week for his physical-training requirement, he wangled tea invitations from Demos and Jaeger and the Bishop of Massachusetts, he attended free evening lectures and readings, he associated himself with Phillips Brooks House and spent two afternoons a week supervising slum boys in a Roxbury redevelopment house. In addition, he had begun to take piano lessons in Brookline. Many days, Orson saw him only at meals in the Union, where the dormitory neighbors, in those first fall months, when their acquaintance was crisp and young and differing interests had not yet scattered them, tended to regroup around a long table. In these months there was often a debate on the topic posed beneath their eyes: Hub's vegetarianism. There he would sit, his tray heaped high with a steaming double helping of squash and lima beans, while Fitch would try to locate the exact point at which vegetarianism became inconsistent. "You eat eggs," he said.

"Yes," Hub said.

"You realize that every egg, from the chicken's point of reference, is a newborn baby?"

"But in fact it is not unless it has been fertilized by a rooster."

"But suppose," Fitch pursued, "as sometimes happens—which I happen to know, from working in my uncle's henhouse in Maine—an egg that *should* be sterile has in fact been fertilized and contains an embryo?"

"If I see it, I naturally don't eat that particular egg," Hub said, his lips making that satisfied concluding snap.

Fitch pounced triumphantly, spilling a fork to the floor with a lurch of his hand. "But *why?* The hen feels the same pain on being parted from an egg whether sterile or fertile. The embryo is unconscious—a vegetable. As a vegetarian, you should eat it with special relish." He tipped back in his chair so hard he had to grab the table edge to keep from toppling over.

"It seems to me," Dawson said, frowning ominously—the merriment of others often spilled him into a bad temper—"that psychoanalysis of hens is hardly relevant."

"On the contrary," Kern said lightly, clearing his throat and narrowing his pink, infected eyes, "it seems to me that there, in the tiny, dim mind of the hen—the minimal mind, as it were—is where the tragedy of the universe achieves a pinpoint focus. Picture the emotional life of a hen. What does she know of companionship? A flock of pecking, harsh-voiced gossips. Of shelter? A few dung-bespattered slats. Of food? Some flecks of mash and grit rudely tossed on the bare ground. Of love? The casual assault of a polygamous cock—cock in the Biblical sense. Then, into this heartless world, there suddenly arrives, as if by magic, an egg. An egg of her own. An egg, it must seem to her, that she and God have made. How she must cherish it, its beautiful baldness, its gentle lustre, its firm yet somehow fragile, softly swaying weight."

Carter had broken up. He bent above his tray, his eyes tight shut, his dark face contorted joyfully. "Puhleese," he gasped at last. "You're making my stomach hurt."

"Ah, Carter," Kern said loftily, "if that were only the worst of it. For then, one day, while the innocent hen sits cradling this strange, faceless, oval child, its little weight swaying softly in her wings"—he glanced hopefully at Carter, but the colored boy bit his lower lip and withstood the jab—"an enormous man, smelling of beer and manure, comes and tears the egg from her grasp. And why? Because *he*"—Kern pointed, arm fully extended, across the table, so that his index finger, orange with nicotine, almost touched Hub's nose—"*he,* St. Henry Palamountain, wants more eggs to eat. 'More eggs!' he cries voraciously, so that brutal steers and faithless pigs can continue to menace the children of American mothers!"

Dawson slammed his silver down, got up from the table, and slouched out of the dining room. Kern blushed. His high spirits had rubbed his roommate the wrong way. In the silence, Petersen put a folded slice of roast beef in his mouth and said, chewing, "Jesus, Hub, if somebody else kills the animals you might as well eat 'em. They don't give a damn any more."

"You understand nothing," Hub said simply.

"Hey, Hub," Silverstein called down from the far end of the table. "What's the word on milk? Don't calves drink milk? Maybe you're taking milk out of some calf's mouth."

Orson felt impelled to speak. "*No,*" he said, and his voice seemed to have burst, its pitch was so unsteady and excited. "As anybody except somebody from New York would know, milch cows have weaned their calves. What I wonder about, Hub, is your shoes. You wear leather shoes."

"I do." The gaiety left Hub's defense of himself. His lips became prim.

"Leather is the skin of a steer."

"But the animal has already been slaughtered."

"You sound like Petersen. Your purchase of leather goods—what about your wallet and belt, for that matter?—encourages the slaughter. You're as much of a murderer as the rest of us. More of one—because you think about it."

Hub folded his hands carefully in front of him, propping them, almost in prayer, on the table edge. His voice became like that of a radio announcer, but an announcer rapidly, softly describing the home stretch of a race. "My belt, I believe, is a form of plastic. My wallet was given to me by my mother years ago, before I became a vegetarian. Please remember that I ate meat for eighteen years and I still have an appetite for it. If there were any other concentrated source of protein, I would not eat eggs. Some vegetarians do not. On the other hand, some vegetarians eat fish and take liver extract. I would not do this. Shoes are a problem. There is a firm in Chicago that makes non-leather shoes for extreme vegetarians, but they're very expensive and not comfortable. I once ordered a pair. They hurt my feet. Leather, you see, 'breathes' in a way no synthetic substitute does. My feet are tender; I have compromised. I apologize. For that matter, when I play the piano—'tickle the ivories,' as they say—I encourage the slaughter of elephants, and in brushing my teeth, which I must do faithfully because a vegetable diet is so heavy in starch, I use a brush of pig bristles. I am covered with blood, and pray daily for forgiveness." He took up his fork and resumed eating the mound of squash.

Orson was amazed; he had been impelled to speak by a kind of sympathy, and Hub had answered as if he alone were a serious enemy. He tried to defend himself. "There are perfectly wearable shoes," he said, "made out of canvas, with crepe-rubber soles."

"I'll look into them," Hub said. "They sound a little sporty to me."

Laughter swept the table and ended the subject. After lunch Orson walked to the library with the beginnings of indigestion; a backwash of emotion was upsetting his stomach. There was a growing confusion inside him he could not resolve. He resented being associated with Hub, and yet felt attacked when Hub was attacked. It seemed to him that Hub deserved credit for putting his beliefs into practice, and that people like Fitch and Kern, in mocking, merely belittled themselves. Yet Hub smiled at their criticism, took it as a game, and fought back in earnest only at Orson, forcing him into a false position. Why? Was it because in being also a Christian he alone qualified for serious rebuke? But Carter went to church, wearing a blue pin-striped suit with a monogrammed handkerchief peaked in the breast pocket, every Sunday; Petersen was a nominal Presbyterian; Orson had once seen Kern sneaking out of Mem Chapel; and even Koshland observed his holidays, by cutting classes and skipping lunch. Why, therefore, Orson asked himself, should Hub pick on him? And why should he care? He had no real respect for Hub. Hub's handwriting was childishly large and careful and his first set of hour exams, even in the course on Plato and Aristotle, had yielded a batch of C's. Orson resented being condescended to by him; the knowledge that at the table he had come off second-best galled him like an unfair grade. His situation with Hub became in his head a diagram in which all his intentions curved off at right angles and his strengths inversely tapered into nothing. Behind the diagram hung the tuck of complacence in Hub's lips, the fishy impudence of his eyes, and the keenly irksome shape and tint of his hands and feet. These images—Hub disembodied—Orson carried with him into the library, back and forth to classes, and along the congested streets around the Square; now and then the glaze of an eye or the flat yellowish nail of a big toe welled up distinctly through the pages of a book or, greatly magnified, slid with Orson into the unconsciousness of sleep. Nevertheless, he surprised himself, sitting one February afternoon in Room 12 with Dawson and Kern, by blurting, "I hate him." He considered what he had said, liked the taste of it, and repeated, "I hate him. I've never hated anybody before in my life." His voice cracked and his eyes warmed with abortive tears.

They had all returned from Christmas vacation to plunge into the odd limbo of reading period and the novel ordeal of midyear exams. This was a dormitory, by and large, of public-school graduates, who feel the strain of Harvard most in their freshman year. The private-school boys, launched by little Harvards like Andover and Groton, tend to glide through this year and to run aground later on strange reefs, foundering in alcohol, or sinking into a dandified apathy. But the institution demands of each man, before it releases him, a wrenching sacrifice of ballast. At Christmas, Orson's mother thought he looked haggard, and set about fattening him up. On the other hand, he was struck by how much his father had aged and shrunk. Orson spent his first days home listening to the mindless music on the radio, hours of it, and driving through farmland on narrow straight roads already banked bright with plowed snow. The South Dakota sky had never looked so open, so clean; he had never realized before that the high dry sun that made even sub-zero days feel warm at noon was a local phenomenon. He made love to his girl again, and again she cried. He said to her he blamed himself, for ineptitude; but in his heart he blamed her. She was not helping him. Back in Cambridge, it was raining, raining in January, and the entryway of the Coop was full of gray footprints and wet bicycles and Radcliffe girls in slickers and sneakers. Hub had stayed here, alone in their room, and had celebrated Christmas with a fast.

In the monotonous, almost hallucinatory month of rereading, outlining, and memorizing, Orson perceived how little he knew, how stupid he was, how unnatural all learning is, and how futile. Harvard rewarded him with three A's and a B. Hub pulled out two B's and two C's. Kern, Dawson, and Silverstein did well; Petersen, Koshland, and Carter got mediocre grades; Fitch flunked one subject, and Young flunked three. The pale Negro slunk in and out of the dorm as if he were diseased and marked for destruction; he became, while still among them, a rumor. The suppressed whistling of the trumpet mouthpiece was no longer heard. Silverstein and Koshland and the basketball crowd adopted Carter and took him to movies in Boston three or four times a week.

After exams, in the heart of the Cambridge winter, there is a grateful pause. New courses are selected, and even the full-year courses, heading into their second half, sometimes put on, like a new hat, a fresh professor. The days quietly lengthen; there is a snowstorm or two; the swimming and squash teams lend the sports pages of the *Crimson* an unaccustomed note of victory. A kind of foreshadow of spring falls bluely on the snow. The elms are seen to be shaped like fountains. The discs of snow pressed by boots into the sidewalk in front of Albiani's seem large precious coins; the brick buildings, the arched gates, the archaic lecterns, and the barny mansions along Brattle Street dawn upon the freshman as a heritage he temporarily possesses. The thumb-worn spines of his now familiar textbooks seem proof of a certain knowingness, and the strap of the green book-bag slung over his shoulder tugs at his wrist like a living falcon. The letters from home dwindle in importance. The hours open up. There is more time. Experiments are made. Courtships begin. Conversations go on and on; and an almost rapacious desire for mutual discovery possesses acquaintances. It was in this atmosphere, then, that Orson made his confession.

Dawson turned his head away as if the words had menaced him personally. Kern blinked, lit a cigarette, and asked, "What don't you like about him?"

"Well"—Orson shifted his weight uncomfortably in the black but graceful, shapely but hard Harvard chair—"it's little things. Whenever he gets a notice from the Portland draft board, he tears it up without opening it and scatters it out the window."

"And you're afraid that this incriminates you as an accessory and they'll put you in jail?"

"No—I don't know. It seems exaggerated. He exaggerates everything. You should see how he prays."

"How do you know how he prays?"

"He shows me. Every morning, he gets down on his knees and *throws* himself across the bed, his face in the blanket, his arms way out." He showed them.

"God," Dawson said. "That's marvellous. It's medieval. It's more than medieval. It's Counter-Reformation."

"I mean," Orson said, grimacing in realization of how deeply he had betrayed Hub, "I pray, too, but I don't make a show of myself."

A frown clotted Dawson's expression, and passed.

"He's a saint," Kern said.

"He's *not*," Orson said. "He's a fake. I'm taking Chem 1 with him, and he's worse than a child with the math. And those Greek books he keeps on his desk, they look worn because he bought them second-hand."

"Saints don't have to be good at math," Kern said. "What saints have to have is energy. Hub has it."

"Look how he wrestles," Dawson said.

"I doubt if he wrestles very *well*," Orson said. "He didn't make the freshman team. I'm sure if we heard him play the piano it'd be awful."

"You seem to miss the point," Kern said, eyes closed, "of what Hub's all about."

"I know goddamn well what he thinks he's all about," Orson said, "but it doesn't go. All this vegetarianism and love of the starving Indian — he's really a terribly cold bastard. I think he's about the coldest person I've ever met in my life."

"I don't think Orson thinks that; do you?" Kern asked Dawson.

"No," Dawson said, and his puppyish smile cleared his cloudy face. "That's not what Orson the Parson thinks."

Kern squinted. "Is it Orson the Parson, or Orson the Person?"

"I think Hub is the nub," Dawson said.

"Or the rub," Kern added, and both burst into grinding laughter. Orson felt he was being sacrificed to the precarious peace the two roommates kept between themselves, and left, superficially insulted but secretly flattered to have been given, at last, a nickname of sorts: Orson the Parson.

Several nights later they went to hear Carl Sandburg read in New Lecture Hall — the four adjacent roommates, plus Fitch. To avoid sitting next to Hub, who aggressively led them into a row of seats up front, Orson delayed, and so sat the farthest away from the girl Hub sat directly behind. Orson noticed her immediately; she had a wide mane of coppery-red hair which hung down loose over the back of her seat. The color of it, and the abundance, reminded him, all at once, of horses, earth, sun, wheat, and South Dakota. From Orson's angle she was nearly in profile; her face was small, with a tilted shadowy cheekbone and a pale prominent ear. Her ear reminded him of Emily; she was Emily with long red hair and Cambridge sophistication. He yearned to see her face, and felt her about to turn. She turned away. Hub had leaned forward and was saying something into her other ear. Fitch overheard it, and gleefully relayed it to Dawson, who whispered to Kern and Orson, *Hub said to the girl, 'You have beautiful hair.'*

Several times during the reading, Hub leaned forward to add something more into her ear, each time springing spurts of choked laughter from Fitch, Dawson, and Kern. Meanwhile, Sandburg, his white bangs as straight and shiny as a doll's wig of artificial fibre, incanted above the lectern and quaintly strummed a guitar. Afterward, Hub walked with the girl into the outdoors. From a distance Orson saw her white face break into a laugh. Hub returned to his friends with the complacent nick in the corner of his mouth deepened, in the darkness, to a gash.

It was not the next day, or the next week, but within the month that Hub brought back to the room a heap of coppery hair. Orson found it lying like an animal corpse on a newspaper spread on his bed. "Hub, what the hell is this?"

Hub was on the floor playing with his spinning wheel. "Hair."

"*Human* hair?"

"Of course."

"Whose?"

"A girl's."

"What happened?" The question sounded strange; Orson meant to ask, "What girl's?"

Hub answered as if he had asked that question. "It's a girl I met at the Sandburg reading; you don't know her."

"This is *her* hair?"

"Yes. I asked her for it. She said she was planning to cut it all off this spring anyway."

Orson stood stunned above the bed, gripped by an urge to bury his face and hands in the hair. "You've been *seeing* her?" This effeminate stridence in his voice: he despised it and only Hub brought it out.

"A little. My schedule doesn't allow for much social life, but my adviser has recommended that I relax now and then."

"You take her to movies?"

"Once in a while. She pays her admission, of course."

"Of *course*."

Hub took him up on his tone. "Please remember I'm here on my savings alone. I have refused all financial assistance from my father."

"Hub"—the very syllable seemed an expression of pain—"what are you going to do with her hair?"

"Spin it into a rope."

"A *rope?*"

"Yes. It'll be very difficult; her hair is terribly fine."

"And what will you do with the rope?"

"Make a knot of it."

"A *knot?*"

"I think that's the term. I'll coil it and secure it so it can't come undone and give it to her. So she'll always have her hair the way it was when she was nineteen."

"Oh, Lord. How did you ever talk this poor girl into it?"

"I didn't talk her into it. I merely offered, and she thought it was a lovely idea. Really, Orson, I don't see why this should offend your bourgeois scruples. Women cut their hair all the time."

"She must think you're insane. She was humoring you."

"As you like. It was a perfectly rational suggestion, and my sanity has never been raised as an issue between us."

"Well, *I* think you're insane. Hub, you're a *nut.*"

Orson left the room and slammed the door, and didn't return until eleven, when Hub was asleep in his eye mask. The heap of hair had been transferred to the floor beside the spinning wheel, and already some strands were entangled with the machine. In time a rope was produced, a braided cord as thick as a woman's little finger, about a foot long, weightless and waxen. The earthy, horsy fire in the hair's color had been quenched in the process. Hub carefully coiled it and with black thread and long pins secured and stiffened the spiral into a disc the size of a small saucer. This he presented to the girl one Friday night. The presentation appeared to satisfy him, for, as far as Orson knew, Hub had no further dates with her. Once in a while Orson passed her in the Yard, and without her hair she scarcely seemed female, her small pale face fringed in curt tufts, her ears looking enormous. He wanted to speak to her; some obscure force of pity, or hope of rescue, impelled him to greet this wan androgyne, but the opening word stuck in his throat. She did not look as if she pitied herself, or knew what had been done to her.

Something magical protected Hub; things deflected from him. The doubt Orson had cast upon his sanity bounced back onto himself. As spring slowly broke, he lost the ability to sleep. Figures and facts churned sluggishly in an insomniac mire. His courses became four parallel puzzles. In mathematics, the crucial transposition upon which the solution pivoted consistently eluded him, vanishing into the chinks between the numbers. The quantities in chemistry became impishly unstable; the unbalanced scales clicked down sharply, and the system of interlocked elements that fanned from the lab to the far stars collapsed. In the history survey course, they had reached the Enlightenment, and Orson found himself disturbingly impressed by Voltaire's indictment of God, though the lecturer handled it calmly, as one more item of intellectual history, neither true nor false. And in German, which Orson had taken to satisfy his language requirement, the words piled on remorselessly, and the existence of languages other than English, the existence of so many, each so vast, with so many arbitrary rules, seemed to prove cosmic dementia. He felt his mind, which was always more steady than quick, grow slower and slower. His chair threatened to adhere to him, and he would leap up in panic. Sleepless, stuffed with information he could neither forget nor manipulate, he became prey to obsessive delusions; he became convinced that his girl in South Dakota had taken up with another boy and was making love to him happily, Orson having shouldered the awkwardness and blame of taking her virginity. In the very loops that Emily's ballpoint pen described in her bland letters to him he read the pleased rotundity, the inner fatness of a satisfied woman. He even knew the man. It was Spotted Elk, the black-nailed Chippewa, whose impassive nimbleness had so often mocked Orson on the basketball court, whose terrible ease and speed of reaction had seemed so unjust, and whose defense—he recalled now— Emily had often undertaken. His wife had become a whore, a squaw; the scraggly mute reservation children his father had doctored in the charity clinic became, amid the sliding transparencies of Orson's mind, his own children. In his dreams—or in those limp elisions of imagery which in the absence of sleep passed for dreams—he seemed to be rooming with Spotted Elk, and his roommate, who sometimes wore a mask, invariably had won, by underhanded means, the affection and admiration that were rightfully his. There was a conspiracy. Whenever Orson heard Kern and Dawson laughing on the other side of the wall, he knew it was about him, and about his most secret habits. His privacy was outrageously invaded; in bed, half relaxed, he would suddenly see himself bodily involved with Hub's lips, Hub's legs, with Hub's veined, vaguely womanish hands. At first he resisted these visions, tried to erase them; it was like trying to erase ripples on water. He learned to submit to them, to let the attack— for it was an attack, with bared teeth and sharp acrobatic movements— wash over him, leaving him limp enough to sleep. These dives became the only route to sleep. In the morning he would awake and see Hub sprawled flamboyantly across his bed in prayer, or sitting hunched at his spinning wheel, or, nattily dressed in his Nehru hat, tiptoeing to the door and with ostentatious care closing it softly behind him; and he would hate him—hate his appearance, his form, his manner, his pretensions— with an avidity of detail he had never known in love. The tiny details of his roommate's physical existence—the wrinkles flickering beside his mouth, the slightly withered look about his hands, the complacently polished creases of his leather shoes—seemed a poisonous food Orson could not stop eating. His eczema worsened alarmingly.

By April, Orson was on the verge of going to the student clinic, which had a department called Mental Health. But at this point Fitch relieved him by having, it seemed, his nervous breakdown for him. For weeks, Fitch had been taking several showers a day. Toward the end he stopped going to classes and was almost constantly naked, except for a towel tucked around his waist. He was trying to complete a humanities paper that was already a month overdue and twenty pages too long. He left the dormitory only to eat and to take more books from the library. One night, around nine, Petersen was called to the phone on the second-floor landing. The Watertown police had picked Fitch up as he was struggling through the underbrush on the banks of the Charles four miles away. He claimed he was walking to the West, where he had been told there was enough space to contain God, and proceeded to talk with wild animation to the police chief about the differences and affinities between Kierkegaard and Nietzsche. Hub, ever alert for an opportunity to intrude in the guise of doing good, went to the hall proctor—a spindly and murmurous graduate student of astronomy engaged, under Harlow Shapley, in an endless galaxy count—and volunteered himself as an expert on the case, and even conferred with the infirmary psychologist. Hub's interpretation was that Fitch had been punished for *hubris*. The psychologist felt the problem was fundamentally Oedipal. Fitch was sent back to Maine. Hub suggested to Orson that now Petersen would need a roommate next year. "I think you and he would hit it off splendidly. You're both materialists."

"I'm *not* a materialist."

Hub lifted his dreadful hands in half-blessing. "Have it your way. I'm determined to minimize friction."

"Damnit, Hub, all the friction between us comes from *you*."

"How? What do I do? Tell me, and I'll change. I'll give you the shirt off my back." He began to unbutton, and stopped, seeing that the laugh wasn't going to come.

Orson felt weak and empty, and in spite of himself he cringed inwardly, with a helpless affection for his unreal, unreachable friend. "I don't know, Hub," he admitted. "I don't know what it is you're doing to me."

A paste of silence dried in the air between them.

Orson with an effort unstuck himself. "I think you're right, we shouldn't room together next year."

Hub seemed a bit bewildered, but nodded, saying, "I told them in the beginning that I ought to live alone." And his hurt eyes, bulging behind their lenses, settled into an invulnerable Byzantine stare.

One afternoon in mid-May, Orson was sitting stumped at his desk, trying to study. He had taken two exams and had two to go. They stood between him and release like two towering walls of muddy paper. His position seemed extremely precarious: he was unable to retreat and able to advance only along a very thin thread, a high wire of sanity on which he balanced above an abyss of statistics and formulae, his brain a firmament of winking cells. A push would kill him. There was then a hurried pounding up the stairs, and Hub pushed into the room carrying cradled in his arm a metal object the color of a gun and the size of a cat. It had a red tongue. Hub slammed the door behind him, snapped the lock, and dumped the object on Orson's bed. It was the head of a parking meter, sheared from its post. A keen quick ache cut through Orson's lower abdomen. "For God's sake," he cried in his contemptible squeaky voice, "what's *that?*"

"It's a parking meter."

"I *know*, I can *see* that. Where the hell did you *get* it?"

"I won't talk to you until you stop being hysterical," Hub said, and crossed to his desk, where Orson had put his mail. He took the top letter, a special delivery from the Portland draft board, and tore it in half. This time, the pain went through Orson's chest. He put his head in his arms on the desk and whirled and groped in the black-red darkness there. His body was frightening him; his nerves listened for a third psychosomatic slash.

A rap sounded on the door; from the force of the knock, it could only be the police. Hub nimbly dashed to the bed and hid the meter under Orson's pillow. Then he pranced to the door and opened it.

It was Dawson and Kern. "What's up?" Dawson asked, frowning as if the disturbance had been created to annoy him.

"It sounded like Ziegler was being tortured," Kern said.

Orson pointed at Hub and explained, "He's castrated a parking meter!"

"I did not," Hub said. "A car went out of control on Mass. Avenue and hit a parked car, which knocked a meter down. A crowd gathered. The head of the meter was lying in the gutter, so I picked it up and carried it away. I was afraid someone might be tempted to steal it."

"Namely, you," Orson said.

"Nobody tried to stop you?" Kern asked.

"Of course not. They were all gathered around the driver of the car."

"Was he hurt?"

"I doubt it. I didn't look."

"You didn't *look!*" Orson cried. "You're a great Samaritan."

"I am not prey," Hub said, "to morbid curiosity."

"Where were the police?" Kern asked.

"They hadn't arrived yet."

Dawson asked, "Well, why didn't you wait till a cop arrived and give the meter to him?"

"Why should I give it to an agent of the state? It's no more his than mine."

"But it *is*," Orson said.

"It was a plain act of Providence that placed it in my hands," Hub said, the corners of his lips dented securely. "I haven't decided yet which charity should receive the money it contains."

Dawson asked, "But isn't that stealing?"

"No more stealing than the state is stealing in making people pay money for space in which to park their own, heavily taxed cars."

"Hub," Orson said, getting to his feet, "you give it back or we'll both go to jail." He saw himself ruined, the scarcely commenced career of his life destroyed, his father the doctor disgraced.

Hub turned serenely. "I'm not afraid. Going to jail under a totalitarian regime is a mark of honor. If you had a conscience, you'd understand."

Petersen and Carter and Silverstein came into the room. Some boys from the lower floors followed them. The story was hilariously retold. The meter was produced from under the pillow and passed around and shaken to demonstrate the weight of pennies it contained. Hub always carried, as a vestige of the lumberjack country he came from, an intricate all-purpose pocket knife. He began to pry open the little money door. Orson came up behind him and got him around the neck with one arm. Hub's body stiffened. He passed the head of the meter and the open knife to Carter, and then Orson experienced sensations of being lifted, of flying, and of lying on the floor, looking up at Hub's face, which was upside down in his vision. He scrambled to his feet and went for Hub again, rigid with anger and yet, in his heart, happily relaxed. Hub's body was tough and quick and satisfying to grip, though, being a wrestler, he somehow deflected Orson's hands and again lifted and dropped him to the black floor. This time, Orson felt a blow as his coccyx hit the wood; yet even through the pain he perceived, gazing into the heart of this forced marriage, that Hub was being as gentle with him as he could be. He saw that he could try in earnest to kill Hub and be in no danger of succeeding.

He renewed the attack and again enjoyed the tense defensive skill that made Hub's body a kind of warp in space through which his own body, after a blissful instant of contention, was converted to the supine position. He got to his feet and would have gone for Hub the fourth time, but his fellow-freshmen grabbed his arms and held him. He shook them off and without a word returned to his desk and concentrated down into his book, turning the page. The type looked extremely distinct, though it was trembling too hard to be deciphered.

The head of the parking meter stayed in the room for one night. The next day, Hub allowed himself to be persuaded (by the others; Orson had stopped speaking to him) to take it to the Cambridge police headquarters in Central Square. Dawson and Kern tied a ribbon around it, and attached a note: "Please take good care of my baby." None of them, however, had the nerve to go with Hub to the headquarters, though when he came back he said the chief was delighted to get the meter, and had thanked him, and had agreed to donate the pennies to the local orphans' home.

In another week, the last exams were over. The freshmen all went home. When they returned in the fall, they were different: sophomores. Petersen and Young did not come back at all. Fitch returned, made up the lost credits, and eventually graduated *magna cum* in history and lit. He now teaches in a Quaker prep school. Silverstein is a biochemist, Koshland a lawyer. Dawson writes conservative editorials in Cleveland, Kern is in advertising in New York. Carter, as if obliged to join Young in oblivion, disappeared between his junior and senior years. The dormitory neighbors tended to lose sight of each other, though Hub, who had had his case shifted to the Massachusetts jurisdiction, was now and then pictured in the *Crimson*, and once gave an evening lecture, "Why I Am an Episcopalian Pacifist." As the litigation progressed, the Bishop of Massachusetts rather grudgingly vouched for him, and by the time of his final hearing the Korean War was over, and the judge who heard the case ruled that Hub's convictions were sincere, as witnessed by his willingness to go to jail. Hub was rather disappointed at the verdict, since he had prepared a three-year reading list to occupy him in his cell and was intending to memorize all four Gospels in the original Greek.

After graduation, he went to Union Theological Seminary, spent several years as the assistant rector of an urban parish in Baltimore, and learned to play the piano well enough to be the background music in a Charles Street cocktail lounge. He insisted on wearing his clerical collar, and as a consequence gave the bar a small celebrity. After a year of overriding people of less strong convictions, he was allowed to go to South Africa, where he worked and preached among the Bantus until the government requested that he leave the country. From there he went to Nigeria, and when last heard from—on a Christmas card, with French salutations and three black Magi, which arrived, soiled and wrinkled, in South Dakota in February—Hub was in Madagascar, as a "combination missionary, political agitator, and soccer coach." The description struck Orson as probably facetious, and Hub's childish and confident handwriting, with every letter formed individually, afflicted him with some of the old exasperation. Having vowed to answer the card, he mislaid it, uncharacteristically.

Orson didn't speak to Hub for two days after the parking-meter incident. By then, it seemed rather silly, and they finished out the year sitting side by side at their desks as amiably as two cramped passengers who have endured a long bus trip together. When they parted, they shook hands, and Hub would have walked Orson to the subway kiosk except that he had an appointment in the opposite direction. Orson received two A's and two B's on his final exams; for the remaining three years at Harvard, he roomed uneventfully with two other colorless pre-med students, named Wallace and Neuhauser. After graduation, he married Emily, attended the Yale School of Medicine, and interned in St. Louis. He is now the father of four children and, since the death of his own father, the only doctor in the town. His life has gone much the way he planned it, and he is much the kind of man he intended to be when he was eighteen. He delivers babies, assists the dying, attends the necessary meetings, plays golf, and does good. He is honorable and irritable. If not as much loved as his father, he is perhaps even more respected. In one particular only— a kind of scar he carries without pain and without any clear memory of the amputation—does the man he is differ from the man he assumed he would become. He never prays.

Dentistry and Doubt

BURTON KNEW what the dentist would notice first: the clerical collar. People always did. The dentist was standing not quite facing the door, as if it had just occurred to him to turn away. His eyes, gray in a rosy, faintly mustached face, clung to Burton's throat a moment too long for complete courtesy before lifting as he said, "Hello!" Shifting his feet, the dentist thrust out an unexpectedly soft hand.

He noticed next that Burton was an American. In Oxford Burton had acquired the habit of speaking softly, but susurration alone could not alter the proportionate emphasis of vowel over consonant, the slight drag at the end of each sentence, or any of the diphthongal peculiarities that betray Americans to the twittering English. As soon as Burton had returned the greeting, with an apology for being late (he did not blame the British buses, though they were at fault), he fancied he could hear the other man's mind register: "U.S.A. . . . pioneer piety . . . RC? Can't be; no black hat . . . nervous smile . . . rather heavy tartar on the incisors."

He motioned Burton to the chair and turned to a sink, where he washed his hands without looking at them. He talked over his shoulder. "What part are you from?"

"Of the States?" Burton enjoyed saying "the States." It sounded so aggregate, so ominous.

"Yes. Or are you Canadian?"

"No, I'm from Pennsylvania." Burton had never had such a good view from a dentist's chair. A great bay window gave on a small back yard. Black shapes of birds fluttered and jiggled among the twigs of two or three trees—willows, he guessed. Except for the birds, the trees were naked. A wet-wash sky hung, it seemed, a few feet behind the net of limbs. A brick wall looked the shade of rust, and patches of sky hinted at blue, but there was little color in any of it.

"Pennsylvania," the dentist mused, the latter syllables of the word amplifying as he drew closer. "That's in the East?"

"It's a Middle Atlantic state. You know where New York City is?"

"Roughly."

"It's a little west of that, more or less. It's an in-between sort of state."

"I see." The dentist leaned over him, and Burton received two wonderful surprises: when he opened his mouth the dentist said "Thank you"; and the dentist had something on his breath that, without being either, smelled sweet as candy and spicy as cloves. Peering in, he bumped a mirror across Burton's teeth. An electric reflector like an eye doctor's was strapped to his head. Outside, the big black birds did stunts among the twigs. The dentist's eyes were not actually gray; screwed up, they seemed more brown, and then, as they flicked toward the tool tray, rather green. The man scraped at an eyetooth, but with such tact that Burton felt nothing. "There's certainly one," he said, turning to make a mark on a clean card.

Burton took the opportunity to rid himself of a remark he had been holding in suspension. "More than ninety percent of the world's anthracite used to come from Pennsylvania."

"Really?" the dentist said, obviously not believing him. He returned his hands, the tools in them, to in front of Burton's chin. Burton opened his mouth. "Thank you," the dentist said.

As he peered and picked and made notations, a measure of serenity returned to Burton. That morning, possibly because of the scheduled visit to a foreign dentist, the Devil had been very active. Skepticism had mingled with the heat and aroma of his bed; it had dripped from the cold ochre walls of his digs; it had been the substance of his dreams. His slippers, his bathrobe, his face in the mirror, his books—black books, brown ones, C. S. Lewis, Karl Barth, *The Portable Medieval Reader*, Raymond Tully, and Bertrand Russell lying together as nonchalantly as if they had been Belloc and Chesterton—stood witness to a futility that undercut all hope and theory. Even his toothbrush, which on good days presented itself as an acolyte of matinal devotion, today seemed an agent of atheistic hygiene, broadcasting the hideous fact of bacteria. Why had God created them, to breed madly and devour one another and cause trouble in the mouths and intestines of higher animals? The faucet's merry gurgle had mocked Burton's sudden prayer that the Devil's voice be silenced.

The scent of candy and cloves lifted. The dentist, standing erect, was asking, "Do you take Novocain?"

Burton hesitated. He believed that one of the lazier modern assumptions was the identification of pain with evil. Indeed, insofar as pain warned us of corruption, it was necessary and good. On the other hand, relieving the pain of others was an obvious virtue—perhaps the *most* obvious virtue. And to court pain was as morbid as to chase pleasure. Yet to flee from pain was clearly cowardice.

The dentist, not hinting by his voice whether he had been waiting for an answer several seconds or no time at all, asked, "Does your dentist at home give you Novocain?"

Ever since Burton was a little boy in crusty dungarees, Dr. Gribling had given him Novocain. "Yes." The answer sounded abrupt, impolite. Burton added, "He says my nerves are exceptionally large." It was a pompous thing to say.

"We'll do the eyetooth, straight off," the dentist said.

Burton's heart beat like a wasp in a jar as the dentist moved across the room, performed an unseeable rite by the sink, and returned with a full hypodermic. A drop of fluid, by some miracle of adhesion, clung trembling to the needle's tip. Burton opened his mouth while the dentist's back was still turned. When at last the man pivoted, his instrument tilting up, a tension beneath his mustache indicated surprise and perhaps amusement at finding things in such readiness. "Open a little wider, please," he said. "Thank you." The needle moved closer. It was under Burton's nose and out of focus. "Now, this might hurt a little." What a kind thing to say! The sharp prick and the consequent slow, filling ache drove Burton's eyes up, and he saw the tops of the bare willow trees, the frightened white sky, and the black birds. As he watched, one bird joined another on the topmost twig, and then a third joined these two and the twig became radically cresent, and all three birds flapped off to where his eyes could not follow them.

"There," the dentist sighed, in a zephyr of candy and cloves.

Waiting for the Novocain to take effect, Burton and the dentist made conversation.

"And what brings you to Oxford?" the dentist began.

"I'm doing graduate work."

"Oh? What sort?"

"I'm doing a thesis on a man called Richard Hooker."

"Oh?" The dentist sounded as incredulous as he had about Pennsylvania's anthracite.

Richard Hooker—"pious, peaceable, primitive," in Walton's phrase—loomed so large in Burton's world that to doubt Hooker's existence was in effect to doubt the existence of Burton's world. But he added the explanatory "An English divine" without the least bit of curtness or condescension. The lesson of humility was one that had come rather easily to Burton. He recognized, however, that in his very thinking of his own humility he was guilty of pride, and his immediate recognition of it as pride was foundation for further, subtler egotism.

He would have harried the sin to its source had not the dentist said, "A divine is a church writer?"

"That's right."

"Could you quote me something he wrote?"

Burton had expected, and was prepared to answer, several questions ("When did he live?" "From 1554 to 1600." "What is the man's claim to fame?" "He attempted to reconcile Christian—that is, Thomist—political theory with the actual state of things under the Tudor monarchy; he didn't really succeed, but he did anticipate a fair amount of modern political thought." "What is your thesis?" "Mostly an attempt to get at reasons for Hooker's failure to come to grips with Renaissance Platonism"), but he was unprepared for this one. Scraps and phrases—"visible Church," "law eternal," "very slender ability," "Popish superstition," the odd word "scrupulosity"—came to mind, but no rounded utterance formed itself. "I can't think of anything right now," he apologized, touching his fingers to his collar and, as still sometimes happened, being taken aback by the hard, unbroken edge they met.

The dentist did not seem disappointed. "Feel numb yet?" he asked.

Burton tested and said, "Yes."

The dentist swung the drilling apparatus into place and Burton opened his mouth. "Thank you." The Novocain had taken. The drilling at the tooth seemed vastly distant, and it hurt no more than the explosion of a star, or the death of an elephant in India, or, Burton realized, the whipping of a child right next door. Pain. The problem presented itself. He slipped into the familiar arguments he used with himself. Creation is His seeking to make souls out of matter. Morally, matter, per se, is neutral—with form imposed upon it, good, but in any case its basic nature is competitive. No two things can occupy the same place at the same time. Hence, pain. But we must act with non-material motives. What was His journey on earth but a flouting of competitive values? And then there is the Devil. But with the Devil the whole cosmos became confused, and Burton's attention, by default, rested on the black birds. They kept falling out of the sky and the treetops, but he noticed few ascending.

The dentist changed his drill. "Thank you." There were things Burton could comprehend. And then there were things he could not, such as

God's aeons-long wait as life struggled up from the atom and the algae. With what emotion did He watch all those preposterous, earnest beasts labor up out of the swamp and aimlessly perish on the long and crooked road to Man? And the stars, so far off, the comedy of waste spaces— theologians had always said infinite, but could they have meant *that* infinite? Once, Burton had asked his father if he believed in purgatory. "Of course I do," he had snapped, jabbing toward the floor with his pipestem. "*This* is purgatory." Remembering the incident so depressed Burton that when the drill broke through the shell of anesthetic and bit his nerve, it came in the shape of an answer, and he greeted the pain with something like ecstasy.

"There," the dentist said. "Would you care to wash out, please?" He swung the drilling apparatus over to one side, so Burton could see it wouldn't be used any more. He was so kind.

"There seem to be a lot of birds in your back yard," Burton said to him.

"We have a feeding station," the dentist said, grinding the silver for the filling in a thick glass cup.

"What are those black birds?"

"Starlings. A greedy bird. They take everything they can away from the wren."

For the first time, Burton noticed some smaller shapes among the branches, quicker, but less numerous and less purposeful than the black birds. He watched one in particular, swivelling on his perch, now a formless blob, like a big bud, the next moment in vivid profile, like a Picasso ceramic. As he watched the bird, his mind emptied itself, and nothing, not even the squeaking of the silver, disturbed it.

When he again became conscious, it was of the objects on the tray before him as things in which an unlimited excitement inhered; the tweezers, the picks, the drill burrs, the celluloid container of cotton, the tiny cotton balls, the metal cup where a flame could burn, the enamelled bowl beside him with its dribble of water, the tiled walls, the window frame, the shapes beyond the window—all travelled to his senses burdened with delight and power. The sensation was one that Burton had frequently enjoyed in his childhood and more and more rarely as he aged. His urge to laugh, or to *do* something with the objects, was repressed, and even the smile he gave the dentist was lost, for the man was concerned with keeping a dab of silver on the end of a golf-club-shaped tool.

Burton received the silver. He thought of the world as being, like all music, founded on tension. The tree pushing up, gravity pulling down, the bird desiring to fill the air, the air compelled to crush the bird. His head brimmed with irrelevant recollections: a rubber Donald Duck he had owned, and abused, as an infant; the grape arbor in his parents' back yard; the touching strange naked look his father wore when he worked in the garden without wearing his clergyman's collar; Shibe Park in sunlight; Max Beerbohm's sentence about there always being a slight shock in seeing an envelope of one's own after it has gone through the post.

The dentist coughed. It was the sound not of a man who has to cough but of one who has done his job, and can cough if he pleases. "Would you like to wash out, please?" He gestured toward a glass filled with pink fluid, which up to this time Burton had ignored. Burton took some of the liquid into his mouth (it was good, but not as good as the dentist's breath), sloshed it around, and, as silently as possible, spat it into the murmuring basin. "I'm afraid three or four trips are called for," the dentist said, studying his card.

"Fine."

The dentist's mustache stretched fractionally. "Miss Leviston will give you the appointments." One by one, he dropped the drill burrs into a compartmented drawer. "Do you have any idea why your teeth should be so, ah, indifferent?"

Burton concentrated. He yearned to thank the man, to bless him even, but since he was not prepared to do that, he would show his gratitude by giving everything the dentist said his closest attention. "I believe Pennsylvania has one of the worst dental records of any state."

"Really? And why should that be?"

"I don't know. We eat sugar doughnuts and sticky buns. I think the Southern states have the best teeth. They eat fish, or turnip tops, or something with lots of calcium in it."

"I see." The dentist moved aside so Burton could climb out of the chair. "Until next time, then."

Burton supposed they would not shake hands twice in one visit. Near the doorway, he turned. "Oh, Doctor, uh . . ."

"Merritt," the dentist said.

"I just thought of a quotation from Hooker. It's very short."

"Yes?"

" 'I grant we are apt, prone, and ready, to forsake God; but is God as ready to forsake us? Our minds are changeable; is His so likewise?' "

Dr. Merritt smiled. The two men stood in the same position they had hesitated in when Burton entered the room. Burton smiled. Outside the window, the wrens and the starlings, mixed indistinguishably, engaged in maneuvers that seemed essentially playful.

A Madman

ENGLAND ITSELF seemed slightly insane to us. The meadows skimming past the windows of the Southampton–London train seemed green deliriously; they were so obsessively steeped in the color that my eyes, still attuned to the exhausted verdure and September rust of American fields, doubted the ability of this landscape to perform useful work. England appeared to exist purely as a context of literature. I had studied this literature for four years, and had been sent here to continue this study. Yet my brain, excited and numbed by travel, could produce only one allusion; "a' babbled of green fields," that inconsequential Shakespearean snippet rendered memorable by a classic typographical emendation, kept running through my mind, "a' babbled, a' babbled," as the dactylic scansion of the train wheels drew us and our six mute, swaying compartment-mates northward into London.

The city overwhelmed our expectations. The Kiplingesque grandeur of Waterloo Station, the Eliotic despondency of the brick row in Chelsea where we spent the night in the flat of a vague friend, the Dickensian nightmare of fog and sweating pavement and besmirched cornices that surrounded us when we awoke—all this seemed too authentic to be real, too corroborative of literature to be solid. The taxi we took to Paddington Station had a high roof and an open side, which gave it to our eyes the shocked, cockeyed expression of a character actor in an Agatha Christie melodrama. We wheeled past mansions by Galsworthy and parks by A. A. Milne; we glimpsed a cobbled eighteenth-century alley, complete with hanging tavern boards, where Dr. Johnson might have reeled and gasped the night he laughed so hard—the incident in Boswell so beautifully amplified in the essay by Beerbohm. And underneath all, underneath Heaven knew how many medieval plagues, pageants, and conflagrations, old Londinium itself like a buried Titan lay smoldering in an abyss and tangle of time appalling to eyes accustomed to view the land as a surface innocent of history. We were relieved to board the train and feel it tug us westward.

The train brought us into Oxford at dusk. We had no place to go. We had made no reservations. We got into a cab and explained this to the driver. Middle-aged, his huge ears frothing with hair, he seemed unable to believe us, as if in all his years he had never before carried passengers who had not already visited their destination. He seemed further puzzled by the discovery that, though we claimed to be Americans, we had never been in Stillwater, or even in Tulsa. Fifteen years ago he had spent some months in the depths of Oklahoma learning to fly Lend-Lease planes. Now he repaid his debt by piloting us down a narrow street of brick homes whose windows—queerly, for this was suppertime—were all dark. "We'll give you a try at the Potts'," he explained briefly, braking. He went with us up to the door and twisted a heavy wrought-iron knob in its center. A remote, rattling ring sounded on the other side of the opaquely stained panes. At length a tall saturnine man answered. Our driver explained to him, "Potty, we've two homeless Yanks here. They don't know the score as yet."

Early in the evening as it was, Mr. Pott wore a muttering, fuddled air of having been roused. The BED AND BREAKFAST sign in his window seemed to commit him to no hospitality. Only after impressing us with the dark difficulty of it, with the unprecedented strain we were imposing upon the arrangements he had made with a disobliging and obtusely technical world, did he lead us upstairs and into a room. The room was large, chill, and amply stocked with whatever demigods it is that supervise sleep. I remember that the deliciously cool sheets and coarse blankets were topped by a purple puff smelling faintly of lavender, and that in the morning, dressing, my wife and I skipped in and out of the radiant influence of the electric heater like a nymph and satyr competing at a shrine. The heater's plug was a ponderous and dangerous-looking affair of three prongs; plugging it in was my first real work of acclimatization. We appeared for breakfast a bit late. Of all the other boarders, only Mr. Robinson (I have forgotten his actual name) had yet to come down. Our places were laid at the dining table, and at my place—I couldn't believe my eyes—was set an insanity, a half of a cooked tomato on a slice of fried bread.

Mr. Robinson came down as Mr. Pott was finishing explaining to us why we must quickly find permanent lodgings. Our room would soon be needed by its regular tenant, an Indian undergraduate. Any day now he would take it into his head to show up. It was a thankless job, keeping students' rooms; they were in and out and up and talking and making music at all hours, and the landlord was supposed to enforce the midnight curfew. "The short of it is," Mr. Pott snarled, "the university wants me to be a nanny and a copper's nark." His voice changed tone. "Ah, Mr. Robinson! Good morning, Professor. We have with us two lovebirds from across the Atlantic."

Mr. Robinson ceremoniously shook our hands. Was he a professor? He was of middle size, with a scholar's delicate hunch and long thinning yellowish-white hair brushed straight back. In speech, he was all courtesy, lucid patter, and flattering attention. We turned to him with relief; after our host's dark hints and dour discontents, we seemed to be emerging into the England of light. "Welcome to Oxford," he said, and from a bright little tension in his cheeks we could see he was about to quote. " 'That home of lost causes, and forsaken beliefs, and unpopular names, and impossible loyalties.' That's Matthew Arnold; if you want to understand Oxford, read Arnold. Student of Balliol, fellow of Oriel, professor of poetry, the highest bird as ever flew with a pedant's clipped wings. Read Arnold, and read Newman. 'Whispering from her towers the last enchantments of the Middle Age'—which he did not *mean*, you know, entirely sympathetically; no, not at all. Arnold was not at all church-minded. 'The Sea of Faith / Was once, too, at the full . . . But now I only hear / Its melancholy, long, *withdrawing* roar, / Retreating, to the breath / Of the night-wind down the vast edges drear / And naked shingles of the world.' Hah! Mr. Pott, what is this I see before me? My customary egg. You are a veritable factotum, a Johannes Factotum, of kindness. Mr. Pott of St. John's Street," he confided to us in his quick, twinkling way, "an institution no less revered by the student body than the church of St. Michael's-at-the-North-Gate, which contains, you should know, and will *see*, the oldest standing structure in"—he cleared his throat, as if to signal something special coming—"Oxnaford: the old Saxon tower, dating from the ninth century at the least. At the *least*, I insist, though in doing so I incur the certain wrath of the more piddling of local archaeologists, if we can dignify them with the title upon which Schliemann and Sir Leonard Woolley have heaped so much indelible honor." He set to his egg eagerly, smashing it open with a spoon.

My wife asked him, "Are you a professor of archaeology?"

"Dear madam," he said, "in a manner of speaking, in a manner of speaking, I have taken all knowledge for my province. Do you know Ann Arbor, in, I believe, the very wooded state of Michigan? No? Have no shame, no shame; your country is so vast, a poor Englishman's head reels. My niece, my sister's daughter, married an instructor in the university there. I learn from her letters that the temperature frequently—*frequently*—drops below zero Fahrenheit. Mr. Pott, will this charming couple be spending the term with us here?" When it was explained to him, more readily than tactfully, that our presence here was an emergency measure, the result of a merciful impulse which Mr. Pott, his implication was, already regretted, Mr. Robinson bent his face low over the table to look up at us. He had perfect upper teeth. "You must know the *way*," he said, "the ins and outs, the little shortcuts and circumlocutions, circumflexions, the *circumstances*; else you will never find a flat. You have waited long, too long; in a few days the Michaelmas term will be upon us and from Woodstock to Cowley there won't be a room to be *had*. But I, *I*"—he lifted one finger and closed one eye sagely—"I may be of help. *'Che tu mi segui,'* as Vergil said to Dante, *'e io sarò tua guida!'* "

We were of course grateful for a guide. The three of us walked down St. John's Street (all the shades were drawn, though this was daylight), up Beaumont past the sooty, leonine sprawl of the Ashmolean, and down Magdalen Street to Cornmarket, where indeed we did see the Saxon tower. Mr. Robinson indicated points of interest continuously. His lower jaw seemed abnormally slender, as if a normal jaw had been whittled for greater flexibility and lightness. It visibly supported only one lower tooth, and that one hardly bigger than a fleck of tobacco, and set in the gum sideways; whereas his upper teeth were strikingly even and complete. Through these mismatched gates he poured an incessant stream of frequently stressed words, broken only when, preparatory to some heightened effort of erudition, he preeningly cleared his throat. "Now we are standing in the center of town, the very hub and beating heart of Oxfordshire, Carfax, derived—uh-uh-*hem*—from the Norman *carrefor*, the Latin *quadrifurcus*, meaning 'four forks,' or 'crossroads.' Do you know Latin? The last international language, the—uh-hem—Esperanto of Christendom." He carried an old paper bag, and we found ourselves in a vast roofed market, surrounded by blood-flecked butcher's stalls and bins of raw vegetables smelling of mud. Mr. Robinson methodically filled his bag with potatoes. He examined each potato, and hesitated with it, as if it would be his last; but then his anxious parchmenty hand would dart out and seize yet another. When the bag could hold no more, he shrugged and began to wander away. The proprietress of the stall shouted in protest. She was fat; her face looked scorched; and she wore a man's boots and numerous unravelling sweaters. Without a word, Mr. Robinson returned and rather grandly dumped all the potatoes back into the bin. Along with the potatoes some papers fluttered out, and these he put back in the bag. He turned to us and smiled. "Now," he said, "it is surely time for lunch. Oxnaford is no town to storm on an empty stomach."

"But," I said, "Mr. Robinson, what about the place we have to find?"

He audibly exhaled, as if he had just tasted a superb wine. "*Aaaaah*. I have not forgotten, I have not forgotten. We must tread cautiously; you do not know, you see, the *way*. The ins and outs, the *circumstances*." He led us to a cafeteria above a furniture store on the Broad and through the chips and custard tried to distract us with a profuse account of Oxford in its medieval heyday—Roger Bacon, Duns Scotus, the "Mad Parliament" of 1256, the town-gown riots of St. Scholastica's Day in 1355. Down on the street once more, he took to plucking our arms and making promises. One more little trip, one harmless excursion that would be *very* useful for us, and then down to business. He escorted us all the way down High Street to the Magdalen Bridge, and thus we received our first glimpse of the Cherwell. No punts were out at this time of year, and swans generally stayed downriver. But, looking back toward the center of town, we were treated to the storybook view of Oxford, all spires and silhouette and flaking stone, under a sky by John Constable, R.A.

Weak, distraught, I felt myself succumb; we surrendered the day to Mr. Robinson. Triumphantly sensing this, he led us down Rose Lane, through the botanic gardens orange and golden with fall flowers, along Merton Field, and back through a series of crooked alleys to the business district. Here he took us into a bookstore and snatched a little newspaper, the Oxfordshire weekly, out of a rack and indicated to the man behind the counter that I would pay for it. While I rummaged the fourpence out of my pocket, Mr. Robinson pranced to the other wall and came back holding a book. It was a collection of essays by Matthew Arnold. "Don't buy this book," he told me. "*Don't buy it*. I have it in a superior edition, and will lend it to you. Do you understand? I will *lend* it to you." I thanked him and, as if all he had wanted from us was a little gratitude, he announced that he would leave us now. He tapped the paper in my hand. He winked. "Your problems—and don't think, *don't* think they have not been painfully on my mind—are solved; you will find your rooms in here. Very few, *very* few people know about this paper, but all the locals, *all* the locals with *good* rooms advertise in here; they don't *trust* the regular channels. You must know the *way*, you see, the ins and outs." And he left us, as at the edge of Paradise.

It was growing dark, in that long, slow, tea-shoppe-lit style of English afternoons, and we had tea to clear our heads. Then there seemed nothing to do but return to Mr. Pott's house, on St. John's Street. Now we noticed for the first time students in the streets, whirring along on their bicycles like bats, their black gowns fluttering. Only we lacked a roost. My wife lay down on top of our purple puff and silently cried. Her legs ached from all the walking. She was—our heavy secret—three months pregnant. We were fearful that if this became known not a landlord in Oxford would have us. I went out in the dusk with my newspaper to a phone booth. In fact, there were few flats advertised in the weekly, and all but one lacked a kitchen; this one was listed as on St. Aldate's Street. I called the number and a woman answered. When she heard my voice, she asked, "Are you an American?"

"I guess, yes."

"I'm sorry. My husband doesn't like Americans."

"He doesn't? Why not?" It had been impressed upon me, with the award of my fellowship, that I was to act as an ambassador abroad.

There was a pause, then she said, "If you must know, our daughter's gone and married an airman from your base at Brize Norton."

"Oh—well, I'm not an airman. I'm a student. And I'm already married. It would just be me and my wife, we have no children."

"Hooh, Jack!" The exclamation sounded off focus, as if she had turned her mouth from the receiver. Then she returned close to my ear, confidential, murmurous. "My husband's this minute come in. Would you like to talk to him?"

"No," I said, and hung up, shaky but pleased to have encountered a conversation I could end.

The next morning, Mr. Robinson had reached the breakfast table before us. Perhaps it had cost him some sleep, for his hair was mussed and its yellow tinge had spread to his face. His eagerness in greeting us was now tipped with a penetrating whine. The falseness of his upper teeth had become painfully clear; spittle sparked from his mouth with the effort of keeping the plate in place. " 'Noon strikes on England,' " he recited at our appearance, " 'noon on Oxford town, / Beauty she was statue cold, there's blood upon her gown, / Proud and godly kings had built her long ago, / With her towers and tombs and statues all arow, / With her fair and floral air / And the love that lingers there, / And the streets where the great men go.' "

"I thought this morning," I told him, "I'd go to my college and see if they could help."

"Which college?" he asked. His face became jealously alert.

"Keble."

"Ah," he crowed, "they won't help. *They won't help.* They know *nothing.* They *wish* to know nothing. *Nihil ex nihilo.*"

"It's a game they play," Mr. Pott muttered sourly, "called Hands Off."

"Really?" my wife said, her voice brimming.

"Nevertheless," I insisted, "we have to begin somewhere. That weekly you got for us had only one possibility, and the woman's husband didn't like Americans."

"Your ruddy airmen," Mr. Pott explained, "from out Norton way have given you a name. They come into town with their powder-blue suits and big shoulders, some of 'em black as shoe polish, and give the local tarts what-for."

My mention of the weekly had set off a sequence in Mr. Robinson's mind, for now he clapped his hands to his head and said, "That book. I promised to lend you that book. Forgive, for*give* a rattlebrained old man. I will get it for you *instanter.* No protest, no protest. Youth must be served."

He went upstairs to his room, and we glanced at Mr. Pott inquisitively. He nodded. "I'd beat it now, in your shoes," he said.

We had made three blocks and felt safely lost in the crowd along Corn-market when Mr. Robinson caught up with us. He was panting and wearing his bedroom slippers. "Wait," he whined, *"wait,* you don't *see.* You can't run blind and headlong into these situations, you don't understand the *circumstances."* He carried his paper shopping bag and produced from it a book, which he pressed upon me. It was a turn-of-the-century edition of Arnold's essays, with marbled end papers. Right there, on the jostling pavement, I opened it, and nearly slammed it shut in horror, for every page was a spider's web of annotations and underlinings, in many pencils and inks and a wild variety of handwritings. "Cf.," *"videlicet,"* "He betrays himself here," "19th cent. optmsm."—these leaped at me out of the mad swarm. The annotations were themselves annotated, as his argument with the text doubled and redoubled back on itself. "Is this so?" a firm hand had written in one margin, and below it, in a different slant and fainter pencil, had been added, "Yes it is so," with the "is" triple-underlined; and below this a wobbly ballpoint pen had added, without capitals, "but is it?" It made me dizzy to look into; I shut the book and thanked him.

Mr. Robinson looked at me cleverly sideways. "You thought I had forgotten," he said. "You thought an old man's brain didn't hold water. No shame, no shame; in your circumstances you could hardly think otherwise. But no, what I promise, I fulfill; now I will be your guide. A-hem. Everyman, I will go with thee: hah!" He gestured toward the ancient town hall and told us that during the Great Rebellion Oxford had been the Royalist headquarters.

" 'The king, observing with judicious eyes / The state of both his universities, / To Oxford sent a troop of horse, and why?' " he recited, ending with a sweep of his arm that drew the eyes of passersby to us.

Just as, by being pronounced definitely insane, a criminal curiously obligates the society he has injured, so now Mr. Robinson's hold upon us was made perfect. The slither of his shuffling slippers on the pavement, the anxious snagging stress of periodic syllables, the proud little throat-clearings were so many filaments that clasped us to him as, all but smothered by embarrassment and frustration, we let him lead us. Our route overlapped much of the route of the day before; but now he began to develop a new theme—that all this while he had been subjecting us to a most meticulous scrutiny and we had passed favorably, with *flying* colors, and that he was going to introduce us to some of his friends, the really *important* people, the grand panjandrums, the people who knew where there were rooms and rooms. He would write letters, perform introductions, secure our admission to secret societies. After lunch, at about the hour when on the day before he had introduced us to the paper seller, he shepherded us into the library of the Oxford Union Society and introduced us to the fastidious boy behind the desk. Mr. Robinson's voice, somehow intensified by whispering, carried to every crusty corner and sacrosanct gallery. The young librarian in his agony did not suppress an ironical smile. When his eyes turned to us, they took on a polite glaze that fell a little short of concealing contempt. But with what a deal of delighted ceremony did Mr. Robinson, who evidently really was a member, superintend the signing of our names in a huge old ledger! In return for our signatures we were given, with a sorcerer's flourishes, an application form for membership. There was this to be said for Mr. Robinson: he never left you quite empty-handed.

Returning, frantic and dazed, to our room at the Potts', we were able to place the application blank and the annotated Arnold beside our first trophy, the Oxfordshire weekly. I lay down on the bed beside my wife and read through the lead article, a militant lament on the deterioration of the Norman church at Iffley. When I had regained some purpose in my legs, I walked over to Keble and found it was much as I had been warned. The patterns of paternalism did not include those students tasteless enough to have taken a wife. Flats were to be had, though, the underling asserted, absurdly scratching away with a dip pen in his tiny nook with its one Gothic window overlooking a quad; his desk suggested the Tenniel illustration of all the cards flying out of the pack.

I was newly enough married not to expect that my wife, once I was totally drained of hope, would supply some. She had decided in my absence that we must stop being polite to Mr. Robinson. Indeed, this did seem the one way out of the maze. I should have thought of it myself. We dressed up and ate a heartily expensive meal at a pseudo-French restaurant that Mr. Robinson had told us never, *never* to patronize, because they were brigands. Then we went to an American movie to give us brute strength and in the morning came down to breakfast braced. Mr. Robinson was not there.

This was to be, it turned out, our last breakfast at the Potts'. Already we had become somewhat acclimatized. We no longer, for example, glanced around for Mrs. Pott; we had accepted that she existed, if she existed at all, on a plane invisible to us. The other boarders greeted us by name now. There were two new faces among them—young students' faces, full of bewilderingly pertinent and respectful questions about the United States. The States, their opinion was, had already gone the way that all countries must eventually go. To be American, we were made to feel, was to be lucky. Mr. Pott told us that Karam had written he would be needing his room by the weekend and pushed across the table a piece of paper containing several addresses. "There's a three-room basement asking four pounds ten off Banbury Road," he said, "and if you want to go to five guineas, Mrs. Shipley still has her second floor over toward St. Hilda's."

It took us a moment to realize what this meant; then our startled thanks gushed. "Mr. Robinson," I blurted in conclusion, groping for some idiom suitable to Mr. Pott and not quite coming up with it, "has been leading us all around the Maypole."

"Poor Robbie," said Mr. Pott. "Daft as a daisy." He tapped the bony side of his lean dark head.

My wife asked, "Is he always—like that?"

"Only as when he finds an innocent or two to sink his choppers in; they find him out soon enough, poor Robbie."

"Does he really have a niece in Michigan?"

"Ah yes, he's not all fancy. He was a learned man before his trouble, but the university never quite took him on."

" 'So poetry, which is in Oxford made an art,' " a familiar voice sweetly insisted behind us, " 'in London only is a trade.' Dryden. *Not* a true

Oxonian, but an excellent poet and amateur scholar nevertheless. If you enjoy his jingling style. Mr. Pott. Can that egg be mine?" He sat down and smashed it neatly with his spoon and turned to us jubilantly. Perhaps the delay in his appearance had been caused by an effort of grooming, for he looked remarkably spruce, his long hair brushed to a tallowish lustre, his tie knotted tightly, his denture snug under his lips, and a plaid scarf draped around his shoulders. "Today," he said, "I will devote myself to your cause wholeheartedly, without intermissions, interruptions, or intercessions. I have spent the last hour preparing a wonderful surprise, *mirabile dictu*, as faithful Aeneas said to his natural mother, Aphrodite."

"I think," I said, in a voice constrained by the presence of others around the table, "we really must do other things today. Mr. Pott says that Karam—"

"Wait, *wait*," he cried, becoming agitated and rising in his chair. "You do not understand. You are *innocents*—charming, yes, vastly potential, yes, but innocents, you see. You must know the *way*, the ins, the outs—"

"No, honestly—"

"*Wait.* Come with me now. I will show you my surprise *instanter*, if you insist." And he bustled up from the table, the egg uneaten, and back up the stairs toward his room. My wife and I followed, relieved that what must be done could now be done unwitnessed.

Mr. Robinson was already coming out of his room as we met him on the second-floor landing. In his haste he had left the door open behind him. Over his shoulder I glimpsed a chaos of tumbled books and old magazines and and worn clothes. He held in his hands a sheet of paper on which he had made a list. "I have spent the last hour preparing," he said, "with a care not incomparable to that of—*ih-ih-humm*—St. Jerome transcribing the Vulgate, a list; these are the people that today we will *see*." I read the list he held up. The offices and titles and names at the top meant nothing to me, but halfway down, where the handwriting began to get big and its slant to become inconstant, there was the word "Chancellor" followed by a huge colon and the name "Lord Halifax."

Something in my face made the paper begin to tremble. Mr. Robinson took it away and held it at his side. With the other hand he fumbled with his lapel. "You're terribly kind," I said. "You've given us a *won*derful introduction to Oxford. But today, really, we must go out on our own. Absolutely."

"No, no, you don't seem to comprehend; the *circum*—"

"*Please*," my wife said sharply.

He looked at her, then at me, and an unexpected calm entered his features. The twinkle faded, the jaw relaxed, and his face might have been that of any tired old man as he sighed, "Very well, very well. No shame."

"Thank you so much," my wife said, and made to touch, but did not quite touch, the limp hand that had curled defensively against the breast of his coat.

Knees bent, he stood apparently immobilized on the landing before the door of his room. Yet, as we went down the stairs, he did one more gratuitous thing; he came to the banister, lifted his hand, and pronounced, as we quickened our steps to dodge his words, "God bless. God bless."

Still Life

Leonard Hartz, a slender and earnest American with a rather comically round head, came to the Constable School because it was one of three British art schools approved by the Veterans Administration under the new, pruned GI Bill. He could not imagine what the VA had seen in the place. Constable—"Connie" to the bird-tongued, red-legged girls who composed half its student body—was at once pedantic and frivolous. The vast university museum which, with a gesture perhaps less motherly than absent-mindedly inclusive, sheltered the school in its left wing, was primarily archaeological in interest. Upstairs, room after room was packed with glass cases of Anglo-Saxon rubble; downstairs, a remarkably complete set of plaster casts taken from classical statuary swarmed down corridors and gestured under high archways in a kind of petrified riot. This counterfeit wealth of statues, many of them still decorated with the seams of the casting process and quite swarthy with dust, was only roughly ordered. Beginning in the East with wasp-waisted *kouroi* whose Asiatic faces wore the first faint smile of the Attic dawn, one passed through the jumbled poignance and grandeur of Greece's golden age and ended in a neglected, westerly room where some large, coarse monuments of the Roman-Christian degeneracy rested their hypnotized stares in the shadows. Masterpieces lurked like spies in this mob. His first week, Leonard spent a morning and two afternoons sketching a blackened Amazon leaning half clad from a dark corner, and only at the end of the second day, struck by a resemblance between his sketch and the trademark of an American pencil manufacturer, did he realize that his silent companion had been the Venus de Milo.

For freshmen at the Constable School were to start off banished from the school itself, with its bright chatter and gay smocks, and sent into these dim galleries to "draw from the antique." The newcomers—Leonard and four other resentful American veterans and one wispy English boy and a dozen sturdy English teen-age girls—straggled each morning into the museum, gripping a drawing board under one arm and a bench called a "horse" under the other, and at dusk, which came early to the interior of the museum, returned with their burdens, increased by the weight of a deity pinned to their boards, in time to see the advanced students jostle at the brush-cleaning sink and the nude model, incongruously dressed in street clothes, emerge from her closet. The school always smelled of turpentine at this hour.

Its disconsolate scent lingering in his head, Leonard left the school alone, hurrying down the three ranks of shallow steps just in time to miss his bus. Everywhere he turned, those first weeks, he had this sensation of things evading him. When he did board his bus, and climbed to the second deck, the store fronts below sped backwards as if from pursuit—the chemist's shops that were not exactly drugstores, the tea parlors that were by no means luncheonettes. The walls of the college buildings, crusty and impregnable, swept past like an armada of great gray sails, and the little river sung by Drayton and Milton and Matthew Arnold slipped from under him, and, at right angles to the curving road, red suburban streets plunged down steep perspectives, bristling with hedges and spiked walls and padlocked chains. Sometimes, suspended between the retreating brick rows like puffs of flak, a flock of six or so birds was turning and flying, invariably away. The melancholy of the late English afternoon was seldom qualified for Leonard by any expectation of the night. Of the four other Americans, three were married, and although each of these couples in turn had him over for supper and Scrabble, these meals quickly vanished within his evenings' recurrent, thankless appetite. The American movies so readily available reaffirmed rather than relieved his fear that he was out of contact with anything that might give him strength. Even at the school, where he had decided to place himself at least provisionally under the influence of Professor Seabright's musty aesthetic, he began to feel that indeed there was, in the precise contour of a shoulder and the unique shape of space framed between Apollo's legs, something intensely important, which, too—though he erased until the paper tore and squinted till his eyes burned—evaded him.

Seabright tried to visit the students among the casts once a day. Footsteps would sound briskly, marking the instructor off from any of the rare sightseers, often a pair of nuns, who wandered, with whispers and a soft slithering step, into this section of the museum. Seabright's voice, its lisp buried in the general indistinctness, would rumble from far away, as if the gods were thinking of thundering. In stages of five minutes each, it would draw nearer, and eventually addressed distinctly the student on the other side of the pedestals, a tall English girl named, with a pertness that sat somewhat askew on her mature body, Robin.

"Here, here," Seabright said. "We're not doing silhouettes."

"I thought, you know," Robin replied in an eager voice that to Leonard's American ears sounded also haughty, "if the outline came right, the rest could be fitted in."

"Oh no. Oh no. We don't fit *in;* we build *across* the large form. Otherwise all the little pieces will never read. You see, there, we don't even know where the center of your chest is. Ah—may I?" From the grunts and sighs Leonard pictured Robin rising from straddling her horse and Seabright seating himself. "Dear me," he said, "you've got the outlines so black they rather take my eye. However . . ."

To Leonard it was one of Seabright's charms that, faced with any problem of drawing, he became so engrossed he forgot to teach. He had had to train himself to keep glancing at his watch; else he would sit the whole afternoon attacking a beginner's exercise, frowning like a cat at a mouse hole, while the forgotten student stood by on aching legs.

"There," Seabright sighed reluctantly. "I'm afraid I've spent my time with you. It's just one passage, but you can see here, across the thorax, how the little elements already are turning the large surface. And then, as you'd pass into the rib cage, with these two shadows just touched in at first, you see . . . Perhaps I should do a *bit* more. . . . There, you see. And then we could pass on to the throat. . . . It's a good idea, actually, on these figgers to start with the pit of the throat, and then work the shoulders outwards and go up for the head. . . ."

"Yes, sir," Robin said, a shade impatiently.

"The whole thrust of the pose is in those angles, you see? *Do* you see?"

"Yes, sir, I hope so."

But her hopes were not enough for him; he came around the pedestals and his plump, solemn, slightly feline figure was in Leonard's view when he turned and said apprehensively to the hidden girl, "You understand to use the pencil as lightly as you can? Work up the whole form gradually?"

"Oh, yes. Quite," Robin's pert voice insisted.

Seabright twitched his head and came and stood behind Leonard. "I don't think," he said at last, "we need draw in the casting seams; we can idealize to that extent."

"It seemed to help in getting the intervals," Leonard explained.

"Even though these are exercises, you know, there's no advantage in having them, uh, positively ugly." Leonard glanced around at his teacher, who was not usually sarcastic, and Seabright continued with some embarrassment; his speech impediment was less audible than visible, a fitful effortfulness of the lips. "I must confess you're not given much help by your subject matter." His eyes had lifted to the statue Leonard had chosen to draw, for the reason that it had all four limbs. Completeness was the crude token by which Leonard preferred one statue to another; he was puzzled by Seabright's offended murmur of "Wretched thing."

"Beg pardon, sir?"

"Look here, Hartz," Seabright exclaimed, and with startling aggressiveness trotted forward, stretched up on tiptoe, and slapped the plaster giant's side. "The Roman who copied this didn't even understand how the side here is constricted by this leg taking the weight!" Seabright himself constricted, then blinked abashedly and returned to Leonard's side with a more cautious voice. "Nevertheless, you've carried out parts of it with admirable intensity. Per, uh, perhaps you've been rather *too* intense; relax a bit at first and aim for the swing of the figger—how that little curve here, you see, sets up against this long lean one." Leonard expected him to ask for the pencil, but instead he asked, "Why don't you get yourself a new statue? That charming girl Miss Cox is doing—Diana, really, I suppose she is. At least there you do get some echoes of the Greek grace. I should think you've done your duty by this one."

"O.K. It *was* starting to feel like mechanical drawing." To dramatize his obedience, Leonard began prying out his thumbtacks, but Seabright, his five minutes not used up, lingered.

"You do see some sense in drawing these at the outset, don't you?" Seabright was troubled by his American students; of the five, Leonard knew he must seem the least rebellious.

"Sure. It's quite challenging, once you get into one."

The Englishman was not totally reassured. He hovered apologetically, and confided this anecdote: "Picasso, you know, had a woman come to him for advice about learning to draw, and he told her right off, '*Dessinez antiques.*' Draw from the antique. There's nothing like it, for getting the big forms."

Then Seabright left, pattering past threatening athletes and emperors, through the archway, out of the section altogether, into the brighter room where medieval armor, spurs, rings, spoons, and chalices were displayed. The sound of his shoes died. From behind the hedge of pedestals, quite close to Leonard's ear, Robin's clear voice piped, "Well, isn't Puss in a snorty mood?"

.   .   .

To attack the statue Seabright assigned him, Leonard moved his horse several yards forward, without abandoning the precious light that filtered through a window high behind him. From this new position Robin was in part visible. A plinth still concealed her bulk, but around the plinth's corner her propped drawing board showed, and her hand when it stabbed at the paper, and even her whole head, massive with floppy fair hair, when she bent forward into a detail. He was at first too shy to risk meeting her eyes, so her foot, cut off at the ankle and thus isolated in its blue ballet slipper on the shadowy marble floor, received the brunt of his attention. It was a long foot, with the division of the toes just beginning at the rim of the slipper's blue arc, and the smooth pallor of the exposed oval yielding, above the instep, to the mist-reddened roughness of an Englishwoman's leg. These national legs, thick at the ankles and glazed up to the knees with a kind of weatherproofing, on Robin were not homely; like a piece of fine pink ceramic her ankle kept taking, in Seabright's phrase, his eye.

After an hour Leonard brought out, "Aren't your feet cold, in just those slippers?"

"Rather," she promptly responded and, with the quick skip that proved to be her custom, went beyond the question: "Gives me the shivers all over, being in this rotten place."

It was too quick for him. "You mean the school?"

"Oh, the school's all right; it's these wretched antiques."

"Don't you like them? Don't you find them sort of stable, and timeless?"

"If these old things are timeless, I'd rather be timely by a long shot."

"No, seriously. Think of them as angels."

"Seriously my foot. You Americans are never serious. Everything you say's a variety of joke; honestly, it's like conversing in a monkey-house."

On this severe note Leonard feared they had concluded; but a minute later she showed him his silence was too careful by lucidly announcing, "I have a friend who's an atheist and hopes World War Three blows everything to bits. He doesn't care. He's an atheist."

Their subsequent conversations sustained this discouraging quality, of two creatures thrown together in the same language exchanging, across a distance wider than it seemed, miscalculated signals. He felt she quite misjudged his seriousness and would have been astonished to learn how deeply and solidly she had been placed in his heart, affording a fulcrum by which he lifted the great dead mass of his spare time, which now seemed almost lighter than air, a haze of quixotic expectations, imagined murmurs, easy undressings, and tourist delights. He believed he was coming to love England. He went to a tailor and bought for four guineas a typical jacket of stiff green wool, only to discover, before the smeary mirror in his digs, that it made his head look absurdly small, like one berry on top of a bush; and he kept wearing his little zippered khaki windbreaker to the Constable School.

As an alien, he could not estimate how silly she truly was. She was eighteen, and described looking up as a child and seeing bombs floatingly fall from the belly of a German bomber, yet there was something flat and smooth behind her large eyes that repelled closeness. She seemed to be empty of the ragged, absorbent wisdom of girls at home whose war experiences stopped short at scrap drives. Across Robin's incongruities— between her name and her body, her experiences and her innocence—was braced a determined erectness of carriage, as if she were Britannia in the cartoons; her contours contained nothing erotic but limned a necessarily female symbol of ancient militance. Robin was tall, and her figure, crossing back and forth through the shadows of the casts and the patchy light between, seemed to Leonard to stalk. She was always in and out now. In at nine-thirty, breathless; out at ten for a coffee break; back at eleven; lunch at eleven-thirty; back by one; at two-thirty, out for a smoke; in by three; gone by four. Since the days of their joint attack on that chaste archer the moon goddess, Robin's work habits had grown blithe. She had moved away to another area, to analyze another figure, and he had not been bold enough to follow with his horse, though his next statue took him in her direction. So at least once an hour she appeared before his eyes, and, though the coffee breaks and long lunches forced him to deduce a lively native society, he, accustomed by the dragged-out days of Army life to patience, still thought of her as partly his. It seemed natural when, three weeks before the Michaelmas term ended, Puss—Leonard had fallen in with mocking Seabright—promoted them to still life together.

At the greengrocer's on Monday morning they purchased still-life ingredients. The Constable School owned a great bin of inanimate objects, from which Leonard had selected an old mortar and pestle. His idea was then to buy, to make a logical picture, some vegetables that could be ground, and to arrange them in a Chardinesque tumble. But what, really, *was* ground, except nuts? The grocer did have some Jamaican walnuts.

"Don't be funny, Leonard," Robin said. "All those horrid little wrinkles, we'd be at it forever."

"Well, what else could you grind?"

"We're not going to *grind* anything; we're going to paint it. What we want is something *smooth*."

"Oranges, miss?" the lad in charge offered.

"Oh, oranges. Everyone's doing oranges—looks like a pack of advertisements for vitamin C. What we want . . ." Frowning, she surveyed the produce, and Leonard's heart, plunged in the novel intimacy of shopping with a woman, beat excitedly. "Onions," Robin declared. "Onions are what we want."

"Onions, miss?"

"Yes, three, and a cabbage."

"One cabbage?"

"Here, may I pick it out?"

"But, Robin," Leonard said, having never before called her by name, "onions and cabbages don't go together."

"Really, Leonard, you keep talking as if we're going to *eat* them."

"They're both so round."

"I dare say. You won't get me doing any globby squashes. Besides, Leonard, ours won't get rotten."

"Our globby squashes?"

"Our *still* life, love. Haven't you seen Melissa's pears? Really, if I had to look at those brown spots all day I think I'd go sick."

The lad, in his gray apron and muddy boots, gently pushed a paper bag against her arm. "Tenpence, miss. Five for the onions and four for the head and the bag's a penny."

"Here," Leonard said hoarsely, and the action of handing over the money was so husbandly he blushed.

Robin asked, "Are the onions attractive?"

"Oh yes," the boy said in a level uncomprehending tone that defended him against any intention she might have, including that of "having him on."

"Did you give us attractive onions?" she repeated. "I mean, we're not going to eat them."

"Oh yes. They're good-looking, miss."

The boy's referring to the cabbage simply as "the head" haunted Leonard, and he started as if at a ghost when, emerging with Robin into the narrow street, the head of a passerby looked vividly familiar; it was the handsomely sculpted head alone, for otherwise Jack Fredericks had quite blended in. He was dressed completely in leather and wool, and even the haircut framing his amazed gape of recognition had the heavy British form. Eerie reunions are common among Americans abroad, but Leonard had never before been hailed from this far in the past. It offended him to have his privacy, built during so many painful weeks of loneliness, unceremoniously crashed; yet he was pleased to be discovered with a companion so handsome. "Jack, this is Miss Robin Cox; Robin, Jack Fredericks. Jack is from my home town, Wheeling."

"Wheeling, in what state?" the girl asked.

"West Virginia," Jack smiled. "It's rather like your Black Country."

"More green than black," Leonard said.

Jack guffawed. "Good old literal Len," he told Robin. His small moist eyes sought in vain to join hers in a joke over their mutual friend. He and Leonard had never been on a "Len" basis. Had they been on the streets of Wheeling, neither one would have stopped walking.

"What are you doing here?" Leonard asked him.

"Reading ec at Jesus; but you're the one who baffles me. You're *not* at the university surely?"

"Sort of. We're both at the Constable School of Art. It's affiliated."

"I've never *heard* of it!" Jack laughed out loud, for which Leonard was grateful, since Robin further stiffened.

She said, "It's in a wing of the Ash. It's a very serious place."

"Is it *really?* Well, I must come over sometime and see this remarkable institution. I'm rather interested in painting right now."

Leonard said, feeling safe, "Sure. Come on over. Any time. We have to get back now and make a still life out of these onions."

"Well, aren't you full of tricks? You know," Jack said to the girl, "Len was a year older than I in public school and I'm used to looking up at him."

To this preposterous lie Robin coolly replied with another: "Oh, at Connie we all look up to him."

The Constable School could not afford to waste its precious space on still lifes, and imposed upon the museum's good nature by setting them up in the Well, a kind of basement with a skylight. Here hard-to-classify casts were stashed. Here a great naturalistic boar reclined on his narrow tufted bottom, the Dying Gaul sunned himself in the soft light sifting from above like dust, Winged Victory hoisted her battered feathers; and a tall hermaphrodite, mutilated by Byzantine piety, posed behind a row of brutal Roman portrait busts. The walls were a strange gay blue; even more strangely gay were the five or six students, foreshortened into chipper, quick shapes, chirping around tables of brilliant fruit. As he followed his friend's blond hair down the reverberating iron of the spiral stairs, Leonard felt he had at last arrived at the radiant heart of the school.

Nowhere in the museum was there as much light as in the Well. Their intimacy in the grocer's shop seemed clarified and enhanced here, and pointed by artistic purpose. With minute care they arranged the elements upon a yellow cloth. Robin's white hands fussed imperiously with the cabbage, tearing off leaf after leaf until she had reduced it to a roundness she imagined would be simple to draw. After lunch they began to mark with charcoal their newly bought canvases, which smelled of glue and fresh wood. To have her, some distance from his side, echoing his task, and to know that her eyes concentrated into the same set of shapes, which after a little concentration took on an unnatural intensity, like fruit in Paradise, curiously enlarged his sense of his physical size; he seemed to tower above the flagstones, and his voice, in responding to her erratic exclamations and complaints, resonated in the bright Well. The other students on still life also worked solemnly, and in the afternoon there were few of them. The sounds of museum traffic drifted down from a comparatively dark and cluttered world.

Jack Fredericks paid his visit the very next day. He thumped down the stairs in his little scholar's gown and stared at the still life over Robin's shoulder and asked, "Why are you going to grind onions in a mortar?"

"We're not," she replied in the haughty voice Leonard had first heard.

Jack sauntered over to the hermaphrodite and said, "Good Lord. What happened to *him?*"

Leonard made no earnest effort to put him at his ease. Embarrassed and hence stubborn, Jack lay down on the shallow ledge designed to set off the exhibits, in a place just behind the table supporting the still life, and smiled up quizzically at the faces of the painters. He meant to look debonair, but in the lambent atmosphere he looked ponderous, with all that leather and wool. The impression of mass was so intense Leonard feared he might move and break one of the casts. Leonard had not noticed on the street how big his fellow West Virginian had grown. The weight was mostly in flesh — broad beefy hands folded on his vest, corpulent legs uneasily crossed on the cold stone floor.

Seabright made no pretense of not being startled at finding him there. "What, uh, what are you doing?"

"I guess I'm auditing."

The telltale "guess" put the Puss's back up higher. "We don't generally set aside space for spectators."

"Oh, I've been very unobtrusive, sir. We haven't been saying a word to each other."

"Be that as it may, you're right in these people's vision. If you didn't come down here to look at the statues, I'm really afraid there's nothing here for you."

"Oh. Well. Certainly." Jack, grimacing with the effort, raised his body to his feet. "I didn't know there were all these regulations."

Leonard did not strenuously follow up this victory. His courtship of Robin continued as subtly as before, though twice he did dare ask her to the movies. The second time, she accepted. The delicately tinted Japanese love tale, so queerly stained with murders, seemed to offer a mutually foreign ground where they might meet as equals, but the strict rules of the girls' house where she stayed, requiring them to scamper directly into a jammed bus, made the whole outing, in the end, seem awkward and foolish. He much preferred the days, full of light and time, when their proximity had the grace of the accidental and before their eyes a constant topic of intercourse was poised. He even wondered if through their one date he hadn't lost some dignity in her eyes. The tone of her talk to him in the Well was respectful; the more so since his painting was coming excellently. Something in those spherical shapes and mild colors spoke to him. Seabright was plainly flattered by his progress. "Mmm," he would purr, "delicious tones on the shadow side here. But I believe you're shading a bit too much towards red. It's really a very distinct violet, you know. If I could have your palette a moment . . . And a clean brush?" Lesson by lesson, Leonard was drawn into Seabright's world, a tender, subdued world founded on violet, and where violet—pronounced "vaalet"—at the faintest touch of a shadow, at the slightest hesitation of red or blue, rose to the surface, shyly vibrant. Robin's bluntly polychrome vision caused him to complain, "Really, Miss Cox, I wish you had got the drawing correct before you began filling in the spaces." When Puss had gone back up the spiral stair, Robin would transfer his vexation to Leonard as "Honestly, Len, I can't see all this rotten purple. You'd think my onions were grapes, to see what he's done to them. Tell me, should I scrape his paint right off?"

Leonard walked around to her easel and suggested, "Why don't you try keying in the rest of it around them?"

"Key it in? Key it in!" She seemed to relish the shrill syllables.

"Sure. Make your cabbage kind of greeny-purple, and the yellow cloth browny-purple, and for the mortar, well, try pure turps."

"No," she pouted. "It's not a joke. You're just being a disgusting silly American. You think I'm stupid at paints."

Each day he sank deeper into a fatherly role; he welcomed any secure relationship with her, yet wondered if he wasn't being, perhaps, neutralized. Except on technical matters, she never sought his advice until the day near the end of term when, conceding him in this sense a great stride forward, she asked, "How well do you know your friend Jack Fredericks?"

"Not well at all. I wouldn't call him my friend. He was a year younger in high school, and we weren't really in the same social class either."

"The social classes in America—are they very strong?"

"Well—the divisions aren't as great as here, but there're more of them."

"And he comes from a good class?"

"Fair." He thought reticence was his best tactic, but when she joined him in silence he was compelled to prod. "What makes you ask?"

"Now, Leonard. You mustn't breathe a word; if you do, I'll absolutely shrivel. You see, he's asked me to model for him."

"*Model* for him? He can't paint."

"Yes he can. He's shown me some of his things and they're rather good."

"How does he mean 'model'? Model in what condition?"

"Yes. In the nude." High color burned evenly in her face; she dabbed at the canvas.

"That's ridiculous. He doesn't paint at all."

"But he *does*, Leonard. He's taken it up very seriously. I've *seen* his things."

"What do they look like?"

"Oh, rather abstract."

"I bet."

"*All* you Americans paint in the abstract."

"I don't." He didn't feel this was much of a point to score.

"He says I have a lovely body—"

"Well, *I* could have told you *that*." But he hadn't.

"—and *swears*, absolutely, there would be nothing to it. He's even offered a model's fee."

"Well, I never heard of such an embarrassing, awful scheme."

"Really, Leonard, it's embarrassing only when you talk of it. I *know* he's perfectly serious as a painter."

Leonard added a fleck of black to a mixture on his palette and sighed. "Well, Robin. You do whatever you want. It's your life."

"Oh, I wouldn't *dream* of *do*ing it. Mummy and Daddy would *die*."

His relief was overwhelmed by a sudden fierce sense of being wronged.

He said, "Don't let *them* stand in your way. Why, this may be the start of a whole career for you."

"I mean, I never con*sid*ered it. I was just interested in your opinion of the man."

"My opinion is, he's a *horrible* man. He's a silly spoiled snob and about to get hog fat and I don't see what attracts you in him. Terrible person. Terrible."

"Well, as you say, you don't know him very well."

Leonard and the other unmarried veteran went to Europe during the Michaelmas vacation. On the Channel boat, his thoughts, free for the first time from the bustle of departure, returned to Robin, and the certainty of her turning Fredericks down warmed him on the cold, briny deck. In Paris the idea that she even toyed with such a proposition excited him; it suggested an area of willingness, of loneliness, that Leonard could feasibly invade. In Frankfurt he wondered if actually she would turn his fellow-countryman down—she was staying around the university during vacation, Leonard knew—and by Hamburg he was certain that she had not; she had succumbed. He grew accustomed to this conviction as he and his companion (who was devoting himself to a survey of all the beers of Europe) slowly circled back through the Lowlands. By the time he disembarked at Dover he was quite indifferent to her nakedness.

The school had grown chillier in four weeks. In the Well, the arrangements of fruit had decayed; in case some of the students continued to work during the vacation, the things had not been disturbed. Their own still life was least affected by time. The onions were as immutable as the statues; but the cabbage, peeled by Robin to its solid pale heart, had relaxed in wilting, and its outer leaves, gray and almost transparent, rested on the yellow cloth. His painting, still standing in its easel, preserved the original appearance of the cabbage, but the pigments had dulled, sinking into the canvas; their hardness made the painting seem finished, though there were several uncovered corners and numerous contrasts his fresh eye saw the need of adjusting. He loaded his palette and touched paint to the canvas reluctantly. The Well was so empty on this Monday morning of resumption, he wondered if he had made a mistake, misreading the schedule or taking it too seriously. At the far end, the wispy English boy, who had established himself as the teachers' pet, noisily dismantled groups, crashing vegetable elements into a paper sack.

After eleven o'clock, Robin appeared on the balcony of the spiral stair. She overlooked the Well with her serene Britannia stance—her bosom a brave chest, her hips and legs a firm foundation—and then descended in a flurry. "Leonard. Where have you *been?*"

"I told you, I was going to Europe with Max. We went as far east as Hamburg, and came back through Holland and Belgium."

"You went to *Germany?* Whatever for?"

"Well, I am German, eventually."

Her attention went sideways. "I say, the cabbage has taken it hard, hasn't it?" She lifted her own painting off the easel. "Are you still going at it? Puss has put me back in antique."

"Of all the *crust.*"

"Oh, well. He said to me, 'You're pretty rotten at this, aren't you?' and I agreed. It's the truth."

Leonard resented the implication in this blitheness that he, too, the companion of her futile labors, was easy to give up. His mouth stiff with injury, he sarcastically asked, "How's your posing for Jack Fredericks coming?"

Her blue eyes squared. "Posing for *him?* I did nothing of the sort." Her words might have been "I love you"; his heart felt a sudden draft and he started to say, "I'm glad."

But she went on with surprising vehemence, "Really, Leonard, you refuse to take me *seriously*. I could see all along he was a dreadful bore." Her arm held her canvas captive against her side and with her free hand she impatiently pushed floppy hair back from her forehead—a rigid, aristocratic gesture that swept his stir of hope quite away. He had been stupid. He had been stupid to think that if Fredericks were eliminated he, Leonard Hartz, was left. Over here, he and Jack were two of a kind, and by his own admission he was Jack's social inferior. She was done with the silly strange lot. After all, boyfriends are a serious bit.

Like those flocks of birds seen from the bus window, she had exploded as he watched. Even before she took a backward step, her receding from him seemed so swift he raised his voice in claiming, less in apology than as a fresh basis, "All Americans are bores, I guess."

Home

First, the boat trip home: a downpour in Liverpool, and on the wharf two girls (harlots?) singing "Don't Sit Under the Apple Tree" under a single raincoat held over their heads like a canopy, everyone else huddling beneath the eaves of the warehouses, but these girls coming right down to the edge of the concrete wharf, singing, in effect to the whole ocean liner but more particularly to some person or persons (a pair of sailor lovers?) under the tourist deck. And then Cobh in damp golden sunlight, and an American girl from Virginia coming out on the pilot boat in tight toreador pants and with the Modern Library *Ulysses* ostentatiously under her arm. And then the days of the flawless circular horizon: blackjack with the Rhodes Scholars, and deck tennis with the Fulbrights, and eleven-o'clock bouillon, and the waves folding under by the prow, and the wake wandering behind them like a lime-colored highway. Robert had determined to be not disappointed by the Statue of Liberty, to submit to her cliché, but she disappointed him by being genuinely awesome, in the morning mist of the harbor, with a catch in her green body as if she had just thought to raise the torch, or at least to raise it so high. His baby in her bunting wriggled on his shoulder, and the other young Americans crowded the rail, and he felt obstructed from absorbing a classic effect, the queen of insignia, the trademark supreme. So it was he, prepared to condescend, who was unequal to the occasion.

And then America. Just the raggle-taggle of traffic and taxis that collects at the west end of the Forties when a liner comes in, but his, his fatherland. In the year past, the sight of one of these big grimacing cars shouldering its way through the Oxford lanes had been to him a breathing flag, a bugle blown across a field of grain, and here they were, enough of them to create a traffic jam, honking and glaring at each other in the tropical-seeming heat, bunched like grapes and as blatantly colored as birds of paradise. They were outrageous, but made sense; they fitted his eyes. Already England seemed a remote, gray apparition. It seemed three years and not three months since he had sat alone in the two-and-six seats of the American-style cinema in Oxford and cried. Joanne had just had the baby. She slept a tuppenny bus ride away, in a hospital bed, to whose foot was attached a basket containing Corinne. All the mothers in the ward seemed to have something wrong with them. They were Irish or American, unwed or unwell. One garrulous crone, tubercular, was frequently milked by a sputtering machine. In the bed beside Joanne, a young colleen wept all day long because her immigrating husband had not yet found work. In visiting hours he nested his snub face on the sheets beside her and they cried together. Joanne had cried when they told her that in this country healthy women were asked to have their babies at home; their home was a dank basement flat in which they leaped from one shin-roasting island of heat to another. She had burst into tears, right there at the head of the queue, and the welfare state had clasped her to its drab and ample bosom. They gave her coupons to trade for powdered orange juice. They wrapped the newborn baby in swaddling bands. All he could see of Corinne was her head, a bright-red ball, blazing with his blood. It was all very strange. At sunset a parson came into the ward and led an Anglican service that made the mothers weep. Then the husbands came, carrying little bags of fruit and candy bars. Bunched in the waiting room, they could see their wives primping in their cranked-up beds. Then the seven-o'clock bells rang, now here, now there, all over the city. When the eight-o'clock bells rang, Joanne gave Robert a passionate kiss, hard with panic yet soft with the wish to sleep. She slept, and a mile away he watched a Doris Day movie about that mythical Midwestern town that Hollywood keeps somewhere among its sets. The houses were white, the porches deep, the lawns green, the sidewalks swept, the maples dark and blowzy against the streetlights. Doris Day's upper lip lifted in just that apprehensive but spunky small-town way; her voice cracked. Abruptly, right there in the midst of the rustling Kit Kat bars and stunted shopgirl doxies and young British toughs in their sinister liveries of black, he discovered himself, to his amazement and delight, crying, crying hot honest tears for his lost home.

And then the gritty snarl of customs, and watching the baggage slide piece by piece down the roller ramp, and trying to soothe the fussy infant, who had never known such heat. The badged cherubim guarding the gate to the nation allowed him to pass through and give the child to the grandparents and great-aunts and cousins that waited on the other side.

His mother rose and kissed him on the cheek, and with an averted glance his father shook his hand, and his parents-in-law mimicked them, and the other relatives made appropriate motions of affection, and then they all wandered about the dismal, echoing waiting room in the desperate little circles of delay. While he had been abroad, his mother's letters—graceful, witty, informative, cheerful—had been his main link with home, but now that he saw his parents in the flesh, it was his father who interested him. There had been nothing like him in Europe. Old, sadly old—he had had all sixteen remaining teeth pulled while Robert was away, and his face seemed jaundiced with pain and his false teeth huge and square—he still stood perfectly erect, like a child that has just learned to stand, his hands held limply, forward from his body, at the level of his belt. Unwilling, or unable, to look long at his only son or his infant granddaughter, he explored the waiting room, studying the water fountain, and a poster for Manischewitz wine, and the buttons on the coat of a colored porter, as if each might contain the clue to something he had lost. Though for thirty years a public-school teacher, he still believed in education. Now he engaged the porter in conversation, gesturing sadly with his hands, asking questions, questions that Robert could not hear but that he knew from experience could be about anything—the tonnage of great ships, the popularity of Manischewitz wine, the mechanics of unloading luggage. The receipt of any information made his father for a brief moment less mournful. The porter looked up, puzzled and wary at first, and then, the way it usually went, became flattered and voluble. People in passing, for all their haste, turned their heads to stare at the strange duet of the tall, yellow-faced, stubbornly nodding man in rolled-up shirtsleeves and the dissertating little Negro. The porter fetched one of his colleagues over to confirm a point. There was much waving of hands, and their voices began to grow loud. Robert's face smarted with the familiar prickles of embarrassment. His father was always so conspicuous. He was so tall that he had been chosen, on the occasion of another return from Europe, to be Uncle Sam and lead their town's Victory Parade in the autumn of 1945.

At last he rejoined the rest of the family and announced, "That was a very interesting man. He said these signs all around saying 'No Tipping' are strictly baloney. He said his union has been fighting for years to get them taken down." He offered this news with a mild air of hope, forming the words hurriedly around his unaccustomed false teeth. Robert made an exasperated noise and turned his back. There. Not in the country one hour and already he had been rude to his father. He returned to the other side of the gate and completed the formalities.

They maneuvered the baggage into the trunk of his father's brown '49 Plymouth. The little car looked dusty and vulnerable amid the vibrant taxis. A young blond cop came over to protest its illegal position at the curb and ended, so seductive was the appeal of his father's stoic bewilderment, by helping them lift the huge old-fashioned trunk—Robert's mother's at college—into place among the broken jacks and knots of rope and unravelling wheels of basketball tickets his father carried around. The trunk stuck out over the bumper. They tied the door of the car trunk down with frayed ropes. His father asked the policeman how many taxicabs there were in Manhattan and if it was true, as he had read, that the drivers had been robbed so often they wouldn't go into Harlem at night any more. Their discussion continued throughout the farewells. Robert's aunt, with a kiss that smelled of Kool cigarettes and starched linen, went off to catch the train to Stamford. His cousin, her son, walked away under the pillars of the West Side Highway; he lived on West Twelfth Street and worked as an animator for television commercials. His wife's parents herded their little flock of kin toward the parking lot, redeemed their scarlet Volvo, and began the long haul to Boston. Mother got into the front seat of the Plymouth. Robert and Joanne and Corinne arranged themselves in the back. Minutes passed; then his father and the policeman parted, and his father got in behind the wheel. "That was very interesting," he said. "He said ninety-nine out of a hundred Puerto Ricans are honest." With a doleful thump of the clutch, they headed for Pennsylvania.

Robert had a job teaching—his father's harness, but a higher grade of leather—to ex-debutantes at a genteel college on the Hudson. It would begin in September. This was July. For the interval, he and Joanne were to sponge off their parents. His got them first. He had looked forward to this month; it would be the longest he would have been in Pennsylvania with his wife, and he had a memory of something he had wanted to describe, to explain, to her about his home. But exactly what that was, he had forgotten. His parents lived in a small town fifty miles west of Philadelphia, in a county settled by German immigrants a century and a half ago. His mother had been born in the county, on a farm, and felt involved with the land but estranged from its people. His father had come from Elizabeth, New Jersey, and groped after people, but saw no comfort in land. Whereas Robert, who had been born and raised in the small town, where people and land formed a patchwork, thought he loved both; yet, ever since he could remember, he had been planning to escape. The air had seemed too dense, too full of pollen and morality, and apt to choke him. He had made that escape. It had seemed necessary. But it had left him feeling hollow, fragile, transparent—a vial waiting to be filled with tears by the next Doris Day movie. Coming home filled him with strength, a thicker liquid. But each time less full; he sensed this. Both he and the land were altering. The container was narrowing; the thing contained was becoming diluted. In the year past, his mother's letters had often seemed enigmatic and full of pale, foreign matter. So it was with a sense of guilty urgency that he silently willed the car forward, as if the heart of his homeland might give out before he reached it.

His father said, "That cop told me he had studied to be a television repairman but couldn't get any business so he became a cop. He said the field's gotten crowded as hell in the last five years."

"Daddy, hush," said the new grandmother. "The baby wants to go to sleep."

Corinne had been terrorized by the tooting of the tugboats; being passed from arms to arms had sustained her upset. Now she lay on the floor of the car in a cream-colored Carry-Cot they had bought in England. Just looking at its nickel studs and braces made Robert remember the carriage shop on the Cowley Road, with its bright-black rows of stately prams built as if for a lifetime; and indeed the English did wheel their children around until they were immense. Ah, the dear, rosy English: he began, with a soft reversal of blood, to feel homesick for them. Could he never rest?

They undressed Corinne of her woolen clothes and she lay in a diaper, pink with heat, kicking her legs and whimpering. Then the whorls of her face slumped sideways, her star-shaped hands stopped fidgeting, and she fell asleep on the jiggling bosom of the highway. "Honestly, Joanne," Robert's mother said, "I've never seen such a perfect baby. And I'm not just being a mother-in-law when I say that." Her protest was abrasive on several sides; Robert resisted the implication that the baby had been solely Joanne's doing.

"I like her bellybutton," he asserted.

"It's a masterpiece," his mother said, and he felt, in a queer way, confirmed. But even then: the baby's beauty, like all beauty, was self-enclosed, and led nowhere. Their talk stayed shy and tentative. There was gossip between Robert and his parents that his wife could not share; and a growing body of allusions between himself and Joanne to which his parents were foreigners. The widening range and importance of these allusions, which could not by any effort of politeness be completely suppressed, seemed to dwindle and mock his relation with his parents.

He had always, even at college age, smoked *sub rosa*, out of the house, where the sight would not offend his mother. It had been like sex: forgivable but unsightly. But now, as Joanne burned Player after Player in her nervousness at his father's eccentric and preoccupied driving, Robert could not, as her husband and as a man, abstain; and anyway, of the two old sins it had been the lesser, and the fruit of the worse had just been praised. At the scratch of his match, his mother turned her head and looked at him levelly. To her credit, there was not a tremor of reproach. Yet after that level look he was painfully conscious of the smoke that drifted forward and encircled her head, and of the patient way she kept brushing it from her face with her hand. Her hand was freckled on the back and her wedding ring cut deeply into the flesh of the third finger, giving her quietest gesture a passive, wounded eloquence.

It seemed a point scored for her side when Joanne, panicked that her father-in-law would bungle the turnoff for the Pulaski Skyway, shattered the tip of her cigarette against the back of the seat and a live ash fell on the baby's belly. It went unnoticed for a second, until Corinne screamed; then they all saw it, a little flea of fire glowing beside the perfect navel. Joanne jumped, and squealed with guilt, and flapped her hands and stamped her feet and hugged the baby against her, but the evidence could not be destroyed: a brown dot of char on the globe of immaculate skin. Corinne continued her screams, splicing them with shrill hard gasps of intake, while everyone rummaged through purses and pockets for Vaseline, butter, toothpaste—anything for an unguent. Mother had a tiny bottle of toilet water given her in a department store; Joanne dabbed some of this on, and in time Corinne, shaken by more and more widely spaced spasms of sobbing, mercifully dragged her injury with her into the burrow of sleep.

The incident was so like the incident of the penny that Robert had to tell them about it. On the boat, he had gone down to their cabin, where Corinne was sleeping, to get his wallet from his other coat. The coat was hanging on a hook over her crib. The tourist cabins on these big liners, he explained, are terribly cramped—everything on top of everything else.

His father nodded, swallowing a fact. "They don't give you much space, huh?"

"They *can't*," Robert told him. "Anyway, in my hurry or something, when I took out the wallet I flipped an English penny out with it and it flew and hit Corinne right in the center of her forehead."

"Why, Robert!" his mother said.

"Oh, it was awful. She cried for an hour. Much longer than just now, with the spark."

"She must be getting used to our dropping things on her," Joanne said.

With a possibly pointed tact, his mother declined to agree with this suggestion, and expressed politely exaggerated interest in the English penny they showed her. Why, it *is* heavy! And is this the *smallest* denomination? They eagerly showed her other British coins. But there were elements in the story that had been suppressed: they had needed his wallet because they had used up all their change in an uproarious orgy of blackjack and beer. And from Joanne, even, Robert had this secret: the reason for his haste in retrieving the wallet was his hurry to get back to the invigorating company of the flashy girl from Virginia who had boarded the boat at Cobh. In the dim cabin lit by a blue bulb and warmed by his overheated body, the weird flight of the penny had seemed a judgment.

So the accident, and the anecdote, reinforced the constraint. The dear roadside ice-cream stands, the beloved white frame houses, the fervently stocked and intimately cool drugstores unfurled behind car windows smeared with sullen implications of guilt, disappointment, apology, and lost time. Robert looked to his parents to break the spell. Married, employed, in a narrow way learned, himself a father, he was still childish enough to expect his parents to pierce the many little mysteries that had been deposited between them. He blamed them for failing to do it. In their infinite power they had only to stretch out a hand. Spitefully he began to look forward to the month in Boston they would spend with Joanne's parents.

They came west across New Jersey, crossed the Delaware where Washington had once crossed it, and on a southwesterly curve penetrated into Pennsylvania. The towns along the route changed from the flat, wooden New Jersey sort into a stiffer, more Teutonic type, braced against hills with stone and brick, laid out stubbornly on the plan of a grid, though this dogmatism compelled extensive sustaining walls that rose and fell with the land, damming brief domed lawns crowned with narrow brick houses whose basement windows were higher than the top of their car. The brutal sun passed noon; the trunk lid rattled and bobbed as the ropes loosened. They came to the border of the twenty square miles that Robert knew well. In this town he had gone each fall to a football game, and in this one he had attended a fair where the girls in the tents danced wearing nothing but high-heeled shoes.

A web began to clog Robert's throat. He sneezed. "Poor Bobby," his mother said. "I bet he hasn't had hay fever since the last time he was home."

"I didn't know he got hay fever," Joanne said.

"Oh, terribly," his mother said. "When he was a little boy, it used to break my heart. With his sinuses, he really shouldn't smoke."

They all swayed; a car at the curb had unexpectedly nosed out into their path. Robert's father, without touching the brake, swung around it; it was a long green car, glitteringly new, and the face at the driver's window, suspended for a moment on the wave of their swerve, was startled and pink. Robert noticed this dully. His eyes were watering allergically. They drove on, and a half-mile passed before the swelling honking behind them dawned on him as aimed at them.

The green car was speeding to catch them; it rode a few yards behind their bumper while the driver leaned on the horn. Robert turned and through the rear window read, between the triple headlights hooded under twirled eyebrows of metal, the tall letters OLDSMOBILE embodied in the grille. The car surged into the next lane and slowed to their speed; its streamlined sweepback windshield gave it the look of losing its hat. The little pink driver screamed over through the passenger's window. The man's middle-aged wife, as if she were often a partner in this performance, expertly pulled back her head to let his words fly past, but they were indistinguishable in the rush of wind and whirling rubber.

Daddy turned to Mother; he was squinting in pain. "What's he saying, Julia? I can't hear what he's saying." He still looked to his wife as his interpreter in this region, though he had lived here more than thirty years.

"He's saying he's an angry man," Mother said.

Robert, his brain fogged by the gathering gasps of a sneeze, stamped on the floor, to make their car travel faster and outrace their assailant. But his father slowed and braked to a stop.

The Olds was taken by surprise, and travelled a good distance beyond them before it, too, pulled over to the side of the road. They were outside the town; trim farmland, hazy with pollen, undulated in the heat on either side of the highway. The car up ahead spat out its driver. At a fat little trot a short perspiring man jogged back along the gravel shoulder toward them. He wore a flowered Hawaiian shirt, and words were spilling from his mouth. The motor of the old Plymouth, too hot to idle after hours of steady running, throbbed and stalled. The man's head arrived at the side window; he had a square skull, with ridges of cartilage above the neat white ears, and his skin, flushed and puckered as it was by raving, gave an impression of translucent delicacy, like the skin on a sausage. Even before the man regained his breath to speak, Robert recognized him as a prime specimen of the breed that the outside world fondly calls the Pennsylvania Dutch. And then, in the first shrill cascade of outrage, the juicy *ch*'s and misplaced *w*'s of the accent seemed visually distinct, like letters stamped on shattered crates sliding down a waterfall. As the wild voice lowered and slowed, whole strings of obscenities were explicit. Consecutive sentences could be understood. "You hat no right to cut me off like that. Youff no right to go through town like that."

Robert's father, whose hearing had deteriorated along with his teeth, made no answer; this refusal whipped the little stout man into a new spin of fury: his skin shining as if to burst, he thrust his face into their window; he shut his eyes and his eyelids swelled; the wings of his nostrils whitened with pressure. His voice broke, as if frightened of itself, and he turned his back and walked a step away. His movements in the brilliant air seemed managed against a huge and impelling rigidity.

Robert's father mildly called after him, "I'm trying to understand you, mister, but I can't catch your meaning. I can't get your point."

This gave the top another turn, more furious still, but of shorter duration. Mother brushed some smoke from her face, relieving a long paralysis. The baby whimpered, and Joanne moved to the edge of the seat, trying to confront the source of the disturbance. Perhaps these motions from the women stirred feelings of guilt in the Dutchman; he released, like an ancillary legal argument, another spasm of lavatory-wall words, and his hands did a galvanized dance among the flowers of his shirt, and he actually, like a dervish, whirled completely around. Mournfully Robert's father gazed into the vortex, the skin of his face going increasingly yellow, as if with repeated extractions. In profile his lips clamped stubbornly over his clumsy new teeth, and his eye was a perfect diamond of undeviating interest. This attentiveness dragged at the Dutchman's indignant momentum. The aggrieved and obscene voice, which in the strange acoustics of the noon seemed to be echoing off the baking blue sky above them all, halted with a scratch of friction.

As if the spark had just struck her belly, Corinne began to scream. Joanne crouched down and shouted toward the front window, "You've woken up the baby!"

Robert's legs ached, and, partly to stretch them, partly to show some fight, he opened his door and got out. He felt his slender height, encased in his pin-striped English suit, unfold like an elegant and surprising weapon. The enemy's beaded forehead puckered doubtfully. "Wha-wereya trine to pull aat in front of us for?" Robert asked him in the slouching accents of home. His voice, stoppered by hay fever and dwindled by the blatant sunlight, seemed less his own than that of an old acquaintance.

His father opened his door and got out also. At the revelation of this even greater, more massive height, the Dutchman spat on the asphalt, taking care not to hit any shoes. Still working against that invisible resistance in the air, he jerkily pivoted and began to strut toward his car.

"No, wait a minute, mister," Robert's father called, and began to stride after him. The pink face, abruptly drained of fury, flashed above the soaked shoulder of the Hawaiian shirt. The Dutchman went into his trot. Robert's father, in his anxiety at seeing a conversation broken off, gave chase; his lengthening stride lifted his body off the ground with an awesome, floating slow motion. Under the shimmer of the road his shadow seemed to be falling away from his feet. His voice drifted faintly down the glaring highway. "Wait a minute, mister. I want to ask you something." As the perspective closed the distance between them, the Dutchman's legs twittered like a pinioned insect's, but this was an illusion; he was not caught. He arrived at the door of his Oldsmobile, judged he had time to utter one more curse, uttered it, and dodged into the glistening green shell. Robert's father arrived at the bumper as the car pulled out. The tense wrinkles on the back of his shirt implied an urge to hurl himself upon the fleeing metal. Then the wrinkles relaxed as he straightened his shoulders.

Erect with frustration, arms swinging, he marched down the side of the road just as, fifteen years before, in spats and a top hat made of cardboard, he had marched at the head of that parade.

Inside the car, Joanne was jiggling the baby and beaming. "That was wonderful," she said.

With an effort of contraction Daddy shrank into his place behind the steering wheel. He started the car and turned his big head sadly to tell her, "No. That man had something to say to me and I wanted to hear what it was. If I did something wrong, I want to know about it. But the bastard wouldn't talk sense. Like everybody else in this county—I can't understand them. They're Julia's people."

"I think he thought we were Gypsies," Mother said. "On account of the old trunk in the back. Also, the lid was up and he couldn't see our

Pennsylvania license plate. They're very anxious, you know, to keep the 'impure races' out of this section. Once the poor fellow heard us talk, he was satisfied, and I think embarrassed."

"He seemed awfully mad about nothing," Joanne said.

Mother's voice quickened, became fluid. "Well, that's how they *are*, Joanne. The people in this part of the country are just mad all the time. God gave them these beautiful valleys and they're hopping mad. I don't know why. I think there's too much starch in their diet." Her dietary theories were close to her heart; her touching on them conferred on Joanne a daughter's status.

Robert called forward, "Daddy, I don't think he really had any information to share." He spoke partly to hear his old voice again, partly to compete for attention with his newly created sibling, and partly in a vain hope of gathering to himself some of the glory his father now and then won in the course of his baffled quest for enlightenment. Primarily, Robert spoke to show his wife how accustomed he was to such scenes, how often such triumphant catastrophes had entered his life at home, so that he could be quite blasé about them. This was not true: he was intensely excited, and grew even more so as in folds of familiarity the land tightened around him.

Who Made Yellow Roses Yellow?

OF THE THREE TELEPHONES in the apartment, the one in the living room rested on a tabouret given to Fred Platt's grandmother by Henry James, who considered her, the Platts claimed, the only educated woman in the United States. Above this cherrywood gift hung an oval mirror, its frame a patterned involvement of cherubs, acanthus leaves, and half-furled scrolls; its gilt, smooth as butter in the valleys between figures, yielded on the crests of the relief to touches of Watteau brown. Great-Uncle Randy, known for his whims and mustaches, had rescued the mirror from a Paris auction. In the capacious room there was nothing of no intrinsic interest, nothing that would not serve as cause for a narrative, except the three overstuffed pieces installed by Fred's father—two chairs, facing each other at a distance of three strides, and a crescent-shaped sofa, all covered in spandy-new, navy-blue leather. This blue, and the dark warm wood of inherited cabinets, the twilight colors of aged books, the scarlet and purple of the carpet from Cairo (where Charlotte, Uncle Randy's wife, had caught a bug and died), and the dismal sonorities of the Seicento Transfiguration on the west wall vibrated around the basal shade of plum. Plum: a color a man can rest in, the one toward which all dressing gowns tend. Reinforcing the repose and untroubled finality of the interior were the several oval shapes. The mirror was one of a family, kin to the feminine ellipse of the coffee table; to the burly arc of Daddy's sofa, as they never failed to call it; to the ovoid, palely painted base of a Florentine lamp; to the plaster medallion on the ceiling—the one cloud in the sky of the room—and the recurrent, tiny gold seal of the Oxford University Press, whose books, monochrome and Latinate as dons, were among the chief of the senior Platt's plum-colored pleasures.

Fred, his only son, age twenty-five, dialled a JUdson number. He listened to five burrs before the receiver was picked up, exposing the tail end of a girl's giggle. Still tittery, she enunciated, "Carson Chem-i-cal."

"Hello. Is—ah, Clayton Thomas Clayton there, do you know?"

"Mr. Thomas Clayton? Yes, he is. Just one moment, please." So poor Clayton Clayton had finally got somebody to call him by his middle name, that "Thomas" which his parents must have felt made all the difference between the absurd and the sublime.

"Mr. Clayton's of-fice," another young woman said. "About what was it you wished to speak to him?"

"Well, nothing, really. It's a friend."

"Just one moment, please."

After a delay—purely disciplinary, Fred believed—an unexpectedly deep and even melodious voice said, "Yes?"

"Clayton Clayton?"

A pause. "Who is this?"

"Good morning, sir. I represent the Society for the Propagation and Eventual Adoption of the A. D. Spooner Graduated Income Tax Plan. As perhaps you know, this plan calls for an income tax which increases in inverse proportion to income, so that the wealthy are exempted and the poor taxed out of existence. Within five years, Mr. Spooner estimates, poverty would be eliminated: within ten, a thing not even of memory. Word has come to our office—"

"It's Fred Platt, isn't it?"

"Word has come to our office that in recent years Providence has so favored thee as to incline thy thoughts the more favorably to the Plan."

"Fred?"

"Congratulations. You now own the Motorola combination phonograph-and-megaphone. Do you care to try for the Bendix?"

"How long have you been in town? It's damn good to hear from you."

"Since April first. It's a prank of my father's. Who are all these girls you live in the midst of?"

"Your father called you back from Europe?"

"I'm not sure. I keep forgetting to look up 'wastrel' in the dictionary."

That made Clayton laugh. "I thought you were studying at the Sorbonne."

"I was, I was."

"But you're not now."

"I'm not now. *Moi et la Sorbonne, nous sommes kaput.*" When the other was silent, Fred added, *"Beaucoup kaput."*

"Look, we should get together," Clayton said.

"Yes. I was wondering if you eat lunch."

"When had you thought?"

"Soon?"

"Wait. I'll check." Some muffled words—a question with his hand over the mouthpiece. A drawer scraped. "Say, Fred, this is bad. I have something on the go every day this week."

"So. Well, what about June 21? They say the solstice will be lovely this year."

"Wait. What about today? I'm free today, they just told me."

"Today?" Fred had to see Clayton soon, but immediately seemed like a push. "*Comme vous voulez, monsieur.* One-ish?"

"All right, uh—could you make it twelve-thirty? I have a good bit to do. . . ."

"Just as easy. There's a Chinese place on East Forty-ninth Street run by Australians. Excellent murals of Li Po embracing the moon in the Yalu, *plus* the coronation of Henri Quatre."

"I wonder, could that be done some other time? As I say, there's some stuff here at the office. Do you know Shulman's? It's on Third Avenue, a block from here, so that—"

"Press of work, eh?"

"You said it," Clayton said, evidently sensing no irony. "Then I'll see you then."

"In all the old de dum de dumpty that this heart of mine embraces."

"Pardon?"

"See you then."

"Twelve-thirty at Shulman's."

"Absolutely."

"So long."

"*À bientôt. Très bientôt, mon chéri.*"

The first impulse after a humiliation is to look into a mirror. The heavy Parisian-looking glass, hung on two long wires, leaned inches from the wall. A person standing would see reflected in it not his head but the carpet, some furniture, and perhaps, in the upper portion of the oval, his shoes and cuffs. By tilting his chair Fred could see his face; thus a momentary escapee from a hectic cocktail party checks his flushed mask in the bathroom mirror. Here, in this silent overstuffed room, his excited appearance annoyed him. Between his feverish attempt to rekindle friendship—his mind skidding, his tongue wagging—and Clayton's response an embarrassing and degrading disproportion had existed.

Until now it had seemed foolishly natural for Clayton to offer him a job. Reportedly he had asked Bim Blackwood to jump Harcourt for a publicity job at Carson Chemical. Bim had said, without seeing anything funny in the word, that Clayton had lots of "power" at Carson. "In just three years, he's near the top. He's a *killer*. Really."

It had been hard to gather from Bim's description exactly what Clayton did. As Bim talked on, flicking at the stiff eave of brown hair that overhung his forehead with a conceited carelessness, he would say anything to round out a sentence, never surrendering his right to be taken seriously. "It's an octopus," he had asserted. "You know, *every*thing is chemicals *ult*imately. Clayton told me the first thing he was given to do was help design the wrapper for an ammoniated chewing gum they were just putting out. He said the big question was whether chalk-white or mint-green suggested better a clean feeling in the mouth. They had a survey on it; it cost thousands and *thousands*—thousands of little men going inside people's mouths. Of course he doesn't draw any more; he consults. Can you imagine doing nothing all day but *consult*? On pamphlets, you know, and 'flyers'—what *are* flyers anyway?—and motion pictures to show to salesmen to show them how to explain the things they sell. He's *ter*ribly involved with *tele*vision; he told me a *hor*rible story about a play about Irish peasants the *Carson Chemical Hour* was putting on and at the last minute it dawned on everybody that these people were *organic farmers*. Clayton Clayton saw it through. The killer instinct."

Clayton hadn't had to go into the Army. Shadowy lungs, or something. That was the thing about poor children: they acquired disabilities which give them the edge in later life. It's unjust, to expect a man without a handicap to go far.

Fred's position was not desperate. An honorable place in the family investments firm was not, as Father had said, with his arch way of trotting out clichés as if they were moderately obscure literary quotations, "the fate worse than death." Furthermore—he was a great man for furthermores—anyone who imagined that the publicity arm of Carson Chemical was an ivory tower compared with Brauer, Chappell & Platt lived in a fool's paradise.

Yet, viewed allegorically, the difference seemed great. Something about all this, perhaps the chaste spring greenery of Central Park, which from these windows was spread out with the falcon's-eye perspective of a medieval map, suggested one of those crossroads in *The Faerie Queene*. Fred had loved *The Faerie Queene*—its tiny type, its archaic spellings, its perfect uselessness.

Besides, he had been very kind to Clayton—gotten him onto the *Quaff*, really. Sans *Quaff*, where would Clayton be? Not that Clayton need consider any of this. Hell, it wasn't as if Fred were asking for something; he was offering something. He pushed back the chair a few feet— so a full view of himself was available in the tilted mirror: a tall, ascetic youth, dressed in darkest gray. An unchurched Episcopalian, Fred was half in love with the clergy.

Entering, late, the appointed restaurant, he instantly spotted Clayton Clayton standing at the bar. That three years had passed, that the place was smoky and crowded with interchangeable men, did not matter; an eclipsing head bowed, and the fragment of cheek then glimpsed, though in itself nothing but a daub of white, not only communicated to Fred a single human identity but stirred in him warm feelings for the *Quaff*, college, his youth generally, and even America, with its freedom from Europe's stony class distinctions. Fred had inherited that trick of the rich of seeming to do everything out of friendship, but he was three generations removed from the founding of the wealth, and a manner of business had become, in him, a way of life; his dealings were in fact at the mercy of his affections. Grotesquely close to giggling, he walked up to his man and intoned, *"Ego sum via, vita, veritas."*

Clayton turned, grinned, and pumped Fred's hand. "How *are* you, Fred?"

Members of the *Quaff* did not ask one another how they were; Fred had supposed ex-members also did not. Finding they did baffled him. He could not think of the joke to turn such a simple attack aside. "Pretty well," he conceded and, as if these words were an exorcism enabling the gods of fatuity to descend and dwell in his lips, heard himself add, in what seemed full solemnity, "How are *you?*"

"I'm doing"—Clayton paused, nodding once, giving the same words a new import—"pretty well."

"Yes, everybody says."

"I was glad I could make it today. I really am up to my ears this week." Confidingly: "I'm in a crazy business."

On one wall of the restaurant were Revolutionary murals, darkened perhaps by smoke and time but more likely by the painter's belief that history is murky. "Ah," said Fred, gesturing. "The Renaissance Popes in Hell."

"Would you like one of these?" Clayton touched the glass in front of him; it contained that collegiate brew, beer.

How tender of Clayton still to drink beer! By a trick of vision the liquid stood unbounded by glass. The sight of that suspended amber cylinder, like his magic first glimpse of Clayton's face, conjured in Fred an illusion of fondness. This time he curbed his tendency to babble and said, anxious to be honest, certain that the merest addition of the correct substance—the simple words exchanged by comrades—would reform the alchemy of the relationship, "Yes. I would like one. Quite a bit."

"I tell you. Let's grab a table and order from there. They'll let us stand here all day."

Fred felt not so much frustrated as deflected, as if the glass that wasn't around the beer was around Clayton.

"There's a table." Clayton picked up his stein, placed a half-dollar in the center of the circle its base had occupied, and shouldered away from the bar. He led the way into a booth, past two old men brandishing their topcoats. Inside, the high partitions shielded them from much of the noise of the place. Clayton took two menus from behind the sugar and handed one to Fred. "We had better order the food first, then ask for the beer. If you ask for the drinks first, they just run off." He was perfect: the medium-short dry-combed hair, the unimpeachable medium-gray suit, the buttonless collar, the genially dragged vowels, the little edges of efficiency bracing the consonants. A few traces of the scholarship freshman from some Maryland high school who had come down to the *Quaff* on Candidates' Night with an armful of framed sports cartoons remained—the not smoking, the tucked-in chin and the attendant uplook of the boyishly big eyes, and the skin condition that placed on the flank of each jaw a constellation of red dots. Even these vestiges fitted into the picture, by lending him the unthreatening youthful look desired in New York executives. It was just this suggestion of inexperience that in his genuine inexperience Clayton was working to suppress. "See anything you like," he asked with a firmness not interrogative.

Fred decided to make a meal of it. The family apartment was low on provender.

"I think maybe a lamb chop."

"I don't see them on the menu."

"I don't either."

Raising his hand to the level of his ear and snapping his fingers, Clayton summoned a waiter. "This gentleman wants a lamb chop. Do you have them?"

The waiter didn't bother to answer, just wrote it down.

"I think I might try," Clayton went on, "the chopped sirloin with mushroom sauce. Beans instead of the peas, if you will. And I'm having another glass of Ballantine. Shall I make that two, Fred?"

"Do you have any decent German beer? Würzburger? Or Löwenbräu?"

The request materialized the man, who had been serving them with only his skimpy professional self. Now he smiled, and stood bodied forth as a great-boned Teuton in the prime of his fifties, with a segmented shining bald head and portentous ears covered by a diaphanous fuzz that brought to the dignity his head already possessed a certain silky glamour. "I believe, sir, we have the Löwenbräu. I don't think we stock the Würzburger, sir."

"O.K. Whatever you do stock, then."

Though Fred wanted this to be Clayton's show, he had called into being a genie—cloying, zealous, delighted to have his cavernous reserve of attentiveness tapped. The waiter bowed and indeed whispered, making an awkward third party of Clayton, "If not the Löwenbräu, would an English stout do? A nice Guinness, sir?"

"The Löwenbräu will be fine." Trying to bring Clayton back into it, Fred asked him, "Do you want to try one? Fewer bubbles than Ballantine. Less tingle for more ferment."

Clayton's answering laugh would have been agreeable if he had not, while uttering it, lowered his eyelids, showing that he conceived of this as a decision whereby he stood to gain or lose. "No, I think I'll stick to Ballantine." He looked Fred needlessly in the eyes. When Clayton felt threatened, the middle sector of his face clouded over; the area between his brows and nostrils became sulky.

Fred was both repelled and touched. The expression was exactly that worn by the adolescent Clayton at the *Quaff* candidates' punches, when all the dues members, dead to the magazine, showed up resplendent in elbow-patched tweeds and tight collar pins, eager for martinis, as full of chatter and strut as a flock of whooping cranes bent on proving they were not extinct yet. Fred pitied Clayton, remembering the days when Fred alone, a respected if sophomore member, was insisting that the kid with the gag name be elected to the *Quaff*. The point was he could draw. Wonky, sure. He was right out of the funny papers. But at least his hands had fingers you could count. Pathetic, of course, to have the drawings framed, but his parents put him up to that—anybody who'd call a defenseless baby Clayton Clayton. . . . He wore cocoa-colored slacks and sport shirts. They'd wear out. If he was sullen, he was nervous. The point was, If we don't get anybody on the magazine who can draw we'll be forced to run old daguerreotypes of Chester Arthur and the Conkling Gang.

"Do you see much of Anna Spooner?" Clayton asked, referring back, perhaps unconsciously, to Fred's earlier mistake, his mention of the bad-taste income-tax plan of their friend A. D. Spooner, nicknamed "Anno Domini" and eventually "Anna."

"Once or twice. I haven't been back that long. He said he kept running into you at the Old Grads' Marching Society."

"Once in a while."

"You don't sound too enthusiastic."

"I hadn't meant to. I mean I hadn't meant not to. He's about the same. Same tie, same jokes. He never thanks me when I buy him a drink. I don't mean the money bothers me. It's one of those absurd little things. I shouldn't even mention it."

The waiter brought the beers. Fred stared into his Löwenbräu and breathed the word "Yeah."

"How long *have* you been back?"

"Two weeks, I guess."

"That's right. You said. Well, tell me about it. What've you been doing for three years?" His hands were folded firmly on the table, conference-style. "I'm interested."

Fred laughed outright at him. "There isn't that much. In the Army I was in Germany in the Quartermaster Corps."

"What did you do?"

"Nothing. Typed. Played blackjack, faro, Rook."

"Do you find it's changed you much?"

"I type faster. And my chest now is a mass of pornographic tattoos."

Clayton laughed a little. "It just interests me. I know that psychologically the effect on me of *not* going in is—is genuine. I feel not exactly guilty, but it's something that most of the men of our generation have gone through. Not to seems incom*plete*."

"It should, it should. I bet you can't even rev out a Bowling Bunting H-4 jet-cycle tetrameter. As for shooting a bazooka! Talk of St. Teresa's spiritual experiences—"

"It's impressive, how little it's changed you. I wonder if I'm changed. I do like the work, you know. People are always slamming advertising, but I've found out it's a pretty damn essential thing in our economy."

. . .

When the waiter came and set their platters before them, Clayton set to with a disconcerting appetite, forking in the food as often with his left hand as his right, pausing only to ask questions. "Then you went back to Europe."

"Then I went back to Europe."

"Why? I mean what did you do? Did you do any writing?"

In recent years Fred's literary intelligence had exerted itself primarily in the invention of impeccable but fruitless puns. Parcel Proust. Or Supple Simon. *Supple Simon met a Neiman / Fellow at the Glee Club, gleamin'. / Said Supple Simon, "Tell me, Fellow / Who made yellow roses yellow?"*

"Why, yes," Fred told Clayton. "Quite a bit. I've just completed a three-volume biography of the great Hungarian actress, Juxta Pose."

"No, actually. What did you do in Paris?"

"Actually, I sat in a chair. The same chair whenever I could. It was a straw chair in the sidewalk area of a restaurant on the Boulevard Saint-Germain. In the summer and spring the tables are in the open, but when it gets cold they enclose the area with large windows. It's best then. Everybody except you sits inside the restaurant, where it's warm. It's best of all at breakfast, around eleven of a nippy morning, with your *café* and *croissant avec du beurre* and your—what's the word?—*coude* all on a little table the size of a tray, and people outside the window trying to sell *ballons* to Christmas tourists."

"You must know French perfectly. It annoys the hell out of me that I don't know any."

"*Oui, pardon, zut!* and *alors!* are all you need for ordinary conversation. Say them after me: *oui*—the lips so—*par-don*—"

"The reason you probably don't write more," Clayton said, "is that you have too much taste. Your critical sense is always a jump ahead of your creative urge." Getting no response, he went on, "I haven't been doing much drawing either. Except roughing out ideas. But I plan to come back to it."

"I know you do. I know you will."

That was what Clayton wanted to hear. He loved work; it was all he knew how to do. His type saw competition as the spine of the universe. His *Quaff* career had been all success, all adaptation and good sense, so that in his senior year Clayton was president, and everybody said he alone was keeping silly old *Quaff* alive, when in fact the club, with its delicate ethic of frivolity, had withered under him. The right sort had stopped showing up.

Clayton had a forkful of hamburger poised between the plate and his mouth. "What does your father want?" In went the hamburger.

"My father seems to fascinate you. He is a thin man in his late fifties. He sits at one end of an enormous long room filled with priceless things. He is wearing a purple dressing gown and trying to read a book. But he feels the room is tipping. So he wants me to get in there with him and sit at the other end to keep the balance."

"No. I didn't mean—"

"He wants me to get a job. Know of one?" So the crucial question was out, stated like a rebuke.

Clayton carefully chewed. "What sort?"

"I've already been offered a position in Brauer, Chappell & Platt. A fine old law firm. I'd have to go to law school, a three-year slog. I'm looking for something with a lower entry bar."

"In publishing?"

Stalling, stalling. "Or advertising."

Clayton set down his fork. "Gee. You should be able to get something."

"I wouldn't know why. I have no experience. I can't use my father's contacts, that wouldn't be the game. Using him to pull out."

"I wish you had been here about six months ago. There was an opening up at Carson, and I asked Bim Blackwood, but he didn't want to make the jump. Speaking of Bim, he's certainly come along."

"Come along? Where to?"

"You know. He seems more mature. I feel he's gotten a hold of himself. His view of things is better proportioned."

"That's very perceptive. Who else do we know who's come along?"

"Well, I would say Harry Ducloss has. I was talking last week with a man Harry works for."

"He said he's come along?"

"He said he thought highly of him."

" 'Thought highly,' " Fred said. "Fermann was always thinking highly of people."

"I saw Fermann in the street the other day. Boy!"

"Not coming along?"

Clayton lifted his wrists so the waiter could clear away his plate. "It's just, it's"—with a peculiar intensity, as if Fred had often thought the same thing but never so well expressed it—"*something* to see those tin gods again."

"Would you young men like dessert?" the waiter asked. "Coffee?" To

Fred: "We have nice freshly baked *Apfelstrudel*. Or *Bienenstiche*. Very nice. They are made right in the kitchen ovens."

Fred deferred to Clayton. "Do you have time for coffee?"

Clayton craned his neck to see the clock. "Eight of two." He looked at Fred apologetically. "To tell the truth—"

"No coffee," Fred told the waiter.

"Oh, let's have it. It'll take just a few minutes."

"No. I have all afternoon but I don't want to delay a workingman."

"They won't miss me. I'm not *that* indispensable. Are you sure you don't want any?"

"Positive."

"All ri-i-ght," Clayton said in the dragged-out, musical tone of a parent acceding to a demand that will only do the child harm. "Could I have the check, please, waiter?"

"Certainly, sir." The something sarcastic about that "sir" was meant for Fred to see.

The check came to $3.79. When Fred reached for his wallet, Clayton said, "Keep that in your pocket. This is on me."

"Don't be a fool. The lunch was my idea."

"No, please. Let me take this."

Fred dropped a five-dollar bill on the table.

"No, look," Clayton said. "I know you have the money—"

"Money! We *all* have money."

Clayton, at last detecting anger, looked up timidly, his irises in the top of his too-big eyes, his chin tucked in. "Please. You were always quite kind to me. You went out on a limb for me. I knew that."

It was like a plain girl opening her mouth in the middle of a kiss. Fred wordlessly took back his five. Clayton handed four ones and two quarters to the waiter and said, "That's right."

"Thank *you*, sir."

"Thanks a lot," Fred said to Clayton as they moved toward the door.

"It's—" Clayton shook his head slightly. "You can get the next one."

"*Merci beaucoup, monsieur.*"

"I hope you didn't mind coming to this place."

"A great place. Vy, sey sought I vuss Cherman."

Outside, the pavement glittered as if cement were precious; Third Avenue, disencumbered of the el, seemed as spacious and queenly as a South American boulevard. In the harsh light of the two-o'clock sun, blemishes invisible in the shadows of the restaurant could be noticed on the skin of Clayton's face—an uneven redness on the flesh of the nose, two spots on his forehead, a flaky area partially hidden beneath an eyebrow. Clayton's feet tended to shuffle backward; he was conscious of his skin, or anxious to get back to work. Fred stood still, making it clear he was travelling in the other direction. Clayton did not feel free to go. "You really want a job in advertising?"

"Forget it. I don't really."

"I'll keep on the lookout."

"Don't go to any trouble, but thanks anyway."

"Thank *you*, for heaven's sake. I really enjoyed this. It's been good. Those were great old days."

For a moment Fred felt regret; he had an impulse to walk a forgiving distance with Clayton.

But his *Quaff* mate, helplessly offensive, sighed and said, "Well. Back to the salt mines."

"Well put." Fred lifted his hand in a benign ministerial gesture. "Ye are the salt of the earth. *La lumière du monde.* The light of the world. *Fils de St. Louis, montez au ciel!*"

Clayton, bewildered by the foreign language, backed a step away and with an uncertain jerk of his hand affirmed, "See you."

"*Oui. Le roi est un bon homme. Le crayon de ma tante est sur la table de mon chat. Baisez mes douces fesses. Merci. Merci.* Meaning thank you. Thanks again."

His Finest Hour

FIRST THEY HEARD, at eight p.m., the sound of a tumbler shattering. It was a distinct noise, tripartite: the crack of the initial concussion, the plump, vegetal *pop* of the disintegration, and the gossip of settling fragments. The glass might have been hurled within their own living room. To George this showed how thin the walls were. The walls were thin, the ceiling flaked, the furniture smelled ratty, the electricity periodically failed. The rooms were tiny, the rent was monstrous, the view was dull. George Chandler hated New York City. A native of Arizona, he felt that the unclean air here was crowded with spirits constantly cheating him. As the sincere Christian examines each occurrence for the fingerprints of the Providential hand, George read into each irregular incident—a greeting in the subway, an unscheduled knock on the door—possible financial loss. His rule was, Sit tight. This he did, not raising his eyes from the book with which he was teaching himself Arabic.

Rosalind, taller than her husband and less cautious, uncrossed her long legs and said, "Mrs. Irva must have dropsy."

George didn't want to talk about it, but he could seldom resist correcting her. "That wasn't dropped, honey. It was thrown."

Within the Irvas' rooms something wooden overturned, and it seemed a barrel was being rocked. "What do you suppose is wrong?" Rosalind had no book in her hand; evidently she had just been sitting there on the edge of the easy chair, waiting for something to listen to. She minded New York less than George. He hadn't noticed when she had come in from doing the dishes in the kitchenette. After supper every evening, he had his Arabic hour; during it he liked to be undisturbed. "Do you suppose something's the matter?" Rosalind persisted, slightly rephrasing her question in case he had heard it the first time.

George lowered his book with ostensible patience. "Does Irva drink?"

"I don't know. He's a chef."

"You think chefs don't drink. Just eat."

"I hadn't meant the two to be connected." Rosalind made the reply blandly, as if he had simply misunderstood.

George returned to his book. *The imperfect with the perfect of another verb expresses the future perfect: "Zaid will have written."* (Another glass was smashed, this time in a subdued way. A human voice could be heard, though not understood.) *When it is an independent verb, the subject is in the nominative and the complement in the accusative: "The apostle will be a witness against you."*

"Listen," Rosalind said with the doomsday hiss of a wife who at night smells gas. He listened, hearing nothing. Then Mrs. Irva began to scream.

George immediately hoped that the woman was joking. The noises she made might have meant anything: fear, joy, anger, exuberance. They might have been produced mechanically, by the rhythmic friction of a huge and useful machine. It seemed likely that they would stop.

"What are you going to do?" Rosalind asked him. She had risen and was standing close to him, giving off an oppressive aroma of concern.

"Do?"

"Is there anyone we could get?"

Their janitor, a slender, blue-jawed Pole, was in charge of three other buildings and a grammar school, and made his visitations around dawn and midnight. Their landlady, a grim Jewish widow, lived across the Park, at a more acceptable address. Their only neighbor other than the Irvas was a young Chinese student in a room at the back of the building, behind the Chandlers' bedroom; his examinations over, he had inked, in a beautiful black calligraphy, an Ohio forwarding address onto the wall above his mailbox, and left.

"No, Karl! Decency!" Mrs. Irva shouted. Her voice, mingled with confused tumbling effects, had lost its early brilliance. Now hoarse, now shrill, her mouthings were frantic. "No, no, no, no, please God no!"

"He's killing her, George. George, what *are you doing?*"

"Doing?"

"Must *I* call the police?" She glared at him with an icy contempt that her good nature melted in seconds. She went to the wall and leaned against it gracefully, her mouth wide open. "They're turning on the faucet," she whispered.

George asked, "You think we should interfere?"

"Wait. They're so quiet now."

"They—"

"*Sh-h-h!*"

George said, "She's dead, honey. He's washing the blood off his hands." Even in these taut circumstances, he could not resist kidding her. In her excitement she fell right in with it.

"He has, hasn't he?" she agreed. Then, seeing his smile, she said, "You don't think he has."

He squeezed her soft forearm kindly.

"George, he really has killed her," Rosalind said. "That's why there's no noise. Break in!"

"Stop and think, honey. How do you know they're not—?"

Her eyes widened as the thought dawned on her. "Are there really people like that?" She was confused; the room beyond the wall was silent; it seemed to George that he had brought the incident to a conclusion.

"Help, please help," Mrs. Irva called, rather calmly. Evidently this enraged her attacker, for in a moment she screamed with an intensity that choked her, as a baby at the height of a tantrum will nearly strangle. The noise, so irrational, such a poor reward for his patience, infuriated George; maddened into bravery, he opened his door and stepped out on the square of uncarpeted boards that served as an entrance hall to the three apartments. Standing there in its center, he seemed to see himself across a great span of time, as if he were an old man recalling a youthful exploit, recounting his finest hour. Fearless and lucid, he rapped his knuckles below the tacked card: *Mr. and Mrs. Karl Irva.* He sang out, "Everybody all right in there?"

"Be careful," Rosalind pleaded, at the same time resting her hands on his back, threatening a shove forward. He turned to rebuke her and was offended to discover that, because of his crouching and her tiptoeing, her eyes were much higher than his.

"Do you want to run in yourself?" he snapped and, without thinking, turned the knob of the Irvas' door. It had not been locked.

He swung the door in timidly, gaining an upright slice of an American interior: dimly figured carpet, a slice of easy chair, a straw wastebasket beneath a television set seen sidewise, a bamboo lamp, a propped-up photograph, ochre wall, bad green ceiling. Nothing reflected disturbance. From the large unseen portion of the room, Mrs. Irva called, "Go away—he has a knife!" At the sound of her voice George slammed the door shut instinctively, keeping his hand on the knob, as if the door were his shield.

"We must help her," Rosalind insisted.

"Get off my back," he said.

"Lord," Mrs. Irva moaned. George pushed open the door again, far enough to see one trace of disorder—an undershirt on a sofa arm. "Stay out!" the unseen woman called. "Get some help!" Again George closed the door.

A voice unmistakably Mr. Irva's asked without inflection, "Who have you fetched?" No answer was made. George was relieved. Though he had not seen Mrs. Irva, she might have supposed who he was. Footsteps unexpectedly thumped toward them, and the young couple fled to their own apartment, Rosalind skinning her husband's arm as she shut and bolted their door.

Here George, in telling the story, would hold his elbow outward and with the stiffened fingers of his other hand indicate precisely how the metal edge of the lock projection caught the flat area on the side of his forearm and scraped the skin blue, right through his shirt—ripped the shirt, too. A four-dollar shirt. His emphasis on this detail was clearly for his wife's benefit, but she failed to consider herself chided, and her wide triangular face expressed only a pretty anxiety to have the narrative continue. Rosalind, the daughter of a self-made Topeka contractor, was, unlike her husband, optimistic and un-self-conscious. Her gaps in judgment were startling. Over her tall and generous figure she wore noisy, big-patterned dresses. She mispronounced even simple names—Sart-er, Hāzlitt, Maughhum. In time, anticipating George's embarrassed correction, she came to pause and smile considerately at company before blundering. "And what I liked best were some pink fish and stick figures by a wonderful painter called . . . Klēē?" Yet she remembered some things excellently: shops and streets, characters in novels she had enjoyed, infielders, minor movie actors. When George's arm-scraping demonstration was completed, she would say, "One of the policemen who finally came looked just like John Ireland. Only younger, and not so nice."

It had been Rosalind who had called them; George was in the bathroom dabbing boric acid on his wound. Following the instructions on page one of the telephone directory, she dialed zero and said, "I want a policeman."

The operator, mistaking Rosalind for a teen-ager, asked, "You're sure now, honey?" She was always being called "honey."

"I really do."

The two cops who came twelve minutes later were young, and plainly in process of being wised up. They stood frowning in the Chandlers' doorway, shoulder to shoulder, just two decent ex-MPs trying to make an honest buck in a rotten world. First off, their eyes were very interested in the third finger of Rosalind's left hand. As soon as the one that looked a little like John Ireland saw the glint of gold there, he turned his attention to George, but the other one kept at it, trying to get his eyes around the ring, under it, giving it the acid bath.

"We were given this apartment number," John said. He looked at a slip of paper and read each figure separately, "Five, four, A."

"That door there," George said, unnecessarily pointing over the cop's shoulder. He was frightened; his hand shook badly. The cops took this in. "We heard a glass break about two hours ago, around eight o'clock."

"It's nine-oh-five now," the other cop said, looking at his wristwatch.

"It seems later," Rosalind said. The eyes of both policemen focused on her lips. The suspicious one grimaced with the effort of letting nothing about her voice—Midwestern, less snappy than the voices of most tarts— escape him.

George took courage from his wife's reminder that he had been given bad service. With new authority he described the sounds and screams they had heard. "There's been some rumpus after we called you, but for the last six minutes or so there's been no noise. We would have heard if there had been—these walls are so goddamn thin." He smiled slightly, to go with the swearing, but it won him no friends.

The other cop wrote scrunchily in a little pad. "Six minutes or *so*," he muttered. George had no idea why he had said six minutes instead of five. It did sound fishy. "Since you called us, you stayed in your room?"

"We didn't want to enrage him," George said.

John Ireland, his needle nose in the air, rapped delicately on the Irvas' door. Getting no answer, he toed it open. They all followed him in. The room was empty. One chair was overturned. Flakes and shards of glass glittered on the carpet. The disorder in the room was less than it should have been; the Chandlers were disappointed and shamed.

Yet now, when they seemed to themselves most vulnerable, the policemen failed to bully them. John Ireland undid the little snap on his holster. The other one said, "Blood on the sofa arm." Moving into the kitchenette, he said, in a murmur that carried, "Blood in the sink."

Blood in the sink! "Her cries became more and more frantic," George said.

John Ireland stuck his head out of a window.

The other cop asked, "Miss, is there a phone in here?"

"We never hear it ring," Rosalind said.

"We have a phone in our apartment," George told them. He was eager to succeed in his new role of cops' ally. That they all faced a common enemy was clear now. Perhaps Irva was behind the shower curtain, or stood outside the window, on the tiny concrete balcony, advertised as "terrace," which the Chandlers could see when they risked stepping out on their own. A sense of danger spread through the room like iodine in water. John Ireland moved quickly away from the window. The other cop came in from the kitchen. The three men gathered around the door, waiting, with a strained courtesy, for Rosalind to go first.

She stepped into the little hall and screamed; astounded, George leaped and embraced her from behind. The cops came after. On the first landing of the stairs going up to the next floor, at the level of their heads, Mrs. Irva crouched on all fours, staring at them, in her eyes an obscure and watery emotion. Her right forearm was solidly red with blood. How bright blood is! The right side of her slip was torn, exposing one breast. She said nothing.

What had happened, the Chandlers later decided, was that, after Mr. Irva left (they wondered in retrospect if a door hadn't slammed), Mrs. Irva, afraid, had run up the stairs and then, feeling weak, or curious about the conversations downstairs, had begun to crawl down again. There was a lot this didn't explain. Why should she have left the room *after* her husband had gone? On the other hand, if he had chased her up the stairs, why wasn't he still up there with her? One cop had gone up and looked and found nothing. Perhaps Irva had been up there when the police arrived and had sneaked down when they were all in his apartment. He could even have taken the elevator down, though this seemed a cool thing to do. The elevator in the building was self-service, and if anybody on a lower floor had rung, the elevator, with the criminal in it, would have stopped to let him on. Yet weren't the walls thin enough for them to have heard Mr. Irva's footsteps?

Mrs. Irva shed no light. She looked so bloody and dazed no one pressed her for information. The cops led her into the Chandlers' apartment and had her lie on the odorous sofa that had come with the place. John Ireland told Rosalind to bring two towels from the bathroom and asked George if there was any hard liquor around. When Rosalind brought the towels (guest towels, George saw), John tore one lengthwise to make a tourniquet. The Chandlers drank seldom, being both thrifty and health-minded, but they did have some sherry in the kitchen cabinet, behind a loaf of Pepperidge Farm bread. George poured some into a tumbler and handed it timidly to Mrs. Irva, by now rather dapper in her tourniquet.

Her broken slip strap had been knotted. She politely took a sip and said "Fine," though she drank no more. Rosalind brought in a yellow blanket from the bedroom. She spread it over Mrs. Irva, then went into the kitchen and began to heat water.

"What are you doing?" George asked her.

"He told me to make coffee," she said, nodding toward the cop who did not look like any movie star.

The one who did came and stood by George; having this blue uniform brush against him made George feel arrested. "Takes all types," he muttered uneasily.

"Buddy, this is nothing," the policeman answered. "This is tame. Stuff worse than this happens every minute in this city."

George began to like him. "I believe it," he said. "Hell, I was in the subway two weeks ago and a young kid took a swing at me."

John shook his head. "Buddy, that's nothing compared to what I see every day. Every day of the week."

The ambulance came before the coffee water boiled. Two Negroes were admitted. One was dressed in crisp white and carried a folded stretcher, which he unravelled with a conjurer's zest. The other, taller, logier, and perhaps recently from the South, wore a maroon sports jacket over the thin coat of his uniform. They eased Mrs. Irva into the stretcher; she was passive, but her mouth worked with fright when she felt herself being lifted. "Eeasy theah," the tall bearer said. The ambulance men had noticed on the way up that the elevator was too small for the stretcher; they had to walk down four flights, the front one holding the handles at shoulder height, both of them murmuring to their living burden.

The policemen lingered a moment in the elevator, facing the Chandlers, who hung together in the doorway like the host couple after a shindig. "O.K.," John said threateningly. "We've got statements." The elevator door sucked shut, and the cops dropped from view.

From their window George and Rosalind could see the pavement, dotted with foreshortened spectators. These human beings made an aisle down which the four public servants with their burden passed. Mrs. Irva, a yellow rectangle from five stories up, was inserted into the gray rectangle of the ambulance. The policemen got into their green-and-white-and-black Ford, and the two vehicles pulled away from the curb precisely together, like nightclub dancers. The ambulance moaned irritably and didn't begin to wail until it was down the block, out of sight.

George tried to return to his Arabic, but his wife was too excited, and they stayed awake until one o'clock, twisting and talking in bed. For the sixth time Rosalind regretted that she had not seen the one policeman tie Mrs. Irva's slip strap. Again George objected that most likely she tied it herself.

"With her arm cut to the bone?"

"It wasn't cut to the bone, honey. It was just a nick."

She pounded her pillow and dropped her head into it. "I know he did it. That would have been just like him. The one with the blunt nose was much sweeter."

"After the way he looked at you at the door? Didn't you see him look at your wedding ring?"

"At least he paid some attention to me. The other one was in love with *you*." Rosalind saw homosexuals everywhere.

Next morning, they could hear Mrs. Irva in her apartment, vacuuming. Several days later, George went down in the elevator with her. He asked her how she was feeling. No bandage showed; she was wearing long sleeves.

She beamed. "Very decent. And how's yourself and your lovely wife?"

"All right," George said, nettled to have his question taken as a pleasantry. He prodded her with "You got home all right?"

"Oh, yes," she said. "They were such nice men."

George didn't understand. The policemen? The doctors at the hospital? The fourth, the third, the second floors passed them in silence.

"My husband—" Mrs. Irva began. They had reached the ground floor; the door drew open.

"What about your husband?"

"Yes, he doesn't blame you and your wife in the slightest," she said, and then smiled as if she had just uttered a gracious invitation. And she hadn't even mentioned his blanket.

George missed that yellow blanket. For him, May nights in New York were chilly. He was here looking for a job that would take him to Arabia or some other Moslem place. The quest led him into the sinister, lavishly carpeted Embassies of Middle Eastern principalities, and into the sour waiting rooms of oil companies, export outfits, shippers, banks with overseas branches. Receptionists were impolite. Personnel men, pressing their fingertips together, pondered. George puzzled them. There was no space on their forms where Arabophilia could be entered.

It *was* hard to coördinate this passion for the desert with George's plump, stodgy face and wary personality. He seldom explained. But late in an evening spent with friends he might blurt out a description of how the Danakil fish for trocas in the Red Sea. "It's fantastic. They walk around on these reefs and dip their whole bodies underwater whenever they see one of these big snails. Then the wind coming down from Egypt dries them so their entire bodies are white with salt. The stuff they're walking on is brittle, and when it breaks through it scrapes the skin off their legs. Then poisonous jellyfish sting them, so as they move along they sing at the top of their lungs to scare them away. You can smell one of these fishing boats six miles away on account of the rotting snails in the hold. At night, they sleep on these little boats with millions of black flies getting into their food. Fifty miles away is the Arabian coast with nothing on it but pirates. And here are these guys singing to keep the poisonous jellyfish away. You wonder— I know what you're thinking." Nobody knew what George was thinking, but an expression on one of the faces turned toward him would make him think he was making a fool of himself.

He might, at another time, lambaste modern housing—the outskirts of Topeka covered with ugly pastel boxes arranged on phony curving streets; the supermarkets, the widening highways, the land going under all over. This was more like George: he advanced his intellect negatively, by extending his contempt. All movies were lousy, all politicians were crooked, public education in America was the world's worst, most novels were a waste of time, everybody on television was out for your money. George was proud of these perceptions; he had not discovered that at the "good" colleges (he was eager to admit that his own college had been no good) one liked everything—Western movies, corny music, trashy books, crooked politicos—and reserved distaste for great men.

A friend looking through the Chandlers' library (mostly old political-science textbooks, and paperback mysteries, which Rosalind chain-read) might pull down, because it alone suggested Arabia, *Hashish*, by Henri de Monfreid, and find underlined—the underlining, thick soft pencil, was unmistakably George—the sentence *The heat of the day breathed out from the walls and ground like an immense sigh of relief.* But, facing a preoccupied executive across a glass-topped desk, George could only say, with a compromising snicker, "I guess it *is* silly, but ever since I was a kid I've been fascinated by those places."

"No, I don't think it's silly," would be the answer.

A month after the Irvas' fight, Rosalind stood outside their door and greeted George at his homecoming with, "The most wonderful thing has happened!"

"I bet." He was coming up the stairs; a woman who lived on the third floor had stepped into the elevator with him, and since the machine tended to return to the ground floor after one stop, he had got out with her and walked up two flights. His day had been frustrating. The most promising possibility, working with the United States delegation to a trade fair in Basra, appeared to have fallen through. It had taken him three-quarters of an hour to see Mr. Guerin again, and then he was told nothing but that funds were limited. He was so depressed that he had gone into a thirty-eight-cent movie, but it was something old with Barbara Stanwyck and so bad he had to leave, feeling sick. In a luncheonette on East Thirty-third Street he was charged $1.10 for a turkey sandwich, a glass of milk, and a cup of coffee. When he gave the cashier a five-dollar bill, she insisted that he also produce a dime and three pennies for tax, and then dealt the four dollars change not into his waiting hand but, rudely, onto the counter. As if he were covered with germs. On his way home, the mobs choking the subways, clustering at intersections, dodging, shoving, avoiding eye contact, seemed one huge contamination. It was his eleventh week of hunting. Rosalind's department-store job, which was for only six hours a day now that the Easter rush had subsided, did not quite take care of rent and food. The Chandlers were eating into their savings at the rate of fifty dollars a month.

Rosalind stood between him and their door. This annoyed George; he was tired. "Wait," Rosalind said. Holding up a palm, she prolonged her own delight. "Have you seen either of the Irvas lately? Think."

"I never see *him*. Once in a while Mrs. and I get caught in the elevator together." After his first conversation, he had not tried to sound Mrs. Irva out on the incident, and there seemed to be so little connection between the crazed and half-naked sufferer of that night and this compact little woman, with her hair going white in stripes and black buttons down the front of her blouse and an orange mouth painted up over the natural edge of her upper lip, that it was easy for George to discuss with her the weather and the poor way the building was run, as if they had nothing more important between them.

"What *is* this routine?" George asked after Rosalind had stood silent for a moment, on her face a great, loving smile.

"Behold, effendi," she said, opening the door.

Inside the room George saw flowers everywhere, white, pink, yellow, tall flowers, motionless, in vases, pitchers, and wastebaskets, lying in bundles on tables and chairs and on the floor. George never knew the names of flowers, but these were a public sort, big and hardy. Benevolence breathed from their long, ignorant, complex faces. The air in the room had a flower-shop coolness.

"They came in a station wagon. Mrs. Irva said they were used to decorate a banquet last night, and the man in charge said the chef should have them. Mr. Irva thought it would be nice to give them to us. To show that everything was right between our families, Mrs. Irva said."

George was puzzled, stopped. His mind, swept clean of assertion, knew nothing but the flowers; they poured through his eyes. Later, in the stink and strangeness of Basra, whenever the homesick couple tried to recall America, the image that first and most vividly came to George was that of those massed idiot beauties.

A Trillion Feet of Gas

OLD MAN FRAELICH, as soon as they entered his room, rose in his pearl-pale suit and intoned flatulently, "John, let's you and I go downstairs."

Another man, in black, got to his feet.

"That would be rude," Mrs. Fraelich stated, more as a simple fact than as a reprimand, though it might have been her influence—it was hard to guess how much power she had over her husband—that induced Fraelich to shake hands with his three young guests, listening to their names and gazing above their heads while his puffy, beringed hand, apparently cut off from his brain and acting on its own decent instincts, floated forward from his vest. Under those averted eyes Luke felt like a rich pastry mistakenly offered to an ill man. Had Fraelich forgotten the several times they had met before?

Kathy, introducing her guests to her father-in-law with the angular exaggerations of a girl whose beauty is her sole defense, also implied they were strangers. "Father, this is Elizabeth Forrest, and Luther Forrest."

"You remember Luke from school," Tim told him.

"Of course I have," Fraelich said evenly, changing his son's verb and tilting back his head, as if into a pillow, so that he looked sicker than ever; his complexion had the sheen of a skin sweating out a fever. Luke suddenly got the idea that Liz's being pregnant had offended him.

"And Mr. Boyce-King from England," Kathy continued.

"Just King," Donald corrected, blushing quickly. "Don King. *Bryce* is the middle name."

"*Not* a hyphen!" Kathy cried, insisting, in the midst of her in-laws and her husband's friends, on her right to be natural and gay. Fatigue added to her lean charm all the romantic suggestions of exhaustion. Luke had been told she was undergoing analysis. "Pardon *me*. I only heard your name once over the phone."

"It's awfully good of you to have me," Donald said mechanically.

"He looks like a hyphen person, doesn't he?" Liz said, helping the other girl out, and unwittingly reflecting the ironic discussions she and Luke had had about their English guest in the few hours since Monday when Donald had not been with them. "I think it's his eyebrows."

In the background Mrs. Fraelich had got to her feet, swinging her arms in boredom or exasperation. As she did so, the décolletage of her dress—a tube of soft blue cloth with big holes cut for the throat and arms, as in old copies of *Vanity Fair*—wandered alarmingly over her gaunt, freckled chest. She offered her second fact to the group. "Here is Mr. Born."

For the first time Fraelich showed animation. "Yes," he announced, and his voice ballooned, "we can't forget John Born." The man in black, stout but solid, gave each of the young people a firm handshake and a grunt of pleasure. His suit and mustache were identically dark. Luke was delighted that Donald was meeting, even wordlessly, an authentic specimen of the Manhattan rich. Fraelich was rich but scarcely authentic.

The old people scattered to other quarters of the duplex, and the young people were left alone with the bulwark-style leather furniture, Mrs. Fraelich's Japanese watercolors, and the parabolic sub-ceiling suspended and glowing *à la* restaurant.

"Please forgive the hyphen; it's a fantasy of mine that all Englishmen have double names," Kathy said to Donald, who, with the abrupt ease of the British, was examining, his head atilt, the spines of the books on the shelves.

"Not at all. I enjoyed it."

The smug inappropriateness of the remark tipped them into a difficult silence. An awkward evening seemed foreshadowed. Most of the strands of acquaintance between the five were tenuous. Luke had known Tim at college, and had met Donald in England, and the two wives were, considering the slightness of their acquaintance, fond of each other. They made the best of it, chatting and sipping alcoholic drinks just like grownups. Luke kept wanting to suggest that they play Monopoly. Fraelich must have a set, and it would be a good American game for Donald to learn. Dinner evidently would be quite late. A new factor, hunger, was added to the nervous unrest in Luke's stomach.

He talked to Tim of common friends. Neither had heard anything from Irv. Preston Wentworth, Tim thought, was on the West Coast. Leo Bailley *had* been in town. It was strange how completely you could lose sight of men you saw every day in college. Our generation just doesn't write letters, Luke offered.

Donald said he thought that Americans phoned everywhere, or had little boys in wingèd boots carrying singing messages.

Kathy asked Liz how she felt. Liz said that she felt just the same, but clumsier; that it was surprising how much you felt like your old self; and that she was looking forward to the contented-cow stage mentioned in the motherhood books. Donald laughed at "motherhood books." Luke saw Kathy send Liz, by wingèd facial expression, a message that probably read, "We're thinking about babies, too, but Timothy . . ." "How nice or sad," Liz's face sent back. Donald, trapped near the intersection of these baby-looks, experienced another flash of discomfiture and blushed stuffily. He had the oval slant eyes and full-fleshed lips of the British intellectual, and the raw sloping forehead.

Tim Fraelich, sensing that his three guests had been together so much that in relation to each other they were speechless, assumed the role of topic starter. He mentioned the Olympic Games. Luke joined in gratefully. Since his interceding with, "You remember Luke from school," Luke loved Tim, his slow considerate mind and his ugly laborer's face. The blessing of money, in combination with modest endowments otherwise, had made Tim very gentle. In the Areté Club—he had been president when Luke was a sophomore—he had hated that anyone must be blackballed, whereas Luke, who knew that his own election had been close, proudly and recklessly wielded the veto.

The Olympic discussion died soon. Luke couldn't think of any stars except Perry O'Brien, and the vaulting preacher Richards, and the young Negro—what was his name?—who jumped seven feet.

Swift and strong Americans, Donald said, appeared on the scene like waves of industrial produce.

But it was the Commonwealth, they hastened to assure him, that demolished the four-minute mile. The Forrests, their year in Oxford, had lived a block away from the Iffley track, where Bannister had run the first one. Donald had been at Oxford at the time but naturally hadn't bothered to attend the meet. He seemed to feel a certain distinction lay in this.

Tim asked his English guest what he had seen of New York so far—if he had seen such-and-such an interesting place. Lamentably, nothing Tim named had Donald seen. The Forrests had been poor guides, though they had worked hard. Preceded by a radiogram, Donald had arrived on a Dutch liner, penniless and in the show-me mood of a cultural delegation. With the politico-literary precocity of Oxford youth, he had already been published in one of the British liberal weeklies, and he seemed to imagine that visiting the transatlantic land mass would constitute a scoop, Mrs. Trollope alone preceding him. Cruelly harried by their sense of official responsibility, the Forrests, after displaying to him their own selves— typical of the rising generation, he with a job in media and she with Scandinavian tastes, favoring natural wood and natural childbirth—had arranged parties and suppers where the allegorical figures of Graduate Student, Unwed Secretary, Struggling Abstract Painter, Intellectual Catholic, Jewish Would-Be Actress, and Fledgling Corporation Lawyer filed across the stage of their visitor's preconceptions. Luke described in sociological detail his childhood in a small Ohio town, and Liz contributed what she knew of the caste system in Massachusetts. Donald, though polite, was rarely moved. Luke and Liz whispered guiltily in bed at night if, when the guests were gone, Donald did not withdraw his notebook from his coat pocket and take it to the sofa with a pencil and his final drink of the day. He drank steadily and soberly. In the daytime, Liz, saying that pregnant women should walk lots anyway, took Donald hunting for useful sights. She led him through Chinatown, the Village, Wall Street, the Lower East Side, and at Luke's evening homecoming complained, as Donald sat sipping joylessly, his silence lending assent, that everything is just buildings and cars, that she felt so sorry for Donald, being stuck with them.

Their guest claimed he did plan to leave. He wanted to see the "Southland," and especially "your plains." But no trip could begin until a money order arrived from somewhere—Canada, they thought he said. The Forrests had nicknamed it "the packet from France." In the close company the three kept, the joke had come into the open. For several breakfasts, Luke had asked, "The packet from France arrive?" Liz, noting Donald's diminishing response, warned her husband that he gave the impression of hinting. Luke said it wasn't a hint, it was a pleasantry, and anyway, it didn't look to him as if Donald was very sensitive to hints or indeed to anything.

It was true, the Englishman's calm—so cheering in Oxford, so strong that, even meeting him on High Street, against a background of steelworkers on bicycles and whey-faced bus queues, you smelled pipe smoke, and felt the safety of his room in Magdalen, with the old novels in many thin volumes and the window giving onto the deer park and the drab London magazines stacked like dolls' newspapers on the mantel—in America had become a maddening quiescence, as if the thicker sunlight of this more southern country were a physical weight on his limbs. He had protested the bother of being included in this dinner engagement, but he had not suggested, as they had hoped, that he could manage a night on his own.

"No," he was saying to Tim, "they haven't taken me to Louie's. You say it's an interesting place. Does it have lots of ethos? You Americans are always talking about ethos. Margaret Mead is something of your White Goddess over here, isn't she?"

"Mamie is," Kathy suddenly said, thrusting her fingers into the hair at her temples and laughing when the others did.

Donald said that once again the American people had proven themselves idiots in the eyes of the world. Luke said it would be a different story in 1960. "Wait till 'sixty, wait till 'sixty," Donald said. "That's all you people think about. The 1960 model of Plymouth car; the population in 1960. You're in love with the future." He touched, in an unconscious gesture, the breast of his coat, to make sure the stiffness of the notebook was there. Luke smiled and saw them all through Donald's eyes: the mild, homely heir; his fretful, leggy wife; Liz with her half-formed baby; Luke himself with his half-baked success—pale, pale. Poor Americans, these, for the *New Statesman & Nation*. What Donald couldn't see that Luke could was how well he, Donald, his sensible English shoes cracked and his wool clothes frazzled, blended into their pastel frieze.

The man introduced to them as Mr. Born walked into the room. "Looks like Ah'll be getting a ride," he said to Tim. "With your pa and ma." His voice, as Luke had expected, was rich and grainy, but the accent forced a slight revision of his first idea of the man. He was not a New Yorker. In the black suit, Born's body, solid as a barrel, stood out with peculiar force against the linen-covered wall, where Mrs. Fraelich's Japanese prints made patches of vague color.

"Would you like a Scotch-and-water, John?" Tim asked. "Or cognac?" Mr. Born shook his massive head—severed from his body, it might have weighed forty pounds—and held up his square, exquisitely clean hand to halt all liquor traffic. In the other he gripped a heavy cigar, freshly lighted.

"We've been chewing over the election," Tim said.

"You desahd who won it?"

The young people made a fragile noise of laughter.

"We've been deciding who should have won it," Donald said, cross spots appearing on his cheekbones and forehead.

"Yeass," Mr. Born said, simultaneous with the hissing of the cushions as he settled into a leather armchair. "There was never any doubt about the way it would go in Texas. The betting in Houston wasn't on *who*"—his lips pushed forward on the prolonged "who"—"would get it but at what *taam* the other fella would con*cede*." He rotated the cigar a half-circle, so the burning end was toward himself. "A lotta money was lost in Houston while Adlai was making that speech so good. They thought, you see, it would be *soon*er."

"How did *you* do?" Donald asked tactlessly, as if this were an exhibit they had arranged for him.

"Noo." The Texan scratched his ear fastidiously and beamed. "I had no money on it."

"What *is* the situation out there? Politically? One reads the Democrats are in bad shape," Donald said.

The broad healthy face bunched as he pleasantly studied the boy. "What they say, Lyndon didn't show up too good at the convention. We aren't all that proud of him. As I heard it expressed, the feeling was, Let those two run and get killed and get rid of 'em that way. That's the way I've heard it expressed: Run those two, and let 'em get killed."

"Really!" Kathy exclaimed. Then, surprised at herself, she bit her lower lip coquettishly and crossed her legs, calling attention to them. Luke liked her legs because above the lean and urban ankles the calves swelled to a country plumpness.

"The American scramble," Donald murmured.

Luke, afraid Mr. Born would feel hostility in the air, asked why the South hadn't pushed someone like Gore instead of Kennedy.

"Gore's not *pop*ular. The answer's very simple: The South doesn't have anyone big enough. 'Cept Lyndon. And he's sick. Heart attack. No, they're in a bad way down there. They got the leaders of both houses, and they're in a bad way."

"Wouldn't there be a certain amount of anti-Catholic sentiment stirred up if Kennedy were to run?" Tim asked. His mother, for a period in her youth, had been a convert to the Church.

Mr. Born puffed his cigar and squinted at his friend's son through the smoke. "I think we've outgrown that. I think we've outgrown that."

The rough bulge of Donald's forehead burned with political antagonism. He blurted, "You're pleased with the way things went?"

"Well. I voted for Aahk. Not particularly proud of it, though. Not particularly proud of it. He vetoed our gas bill." Everyone laughed, for no clear reason. "If he had it to do over again, he wouldn't *do* it."

"You think so?" Donald asked.

"I know it for a *faact*. He's said so. He wants the bill. And Adlai, he wouldn't promise if he got in he wouldn't try to get the Lands back to Washington. So we voted Aahk in; he was the best we could get."

Donald pointed at him gingerly. "You, of course, don't want the Tidelands to revert to the federal government."

"They *cain't*. There won't be any gas. It's off twelve percent from last year now, for the *needs*. You see— Are you all interested in this?"

The group nodded hastily.

"I have a trillion feet of gas. It's down there. In the ground. It's not gone to go away. Now, I made a contract to sell that gas at eighteen cents in Chicago. In the city of Chicago there are maybe twelve thousand meters now that don't have adequate supply. I wanted to pipe it up, from Texas. That was two years ago. They won't let me do it. I've been in Washington, D.C., for most of those two years, trying to see a bill passed that'll *let* me do it." He released some smoke and smiled. Washington, the implication was, had agreed with him.

Donald asked why they wouldn't let him do it. Mr. Born explained in detail—clearly and kindly, and even got to his feet to explain—federal agencies, state commissions, wellhead quotas, costs of distillate, dry holes ("They don't allow you for drah holes *after*; the ones up *to*, O.K., but then they don't recognize 'em"), and the Socialist color of thinking in Washington. On and on it went, a beautiful composition, vowel upon vowel, occasional emphasis striking like an oboe into a passage of cellos. The coda came too soon: "But the point, the point is this: If they *do* pass it, then fine. I'm contracted out; I'm willing to stick by it. But if they *don't*— if they don't, then I sell it for more *insaahd Texas*. That's how demand is gone up."

Luke realized with delight that here, not teen feet away, walked and talked a bugaboo—a Tidelands lobbyist, a States' Righter, a Purchaser of Congressmen, a Pillar of Reaction. And what had he proved to be, this stout man holding his huge head forward from his spine, bisonlike? A companion all simplicity and courtesy, bearing without complaint—and all for the sake, it seemed, of these young people—the unthinkable burden of a trillion feet of gas. Luke could not remember the reasons for governmental control of big business any better than he could recall when drunk the defects of his own personality. With a gentle three-finger grip on his cigar, Mr. Born settled back into the armchair, the viewpoints alternative to his hanging vaporized in the air around him, a flattering haze.

The next minute, Mr. and Mrs. Fraelich came and took John Born away, though not before old man Fraelich, his bulbous gray voice droning anxiously, exuded every fact he knew about the natural-gas industry. Mr. Born listened politely, tilting his stogie this way and that. The possibility occurred to Luke that, as Mr. Born owned a trillion feet of gas, Mr. Fraelich owned John Born.

"He's really a hell of a nice guy," Tim said when the older people had gone.

"Oh, he was wonderful!" Liz said. "The way he stood there, so big in his black suit—" She encircled an area with her arms and, without thinking, thrust out her stomach.

Kathy asked, "Did he mean a trillion feet of gas in the pipe?"

"No, no, you fluff," Tim said, giving her a bullying hug that jarred Luke. "*Cubic* feet."

"That still doesn't mean anything to me," Liz said. "Can't you compress gas?"

"Where does he keep it?" Kathy asked. "I mean have it."

"In the *ground*," Luke said. "Weren't you listening?" But she wasn't his to scold.

Kathy kept at it. "Gas like you burn?"

"A trillion," Donald said, tentatively sarcastic. "I don't even know how many ciphers are in it."

"Twelve in America," Luke told him. "In Britain, more. Eighteen."

"You Americans are so good at figgers. Yankee ingenuity."

"Watch it, Boyce-King. If you British don't learn how to say 'figures' we'll pipe that gas under your island and float it off into space."

Though no one else laughed, Luke himself did, at the picture of England as a red pieplate skimming through space, fragments chipping off until nothing remained but the dome of St. Paul's. And after they had sat down to dinner, he continued, he felt, to be quite funny, frequently at the expense of "Boyce-King." He felt back in college, full of novel education and undulled ambition. Kathy Fraelich laughed until her hand shook over the soup. It was good to know he could still, impending fatherhood or not, make people laugh. ". . . but the *great* movies are the ones where an idol teeters, you know, all grinning and bug-eyed"—he wobbled rigidly in his chair and then with horrible slow menace fell forward, breaking off the act just as his nose touched the rim of the water glass— "and then crumbles all over the screaming worshippers. They don't make scenes like that in British movies. They save their idols and pawn them off as Druid shrines. Or else scratch 'Wellington' across the front. Ah, you're a canny race, Boyce-King."

After dinner they watched two television plays, which Luke ingeniously defended as fine art at every turn of the action, Donald squirming and blinking and the others not even listening but attending to the screen. Liz in her passive pregnant state didn't resist TV. The young Fraelichs nuzzled together in one fat chair. The black-and-white figures— Luke kept saying "figgers"—were outlined on Fraelich's costly color set with rainbows.

Luke, at the door, thanked their hosts enthusiastically for the excellent meal, the educational company, the iridescent dramas. The two couples expanded the last goodbye with a discussion of where to live eventually. They decided, while Donald nodded and chuckled uneasily on the fringe of the exchange, that nothing was as important as the children's feeling secure in a place.

In the taxi, Luke, sorry that in the end Donald had seemed an extra party, said to him, "Well, we've shown you the Texas Billionaire. You've gazed into the heart of a great nation."

"Did you notice his hands?" Liz asked. "They were really beautiful." She was in a nice, tranquil mood, bathed in maternal hormones.

"It was extraordinary," Donald said, squeezed in the middle and uncertain where his arms should go, "the way he held you all, with his consistently selfish reasoning."

Luke put his arm on the back of the seat, including his visitor in a non-tactile embrace and touching Liz's neck with his fingers. The packet from France, he reckoned, was on the way. The head of the cabby jerked as he tried to make out his passengers in the rearview mirror. "You're afraid," Luke said loudly, so the cabbie, democratically, could hear, "of our hideous vigor."

Dear Alexandros

TRANSLATION *of a letter written by Alexandros Koundouriotis, Needy Child No. 26,511 in the records of Hope, Incorporated, an international charity with headquarters in New York.*

July, 1959

Dear Mr. and Mrs. Bentley:

Dear American Parents, first of all I want to inquire about your good health, and then, if you ask me, tell you that I am keeping well, for which I thank God, and hope that it is the same with you. May God keep you always well, and grant you every happiness and joy. With great eagerness I was looking forward again this month to receiving a letter from you, but unfortunately I have again not received one. So I am worried about you, for I am longing to hear about you, dear American Parents. You show such a great interest in me, and every month I receive your help. Over here it is very hot at this time of the year, for we are in the heart of the summer. The work out in the fields is very tiring, as I hear the older people saying. As for me, when I have no work at home I go down to the sea for a swim, and enjoy the sea with my friends. For at this time of the year the sea is lovely. So much for my news. Vacations continue, until it is time for the schools to reopen, when with new strength and joy we shall begin our lessons again. Today that I am writing to you I received again the $8.00 that you sent me, for the month of July, and I thank you very much. With this money I shall buy whatever I need, and we shall also buy some flour for our bread. In closing, I send you greetings from my granny and my sister, and hope that my letter finds you in good health and joy. I shall be looking forward to receiving a letter from you, to hear about you and how you are spending your summer. I greet you with much affection.

Your son,
Alexandros

Reply from Kenneth Bentley, American Parent No. 10,638.

September 25

Dear Alexandros:

We are all sorry that you should worry about us because you have not received a letter from us. I fear we are not as regular in writing as you are, but the grandly named organization which delivers our letters seems to be very slow, they take about three months to deliver. Perhaps they send them by way of China.

You describe the Greek summer very beautifully. It is autumn now in New York City. The sad little trees along the somewhat sad little street where I live now are turning yellow, the ones that are not already dead. The pretty girls that stride along the broad avenues are putting on hats again. In New York the main streets run north and south so that there is usually a sunny side and a shady side and now people cross the street to be on the sunny side because the sun is no longer too warm. The sky is very blue and some evenings, after I eat in a drugstore or restaurant, I walk a few blocks over to the East River to watch the boats and look at Brooklyn, which is another section of this excessively large city.

Mrs. Bentley and I no longer live together. I had not intended to tell you this but now the sentence is typed and I see no harm in it. Perhaps already you were wondering why I am writing from New York City instead of from Greenwich, Connecticut. Mrs. Bentley and little Amanda and Richard all still live in our nice home in Greenwich and the last time I saw them looked very well. Amanda now is starting kindergarten and was very excited and will never wear dungarees or overalls any more but insists on wearing dresses because that is what makes little girls look nice, she thinks. This makes her mother rather angry, especially on Saturdays and Sundays when Amanda plays mostly in the dirt with the neighbor children. Richard walks very well now and does not like his sister teasing him. As who does? I go to see them once a week and pick up my mail and your last letter was one of the letters I picked up and was delighted to read. Mrs. Bentley asked me to answer it, which I was delighted to do, because she had written you the last time. In fact I do not think she did, but writing letters was one thing she was not good at, although it was her idea for us to subscribe to Hope, Incorporated, and I know she loves you very much, and was especially happy to learn that you plan to begin school with "new strength and joy."

There has been much excitement in the United States over the visit of the head of Soviet Russia, Mr. Khrushchev. He is a very talkative and self-confident man and in meeting some of our own talkative and self-confident politicians there has been some friction, much of it right on television where everybody could see. My main worry was that he would be shot but I don't think he will be shot any more. His being in the country has been a funny feeling, as if you have swallowed a penny, but the American people are so anxious for peace that they will put up with small discomforts if there is any chance it will do any good. The United States, as perhaps you will learn in school, was for many years an isolated country and there still is a perhaps childish belief that if other nations, even though we are a great power, leave us alone, then the happiness will return.

That was not a very good paragraph and perhaps the man or woman who kindly translates these letters for us will kindly omit it. I have a cold in my chest that mixes with a great deal of cigarette smoke and makes me very confused, especially after I have been sitting still for a while.

I am troubled because I imagine I hear you asking, "Then were Mr. and Mrs. Bentley, who sent me such happy letters from America, and photographs of their children, and a sweater and a jackknife at Christmas, telling lies? Why do they not live together any more?" I do not wish you to worry. Perhaps in your own village you have husbands and wives who quarrel. Perhaps they quarrel but continue to live together but in America where we have so much plumbing and fast automobiles and rapid highways we have forgotten how to live with inconveniences, although I admit that my present mode of life is something of an inconvenience to me. Or perhaps in your schooling, if you keep at it, and I hope you will, the priests or nuns will have you read the very great Greek poem the Iliad, in which the poet Homer tells of Helen who left her husband to live with Paris among the Trojans. It is something like that with the Bentleys, except that I, a man, have gone to live among the Trojans, leaving my wife at home. I do not know if the Iliad is a part of your schooling, and would be curious to know. Your nation should be very proud of producing masterpieces which the whole world can enjoy. In the United States the great writers produce works which people do not enjoy, because they are so depressing to read.

But we were not telling lies: Mrs. Bentley and Amanda and Richard and I were very happy and to a degree are yet. Please continue to send us your wonderful letters, they will go to Greenwich, and we will all enjoy them. We will continue to send you the money for which you say you are grateful, though the money we give you this way is not a tenth of the money we used to spend for alcoholic drinks. Not that Mrs. Bentley and I drank all these alcoholic drinks. We had many friends who helped us, most of them very tedious people, although perhaps you would like them more than I do. Certainly they would like you more than they presently like me.

I am so happy that you live near the sea where you can swim and relax from the tiring work of the fields. I was born far inland in America, a thousand miles from any ocean, and did not come to love the sea until I was grown up and married. So in that sense you are luckier than I. Certainly to be near the sea is a great blessing, and I remember often thinking how nice it was that my own children should know what it was to run on the sand of the pretty though not large beach at Greenwich, and to have that invigorating, cold, "wine-dark," as your Homer writes, other world to contemplate.

Now I must end, for I have agreed to take a young woman out to dinner, a young woman who, you will be interested to hear, is herself partially Greek in origin, though born in America, and who has much of the beauty of your race. But I have already cruelly burdened our translator. My best wishes to your granny, who has taken such good care of you since your mother died, and to your sister, whose welfare and good health is such a large concern in your heart.

Sincerely,
Kenneth Bentley

P.S.: In looking back at the beginning of my letter I see with regret that I have been unkind to the excellent organization which has made possible our friendship with you, which has produced your fine letters, which we are always happy to receive and which we read and reread. If we have not written as often as we should have it is our fault and we ask you to forgive us.

The Doctor's Wife

"SHARKS?" The tip of the doctor's wife's freckled nose seemed to sharpen in the sparkling air. Her eyes, momentarily rendered colorless by thought, took up the green of the Caribbean; the plane of the water intersected her throat. "Yes, we have some. Big dark fellows, too."

Ralph, hanging beside her, squatting on buoyance, straightened up, splashing, and tried to survey the beryl depths around him. His sudden movements rendered even the immediate water opaque. The doctor's wife's surprisingly young laughter rang out.

"You Americans," she said, "so nervy," and with complacence pushed a little deeper into the sea, floating backward while the water gently bubbled around her mouth. She had a small face, gone freckled and rosy in this climate; her stringy auburn hair had been bleached by daily sea-bathing. "They rarely come in this far," she said, tilting her face upward and speaking to the sky. "Only in the turtle-killing season, when the blood draws them in. We're fortunate. Our beaches go out shallowly. Over in St. Martin, now, the offshore water is deep, and they must be careful."

She turned and, with the casual paddling stroke of a plump woman who floats easily, swam smiling toward him. "A shame," she said, her voice strained by the effort of curving her throat to keep her lips free, "Vic Johnson is gone. He was a dear soul. The old Anglican vicar." She pronounced "vicar" rather harshly, perhaps humorously. She stood up beside Ralph and pointed to the horizon. "Now, *he*," she said, "used to swim far out into the bay, he and his great black dog, Cato. Vic would swim straight out, until he couldn't move a muscle, and then he would float, and grab Cato's tail, and the dog would pull him in. Honestly, it was a sight, this fat old Englishman, his white hair streaming, coming in on the tail of a dog. He never gave a thought to sharks. Oh, he'd swim *way* out, until he was just a dot."

They were waist-deep in the sea, and at a motion from Ralph they walked toward shore together. The calm warm water leaped from their strides. She was small beside him, and her voice piped at his shoulder. "I'm sorry he's gone," she said. "He was a lovely old gentleman. He had been here forty years. He loved the island."

"I can see why he would," Ralph said. He turned his head to review the crescent of landscape around the beach, as if through his fresh eyes the doctor's wife could renew—what seemed to him to need renewing—her sense of the island's beauty. The white beach was empty. The natives used it only as a path. Their homes were set behind the ragged hedge of sea grape that rimmed the sand. Bits of tarpaper, pink-painted cement, corrugated roofing reddened by rust, wooden walls weathered to silver and patched by flattened kerosene tins, shacks on stilts, and unfinished cinderblock shells peeped above the dull, low foliage. There were few flowers. This was January. But the clusters of coconuts nested under the shuffling branches of the palms, and the high small puffy clouds, like the quick clouds of spring in his own climate, suggested that here the season of bloom and the season of harvest were parallel and perpetual: germination and fruition ceaselessly intertwined. There were no mountains in the view. The island was low; when they came in on the airplane, it seemed a two-dimensional twin, or sketch, of St. Martin, which thrust from the sea like a set of Vermont mountaintops. There, the beaches were steep and dangerous; here, they were safe. There, Dutchmen and Frenchmen built bustling hotels and restaurants to entice American dollars; here, strangers rarely came. Here, even the place names were bestowed without enterprise or effort. East End, West End, The Road, The Forest—thus the island was geographically divided. The uninhabited ridge of scrub and coral rubble that formed one side of the bay was named High Hill. The village was called The Bay. The orange cliffs on the other side of the bay were called The Cliffs. During these short winter days the sun set on a diagonal above them and, between six and seven o'clock, touched the sea at the fingertips of the most distant arm of land. Yet, after the sun had drowned, light, itself lazy, lingered among the huts and the oleander bushes. Now it was late afternoon; the tiny tropical sun, not yet swollen to red, patiently poured white brilliance down through the hushed air. The air was as soft, as kind, as the water; there was no hostility in either. The two elements, as Ralph came out of one into the other, seemed tints of a single enveloping benevolence.

"Oh, yes, but not merely that," the doctor's wife said. "He loved the people. He built them three churches and, oh, did all manner of good works. We're talking of Reverend Johnson," she explained to Eve, who had remained on the beach with the children. "The Anglican padre. He retired last year and went back to England. Sussex, I think."

"He loved the people?" Eve asked. She had heard. Voices carried well in the air, disturbed, during the day, by only the whispering beat of the surf and infrequent voices calling in English made musical by an unintelligible lilt.

The doctor's wife dropped down on the sand. "These are my children," she intoned gruffly. She chased the abrupt parody away with her sharp laughter. "Oh, yes, he loved them. He gave his life to them." The youthful excitement of her voice and the innocent clarity of her eyes went queerly with her body, which was middle-aged. Her plump legs had gone lumpy and sodden, and her small face was finely wrinkled, each wrinkle accented by a line of white where the pinched skin had evaded the sun. "He didn't have any children of his own," she thought to add. "Just this dreadful dog Cato. Such a funny old man. You might have liked him. I'm sure you never see his kind in America."

"I know we would have liked him," Eve said. "Hannah often mentions Reverend Johnson." Hannah was their cook, a woman of over thirty yet as shy and subtle as a girl. Her skin was always shining as if in embarrassment, but she had a jaunty way of crooning hymns to herself in the kitchen. The children, at first timid of her color, adored her, and listened with eyes rounded by delight when she held up a two-tone forefinger and told them to be good. Goodness had never before been presented to them seriously.

Ralph and Eve had not expected a servant. Prepared to rough it on a family vacation, they had picked the most obscure island they could find. But Hannah came with the house; the owner, a svelte widow who had children in Florida, Peru, and Antigua, assumed they would need her. As it turned out, they did. They could never have unravelled alone all the riddles of this novel world. Eve could never have managed the shopping, which was carried on by gossip—invisible voices as liquid as the wind, telling who had just slaughtered a pig, and whose fishing boat had come in with a catch. The village was full of stores; almost every shack at least sold—for disturbingly discrepant prices—American cigarettes smuggled from St. Martin. But even the business hours of the most official store, a cement corridor of shelves attached to the customs office, had proved a mystery the Americans were unable to crack. They always found barred the large green door bearing in wobbly chalk script the ancient announcement "Attention Members! Attention Friends! This Store will be CLOSED Thursday afternoon."

"Oh, Hannah. She's a good girl," the doctor's wife said, and rolled over on her stomach. The corrugated backs of her thighs were frosted with sand like wet sugar.

"She is, you know," Eve said. "She's lovely. I think they're all lovely. They've all been lovely to us." Such insistence was unlike his wife. Ralph wondered what was between the two women, who had just met a day ago. "I can see why Reverend Johnson loved the people," Eve added in a deliberate, though cautiously soft, voice. "The people" were all around them; their huts came down to the edge of the sand, and, windows shuttered, the patched walls seemed to be listening.

The doctor's wife rolled over again and returned to a sitting position. What was making her so restless?

"Yes," she said, and an especially heavy curl of surf foamed up the white slope and soaked in just short of their feet. The sand was porous; innumerable punctures dotted it, the breathing holes of crabs. The doctor's wife's eyes fixed on the horizon and became, from the side, colorless lenses. Her nose in profile turned sharp. "They're simple souls," she said.

The doctor's wife was a queen here. She was the only fully white woman resident on the island. When the rare British official and the rarer, fantastically minor member of royalty came to grace this most remote and docile scrap of empire with a visit, she was the hostess. When she roared along the dirt roads in her spattered English Ford—its muffler had long ago rotted away—the older natives touched their foreheads ironically and the children flapped their arms in her wake of dust. When she and the doctor condescended to call upon the American family staying three weeks in The Bay, Hannah had trembled with pride and broken a cup in the kitchen. The doctor was a slight, rapid-voiced man with a witty air of failure. His fingertips were dyed deep yellow by smuggled cigarettes. He preferred Camels, but Chesterfields were all that were coming through now. Camels had more scratch in them. He had never seen a filtered cigarette. He and his wife had been ten years in the tropics—B.G., Trinidad, Barbados, now this. He had some vague scheme of getting to America and making a fortune and retiring to a Yorkshire village. He was off for the day to St. Martin.

"In America, now," the doctor's wife said, vehemently brushing sand from her knees, "are the coloreds well cared for?"

"How do you mean?" Eve asked.

"Are they well off?"

"Not really," Ralph said, because he sensed that it would be better if he, rather than Eve, answered. "In some parts better than others. In the South, of course, they're openly discriminated against; in the North they by and large have to live in the city slums but at least they have full legal rights."

"Oh, dear," the doctor's wife said. "It is a problem, isn't it?"

Eve's face flashed up from studying a shell. "Whose problem?" she asked. She was a graduate of one of those female colleges where only a member of a racial minority or a physically handicapped person is ever elected class president. News from South Africa made her voice thrash, and she was for anyone—Castro, Ben-Gurion, Martin Luther King— who in her mind represented an oppressed race.

The doctor's wife returned her gaze to the horizon, and Ralph wondered if they had been rude. In the woman's pointed profile there was a certain purposely silent thrust. But, the hostess, she relented and tried to make the conversation go again. She turned her head, shading her eyes with a quick hand and exposing her neat white teeth in a tense smile. "The schools," she said. "Can they go to your schools?"

"Of course," Ralph said swiftly, at the same time realizing that for her there was no "of course" to it. She knew nothing about his country. He felt firmer, having gauged her ignorance, and having moved to the hard ground of information. "Nobody denies them schools. In the South the schools are segregated. But in the North, and the West, and so on, there's no problem." He hunched his shoulders, feeling at his back Eve's disapproval of his saying "problem."

"But"—the doctor's wife's freckles gathered under her eyes as she squinted into the heart of the issue—"would *your* children go to school with them?"

"Sure. Good heavens. Why not?" He was relieved to clear this up, to lock this door. He hoped the doctor's wife would now turn away and talk of something else.

She sighed. "Of course, you in America have lived with the problem so long. In England, now, they're just waking up; the blacks are *pouring* into London."

A wave, pushed by one behind it, slid so far up the slant of sand that their feet were unexpectedly soaked. For a few seconds their ankles glittered in rippling sleeves of retreating water. Eve said slowly, "You talk as if they had asked to be made slaves and brought here."

"Mommy, look! Mommy, look!" Kate's voice, mingling with Larry's babyish yips of excitement, came from far down the beach. Their little silhouettes were jiggling around something dark at their feet, and out of the sea grape an old woman in a kerchief and a young man with a naked chest had emerged to watch them, amused to see what amused these exotic children. Eve rose, casting down, for Ralph to see, a startled and indignant look at the doctor's wife's body, as if it were an offensive piece of rubbish washed up on the pure sands of her mind.

As Eve walked away, the doctor's wife said, "Doesn't she take a tan beautifully?"

"Yes, she always does. She's part French." With his wife out of earshot, Ralph relaxed into the sand. Mediating between the two women had demanded an exhausting equilibrium. He resigned himself to listening; he knew the doctor's wife's tongue would be loosened. The presence of another white queen inhibited her, diluted her authority.

"Do you want to hear a frightening story?"

"Sure." He acquiesced uneasily. The attention of the houses behind them seemed to grow more intense. He felt that he and his family were liked in the village; the doctor's wife, driving down from the center of the island to enjoy their beach, assumed an incriminating alliance which he did not wish to exist. For, when the sun went down, she would go home, leaving them alone in the village with the night and its noises. Their tilly lamps hissed; black bugs droned into the lamps and fell crackling onto the table. Far up the road a boy practiced on his lonely steel drum, and next door, in an unpainted cabin that was never unshuttered, a woman wailed and a man infrequently growled a brief, dangerous complaint.

"When Vic Johnson left," the doctor's wife said, lowering her voice and sinking back on her elbow, to bring her face closer to Ralph's, "they had a party to greet the new parson, a very nice young colored boy from St. Kitts. *Very* nice, I must say, and they say very intelligent, though I haven't heard him preach. Well, the Warden—you haven't met him, and I dare say you won't, a big smooth Jamaican, takes himself, oh, *ever* so seriously—the Warden makes this little speech. He of course mentions Vic, forty years and so on, but right at the end he says that he knows we will not miss Reverend Johnson, because the new vicar is such a fine young man, comes to us with such an excellent record of study, and the rest of it, and furthermore, *furthermore*, what makes us especially happy and proud, he is one of us. Imagine! One of us! Of course, the young parson was embarrassed to death. It made me so mad I would have jumped up and left if the doctor hadn't held my hand. *One of us!* Vic had given his life to these people."

Her voice had become shrill; Ralph spoke in the hope of restraining it. "It seems unnecessary to spell out, but natural," he said.

"I don't see anything natural about it. *Un*natural, in my book. Unnatural, childish ingratitude. You just don't know how unnatural these people are. If you could see one-tenth of the antics, and then the selfishness, the doctor puts up with. At two in the morning, 'Doctor, Doctor, come save my child,' and then, a week later, when he tries to collect his poor little dollar or two, they don't *remember*. They don't remember at all. And if he insists—'The white people are stealing our money.' Oh. I hate them. God forgive me, I've come to hate them. They're *not* natural. They're not fully human." Seeing his hand begin a protesting movement, she added, "And for that matter, do you know what they say about you and your wife?" It was as if a shadow cruising through her words now made its lunge.

"No. Do they say something?"

"This is just to show how malicious they are. They say your wife has a touch of the brush." It took Ralph a moment to expand "brush" into "tar brush." He laughed; what else?

The doctor's wife laughed, too; but under the blond eyebrows her blue eyes, the pupils pinpricks in the sun, were fixed on his face. She expected his face to crack and the truth to escape. "You see how dark she is," she explained. "How tan." He watched her tongue tick as she suspensefully pronounced the last two words.

Blood rushed through his body; the wound was confused; his anger entangled him with his attacker. He was supplying an absurd assault with teeth out of himself. "She's always taken a good tan."

"And you see," the doctor's wife went on, still not unpinning her eyes from his face, "that's why they say you came here. No tourists come here, least of all with children. They say your wife's being part Negro has kept you out of the hotels on the better islands."

He felt certain that this ingenious argument was wholly her own. "We came here because it was cheap," he said.

"Of *course*," she said, "of *course*. But they can't believe that. They believe, you see, that all Americans are *rich*." Which was just what, Ralph suspected, she and the doctor believed.

He stood up, wet sand collapsing from his legs. In an effort to control his excitement, he threw several unrelated laughs, as if out of a renewed apprehension of absurdity, into the air. He looked down at the woman and said, "Well, that explains why they seem to like her better than me."

The doctor's wife, having strained her neck to squint up at him, collapsed the rest of the way. She pillowed her head with one arm and threw the other over her eyes. Without her eyes her lips seemed vague and numb. "Oh, no," she said. "They hate her for getting away with it."

His laughter this time was totally vacant. "I think I'll go in again," he said. "Before the sun fades."

"It won't fade," was the faint, withdrawing answer.

From the safety of the water he watched his tan wife herd his two pale, burned children up the beach, toward the doctor's wife. He had an urge to shout a warning, then smiled, imagining the amused incredulity that would greet this story when they were back home, at a cocktail party, secure among their own. Abruptly, he felt guilty in relation to his wife. He had betrayed her; his defensiveness had been unworthy of her. She would have wanted him to say something like yes, her great-grandfather picked cotton in Alabama, in America these things are taken for granted, we have no problem. But he saw, like something living glimpsed in a liquid volume, that his imaginary scenarios depended upon, could only live within, a vast unconscious white pride; he and the doctor's wife were in this together. There was no bottom to his guilt, its intricacy was as dense as a liquid mass. He moved backward in the ocean, touching the ribbed bottom with his toes, until the water wrapped around his throat. Something—seaweed or the pulse of a current—touched Ralph's calf. He thrashed, and peered down, but saw nothing. He was afraid of the sharks, and he was afraid of the doctor's wife, so he hung there between them, bleeding shame.

At a Bar in Charlotte Amalie

BLOWFISH with lightbulbs inside their dried skins glowed above the central fortress of brown bottles. The bar was rectangular; customers sat on all four sides. A slim schoolteacherish-looking girl, without much of a tan and with one front tooth slightly overlapping the other, came in, perched on a corner stool, and asked for a daiquiri-on-the-rocks. She wore a yellow halter, turquoise shorts, and white tennis sneakers. The white bartender, who was not visibly malformed, nevertheless moved like a hunchback, with a sideways bias and the scuttling nimbleness peculiar to cripples. He wore a powder-blue polo shirt, and now and then paused to take a rather avid sip from a tall glass containing perhaps orange juice; his face was glazed with sweat and he kept peering toward the outdoors, as if expecting to be relieved of duty. The green sea was turning gray under round pink clouds. A boat dully knocked against the cement wharf, and suddenly the noise had the subtle importance noises in these latitudes assume at night. A member of the steel band, a tall, long-jawed Negro, materialized in the rear of the place, on a shallow shadowy platform where the cut and dented steel drums were stacked. After unstacking and mounting them, this Negro, who wore a tattered red shirt and held a dead cigarette in the center of his lips, picked up a mallet and experimentally tapped into the air a succession, a cluster, an overlapping cascade of transparent notes that for a moment rendered everyone at the bar silent.

Then a homosexual with a big head turned to the schoolteacherish girl, who had been served, and said, "See my pretty hat?" His head seemed big because his body was small, a boy's body, knobby and slack and ill-fitted to his veined man's hands and to his face. His eyes were rather close together, making him seem to concentrate, without rest, upon a disagreeable internal problem, and his lips—which in their curt cut somehow expressed New York City—were too quick, snapping in and out of a grin as if he were trying to occupy both sides of his situation, being both the shameless clown and the aloof, if amused, onlooker. He had been talking about his hat, half to himself, since four o'clock this afternoon, and when he held it out to the girl an eddy of sighs and twisted eyebrows passed through the faces in the yellow darkness around the bar. The hat was a cheap broadweave straw with a bird's nest of artificial grass set into the crown, a few glass eggs fixed in the nest, and several toy birds suspended on stiff wires above it, as if in flight. "I designed it myself," he explained. "For the carnival this weekend. Isn't it marvellously uninhibited?" He glanced around, checking on the size of his audience.

He was well known here. If he had scraped, from the surface of indifference, a few shreds of attention, it was because of the girl. Her coming in here, at this twilight hour, alone, bearing herself with such prim determined carelessness, was odd enough to attract notice, even at a tropical bar, where everything is permitted to happen.

"It's lovely," she said, of the hat, and sipped her drink.

"Do you want to put it on? Please try it."

"I don't think so, thank you."

"I designed it myself," he said, looking around and deciding to make a speech. "That's the way I am. I just give my ideas away." He flung up his hands in a gesture of casting away, and a breeze moved in from the street as if to accept his gift. "If I were like other people, I'd make money with my ideas. Money, mo*nnn*ey. It's excrement, but I love it." A brief anonymous laugh rose and was borne off by the breeze. The homosexual returned to the girl with a tender voice. "You don't have to put it on," he told her. "It's not really finished. When I get back to my room, where I've been meaning to go all day, if that *fiend*"—he pointed at the bartender, who with his slightly frantic deftness was pouring a rum Collins—"would let me go. He says I owe him mo*nnn*ey! When I get back to my room, I'm going to add a few touches, here, and here. A few spangly things, just a few. It's for the carnival this weekend. Are you down here for the carnival?"

"No," the girl said. "I'm flying back tomorrow."

"You should stay for the carnival. It's wonderfully uninhibited."

"I'd like to, but I must go back." Slightly blushing, she lowered her voice and murmured something containing the word "excursion."

The homosexual slapped the bar. "Forgive me, forgive me, dear Lord above"—he rolled his eyes upward, to the glowing blowfish and the great roaches and tarantulas of straw which decorated the walls—"but I *must* see how my hat looks on you, you're so pretty."

He reached out and set the hat with its bright hovering birds on her head. She took another sip of her drink, docilely wearing the hat. A child laughed.

The homosexual's eyes widened. This unaccustomed expression was painful to look at; it was as if two incisions were being held open by clamps. The child who had laughed was looking straight at him: a bright round face fine-featured as the moon, rising just barely to the level of the bar and topped by hair so fair it was white. The little boy sat between his parents, a man and a woman oddly alike, both wearing white cotton and having stout sun-browned arms, crinkled weather-whipped faces, and irises whose extremely pale blue seemed brittle, baked by days of concentration on a glaring sea. Even their hair matched. The man's had not been cut in months, except across his forehead, and was salt-bleached in great tufts and spirals, like an unravelling rope of half-dark strands. The woman's, finer and longer, was upswept into a tumultuous blond crown that had apparently sheltered the roots enough to leave them, for an inch or two, dark. They looked, this husband and wife, like two sexless chieftains of a thickset, seagoing Nordic tribe. As if for contrast, they were accompanied by a gaunt German youth with swarthy skin, watchful eyes, close-cropped hair, and protruding ears. He stood behind and between them, a shadow uniting three luminaries.

The homosexual crouched down on the bar and fiddled his fingers playfully. "Hi," he said. "Are you laughing at me?"

The child laughed again, a little less spontaneously.

His parents stopped conversing.

"What a gorgeous child," the homosexual called to them. "He's so— so *fresh*. So uninhibited. It's wonderful." He blinked; truly he did seem dazzled.

The father smiled uneasily toward the wife; the pale creases around his eyes sank into his tan, and his face, still young, settled into what it would become—the toughened, complacent, blind face of an old Scandinavian salt, the face that, pipe in teeth, is mimicked on carved bottle-stoppers.

"No, really," the homosexual insisted. "He's darling. You should take him to Hollywood. He'd be a male Shirley Temple."

The child, his tiny pointed chin lifting in mute delight, looked upward from one to the other of his parents. His mother, in a curious protective motion, slipped from her stool and placed a sandalled foot on the rung of her child's stool, her tight white skirt riding up and exposing half her thigh. It was thick yet devoid of fat, like the trunk of a smooth-skinned tree.

The father said, "You think?"

"I *think?*" the homosexual echoed eagerly, crouching farther forward and touching his chin to his glass. "I *know.* He'd be a male Shirley Temple. My judgment is infallible. If I was willing to leave all you lovely people and go dig in the dung, I'd be a stinking-rich talent scout living in Beverly Hills."

The father's face collapsed deeper into its elderly future. The mother seized her thigh with one hand and ruffled the child's hair with the other. The dark German boy began to talk to them, as if to draw them back into their radiant privacy. But the homosexual had been stirred. "You know," he called to the father, "just looking at you I can feel the brine in my face. You both look as if you've been on the ocean all of your life."

"Not quite," the father said, so tersely it wasn't heard.

"I beg your pardon?"

"I haven't been on the sea all my life."

"You know, I *love* sailing. I love the life of the open sea. It's so"—his lips balked, rejecting "uninhibited"—"it's so free, so pure, all that wind, and the waves, and all that jazz. You can just be yourself. No, really. I think it's wonderful. I love Nature. I used to live in Queens."

"Where do you live now?" the girl beside him asked, setting his hat on the bar between them.

The homosexual didn't turn his head, answering as if the sailing couple had asked the question. "I live here," he called. "In dear old St. Thomas. God's own beloved country. Do you need a cook on your boat?"

The child tugged at his mother's waist and pulled her down to whisper something into her ear. She listened and shook her head; a brilliant loop of hair came undone. The father drank from the glass in front of him and in a freshened voice called across, "Not at the moment."

"I wish you did, I wish to Heaven you did, I'm a beautiful cook, really. I make the *best* omelets. You should see me; I just put in the old eggs and a little bit of milk and a glass of brandy and some of those little green things—what are they called?—chives, I put in the chives and stir until my arm breaks off and it comes out just *won*derful, so light and fluffy. If I cared about money, I'd be a chef in the Waldorf."

The child's whispered request seemed to recall the group to itself. The father turned and spoke to the German boy, who, in the instant before bowing his head to listen, threw, the whites of his eyes glimmering, a dark glance at the homosexual. Misunderstanding, the homosexual left his stool and hat and drink and went around the corner of the bar toward them. But, not acknowledging his approach, they lifted the child and walked away toward the rear of the place, where there was a jukebox. Here they paused, their brilliant hair and faces bathed in boxed light.

The homosexual returned to his stool and watched them. His head was thrown back like that of a sailor who has suffered a pang at the sight of land. "Oh dear," he said aloud, "I can't decide which I want to have, the man or the woman."

The schoolteacherish girl sipped her daiquiri, dipping her head quickly, as if into a bitter birdbath. One stool away from her down the bar, there sat a beefy unshaven customer, perhaps thirty years old, drinking a beer and wearing a T-shirt with a ballpoint pen clipped to the center of the sweat-soaked neckline. Squinting intently into space and accenting some inner journey with soft grunts, he seemed a truck driver transported, direct and intact, from the counter of an Iowa roadside diner. Next to him, across a space of empty stools, behind an untouched planter's punch, sat a very different man of about the same age, a man who, from his brick-red complexion, his high burned forehead, the gallant immobility of his posture, and the striking corruption of his teeth, could only have been English.

Into the space of three stools between them there now entered a dramatic person—tall, gaunt, and sandy. He displayed a decrepit Barrymore profile and a gold ring in one ear. He escorted a squat powdered woman who looked as though she had put on her lipstick by eating it. She carried a dachshund under one arm. The bartender, unsmiling, awkwardly pivoting, asked, "How's the Baron?"

"Rotten," the Baron said; and as he eased onto his stool his stiff wide shoulders seemed a huge coat hanger left, out of some savage stubbornness, in his coat. The woman set the dachshund on the bar. When their drinks came, the dog lapped hers, which was a lime rickey. When he tried to lap the Baron's—a straight Scotch—the man gripped the dachshund's thirstily wagging rump, snarled "Damn alcoholic," and sent him skidding down the bar. The dog righted himself and sniffed the truck driver's beer; a placid human paw softly closed over the mouth of the glass, blocking the animal's tongue. His nails clicking and slipping on the polished bar, the dog returned to his mistress and curled up at her elbow like a pocketbook. The girl at the corner shyly peeked at the man beside her, but he had resumed staring into space. The pen fixed at his throat had the quality of a threat, of a scar.

The blond family returned from having put a quarter into the jukebox, which played "Loco Motion," by Little Eva; "Limbo Rock," by Chubby Checker; and "Unchain My Heart," by Ray Charles. The music, like an infusion of letters from home, froze the people at the bar into silence. Beyond the overhang that sheltered the tables, night dominated. The bar lit up a section of pavement where pedestrians flitted like skittish actors from one wing of darkness into the other. The swish of traffic on the airport road had a liquid depth. The riding lights of boats by the wharf bobbed up and down, and a little hard half-moon rummaged for its reflection in the slippery sea. The Baron muttered to the painted old woman an angry and long story in which the obscene expressions were peculiarly emphasized, so that only they hung distinct in the air, the connecting threads inaudible. The Englishman at last moved his forearm and lowered the level of his planter's punch by a fraction of an inch, making a stoic face afterward, as if the sweetness had hurt his teeth. The homosexual, nettled by the attention received by the drinking dachshund, took off his hat and addressed the ceiling of the bar as if it were God. "Hey there, Great White Father," he said. "You haven't been very good to me this month. I know You love me—how could You help it, I'm so beautiful—but I haven't seen any money coming out of the sky. I mean, really, You put us down here in the manure and we need it to live, like. You know? I mean, don't get too uninhibited up there. Huh?" He listened, and the Baron, undistracted, set another blue word burning in the hushed air. "That's O.K.," the homosexual continued. "You've kept the sun shining, and I appreciate it. You just keep the sun shining, Man, and don't send me back to Queens." At prayer's end, he put the hat on his head and looked around, his curt lips pursed defiantly.

Five Negroes, uncostumed, in motley clothes and as various in size as their instruments, had assembled on the shadowy platform, kidding and giggling back and forth and teasing the air with rapid, stop-and-start gusts of tuning up. Abruptly they began to play. The ping-pong, the highest pan, announced itself with four harsh solo notes, and on the fifth stroke the slightly deeper guitar pans, the yet deeper cello pans, and the bass boom, which was two entire forty-four-gallon oil drums, all at once fell into the tune, and everything—cut and peened drums, rubber-tipped sticks, tattered shirtsleeves, bobbing heads, munching jaws, a frightened-looking little black child whipping a triangle as fast as he could—was in motion, in flight. The band became a great loose-jointed bird feathered in clashing, rippling bells. It played "My Basket," and then, with hardly a break, "Marengo Jenny," "How You Come to Get Wet?," and "Madame

Dracula." Nobody danced. It was early, and the real tourists, the college students and Bethlehem Steel executives and Westchester surgeons, had not yet come down from dinner in the hills to sit at the tables. There was a small dance floor on one side of the bar. A young Negro appeared here. He wore canary-yellow trousers and a candy-striped jersey with a boat neck and three-quarter sleeves. He had a broad, hopeful face and an athletic, wedge-shaped back. From his vaguely agitated air of responsibility, he seemed to be associated with the establishment. He asked the schoolteacherish girl, who looked alone and lost, to dance; but she, with a pained smile and a nervous dip of her head into her second daiquiri, refused. The young Negro stood stymied on the dance floor, clothed only, it seemed, in music and embarrassment, his pale palms dangling foolishly. When the band, in a final plangent burst cut short as if with a knife, stopped, he went to the leader, the long-jawed red shirt on the Ping-Pong, and said, "Ey, mon, le peo-*ple* wan I bet 'Yel*low* Bird.' " He phrased it, as the West Indian accent phrases all statements, like a question.

The leader took offense. He answered deliberately, unintelligibly, as if, the music still ringing in the pan of his skull, he were softly tapping out a melody with his tongue. The man on the bass boom, a coarse thick-lipped mulatto in a blue work shirt unbuttoned down to his navel, joined in the argument and gave the young man a light push that caused him to step backward off the platform. The bass-boom man growled, and the strip of hairy cocoa skin his shirt exposed puffed up like a rooster's throat. No one had danced; the band was defensive and irritable. The leader, biting the butt of his cigarette, rattled a venomous toneless tattoo on the rim of his ping-pong. Then the shadow manning the cello pans—he had a shaved head, and was the oldest of them—spoke an unheard word, and all the Negroes, including the boy with the wedge-shaped back, broke into disjointed laughter.

When the band resumed playing, they began with "Yellow Bird"—played flat, at a grudging, slow tempo. The young Negro approached the blonde mother of the little boy. She came with him into the center of the floor and lifted her fat fair arms. They danced delicately, sleepily, the preening shuffle of the mambo, her backside switching in its tight white dress, his broad face shining as his lips silently mouthed the words: *Ye-ell-o-oh bi-ird, up in the tree so high, ye-ell-o-oh bi-ird, you sit alone like I.* Her thick waist seemed at home in the wide clasp of his hand.

When the song finished, he bowed thank you and she returned to her family by the bar and, as if sighing, let down her hair. Apparently it had been held by one pin; she pulled this pin, and the fluffy sun-bleached crown on the top of her head cascaded down her back in a loosening stream, and she looked, with her weather-pinched face, like a negative of a witch, or what relates to witches as angels relate to devils. The little boy, as if his heart were climbing the golden rope she had let down, whispered up to her, and she, after bowing her head to listen, glanced up at the homosexual, who was complaining to the bartender that his vodka-and-tonic had gone watery.

"You owe me," the bartender said, "a dollar fifty, and if you let the drink sit there hour after hour, damn right the ice'll melt."

"I don't have a dollar fifty," was the answer. "I have washed my hands, forever and ever, amen, of filthy lucre. People want me to get a job but I won't; that's the way I am. It's a matter of principle with me. Why should I work all day for a pittance and starve when I can do nothing whatsoever and starve anyway?"

Now the whole blond family was staring at him fascinated. The glow of their faces caught the corner of his eye, and he turned toward them inquisitively; memory of the snub they had given him made his expression shy.

"I want one dollar and fifty cents from you," the bartender insisted, with unconvincing emphasis; his anxious sweat and obscurely warped posture seemed that of a warden trapped in his own prison, among inmates he feared. He gulped some orange from his glass and looked toward the outdoors for relief. Pale square clouds rested above the sea, filtering stars. Laughter like spray was wafted from a party on a yacht.

The homosexual called, "Really, he is the most cunning little boy I have ever seen in all my *life*. In Hollywood he could be a male Shirley Temple, honestly, and when he grows up a little he could be a male what's-her-name—oh, what *was* her name? Jane Withers. I have a beautiful memory. If I cared, I could go back to New York and get on a quiz show and make a million dollars."

The German boy spoke for the group. "He vunts—your hatt."

"Does he? Does he really? The little angel wants to wear my hat. I designed it myself for the carnival this weekend." He left his stool, scrambled around the corner, set the hat with its glade of decoration squarely on the child's spherical head, and, surprisingly, knelt on the floor. "Come on," he said, "come on, darling. Get on my shoulders. Let's go for a ride."

The father looked a question at his wife, shrugged, and lifted his son onto the stranger's shoulders. The birds on their wires bobbed unsteadily, and fear flickered not only in the child's face but in the grown face to which he clung. The homosexual, straightening up, seemed startled that the child was a real weight. Then, like a frail monster overburdened with two large heads, one on top of the other and the upper one sprouting a halo of birds, he began to jog around the rectangular bar, his shaved legs looking stringy and bony in their shorts. The steel band broke into a pachanga. Some tourist families had come down from the hills to occupy the tables, and the athletic young Negro, whose flesh seemed akin to rubber, successfully invited a studiously tanned girl with orange hair, a beauty, to dance. She had long green eyes and thin lips painted paler than her skin, and an oval of nakedness displayed her long brown collarbones. The Baron cursed and yanked his own lady onto the floor; as they danced, the dachshund nipped worriedly at their stumbling feet. The Baron kicked the dog away, and in doing so turned his head, so that, to the dizzy little boy riding by, the gold ring in his ear flashed like the ring on a merry-go-round. A stately bald man, obviously a North American doctor, rose, and his wife, a midget whose Coppertone face was wrinkled like a walnut, rose to dance with him. The homosexual's shoulders hurt. He galloped one last lap around the bar and lifted the child back onto the stool. The airy loss of pressure around his neck led him to exhale breathlessly into the bright round face framed by straw, "You know, Mark Twain wrote a lovely book *just* about you." He took the hat from the child's head and replaced it on his own. The child, having misunderstood the bargain, burst into tears, and soon his mother carried him from the bar and into the night, their blond heads vanishing.

The dancing gathered strength. The floor became crowded. From her high vantage at the corner of the bar, the schoolteacherish girl studied with downcast eyes the dancing feet. They seemed to be gently tamping smooth a surface that was too hot to touch for more than an instant. Some females, of both races, had removed their shoes; their feet looked ugly and predatory, flickering, spread-toed, in and out of shadows and flashes of cloth. When the music stopped, black hands came and laid, on the spot of floor where her eyes were resting, two boards hairy with upright rusty nails. A spotlight was focused on them. The band launched into a fierce limbo. The young Negro with the handsome rubbery back leaped, nearly naked, into the light. His body was twitching in rhythm, he was waving two flaming torches, and he was clad in knit swimming trunks and orange streamers representing, she supposed, Caribbean slave dress. His eyes shut, he thrust the torches alternately into his mouth and spat out flame. Indifferent applause rippled through the tables.

The Baron, drunker than anyone had suspected, pushed off from the bar and, as the young Negro lay down on a board of nails and stroked the skin of his chest with the sticks of fire, lay down beside him and kicked his trousered legs high in parody. No one dared laugh, the Baron's face was so impassive and rapt. The young Negro, his back resting on the nails, held one torch at arm's length, so that the flame rested on the Baron's coat lapel and started a few sparks there; but the Baron writhed on obliviously, and the smoldering threads winked out. When the Negro stood, now clearly shaken, and with a great mock-primitive grimace leaped on one board of nails with his bare feet, the Baron leaped in his sandals on the other, and through sandy eyelashes blindly peered into the surrounding darkness of applause, his earring glinting, his shoulders still seeming to have a coat hanger in them. Two black waiters, nervous as deer, ventured into the spotlight and seized his upraised arms; as they led him out of the light, the tall figure of the white man, gasping as if he had surfaced after a shipwreck, yet expressed, in profile, an incorrigible dignity. There was murmuring at the tables as the tourists wondered if this had been part of the act.

The music pitched into an even fiercer tempo. The young Negro, handing away his torches, was given a cloth sack, which he dropped on the floor. It fell open to reveal a greenish heap of smashed bottles. He trod on the heap with both feet. He got down and rolled in it as a dog rolls ecstatically in the rotten corpse of a woodchuck. He rested his back on the pillow of shards and the heavy mulatto left the bass boom and stood on his chest. There was applause. The mulatto jumped off and walked away. The Negro got up on his knees, cupped a glittering quantity of broken glass in his palms, and scrubbed his face with it. When he stood to take the applause, the girl observed that his back, which gleamed, heaving, a foot from her eyes, indeed did bear a few small fresh cuts. The applause died, the music halted, and the bright lights went on before the pseudo-slave, hugging his nail-boards and bag of glass, had reached the haven of the door behind the platform. As he passed among them, the members of the steel band cackled.

Now there was an intermission. The bartender, his hands trembling and his eyes watering, it seemed, on the edge of tears, scuttled back and forth mixing a new wave of drinks. More tourists drifted in, and the families containing adolescents began to leave. The traffic on the airport road had diminished, and the bumping of the boats on the wharf, beneath the moon that had lost its reflection, regained importance. The people on the decks of these boats could see the windows burning in the dry hills above Charlotte Amalie, lights spread through the middle of the night sky like a constellation about to collide with our planet but held back, perpetually poised in the just-bearable distance, by that elusive refusal implicit in tropical time, which like the soft air seems to consist entirely of circles. Within the bar, the German boy wandered over and spoke to the homosexual, who looked up from under the brim of his antic hat with alert lips and no longer preoccupied eyes, all business. The German boy put two dollar bills on the bar, to cover the unpaid drink. The very English-appearing man left his place behind the undiminishing planter's punch, sauntered around the bar, and commenced a conversation with the now deserted Nordic father; the Englishman's first words betrayed a drawling American accent. The Baron laid his handsome head on the bar and fell asleep. The dachshund licked his face, because it smelled of alcohol. The woman slapped the dog's nose. The beefy man abruptly pulled the pen from the neck of his T-shirt, removed the cardboard coaster from under his beer, and wrote something on it, something very brief—one word, or a number. It was as if he had at last received a message from the ghostly trucking concern that had misplaced him here. The ping-pong sounded; the music resumed. The young Negro, changed out of costume back into his yellow pants and candy-striped boat-necked shirt, returned. Flexing his back and planting his palms on his hips, he again asked the strange girl at the corner of the bar to dance. This time, with a smile that revealed her slightly overlapping front teeth, she accepted.

MARRIED LIFE

Toward Evening

WAITING for a number 5 bus in front of St. Patrick's Cathedral, Rafe was tired and hence dreamy. When the bus at last came and a short fatty woman in black bounced in front of him and then stopped, apparently paralyzed, right at the open doors, with the bus driver tapping the wheel and Rockefeller's towers gathered above them like a thunderhead, Rafe was not very much surprised. The woman made metallic, agitated noises. She seemed unable to step up, to grab the vertical bar, to move away, to do anything. Her hat, black straw strewn with purple berries, quivered, whether with indignation or fright, there was no telling. "Here we go," Rafe said, grabbing her a few inches below the armpits and hoisting. The woman was filled with sand. The only thing that worried Rafe was, he was carrying in one hand, by a loop of string, a box containing a mobile for the baby and didn't want it crushed.

"Oh, thank you!" a chirping voice beneath the hat cried even before she was safe on the step. "Thank you so much, whoever you are." His face seemed to be in her hat; he could see little else. The cloth beneath his fingers turned moist and kept slipping; Rafe had the frightening notion that something would break, and the sack spill, and the woman angrily sink to the pavement as a head in a nest of vacant clothing, like Ray Bolger in *The Wizard of Oz*. Suddenly, when her ascension seemed impossible, she was up, and his freed hands jerked, as if birds had flown from them.

"Wasn't that kind?" the woman asked the bus driver, not turning, though, and never showing Rafe her face.

"Move to the rear," the driver said in the soft level tones of a poor disciplinarian. Holding the box close to his chest, Rafe edged through the bodies, hunting a porcelain loop. The woman in black had disappeared, yet she couldn't have found a seat. And in the rear of the bus, where there was ample standing space, a beautiful girl stood. Two ash-blue streaks had been symmetrically dyed into her brandy-colored hair. Her topcoat, box-style and black, hung open, half sheathing her body. Her feet, in gray heels, were planted on the sides of an invisible *V*. Numberless *V*'s were visible wherever two edges of the pencil-stripe fabric of her suit met: in a straight seam down her back, along her sleeves, within her lapels, at the side of her skirt (very acute, these). At the base of her throat, where a *V* seemed promised, something more complex occurred, involving the sheathed extremities of opposed collarbones, the tapered shelves of their upper edges, the two nervous and rather thoroughbred cords of her neck, and between them a hollow where you could lay a teaspoon. She was less tall than her thinness made her appear; her forehead was level with Rafe's chin.

The bus veered. The standees swung, and her face, until then averted, turned toward his—a fine face, lucid. The kind of mouth you felt spoke French. If her nose had been smaller it would have been too small. The indentation in the center of the upper lip—the romantic dimple, Rafe's mother had called it, claiming, in the joking, sentimental way she had assumed to raise a child, that in its depth the extent of sexual vigor could be read—was narrow and incisive. Rafe was wondering about her eyes when she turned them up from her book to stare at him for staring, and he lowered his lids too quickly to gain any prize but a meagre impression of bigness. The book in her hand was *À l'ombre des jeunes filles en fleurs*.

After a few moments, he felt that even studying her hand was an intrusion in the ellipse of repose focused on the twin points of face and book. Rafe hugged the box containing the mobile and, stooping down, looked out of the bus window. They had rounded Columbus Circle and were headed up Broadway. The clearly marked numbers on the east side of the street ran: 1832, 1836, 1846, 1850 (Wordsworth dies), 1880 (great Nihilist trial in St. Petersburg), 1900 (Rafe's father born in Trenton), 1902 (Braque leaves Le Havre to study painting in Paris), 1914 (Joyce begins *Ulysses*; war begins in Europe), 1926 (Rafe's parents marry in Ithaca), 1936 (Rafe is four years old). Where the present should have stood, a block was torn down, and the numbering began again with 2000, a boring progressive edifice. Rafe diverted his attention from the window to the poster above it. The poster ingeniously advertised Jomar Instant Coffee. The gimmick was a finely corrugated cellulose sheet in which had been embedded two positions of a depicted man's eyeball, arm, and lips. Ideally, from one angle the man was seen holding a cup of coffee to his mouth, smiling, and in flavorful ecstasy rolling his iris to the top of his egg-shaped eye; from another angle he appeared with the cup lowered, his eyeball also lowered, and his lips parted in downright laughter. Rafe's closeness and the curvature of the bus roof prevented the illusion from working with complete success. Both arms, both eyeballs were always present, though with seesaw intensity as Rafe ducked his head up and down. Either the Jomar man's openmouthed grin was intersected by the ghost of his closed-mouthed smile, or the latter was surrounded by the shadow of the former. Rafe began to feel bus-sick. The bus had swung down Seventy-second Street and up Riverside Drive.

He returned to the girl. She was there, beside him, but leaving. Proust jutted from her pocketbook. Her face wore the enamelled look of a person who has emerged from a piece of fiction into the world of real decisions. With a whispering touch, her backside eased past his. Having pulled the green cord, she waited in front of the side doors, her profile a brilliant assault on the daylight. The double-jointed doors flapped open. Pursing her mouth, she managed the step, walked south, and was gone.

The entry of some new passengers forced Rafe deeper into the rear of the bus, yards away from where he had stood with the girl. Bit by bit, in confused order, as word of a disaster first filters in over the wires, he became conscious of the young Negress seated beneath him. Her baby-flat nose was a good glossy place for his attention to rest. When she recrossed her legs, he noticed the unpatterned breadth of turquoise skirt, the yellow coat clashing with it, the tense henna-tinged hair painfully pulled straight, the hard-to-read foreshortened curves of her face, the hands folded, with an odd precision, in her turquoise lap. She was wearing blue half-gloves; they stopped at the base of her thumbs. It was the hint of grotesqueness needed to make Rafe lustful. Yet the woman, in becoming so desirable, became inaccessible. If Rafe looked at her more steadily than at his previous love, it was because her armor of erotic power rendered her tactually insensitive to long looks. Likewise, because his imaginings concerning himself and the girl were so plainly fantastic, he could indulge them without limit.

The pure life of the mind, for all its quick distances, is soon tedious. Rafe, dwelling again on the actual Negress, observed the prim secretarial carriage of her head, the café-au-lait skin, the sarcastic Caucasian set of her lips. Dress women in sea and sand or pencil lines, they were chapters on the same subject, no more unlike than St. Paul and Paul Tillich. In the end, when he alighted at Eighty-fifth Street, the Negress had dwindled to the thought that he had never seen gloves like that before.

Behind him the bus doors closed: pterodactyl wings. A woman standing on the deserted pavement stared at the long box, never guessing a mobile for a baby was in it. The warm air, moistened by the Hudson, guaranteed spring. Rafe went up the rounded, coral-colored steps, across the checkered lobby floor, and into the tiny scarlet elevator, which was nearly always waiting for him, like a loyal but not slavish dog. Inside his apartment, the baby had just been fed and was laughing; her mother, flushed and sleepy, lay in a slip on the sofa bed.

That invisible gas, goodness, stung Rafe's eyes and made him laugh, strut, talk nonsense. He held the baby at arm's height, lowered her until her belly rested on the top of his head, and walked rapidly around the room singing, "I have a little babe, her name is Liz, I think she's better than she really is, I think she's better than she ever will be, what ev-er will become of me?"

The baby laughed, "Gkk, ngk!"

The mobile was not a success. His wife had expected a genuine Calder, made of beautiful polished woods, instead of seven rubber birds, with celluloid wings, hung from a piece of coarse wire. Elizabeth wanted to put the birds in her mouth and showed no interest in, perhaps did not even see, their abstract swinging, quite unlike the rapt infant shown on the box.

The baby went to sleep and his wife prepared the dinner in an atmosphere of let-down.

"I saw some funny gloves today," Rafe called. There was no answer from the kitchen, just the sound of pans.

When dinner came, it was his favorite everything—peas, hamburger, baked potato, cooked to avoid his allergies, served on the eccentric tilting plates in which, newly married, they had sailed the clean seas of sophistication.

It was growing dark, spottily. A curious illusion was unexpectedly created: his wife, irritated because he had failed to answer some question of hers—her questions about his life at the office, so well meant, so understandable in view of her own confined existence, numbed his mind to the extent that not only his recent doings but her questions themselves were obliterated—dropped a triangular piece of bread from her fingers, and the bread, falling to her lap through a width of light, twirled and made a star.

From where he sat, dinner done, smoking a cigarette, Rafe could look across the Hudson to the Palisades, surmounted by seeming villages. A purple sky was being lowered over a yellow one. The Spry sign came on. The sign, which by virtue of brightness and readability dominated their night view, had three stages: Spry (red), Spry (white) FOR BAKING (red), and Spry (white) FOR FRYING (red). Rafe sometimes wondered how it had come to be there. Some executive, no doubt, had noticed the bare roof of the newly acquired waterfront plant. "We could use a Spry sign there," he murmured to his secretary, whom he had kept late at the office and was driving to her home in Riverdale. The following Monday, the secretary made an interdepartmental memo of J.G.'s remark. The man second in charge of Public Relations (the man first in charge was on vacation in the Poconos), new at the job, seven years out of Yale, and not bold enough to take J.G. with a grain of salt, told a man in the Creative End to draw up a sketch. After three days, the man in Creative did this, basing his sketch upon a 186-pound file of past Spry ads. The man in Public Relations had a boy take it into the head office. J.G., flattered to have his suggestion followed up, wrote on the back, "Turn it slightly south. Nobody at Columbia cooks," and passed it on, O.K.'ed. The two other executives who saw the sketch (both of whom, by an almost supernatural coincidence, had daughters at Sarah Lawrence threatening marriage) suspected that J.G. was developing power among the stockholders and shrewdly strung along. Bids were requested and submitted. One was accepted. The neon people shaped the tubes. Metalworkers constructed a frame. On a November Tuesday, the kind of blowy day that gives you earache, the sign was set in place by eighteen men, the youngest of whom would some day be an internationally known film actor. At three-thirty, an hour and a half before they were supposed to quit, they knocked off and dispersed, because the goddamn job was done. Thus the Spry sign (thus the river, thus trees, thus babies and sleep) came to be.

Above its winking, the small cities had disappeared. The black of the river was as wide as that of the sky. Reflections sunk in it existed dimly, minutely wrinkled, below the surface. The Spry sign occupied the night with no company beyond the also uncreated but illegible stars.

Snowing in Greenwich Village

THE MAPLES had moved just the day before to West Thirteenth Street, and that evening they had Rebecca Cune over, because now they were so close. A tall, always slightly smiling girl with an absent-minded manner, she allowed Richard Maple to slip off her coat and scarf even as she stood gently greeting Joan. Richard, moving with an extra precision and grace because of the smoothness with which the business had been managed—though he and Joan had been married nearly two years, he was still so young-looking that people did not instinctively lay upon him hostly duties; their reluctance worked in him a corresponding hesitancy, so that often it was his wife who poured the drinks, while he sprawled on the sofa in the attitude of a favored and wholly delightful guest—entered the dark bedroom, entrusted the bed with Rebecca's clothes, and returned to the living room. Her coat had seemed weightless.

Rebecca, seated beneath the lamp, on the floor, one leg tucked under her, one arm up on the Hide-a-Bed that the previous tenants had not as yet removed, was saying, "I had known her, you know, just for the day she taught me the job, but I said O.K. I was living in an awful place called a hotel for ladies. In the halls they had typewriters you put a quarter in."

Joan, straight-backed on a Hitchcock chair from her parents' home in Amherst, a damp handkerchief balled in her hand, turned to Richard and explained, "Before her apartment now, Becky lived with this girl and her boyfriend."

"Yes, his name was Jacques," Rebecca said.

Richard asked, "You lived with them?" The arch composure of his tone was left over from the mood aroused in him by his successful and, in the dim bedroom, somewhat poignant—as if he were with great tact delivering a disappointing message—disposal of their guest's coat.

"Yes, and he insisted on having his name on the mailbox. He was terribly afraid of missing a letter. When my brother was in the Navy and came to see me and saw on the mailbox"—with three parallel movements of her fingers she set the names beneath one another—

"Georgene Clyde,
Rebecca Cune,
Jacques Zimmerman,

he told me I had always been such a nice girl. Jacques wouldn't even move out so my brother would have a place to sleep. He had to sleep on the floor." She lowered her lids and looked in her purse for a cigarette.

"Isn't that wonderful?" Joan said, her smile broadening helplessly as she realized what an inane thing it had been to say. Her cold worried Richard. It had lasted seven days without improving. Her face was pale, mottled pink and yellow; this accentuated the Modiglianiesque quality established by her oval blue eyes and her habit of sitting to her full height, her head quizzically tilted and her hands palm upward in her lap.

Rebecca, too, was pale, but in the consistent way of a drawing, perhaps— the weight of her lids and a certain virtuosity about the mouth suggested it—by da Vinci.

"Who would like some sherry?" Richard asked in a deep voice, from a standing position.

"We have some hard stuff if you'd rather," Joan said to Rebecca; from Richard's viewpoint the remark, like those advertisements which from varying angles read differently, contained the quite legible declaration that this time *he* would have to mix the old-fashioneds.

"The sherry sounds fine," Rebecca said. She enunciated her words distinctly, but in a faint, thin voice that disclaimed for them any consequence.

"I think, too," Joan said.

"Good." Richard took from the mantel the eight-dollar bottle of Tio Pepe that the second man on the Spanish-sherry account had stolen for him. So all could share in the drama of it, he uncorked the bottle in the living room. He posingly poured out three glasses, half full, passed them around, and leaned against the mantel (the Maples had never had a mantel before), swirling the liquid, as the agency's wine expert had told him to do, thus liberating the esters and ethers, until his wife said, as she always did, it being the standard toast in her parents' home, "Cheers, dears!"

Rebecca continued the story of her first apartment. Jacques had never worked. Georgene never held a job more than three weeks. The three of them contributed to a kitty, to which all enjoyed equal access. Rebecca had a separate bedroom. Jacques and Georgene sometimes worked on television scripts; they pinned the bulk of their hopes onto a serial titled *The IBI*—*I* for Intergalactic, or Interplanetary, or something—*in Space and Time.* One of their friends was a young Communist who never washed and always had money because his father owned half of the West Side. During the day, when the two girls were off working, Jacques flirted with a young Swede upstairs who kept dropping her mop onto the tiny balcony outside their window. "A real bombardier," Rebecca said. When Rebecca moved into a single apartment for herself and was all settled and happy, Georgene and Jacques offered to bring a mattress and sleep on her floor. Rebecca felt that the time had come for her to put her foot down. She said no. Later, Jacques married a girl other than Georgene.

"Cashews, anybody?" Richard said. He had bought a can at the corner delicatessen, expressly for this visit, though if Rebecca had not been coming he would have bought something else there on some other excuse, just for the pleasure of buying his first thing at the store where in the coming years he would purchase so much and become so familiar.

"No thank you," Rebecca said. Richard was so far from expecting refusal that out of momentum he pressed them on her again, exclaiming, "Please! They're so good for you." She took two and bit one in half.

He offered the dish, a silver porringer given to the Maples as a wedding present, to his wife, who took a greedy handful of cashews and looked so pale and mottled that he asked, "How do you feel?", not so much forgetting the presence of their guest as parading his concern, quite genuine at that, before her.

"Fine," Joan said edgily, and perhaps she did.

Though the Maples told some stories—how they had lived in a log cabin in a YMCA camp for the first three months of their married life; how Bitsy Flaner, a mutual friend, was the only girl enrolled in Bentham Divinity School; how Richard's advertising work brought him into glancing contact with Yogi Berra, who was just as funny as the papers said— they did not regard themselves (that is, each other) as raconteurs, and Rebecca's slight voice dominated the talk. She had a gift for odd things.

Her rich uncle lived in a metal house, furnished with auditorium chairs. He was terribly afraid of fire. Right before the Depression he had built an enormous boat to take himself and some friends to Polynesia. All his friends lost their money in the crash. He did not. He made money. He made money out of everything. But he couldn't go on the trip alone, so the boat was still waiting in Oyster Bay, a huge thing, rising thirty feet out of the water. The uncle was a vegetarian. Rebecca had not eaten turkey for Thanksgiving until she was thirteen years old because it was the family custom to go to the uncle's house on that holiday. The custom was dropped during the war, when the children's synthetic heels made black marks all over his asbestos floor. Rebecca's family had not spoken to the uncle since. "Yes, what got me," Rebecca said, "was the way each new wave of vegetables would come in as if it were a different course."

Richard poured the sherry around again and, because this made him the center of attention anyway, said, "Don't some vegetarians have turkeys molded out of crushed nuts for Thanksgiving?"

After a stretch of silence, Joan said, "I don't know." Her voice, unused for ten minutes, cracked on the last syllable. She cleared her throat, scraping Richard's heart.

"What would they stuff them with?" Rebecca asked, dropping an ash into the saucer beside her.

Beyond and beneath the window there arose a clatter. Joan reached the windows first, Richard next, and lastly Rebecca, standing on tiptoe, elongating her neck. Six mounted police, standing in their stirrups, were galloping two abreast down Thirteenth Street. When the Maples' exclamations had subsided, Rebecca remarked, "They do it every night at this time. They seem awfully jolly, for policemen."

"Oh, and it's snowing!" Joan cried. She was pathetic about snow; she loved it so much, and in these last years had seen so little. "On our first night here! Our first *real* night." Forgetting herself, she put her arms around Richard, and Rebecca, where another guest might have turned away, or smiled too broadly, too encouragingly, retained without modification her sweet, absent look and studied, through the embracing couple, the scene outdoors. The snow was not taking on the wet street; only the hoods and tops of parked automobiles showed an accumulation.

"I think I'd best go," Rebecca said.

"Please don't," Joan said with an urgency Richard had not expected; clearly she was very tired. Probably the new home, the change in the weather, the good sherry, the currents of affection between herself and her husband that her sudden hug had renewed, and Rebecca's presence had become in her mind the inextricable elements of one enchanted moment.

"Yes, I think I'll go because you're so snuffly and peakèd."

"Can't you just stay for one more cigarette? Dick, pass the sherry around."

"A teeny bit," Rebecca said, holding out her glass. "I guess I told you, Joan, about the boy I went out with who pretended to be a headwaiter."

Joan giggled expectantly. "No, honestly, you never did." She hooked her arm over the back of the chair and wound her hand through the slats, like a child assuring herself that her bedtime has been postponed. "What did he do? He imitated headwaiters?"

"Yes, he was the kind of guy who, when we get out of a taxi and there's a grate giving off steam, crouches down"—Rebecca lowered her head and lifted her arms—"and pretends he's the Devil."

The Maples laughed, less at the words themselves than at the way Rebecca had evoked the situation by conveying, in her understated imitation, both her escort's flamboyant attitude and her own undemonstrative nature. They could see her standing by the taxi door, gazing with no expression as her escort bent lower and lower, seized by his own joke, his fingers writhing demonically as he felt horns sprout through his scalp, flames lick his ankles, and his feet shrivel into hoofs. Rebecca's gift, Richard realized, was not that of having odd things happen to her but that of representing, through the implicit contrast with her own sane calm, all things touching her as odd. This evening, too, might appear grotesque in her retelling: "Six policemen on horses galloped by and she cried 'It's snowing!' and hugged him. He kept telling her how sick she was and filling us full of sherry."

"What else did he do?" Joan eagerly asked.

"At the first place we went to—it was a big nightclub on the roof of somewhere—on the way out he sat down and played the piano until a woman at a harp asked him to stop."

Richard asked, "Was the woman *playing* the harp?"

"Yes, she was strumming away." Rebecca made circular motions with her hands.

"Well, did he play the tune she was playing? Did he *accompany* her?" Petulance, Richard realized without understanding why, had entered his tone.

"No, he just sat down and played something else. I couldn't tell what it was."

"Is this *really* true?" Joan asked, egging her on.

"And then, at the next place we went to, we had to wait at the bar for a table and I looked around and he was walking among the tables asking people if everything was all right."

"Wasn't it *awful*?" said Joan.

"Yes. Later he played the piano there, too. We were sort of the main attraction. Around midnight he thought we ought to go out to Brooklyn, to his sister's house. I was exhausted. We got off the subway two stops too early, under the Manhattan Bridge. It was deserted, with nothing going by except black limousines. Miles above our head"—she stared up, as though at a cloud, or the sun—"was the Manhattan Bridge, and he kept saying it was the el. We finally found some steps and two policemen who told us to go back to the subway."

"What does this amazing man do for a living?" Richard asked.

"He teaches school. He's quite bright." She stood up, extending in stretch a long, silvery-white arm. Richard got her coat and scarf and said he'd walk her home.

"It's only three-quarters of a block," Rebecca protested in a voice free of any insistent inflection.

"You must walk her home, Dick," Joan said. "Pick up a pack of cigarettes." The idea of his walking in the snow seemed to please her, as if she were anticipating how he would bring back with him, in the snow on his shoulders and the coldness of his face, all the sensations of the walk she was not well enough to risk.

"You should stop smoking for a day or two," he told her.

Joan waved them goodbye from the head of the stairs.

The snow, invisible except around streetlights, exerted a fluttering pressure on their faces. "Coming down hard now," he said.

"Yes."

At the corner, where the snow gave the green light a watery blueness, her hesitancy in following him as he turned to walk with the light across Thirteenth Street led him to ask, "It *is* this side of the street you live on, isn't it?"

"Yes."

"I thought I remembered from the time we drove you down from Boston." The Maples had been living in the West Eighties then. "I remember I had an impression of big buildings."

"The church and the butcher's school," Rebecca said. "Every day about ten when I'm going to work the boys learning to be butchers come out for an intermission all bloody and laughing."

Richard looked up at the church; the steeple was fragmentarily silhouetted against the scattered lit windows of a tall apartment building on Seventh Avenue. "Poor church," he said. "It's hard in this city for a steeple to be the tallest thing."

Rebecca said nothing, not even her habitual "Yes." He felt rebuked for being preachy. In his embarrassment he directed her attention to the first next thing he saw, a poorly lettered sign above a great door. "Food Trades

Vocational High School," he read aloud. "The people upstairs told us that the man before the man before *us* in our apartment was a wholesale-meat salesman who called himself a Purveyor of Elegant Foods. He kept a woman in the apartment."

"Those big windows up there," Rebecca said, pointing up at the top story of a brownstone, "face mine across the street. I can look in and feel we are neighbors. Someone's always there; I don't know what they do for a living."

After a few more steps they halted, and Rebecca, in a voice that Richard imagined to be slightly louder than her ordinary one, said, "Do you want to come up and see where I live?"

"Sure." It seemed far-fetched to refuse.

They descended four concrete steps, opened a shabby orange door, entered an overheated half-basement lobby, and began to climb flights of wooden stairs. Richard's suspicion on the street that he was trespassing beyond the public gardens of courtesy turned to certain guilt. Few experiences so savor of the illicit as mounting stairs behind a woman's fanny. Three years ago, Joan had lived in a fourth-floor walkup, in Cambridge. Richard never took her home, even when the whole business, down to the last intimacy, had become routine, without the fear that the landlord, justifiably furious, would leap from his door and devour him as they passed.

Opening her door, Rebecca said, "It's hot as hell in here," swearing for the first time in his hearing. She turned on a weak light. The room was small; slanting planes, the underside of the building's roof, intersected the ceiling and walls and cut large prismatic volumes from Rebecca's living space. As he moved farther forward, toward Rebecca, who had not yet removed her coat, Richard perceived, on his right, an unexpected area created where the steeply slanting roof extended itself to the floor. Here a double bed was placed. Tightly bounded on three sides, the bed had the appearance not so much of a piece of furniture as of a permanently installed, blanketed platform. He quickly took his eyes from it and, unable to face Rebecca at once, stared at two kitchen chairs, a metal bridge lamp around the rim of whose shade plump fish and helm wheels alternated, and a four-shelf bookcase—all of which, being slender and proximate to a tilting wall, had an air of threatened verticality.

"Yes, here's the stove on top of the refrigerator I told you about," Rebecca said. "Or did I?"

The top unit overhung the lower by several inches on all sides. He touched his fingers to the stove's white side. "This room is quite sort of nice," he said.

"Here's the view," she said. He moved to stand beside her at the windows, lifting aside the curtains and peering through tiny flawed panes into the apartment across the street.

"That guy *does* have a huge window," Richard said.

She made a brief agreeing noise of *n*'s.

Though all the lamps were on, the apartment across the street was empty. "Looks like a furniture store," he said. Rebecca had still not taken off her coat. "The snow's keeping up."

"Yes. It is."

"Well"—this word was too loud; he finished the sentence too softly— "thanks for letting me see it. I— Have you read this?" He had noticed a copy of *Auntie Mame* lying on a hassock.

"I haven't had the time," she said.

"I haven't read it either. Just reviews. That's all I ever read."

This got him to the door. There, ridiculously, he turned. It was only at the door, he decided in retrospect, that her conduct was quite inexcusable: not only did she stand unnecessarily close, but, by shifting the weight of her body to one leg and leaning her head sidewise, she lowered her height several inches, placing him in a dominating position exactly suited to the broad, passive shadows she must have known were on her face.

"Well—" he said.

"Well." Her echo was immediate and possibly meaningless.

"Don't, don't let the b-butchers get you." The stammer of course ruined the joke, and her laugh, which had begun as soon as she had seen by his face that he would attempt something funny, was completed ahead of his utterance.

As he went down the stairs she rested both hands on the banister and looked down toward the next landing. "Good night," she said.

"Night." He looked up; she had gone into her room. Oh but they were close.

Sunday Teasing

SUNDAY MORNING: waking, he felt long as a galaxy, and just lacked the will to get up, to unfurl the great sleepy length beneath the covers and go be disillusioned in the ministry by some servile, peace-of-mind-peddling preacher. If it wasn't peace of mind, it was the integrated individual, and if it wasn't the integrated individual, it was the power hidden within each one of us. Never a stern old commodity like sin or remorse, never an open-faced superstition. So Arthur decided, without pretending that it was the preferable course as well as the easier, to stay home and read St. Paul.

His wife fussed around the apartment with a too-determined silence; whenever he read the Bible, she acted as if he were playing solitaire without having first invited her to play rummy, or as if he were delivering an oblique attack on Jane Austen and Henry Green, whom she mostly read. Trying to bring her into the Sunday-morning club, he said, "Here's my grandfather's favorite passage: First Corinthians eleven, verse three. 'But I would have you know, that the head of every man is Christ; and the head of the woman is the man; and the head of Christ is God.' He loved reading that to my mother. It infuriated her."

A mulish perplexity ruffled Macy's usually smooth features. "*What?* The head? The head of every man. What does 'the head' mean exactly? I'm sorry, I just don't understand."

If he had been able to answer her immediately, he would have done so with a smile, but, though the sense of "head" in the text was perfectly clear, he couldn't find a synonym. After a silence he said, "It's so obvious."

"Read me the passage again. I really didn't hear it."

"No," he said.

"Come on, please. 'The head of the man is God . . . ' "

"No."

She abruptly turned and went into the kitchen. "All you do is tease," she said from in there. "You think it's so funny." He hadn't been teasing her at all, but her saying it put the idea into his head.

They were having a friend to the midday meal that Sunday, Leonard Byrne, a Jewish friend who, no matter what the discussion was about, turned it to matters of the heart and body. "Do you realize," he said halfway through the salad, a minute after a round of remarks concerning the movie *Camille* had unexpectedly died, "that in our home it was nothing for my father to kiss me? When I'd come home from summer camp, he'd actually em*brace* me — physically embrace me. No inhibitions about it at all. In my home, it was *nothing* for men physically to show affection for one another. I remember my uncle when he came to visit had *no* inhibitions about warmly embracing my father. Now, that's one thing I find repugnant, personally re*pug*nant to me, about the American home. That there is none of that. It's evident that the American male has some innate fear of being mistaken for a homosexual. But *why*, that's the interesting thing, *why* should he be so protective of his virility? Why shouldn't the American father kiss the American son, when it's done in Italy, in Russia, in France?"

"It's the pioneer," Macy said; she seldom volunteered her opinions, and in this case, Arthur felt, did it only to keep Leonard from running on and on and embarrassing himself. Now she was stuck with the words "It's the pioneer," which, to judge from her face, were beginning to seem idiotic to her. "Those men *had* to be virile," she gamely continued, "they were out there alone, with Indians and bears."

"By the way," Leonard said, resting his elbow on the very edge of the table and tilting his head toward her, for suaveness, "do you know, it has been established beyond all doubt that the American pioneer was a drunkard? But that's not the point. Yes, people say, 'the pioneer,' but I can't quite see how that affects me, as a second-generation American."

"That's it," Arthur told him. "It doesn't. You just said yourself that your family wasn't American. They kissed each other. Now, take me. *I'm* an American. Eleventh-generation German. White, Protestant, Gentile, small-town, middle-class. I am *pure* American. And do you know, I have never seen my father kiss my mother. Never."

Leonard, of course, was outraged ("That's shocking," he said. "That is truly shocking"), but Macy's reaction was what Arthur had angled for. It was hard to separate her perturbation at the announcement from the perturbation caused by her not knowing if he was lying or not. "That's not true," she told Leonard, but then asked Arthur, "Is it?"

"Of course it's true," he said, talking more to Leonard than to Macy. "Our family dreaded body contact. Years went by without my touching my mother. When I went to college, she got into the habit of hugging me goodbye, and now does it whenever we go home. But in my teens, when she was younger, there was nothing of the sort."

"You know, Arthur, that really frightens me," Leonard said.

"Why? Why should it? It never occurred to my father to manhandle me. He used to carry me when I was little, but when I got too heavy, he stopped. Just like my mother stopped dressing me when I could do it myself." Arthur decided to push the proposition further, since nothing he had said since "I have never seen my father kiss my mother" had aroused as much interest. "After a certain age, the normal American boy is raised by people who just see in him a source of income—movie-house managers, garage attendants, people in luncheonettes. The man who ran the luncheonette where I ate did nothing but cheat us out of our money and crab about the noise we made, but I loved that man like a father."

"That's *terrible*, Arthur," Leonard said. "In my family we didn't really trust anybody outside the family. Not that we didn't have friends. We had lots of friends. But it wasn't quite the *same*. Macy, your mother kissed you, didn't she?"

"Oh, yes. All the time. And my father."

"Ah, but Macy's parents are atheists," Arthur said.

"They're Unitarians," she said.

Arthur continued, "To go back to your *why* this should be so. What do we know about the United States other than the fact that it was settled by pioneers? It is a Protestant country, perhaps the only one. It and Norway. Now, what *is* Protestantism? A vision of attaining God with nothing but the mind. Nothing but the mind alone on a mountaintop."

"Yes, yes, of course. We know that," Leonard said, though in truth Arthur had just stated (he now remembered) not a definition of Protestantism but Chesterton's definition of Puritanism.

"In place of the bureaucratic, interceding Church," Arthur went on, trying to correct himself, flushing because his argument had chased him into the sacred groves of his mind, "Luther's notion of Christ is substituted. The reason why in Catholic countries everybody kisses each other is that it's a huge family—God is a family of three, the Church is a family of millions, even heretics are kind of black sheep of the family. Whereas the Protestant lives all by himself, inside of himself. *Fide sola*. Man *should* be lonely."

"Yes, yes," Leonard said, puzzling Arthur; he had meant the statements to be debatable.

Arthur felt his audience was bored, because they were eating again, picking at the anchovies and croutons. He said, as a punch line, "I know when we have kids I'm certainly not going to kiss Macy in front of them."

It was too harsh a thing to say, too bold; he was too excited. Macy said nothing, did not even look up, but her face was tense with an accusatory meekness.

"No, I don't mean that," Arthur said. "It's all lies, lies, lies, lies. My family was very close."

Macy said to Leonard softly, "Don't you believe it. He's been telling the truth."

"I know it," Leonard said. "I've always felt that about Arthur's home ever since I met him. I really have."

And though Leonard could console himself with this supposed insight, something uncongenial had been injected into the gathering, and he became sullen; his mood clouded the room, weighed on their temples like smog, and when, hours later, he left, both Arthur and Macy were unwilling to let him go because he had not had a good time. In a guilty spurt of hospitality, they chattered to him of future arrangements. Leonard walked down the stairs with his hat at an angle less jaunty than when he had come up those stairs—a somehow damp angle, as if he had confused his inner drizzle with a state of outer weather.

Suppertime came. Macy said that she didn't feel well and couldn't eat a bite. Arthur put Benny Goodman's 1938 Carnegie Hall concert on the record-player and, rousing his wife from the Sunday *Times*, insisted that she, who had been raised on Scarlatti and Purcell, take notice of Jess Stacy's classic piano solo on "Sing, Sing, Sing," which he played twice, for her benefit. He prepared some chicken-with-rice soup for himself, mixing the can with just half a can of water, since it would be for only one person and need not be too much thinned. The soup, heated to a simmer, looked so wholesome that he asked Macy if she really didn't want any. She looked up and thought. "Just a cupful," she said, which left him enough to fill a large bowl—plenty, though not a luxurious plenitude.

"Mm. That was so good," she said after finishing.

"Feel better?"

"Slightly."

Macy was reading through a collection of short stories, and Arthur brought the rocking chair from the bedroom and joined her by the lamp, with his paperback copy of *The Tragic Sense of Life*. Here again she misunderstood him; he knew that his reading Unamuno depressed her, and he was reading the book not to depress her but to get the book finished and depress her no longer. She knew nothing of the contents except for his remark one time that according to the author the source of religion is our unwillingness to die; yet she was suspicious.

"Why don't you ever read anything except scary philosophy?" she asked him.

"It isn't scary," he said. "The man's a Christian, sort of."

"You should read some fiction."

"I will, I will, as soon as I finish this."

Perhaps half an hour passed. "Oh," Macy said, dropping her book to the floor. "That's *so* terrible, it's so *aw*ful."

He looked at her inquiringly. She was close to tears. "There's a story in here," she explained. "It just makes you sick. I don't want to think about it."

"See, if you'd read Kierkegaard instead of squalid fiction—"

"No, really. I don't even think it's a good story, it's so awful."

He read the story himself, and Macy moved into the sling chair facing him. He was conscious of her body as clouds of pale color beyond the edge of the page, like a dawn, stirring with gentle unease. "Very good," Arthur said when he was done. "Quite moving."

"It's so horrible," Macy said. "Why was he so awful to his wife?"

"It's all explained. He was out of his caste. He was trapped. A perfectly nice man, corrupted by bad luck."

"How can you *say* that? That's so ridiculous."

"Ridiculous! Why, Macy, the whole pathos of the story lies in the fact that the man, for all his selfishness and cruelty, loves the woman. After all, *he's* telling the story, and if the wife emerges as a sympathetic character, it's because that's the way he sees her. The description of her at the train—here—'As the train glided away she turned toward me her face, calm and so sweet and which, in the instant before it vanished, appeared a radiant white heart.'" The story, clumsily translated from the French, was titled "Un Cœur blanc." "And then, later, remembering—'It gladdens me that I was able then to simulate a depth of affection that I did not at that time feel. She too generously repaid me, and in that zealous response was there not her sort of victory?' That's absolutely sympathetic, you see. It's a terrific image—this perceptive man caged in his own weak character."

To his surprise, Macy had begun to cry. Tears mounted from the lower lids of eyes still looking at him. "Macy," he said, kneeling by her chair and touching his forehead to hers. He ardently wished her well at that moment, yet his actions seemed hurried and morbid. "What is it? Of course I feel sorry for the woman."

"You said he was a *nice* man."

"I didn't mean it. I meant that the horror of the story lies in the fact that the man *does* understand, that he does love the woman."

"It just shows, it shows how *different* we are."

"No we're not. We're exactly alike. Our noses"—he touched hers, then his—"are alike as two peas, our mouths like two turnips, our chins like two hamsters." She laughed sobbingly, but the silliness of his refutation tended to confirm the truth of her remark.

He held her as long as her crying remained strenuous, and when it relented, she moved to the sofa and lay down, saying, "It's awful when you have an ache and don't know if it's your head or your ear or your tooth."

He put the palm of his hand on her forehead. He could never tell about fevers. Her skin felt warm, but then human beings were warm things. "Have you taken your temperature?"

"I don't know where the thermometer is. Broken, probably." She lay in a forsaken attitude, with one arm, the bluish underside uppermost, extended outward, supported in midair by the limits of its flexure. "Oog," she said, sticking out her tongue. "This room is a mess." The Bible had never been replaced in the row of books; it lay on its side, spanning four secular volumes. Several glasses, drained after dinner, stood like castle sentries on the windowsill, the mantel, and the lowest shelf of the bookcase. Leonard had left his rubbers under the table. The jacket of the Goodman record lay on the rug, and the Sunday *Times*, that manifold summation of a week's confusion, was oppressively everywhere. Arthur's soup bowl was still on the table; Macy's cup, cockeyed in the saucer, rested by her chair, along with Unamuno and the collection of short stories. "It's always so awful," she said. "Why don't you ever help to keep the room neat?"

"I will, I will. Now you go to bed." He guided her into the other room and took her temperature. She kept the thermometer in her mouth as she undressed and got into her nightgown. He read her temperature as 98.8°. "Very, very slight," he told her. "I prescribe sleep."

"I look so pale," she said in front of the bathroom mirror.

"We never should have discussed *Camille*." When she was in bed, her face pink against the white pillow and the rest of her covered, he said, "You and Garbo. Tell me how Garbo says, 'You're fooling me.' "

"You're fooling me," she said in a fragile Swedish whisper.

Back in the living room, Arthur returned the books to the shelves, tearing neat strips from the *Times* garden section as bookmarks. He assembled the newspaper and laid it in the kitchen next to the trash can. He stood holding Leonard's rubbers for ten seconds, then dropped them in a corner. He took the record off the phonograph, slipped it into its envelope, and hid it in the closet with the others.

Lastly, he collected the dishes and glasses and washed them. As he stood at the sink, his hands in water which, where the suds thinned and broke, showed a silvery gray, the Sunday's events repeated themselves in his mind, bending like nacreous flakes around a central infrangible irritant, becoming the perfect and luminous thought: *You don't know anything.*

Incest

"I WAS IN A MOVIE HOUSE, fairly plush, in a sort of mezzanine, or balcony. It was a wide screen. On it there were tall people—it seemed to be at a dance or at least *function*—talking and bending toward each other gracefully, in that misty Technicolor Japanese pictures have. I *knew* that this was the movie version of *Remembrance of Things Past*. I had the impression sitting there that I had been looking forward to it for a long time, and I felt slightly guilty at not being home, you know. There was a girl sitting down one row, catty-corner from me. She had a small head with a thin, rather touching neck, like Moira Bryer, but it wasn't her, or anyone we know. At any rate there was this feeling of great affection toward her, and it seemed, in the light of the movie—the movie was taking place entirely in a bright-yellow ballroom, so the faces of the audience were clear—it seemed somehow that the entire chance to make my life good was wrapped up in this girl, who was strange to me. Then she was in the seat beside me, and I was giving her a back rub."

"*Uh*-oh," his wife said, pausing in her stooping. She was grazing the carpet, picking up the toys, cards, matches, and spoons scattered by their daughter, Jane, a year and seven months old. Big Jane, as she had dreaded being called when they named the child, held quite still to catch what next he had to tell. Lee had begun the account ironically, to register his irritation with her for asking him, her own day had been so dull and wearing, to talk, to tell her of *his* day. Nothing interested him less than his own work day, done. It made his jaws ache, as with a smothered yawn, to consider framing one sentence about it. So, part desperation, part admonishment, he had begun to describe the dream he had been careful to keep from her at breakfast. He protected his wife here, at the place where he recalled feeling his hands leave the lean girl's comforted shoulder blades and travel thoughtfully around the cool, strait, faintly ridged sides of the rib case to the always surprising boon in front—sensations momentarily more vivid in the nerves of his fingers than the immediate texture of the bamboo chair he occupied.

"Through the blouse."

"Good," she said. "Good for you both."

Jane appeared so saucy saying this he was emboldened to add a true detail: "I think I did undo her bra strap. By pinching through the cloth." To judge by his wife's expression—tense for him, as if he were bragging before company—the addition was a mistake. He hastened on. "Then we were standing in back of the seats, behind one of those walls that come up to your chest, and I was being introduced to her father. I had the impression he was a doctor. He was rather pleasant, really: gray hair, and a firm grip. He seemed cordial, and I had a competent feeling, as if I couldn't help making a good impression. But behind this encounter—with the girl standing off to one side—there was the sadness of the movie itself continuing on the screen; the music soared; Proust's face was shown—a very young face—with the eyelids closed, and this shimmered and spun and turned into a slow pink vortex that then solidified into a huge motionless rose, filling the whole screen. And I thought, *Now I know how the book ends*."

"How exciting, sweetie! It's like 'The Dream of the Rood.' " Jane resumed cleaning up after her daughter. Lee was abruptly oppressed by a belief that he had made her life harder to bear.

He said, "The girl must have been you, because you're the only person I know who likes to have their back rubbed."

"You find my neck touching?"

"Well, for God's sake, I can't be held accountable for the people I meet in dreams. *I* don't invite them." He was safe, of course, as long as they stayed away from the real issue, which was why he had told her the dream at all. "That girl means nothing to me now. In the dream obviously I was still in high school and hadn't met you. I remember sitting there and wondering, because it was such a long movie, if my mother would give me hell when I got back."

"I say, it's a very exciting dream. How far *are* you in Proust?"

"*Sodom and Gomorrah.*" It occurred to him, what a queer mediocre thing it was, to scorn the English title yet not dare pronunciation of the French, and apropos of this self-revelation he said, "I'll never get out. I'm just the sort of person who begins Proust and can't finish. Lowest of the low. Won't even tell his wife what his day at work was like." He changed his tone. "Which is better—to finish *Remembrance of Things Past,* or to never begin it?"

Unexpectedly, so profound was her fatigue, she did not recognize the question as a piece of sport rhetoric, and, after a moment's thought, seriously answered, "To finish it."

Then she turned, and her lovely pale face—in photographs like a white water-smoothed stone, so little did the indentations and markings of it have harshness—lengthened, and the space between her eyebrows creased vertically; into the kitchen she shouted, *"Jane!* What are you *doing?"*

While they had been talking, the child had been keeping herself quiet with the sugar bowl. It was a new trick of hers, to push a chair and climb up on it; in this way a new world, a fresh stratum of things, was made available to her curiosity. The sugar bowl, plump modern pewter, lived casually on the counter of a waist-high cabinet, near the wall. Little Jane had taken and inverted it and, with an eerie, repetitious, patient dabbling motion had reduced the one shining Alp to a system of low ranges. She paid no attention to her mother's shout, but when her parents drew closer and sighed together, she quickly turned her face toward them as if for admiration, her chin and lips frosted. Her upper lip, when she smiled, curved like the handlebar of a bicycle. The sight of her little, perfect, blue, inturned teeth struck joy into Lee's heart.

With an audience now, little Jane accelerated her work. Her right hand, unattended by her eyes, which remained with her parents, scrabbled in a panicky way among the white drifts and then, palm down, swept a quantity onto the floor, where it hit with a sound like one stroke of a drummer's brush. On the spatter-pattern linoleum the grains of sugar were scarcely visible. The child looked down, wondering where they had gone.

"Damn you," his wife said to Lee, "you never do a damn thing to help. Now, why can't you play with her a minute? You're her father. *I'm* not going to clean it up." She walked out of the kitchen.

"I *do* play with her," he said, helplessly amiable (he understood his wife so well, divined so exactly what confused pain the scattered sugar caused her, she whose mother was a fanatic housekeeper), although he recognized that in her distraught state his keeping cheerful figured as mockery of her, one more cross to carry toward the day's end.

Lee asked his daughter, "Want to run around?"

Jane hunched her shoulders and threw back her head, her sugar-gritty teeth gleefully clenched. "Pay roun," she said, wagging her hand on her wrist.

He made the circular motion she had intended, and said, "In a minute. Now we must help poor Mommy." With two sheets of typing paper, using one as a brush and the other as a pan, he cleaned up what she had spilled on the counter, reaching around her, since she kept her position standing on the chair. Her breath floated randomly, like a butterfly, on his forearms as he swept. They had become two conspirators. He folded the pan into a chute and returned the sugar to the bowl. Then there was the sugar on the floor—when you moved your feet, atoms of it crackled. He stooped, the two pieces of paper in his hands, knowing they wouldn't quite do.

Jane whimpered and recklessly jogged her body up and down on her legs, making the chair tip and slap the cabinet. "*Jane*," he said.

"Pay roun," the girl whined feebly, her strength sapped by frustration.

"*What?*" his wife answered from the living room in a voice as cross as his. She had fought giving the baby her name, but he had insisted; there was no other woman's name he liked, he had said.

"Nothing, I was scolding the kid. She was going to throw herself off the chair. She wants to play Round."

"Well, why don't you? She's had an awfully dismal day. I don't think we make her happy enough."

"O.K., damn it. I will." He crumpled the sheets of paper and stuffed them into the wastepaper can, letting the collected sugar fly where it would.

Round was a simple game. Jane ran from the sofa in one room to the bed in the other, through the high white double doorway, with pilasters, that had persuaded them to take the small apartment. He chased her. When his hands nicked her bottom or touched her soft baby waist, she laughed wildly her double laugh, which originated deep in her lungs and ricocheted, shrill, off her palate. Lee's problem was to avoid overtaking her, in the great length of his strides, and stepping on her. When she wobbled or slowed, he clapped twice or thrice, to give her the sense of his hands right behind her ears, like two nipping birds. If she toppled, he swiftly picked her up, tickling her briefly if she seemed stunned or indignant. When she reached the bed—two low couches, box springs on short legs, set side by side and made up as one—he leapfrogged over her and fell full-length on the mattresses. This, for him, was the strenuous part of the game. Jane, finding herself between her father's ankles after the rush of his body above her head, laughed her loudest, pivoted, and ran the other way, flailing her arms, which she held so stiffly the elbows were indentations. At the sofa end of the track there could be no leapfrogging. Lee merely stopped and stood with his back toward her until the little girl calculated she dare make a break for it. Her irises swivelled in their blue whites; it was the first strategy of her life. The instant she decided to move, her bottled excitement burst forth; as she clumped precipitately toward the high white arch, laughter threatened to upend her world. The game lasted until the child's bath. Big Jane, for the first time that day free of her daughter, was not hurrying toward this moment.

After four times back and forth, Lee was exhausted and damp. He flopped on the bed the fifth time and instead of rising rolled onto his back. This was ruining the crease in his suit pants. His daughter, having started off, felt his absence behind her and halted. Her mother was coming from the kitchen, carrying washed diapers and a dust brush. Like her own mother, big Jane held a cigarette in the left corner of her mouth. Her left eye fluttered against the smoke. Lee's mother-in-law was shorter than his wife, paler, more sarcastic—very different, he had thought. But this habit was hers right down to the tilt of the cigarette and the droop of the neglected ash. Looking, Lee saw that, as Jane squinted, the white skin at the outside corner of her eye crinkled finely, as dry as her mother's, and that his wife's lids were touched with the lashless, grainy, desexed quality of the lids of the middle-aged woman he had met not a dozen times, mostly in Indianapolis, where she kept a huge brick house spotlessly clean and sipped vermouth from breakfast to bed. All unknowing he had married her.

Jane, as she passed him, glanced down with an untypical, sardonic, cigarette-stitched expression. By shifting his head on the pillow he could watch her in the bathroom. She turned her back to hang the diapers on a brown cord strung between mirror and window. This was more his Jane: the wide rounded shoulders, the back like two halves of a peach, the big thighs, the narrow ankles. In the mirror her face, straining up as she attached the clothespins, showed age and pallor. It was as if there could exist a coin one side of which wears thin while the other keeps all the gloss and contour of the minting.

"Da-*tee*." A coral flush had overspread his daughter's face; in another moment she would whimper and throw herself on the floor.

With an ostentatious groan—he didn't know which of his females he was rebuking—Lee rose from the bed and chased his daughter again. Then they played in the living room with the bolsters, two prism-shaped pieces of foam rubber that served as a back to the sofa, an uncomfortable modernist slab that could, when a relative visited, be used for sleeping. Stood on end, the stiff bolsters were about the toddler's height, and little Jane hugged them like brothers, and preferred them to dolls. Though her size, they were light enough for her to lift and manipulate. Especially she loved to unzip the skin of gray fabric and prod with her finger the colorless, buoyant flesh beneath.

Catching them at this, big Jane said, "It kills me, it just is more depressing than anything she does, the way she's always trying to undress those bolsters. Don't en*courag*e her at it."

"I don't. It's not my idea. It was *you* who took the covers to the Launderette so she saw the bolsters naked. It made a big impression. It's a state of primal innocence she wants to get them back to."

Wavering between quarrel and honest discussion—that there was a way of "talking things out" was an idea she had inherited from her father, a rigorously liberal civic leader and committeeman—she chose discussion. "It's not just those bolsters, you know. About three times a day she takes all the books out of their jackets. And spills matches in a little heap. You have no idea how much cleaning up I have to do to keep this place from looking like a pigpen. Yesterday I was in the bathroom washing my hair and when I came out she had gotten our camera open. I guess the whole roll's exposed. I put it back. Today she wanted to get the works out of the music box and threw a tantrum. And I don't know how often she brings those nasty frustrating little Chinese eggs you got her to me and says, 'Opo. Opo.' "

Reminded of the word, little Jane said, of a bolster, "Opo, opo." The zipper was stuck.

"Japanese," Lee said. "Those eggs were made in Genuine Occupied Japan. They're antiques." The child's being balked by the zipper preyed on his nerves. He hated fiddling with things like zippers caught on tiny strips of cloth; it was like squinting into a narrow detail of Hell. Further, as he leaned back on the bolsterless sofa to rest his neck against the wall, he infuriatingly felt the glass-capped legs skid on the uneven floor. "It's a very healthy instinct," he went on. "She's an empiricist. She's throwing open doors long locked by superstition."

Jane said, "I looked up 'unwrapping instinct' in Spock and the only thing in the index was 'underweight.' " Her tone was listless and humorous, and for the moment this concession put the family, to Lee's mind, as right as three Japanese eggs, each inside the other.

. . .

His wife gave his daughter her bath as day turned to evening. He had to go into the bathroom himself and while there studied the scene. The child's silky body, where immersed, was of a graver tint than that of her skin smarting in air. Two new cakes of unwrapped soap drifted around her. When her mother put a washrag to her face, blinding and scratching her, her fingers turned pale green with the pressure of her grip on the edge of the tub. She didn't cry, though. "She seems to like her bath better now," he said.

"She loves it. From five on, until you come, she talks about it. Daddy. Bath. Omelet."

"Omma net," his daughter said, biting her lower lip in a smile for him.

It had become, in one of those delicate mutations of routine whereby Jane shifted duties to him, his job to feed the little girl. The child's soft mouth had been burned and she was wary; the sample bites Lee took to show her that the food was safe robbed of sharpness his appetite for his own dinner. Foreknowledge of the emotion caused in his wife by the sight of half-clean plates and half-full cups led him to complete little Jane's portion of tomato juice, omelet-with-toast, and, for dessert, apple-sauce. Handling the tiny cup and tiny knife and fork and spoon set his stomach slightly on edge. Though not fussy about food, he was disturbed by eating implements of improper weight or length. Jane, hidden in the kitchen, was unable to see or, if she had seen, to appreciate—for all their three years of marriage, she had a stunted awareness of his niceties—the discomfort he was giving himself. This annoyed him.

So he was unfortunately brusque with little Jane's bottle. Ideally the bottle was the happiest part of the meal. Steaming and dewy, it soared, white angel, out of the trembling pan, via Mommy's hands, with a kiss, into hers. She grabbed it, and Lee, his hand behind her head, steered her toward the bedroom and her crib.

"Nice maugham," she said, conscientiously echoing the infinity of times they had told her that the bottle was nice and warm.

Having lifted her into the crib and seen her root the bottle in her mouth, he dropped the fuzzy pink blanket over her and left quickly, gently closing the doors and sealing her into the darkness that was to merge with sleep. It was no doubt this quickness that undid the process. Though the child was drugged with heated milk, she still noticed a slight.

He suspected this at the time. When, their own meal barely begun, the crib springs creaked unmistakably, he said, "Son of a bitch." Stan Lomax, on their faint radio, was giving an account of Ted Williams' latest verbal outrage; Lee was desperate to hear every word. Like many Americans, he was spiritually dependent on Ted Williams. He asked his wife, "God damn it, doesn't that kid do anything in the day? Didn't you take her to the park? Why isn't she worn out?"

The one answer to this could be his own getting up, after a silence, and going in to wait out the baby's insomnia. The hollow goodness of the act, like a coin given to a beggar with a scowl, infuriated his tongue: "I work like a fool all day and come home and run the kid up and down until my legs ache and I have a headache and then I can't even eat my pork chop in peace."

In the aquarium of the dark room the child's face floated spectrally, and her eyes seemed discrete pools of the distant, shy power that had put them all there, and had made these walls, and the single tree outside, showing the first stages of leaf under the tawny night sky of New York. "Do you want to go on the big bed?"

"Big—*bed!*"

"O.K."

"Ogay."

Adjusting to the lack of light, he perceived that the bottle, nested in a crumpled sheet, was drained. Little Jane had been standing in her crib, one foot on the edge, as if in ballet school. For two weeks she had been gathering nerve for the time she would climb the crib's wall and drop free outside. He lifted her out, breathing "Ooh, *heavy*," and took her to the wide low bed made of two beds. She clung to the fuzzy blanket—with milk, her main soporific.

Beside her on the bed, he began their story. "Once upon a time, in the big, big woods—" She flipped ecstatically at the known cadence. "Now, you relax. There was a tiny little creature name of Barry Mouse."

"Mouff!" she cried, and sat straight up, as if she had heard one. She looked down at him for confirmation.

"Barry Mouse," he said. "And one day, when Barry Mouse was walking through the woods, he came to a great big tree, and in the top of the great big tree what do you think there was?"

At last she yielded to the insistent pressure of his hand and fell back, her heavy blond head sinking into the pillow. He repeated, "What do you think there was?"

"Owl."

"That's right. Up at the top of the tree there was an owl, and the owl said, 'I'm going to eat you, Barry Mouse.' And Barry Mouse said, 'No, no.' So Owl said, 'O.K., then why don't you *hop* on my *back* and we'll *fly* to the *moon?*' And so Barry Mouse hopped on Owl's back and awaay they went—"

Jane turned on her side, so her great face was an inch from his. She giggled and drummed her feet against his abdomen, solidly. Neither Lee nor his wife, who shared the one bedtime story, had ever worked out what happened on the moon. Once the owl and the mouse were aloft, their imaginations collapsed. Knowing his voice daren't stop now, when the child's state was possibly transitional and he felt as if he were bringing to his lips an absolutely brimful glass of liquid, he continued with some nonsense about cinnamon trees and Chinese maidens, no longer bothering to keep within the child's vocabulary. Little Jane began touching his face with her open mouth, a sure sign she was sleepy. "Hey," he murmured when one boneless moist kiss landed directly on his lips. "Jane is so sleepy," he said, "because Daddy is sleepy, and Mommy is sleepy, and Bear is ssleepy, and Doll is sssleeepy. . . ."

She lay quiet, her face in shadow, her fine straight yellow hair fanned across the pillow. Neither he nor his wife was blond; they had brown hair, rat-color. There was little blondness in either family: just Jane's Aunt Ruth, and Lee's sister, Margaret, eight years older than he and married before he had left grade school. She had been the good one of the children and he the bright, difficult one.

Presuming his daughter asleep, he lifted himself on one elbow. She kicked his belly, rolled onto her back, and said in a voice loud with drowsiness, "Baaiy Mouff."

Stroking her strange hair, he began again, "Once upon a time, in the deep, deep woods, there lived a little creature . . ." This time, he seemed to succeed.

As he lowered her into her crib, her eyes opened. He said, "O.K.?"

She pronounced beautifully, "O.K."

"Gee, she's practically epileptic with energy," he said, blinded by the brilliant light of the room where his wife had remained.

"She's a good child," Jane affirmed, speaking out of her thoughts while left alone rather than in answer to his remark. "Your dessert is on the table." She had kept hers intact on the sofa beside her, so they could eat their raspberry whip together. She also had beside her an orange-juice glass half full of vermouth.

When the clock said seven-fifty, he said, "Why don't you run off to the movie? You never have any fun."

"All right," she said. "Go ahead. Go."

"No, I don't mean that. I mean you should go." Still, he smiled.

"You can go as a reward for putting her to sleep."

"Venus, I don't *want* to go," he said, without great emphasis, since at that moment he was rustling through the paper. He had difficulty finding the theatre section, and decided. "No, if you're too tired, no one will. I can't leave you. You need me too much."

"If you want to, go; don't torment me about it," she said, drawing on her vermouth and staring into *The New Republic*.

"Do you think," he asked, "when Jane is sixteen, she'll go around in the back seat of Chevrolets and leave her poor old daddy?"

"I hope so," Jane said.

"Will she have your bosom?"

"She'll think it's her own."

He earnestly tried to visualize his daughter matured, and saw little but a charm bracelet on a slim, fair wrist. The forearms of teen-age girls tapered amazingly, toward little cages of bird bones. Charm bracelets were *démodé* already, he supposed.

Lee, committed to a long leisured evening at home, of the type that seemed precious on the nights when they had to go out, was unnerved by its wide opportunities. He nibbled at the reading matter closest to hand—an article, "Is the Individual a Thing of the Past?," and last Sunday's comic section. At *Alley Oop* he checked himself and went into the kitchen. Thinking of the oatmeal cookies habitual in his parents' home, he opened the cupboard and found four kinds of sugar and seven of cereal, five infants' and two adults'. Jane was always buying some esoteric grind of sugar for a pastrymaking project, then discovering she couldn't use it. He smiled at this foible and carried his smile like an egg on a spoon into the living room, where his wife saw it but of course not the point of it, that it was a smile generated by love of her. He leaned his forehead against the bookcase, by the anthology shelf, and considered all the poetry he had once read evaporating in him, a vast dying sea.

As he stood there, his father floated from behind and possessed him, occupying specifically the curved area of the jawbone. He understood perfectly why that tall stoical man was a Mason, church-council member, and Scout-troop leader, always with an excuse for leaving the house.

Jane, concentrating all the pleasures her day had withheld into the hour remaining before she became too drowsy to think, put Bach on the record-player. As she did so, her back and arms made angles reminding him of her more angular, less drowsy college self.

When she returned to the sofa, he asked, "What makes you so pretty?" Then, having to answer it himself, he said, "Childbearing."

Preoccupied with some dim speckled thinker in her magazine, she fondled the remark briefly and set it aside, mistakenly judging it to be a piece of an obscure, ill-tempered substance—him "getting at" her. He poured a little vermouth for himself and struck a pose by the mantel, trying to find with his legs and shoulders angles equivalent in effect to those she had made putting on the record. As she sat there, studious, he circumscribed her, every detail, with the tidal thought *Mine, mine.* She wasn't watching. She thought she knew what to expect from him, tonight at least.

Later, he resolved, and, in a mood of resolution, read straight through the Jones Very section of F. O. Matthiessen's anthology of American poetry. The poet's stubborn sensibility aroused a readerly stubbornness; when Lee had finished, it was too late, the hour had slipped by. By the clock it was ten-thirty; for his wife, having risen with little Jane, it was after one. Her lids were pink. This was one of those days when you sow and not reap.

Two hissing, clattering elves working a minor fairy-tale transposition, together they lifted the crib containing the sleeping girl and carried it into the living room, and shut the doors. Instead of undressing, Jane picked up odds and ends of his—spare shoes and the socks he had worn yesterday and the tie he had worn today. Next she went into the bathroom and emerged wearing a cotton nightie. In bed beside him she read a page of *Swann's Way* and fell asleep under the harsh light. He turned it off and thought furiously, the family's second insomniac. The heat of Jane's body made the bed stuffy. He hated these low beds; he lay miles below the ceiling, deep in the pit. The radiator, hidden in the windowsill by his head, breathed lavishly. High above, through a net of crosses, a few stars strove where the brownish glow of New York's night sky gave out. The child cried once, but, thank God, in her sleep.

He recalled what he always forgot in the interval of day, his insomnia game. Last night he had finished *D* in a burst of glory: Yvonne Dionne, Zuleika Dobson. He let the new letter be *G.* Senator Albert Gore. Benny Goodman, Constance Garnett, *David* Garnett, Edvard Grieg. Goethe was Wolfgang and Gorki was Maxim. Farley Granger, Graham Greene (or Greta Garbo, *or* George Gobel), Henry Green. *I* was always difficult. You kept thinking of Ilka Chase. He wrestled and turned and cursed his wife, her heedless rump way on his side. To ward off the temptation to nudge her awake, he padded after a glass of water, grimacing into the mirror. As he returned his head to the cooled pillow, it came to him, first name and surname both at once: Ira Gershwin. Ira Gershwin: he savored it before proceeding. John Galsworthy, Kathryn Grayson . . . Lou Gehrig, poor devil . . .

He and Jane walked along a dirt road, in high, open-field country, like the farm owned by Mark, his mother's brother. He was glad that Jane was seeing the place, because while he was growing up it had given him a sense of wealth to have an uncle attached to a hundred such well-kept acres. His relationship with Jane seemed to be at that stage when it was important for each side of the betrothal to produce external signs of respectability. "But *I* am even richer," he abruptly announced. She appeared not to notice. They walked companionably but in silence, and seemed responsible for the person with them, a female their height. Lee gathered the impression, despite a veil against his eyes, that this extra girl was blonde and sturdy and docile. His sense of her sullenness may have been nothing but his anxiety to win her approval, reflected. Though her features were hard to make out, the emotion he bore her was precise: the coppery, gratified, somewhat adrift feeling he would get when physically near girls he admired in high school. The wind had darkened and grown purposeful.

Jane went back, though the countryside remained the same, and he was dousing, with a lawn hose attached to the side of the house, the body of this third person. Her head rested on the ground; he held her ankles and slowly, easily turned the light, stiff mass, to wet every area. It was important that water wash over every bit of skin. He was careful; the task, like rinsing the suds off of an automobile, was absorbing, rather than pleasant or unpleasant.

A Gift from the City

LIKE MOST HAPPY PEOPLE, they came from well inland. Amid this city's mysteries, they had grown very close. When the phone on his desk rang, he knew it was she. "Jim? Say. Something awful has happened."

"What?" His voice had contracted and sounded smaller. He pictured his wife and small daughter attacked by teen-agers, derelicts, coal men, beneath the slender sparse trees of Tenth Street; oh, if only love were not immaterial! If only there were such a thing as enchantment, and he could draw, with a stick, a circle of safety around them that would hold, though they were on Tenth near Sixth and he forty blocks north.

"I guess it shouldn't be awful but it's so upsetting. Martha and I were in the apartment, we had just come back from the park, and I was making tea for her tea party—"

"Nnn. And?"

"And the doorbell rang. And I didn't know who could be calling, but I pressed the buzzer and went to the stairs, and there was this young Negro. It seemed strange, but then he looked awfully frightened and really smaller than I am. So I stood at the banister and he stood on the middle of the stairs, and he told me this story about how he had brought his family up from North Carolina in somebody else's truck and they had found a landlord who was giving them a room but they had no furniture or food. I couldn't understand half of what he said." Her voice broke here.

"Poor Liz. It's all right, he didn't expect you to."

"He kept saying something about his wife, and I *couldn't* understand it."

"You're O.K. now, aren't you?"

"Yes, I'm O.K., let me finish."

"You're crying."

"Well, it was awfully strange."

"What did he *do?*"

"He didn't *do* anything. He was very nice. He just wanted to know if there were any odd jobs I could let him do. He'd been all up and down Tenth Street just ringing doorbells, and nobody was home."

"We don't have any odd jobs."

"That's what I said. But I gave him ten dollars and said I was sorry but this was all I had in the house. It's all I did have."

"Good. That was just the right thing."

"Was it all right?"

"Sure. You say the poor devil came up in a truck?" James was relieved: the shadow of the coal man had passed; the enchantment had worked. It had seemed for a moment, from her voice, that the young Negro was right there in the apartment, squeezing Martha on the sofa.

"The point is, though," Liz said, "now we don't have any money for the weekend, and Janice is coming tomorrow night so we can go to the movies, and then the Bridgeses on Sunday. You know how she eats. Did you go to the bank?"

"Damn it, no. I forgot."

"Well, *dar*ling."

"I keep thinking we have lots of money." It was true; they did. "Never mind, maybe they'll cash a check here."

"You think? He was really awfully pathetic, and I couldn't tell if he was a crook or not."

"Well, even if he was he must have needed the money; crooks need money, too."

"You think they *will* cash a check?"

"Sure. They love me."

"The really awful thing I haven't told you. When I gave him the ten dollars he said he wanted to thank you—he seemed awfully interested in you—and I said, Well, fine, but on Saturdays we were in and out all day, so he said he'd come in the evening. He really wants to thank you."

"He does."

"I told him we were going to the movies and he said he'd come around before we went."

"Isn't he rather aggressive? Why didn't he let *you* thank me for him?"

"Darley, I didn't know *what* to say."

"Then it's not the Bridgeses we need the money for; it's him."

"No, I don't think so. You made me forget the crucial part: he said he has gotten a job that starts Monday, so it's just this weekend he needs furniture."

"Why doesn't he sleep on the floor?" James could imagine himself, in needful circumstances, doing that. In the Army he had done worse.

"He has this *family*, Jim. Did you want me not to give him anything— to run inside and lock the door? It would have been easy to do, you know."

"No, no, you were a wonderful Christian. I'm proud of you. Anyway, if he comes before the movie he can't very well stay all night."

This pleasant logic seemed firm enough to conclude on, yet, when she had hung up and her voice was gone, the affair seemed ominous again. It was as if, with the click of the receiver, she had sunk beneath an ocean. His own perch, twelve stories above Madison Avenue, swayed slightly, with the roll of too many cigarettes. He ground his present one into a turquoise ashtray, and looked about him, but his beige office at Dudevant & Smith, Industrial and Package Design, offered an inappropriate kind of comfort. His youth's high hopes—he had thought he was going to be a painter—had been distilled into a few practical solids: a steel desk, an adjustable office chair, a drawing board the size of a dining table, infinitely adjustable lighting fixtures, abundant draftsman's equipment, and a bulletin board so fresh it gave off a scent of cork. Oversized white tacks fixed on the cork several flattering memos from Dudevant, a snapshot, a studio portrait of Liz, and a four-color ad for the Raydo shaver, a shaver that James had designed, though an asterisk next to the object dropped the eye to the right-hand corner, to the firm's name, in modest sans-serif. This was all right; it was in the bargain. James's anonymity had been honestly purchased. Indeed, it seemed they couldn't give him enough; there was always some bonus or adjustment or employee benefit or Christmas present appearing on his desk, in one of those long blue envelopes that spelled "money" to his mind as surely as green engravings.

His recent fortunes had been so good, James had for months felt that some harsh blow was due. Cautious, he gave Providence few opportunities to instruct him. Its last chance, except for trips in the car, had been childbirth, and Liz had managed that twenty months ago, one Thursday at dawn, as if it were the most natural thing in the world. As the months passed harmlessly, James's suspicion increased that the city itself, with its aging Art Deco surfaces, its black noon shadows, its godless millions, was poised to strike. He placated the circumambient menace the only way he knew—by giving to beggars. He distributed between one and two dollars a day to Salvation Army bell ringers, sidewalk violinists, husky blind men standing in the center of the pavement with their beautiful German shepherds, men on crutches offering yellow pencils, mumbling drunks anxious to shake his hand and show him the gash beneath their hats, men noncommittally displaying their metal legs in subway tunnels. Ambulatory ones, given the pick of a large crowd, would approach him; to their vision, though he dressed and looked like anyone else, he must wear, with Byzantine distinctness, the aureole of the soft touch.

Saturday was tense. James awoke feeling the exact shape of his stomach, a disagreeable tuber. The night before, he had tried to draw from Liz more information about her young Negro. "How was he dressed?"

"Not badly."

"Not badly!"

"A kind of sport coat with a red wool shirt open at the neck, I think."

"Well, why is he all dolled up if he has no money? He dresses better than I do."

"It didn't seem *terribly* strange. He *would* have *one* good outfit."

"And he brought his wife and *seven* children up here in the cab of a truck?"

"I said seven? I just have the feeling it's seven."

"Sure. Seven dwarfs, seven lively arts, seven levels of Purgatory . . ."

"It couldn't have been in the cab, though. It must have been in the truck part. He said they had no furniture or anything except what they wore."

"Just the rags on their backs. Son of a bitch."

"This is so unlike you, darling. You're always sending checks to Father Flanagan."

"He only asks me once a year, and at least he doesn't come crawling up the stairs after my wife."

James was indignant. The whole tribe of charity seekers, to whom he had been so good, had betrayed him. On Saturday morning, down on Eighth Street buying a book, he deliberately veered away, off the curb and into the gutter, to avoid a bum hopefully eyeing him. At lunch the food lacked taste. The interval between the plate and his face exasperated him; he ate too fast, greedily. In the afternoon, all the way to the park, he maintained a repellent frown. When Liz seemed to dawdle, he took over the pushing of the carriage himself. A young colored man in Levi's descended the steps of a brick four-story and peered up and down the street uncertainly. James's heart tripped. "There he is."

"Where?"

"Right ahead, looking at you."

"Aren't you scary? That's not him. Mine was really short."

At the park his daughter played in the damp sand by herself. No one seemed to love her; the other children romped at selfish games. The slatted shadow of the fence lengthened as the sun drew closer to the tops of the NYU buildings. Beneath this orange dying ball on an asphalt court, a yelping white played tennis with a tall, smooth-stroking black man with a Caribbean accent. Martha tottered from the sandbox to the seesaw to the swings, in her element and fearless. Strange, the fruit of his seed was a native New Yorker; she had been born in a hospital on West Eleventh Street. He rescued her at the entry to the swing section, lifted her into one, and pushed her from the front. Her face dwindled and loomed, dwindled and loomed; she laughed, but none of the other parents or children gave a sign of hearing her. The metal of the swing was icy. This was September; a chill, end-of-summer breeze weighed on the backs of his hands.

When they returned to the apartment, after four, safe, and the Negro was not there, and Liz set about making tea as on any other day, his fears were confounded, and he irrationally ceased expecting anything bad to happen. They gave Martha her bath and ate their dinner in peace; by pure will he was keeping the hateful doorbell smothered. And when it did ring, it was only Janice their baby-sitter, coming up the stairs with her grandmotherly slowness.

He warned her, "There's a slight chance a young Negro will be coming here to find us," and told her, more or less, the story.

"Well, don't worry, I won't let him in," Janice said in the tone of one passing on a particularly frightening piece of gossip. "I'll tell him you're not here and I don't know when you'll be back." She was a good-hearted, unfortunate girl, with dusty tangerine hair. Her mother in Rhode Island was being filtered through a series of hopeless operations. Most of her weekends were spent up there, helping her mother die. The salary Janice earned as a stenographer at NBC was consumed by train fares and long-distance phone calls; she never accepted her fee at the end of a night's sitting without saying, with a soft one-sided smile wherein ages of Irish wit were listlessly deposited, "I hate to take it, but I need the money."

"Well, no, don't be rude or anything. Tell him—and I don't think he'll come, but just in case—we'll be here Sunday."

"The Bridgeses, too," Liz pointed out.

"Yeah, well, I don't think he'll show. If he's as new here as you said he said he was, he probably can't find the place again."

"You know," Janice said to Liz, "you really can't be so softhearted. I admire you for it, and I feel as sorry for these people as you do, but in this town, believe me, you don't dare trust anybody, literally *any*body. A girl at work beside me knows a man who's as healthy as you or me, but he goes around on crutches and makes a hundred and twenty dollars a week. Why, that's more than any of us who work honestly make."

James smiled tightly, insulted twice; he made more than that a week, and he did not like to hear he was being defrauded by pitiable souls on the street who he could see were genuinely deformed or feeble-minded or alcoholic.

After a pause, Liz gently asked the girl, "How is your mother?"

Janice's face brightened and was not quite so overpowered by the orange hair. "Oh, on the phone last night she sounded real high and mighty. The P.-T.A. has given her some job with a drive for funds, something she could do with pencil and paper, without getting up. I've told you how active she had been. She was all for getting out of bed. She said she can feel, you know, that it's out of her body now. But when I talked to the doctor last Sunday, he said we mustn't hope too much. But he seemed very proud of the operation."

"Well, good luck," James said, jingling the change in his pocket.

Janice shook her finger. "You have a good time. He isn't going to get in if I'm here, *that* you can depend on," she assured them, misunderstanding, or perhaps understanding more than necessary.

The picture was excellent, but just at the point where John Wayne, after tracking the Comanches from the snowbound forests of Montana to the blazing dunes of Border Country, was becoming reconciled to the idea of his niece's cohabiting with a brave, James vividly remembered the bum who had wobbled toward him on Eighth Street—the twisted eye, the coat too small to button, the pulpy mouth with pathetic effort trying to frame the first words. The image made him squirm in his seat and pull away from Liz's hand. She, as the credits rolled, confided that her eyes smarted from the VistaVision. They were reluctant to go home so early; Janice counted on them to stay away during the easy hours when Martha was asleep. But the bar at the White Horse Tavern was crowded and noisy—it had become a tourist trap—and the main streets of the Village, thronged with gangsters and hermaphrodites, seemed to James a poor place to stroll with his wife. Liz with her innocent open stare caught the attention of every thug and teen-ager they passed. "Stop it," he said. "You'll get me knifed."

"Darling. There's no law against people's eyes."

"There should be. They think you're a whore out with her pimp. What makes you stare at everybody?"

"Faces are *interesting.* Why are you so uninterested in people?"

"Because every other day you call up the office and I have to come rescue you from some damn spook you've enticed up the stairs. No wonder Dudevant is getting set to fire me."

"Let's go home if you want to rave."

"We can't. Janice needs the money, the bloodsucker."

"It's nearly ten. She charges a dollar an hour, after all."

As they advanced down Tenth from Fifth he saw a slight blob by their gate which simply squinting did not erase. He did not expect ever to see Liz's Negro, who had had his chance at dinner. Yet, when it was clear that a man *was* standing there, wearing a hat, James hastened forward, glad at last to have the enemy life-sized and under scrutiny. They seemed to know each other well; James said "Hi!" and grasped the quickly offered hand. The palm felt waxy and cool, like a synthetic fabric.

"I just wanted . . . *thank* . . . such a fine gentleman," the Negro said, in a voice incredibly thin-spun, the thread of it always breaking.

"Have you been waiting long?" Liz asked.

"No, well . . . the lady upstairs, she said you'd be back. When the man in the taxi let me go from the station . . . came on back to thank such wonderful people."

"I'm awfully sorry," James told him. "I thought you knew we were going off to the movies." His own voice sounded huge—a magnificent instrument. He must not be too elaborately courteous. Since his New York success, Liz was sensitive to any sign in him of vanity or condescension. She was unfair; his natural, heartfelt impulse at this moment was toward elaborate courtesy.

"You were at the police station?" Liz asked. Their previous encounter seemed to have attuned her to the man's speech.

". . . how I do appreciate." He was still speaking to James, ignoring Liz completely. This assumption that he, as head of the family, superseded all its other elements, and that in finding him the Negro had struck the fountainhead of his good fortune, panicked James. He had been raised to believe in strong women and recessive husbands. Further, the little intruder seemed to need specifically maternal attention. He trembled under his coat, and it was not that cold; the night was warmer than the late afternoon had been.

The man's clothes, in the dimness of outdoors, did not look as shabby as James would have liked. As for his being young, there were few marks of either youth or age.

"Well, come on inside," James said.

"Aaaah . . . ?"

"Please," Liz said.

They entered the little overheated vestibule, and immediately the buzzer rasped at the lock, signalling that Janice had been watching from the window. She ran to the banister and shouted down in a whisper, "Did he get in? Has he told you about the taxi driver?"

James, leading the group, attained the top of the stairs. "How was Martha?" he asked, rather plainly putting first things first.

"An absolute angel. How was the movie?"

"Quite good, really. It really was. Long, though."

"I was honestly afraid he'd kill him."

They shuffled each other into the room. "I gather you two have met, then," James said to Janice and the Negro. The girl bared her teeth in a kindly smile that made her look five years older, and the Negro, who had his hat already in his hands and was therefore unable to tip it, bent the brim slightly and swiftly averted his head, confronting a striped canvas Liz had done in art school, titled *Swans and Shadows*.

At this juncture, Liz deserted him, easing into the bedroom. She was bothered by fears that Martha would stop breathing among the blankets. "Before the doorbell rang, even," Janice talked on, "I could hear the shouting on the street— Oh, it was something. These terrible things being shouted. And then the bell rang, and I answered it, like you had said to, and *he* said—" She indicated the Negro, who was still standing, in a quiet plaid sport coat.

"Sit down," James told him.

"—and *he* said that the taxi driver wanted money. *I* said, 'I don't have any. I don't have a red cent, honestly.' You know, when I come over I never think to bring my purse." James recalled she could never make change, creating an amount she was left owing them, "toward next time."

"I *tol* him," the Negro said, "there were these fine people, in this house here. The lady in there, she tol me you'd be *here*."

James asked, "Where did you take a taxi *from?*"

The Negro sought refuge in contemplation of his hat, pendent from one quivering hand. "Please, mister . . . the lady, she knows about it." He looked toward the bedroom door.

Janice rescued him, speaking briskly: "He told me the driver wanted two thirty, and I said, 'I don't have a cent.' Then I came in here and hunted, you know, to see if you left any around—sometimes there's some tens under the silver bowl."

"Oh, yes," James said. "I suppose there are."

"Then I went to the window to signal—I'm scared to death of going downstairs and locking myself out—and down on the street there was this crowd, from across the street at Alex's, and it looked like, when he went back to tell the driver, the driver grabbed him; there was a lot of shouting, and some woman kept saying 'Cop. Call a cop.' "

Liz reëntered the room.

"He grab me here," the Negro humbly explained. He touched with his little free hand the open collar of his red wool shirt.

"So I guess then they went to the police station," Janice concluded lamely, disappointed to discover that her information was incomplete.

Liz, assuming that the police-station part of the story had been told when she was out of the room, took this to be the end, and asked, "Who wants some coffee?"

"No thanks, Betty," Janice said. "It keeps me awake."

"It keeps everybody awake," James said. "That's what it's supposed to do."

"Oh, no, ma'am," the Negro said. "I couldn't do that." Uneasily shifting his face toward James, though he kept his eyes on the lamp burning above Janice's head, he went on, "I *tol*em at the station how there were these people. I had your address, 'cause the lady wrote it down on a little slip."

"Uh-huh." James assumed there was more to come. Why wasn't he still at the police station? Who paid the driver? The pause stretched. James felt increasingly remote; it scarcely seemed his room, with so strange a guest in it. He tilted his chair back, and the Negro sharpened as if through the wrong end of a telescope. There was a resemblance between the Negro's head and the Raydo shaver. The inventive thing about that design—the stroke of mind, in Dudevant's phrase—had been forthrightly paring away the space saved by the manufacturer's improved, smaller motor. Instead of a symmetrical case, then, in form like a tapered sugar sack, a squat, asymmetrical shape was created, which fitted, pleasingly weighty, in the user's hand like a religious stone, full of mana. Likewise, a part of the Negro's skull had been eliminated. His eyes were higher in his head than drawing masters teach, and had been shallowly placed on the edges, where the planes of the face turned sideways. With a smothered start James realized that Janice, and Liz leaning in the doorway of the kitchen, and the Negro, too, were expecting him to speak—

the man of the situation, the benefactor. "Well, now, what *is* your trouble?" he asked brutally.

The coffee water sang in its kettle, and Liz, after wrinkling her expressive high forehead at him, turned to the stove.

The Negro feebly rubbed the slant of his skull. "Aaaah? . . . appreciate the kindness of you and the lady . . . generous to a poor soul like me nobody wanted to help."

James prompted. "You and your wife and—how many children?"

"Seven, mister. The oldest boy ten."

"—*have* found a place to live. Where?"

"Yes, sir, the man say he give us this room, but he say he can't put no beds in it, but I found this other man willing to give us on loan, you know, until I go to my job. . . . But the wife and children, they don't have no bed to rest their heads. Nothing to eat. My children are tired. They're gettin' sick, they so tired."

James put a cigarette in the center of his mouth and said as it bobbled, "You say you *have* a job?"

"Oh, yes, mister, I went to this place where they're building the new road to the tunnel, you know, and *he* tol *me* as soon as I get in one day's work he can give me that money, toward my pay. He ast if I could do the work and I said, 'Yes, sir, any kind of work you give I can do.' He said the pay was two dollar seventy cents for every hour you work."

"Two seventy? For Heaven's sake. Twenty dollars a day just laboring?"

"Yes, pushing the wheelbarrow . . . he said two seventy. I said, 'I can do any kind of work you give. I'm a hard worker.' "

To James he looked extremely frail, but the notion of there existing a broad-shouldered foreman willing to make this hapless man a working citizen washed all doubts away. James smiled and insisted, "So it's really just this weekend you need to get over."

"Thas right. Starting Monday I'll be making two seventy every hour. The wife, she's as happy as anybody could be."

The wife seemed to have altered underfoot, but James let it pass; the end was in sight. He braced himself to enter the realm of money. Here Janice, the fool, who should have left the minute they came home, interrupted with, "Have you tried any agencies, like the Salvation Army?"

"Oh, yes, miss. All. They don't care much for fellas like me. They say they'll give us money to get *back*, but as for us staying—they won't do a damn thing. Boy, you come up here in a truck, you're on your own. Nobody help me except these people."

The man he probably was with his friends and family was starting to show. James was sleepy. The hard chair hurt; the Negro had the comfortable chair. He resented the man's becoming at ease. But there was no halting the process; the women were at work now.

"Isn't that awful," Janice said. "You wonder why they have these agencies."

"You say you need help, your wife ain't got a place to put her head, they give you money to go *back*."

Liz entered with two cups of coffee. Hers, James noticed, was just half full; he was to bear the larger burden of insomnia. The cup was too hot to hold. He set it on the rug, feeling soft-skinned and effeminate in the eyes of this hard worker worth twenty dollars a day.

"Why did you decide to leave North Carolina?" Liz asked.

"Missis, a man like me, there's no chance there for him. I worked in the cotton and they give me thirty-five cents an hour."

"Thirty-five cents?" James said. "That's illegal, isn't it?"

The Negro smiled sardonically, his first facial expression of the evening. "Down there you don't tell them what's legal." To Liz he added, "The wife, ma'am, she's the bravest woman. When I say, 'Less go,' she say, 'Thas right, let's give oursels a chance.' So this man promise he'd take us up in the cab of the truck he had. . . ."

"With all seven children?" James asked.

The Negro looked at him without the usual wavering. "We don't have anybody to leave them behind."

"And you have no friends or relatives here?" Liz asked.

"No, we don't have no friends, and until you were so kind it didn't look like we'd find any either."

Friends! In indignation James rose and, on his feet, had to go through the long-planned action of placing two ten-dollar bills on the table next to the Negro. The Negro ignored them, bowing his head. James made his speech. "Now, I don't know how much furniture costs—my wife gave me the impression that you were going to make the necessary payment with the ten. But here is twenty. It's all we can spare. This should carry you over until Monday, when you say you can get part of your salary for working on the Lincoln Tunnel. I think it was very courageous of you to bring your family up here, and we want to wish you lots of luck. I'm sure you and your wife will manage." Flushing with shame, he resumed his post in the hard chair.

Janice bit her lip to cure a smile and looked toward Liz, who said nothing.

The Negro said, "Aeeh . . . Mister . . . can't find words to press, such fine *people*." And, while the three of them sat there, trapped and stunned, he tried to make himself cry. He pinched the bridge of his nose and shook his head and squeezed soft high animal sounds from his throat, but when he looked up, the grainy whites of his eyes were dry. Uncoördinated with this failure, his lips writhed in grief. He kept brushing his temple as if something were humming there. "Gee," he said. "The wife . . . she *tol* me, You got to go back and thank that man. . . ."

The Negro's sense of exit seemed as defective as his other theatrical skills. He just sat there, shaking his head and touching his nose. The bills on the table remained ignored—taboo, perhaps, until a sufficiently exhausting ritual of gratitude was performed. James, to whom rudeness came hard, teetered in his chair, avoiding all eyes; at the root of the Negro's demonstration there was either the plight he described or a plight that had made him lie. In either case, the man must be borne. Yet James found him all but unbearable; the thought of his life as he described it, swinging from one tenuous vine of charity to the next—the truck driver, the landlord, Liz, the furniture man, the foreman, now James—was sickening, giddying. James said courteously, "Maybe you'd better be getting back to her."

"Iiih," the Negro sighed, on an irrelevant high note, as if he produced the sound with a pitch pipe.

James dreaded that Liz would start offering blankets and food if the Negro delayed further—as he did, whimpering and passing the hat brim through his hands like an endless rope. While Liz was in the kitchen filling a paper bag for him, the Negro found breath to tell James that he wanted to bring his wife and all his family to see him and his missis, tomorrow, so they could all express gratitude. "Maybe there's some work . . . washing the floors, anything, she's so happy, until we can pay back. Twenty, gee." His hand fled to his eyes.

"No, don't you worry about us. That thirty dollars"—the first ten seemed already forgotten—"you can think of as a gift from the city."

"Oh, I wouldn't have it no other way. You let my wife do all your work tomorrow."

"You and she get settled. Forget us."

Liz appeared with an awkward paper bag. There were to be no blankets, he deduced; she wasn't as soft as he feared.

Talkative as always when a guest was leaving, James asked, "Now, do you know how to get back? For Heaven's sake, don't take a taxi again. Take a bus and then the subway. Where is your place?"

"Aaaah . . . right near where that Lexington Avenue is."

"Where on Lexington? What cross street?"

"Beg pardon, mister? I'm sorry, I don't make sense I'm so thrilled."

"What cross street? How far *up* on Lexington?"

"The, ah, Hundred Twenty-nine."

As James, with an outlander's simple pride in "knowing" New York, gave detailed instructions about where to board the Fourteenth Street bus, where to find the subway kiosk, and how to put the token in the turnstile, the words seemed to bounce back, as if they were finding identical information already lodged in the Negro's brain. He concluded, "Just try to resist the temptation to jump in a taxicab. That would have cost us two thirty if we'd been home. Now, here, I'll even give you bus fare and a token." Dredging a handful of silver from his coat pocket, he placed a nickel and a dime and a token in the svelte little palm and, since the hand did not move, put two more dimes in it, then thought, *Oh, hell,* and poured all the coins in—over a dollar's worth.

"Now I'm penniless," he told the colored man.

"Thank eh, you too Missis, so much, and you, miss."

They wished him luck. He shook hands all around, hoisted the bag with difficulty into his arms, and walked murmuring through the door James held open for him.

"Four blocks up, to Fourteenth Street," James called after him, adding in a normal voice, "I know damn well he'll take a taxi."

"It's awfully good-hearted of you," Janice said, "but about giving all that money, I—don't—know."

"Ah, well, money is dross," said James, doing a small dance step, he was so relieved the Negro was out the door.

Liz said, "I *was* surprised, darley, that you gave him *two* bills."

"You *were?* These are times of inflation. You can't buy seven air-conditioned Beautyrest mattresses for ten dollars. He's shown a great gift for spending; he ran through your ten like a little jackrabbit. We never did find out where it went to."

Janice, Irishly strict, still grappled with the moral issue. She spoke more to Liz than to him. "I don't doubt he needs the money— Oh, you should have heard the things that cabby said, or maybe you shouldn't. But then who doesn't need money? You and I need money, too."

"Which reminds me," James said. He looked at the electric clock in the kitchen: 11:20. "We came home, didn't we, around ten? Seven-thirty to ten—two and a half. Two and a half dollars. You can't change a ten, can you?"

The girl's face fell. "Honestly, I never remember to bring my purse. But you could owe me to next time. . . ."

"I hate to do that. You need the money." He couldn't believe the girl would take a surplus of $7.50 from him.

"That—I—do," Janice admitted cheerfully, gathering up her coat and a limp black book stamped simply with a cross. *Her mother*, James thought, and felt the night's prayers still circling the room.

"Wait," Liz said. "I think in my purse. I lied to him when I said I had nothing in the house but the ten." They found the purse and were indeed able to piece together, out of paper and silver, the fee.

Spited, Janice said, "For your sakes, I sure hope he doesn't bother you again. This little island has more different kinds of crooks on it than you or I could imagine existed. Some of them could out-act old Larry Olivier himself."

"I really don't see how he can do this laboring job," Liz said, with a tactful appearance of agreeing. "Why, just that little bag I gave him almost knocked him over." When Janice was gone, she asked, "Do you think she expected us to pay her for the hour and a half she stayed to watch the Negro?"

"Heaven knows. I feel vile."

"Where?"

"Everywhere. I feel like a vile person."

"Why? You were fine. Jim, you were awfully, awfully good."

From her hasty kiss on his cheek he gathered that, surprisingly, she meant it.

Sunday, husk among days, was full of fear. Even in happy times James felt on this day like a nameless statue on an empty plaza. Now he dared not go out, either to church or to the newsstand. Last night's episode had the color of a public disgrace. James holed up in his inadequate cave. The walls seemed transparent, the floors sounding boards. The Negro's threat to return had smashed the windows and broken the burglar locks. Never on a morning had he wished so intensely to be back in his home town, in Minnesota. The town had over seven thousand residents now, and a city manager instead of a mayor, and since the war its main drag had been robbed of its Indian name and called Douglas MacArthur Avenue; but the cars still parked at will on the elm-shaded streets, and he would still have a place, his father's son.

On West Tenth Street, Liz and James lived four doors down from an Episcopal church. There was not an inch of air between the masonry of any of the buildings. When the church bells rang, their apartment quivered. Enveloped in this huge dead hum, he fought the picture of seven woolly-haired children squeezed into the cab of a truck, roadside lights flickering in their faces, the dark of the Carolina fields slipping away, great whoring cities bristling and then falling back, too, and then the children dozing, except for the oldest, a boy of ten, who remained awake to stare unblinking at the bent-necked blue lights of the Jersey Turnpike, the jet carpet carrying them to the sorcerer's palace, where Harlem was choked with Cadillacs, and white men on subways yielded their seats to colored ladies. James hated the Negro chiefly because he was tactless. Janice's mother, the scores of street beggars—this was misery, too, but misery that knew its limits, that kept an orbit and observed manners. But in his perfect ignorance the Negro was like one of those babies born with their hearts in front of their ribs. He gave no protection. You touched him and you killed him. Now that he had found this Northern man—the promised man—so free with money, he would be back today, and again tomorrow, with an even greater gift of mumbled debts. Why not? Thirty was nothing to James. He could give away a flat three thousand, and then thirty every week—more than thirty, fifty—and he and Liz would still be comfortable. Between him and the Negro the ground was unimpeded, and only a sin, a lack of charity, could be placed there as barrier.

By afternoon the focus of James's discomfort had shifted from the possibility that the Negro had told the truth to the possibility that he had not. Reliving his behavior in this light was agonizing. He shuddered above the depths of fatuity the Negro must have seen in his clumsy kindness. If the story had been a fraud, the impatience of James's charity was its one saving grace. The bits of abruptness, the gibes about the taxi shone in memory like jewels among refuse. The more he thought, the more he raged, aloud and privately. And the angrier he grew at the Negro, the less he wanted to see him, the more he dreaded him, an opponent invincibly armed with the weapon of having seen him as a fool. And those seven clambering children, and the wife bullying Liz while pretending to clean the apartment.

He only wanted to hide his head in the haven of the Bridgeses' scheduled visit. They saw him as others saw him and knew his value. He would bask in their lucid external view.

Then, mercifully, it *was* dark, and his friends had come.

Rudy Bridges was also from Ontauk, Minnesota. He had been two classes ahead of James in the high school, a scholastic wonder, the more so because his father was a no-account who died of tuberculosis the year Rudy graduated. In the nine years since, Rudy's fair hair had thinned severely, but the spherical head and the chubby lips of the prig had remained constant. *His* great hopes had been boiled down to instructing three sections of Barnard girls in American history. His wife came from Maryland. Augustina was a pale and handsome woman with an uncompromising, uptilted nose that displayed its nostrils. She wore her abundant chestnut hair strictly parted in the middle—a madonna for the Piston Age. They had no children, and, with elaborate managing, just enough money. James loved them as guests. In their own home, Rudy talked too much about his special field, U.S. domestic fiscal policy between Grant and Wilson, a desert of dullness where the lowliest scholar could be king. And Augustina, careful of the budget, went hungry and thirsty and inhibited everyone. Away from home she drank and ate beautifully, like the Rockville belle she was.

James tiptoed into the bedroom with their heavy coats. Martha was cased in her crib like a piece of apparatus manufacturing sleep. He heard Liz talking and, returning, asked, "Is she telling you about how we're running the Underground Railway?"

"Why, no, James," Augustina said slowly.

"I was telling them the accident Martha had in the park," Liz said.

"Yeah, the poor kid just ran right into the swings," he said, no doubt duplicating the story.

"Now, James," Rudy said, "what is this mad tale about the Underground Rail*road?*" Years of teaching had perfected his speech habit of pronouncing everything, clichés and all, with artificial distinctness. Throughout James's recital of the Negro story he kept saying "Ah, yes," and when it was over and, like Janice the night before, James seemed to have reached an insufficient conclusion, Rudy felt compelled to clarify: "So the chances are these seven children are going to show up in the middle of supper."

"Oh dear," Augustina said with mock alarm. "Do you have enough food?"

Rudy, beside her on the sofa, attacked the tale pedantically. "Now. You say he was well dressed?"

"Sort of. But after all it was Saturday night." James didn't get the smile he expected.

"Did you look at his shoes?"

"Not much."

"Would you say his accent was Southern or neutral?"

"Well, your wife's the only Southerner I know. His speech was so peculiar and high, I couldn't tell. Certainly he didn't talk like you. Or me."

"And at one point he used the word 'thrilled.' "

"Yeah, that got me, too. But look: there were odd things, but when a man is in such a dither anyway—"

Augustina broke in, addressing Liz. "Did James *really* just hand him twenty dollars?"

"Twenty-one and a token," James corrected.

Rudy laughed excessively—he had no sense of humor, so when he laughed it was too hard—and lifted his golden glass in toast. Augustina, to back him up, gripped hers, which was already empty. "James," Rudy said, "you're the soul of generosity."

It was flattering, of course, but it wasn't the way he thought they should take it. The point really wasn't the twenty dollars at all; hard as it was to explain without seeming to ridicule Rudy's salary, twenty dollars was not much.

"It doesn't seem to *me*," he said, "that he would have such an unlikely story, with so many authentic overtones, unless it were true. He didn't look at all like a Harlem Negro—his head was uncanny—and he seemed to know about North Carolina and the relief agencies—"

"Nonsense, James. There are a hundred—a thousand—ways of obtaining such information. For instance: he quoted thirty-five cents an hour as his old wage. Well, *you* could research that. *Is* thirty-five cents an hour standard pay in the cotton belt? To be frank, it sounds low to me."

"That was the thing," Liz said, "that made me begin to wonder."

James turned on her, surprised and stung. "Damn it, the trouble with people like you, who are passed from one happy breadwinner to the next without missing a damn meal, is you refuse to admit that outside your own bubble anybody can be dirt-poor. Of *course* people starve. Of *course* a man will pay a quarter an hour if nobody makes him pay more. Jesus."

In the shocked hush, Augustina softly offered, "In the Deep South, I know, black people can just show up and attach themselves to you. It's a leftover from slavery."

"However," Rudy went doggedly on, "mere dollar-and-cents quotations mean very little; the relative value, purchasewise, of, for instance, ten cents, 'a thin dime'—"

James's harangue had agitated Augustina; her nostrils darted this way and that, and when she heard her husband's voice drone, she turned those marvellous staring apertures directly on him. Not totally insensitive, he slowly climbed out of his brain, sensed the heat in the room, and, the worst thing possible, fell silent.

The silence went on. Liz was blushing. James held his tongue, by way of apology to her. Rudy's brittle gears shifted, his mouth flipped open, and he considerately said, "No, joke about it as we will, a problem in sheer currency can very seriously affect real people. To take an example, in the states of the Confederacy in the decade after the surrender of Appomattox—that is, from the year eighteen sixty-five to the year eighteen seventy-*four* . . ."

On Monday, James's office was waiting for him. The white-headed tacks made his personal constellation on the cork. The wastebasket had been emptied. A blue envelope lay on the steel desk. Otherwise, not so much as a pen nib had been disturbed; the sketch he had been working on when Liz called still lay by the telephone, its random placement preserved like the handiwork of a superbly precious being.

He did his work all day with great precision, answering letters, making order. His office encouraged the illusion that each episode of life occupied a separate sheet, and could be dropped into the wastebasket, and destroyed by someone else in the night. One job that he gave his mind was to keep the phone from ringing. Whether the Negro came or not, with his tattered children or not, from ten to six let the problem belong to Liz. It was of her making, after all. There should be, in a man's life, hours when he has never married, and his wife walks in magic circles she herself draws. It was little enough to ask; he had sold his talent for her sake. The phone did not ring, except once: Dudevant, effusive. The envelope contained a bonus.

As James made his way home, through indifferent crowds, the conviction grew that Liz had wanted to call and had been balked by the cold pressure he had applied at the other end of the line. He would find her clubbed, and Martha hacked in two. He wondered if he would be able to give a good enough description of the Negro to the police. He saw himself in the station stammering, blushing, despised by the policemen; had it been their families, they would have been there, knotting their fists, baring their teeth. Through this daydream ran the cowardly hope that the killer would not still be there, lingering stupidly, so that James would have to struggle with him, and be himself injured.

Liz waited until he was in the apartment and his coat was off before she communicated her news. Her tone was apprehensive. "He came again, when Martha was having her nap. I went to the stairs—I was terribly busy cleaning up. He said the man who promised to sell him the furniture wouldn't give him the beds if he didn't give him ten dollars more, and I asked him why he wasn't at his job, and he said something about Wednesday, I don't know. I told him we had given him all we could, and I didn't have a dollar—which was true; you went off with the money and we have nothing for supper. Anyway, he seemed to have expected it, and was really very nice. So I guess he was a crook."

"Thank God," he said, and they never saw the Negro again, and their happiness returned.

Walter Briggs

COMING BACK FROM BOSTON, Jack drove, his baby son slept in a Carry-Cot on the front seat beside him, and in the back seat Claire sang to their girl, Jo, age two.

"When the pie was open, the birds began to—?"

"King," the child said.

"Wasn't that a dainty dish, to set before the—?"

"King!"

"That's right."

"Sing birdy nose song."

"Sing birdy nose song? I don't know the birdy nose song. *You* sing the birdy nose song. How does it go?"

"How does go?"

"I'm asking you. Who sings you the birdy nose song? Did Miss Duni do that?"

Jo laughed at the old joke; "Miss Duni" was a phrase that had popped magically from her mouth one day. "Who's Miss Duni?" she asked now.

"*I* don't know who Miss Duni is. You're the one who knows Miss Duni. When did she teach you the birdy nose song?"

"Birdy nose, birdy nose, knock knock knock," the little girl chanted lightly.

"What a *good* song! I wish Miss Duni would teach it to me."

"It's the second stanza of the blackbird song," Jack said. "Down came a blackbird and picked off her nose."

"I've *never* sung it to her," Claire vowed.

"But you know it. It's in your genes."

In ten minutes—the trip took fifty—the child fell asleep, and Claire eased this weight off her lap. Then, turning from a mother into a wife, she rested her chin on the back of the front seat, near Jack's shoulder, and breathed on the right side of his neck.

"Who did you like best at the party?" he asked.

"I don't know, really. It's hard. I'll say Langmuir, because he saw what I meant about Sherman Adams."

"Everybody saw what you meant; it's just that everybody saw it was beside the point."

"It wasn't."

"Who's best," he asked her, "Langmuir or Behnie?" This game, Who's Best?, was one of their few devices for whiling away enforced time together. A poor game, it lacked the minimal element of competition needed to excite Jack.

"I suppose Langmuir," Claire said, after taking thought.

"Knifing poor old Behnie in the back. And he loves you so."

"He *is* kind; I hate myself. Uh—who's best, Behnie, or the boy with the cleft chin and the help-me eyes?"

"The boy with the help-me eyes," he promptly answered. "Oh, he's awful. What *is* his name?"

"Crowley? Cra— Crackers?"

"Something like that. Graham Crackers. What was the name of the girl he was with with the big ears who was so lovely?"

"The poor thing, whatever makes her think she can wear those bobbly gold gypsy hoops?"

"She's not ashamed of her ears. She's proud. She thinks they're grand. Which they are—a lovely girl. To think, I may never see her again."

"*Her* name had *o*'s in it."

"Orlando. Ooh-Ooh Orlando, the soap-bubble queen."

"Not quite."

The highway made a white pyramid in the headlights; the murmur of the motor sounded lopsided, and occasionally a whiff of gasoline haunted the car's interior. *Fuel pump*, he thought, and visualized jets of explosive fluid spraying the piping-hot metal. Pieces of dirt had always been getting into the fuel pump of his father's old Buick, and the car would flood and stall. "This car is going to start costing us money soon," he said, and got no response. He glanced at the speedometer and said, "Forty-three thousand miles it's travelled for us." He added, "Birdy nose, birdy nose, knock knock knock."

Claire laughed abruptly, at something she had thought of. "I know. What was the name of that fat man at Arrow Island who stayed the whole summer and played bridge every night and wore a droopy fisherman's hat?"

He laughed, too, at her recalling this man. The first three months of their married life, five years ago, had been spent at a YMCA family camp on an island in a New Hampshire lake. Jack had worked as registrar, and his bride had run the camp store. "Walter," he began confidently. "Then something monosyllabic. He was always fishing down by that row of men's tents and was there when we got there and stayed after we left, to help them take the metal pier down." He could see everything about the man: his sly cat's smile, the peak of hair at the back of his head, his hemispherical stomach, his candy-striped T-shirt, and his crepe-soled shoes.

"Give me," Claire went on, "Mrs. Young's first name." Young, a chain-smoking failed minister, had been in charge of the camp; his wife was a short thick-necked woman with a square face and alert green eyes and, like so many wives of "good" men, a rather tart tongue. Once, she had called up from the mainland with an excursion of children, and Jack, overworked, had forgotten to tell the Dartmouth boy who ran the launch, and when she called an hour later, still waiting with these whiny children on the hot mainland, Jack had exclaimed into the faint telephone (the underwater cable was all but eaten away), "How ghastly!" After that, all summer, she called him How Gawstly. Coming into the office, she would rasp, "And how's old How Gawstly today?" and Jack would blush.

"Marguerite," he said.

"Right," Claire said. "Now their two girls."

"One was Muffie, she was the tractable one. And the other—"

"*I* know."

"Wait. Muffie and—it kind of rhymed. Muffie and Toughie."

"Audrey. She had a chipped front tooth."

"*Very* good. Now let's think about that fat man. It began with *B*. Baines. Bodds. Byron. They went together, so you never thought of him as one name or the other but as both run together. Walter Buh, buh— isn't that maddening?"

"Byron sounds close. Remember he was so good at shuffleboard, and organized the tournaments every week?"

"He played cards at night, in the rec hall. I can just *see* him, sitting there, on a brown, steel, folding chair."

"Didn't he live the rest of the year in Florida?" she asked, laughing at the idea of a man spending his entire year in vacation spots, and laughing further because, if you tried to imagine such a man, who could he be but lazy, complacent Walter Somebody?

"He used to sell plumbing equipment," Jack said with triumph. "He was retired." But this avenue, like the others, queerly failed to lead to the sanctum where the man's name was hidden. "I can remember their professions but not their names," he said, anxious to score something in his own favor, for he felt his wife was getting ahead of him at this game. "I should remember them all," he went on. "I wrote all their names down on those damn registration cards."

"Yes, you should. Who was that girl who had to leave the island because she started throwing stones at people?"

"God, yes. Mentally disturbed, and *aw*fully good-looking. And never said anything."

"She used to stand under trees and brood."

"Oh, how Young worried with her! And that other Special Case, who was always coming back on the train, and said his brother in Springfield would pay, and the Y had this special fund he thought was all for him. . . ."

"He loved chess so. Checkers. I guess you tried to teach him chess."

"Everything you'd show him on the board, he'd say, 'Pretty neat,' or 'You're a mighty smart fella.' "

"And every time you'd say anything he'd sense you thought was funny, he'd laugh hysterically, that high laugh. He loved us, because we were nice to him."

"Robert—"

"*Roy*, darling; how could you forget Roy? And then there was Peg Grace."

"Peg, Grace. Those huge eyes."

"And that tiny long nose with the nostrils shaped like water wings," Claire said. "Now: tell me the name of her pasty-faced boyfriend."

"With the waxy blond hair. Lord. I can't *conceiv*ably hope to remember his name. He was only there a week."

"I always remember him coming up from the lake after swimming. That long white body and then those tiny black bathing trunks: sexy. Oogh."

"He *was* white. But not unpleasant. In retrospect," Jack announced pompously, "I like them all, except the German kitchen boy with curly hair he thought was so cute and apoplectic cheeks."

"You didn't like him because he was always making eyes at me."

"Was he? Yes, he was, now that I think. The thing I really had against him, though, was that he beat me so badly in the broad jump. Then the Peruvian beat him, happily."

"Escobar."

"*I* knew his name. He was always trying to play basketball with his head."

"And then Barbara, the gay divorcee."

"Walter Barbara. Walter Ba, Be, Bi, Bo, Bu. He had a monstrous bill at the end of the summer, I remember that."

But Claire was no longer waiting for the fat man. She danced ahead, calling into color vast faded tracts of that distant experience: the Italian family with all the empty beer cans, the tall deaf-mute who went around barefoot and punctured the skin of his foot on a chopped root in the east path, the fire hazard until those deadly August rains, the deer on the island that they never saw. The deer had come over on the ice in the winter and the spring thaw had trapped them. It made him jealous, her store of explicit memories—the mother at dusk calling "Beryl, Beryl," the gargantuan ice-cream cones the boys on Murray's crew served themselves—but she moved among her treasures so quickly and gave them so generously he had to laugh at each new face and scene offered him, because these were memories they had collected together and he was happy that they had discovered such a good game for the car just when he feared there were no more games for them. They reached the region of small familiar roads, and he drove a long way around, to prolong the trip a minute.

Home, they carried the children to bed—Claire the tiny boy, as fragile as a paper construction, and Jack the heavy, flushed girl. As he lowered her into the crib, she opened her eyes in the darkness.

"Home," he told her.

"Whezouh dirt?" A new road was being bulldozed not far from their house, and she enjoyed being taken to see the mounds of earth.

"Dirt in the morning," Jack said, and Jo accepted this.

Downstairs, the two adults got the ginger ale out of the refrigerator and watched the eleven-o'clock news on provincial television, Governor Furcolo and Archbishop Cushing looming above Khrushchev and Nasser, and went to bed hastily, against the children's morning rising. Claire fell asleep immediately, after her long day of entertaining them all.

Jack felt he had made an unsatisfactory showing. Their past was so much more vivid to her presumably because it was more precious. Something she had mentioned nagged him. The German boy's making eyes at her. Slowly this led him to remember how she had been, the green shorts and the brown legs, holding his hand as in the mornings they walked to breakfast from their cabin, along a lane that was two dusty paths for the wheels of the camp Jeep. Like the deaf-mute, Claire had gone around barefoot, and she walked between the paths, on the soft broad mane of weeds. Her hand had seemed so small, her height so sweetly adjusted to his, the fact of her waking him so strange. She always heard the breakfast bell, though it rang far away. Their cabin was far from the center of things; its only light had been a candle. Each evening (except Thursday, when he played right field for the staff softball team), in the half-hour between work and dinner, while she made the bed within, he had sat outside on a wooden chair, reading in dwindling daylight *Don Quixote*. It was all he had read that summer, but he had read that, in half-hours, every dusk, and in September cried at the end, when Sancho pleads with his at last sane master to rise from his deathbed and lead another quest, and perhaps they shall find the Lady Dulcinea under some hedge, stripped of her enchanted rags and as fine as any queen. All around the cabin had stood white pines stretched to a cruel height by long competition, and the cabin itself had no windows, but broken screens. Pausing before the threshold, on earth littered with needles and twigs, he unexpectedly found what he wanted; he lifted himself on his elbow and called "Claire" softly, knowing he wouldn't wake her, and said, "Briggs. Walter Briggs."

The Crow in the Woods

ALL THE WARM NIGHT the secret snow fell so adhesively that every twig in the woods about their little rented house supported a tall slice of white, an upward projection which in the shadowless glow of early morning lifted depth from the scene, made it seem Chinese, calligraphic, a stiff tapestry hung from the gray sky, a shield of lace interwoven with black thread. Jack wondered if he had ever seen anything so beautiful before. The snow had stopped. As if it had been a function of his sleep.

He was standing in his bathrobe by the window at dawn because last evening, amid an intricate and antique luxury, he and his wife had dined with their landlords. Two wines, red and darker red, had come with the dinner. Candles shuddered on the long table. Two other couples—older, subtly ravaged—expertly made small talk. Dinner over, the men and women separated and then, the men's throats rasped by brandy and cigars, rejoined in a large room whose walls were, astoundingly, green silk. The mixed sexes chattered immersed in an incoherent brilliance like chandelier facets clashing. And at the end (the clock on the gray marble mantel stating the precipitate hour with golden hands whose threadlike fineness itself seemed a kind of pointed tact), all swooped, in a final and desperate-feeling flight, up the curving stairs and into the chamber where in daytime hours the white-haired hostess conducted her marvellous hobby of *cartonnage*. She had fashioned a pagoda of cut colored papers. On the walls there were paper bouquets of flowers, framed. On the worktable stood the most immense, the most triumphantly glossy and nozzled bottle of Elmer's Glue that Jack had ever seen; he had never dreamed such a size could exist. The blue bull impressed on the bottle jubilantly laughed. Servants came and wrapped their coats around them. On the front porch the departing guests discovered at midnight a world thinly disguised in snow. The universal descent of snow restricted the area of their vision;

outdoors had a domed intimacy. The guests carolled praise. The host, a short and old man, arthritic, preened: his dinner, his wine, his wife's *cartonnage*, and now his snow. Looped, the young couple returned to the little rented house that even was his. They satisfied the sitter, dismissed her into the storm like a disgrace, and, late as it was, made love. So, in a reflex of gratitude, when six hours later their child cried, the man arose instead of his wife, and administered comfort.

The soaked diaper released an invisible cloud of ammonia that washed tears into his eyes. The whiteness edging the windows made decisive and cutting the light of the sun, burning behind the sky like a bulb in a paper lampshade. The child's room had become incandescent; the wallpaper, flowered with pale violets, glowed evenly, so that even the fluff-cluttered corners brimmed with purity.

The wordless girl, stripped and puzzled, studied the unusual figure of her father, out of season at this hour. The purple bathrobe's wool embrace and the cold pressure of the floor on his feet alike felt flattering, magnifying him. His naked giant's thighs kept thrusting between the leaves of the bathrobe into the white air. He saw them, saw everything, through three polished sheets of glass: the memory of his drunkenness, his present insufficiency of sleep, and the infiltrating brilliance of the circumambient snow. As his impressions were sharp, so he was soft. The parallel floor-cracks, the paint's salmon sheen, his daughter's somber and intent gaze like the gaze of a chemically distended pupil—these things, received through an instrument which fatigue had wiped clean of distractions, bit deeply into him and pressed, with an urgency not disagreeable, on his bowels.

Though the house was small, it had two bathrooms. He used the one attached to his daughter's room, where the square shower-curtain rod wobbled and tipped from the repeated weight of wet diapers. Around its bolted root the ceiling plaster had turned crumby. He stood for some seconds looking down at the oval of still water in which floated his several feces like short rotten sticks, strangely burnished.

The toilet flushed; the whole illuminated interior of the little house seemed purged into action. He dressed his daughter's tumblesome body deftly and carried her to the stairs. The top landing gave on the door to his bedroom; he looked in and saw that his wife had changed position in the broadened bed. Her naked arms were flung out of the covers and rested, crook'd, each to a pillow. One breast, lifted by the twist of her shoulders and shallow in her sleep, was with its budded center exposed. The sun, probing the shredding sky, sent low through the woods and windowpanes a diluted filigree, finer than color, that spread across her and up the swarthy oak headboard a rhomboidal web. Like moths alighting on gauze, her blue eyes opened.

Discovered, he hid downstairs. The child absent-mindedly patted the back of his neck as they descended the tricky narrow steps. These weak touches made his interior tremble as if with tentative sunshine. Downstairs was darker. The reflection of the snow was absorbed by the dank and porous rented furniture. Good morning, Mr. Thermostat. The milkman would be late today, chains slogging a tune on his stout tires: glory be. The childbearing arm of him ached.

He was unable to find the box of child's cereal. The cupboards held confectioners' sugar and plastic spoon sets sprawling in polychrome fans. The catch of the tray of the high chair snagged; the girl's legs were hinged the wrong way. With multiplying motions of uncertainty he set water to heating in a cold-handled pan. Winter. Warm cereal. Where? The ceiling rumbled; the plumbing sang.

Down came the wife and mother, came, wrapped in a blue cocoon that made her body shapeless, her face by the contrast white. She complained she had not been able to go back to sleep after he had left the bed. He knew this to be a lie, but unintentional. He had witnessed her unwitting sleep.

Proud, relieved, he sat at the small pine table burnished with linseed oil. Gerber's wheat-dust came to smoke in the child's tray. Orange juice, bright as a crayon, was conjured before him. Like her sister the earth, the woman puts forth easy flowers, fresh fruits. As he lifted the glass to his lips he smelled her on his fingertips.

And now, released to return to his companion through the window, he again stared. The woods at their distance across the frosted lawn were a Chinese screen in which an immense alphabet of twigs lay hushed: a black robe crusted with white braid standing of its own stiffness. Nothing in it stirred. There was no depth, the sky a pearl slab, the woods a fabric of vision in which vases, arches, and fountains were hushed.

His wife set before him a boiled egg smashed and running on a piece of toast on a pink plate chipped and gleaming on the oblique placemat of sunlight flecked with the windowpane's imperfections.

Something happened. Outdoors a huge black bird came flapping with a crow's laborious wingbeat. It banked and, tilted to fit its feet, fell toward the woods. His heart halted in alarm for the crow, with such recklessness assaulting an inviolable surface, seeking so blindly a niche for its strenuous bulk where there was no depth. It could not enter. Its black shape shattering like an instant of flak, the crow plopped into a high branch and sent snow showering from a sector of lace. Its wings spread and settled. The vision destroyed, his heart overflowed. "Claire!" Jack cried.

The woman's pragmatic blue eyes flicked from his face to the window, where she saw only snow, and rested on the forgotten food steaming between his hands. Her lips moved:

"Eat your egg."

Should Wizard Hit Mommy?

IN THE EVENINGS and for Saturday naps like today's, Jack told his daughter Jo a story out of his head. This custom, begun when she was two, was itself now nearly two years old, and his head felt empty. Each new story was a slight variation of a basic tale: a small creature, usually named Roger (Roger Fish, Roger Squirrel, Roger Chipmunk), had some problem and went with it to the wise old owl. The owl told him to go to the wizard, and the wizard performed a magic spell that solved the problem, demanding in payment a number of pennies greater than the number Roger Creature had but in the same breath directing the animal to a place where the extra pennies could be found. Then Roger was so happy he played many games with other creatures, and went home to his mother just in time to hear the train whistle that brought his daddy home from Boston. Jack described their supper, and the story was over. Working his way through this scheme was especially fatiguing on Saturday, because Jo never fell asleep in naps any more, and knowing this made the rite seem futile.

The little girl (not so little; the bumps her feet made under the covers were halfway down the bed, their big double bed that they let her be in for naps and when she was sick) had at last arranged herself, and from the way her fat face deep in the pillow shone in the sunlight sifting through the drawn shades, it did not seem fantastic that something magic would occur, and she would take her nap as she used to. Her brother, Bobby, was two, and already asleep with his bottle. Jack asked, "Who shall the story be about today?"

"Roger . . ." Jo squeezed her eyes shut and smiled to be thinking she was thinking. Her eyes opened, her mother's blue. "Skunk," she said firmly.

A new animal; they must talk about skunks at nursery school. Having a fresh hero momentarily stirred Jack to creative enthusiasm. "All right," he said. "Once upon a time, in the deep dark woods, there was a tiny little creature name of Roger Skunk. And he smelled very bad—"

"Yes," Jo said.

"He smelled so bad none of the other little woodland creatures would play with him." Jo looked at him solemnly; she hadn't foreseen this. "Whenever he would go out to play," Jack continued with zest, remembering certain trials of his own childhood, "all of the other tiny animals would cry, 'Uh-oh, here comes Roger Stinky Skunk,' and they would run away, and Roger Skunk would stand there all alone, and two little round tears would fall from his eyes." The corners of Jo's mouth drooped down and her lower lip bent forward as Jack traced with a forefinger along the side of her nose the course of one of Roger Skunk's tears.

"Won't he see the owl?" she asked in a high and faintly roughened voice.

Sitting on the bed beside her, Jack felt the covers tug as her legs switched tensely. He was pleased with this moment—he was telling her something true, something she must know—and had no wish to hurry on. But downstairs a chair scraped, and he realized he must get down to help Claire paint the living-room woodwork.

"Well, he walked along very sadly and came to a very big tree, and in the tiptop of the tree was an enormous wise old owl."

"Good."

" 'Mr. Owl,' Roger Skunk said, 'all the other little animals run away from me because I smell so bad.' 'So you do,' the owl said. 'Very, very bad.' 'What can I do?' Roger Skunk said, and he cried very hard."

"The wizard, the wizard," Jo shouted, and sat right up, and a Little Golden Book spilled from the bed.

"Now, Jo. Daddy's telling the story. Do you want to tell Daddy the story?"

"No. You me."

"Then lie down and be sleepy."

Her head relapsed onto the pillow and she said, "Out of your head."

"Well. The owl thought and thought. At last he said, 'Why don't you go see the wizard?' "

"Daddy?"

"What?"

"Are magic spells *real*?" This was a new phase, just this last month, a reality phase. When he told her that spiders eat bugs, she turned to her mother and asked, "Do they *really*?" and when Claire told her that God was in the sky and all around them, she turned to her father and insisted, with a sly yet eager smile, "Is He *really?*"

"They're real in stories," Jack answered curtly. She had made him miss a beat in the narrative. "The owl said, 'Go through the dark woods, under the apple trees, into the swamp, over the crick—' "

"What's a crick?"

"A little river. 'Over the crick, and there will be the wizard's house.' And that's the way Roger Skunk went, and pretty soon he came to a little white house, and he rapped on the door." Jack rapped on the windowsill, and under the covers Jo's long body clenched in babyish delight. "And then," Jack went on, "a tiny little old man came out, with a long white beard and a pointed blue hat, and said, 'Eh? Whatzis? Whatcher want? You smell awful.' " The wizard's voice was one of Jack's own favorite effects; he did it by scrunching up his face and somehow whining through his eyes, which felt for the interval rheumy. He felt being an old man suited him.

" 'I know it,' Roger Skunk said, 'and all the little animals run away from me. The enormous wise owl said you could help me.'

" 'Eh? Well, maybe. Come on in. Don't git too close.' Now, inside, Jo, there were all these magic things, all jumbled together in a big dusty heap, because the wizard did not have any cleaning lady."

"Why?"

"Why? Because he was a wizard, and a very old man."

"Will he die?"

"No. Wizards don't die. They just get more and more cranky. Well, he rummaged around and found an old stick called a magic wand and asked Roger Skunk what he wanted to smell like. Roger thought and thought and said, 'Roses.' "

"Yes. Good," Jo said smugly.

Jack fixed her with a trancelike gaze and chanted in the wizard's elderly irritable voice:

> " 'Abracadabry, hocus-poo,
> Roger Skunk, how do you do,
> Roses, boses, pull an ear,
> Roger Skunk, you never fear:
> *Bingo!*' "

He paused as a rapt expression widened out from his daughter's nostril wings, forcing her eyebrows up and her lower lip down in an expression of mute exclamation, an expression in which Jack was startled to recognize his wife feigning pleasure at cocktail parties. "And all of a sudden," he whispered, "the whole inside of the wizard's house was full of the smell of—*roses!* 'Roses!' Roger Fish cried. And the wizard said, very cranky, 'That'll be seven pennies.' "

"Daddy."

"What?"

"Roger *Skunk*. You said Roger Fish."

"Yes. Skunk."

"You said Roger *Fish*. Wasn't that silly?"

"Very silly of your stupid old daddy. Where was I? Well, you know about the pennies."

"Say it."

"O.K. Roger Skunk said, 'But all I have is four pennies,' and he began to cry." Jo made her crying face again, but insincerely, as a piece of acting. This annoyed Jack. Downstairs some more furniture rumbled. Claire shouldn't move heavy things; she was six months pregnant. It would be their third.

"So the wizard said, 'Oh, very well. Go to the end of the lane and turn around three times and look down the magic well and there you will find three pennies. Hurry up.' So Roger Skunk went to the end of the lane and turned around three times and there in the magic well were *three pennies!* So he took them back to the wizard and was very happy and ran out into the woods and all the other little animals gathered around him because he smelled so good. And they played tag, baseball, football, basketball, lacrosse, hockey, soccer, and pick-up-sticks."

"What's pick-up-sticks?"

"It's a game you play with sticks."

"Like the wizard's magic wand?"

"Kind of. And they played games and laughed all afternoon and then it began to get dark and they all ran home to their mommies."

Jo was starting to fuss with her hands and look out of the window, at the crack of daylight that showed under the shade. She thought the story was all over. Jack didn't like women when they took anything for granted; he liked them apprehensive, hanging on his words. "Now, Jo, are you listening?"

"Yes."

"Because this is very interesting. Roger Skunk's mommy said, 'What's that awful smell?' "

"Wha-a-at?" He had surprised her.

He went on, "And Roger Skunk said, 'It's me, Mommy. I smell like roses now.' And she said, 'Who made you smell like that?' And he said, 'The wizard,' and *she* said, 'Well, of all the nerve. You come with me and we're going right back to that very awful wizard.' "

Jo sat up, her hands dabbling in the air with genuine fright. "But, Daddy, then he said about the other little animals run *away!*" Her hands skittered off, into the imaginary underbrush.

"All right. He said, 'But, Mommy, all the other little animals run *away.*' She said, 'I don't care. You smelled the way a little skunk should have and I'm going to take you right back to that wizard,' and she took an umbrella and went back with Roger Skunk and hit that wizard right over the head."

"No," Jo said, and put her hand out to touch his lips, yet even in her agitation did not quite dare to stop the source of the narrative. Inspiration came to her. "Then the wizard hit *her* on the head and did not change that little skunk back."

"No," he said. "The wizard said 'O.K., maybe you're right,' and Roger Skunk did not smell of roses any more. He smelled very bad again."

"But the other little amum—*oh!*—amumals—"

"Joanne. It's Daddy's story. Shall Daddy not tell you any more stories?" Her broad face looked at him through sifted light, astounded. "This is what happened, then. Roger Skunk and his mommy went home and they heard *Woo-oo, woooo-oo,* and it was the choo-choo train bringing Daddy Skunk home from Boston. And they had lima beans, pork chops, celery, liver, mashed potatoes, and Pie-Oh-My for dessert. And when Roger Skunk was in bed, Mommy Skunk came up and hugged him and said he smelled like her little baby skunk again and she loved him very much. And that's the end of the story."

"But Daddy."

"What?"

"Then did the other little ani-mals run away?"

"No, because eventually they got used to the way he was and did not mind it at all. Or did not mind it very much."

"What's evenshiladee?"

"In a little while."

"That was a stupid mommy."

"It was *not*," he said with rare emphasis, and believed, from her expression, that she realized he was defending his own mother to her, or something as odd. "Now I want you to put your big heavy head in the pillow and have a good long nap." He adjusted the shade so not even a crack of day showed, and tiptoed to the door, in the pretense that she was already asleep. But when he turned, she was crouching on top of the covers and staring at him. "Hey. Get under the covers and fall *faaast* asleep. Bobby's asleep."

She stood up and bounced gingerly on the springs. "Daddy."

"What?"

"Tomorrow, I want you to tell me the story that that wizard took that magic wand and hit that mommy"—her plump arms chopped fiercely— "right over the head."

"No. That's not the story. The point is that the little skunk loved his mommy more than he loved *aaalll* the other little animals and she knew what was right."

"No. Tomorrow you say he hit that mommy. Do it." She kicked her legs up and sat down on the bed with a great heave and complaint of springs, as she had done hundreds of times before, except that this time she did not laugh. "Say it, Daddy."

"Well, we'll see. Now, at least have a rest. Stay on the bed. You're a good girl. A wonderful girl."

He closed the door and went downstairs. Claire had spread the news-papers and opened the paint can and, wearing an old shirt of his on top of her maternity smock, was stroking the chair rail with a dipped brush. Above him footsteps vibrated and he called, "*Joanne*. Shall I come up there and spank you?" The footsteps hesitated.

"That was a long story," Claire said.

"The poor kid," he answered, and with utter weariness watched his wife labor. The woodwork, a cage of moldings and rails and baseboards all around them, was half old tan and half new ivory and he felt caught in an ugly middle position, and though he as well felt his wife's presence in the cage with him, he did not want to speak with her, work with her, touch her, anything.

Wife-Wooing

OH MY LOVE. Yes. Here we sit, on warm broad floorboards, before a fire, the children between us, in a crescent, eating. The girl and I share one half-pint of French-fried potatoes; you and the boy share another; and in the center, sharing nothing, making simple reflections within himself like a jewel, the baby, mounted in an Easybaby, sucks at his bottle with frowning mastery, his selfish, contemplative eyes stealing glitter from the center of the flames. And you. You. You allow your skirt, the same black skirt in which this morning you with woman's soft bravery mounted a bicycle and sallied forth to play hymns in difficult keys on the Sunday school's old piano—you allow this black skirt to slide off your raised knees down your thighs, slide *up* your thighs in your body's absolute geography, so the parallel whiteness of their undersides is exposed to the fire's warmth and to my sight. Oh. There is a line of Joyce. I try to recover it from the legendary, imperfectly explored grottoes of *Ulysses:* a garter snapped, to please Blazes Boylan, in a deep Dublin den. What? Smackwarm. That was the crucial word. Smacked smackwarm on her smackable warm woman's thigh. Something like that. A splendid man, to feel that. Smackwarm woman's. Splendid also to feel the curious and potent, inexplicable and irrefutably magical life language leads within itself. What soul took thought and knew that adding *wo* to man would make a woman? The difference exactly. The wide *w*, the receptive *o*. Womb. In our crescent the children for all their size seem to come out of you toward me, wet fingers and eyes, tinted bronze. Three children, five persons, seven years. Seven years since I wed wide warm woman, white-thighed. Wooed and wed. Wife. A knife of a word that for all its final bite did not end the wooing. To my wonderment.

We eat meat, meat I wrested warm from the raw hands of the hamburger girl in the diner a mile away, a ferocious place, slick with grease, sleek with chrome; young predators snarling dirty jokes menaced me, old men reached for me with coffee-dark paws; I wielded my wallet, and won my way back. The fat brown bag of buns was warm beside me in the cold car; the smaller bag holding the two cartons of French fries emitted an even more urgent heat. Back through the black winter air to the fire, the intimate cave, where halloos and hurrahs greeted me, the deer, mouth agape and its cotton throat gushing, stretched dead across my shoulders. And now you, beside the white *O* of the plate upon which the children discarded with squeals of disgust the rings of translucent onion that came squeezed in the hamburgers—you push your toes an inch closer to the blaze, and the ashy white of your thigh's inner side is lazily laid bare, and the eternally elastic garter snaps smackwarm against my hidden heart.

Who would have thought, wide wife, back there in the white tremble of the ceremony (in the corner of my eye I held, despite the distracting hail of ominous vows, the vibration of the cluster of stephanotis clutched against your waist), that seven years would bring us no distance, through all those warm beds, to the same trembling point, of beginning? The cells change every seven years, and down in the atom, apparently, there is a strange discontinuity; it is as if God wills the universe anew every instant. (Ah God, dear God, tall friend of my childhood, I will never forget you, though they say dreadful things. They say rose windows in cathedrals are vaginal symbols.) Your legs, exposed as fully as by a bathing suit, yearn deeper into the amber wash of heat. Well: begin. A green jet of flame spits out sideways from a pocket of resin in a log, crying, and the orange shadows on the ceiling sway with fresh life. Begin.

"Remember, on our honeymoon, how the top of the kerosene heater made a great big rose window on the ceiling?"

"Vnn." Your chin goes to your knees, your shins draw in, all is retracted. Not much to remember, perhaps, for you: blood badly spilled, clumsiness of all sorts. "It was cold for June."

"Mommy, what was cold? What did you say?" the girl asks, enunciating angrily, determined not to let language slip on her tongue and tumble her so that we laugh.

"A house where Daddy and I stayed one time."

"I don't like dat," the boy says, and throws a half-bun painted with chartreuse mustard onto the floor.

You pick it up and with beautiful somber musing ask, "Isn't that funny? Did any of the others have mustard on them?"

"I *hate* dat," the boy insists; he is two. Language is to him thick vague handles swirling by; he grabs what he can.

"Here. He can have mine. Give me his." I pass my hamburger over, you take it, he takes it from you, there is nowhere a ripple of gratitude. There is no more praise of my heroism in fetching Sunday supper, saving you labor. Cunning, you sense, and sense that I sense your knowledge, that I had hoped to hoard your energy toward a more primal spending. We sense everything between us, every ripple, existent and nonexistent; it is tiring. Courting a wife takes tenfold the strength of winning an ignorant girl. The fire shifts, shattering fragments of newspaper that carry in lighter gray the ghost of the ink of their message. You huddle your legs and bring the skirt back over them. With a sizzling noise like the sighs of the exhausted logs, the baby sucks the last from his bottle, drops it to the floor with its distasteful hoax of vacant suds, and begins to cry. His egotist's mouth opens; the delicate membrane of his satisfaction tears. You pick him up and stand. You love the baby more than me.

Who would have thought, blood once spilled, that no barrier would be broken, that you would be each time healed into a virgin again? Tall, fair, obscure, remote, and courteous.

We put the children to bed, one by one, in reverse order of birth. I am limitlessly patient, paternal, good. Yet you know. We watch the paper bags and cartons ignite on the breathing pillow of embers; we read, watch television, eat crackers, it does not matter. Eleven comes. For a tingling moment you stand on the bedroom rug in your underpants, untangling your nightie; oh, fat white sweet fat fatness. In bed you read. About Richard Nixon. He fascinates you; you hate him. You know how he defeated Jerry Voorhis, martyred Mrs. Douglas, how he played poker in the Navy despite being a Quaker, every fiendish trick, every low adaptation. Oh my Lord, let's let the poor man go to bed. We're none of us perfect. "Hey, let's turn out the light."

"Wait. He's just about to get Hiss convicted. It's very strange. It says he acted honorably."

"I'm sure he did." I reach for the switch.

"No. Wait. Just till I finish this chapter. I'm sure there'll be something at the end."

"Honey, Hiss was guilty. We're all guilty. Conceived in concupiscence, we die unrepentant." Once my ornate words wooed you.

I lie against your filmy convex back. You read sideways, a sleepy trick. I see the page through the fringe of your hair, sharp and white as a wedge of crystal. Suddenly it slips. The book has slipped from your hand. You are asleep. Oh, cunning trick, cunning. In the darkness I consider. Cunning. The headlights of cars accidentally slide fanning slits of light around our walls and ceiling. The great rose window was projected upward through the petal-shaped perforations in the top of the black kerosene stove, which we stood in the center of the floor. As the flame on the circular wick flickered, the wide soft star of interlocked penumbrae moved and waved as if it were printed on a silk cloth being gently tugged or slowly blown. Its color soft blurred blood. We pay dear in blood for our peaceful homes.

In the morning, to my relief, you are ugly. Monday's wan breakfast light bleaches you blotchily, drains the goodness from your thickness, makes the bathrobe a limp stained tube flapping disconsolately, exposing sallow décolletage. The skin between your breasts a sad yellow. I feast with the coffee on your drabness, every wrinkle and sickly tint a relief and a revenge. The children yammer. The toaster sticks. Seven years have worn this woman.

The man, he arrows off to work, jousting for right-of-way, veering on the thin hard edge of the legal speed limit. Out of domestic muddle, softness, pallor, flaccidity: into the city. Stone is his province. The winning of coin. The maneuvering of abstractions. Making heartless things run. Ah, the inanimate, adamant joys of a job!

I return with my head enmeshed in a machine. A technicality it would take weeks to explain to you snags my brain; I fiddle with phrases and numbers all the blind evening. You serve me supper as a waitress—as less than a waitress, for I have known you. The children touch me timidly, as they would a steep girder bolted into a framework whose height they can't comprehend. They drift into sleep securely. We survive their passing in calm parallelity. My thoughts rework in chronic right angles the same snagging circuits on the same professional grid. You rustle the book about Nixon; vanish upstairs into the plumbing; the bathtub pipes cry. In my head I seem to have found the stuck switch at last: I push at it; it jams; I push; it is jammed. I grow dizzy, churning with cigarettes. I circle the room aimlessly.

So I am taken by surprise at a turning when at the meaningful hour of ten you come with a kiss of toothpaste to me moist and girlish and quick; an expected gift is not worth giving.

Unstuck

IN HIS DREAM, Mark was mixing and mixing on an oval palette a muddy shade of gray he could not get quite right, and this shade of gray was both, in that absurd but deadpan way of dreams, his marriage and the doctrinal position of the local Congregational church, which was resisting the nationwide merger with the Evangelical and Reformed denominations. He was glad to wake up, though his wife's body, asleep, silently rebuked his. They had made love last night and again she had failed to have her climax.

As the webs of gray paint lifted and the oppressive need to get *the exact precise shade* dawned upon him as unreal, a color from childhood infiltrated his eyes. The air of his bedroom was tinted blue. The ceiling looked waxy. The very sheen on the wallpaper declared: snow. He remembered that it had begun to spit late yesterday afternoon and was streaming in glittering parallels through the streetlamp halo when, an hour earlier than usual, they went to bed.

A car passed, its chains chunking. Farther away, a stuck tire whined. The bedside clock, whose glassy face gleamed as if polished by the excitement in the air, said six-fifty-five. The windowpanes were decorated with those concave little dunes that Mark had often counterfeited in cotton. By profession he was a window decorator, a display man, for a department store in a city fifteen miles away. He eased from the bed and saw that the storm was over: a few final dry flakes, shaken loose by an afterthought in the top twigs of the elm, drifted zigzag down to add their particles to the white weight that had transformed the town—bewigged roofs, bearded clapboards, Christmas-card evergreens, a Stop sign like a frosted lollipop—into one huge display.

The steeple of the Congregational church, painted white, looked spotlit against the heavy grayness that was fading northward into New Hampshire, having done its work here. Over a foot, he guessed. On the street below their windows the plows had been busy; perhaps it had been their all-night struggle that had made his dreams so grating. Scraped streaks of asphalt showed through, and elsewhere the crust had been rutted and beaten into a gloss by the early traffic. So the roads were all right; he could get to work if he could get the car out of the driveway.

Now, at seven, the town fire horn blew the five spaced blasts that signalled the cancellation of school for the day—a noise that blanketed the air for miles around. Mark's wife opened her eyes in alarm, and then relaxed. They had not been married long and had no children. "What fun," she said. "A real storm. I'll make waffles."

"Don't be too ambitious," he said, sounding more sour than he had meant to.

"I want to," she insisted. "Anyway, the bacon's been in the fridge for weeks and we ought to use it up."

She wanted to make a holiday of it. And she wanted, he thought, to bury the aftertaste of last night. He showered and dressed and went out to rescue his car, which was new. Last evening, after watching the forecast on television, he had prudently reparked it closer to the road, its nose pointed outward. No garage had come with this big old house they had recently bought. Their driveway curved in from Hillcrest Road at the back of the yard. The plows had heaped a ridge of already dirty, lumpy snow between his bumper and the cleared street. The ridge came up to his hips, but he imagined that, with the momentum his rear tires could gather on the bare patch beneath the car body, he could push through. Snow is, after all, next to nothing; Mark pictured those airy six-sided crystals so commonly employed as a decorative motif in his trade.

But, getting in behind the steering wheel, he found himself in a tomb. All the windows were sealed by snow. The motor turned over readily and this was a relief. As the motor idled, he staggered around the automobile, clearing the windows with the combination brush and scraper the car dealer had given him. When he cleared the windshield, the wipers shocked him by springing to life and happily flapping. He had left them turned on last night. He got back in behind the wheel and turned them off. Through the cleared windshield, the sky above his neighbor's rooftop was enamelled a solid blue. The chimney smoked a paler blue, and a host of small brown birds scuffled and settled for warmth in the dark bare patch in its lee. His neighbor herself, a woman wearing a checkered apron, came out of the front door and began banging a broom around on her porch. She saw Mark through the windshield and waved; he grudgingly waved back. She was middle-aged, lacked a husband, wore her lip-stick too thick, and seemed a bit too willing to be friendly to this young couple new in the neighborhood.

Mark put the car into first gear. Snow had blown in beneath the sides of the automobile, so the momentum he had hoped to achieve was slug-gish in coming. Though his front tires broke through the ridge, the underside dragged and the back tires slithered to a stop in the shallow gutter that ran down the side of Hillcrest Road. He tried reverse. The rear of the car lifted a fraction and then sagged sideways, the wheels spin-ning in a void. He returned to first gear, and touched the accelerator lightly, and gained for his tact only a little more of that sickening side-ways slipping. He tried reverse again and this time there was no motion at all; it was as if he were trying to turn a doorknob with soapy hands. An outraged sense of injustice, of being asked to do too much, swept over him. "Fuck," he said. He had messed up again. He tried to push open the door, discovered that snow blocked it, shoved savagely, and opened a gap he could worm through backwards. Stepping out, he took an icy shock of snow into his loose galosh.

His neighbor across the street called, "Good morning!" The sound, it seemed, made a strip of snow fall from a telephone wire.

"Isn't it lovely?" were her next words.

"Sure is," was his answer. His voice sounded high, with a croak in it.

Her painted lips moved, but the words "If you're young" came to him faint and late, as if, because of some warping aftereffect of the storm, sound crossed the street from her side against the grain.

Mark slogged down through his back yard, treading in his own footsteps to minimize his desecration of the virgin snow. The bushes were bowed and splayed like bridesmaids overwhelmed by flowers. Chickadee feet had crosshatched the snow under the feeder. The kitchen air struck his face with its warmth and the smells of simmering bacon and burning waf-fle mix. He told his wife, "I got the damn thing stuck. Get out of your nightie and come help."

She looked querulous and sallow in her drooping bathrobe. "Can't we eat breakfast first? You're going to be late anyway. Shouldn't you be call-ing the store? Maybe it won't be open today."

"It'll be open, and anyway even if it isn't I should be there. Easter won't wait." The precise shade of gray he had been mixing in his dream perhaps belonged to some beaverboard cutouts of flowering trees he was prepar-ing for windows of the new spring fashions.

"The *schools* are closed," she pointed out.

"Well, let's eat," he conceded, but ate in his parka, to hurry her. As he swallowed the orange juice, the snow in his galosh slipped deeper down his ankle. Mark said, "If we'd bought that ranch house you were too damn sophisticated for, we'd have a garage and this wouldn't happen. It takes years off the life of a car, to leave it parked in the open."

"It's smoking! Turn the little thing! On the left, the left!" She told him, "I don't know *why* I bother to try to make you waffles; that iron your mother gave us has never worked. Never, never."

"Well, it should. It's not cheap."

"It sticks. It's awful. I hate it."

"It was the best one she could find. It's supposed to be self-greasing, or some damn thing, isn't it?"

"I don't know. I don't understand it. I never have. I was trying to make them to be nice to *you*."

"Don't get so upset. The waffles are terrific, actually." But he ate them without tasting them, he was so anxious to return to the car and erase his error. If a plow were to come along, his car would be jutting into its path, evidence of ineptitude. Young husbands, young car-owners. He wondered if the woman across the street had been laughing at him, getting it stuck. Just that little ridge to push through. He had been so sure he could do it. "I don't suppose," he said, "this will cancel the damn church thing tonight."

"Let's not go," she said, scraping the last batch into the garbage, poking the crusts from the waffle grid with a fork. "Why do we have to go?"

"Because," Mark stated firmly. "These Reformeds, you know, are high-powered stuff. They're very strict about things like the divinity of Christ."

"Well, who isn't? I mean, you either believe it or you don't, I would think."

He winced, feeling himself to blame. If he had given her a climax, she wouldn't be so irreligious. "This is a wonderful breakfast," he said. "How do you make the bacon so crisp?"

"You put it on a paper bag for a minute," she said. "Did you *really* get the car stuck? Maybe you should call the man at the garage."

"It just needs a little push," he promised. "Come on, bundle up. It'll be fun. Old Mrs. Whatsername across the street is out there with the birds, sweeping her porch. It's beautiful."

"I *know* it is," she said. "I used to *love* snowstorms."

"But not now, huh?" He stood and asked her, "Where's the fucking shovel?"

She went upstairs, the belt of her sad bathrobe trailing, and he found the snow shovel in the basement. The furnace, whirring and stinking to itself, reminded him pleasantly that snow on the roof reduced the fuel bill. The old house needed insulation. Everything needed something. On his way out through the kitchen he noticed a steaming cup of coffee she had poured for him, like one of those little caches one explorer leaves behind for another. To appease her, he took two scalding swallows before heading out into the wilderness of his brilliant back yard.

By the time Mark's wife joined him, looking childish and fat and merry in her hood and mittens and ski leggings and fur-topped boots, he had shovelled away as much of the snow underneath and around the car as he could reach. The woman across the street had gone back into her house, the birds on her roof had flown away, and a yellow town truck had come down Hillcrest Road scattering sand. He had leaned on the shovel and waved at the men on the back as if they were all comrades battling together in a cheerful war.

She asked, "Do you want me to steer?"

"No, you push. It'll just take a tiny push now. I'll drive, because I know how to rock it." He stationed her at the rear right corner of the car, where there happened to be a drift that came up over her knees. He felt her make the silent effort of not complaining. "The thing is," he told her, "to keep it from sloughing sideways."

"Sluing," she said.

"Whatever it is," he said, "keep it from doing that."

But slue was just what it did; though he rammed the gearshift back and forth between first and reverse, the effect of all that rocking was—he could feel it—to work the right rear tire deeper into the little slippery socket on the downhill side. He assumed she was pushing, but he couldn't see her in the mirror and he couldn't feel her.

His stomach ached, with frustration and maple syrup. He got out of the car. His wife's face was pink, exhilarated. Her hood was back and her hair had come undone. "You're closer than you think," she said. "Where's the shovel?" She dabbled with it around the stuck tire, doing no good that he could see.

"It's that damn little gutter," he said, impotently itching to grab the shovel from her. "In the summer you're not even conscious of its being there."

She thrust the shovel into a mound so it stood upright and told him, "Sweetheart, now you push. You're stronger than I am."

Grudgingly, he felt flattered. "All right. We'll try it. Now, with the accelerator—don't gun it. You just dig yourself deeper with the spinning tires."

"That's what *you* were doing."

"That's because you weren't pushing hard enough. And steer for the middle of the street, and rock it back and forth gently, back and forth; and don't panic."

As she listened to these instructions, a dimple beside the corner of her mouth kept appearing and disappearing. She got into the driver's seat. A little shower of snow, loosened by the climbing sun, fell rustling through a nearby tree, and the woman across the street came onto her porch without the broom, plainly intending to watch. Her lipstick at this distance was like one of those identifying spots of color on birds.

Mark squatted down and pressed his shoulder against the trunk and gripped the bumper with his hands. A scratch in the paint glinted beneath his eyes. How had that happened? He still thought of their car as brand-new. Snow again insinuated its chill bite into his galosh. Nervous puffs of dirty smoke rippled out of the exhaust pipe and bounced against his legs. He was aware of the woman on the porch, watching. He felt all the windows of the neighborhood watching.

The woman in the driver's seat eased out the clutch. The tires revolved, and the slippery ton of the automobile's rear end threatened to slide farther sideways; but he fought it, and she fed more gas, and they seemed to gain an inch forward. Doing what she had told him, she rocked the car back, and at the peak of its backward swing gunned it forward again, and he felt their forward margin expand. *Good girl.* He heaved; they paused; the car rocked back and then forward again and he heaved so hard the flat muscles straddling his groin ached. Mark seemed to feel, somewhere within the inertial masses they were striving to manage, his personal strength register a delicate response, a flicker in the depths. The car relaxed backwards, and in this remission he straightened and saw through the rear window the back of the driver's head, her hood down, her hair loosened. The wheels spun again, the car dipped forward through the trough it had worn, and its weight seemed to hang, sustained by his strength, on the edge of release. "Once more," he shouted, trembling through the length of his legs. The car sagged back through an arc that had noticeably distended, and in chasing its forward swing with his pushing he had to take steps, one, two . . . *three!* The rear tires, frantically excited and in their spinning spitting snow across his lower half, slithered across that invisible edge he had sensed. The ridge was broken through, and if he continued to push, it was with gratuitous exertion, adding himself through sheer affection to an irresistible momentum. They were free.

Feeling this also, she whipped the steering wheel to head herself downhill and braked to a stop some yards away. The car, stuttering smoke from its exhaust pipe, perched safe in the center of the sand-striped width of Hillcrest Road. It was a 1960 Plymouth SonoRamic Commando V-8, with fins. Its driver, silhouetted with her nose tipped up, looked much too frail to have managed so big a thing.

Mark shouted "Great!" and leaped over the shattered ridge, brandishing the shovel. The woman on the porch called something to him he couldn't quite catch but took kindly. He walked to his car and opened the door and got in beside his wife. The heater had come on; the interior was warm. He repeated, "You were great." He was still panting.

She rosily smiled and said, "So were you."

Giving Blood

THE MAPLES had been married now nine years, which is almost too long. "Goddamn it, goddamn it," Richard said to Joan, as they drove into Boston to give blood, "I drive this road five days a week and now I'm driving it again. It's like a nightmare. I'm exhausted. I'm emotionally, mentally, physically exhausted, and she isn't even an aunt of mine. She isn't even an aunt of *yours*."

"She's a sort of cousin," Joan said.

"Well, hell, every goddamn body in New England is some sort of cousin of yours; must I spend the rest of my life trying to save them *all?*"

"Hush," Joan said. "She might die. I'm ashamed of you. Really ashamed."

It cut. His voice for the moment took on an apologetic pallor. "Well, I'd be my usual goddamn saintly self if I'd had any sort of sleep last night. Five days a week I bump out of bed and stagger out the door past the milkman, and on the one day of the week when I don't even have to truck the brats to Sunday school you make an appointment to have me drained dry thirty miles away."

"Well, it wasn't *me*," Joan said, "who had to stay till two o'clock doing the Twist with Marlene Brossman."

"We weren't doing the Twist. We were gliding around very chastely to *Hits of the Forties*. And don't think I was so oblivious I didn't see you snoogling behind the piano with Harry Saxon."

"We weren't behind the piano, we were on the bench. And he was just talking to me because he felt sorry for me. Everybody there felt sorry for me; you could have at *least* let somebody else dance *once* with Marlene, if only for show."

"Show, show," Richard said. "That's your mentality exactly."

"Why, the poor Matthews or whatever they are looked absolutely horrified."

"Matthiessons," he said. "And that's another thing. Why are idiots like that being invited these days? If there's anything I hate, it's women who keep putting one hand on their pearls and taking a deep breath. I thought she had something stuck in her throat."

"They're a perfectly pleasant, decent young couple. The thing you resent about their being there is that their relative innocence shows us what we've become."

"If you're so attracted," he said, "to little fat men like Harry Saxon, why didn't you marry one?"

"My," Joan said calmly, and gazed out the window away from him, at the scudding gasoline stations. "You honestly *are* hateful. It's not just a pose."

"Pose, show, my Lord, who are you performing for? If it isn't Harry Saxon, it's Freddie Vetter—all these dwarfs. Every time I looked over at you last night it was like some pale Queen of the Dew surrounded by a ring of mushrooms."

"You're too absurd," she said. Her hand, distinctly thirtyish, dry and green-veined and rasped by detergents, stubbed out her cigarette in the dashboard ashtray. "You're not subtle. You think you can match me up with another man so you can swirl off with Marlene with a free conscience."

Her reading his strategy so correctly made his face burn; he felt again the tingle of Mrs. Brossman's hair as he pressed his cheek against hers and in this damp privacy inhaled the perfume behind her ear. "You're right," he said. "But I want to get you a man your own size; I'm very loyal that way."

"Let's not talk," she said.

His hope, of turning the truth into a joke, was rebuked. Any implication of permission was blocked. "It's that *smug*ness," he explained, speaking levelly, as if about a phenomenon of which they were both disinterested students. "It's your smugness that is really intolerable. Your knee-jerk liberalism I don't mind. Your sexlessness I've learned to live with. But that wonderfully smug, New England— I suppose we needed it to get the country founded, but in the Age of Anxiety it really does gall."

He had been looking over at her, and unexpectedly she turned and looked at him, with a startled but uncannily crystalline expression, as if her face had been in an instant rendered in tinted porcelain, even to the eyelashes.

"I asked you not to talk," Joan said. "Now you've said things that I'll never forget."

Plunged fathoms deep into the wrong, feeling suffocated by his guilt, he concentrated on the highway and sullenly steered. Though they were moving at sixty in the sparse Saturday traffic, Richard had travelled this road so often its distances were all translated into time the car seemed to him to be moving as slowly as a minute hand from one digit to the next. It would have been strategic and dignified of him to keep the silence; but he could not resist believing that just one more pinch of syllables would restore the marital balance that with each wordless mile slipped increasingly awry. He asked, "How did Bean seem to you?" Bean was their baby. They had left her last night, to go to the party, with a fever of 102°.

Joan wrestled with her vow to say nothing, but maternal concern won out. She said, "Cooler. Her nose is a river."

"Sweetie," Richard blurted, "will they hurt me?" The curious fact was that he had never given blood before. Asthmatic and underweight, he had been 4-F, and at college and now at the office he had, less through his own determination than through the diffidence of the solicitors, evaded pledging blood. It was one of those tests of courage so trivial that no one had ever thought to make him face up to it.

Spring comes reluctantly to Boston. Speckled crusts of ice lingered around the parking meters, and the air, grayly stalemated between seasons, tinted the buildings along Longwood Avenue with a drab and homogeneous majesty. As they walked up the drive to the hospital entrance, Richard wondered aloud if they would see the King of Arabia.

"He's in a separate wing," Joan said. "With four wives."

"Only four? What an ascetic." And he made bold to tap his wife's shoulder. It was not clear if, under the thickness of her winter coat, she felt it.

At the desk, they were directed down a long corridor floored with cigar-colored linoleum. Up and down, right and left it went, in the secretive, disjointed way peculiar to hospitals that have been built annex by annex. Richard felt like Hansel orphaned with Gretel; birds ate the bread crumbs behind them, and at last they timidly knocked on the witch's door, which said BLOOD DONATION CENTER. A young man in white opened the door a crack. Over his shoulder Richard glimpsed—horrors!—a pair of dismembered female legs stripped of their shoes and laid parallel on a bed. Glints of needles and bottles pricked his eyes. Without widening the crack, the young man passed out to them two long forms. In sitting side by side on the waiting bench, spelling out their middle names and recalling their childhood diseases, Mr. and Mrs. Maple were newly defined to themselves. He fought down that urge to giggle and clown and lie that threatened him whenever he was asked—like a lawyer appointed by the court to plead a hopeless case—to present, as it were, his statistics to eternity. It seemed to mitigate his case slightly that a few of these statistics (present address, date of marriage) were shared by the hurt soul scratching beside him. He looked over her shoulder. "I never knew you had whooping cough."

"My mother says. I don't remember it."

A pan crashed to a distant floor. An elevator chuckled remotely. A woman, a middle-aged woman top-heavy with rouge and fur, stepped out of the blood door and wobbled a moment on legs that looked familiar. They had been restored to their shoes. The heels of these shoes clicked firmly as, having raked the Maples with a dazed, defiant glance, she turned and disappeared around a bend in the corridor. The young man appeared in the doorway holding a pair of surgical tongs. His noticeably recent haircut made him seem an apprentice barber. He clicked his tongs and smiled. "Shall I do you together?"

"Sure." It put Richard on his mettle that this callow fellow, to whom apparently they were to entrust their liquid essence, was so distinctly younger than they. But when Richard stood, his indignation melted and his legs felt diluted under him. And the extraction of the blood sample from his middle finger seemed about the nastiest and most needlessly prolonged physical involvement with another human being he had ever experienced. There is a touch that good dentists, mechanics, and barbers have, and this intern did not have it; he fumbled and in compensation was too rough. Again and again, an atrociously clumsy vampire, he tugged and twisted the purpling finger in vain. The tiny glass capillary tube remained transparent.

"He doesn't like to bleed, does he?" the intern asked Joan. As relaxed as a nurse, she sat in a chair next to a table of scintillating equipment.

"I don't think his blood moves much," she said, "until after midnight."

This stab at a joke made Richard in his extremity of fright laugh loudly, and the laugh at last seemed to jar the panicked coagulant. Red seeped upward in the thirsty little tube, as in a sudden thermometer.

The intern grunted in relief. As he smeared the samples on the analysis box, he explained idly, "What we ought to have down here is a pan of warm water. You just came in out of the cold. If you put your hand in hot water for a minute, the blood just pops out."

"A pretty thought," Richard said.

But the intern had already written him off as a clowner and continued calmly to Joan, "All we'd need would be a baby hot plate for about six dollars, then we could make our own coffee, too. This way, when we get a donor who needs the coffee afterward, we have to send up for it while we keep her head between her knees. Do you think you'll be needing coffee?"

"*No,*" Richard interrupted, jealous of their rapport.

The intern told Joan, "You're O."

"I know," she said.

"And he's A positive."

"Why, that's very good, Dick!" she called to him.

"Am I rare?" he asked.

The boy turned and explained, "O positive and A positive are the most common types. Who wants to be first?"

"Let me," Joan said. "He's never done it before."

"Her full name is Joan of Arc," Richard explained, angered at this betrayal, so unimpeachably selfless and smug.

The intern, threatened in his element, fixed his puzzled eyes on the floor between them and said, "Take off your shoes and each get on a bed." He added, *"Please,"* and all three laughed, one after the other, the intern last.

The beds were at right angles to one another along two walls. Joan lay down and from her husband's angle of vision was novelly foreshortened. He had never before seen her quite this way, the combed crown of her hair so poignant, her bared arm so silver and long, her stocking feet toed in so childishly and helplessly. There were no pillows on the beds, and lying flat made him feel tipped head down; the illusion of floating encouraged his hope that this unreal adventure would soon dissolve, as dreams do. "You O.K.?"

"Are you?" Her voice came softly from the tucked-under wealth of her hair. Her parting was so straight it seemed a mother had brushed it. He watched a long needle sink into the flat of her arm and a piece of moist cotton clumsily swab the spot. He had imagined their blood would be drained into cans or bottles, but the intern, whose breathing was now the only sound within the room, brought to Joan's side what looked like a miniature plastic knapsack, all coiled and tied. His body cloaked his actions. When he stepped away, a plastic cord had been grafted, a transparent vine, to the flattened crook of Joan's extended arm, where the skin was translucent and the veins were faint blue tributaries shallowly buried. It was a tender, vulnerable place where in courting days she had liked being stroked. Now, without visible transition, the pale tendril planted here went dark red. Richard wanted to cry out.

The instant readiness of her blood to leave her body pierced him like a physical pang. Though he had not so much as blinked, its initial leap had been too quick for his eye. He had expected some visible sign of flow, but from the mere appearance of it the tiny looped hose might be pouring blood *into* her body or might be a curved line added, like an impudent mustache, to a painting. The fixed position of his head gave what he saw a certain flatness.

And now the intern turned to him, and there was the tiny felt prick of the Novocain needle, and then the coarse, half-felt intrusion of something resembling a medium-weight nail. Twice the boy mistakenly probed for the vein and the third time taped the successful graft fast with adhesive tape. All the while, Richard's mind moved aloofly among the constellations of the stained, cracked ceiling. What was being done to him did not bear contemplating. When the intern moved away to hum and tinkle among his instruments, Joan craned her neck to show her husband her face and, upside down in his vision, grotesquely smiled, her mouth where her eyes should have been, her eyes a broken, blinking mouth.

It was not many minutes that they lay there at right angles together, but the time passed as something beyond the walls, as something mixed with the faraway clatter of pans and the approach and retreat of footsteps and the opening and closing of unseen doors. Here, conscious of a pointed painless pulse in the inner hinge of his arm but incurious as to what it looked like, he floated and imagined how his soul would float free when all his blood was underneath the bed. His blood and Joan's merged on the floor, and together their spirits glided from crack to crack, from star to star on the ceiling. Once she cleared her throat, and the sound was like the rasp of a pebble loosened by a cliff-climber's boot.

The door opened. Richard turned his head and saw an old man, bald and sallow, enter and settle in a chair. He was one of those old men who hold within an institution an ill-defined but secure place. The young doctor seemed to know him, and the two talked, quietly, as if not to disturb the mystical union of the couple sacrificially bedded together. They talked of persons and events that meant nothing—of Iris, of Dr. Greenstein, of

Ward D, again of Iris, who had given the old man an undeserved scolding, of the shameful lack of a hot plate to make coffee on, of the rumored black bodyguards who kept watch with scimitars by the bed of the glaucomatous king. Through Richard's tranced ignorance these topics passed as clouds of impression, iridescent, massy—Dr. Greenstein with a pointed nose and almond eyes the color of ivy, Iris eighty feet tall and hurling sterilized thunderbolts of wrath. As in some theologies the proliferating deities are said to exist as ripples upon the featureless ground of Godhead, so these inconstant images lightly overlay his continuous awareness of Joan's blood, like his own, ebbing. Linked to a common loss, they were chastely conjoined; the thesis developed upon him that the hoses attached to them met somewhere out of sight. Testing this belief, he glanced down and saw that indeed the plastic vine taped to the flattened crook of his arm was the same dark red as hers. He stared at the ceiling to disperse a sensation of faintness.

Abruptly the young intern left off his desultory conversation and moved to Joan's side. There was a chirp of clips. When he moved away, she was revealed holding her naked arm upright, pressing a piece of cotton against it with the other hand. Without pausing, the intern came to Richard's side, and the birdsong of clips repeated, nearer. "Look at that," he said to his elderly friend. "I started him two minutes later than her and he's finished at the same time."

"Was it a race?" Richard asked.

Clumsily firm, the boy fitted Richard's fingers to a pad and lifted his arm for him. "Hold it there for five minutes," he said.

"What'll happen if I don't?"

"You'll mess up your shirt." To the old man he said, "I had a woman in here the other day, she was all set to leave when, all of a sudden—pow!—all over the front of this beautiful linen dress. She was going to Symphony."

"Then they try to sue the hospital for the cleaning bill," the old man muttered.

"Why was I slower than him?" Joan asked. Her upright arm wavered, as if vexed or weakened.

"The woman generally is," the boy told her. "Nine times out of ten, the man is faster. Their hearts are so much stronger."

"Is that really so?"

"Sure it's so," Richard told her. "Don't argue with medical science."

"Woman up in Ward C," the old man said, "they saved her life for her out of an auto accident and now I hear she's suing because they didn't find her dental plate."

Under such patter, the five minutes eroded. Richard's upheld arm began to ache. It seemed that he and Joan were caught together in a classroom where they would never be recognized, or in a charade that would never be guessed, the correct answer being Two Silver Birches in a Meadow.

"You can sit up now if you want," the intern told them. "But don't let go of the venipuncture."

They sat up on their beds, legs dangling heavily. Joan asked him, "Do you feel dizzy?"

"With my powerful heart? Don't be presumptuous."

"Do you think he'll need coffee?" the intern asked her. "I'll have to send up for it now."

The old man shifted forward in his chair, preparing to heave to his feet.

"I do *not* want any *cof*fee"—Richard said it so loud he saw himself transposed, a lesser Iris, into the firmament of the old man's aggrieved gossip. *Some dizzy bastard down in the blood room, I get up to get him some coffee and he damn near bit my head off.* To demonstrate simultaneously his essential good humor and his total presence of mind, Richard gestured toward the blood they had given—two square plastic sacks filled solidly fat—and declared, "Back where I come from in West Virginia sometimes you pick a tick off a dog that looks like that." The men looked at him amazed. Had he not quite said what he meant to say? Or had they never seen anybody from West Virginia before?

Joan pointed at the blood, too. "Is that us? Those little doll pillows?"

"Maybe we should take one home to Bean," Richard suggested.

The intern did not seem convinced that this was a joke. "Your blood will be credited to Mrs. Henryson's account," he stated stiffly.

Joan asked him, "Do you know anything about her? When is she— when is her operation scheduled?"

"I think for tomorrow. The only thing on the tab this after is an open heart at two; that'll take about sixteen pints."

"Oh . . ." Joan was shaken. "Sixteen . . . that's a full person, isn't it?"

"More," the intern answered, with the regal handwave that bestows largesse and dismisses compliments.

"Could we visit her?" Richard asked, for Joan's benefit. ("Really ashamed," she had said; it had cut.) He was confident of the refusal.

"Well, you can ask at the desk, but usually before a major one like this it's just the nearest of kin. I guess you're safe now." He meant their punctures. Richard's arm bore a small raised bruise; the intern covered it with one of those ample salmon, unhesitatingly adhesive bandages that only hospitals have. That was their specialty, Richard thought—packaging.

They wrap the human mess for final delivery. Sixteen doll's pillows, uniformly dark and snug, marching into an open heart: the vision momentarily satisfied his hunger for order.

He rolled down his sleeve and slid off the bed. It startled him to realize, in the instant before his feet touched the floor, that three pairs of eyes were fixed upon him, fascinated and apprehensive and eager for scandal. He stood and towered above them. He hopped on one foot to slip into one loafer, and then on this foot to slip into the other loafer. Then he did the little shuffle-tap, shuffle-tap step that was all that remained to him of dancing lessons he had taken at the age of seven, driving twelve miles each Saturday into Clarksburg. He made a small bow toward his wife, smiled at the old man, and said to the intern, "All my life people have been expecting me to faint. I have no idea why. I haven't fainted yet."

His coat and overcoat felt a shade queer, a bit slithery and light, but as he walked down the length of the corridor, space seemed to adjust snugly around him. At his side, Joan kept an inquisitive and chastened silence. They pushed through the great glass doors. A famished sun was nibbling through the overcast. Above and behind them, the King of Arabia lay in a drugged dream of dunes and Mrs. Henryson upon her sickbed received, like the comatose mother of twins, their identical packets of blood. Richard hugged his wife's shoulders and as they walked along leaning on each other whispered, "Hey, I love you. Love love *love* you."

Romance is, simply, the strange, the untried. It was unusual for the Maples to be driving together at eleven in the morning. Almost always it was dark when they shared a car. The oval of her face clung in the corner of his eye. She was watching him, alert to take the wheel if he suddenly lost consciousness. He felt tender toward her in the eggshell light, and curious toward himself, wondering how far beneath his brain the black pit did lie. He felt no different; but, then, the quality of consciousness perhaps did not bear introspection. Something surely had been taken from him; he was less himself by a pint. Yet the earth, with its signals and buildings and cars and bricks, continued like a pedalled note.

Boston behind them, he asked, "Where should we eat?"

"Should we eat?"

"Please, yes. Let me take you to lunch. Just like a secretary."

"I do feel sort of illicit. As if I've stolen something."

"You, too? But what did we steal?"

"I don't know. The morning? Do you think Eve knows enough to feed them?" Eve was their sitter, a little bony girl from down the street who would, in exactly a year, Richard calculated, be painfully lovely. They lasted three years on the average, sitters; you got them in the tenth grade and escorted them into their bloom and then, with graduation, like commuters who had reached their stop, they dropped out of sight, into college or marriage. And the train went on, and took on other passengers, and itself became older and longer.

"She'll manage," he told her. "What would you like? All that talk about coffee has made me frantic for some."

"At the Pancake House beyond 128 they give you coffee before you even ask."

"Pancakes? Now? Aren't you jolly? Do you think we'll throw up?"

"Do you feel like throwing up?"

"No, not really. I feel sort of insubstantial and gentle, but it's probably psychosomatic. I don't really understand this business of giving something away and still somehow having it. What is it—the spleen?"

"I don't know," she said. "Are the splenetic man and the sanguine man the same?"

"God. I've totally forgotten the humors. What are the others— phlegm and choler?"

"Bile and black bile are in there somewhere."

"One thing about you, Joan. You're educated. New England women are educated."

"Sexless as we are."

"That's right; drain me dry and then put me on the rack." But there was no wrath in his words; indeed, he had reminded her of their earlier conversation so that, in much this way, his words might be revived, diluted, and erased. It seemed to work. The restaurant where they served only pancakes was empty and quiet this early. A bashfulness possessed them both, and a silence while they ate. Touched by the stain her blueberry pancakes left on her teeth, he held a match to her cigarette and said, "Gee, I loved you back in the blood room."

"I wonder why."

"You were so brave."

"So were you."

"But I'm supposed to be. I'm paid to be. It's the price of having a penis."

"Shh."

"Hey. I didn't mean that about your being sexless."

The waitress refilled their coffee cups and gave them the check.

"And I promise never never to do the Twist, the cha-cha, or the schottische with Marlene Brossman."

"Don't be silly. I don't care."

This amounted to permission, but perversely irritated him. That above-it-all quality; why didn't she *fight?* Trying to regain their peace, scrambling uphill, he picked up their check and with an effort of acting, the pretense being that they were out on a date and he was a raw dumb suitor, said handsomely, "I'll pay."

But on looking into his wallet he saw only a single worn dollar there. He didn't know why this should make him so angry, except the fact somehow that it was only *one.* "Goddamn it," he said. "Look at that." He waved it in her face. "I work like a bastard all week for you and those insatiable brats and at the end of it what do I have? One goddamn crummy wrinkled dollar."

Her hands dropped to the pocketbook beside her on the seat, but her gaze stayed with him, her face having retreated, or advanced, into that porcelain shell of uncanny composure. "We'll both pay," Joan said.

Twin Beds in Rome

THE MAPLES had talked and thought about separation so long it seemed it would never come. For their conversations, increasingly ambivalent and ruthless as accusation, retraction, blow, and caress alternated and cancelled, had the final effect of knitting them ever tighter together in a painful, helpless, degrading intimacy. And their lovemaking, like a perversely healthy child whose growth defies every deficiency of nutrition, continued; when their tongues at last fell silent, their bodies collapsed together as two mute armies might gratefully mingle, released from the absurd hostilities decreed by two mad kings. Bleeding, mangled, reverently laid in its tomb a dozen times, their marriage could not die. Burning to leave one another, they left, out of marital habit, together. They took a trip to Rome.

They arrived at night. The plane was late, the airport grand. They had left hastily, without plans; and yet, as if forewarned of their arrival, nimble Italians, speaking perfect English, took their luggage in hand, reserved a hotel room for them by telephone from the airport, and ushered them into a bus. The bus, surprisingly, plunged into a dark rural landscape. A few windows hung lanternlike in the distance; a river abruptly bared its silver breast beneath them; the silhouettes of olive trees and Italian pines flicked past like shadowy illustrations in an old Latin primer. "I could ride this bus forever," Joan said aloud, and Richard was pained, remembering, from the days when they had been content together, how she had once confessed to feeling a sexual stir when the young man at the gas station, wiping the windshield with a vigorous, circular motion, had made the body of the car, containing her, rock slightly. Of all the things she had ever told him, this remained in his mind the most revealing, the deepest glimpse she had ever permitted into the secret woman he could never reach and had at last wearied of trying to reach.

Yet it pleased him to have her happy. This was his weakness. He wished her to be happy, and the certainty that, away from her, he could not know if she were happy or not formed the final, unexpected door barring his way when all others had been opened. So he dried the very tears he had whipped from her eyes, withdrew each protestation of hopelessness at the very point when she seemed willing to give up hope, and their agony continued. "Nothing lasts forever," he said now.

"You can't let me relax a minute, can you?"

"I'm sorry. Do relax."

She stared through the window a while, then turned and told him, "It doesn't feel as if we're going to Rome at all."

"Where are we going?" He honestly wanted to know, honestly hoped she could tell him.

"Back to the way things were?"

"No. I don't want to go back to that. I feel we've come very far and have only a little way more to go."

She looked out at the quiet landscape a long while before he realized she was crying. He fought the impulse to comfort her, inwardly shouted it down as cowardly and cruel, but his hand, as if robbed of restraint by a force as powerful as lust, crept onto her arm. She rested her head on his shoulder. The shawled woman across the aisle took them for lovers and politely glanced away.

The bus slipped from the country dark. Factories and residential rows narrowed the highway. A sudden monument, a massive white pyramid stricken with light and inscribed with Latin, loomed beside them. Soon they were pressing their faces together to the window to follow the Colosseum itself as, shaped like a shattered wedding cake, it slowly pivoted and silently floated from the harbor of their vision. At the terminal, another lively chain of hands and voices rejoined them to their baggage, settled them in a taxi, and carried them to the hotel. As Richard dropped six hundred-lira pieces into the driver's hand, they seemed the smoothest, roundest, most tactfully weighted coins he had ever bestowed. The hotel desk was one flight up. The clerk was young and playful. He pronounced their name several times, and wondered why they had not gone to Naples. The halls of the hotel, which had been described to them at the airport as second-class, were nevertheless of rose marble. The marble floor carried into their room. This and the amplitude of the bathroom and the imperial purple of the curtains blinded Richard to a serious imperfection until the clerk, his heels clicking in satisfaction with the perhaps miscalculated tip he had received, was far down the hall.

"Twin beds," he said. They had always had a double bed.

Joan asked, "Do you want to call the desk?"

"How important is it to you?"

"I don't think it matters. Can you sleep alone?"

"I guess. But—" It was delicate. He felt they had been insulted. Until they finally parted, it seemed impertinent for anything, even a slice of space, to come between them. If the trip were to kill or cure (and this was, for the tenth time, their slogan), then the attempt at a cure should have a certain technical purity, even though—or, rather, all the more because—in his heart he had already doomed it to fail. And also there was the material question of whether he could sleep without a warm proximate body to give his sleep shape.

"But what?" Joan prompted.

"But it seems sort of sad."

"Richard, don't be sad. You've been sad enough. You're supposed to relax. This isn't a honeymoon or anything, it's just a little rest we're trying to give each other. You can come visit me in my bed if you can't sleep."

"You're such a nice woman," he said. "I can't understand why I'm so miserable with you."

He had said this, or something like it, so often before that she, sickened by simultaneous doses of honey and gall, ignored the entire remark, and unpacked with a deliberate serenity. On her suggestion, they walked into the city, though it was ten o'clock. Their hotel was on a shopping street that at this hour was lined with lowered steel shutters. At the far end, an illuminated fountain played. His feet, which had never given him trouble, began to hurt. In the soft, damp air of the Roman winter, his shoes seemed to have developed hot inward convexities that gnashed his flesh at every stride. He could not imagine why this should be, unless he was allergic to marble. For the sake of his feet, they found an American bar, entered, and ordered coffee. Off in a corner, a drunken male American voice droned through the grooves of an unintelligible but distinctly feminine circuit of complaints; the voice, indeed, seemed not so much a man's as a woman's deepened by being played at a slower speed on the phonograph. Hoping to cure the growing dizzy emptiness within him, Richard ordered a "hamburger" that proved to be more tomato sauce than meat. Outside, on the street, he bought a paper cone of hot chestnuts from a sidewalk vender. This man, whose thumbs and fingertips were charred black, agitated his hand until three hundred lire were placed in it. In a way, Richard welcomed being cheated; it gave him a place in the Roman economy. The

Maples returned to the hotel, and side by side on their twin beds fell into a deep sleep.

That is, Richard assumed, in the cavernous accounting rooms of his sub-conscious, that Joan also slept well. But when they awoke in the morning, she told him, "You were terribly funny last night. I couldn't go to sleep, and every time I reached over to give you a little pat, to make you think you were in a double bed, you'd say 'Go away' and shake me off."

He laughed in delight. "Did I really? In my sleep?"

"It must have been. Once you shouted 'Leave me alone!' so loud I thought you must be awake, but when I tried to talk to you, you were snoring."

"Isn't that funny? I hope I didn't hurt your feelings."

"No. It was refreshing not to have you contradict yourself."

He brushed his teeth and ate a few of the cold chestnuts left over from the night before. The Maples breakfasted on hard rolls and bitter coffee in the hotel and walked again into Rome. His shoes resumed their inex-plicable torture. With its strange, almost mocking attentiveness to their unseen needs, the city thrust a shoe store under their eyes; they entered, and Richard bought, from a gracefully reptilian young salesman, a pair of black alligator loafers. They were too tight, being smartly shaped, but they were dead—they did not pinch with the vital, outraged vehemence of the others. Then the Maples, she carrying the Hachette guidebook and he his American shoes in a box, walked down the Via Nazionale to the Victor Emmanuel Monument, a titanic flight of stairs leading nowhere. "What was so great about him?" Richard asked. "Did he unify Italy? Or was that Cavour?"

"Is he the funny little king in *A Farewell to Arms?*"

"I don't know. But nobody could be *that* great."

"You can see now why the Italians don't have an inferiority complex. Everything is so huge."

They stood looking at the Palazzo Venezia until they imagined Mus-solini frowning from a window, climbed the many steps to the Piazza del Campidoglio, and came to the equestrian statue of Marcus Aurelius on the pedestal by Michelangelo. Joan remarked how like a Marino Marini it was, and it was. She was so intelligent. Perhaps this was what made leav-ing her, as a gesture, exquisite in conception and difficult in execution. They circled the square. The portals and doors all around them seemed closed forever, like the doors in a drawing. They entered, because it was open, the side door of the church of Santa Maria in Aracoeli. They discovered themselves to be walking on sleeping people, life-sized tomb-reliefs worn nearly featureless by footsteps. The fingers of the hands folded on the stone breasts had been smoothed to finger-shaped shadows. One face, sheltered from wear behind a pillar, seemed a vivid soul trying to rise from the all-but-erased body.

Only the Maples examined these reliefs, cut into a floor that once must have been a glittering lake of mosaic; the other tourists clustered around a chapel that preserved, in slippers and vestments, behind glass, the child-sized greenish remains of a pope. Joan and Richard left by the same side door and descended steps and paid admission to the ruins of the Roman Forum. The Renaissance had used it as a quarry; broken columns lay everywhere, loaded with perspective, like a de Chirico. Joan was charmed by the way birds and weeds lived in the crevices of this exploded civic dream. A delicate rain began to fall. At the end of one path, they peeked in glass doors, and a small uniformed man with a broom limped forward and admitted them, as if to a speakeasy, to the abandoned church of Santa Maria Antiqua. The pale vaulted air felt innocent of worship; the seventh-century frescoes seemed recently, nervously executed. As they left, Richard read the question in the broom man's smile and pressed a tactful coin into his hand. The soft rain continued. Joan took Richard's arm, as if for shelter. His stomach began to hurt—a light, chafing ache at first, scarcely enough to distract him from the pain in his feet. They walked along the Via Sacra, through roofless pagan temples carpeted in grass. The ache in his stomach intensified. Uniformed guards, old men standing this way and that in the rain like hungry gulls, beckoned them toward further ruins, further churches, but the pain now had blinded Richard to everything but the extremity of his distance from anything that might give him support. He refused admittance to the Basilica of Constantine, and asked instead for the *uscita*, mispronouncing it. He did not feel capable of retracing his steps. The guard, seeing a source of tips escaping, dourly pointed toward a small gate in a nearby wire fence. The Maples lifted the latch, stepped through, and stood on the paved rise overlooking the Colosseum. Richard walked a little distance and leaned on a low wall.

"Is it so bad?" Joan asked.

"Oddly bad," he said. "I'm sorry. It's funny."

"Do you want to throw up?"

"No. It's not like that." His sentences came jerkily. "It's just a . . . sort of gripe."

"High or low?"

"In the middle."

"What could have caused it? The chestnuts?"

"No. It's just, I think, being here, so far from anywhere, with you, and not knowing . . . why."

"Shall we go back to the hotel?"

"Yes. I think if I could lie down."

"Shall we get a taxi?"

"They'll cheat me."

"That doesn't matter."

"I don't know . . . our address."

"We know sort of. It's near that big fountain. I'll look up the Italian for 'fountain.' "

"Rome is . . . full of . . . fountains."

"Richard. You aren't doing this just for my benefit?"

He had to laugh, she was so intelligent. "Not consciously. It has something to do . . . with having to hand out tips . . . all the time. It's really an ache. It's incredible."

"Can you walk?"

"Sure. Hold my arm."

"Shall I carry your shoebox?"

"No. Don't worry, sweetie. It's just a nervous ache. I used to get them . . . when I was little. But I was . . . braver then."

They descended steps to a thoroughfare thick with speeding traffic. The taxis they hailed carried heads in the rear and did not stop. They crossed the Via dei Fori Imperiali and tried to work their way back, against the sideways tug of interweaving streets, to the familiar territory containing the fountain, the American Bar, the shoe store, and the hotel. They passed through a market of bright food. Garlands of sausages hung from striped canopies. Heaps of lettuce lay in the street. He walked stiffly, as if the pain he carried were precious and fragile; holding one arm across his abdomen seemed to ease it slightly. The rain and Joan, having been in some way the pressures that had caused it, now became the pressures that enabled him to bear it. Joan kept him walking. The rain masked him, made his figure less distinct to passersby, and thus less distinct to himself, and so dimmed his pain. The blocks seemed cruelly uphill and downhill. They climbed a long slope of narrow pavement beside the Banca d'Italia. The rain lifted. The pain, having expanded into every corner of the chamber beneath his ribs, had armed itself with a knife and now began to slash the walls in hope of escape. They reached the Via Nazionale, blocks below the hotel. The shops were unshuttered, the distant fountain was dry. He felt as if he were leaning backward, and his mind seemed a kind of twig, a twig that had deviated from the trunk and chosen to be this branch instead of that one, and chosen again and again, becoming finer with each choice, until, finally, there was nothing left for it but to vanish into air. In the hotel room he lay down on his twin bed, settled his overcoat over him, curled up, and fell asleep.

When he awoke an hour later, everything was different. The pain was gone. Joan was lying in her bed reading the Hachette guide. He saw her, as he rolled over, as if freshly, in the kind of cool library light in which he had first seen her; only he knew, calmly, that since then she had come to share his room. "It's gone," he told her.

"You're kidding. I was all set to call up a doctor and have you taken to a hospital."

"No, it wasn't anything like that. I knew it wasn't. It was nervous."

"You were dead white."

"It was too many different things focusing on the same spot. I think the Forum must have depressed me. The past here is so . . . much. So complicated. Also, my shoes hurting bothered me."

"Darley, it's Rome. You're supposed to be happy."

"I am now. Come on. You must be starving. Let's get some lunch."

"Really? You feel up to it?"

"Quite. It's gone." And, except for a comfortable reminiscent soreness that the first swallow of Milanese salami healed, it was. The Maples embarked again upon Rome, and, in this city of steps, of sliding, unfolding perspectives, of many-windowed surfaces of sepia and rose ochre, of buildings so vast one seemed to be outdoors in them, the couple parted. Not physically—they rarely left each other's sight. But they had at last been parted. Both knew it. They became with each other, as in the days of courtship, courteous, gay, and reserved. Their marriage let go like an overgrown vine whose half-hidden stem has been slashed in the dawn by an ancient gardener. They walked arm in arm through seemingly solid blocks of buildings that separated, under examination, into widely different slices of style and time. At one point she turned to him and said, "Darley, I know what was wrong with us. I'm classic, and you're baroque." They shopped, and saw, and slept, and ate. Sitting across from her in the last of the restaurants that like oases of linen and wine had sustained these level elegiac days, Richard saw that Joan was happy. Her face, released from the tension of hope, had grown smooth; her gestures had taken on the flirting irony of the young; she had become ecstatically attentive to everything about her; and her voice, as she bent forward to whisper a remark about a woman and a handsome man at another table, was rapid, as if the very air of her breathing had turned thin and free. She was happy, and, jealous of her happiness, he again grew reluctant to leave her.

Marching through Boston

THE CIVIL-RIGHTS MOVEMENT had a salubrious effect on Joan Maple. A suburban mother of four, she would return late at night from a non-violence class in Roxbury with rosy cheeks and shining eyes, eager to describe, while sipping Benedictine, her indoctrination. "This huge man in overalls—"

"A Negro?" her husband asked.

"Of course. This huge man, with a *very* refined vocabulary, told us if we march anywhere, especially in the South, to let the Negro men march on the outside, because it's important for their self-esteem to be able to protect us. He told us about a New York fashion designer who went down to Selma and said she could take care of herself. Furthermore, she flirted with the state troopers. They finally told her to go home."

"I thought you were supposed to love the troopers," Richard said.

"Only abstractly. Not on your own. You mustn't do *anything* within the movement as an individual. By flirting, she gave the trooper an opportunity to feel contempt."

"She blocked his transference, as it were."

"Don't laugh. It's all very psychological. The man told us, those who want to march, to face our ego-gratificational motives no matter how irrelevant they are and then put them behind us. Once you're in a march, you have no identity. It's elegant. It's beautiful."

He had never known her like this. It seemed to Richard that her posture was improving, her figure filling out, her skin growing lustrous, her very hair gaining body and sheen. Though he had resigned himself, through twelve years of marriage, to a rhythm of apathy and renewal, he distrusted this raw burst of beauty.

The night she returned from Alabama, it was three o'clock in the morning. He woke and heard the front door close behind her. He had been dreaming of a parallelogram in the sky that was also somehow a meteor, and the darkened house seemed quadrisected by the four sleeping children he had, with more than paternal tenderness, put to bed. He had caught himself speaking to them of Mommy as a distant departed spirit, gone to live, invisible, in the newspapers and the television set. The little girl, Bean, had burst into tears. Now the ghost closed the door and walked up the stairs, and came into his bedroom, and fell on the bed.

He switched on the light and saw her sunburned face, her blistered feet. Her ballet slippers were caked with orange mud. She had lived for three days on Coke and dried apricots; at one stretch she had not gone to the bathroom for sixteen hours. The Montgomery airport had been a madhouse—nuns, social workers, divinity students fighting for space on the northbound planes. They had been in the air when they heard about Mrs. Liuzzo.

He accused her: "It could have been you."

She said, "I was always in a group." But she added guiltily, "How were the children?"

"Fine. Bean cried because she thought you were inside the television set."

"Did you see me?"

"Your parents called long-distance to say they thought they did. I didn't. All I saw was Abernathy and King and their henchmen saying, 'Thass right. Say it, man. Thass sayin' it.' "

"Aren't you mean? It was very moving, except that we were all so tired. These teen-age Negro girls kept fainting; a psychiatrist explained to me that they were having psychotic breaks."

"What psychiatrist?"

"Actually, there were three of them, and they were studying to be psychiatrists in Philadelphia. They kind of took me in tow."

"I bet they did. Please come to bed. I'm very tired from being a mother."

She visited the four corners of the upstairs to inspect each sleeping child and, returning, undressed in the dark. She removed underwear she had worn for seventy hours and stood there shining; to the sleepy man in the bed it seemed a visitation, and he felt as people of old must have felt when greeted by an angel—adoring yet resentful, at this flamboyant proof of a level above theirs.

She spoke on the radio; she addressed local groups. In garages and supermarkets he heard himself being pointed out as her husband. She helped organize meetings at which dapper young Negroes ridiculed and abused the applauding suburban audience. Richard marvelled at Joan's public composure. Her shyness stayed with her, but it had become a kind of weapon, as if the doctrine of non-violence had given it point. Her voice, as she phoned evasive local real-estate agents in the campaign for fair housing, grew curiously firm and rather obstinately melodious—a note her husband had not heard in her voice before. He grew jealous and irritable. He found himself insisting, at parties, on the constitutional case for states' rights, on the misfortunes of African independence, on the history of Reconstruction from the South's point of view. Yet she had little trouble persuading him to march with her in Boston.

He promised, though he could not quite grasp the object of the march. All mass movements, of masses or of ideas supposedly embodied in masses, felt unreal to him. Whereas his wife, an Amherst professor's daughter, lived by abstractions; her blood returned to her heart enriched by the passage through some capillarious good cause. He was struck, and subtly wounded, by the ardor with which she rewarded his promise; under his hands her body felt baroque and her skin smooth as night.

The march was in April. Richard awoke that morning with a fever. He had taken something foreign into himself and his body was making resistance. Joan offered to go alone; as if something fundamental to his dignity, to their marriage, were at stake, he refused the offer. The day, dawning cloudy, had been forecast as sunny, and he wore a summer suit that enclosed his hot skin in a slipping, weightless unreality. At a highway drugstore they bought some pills designed to detonate inside him through a twelve-hour period. They parked near her aunt's house in Louisburg Square and took a taxi toward the headwaters of the march, a playground in Roxbury. The Irish driver's impassive back radiated disapproval. The cab was turned aside by a policeman; the Maples got out and walked down a broad brown boulevard lined with barbershops, shoe-repair nooks, pizzerias, and friendliness associations. On stoops and stairways male Negroes loitered, blinking and muttering toward one another as if a vast, decrepit conspiracy had assigned them their positions and then collapsed.

"Lovely architecture," Joan said, pointing toward a curving side street, a neo-Georgian arc suspended in the large urban sadness.

Though she pretended to know where she was, Richard doubted that they were going the right way. But then he saw ahead of them, scattered like the anomalous objects with which Dalí punctuates his perspectives, receding black groups of white clergymen. In the distance, the hot lights of police cars wheeled within a twinkling mob. As they drew nearer, colored girls made into giantesses by bouffant hairdos materialized beside them. One wore cerise stretch pants and the golden sandals of a heavenly cupbearer, and held pressed against her ear a transistor radio tuned to WMEX. On this thin stream of music they all together poured into a playground surrounded by a link fence.

A loose crowd of thousands swarmed on the crushed grass. Bobbing placards advertised churches, brotherhoods, schools, towns. Popsicle vendors lent an unexpected touch of carnival. Suddenly at home, Richard bought a bag of peanuts and looked around — as if this were the playground of his childhood — for friends.

But it was Joan who found some. "My God," she said. "There's my old analyst." At the fringe of some Unitarians stood a plump, doughy man with the troubled squint of a baker who has looked into too many ovens. Joan turned to go the other way.

"Don't suppress," Richard told her. "Let's go and be friendly and normal."

"It's too embarrassing."

"But it's been years since you went. You're cured."

"You don't understand. You're never cured. You just stop going."

"O.K., come *this* way. I think I see my Harvard section man in Plato to Dante."

But, even while arguing against it, she had been drifting them toward her psychiatrist, and now they were caught in the pull of his gaze. He scowled and came toward them, flat-footedly. Richard had never met him and, shaking hands, felt himself as a putrid heap of anecdotes, of detailed lusts and abuses. "I think I need a doctor," he madly blurted.

The other man produced, like a stiletto from his sleeve, a nimble smile. "How so?" Each word seemed precious.

"I have a fever."

"Ah." The psychiatrist turned sympathetically to Joan, and his face issued a clear commiseration: *So he is still punishing you.*

Joan said loyally, "He really does. I saw the thermometer."

"Would you like a peanut?" Richard asked. The offer felt so symbolic, so transparent, that he was shocked when the other man took one, cracked it harshly, and substantially chewed.

Joan asked, "Are you with anybody? I feel a need for group security."

"Come meet my sister." The command sounded strange to Richard; "sister" seemed a piece of psychological slang, a euphemism.

But again things were simpler than they seemed. His sister was plainly from the same batter. Rubicund and yeasty, she seemed to have been enlarged by the exercise of good will and wore a saucer-sized SCLC button in the lapel of a coarse green suit. Richard coveted the suit; it looked warm. The day was continuing overcast and chilly. Something odd, perhaps the successive explosions of the antihistamine pill, was happening inside him, making him feel queerly elongated; the illusion crossed his mind that he was destined to seduce this woman. She beamed and said, "My daughter Trudy and her *best* friend, Carol."

They were girls of sixteen or so, one size smaller in their bones than women. Trudy had the family pastry texture and a darting frown. Carol was homely, fragile, and touching; her upper teeth were a gray blur of braces and her arms were protectively folded across her skimpy bosom. Over a white blouse she wore only a thin blue sweater, unbuttoned. Richard told her, "You're freezing."

"I'm freezing," she said, and a small love was established between them on the basis of this demure repetition. She added, "I came along because I'm writing a term paper."

Trudy said, "She's doing a history of the labor unions," and laughed unpleasantly.

The girl shivered. "I thought they might be the same. Didn't the unions use to march?" Her voice, moistened by the obtrusion of her braces, had a sprayey faintness in the raw gray air.

The psychiatrist's sister said, "The *way* they *make* these poor children *study* nowadays! The *books* they have them *read!* Their *English* teacher *assigned* them *Tropic of Cancer*! I picked it *up* and read *one page*, and Trudy reassured me, 'It's all *right*, Mother, the teacher says he's a transcen*dent*alist!' "

It felt to Richard less likely that he would seduce her. His sense of reality was expanding in the nest of warmth these people provided. He offered to buy them all Popsicles. His consciousness ventured outward and tasted the joy of so many Negro presences, the luxury of immersion in the polished shadows of their skins. He drifted happily through the crosshatch of their oblique, sardonic hooting and blurred voices, searching for the Popsicle vendor. The girls and Trudy's mother had said they would take one; the psychiatrist and Joan had refused. The crowd was formed of jiggling fragments. Richard waved at the rector of a church whose nursery school his children had attended; winked at a folk singer he had seen on television and who looked lost and wan in three dimensions; assumed a stony face in passing a long-haired youth guarded by police and draped in a signboard proclaiming MARTIN LUTHER KING A

TOOL OF THE COMMUNISTS; and tapped a tall bald man on the shoulder. "Remember me? Dick Maple, Plato to Dante, B-plus."

The section man turned, bespectacled and pale. It was shocking; he had aged.

The march was slow to start. Trucks and police cars appeared and disappeared at the playground gate. Officious young seminarians tried to organize the crowd into lines. Unintelligible announcements crackled within the loudspeakers. Martin Luther King was a dim religious rumor on the playground plain—now here, now there, now absent, now present. The sun showed as a kind of sore spot burning through the clouds. Carol nibbled her Popsicle and shivered. Richard and Joan argued whether to march under the Danvers banner with the psychiatrist or with the Unitarians. In the end it did not matter; King invisibly established himself at their head, a distant truck loaded with singing women lurched forward, a far corner of the crowd began to croon, "Which side are you on, boy?," and the marching began.

On Columbus Avenue they were shuffled into lines ten abreast. The Maples were separated. Joan turned up between her psychiatrist and a massive, doleful African wearing tribal scars, sneakers, and a Harvard Athletic Association sweatshirt. Richard found himself in the line ahead, with Carol beside him. Someone behind him, a forward-looking liberal, stepped on his heel, giving the knit of his loafer such a wrench that he had to walk the three miles through Boston with a floppy shoe and a slight limp. He had been born in West Virginia and did not understand Boston. In ten years he had grown familiar with some of its districts, but was still surprised by the quick curving manner in which these districts interlocked. For a few blocks they marched between cheering tenements from whose topmost windows hung banners that proclaimed END DE FACTO SEGREGATION and RETIRE MRS. HICKS. Then the march turned left, and Richard was passing Symphony Hall, within whose rectangular vault he had often dreamed his way along the deep-grassed meadows of Brahms and up the agate cliffs of Strauss. At this corner, from the Stygian subway kiosk, he had emerged with Joan—Orpheus and Eurydice—when both were students; in this restaurant, a decade later, he and she, on three drinks apiece, had decided not to get a divorce that week. The new Prudential Tower, taller and somehow fainter than any other building, haunted each twist of their march, before their faces like a mirage, at their backs like a memory. A leggy nervous colored girl wearing the orange fireman's jacket of the Security Unit shepherded their section of the line, clapping her hands, shouting freedom-song lyrics for a few bars. These songs struggled through the miles of the march, overlapping and eclipsing one another. "Which side are you on, boy, which side are you on . . . like a tree-ee planted by the wah-ha-ter, we shall not be moved . . . this little light of mine, gonna shine on Boston, Mass., this little light of mine . . ." The day continued cool and without shadows. Newspapers that he had folded inside his coat for warmth slipped and slid. Carol beside him plucked at her little sweater, gathering it at her bosom but unable, as if under a spell, to button it. In the line behind him, Joan, secure between her id and superego, stepped along, swinging her arms, throwing her ballet slippers alternately outward in a confident splaying stride. ". . . let 'er shine, let 'er shine . . ."

Incredibly, they were traversing a cloverleaf, an elevated concrete arabesque devoid of cars. Their massed footsteps whispered; the city yawned beneath them. The march had no beginning and no end that Richard could see. Within him, the fever had become a small glassy scratching on the walls of the pit hollowed by the detonating pills. A piece of newspaper spilled down his legs and blew into the air. Impalpably medicated, ideally motivated, he felt, strolling along the curve of the cloverleaf, gathered within an irresistible ascent. He asked Carol, "Where are we going?"

"The newspapers said the Common."

"Do you feel faint?"

Her gray braces shyly modified her smile. "Hungry."

"Have a peanut." A few still remained in his pocket.

"Thank you." She took one. "You don't have to be paternal."

"I want to be." He felt strangely exalted and excited, as if destined to give birth. He wanted to share this sensation with Carol, but instead he asked her, "In your study of the labor movement, have you learned much about the Molly Maguires?"

"No. Were they goons or finks?"

"I think they were either coal miners or gangsters."

"Oh. I haven't studied about anything earlier than Gompers."

"Sounds good." Suppressing the urge to tell Carol he loved her, he turned to look at Joan. She was beautiful, like a poster, with far-seeing blue eyes and red lips parted in song.

Now they walked beneath office buildings where like mounted butterflies secretaries and dental technicians were pressed against the glass. In Copley Square, stony shoppers waited forever to cross the street. Along

Boylston, there was Irish muttering; he shielded Carol with his body. The desultory singing grew defiant. The Public Garden was beginning to bloom. Statues of worthies—Channing, Kosciuszko, Cass, Phillips— were trundled by beneath the blurring trees; Richard's dry heart cracked like a book being opened. The march turned left down Charles and began to press against itself, to link arms, to fumble for love. He lost sight of Joan in the crush. Then they were treading on grass, on the Common, and the first drops of rain, sharp as needles, pricked their faces and hands.

"Did we have to stay to hear every damn speech?" Richard asked. They were at last heading home; he felt too sick to drive and huddled, in his soaked, slippery suit, toward the heater. The windshield wiper seemed to be squeaking *free-dom, free-dom.*

"I wanted to hear King."

"You heard him in Alabama."

"I was too tired to listen then."

"Did you listen this time? Didn't it seem corny and forced?"

"Somewhat. But does it matter?" Her white profile was serene; she passed a trailer truck on the right, and her window was spattered as if with applause.

"And that Abernathy. God, if he's John the Baptist, I'm Herod the Great. 'Onteel de Frenchman go back t'France, onteel de Ahrishman go back t'Ahrland, onteel de Mexican, he go back tuh—' "

"Stop it."

"Don't get me wrong. I didn't mind them sounding like demagogues; what I minded was that god-awful boring phony imitation of a revival meeting. 'Thass right, yossuh. Yos-*suh!*' "

"Your throat sounds sore. Shouldn't you stop using it?"

"*How* could you crucify me that way? *How* could you make this misera- ble sick husband stand in the icy rain for hours listening to boring stupid speeches that you'd heard before anyway?"

"I didn't think the speeches were that great. But I think it was impor- tant that they were given and that people listened. You were there as a witness, Richard."

"Ah witnessed. Ah believes. Yos-suh."

"You're a very sick man."

"I know, I *know* I am. That's why I wanted to leave. Even your pasty psychiatrist left. He looked like a dunked doughnut."

"He left because of the girls."

"I loved Carol. She respected me, despite the color of my skin."

"You didn't have to go."

"Yes I did. You somehow turned it into a point of honor. It was a sexual vindication."

"How you go on."

" 'Onteel de East German goes on back t'East Germany, onteel de Luxembourgian hies hisself back to Luxembourg—' "

"Please stop it."

But he found he could not stop, and even after they reached home and she put him to bed, the children watching in alarm, his voice continued its slurred plaint. "Ah'ze all raht, missy, jes' a tetch o' double pneu*mon*ia, don't you fret none, we'll get the cotton in."

"You're embarrassing the children."

"Shecks, doan min' me, chilluns. Ef Ah could jes' res' hyah foh a spell in de shade o' de watuhmelon patch, res' dese ol' bones . . . Lawzy, dat do feel good!"

"Daddy has a tiny cold," Joan explained.

"Will he die?" Bean asked, and burst into tears.

"Now, effen," he said, "bah some un*foh*-choonut chayunce, mah spirrut should pass owen, bureh me bah de levee, so mebbe Ah kin heeah de singin' an' de banjos an' de cotton bolls a-bustin' . . . an' mebbe even de whaat folks up in de Big House kin shed a homely tear er two. . . ." He was almost crying; a weird tenderness had crept over him in bed, as if he had indeed given birth, birth to this voice, a voice crying for attention from the depths of oppression. High in the window, the late-afternoon sky blanched as the storm lifted. In the warmth of the bed, Richard crooned to himself, and once cried out, "Missy! Missy! Doan you worreh none, ol' Tom'll see anotheh sun-up!"

But Joan was downstairs, talking firmly on the telephone.

Nakedness

"Oh, look," Joan Maple said, in her voice of delight. "We're being invaded!"

Richard Maple lifted his head from the sand.

Another couple, younger, was walking down the beach like a pair of creatures, tawny, maned, their movements made stately by their invisible effort to control self-consciousness. One had to look hard to see that they were naked. A summer's frequentation of the nudist section up the beach, around the point from the bourgeois, bathing-suited section where the Maples lay with their children and their books and their towels and tubes of lotion, had bestowed upon the bodies of this other couple the smooth pelt of an even tan. The sexual signs so large in our interior mythology, the breasts and pubic patches, melted to almost nothing in the middle distance, in the sun. Even the young man's penis seemed incidental. And the young woman appeared a lesser version of the male—the same taut, magnetic stride, the same disturbingly generic arrangement of limbs, abdomen, torso, and skull.

Richard suppressed a grunt. Silence attended the two nudes, pushing out from their advance like wavelets up the packed sand into the costumed people, away from the unnoticing commotion and self-absorbed sparkle of the sea.

"*Well!*": a woman's exclamation, from underneath an umbrella, blew down the beach like a sandwich wrapper. One old man, his dwindled legs linked to a barrel chest by boyish trunks of plaid nylon, stood up militantly, helplessly, drowning in this assault, making an uplifted gesture between that of hailing a taxi and shaking a fist. Richard's own feelings, he noticed, were hysterically turbulent: a certain political admiration grappled with an immediate sense of social threat; pleasure in the sight of the female was swept under by hatred for the male, whose ally she was publicly declaring herself to be; pleasure in the sight of the male fought specific focus on that superadded, boneless bit of him, that monkeyish footnote to the godlike thorax; and envy of their youth and boldness and beauty lost itself in an awareness of his own body that washed over him so vividly he involuntarily glanced about for concealment.

His wife, buxom and pleased and liberal, said, "They must be stoned."

Abruptly, having paraded several hundred yards, the naked couple turned and ran. The girl, especially, became ridiculous, her buttocks out-thrust in the ungainly effort of retreat, her flesh jouncing heavily as she raced to keep up with her mate. He was putting space between them; his hair lifted in a slow spume against the sea's electric blue.

Heads turned as at a tennis match; the spectators saw what had made them run—a policeman walking crabwise off the end of the boardwalk. His uniform made him, too, representative of a species. But as he passed, his black shoes treading the sand in measured pursuit, he was seen as also young, his mustache golden beneath the sad-shaped mirrors of his sunglasses, his arms swinging athletic and brown from his short blue sleeves. Beneath his uniform, for all they knew, his skin wore another uninterrupted tan.

"My God," Richard said softly. "He's one of *them*."

"He is a pretty young pig," Joan stated with complacent quickness.

Her finding a phrase she so much liked irritated Richard, who had been groping for some paradox, some wordless sadness. The Maples found themselves much together this vacation. One daughter was living with a man, one son had a job, the other son was at a tennis camp, and their baby, Bean, hated her nickname and, at thirteen, was made so uncomfortable by her parents she contrived daily excuses to avoid being with them. In their reduced family they were too exposed to one another; the child saw them, Richard feared, more clearly than he and Joan saw themselves. Now, using their freedom from parenting, he suggested, as in college when they were courting he might have suggested that they leave the library and go to a movie, "Let's follow him."

The policeman was a receding blue dot. "Let's," Joan agreed, standing promptly, sand raining from her, the gay alacrity of her acceptance perhaps forced but the lustrous volume of her body, and her gait beside his, which he unthinkingly matched, and the weight of warm sun on his shoulders as they walked, real enough—real enough, Richard thought, for now.

The bathing-suited section thinned behind them. As they turned the point, they saw naked bodies: freckled redheads with slack and milky bellies; swart brunettes standing upright as if to hold their nut-hard faces closer to the sun; sleeping men, their testicles like dropped fruit slowly rotting; a row of buttocks like the scallop on a doily; a bearded man doing yoga on his head, the fork of his legs appearing to implore the sky. Among these Boschian apparitions the policeman moved gently, cumbersome in his belt and gun, whispering, nearly touching the naked listeners, who nodded and began, singly and in groups, to put on their clothes. The couple who had trespassed, inviting this counter-invasion, could not be distinguished from the numerous naked others; all were being punished.

Joan went up to a trio, two boys and a girl, as they struggled into their worn jeans, their widths of leather and sleeveless vests, their sandals and strange soft hats. She asked them, "Are you being kicked off?"

The boys straightened and gazed at her—her conservative bikini, her pleasant plumpness, her sympathetic smile—and said nothing. The penis of one boy, Richard noticed, hung heavy a few inches from her hand. Joan turned and returned to her husband's side.

"What did they tell you?" he asked.

"Nothing. They just stared at me. Like I was a nincompoop."

"There have been two revolutions in the last ten years," he told her. "One, women learned to say 'fuck.' Two, the oppressed learned to despise their sympathizers."

He added, "Or maybe they just resented being approached when they were putting on their pants. It's a touchy moment, for males."

The nudists, paradoxically, brought more clothing to the beach than the bourgeoisie; they distinguished themselves, walking up the beach to the point, by being dressed head to toe, in denim and felt, as if they had strolled straight from the urban core of the counterculture. Now, as the young cop moved among them like a sorrowing angel, they bent and huddled in the obsequious poses of redressing.

"My God," Joan said, "it's Masaccio's *Expulsion from Paradise*." And Richard felt her heart in the fatty casing of her body plump up, pleased with this link, satisfied to have demonstrated once again to herself the relevance of a humanistic education to modern experience.

All that afternoon, as, returned from the beach, he pushed a balky lawn mower through the wiry grass around their rented house, Richard thought about nakedness. He thought of Adam and Eve ("Who told thee that thou wast naked?") and of Noah beheld naked by Ham, and of Susanna and the elders. He thought of himself as a child, having a sun-bath on the second-story porch with his mother, who had been, in her provincial way, an avant-gardist, a health faddist. Yellow jackets would come visit, the porch was so warm. An hour seemed forever; his embarrassment penetrated and stretched every minute. His mother's skin was a pale landscape on the rim of his vision; he didn't look at it, any more than he bothered to look at the hills enclosing their little West Virginia town, which he assumed he would never leave.

He recalled a remark of Rodin's, that a woman undressing was like the sun piercing through clouds. The afternoon's gathering cloudiness slid shadows across the lawn, burnishing the wiry grass. He had once loved a woman who had slept beside a mirror. In her bed the first time, he glanced to his right and was startled to see them both, reflected naked. His legs and hers looked prodigiously long, parallel. She must have felt his attention leave her, for she turned her head; duplicated in the mirror, her face appeared beneath the duplicate of his. The mirror was an arm's length from the bed. What fascinated him in it was not her body but his own—its length, its glow, its hair, its parallel toes so marvellously removed from his small, startled, sheepish head.

There had been, he remembered, a noise downstairs. Their eyes had widened into one another's, the mirror forgotten. He whispered, "What is it?" Milkmen, mailmen, the dog, the furnace.

She offered, "The wind?"

"It sounded like a door opening."

As they listened again, her breath fanned his mouth. A footstep distinctly betrayed itself beneath them. At the same moment as he tugged to pull the sheets over their heads, she sharply flung them aside. She disengaged herself from him, lifting her leg like the near figure in Renoir's *Bathers*. He was alone in the mirror; the mirror had become a screaming witness to the fact that he was where he should not be ("Dirt is matter in the wrong place," his mother used to say) and that he was in no condition for fight or flight. He was jutting out, "sticking up at you like a hatrack," as the phrase went through Molly Bloom's mind. He had hidden on the sunporch with his bunched clothes clutched to his aching front.

He squatted now to cut the stubborn tufts by the boat shed with the hand clippers, and imperfectly remembered a quotation from one of the Japanese masters of *shungā*, to the effect that the phallus in these pictures was exaggerated because if it were drawn in its natural size it would be negligible.

She had returned, his lover, still naked, saying, "Nothing." She had walked naked through her own downstairs, a trespasser from Eden, past chairs and prints and lamps, eclipsing them, unafraid to encounter a burglar, a milkman, a husband; and her nakedness, returning, had been as calm and broad as that of Titian's Venus, flooding him from within like a swallowed sun.

He thought of Titian's Venus, wringing her hair with two firm hands. He thought of Manet's Olympia, of Goya's Maja. Of shamelessness. He thought of Edna Pontellier, Kate Chopin's heroine, walking in the last year of that most buttoned-up of centuries down to the Gulf and, before swimming to her death, casting off all her clothes. *How strange and awful it seemed to stand naked under the sky! How delicious!*

He remembered himself a month ago, coming alone to this same house, this house into whose lightless, damp cellar he was easing, step by step, the balky mower, its duty done. He had volunteered to come alone and open up the house, to test it; it was a new rental for them. Joan had assented easily; there was something in her, these days, that also wanted to be alone. Half the stores on the island were not yet open for the summer. He had bought some days' worth of meals, and lived in rooms of a profound chastity and silence. One morning he had walked through a mile of huckleberry and wild grape to a pond. Its rim of beach was scarcely a stride wide; only the turds and shed feathers of wild swans testified to other presences. The swans, suspended in the sun-irradiated mist upon the pond's surface, seemed gods to him, perfect and infinitely removed. Not a house, not a car looked down from the hills of sand and scrub that enclosed the pond. Such pure emptiness under the sky seemed an opportunity it would be sacrilegious to waste. Richard took off his clothes, all; he sat on a rough warm rock, in the pose of Rodin's *Thinker*. He stood and at the water's edge became a prophet, a baptist. Ripples of light reflected from the water onto his legs. He yearned to do something transcendent, something obscene; he stretched his arms and could not touch the sky. The sun intensified. As mist burned from the surface of the pond, the swans stirred, flapping their wings in aloof, Olympian tumult. For a second, sex dropped from him and he seemed indeed the divinely shaped center of a concentric Creation; his very skin felt beautiful—no, he felt beauty rippling upon it, as if the Creation were loving him, licking him. Then, the next second, glancing down, he saw himself to be less than sublimely alone, for dozens of busy coppery bodies, ticks, were crawling up through the hair of his legs, as happy in his giant warmth as he was in the warmth of the sun.

The sky was an even gray now, weathered silver like the shingles on this island. As he went into the house to reward himself with a drink, he remembered, from an old sociology text, a nineteenth-century American farmer's boasting that though he had sired eleven children he had never seen his wife's body naked. And from another book, perhaps by John Gunther, the assertion, of some port in West Africa, that this was the last city on the coast where a young woman could walk naked down the main street without attracting attention. And from an old *Time* review, years ago, revolutions ago, of the Brigitte Bardot picture that for a few frames displayed her, from behind, bare from head to toe: *Time* had quipped that, though the movie had a naked woman in it, so did most American homes around eleven o'clock at night.

Eleven o'clock. The Maples have been out to dinner; Bean is spending the night with a friend. Their bedroom within this house is white and breezy, white even to the bureaus and chairs, and the ceiling so low their shadows seem to rest upon their heads.

Joan stands at the foot of the bed and kicks off her shoes. Her face, foreshortened in the act of looking down, appears to pout as she undoes the snaps on her skirt and lets the zipper fling into view a white *V* of slip. She lets her skirt drop, retrieves it with a foot, places it in a drawer. Then the jersey lifts, decapitating her and gathering her hair into a cloud, a fist, that collapses when her face is again revealed, preoccupied. A head-toss, profiled. Auto lights from the road caress the house and then forget. An unexpected sequence: Joan pulls down her underpants in a quick shimmy before—with two hands, arms crossed—pulling up her slip. Above her waist, the bunched nylon snags; she halts in the pose of Michelangelo's slave, of Munch's madonna, of Ingres's urn-bearer, seen from the front, unbarbered. The slip unsnags, the snakeskin slides, the process continues. With a squint of effort she uncouples the snaps at her back and flips the bra toward the hamper in the hall. Her half-brown breasts bounce. Toward the bed she says, in her voice of displeasure, "Don't you have something better to do? Than watch me?"

Richard has been lying on the bed half dressed, a strip-show audience of one, holding his applause. He answers truthfully, "No."

He jumps up and finishes undressing, his shadow whirling about his head. The two of them stand close, as close as at the beach when she had returned from being rejected by the young persons, a girl and two boys, one boy's heavy penis hanging inches from her hand. *Like I was a nincompoop.* Her husband had not been sympathetic. They are back on the beach; she is remembering. Again he feels her heart in the fatty casing of her body plump up. She looks at him, her eyes blue as a morning sea, and smiles. *"No,"* Joan says, in complacent firm denial. Richard feels thrilled, invaded. This nakedness is new to them.

FAMILY LIFE

The Family Meadow

THE FAMILY always reconvenes in the meadow. For generations it has been traditional, this particular New Jersey meadow, with its great walnut tree making shade for the tables and its slow little creek where the children can push themselves about in a rowboat and nibble watercress and pretend to fish. Early this morning, Uncle Jesse came down from the stone house that his father's father's brother had built and drove the stakes, with their carefully tied rag flags, that would tell the cars where to park. The air was still, inert with the post-dawn laziness that foretells the effort of a hot day, and between blows of his hammer Jesse heard the breakfast dishes clinking beneath the kitchen window and the younger collie barking behind the house. A mild man, Jesse moved scrupulously, mildly through the wet grass that he had scythed yesterday. The legs of his gray workman's pants slowly grew soaked with dew and milkweed spittle. When the stakes were planted, he walked out the lane with the REUNION signs, past the houses. He avoided looking at the houses, as if glancing into their wide dead windows would wake them.

By nine o'clock Henry has come up from Camden with a carful—Eva, Mary, Fritz, Fred, the twins, and, incredibly, Aunt Eula. It is incredible she is still alive, after seven strokes. Her shrivelled head munches irritably and her arms twitch, trying to shake off assistance, as if she intends to dance. They settle her in an aluminum chair beneath the walnut tree. She faces the creek, and the helpless waggle of her old skull seems to establish itself in sympathy with the oscillating shimmer of the sunlight on the slow water. The men, working in silent pairs whose unison is as profound as blood, carry down the tables from the barn, where they are stacked from one year to the next. In truth, it has been three summers since the last reunion, and it was feared that there might never be another. Aunt Jocelyn, her gray hair done up in braids, comes out of her kitchen to say hello on the dirt drive. Behind her lingers her granddaughter, Karen, in white Levi's and bare feet, with something shadowy and doubtful about her dark eyes, as if she had been intensely watching television. The girl's father—not here; he is working in Philadelphia—is Italian, and as she matures an alien beauty estranges her, so that during her annual visits to her grandparents' place, which when she was a child had seemed to her a green island, it is now she herself, at thirteen, who seems the island. She feels surrounded by the past, cut off from the places—a luncheonette, a civic swimming pool, an auditorium festooned with crepe paper—that represent life to her, the present, her youth. The air around her feels brown, as in old photographs. These men greeting her seem to have stepped from an album. The men, remembering their original prejudice against her mother's marrying a Catholic, are especially cordial to her, so jovially attentive that Jocelyn suddenly puts her arm around the girl, expressing a strange multitude of things—that she loves her, that she is one of them, that she needs to be shielded, suddenly, from the pronged kidding of men.

By ten-thirty Horace's crowd has come down from Trenton, and the Oranges clan is arriving, in several cars. The first car says it dropped Cousin Claude in downtown Burlington because he was sure that the second car, which had faded out of sight behind them, needed to be told the way. The second car, with a whoop of hilarity, says it took the bypass and never saw him. He arrives in a third car, driven by Jimmy and Ethel Thompson from Morristown, who say they saw this forlorn figure standing along Route 130 trying to thumb a ride and as they were passing him Ethel cried, "Why, I think that's Claude!" Zealous and reckless, a true believer in good deeds, Claude is always getting into scrapes like this, and enjoying it. He stands surrounded by laughing women, a typical man of this family, tall, with a tribal boyishness—a stubborn refusal to look his age, to lose his hair. Though his face is pitted and gouged by melancholy, Claude looks closer to forty than the sixty he is, and, though he works in Newark, he still speaks with the rural softness and slide of middle New Jersey. He has the gift—the privilege—of making these women laugh; the women uniformly run to fat and their laughter has a sameness, a quality both naïve and merciless, as if laughter means too much to them. Jimmy and Ethel Thompson, whose name is not the family name, stand off to one side, in the unscythed grass, a fragile elderly couple whose links to the family have all died away but who have come because they received a mimeographed postcard inviting them. They are like those isolated corners of interjections and foreign syllables in a poorly planned cross-word puzzle.

The twins bring down from the barn the horseshoes and the quoits. Uncle Jesse drives the stakes and pegs in the places that, after three summers, still show as spots of depressed sparseness in the grass. The sun, reaching toward noon, domineers over the meadow; the shade of the walnut tree grows smaller and more noticeably cool. By noon, all have arrived, including the Dodge station wagon from central Pennsylvania, the young pregnant Wilmington cousin who married an airline pilot, and the White Plains people, who climb from their car looking like clowns, wearing red-striped shorts and rhinestone-studded sunglasses. Handshakes are exchanged that feel to one man like a knobbed wood carving and to the other like a cow's slippery, unresisting teat. Women kiss, kiss stickily, with little overlapping patches of adhesive cheek and clicking conflicts of spectacle rims, under the white unslanting sun. The very insects shrink toward the shade.

The eating begins. Clams steam, corn steams, salad wilts, butter runs, hot dogs turn, torn chicken shines in the savage light. Iced tea, brewed in forty-quart milk cans, chuckles when sloshed. Paper plates buckle on broad laps. Plastic butter knives, asked to cut cold ham, refuse. Children underfoot in the pleased frenzy eat only potato chips. Somehow, as the first wave of appetite subsides, the long tables turn musical, and a murmur rises to the blank sky, a cackle rendered harmonious by a remote singleness of ancestor; a kind of fabric is woven and hung, a tapestry of the family fortunes, the threads of which include milkmen, ministers, mailmen, bankruptcy, death by war, death by automobile, insanity—a strangely prevalent thread, the thread of insanity. Never far from a farm or the memory of a farm, the family has hovered in honorable obscurity, between poverty and wealth, between jail and high office. Real-estate dealers, schoolteachers, veterinarians are its noblemen; butchers, electricians, door-to-door salesmen its yeomen. Protestant and teetotalling, ironically virtuous and mildly proud, it has added to America's statistics without altering their meaning. Whence, then, this strange joy?

Watermelons smelling of childhood cellars are produced and massively sliced. The sun passes noon and the shadows relax in the intimate grass of this antique meadow. To the music of reminiscence is added the rhythmic chunking of thrown quoits. They are held curiously, between a straight thumb and four fingers curled as a unit, close to the chest, and thrown with a soft constrained motion that implies realms of unused strength. The twins and the children, as if superstitiously, have yielded the game to the older men, Fritz and Claude, Fred and Jesse, who, in pairs, after due estimation and measurement of the fall, pick up their four quoits, clink them together to clean them, and alternately send them back through the air on a high arc, floating with a spin-held slant like that of gyroscopes. The other pair measures, decides, and stoops. When they tap their quoits together, decades fall away. Even their competitive crowing has something measured about it, something patient, like the studied way their shirtsleeves are rolled up above their elbows. The backs of their shirts are ageless. Generations have sweated in just this style, under the arms, across the shoulder blades, and wherever the suspenders rub. The younger men and the teen-age girls play a softball game along the base paths that Jesse has scythed. The children discover the rowboat and, using the oars as poles, bump from bank to bank. When they dip their hands into the calm brown water, where no fish lives, a mother watching from beneath the walnut tree shrieks, "Keep your hands inside the boat! Uncle Jesse says the creek's polluted!"

And there is a stagnant fragrance the lengthening afternoon strains from the happy meadow. Aunt Eula nods herself asleep, and her false teeth slip down, so her face seems mummified and the children giggle in terror. Flies, an exploding population, discover the remains of the picnic and skate giddily on its odors. The softball game grows boring, except to the airline pilot, a rather fancy gloveman excited by the admiration of Cousin Karen in her tight white Levi's. The Pennsylvania and New York people begin to pack their cars. The time has come for the photograph. Their history is kept by these photographs of timeless people in changing costumes standing linked and flushed in a moment of midsummer heat. All line up, from resurrected Aunt Eula, twitching and snapping like a mud turtle, to the unborn baby in the belly of the Delaware cousin. To get them all in, Jesse has to squat, but in doing so he brings the houses into his viewfinder. He does not want them in the picture, he does not want them there at all. They surround his meadow on three sides, raw ranch shacks built from one bastard design but painted in a patchwork of pastel shades. Their back yards, each holding an aluminum clothes tree, come right to the far bank of the creek, polluting it, and though a tall link fence holds back the children who have gathered in these yards to watch the picnic as if it were a circus or a zoo, the stare of the houses— mismatched kitchen windows squinting above the gaping mouth of a two-door garage—cannot be held back. Not only do they stare, they speak, so that Jesse can hear them even at night. *Sell*, they say. *Sell*.

The Day of the Dying Rabbit

THE SHUTTER CLICKS, and what is captured is mostly accident—that happy foreground diagonal, that telling expression forever pinned in mid-flight. Margaret and I didn't exactly intend to have six children. At first, we were trying until we got a boy. Then, after Jimmy arrived, it was half our trying to give him a brother so he wouldn't turn queer under all those sisters, and half our missing, the both of us, the way new babies are. You know how they are—delicate as film, wrapped in bunting instead of lead foil, but coiled with that same miraculous brimming whatever-it-is: *susceptibility*, let's say. That wobbly hot head. Those navy-blue eyes with the pupils set at f/2. The wrists hinged on silk and the soles of the feet as tender as the eyelids: film that fine-grained would show a doghouse roof from five miles up.

Also, I'm a photographer by trade, and one trick of the trade is a lot of takes. In fact, all six kids have turned out pretty well, now that we've got the baby's feet to stop looking at each other and Deirdre fitted out with glasses. Having so many works smoothly enough in the city, where I go off to the studio and they go off to school, but on vacations things tend to jam. We rent the same five-room shack every August. When the cat dragged in as a love-present this mauled rabbit it had caught, it was minutes before I could get close enough even to *see*.

Henrietta—she's the second youngest, the last girl—screamed. There are screams like flashbulbs—just that cold. This one brought Linda out from her murder mystery and Cora up from her Beatles magazine, and they crowded into the corridor that goes with the bedrooms the landlord added to the shack to make it more rentable and that isn't wide enough for two pairs of shoulders. Off this corridor into the outdoors is a salt-pimpled aluminum screen door with a misadjusted pneumatic attachment that snaps like lightning the first two-thirds of its arc and then closes the last third slow as a clock, ticking. That's how the cat got in. It wasn't our cat exactly, just a tattered calico stray the children had been feeding salami scraps to out in the field between our yard and the freshwater pond. Deirdre had been helping Margaret with the dishes, and they piled into the corridor just ahead of me, in time to hear Linda let crash with a collection of those four-letter words that come out of her face more and more. The more pop out, the more angelic her face grows. She is thirteen, and in a few years I suppose it will be liquor and drugs, going in. I don't know where she gets the words, or how to stop them coming. Her cheeks are trimming down, her nose bones edging up, her mouth getting witty in the corners, and her eyes gathering depth; and I don't know how to stop that coming, either. Faces, when you look at them through a lens, are passageways for angels, sometimes whole clouds of them. Jimmy told me the other day—he's been reading books of records, mostly sports—about a man so fat he had been buried in a piano case for a casket, and he asked me what a casket was, and I told him, and a dozen angels overlapped in his face as he mentally matched up casket with fatness, and piano, and earth; and got the picture. Click.

After Linda's swearing, there was the sound of a slap and a second's silence while it developed who had been hit: Henrietta. Her crying clawed the corridor walls, and down among our legs the cat reconsidered its offer to negotiate and streaked back out the screen door, those last ticking inches, leaving the rabbit with us. Now I could see it: a half-grown rabbit huddled like a fur doorstop in the doorway to the bigger girls' room. No one dared touch it. We froze around it in a circle. Henrietta was still sobbing, and Cora's transistor was keeping the beat with static, like a heart stuffed with steel wool. Then God came down the hall from the smaller children's room.

Godfrey is the baby, the second boy. We were getting harder up for names, which was one reason we decided to call it quits vis-à-vis procreation. Another was, the club feet seemed a warning. He was slow to walk after they took the casts off, and at age four he marches along with an unstoppable sort of deliberate dignity, on these undeformed but somehow distinctly rectangular big feet. He pushed his way through our legs and without hesitation squatted and picked up the rabbit. Cora, the most squeamish of the children—the others are always putting worms down her back—squealed, and God twitched and flipped the bunny back to the floor; it hit neck first, and lay there looking bent. Linda punched Cora, and Henrietta jabbed God, but still none of the rest of us was willing to touch the rabbit, which might be dead this time, so we let God try again. We needed Jimmy. He and Deirdre have the natural touch—middle children tend to. But all month he's been out of the shack, out of our way, playing catch with himself, rowing in the pond, brooding on what it means to be a boy. He's ten. I've missed him. A father is like a dog—he needs a boy for a friend.

This time in God's arms, the rabbit made a sudden motion that felt ticklish, and got dropped again, but the sign of life was reassuring, and Deirdre pushed through at last, and all evening there we were, paying sick calls on this shoebox, whispering, while Deirdre and Henrietta alternately dribbled milk in a dropper, and God kept trying to turn it into a Steiff stuffed animal, and Cora kept screwing up her nerve to look the bunny in its left eye, which had been a little chewed, so it looked like isinglass. Jimmy came in from the pond after dark and stood at the foot of Deirdre's bed, watching her try to nurse the rabbit back to health with a dropper of stale milk. She was crooning and crying. No fuss; just the tears. The rabbit was lying panting on its right side, the bad eye up. Linda was on the next bed, reading her mystery, above it all. God was asleep. Jimmy's nostrils pinched in, and he turned his back on the whole business. He had got the picture. The rabbit was going to die. At the back of my brain I felt tired, damp, and cold.

What was it in the next twenty-four hours that slowly flooded me, that makes me want to get the day on some kind of film? I don't know exactly, so I must put everything in, however underexposed.

Linda and Cora were still awake when headlights boomed in the driveway—we're a city block from the nearest house, and a half-mile from the road—and the Pingrees came by. Ian works for an ad agency I've photographed some nudes shampooing in the shower for, and on vacation he lives in boatneck shirts and cherry-red Bermudas and blue sunglasses, and grows a salt-and-pepper beard—a Verichrome fathead, and nearsighted at that. But his wife, Jenny, is nifty. Low forehead, like a fox. Freckles. Thick red sun-dulled hair ironed flat down her back. Hips. And an angle about her legs, the way they're put together, slightly bowed but with the something big and bland and smooth and unimpeachable about the thighs that you usually find only in the fenders of new cars. Though she's very serious and liberal and agitated these days, I could look at her forever, she's such fun for the eyes. Which isn't the same as being photogenic. The few shots I've taken of her show a staring woman with baby fat, whereas some skinny snit who isn't even a name to me comes over in the magazines as my personal version of Eros. The camera does lie, all the time. It has to.

Margaret doesn't mind the Pingrees, which isn't the same as liking them, but in recent years she doesn't much admit to liking anybody; so it was midnight when they left, all of us giddy with drink and talk under the stars, which seem so presiding and reproachful when you're drunk, shouting goodbye in the driveway, and agreeing on tennis tomorrow. I remembered the rabbit. Deirdre, Linda, and Cora were asleep, Linda with the light still on and the mystery rising and falling on her chest, Cora floating above her, in the upper bunk bed. The rabbit was in the shoebox under a protective lean-to of cookout grills, in case the cat came back. We moved a grill aside and lit a match, expecting the rabbit to be dead. Photograph by sulphur-glow: undertakers at work. But though the rabbit wasn't hopping, the whiskers were moving, back and forth no more than a millimeter or two at the tips, but enough to signify breathing—life, hope, what else? Eternal solicitude brooding above us, also holding a match, and burning Its fingers. Our detection of life, magnified by liquor, emboldened us to make love for the first time in, oh, days beyond counting. She's always tired, and says the Pill depresses her, and a kind of arms race of avoidance has grown up around her complaints. Moonlight muted by window screens. Her eyeless eyesockets beneath me, looking up. To the shack smells of mist and cedar and salt we added musk. Margaret slipped into sleep quick as a fish afterward, but for an uncertain length of time—the hours after midnight lose their numbers, if you don't remind them with a luminous dial—I lay there, the thought of the rabbit swollen huge and oppressive, blanketing all of us, a clenching of the nerves snatching me back from sleep by a whisker, the breathing and rustling all around me precarious, the rumbling and swaying of a ship that at any moment, the next or then the next, might hit an iceberg.

Morning. The rabbit took some milk, and his isinglass eye slightly widened. The children triumphantly crowed. Jubilant sun-sparkle on the sea beyond the sand beyond the pond. We rowed across, six in the rowboat and two in the kayak. The tides had been high in the night, delivering debris dropped between here and Portugal. Jimmy walked far down the beach, collecting lightbulbs jettisoned from ships—they are sealed vacuums and will float forever, if you let them. I had put the 135mm telephoto on the Nikon and loaded in a roll of Plus-X and took some shots of the children (Cora's face, horrified and ecstatic, caught in the translucent wall of a breaker about to submerge her; Godfrey, his close-cut blond hair shiny as a helmet, a Tritonesque strand of kelp slung across his shoulders) but most of grass and sand and shadows, close-up, using the ultraviolet filter, trying to get, what may be ungettable, the way the shadow edges stagger from grain to grain on the sand, and the way some bent-over grass blades draw circles around themselves.

Jimmy brought the bulbs back and arranged them in order of size, and before I could get to him had methodically smashed two. All I could see was bleeding feet but I didn't mean to grab him so hard. The marks of my hand were still red on his arm a half hour later. Our fight depressed Henrietta; like a seismograph, she feels all violence as hers. God said he was hungry and Deirdre began to worry about the rabbit: there is this puffy look children's faces get that I associate with guilt but that can also signal grief. Deirdre and Jimmy took the kayak, to be there first, and Linda, who maybe thinks the exercise will improve her bosom, rowed the rest of us to our dock. We walked to the house, heads down. Our path is full of poison ivy, our scorched lawn full of flat thistles. In our absence, the rabbit, still lying on its side, had created a tidy little heap of pelletlike feces. The children were ecstatic; they had a dirty joke and a miracle all in one. The rabbit's recovery was assured. But the eye looked cloudier to me, and the arc of the whisker tips even more fractional.

Lunch: soup and sandwiches. In the sky, the clouding over from the west that often arrives around noon. The level of light moved down, and the hands of the year swept forward a month. It was autumn, every blade of grass shining. August has this tinny, shifty quality, the only month without a holiday to pin it down. Our tennis date was at two. You can picture for yourself Jenny Pingree in tennis whites: those rounded guileless thighs, and the bobbing, flying hair tied behind with a kerchief of blue gauze, and that humorless, utterly intent clumsiness—especially when catching the balls tossed to her as server—that we love in children, trained animals, and women who are normally graceful. She and I, thanks to my predatory net play, took Ian and Margaret, 6–3, and the next set was called at 4–4, when our hour on the court ran out. A moral triumph for Margaret, who played like the swinger of fifteen years ago, and passed me in the alley half a dozen times. Dazzling with sweat, she took the car and went shopping with the four children who had come along to the courts; Linda had stayed in the shack with another book, and Jimmy had walked to a neighboring house, where there was a boy his age. The Pingrees dropped me off at our mailbox. Since they were going back to the city Sunday, we had agreed on a beach picnic tonight. The mail consisted of forwarded bills, pencil-printed letters to the children from their friends on other islands or beside lakes, and *Life*. While walking down our dirt road, I flicked through an overgorgeous photographic essay on Afghanistan. Hurrying blurred women in peacock-colored saris, mud palaces, rose dust, silver rivers high in the Hindu Kush. An entire valley— misted, forested earth—filled the center page spread. The *lenses* those people have! Nothing expensive on earth is as selfless as a beautiful lens.

Entering the shack, I shouted out to Linda, "It's just me," thinking she would be afraid of rapists. I went into her room and looked in the shoe-box. The eye was lustreless and the whiskers had stopped moving, even infinitesimally.

"I think the bunny's had it," I said.

"Don't make me look," she said, propped up in the lower bunk, keeping her eyes deep in a paperback titled *A Stitch in Time Kills Nine*. The cover showed a dressmaker's dummy pierced by a stiletto, and bleeding. "I couldn't *stand it*," she said.

"What should I do?" I asked her.

"Bury it." She might have been reading from the book. Her profile, I noticed, was becoming a cameo, with a lovely gentle bulge to the forehead, high like Margaret's. I hoped being intelligent wouldn't cramp her life.

"Deirdre will want to see it," I argued. "It's her baby."

"It will only make her *sad*," Linda said. "And dis*gust* me. Already it must be *full* of *ver*min."

Nothing goads me to courage like some woman's taking a high tone. Afraid to touch the rabbit's body while life was haunting it, I touched it now, and found it tepid, and lifted it from the box. The body, far from stiff, felt unhinged; its back or neck must have been broken since the moment the cat pounced. Blood had dried in the ear—an intricate tunnel leading brainwards, velvety at the tip, oddly muscular at the root. The eye not of isinglass was an opaque black bead. Linda was right: there was no need for Deirdre to see. I took the rabbit out beyond the prickly yard, into the field, and laid it under the least stunted swamp oak, where any child who wanted to be sure that I hadn't buried it alive could come and find it. I put a marsh marigold by its nose, in case it was resurrected and needed to eat, and paused above the composition—fur, flower, the arty shape of fallen oak leaves—with a self-congratulatory sensation that must have carried on my face back to the shack, for Margaret, in the kitchen loading the refrigerator, looked up at me and said, "Say. I don't mind your being partners with Jenny, but you don't have to toss the balls to her in that cute, confiding way."

"The poor bitch can't catch them otherwise. You saw that."

"I saw more than I wanted to. I nearly threw up."

"That second set," I said, "your backhand was terrific. The Maggie-O of old."

Deirdre came down the hall from the bedrooms. Her eyes seemed enormous; I went to her and knelt to hold her around the waist, and began, "Sweetie, I have some sad news."

"Linda told me," she said, and walked by me into the kitchen. "Mommy, can I make the cocoa?"

"You did everything you could," I called after her. "You were a wonderful nurse and made the bunny's last day very happy."

"I know," she called in answer. "Mommy, I *promise* I won't let the milk boil over this time."

Of the children, only Henrietta and Godfrey let me lead them to where the rabbit rested. Henrietta skittishly hung back, and never came closer than ten yards. God marched close, gazed down sternly, and said, "Get up." Nothing happened, except the ordinary motions of the day: the gulls and stately geese beating home above the pond, the traffic roaring invisible along the highway. He squatted down, and I prevented him from picking up the rabbit, before I saw it was the flower he was after.

Jimmy, then, was the only one who cried. He came home a half-hour after we had meant to set out rowing across the pond to the beach picnic, and rushed into the field toward the tree with the tallest silhouette and came back carrying on his cheeks stains he tried to hide by thumping God. "If *you* hadn't dropped him," he said. "You *ba*by."

"It was nobody's fault," Margaret told him, impatiently cradling her basket of hot dogs and raw hamburger.

"I'm going to kill that cat," Jimmy said. He added, cleverly, an old grievance: "Other kids my age have BB guns."

"Oh, our big man," Cora said. He flew at her in a flurry of fists and sobs, and ran away and hid. At the dock I let Linda and Cora take the kayak, and the rest of us waited a good ten minutes with the rowboat before Jimmy ran down the path in the dusk, himself a silhouette, like the stunted trees and the dark bar of dunes between the sunset and its reflection in the pond. Ever notice how sunsets upside down look like stairs?

"Somehow," Margaret said to me, as we waited, "you've deliberately dramatized this." But nothing could fleck the happiness widening within me, to capture the dying light.

The Pingrees had brought swordfish and another, older couple—the man was perhaps an advertising client. Though he was tanned like a tobacco leaf and wore the smartest summer playclothes, a pleading uncertainty in his manner seemed to crave the support of advertisement. His wife had once been beautiful and held herself lightly, lithely at attention—a soldier in the war of self-preservation. With them came two teen-age boys clad in jeans and buttonless vests and hair so long their summer complexions had remained sallow. One was their son, the other his friend. We all collected driftwood—a wandering, lonely, prehistoric task that frightens me. Darkness descended too soon, as it does in the tropics, where the warmth leads us to expect an endless June evening from childhood. We made a game of popping champagne corks, the kids trying to catch them on the fly. Startling, how high they soared, in the open air. The two boys gathered around Linda, and I protectively eavesdropped, and was shamed by the innocence and long childish pauses of what I overheard: "Philadelphia . . . just been in the airport, on our way to my uncle's, he lives in Virginia . . . wonderful horses, super . . . it's not actually blue, just bluey-green, blue only I guess by comparison . . . was in France once, and went to the races . . . never been . . . I want to go." Margaret and Jenny, kneeling in the sand to cook, setting out paper plates on tables that were merely wide pieces of driftwood, seemed sisters. The woman of the strange couple tried to flirt with me, talking of foreign places: "Paris is so dead, suddenly . . . the girls fly over to London to buy their clothes, and then their mothers won't let them wear them . . . Malta . . . Istanbul . . . life . . . sincerity . . . the *people* . . . the poor Greeks . . . a friend absolutely assures me, the CIA engineered . . . apparently used the NATO contingency plan." Another champagne cork sailed in the air, hesitated, and drifted down, Jimmy diving but missing, having misjudged. A remote light, a lightship, or the promontory of an unmapped continent hidden in daylight, materialized on the horizon, beyond the shushing of the surf. Margaret and Jenny served us. Hamburgers and swordfish full of woodsmoke. Celery and sand. God, sticky with things he had spilled upon himself, sucked his thumb and rubbed against Margaret's legs. Jimmy came to me, furious because the big boys wouldn't Indian-wrestle with him, only with Linda and Cora: "Showing off for their boyfriends . . . whacked me for no reason . . . just because I said 'sex bomb.' "

We sat in a ring around the fire, the heart of a collapsing star, fed anew by paper plates. The man of the older couple, in whose breath the champagne had undergone an acrid chemical transformation, told me about his money—how as a youth just out of business school, in the depths of the Depression, he had made a million dollars in some deal involving Stalin and surplus wheat. He had liked Stalin, and Stalin had liked him.

"The thing we must realize about your Communist is that he's just another kind of businessman." Across the fire I watched his wife, spurned by me, ardently gesturing with the teen-age boy who was not her son, and wondered how I would take their picture. Tri-X, wide open, at $\frac{1}{60}$; but the shadows would be lost, the subtle events within them, and the highlights would be vapid blobs. There is no adjustment, no darkroom trickery, equal to the elastic tolerance of our eyes as they scan.

As my new friend murmured on and on about his money, and the champagne warming in my hand released carbon dioxide to the air, exposures flickered in and out around the fire: glances, inklings, angels. Margaret gazing, the nick of a frown erect between her brows. Henrietta's face vertically compressing above an ear of corn she was devouring. The well-preserved woman's face a mask of bronze with cunningly welded seams, but her hand an exclamatory flash as it touched her son's friend's arm in some conversational urgency lost in the crackle of driftwood. The halo of hair around Ian's knees, innocent as babies' pates. Jenny's hair an elongated flurry as she turned to speak to the older couple's son; his bearded face was a blur in the shadows, melancholy, the eyes seeming closed, like the Jesus on a faded, drooping veronica. I heard Jenny say, ". . . *must* destroy the system! We've forgotten how to *love!*" Deirdre's glasses, catching the light, leaped like moth wings toward the fire, escaping perspective. Beside me, the old man's face went silent, and suffered a deflation wherein nothing held firm but the reflected glitter of firelight on a tooth his grimace had absent-mindedly left exposed. Beyond him, on the edge of the light, Cora and Linda were revealed sitting together, their legs stretched out long before them, warming, their faces in darkness, sexless and solemn, as if attentive to the sensations of the revolution of the earth beneath them. Godfrey was asleep, his head pillowed on Margaret's thigh, his body suddenly wrenched by a dream sob, and a heavy succeeding sigh.

It was strange, after these fragmentary illuminations, to stumble through the unseen sand and grass, with our blankets and belongings, to the boats on the shore of the pond. Margaret and five children took the rowboat; I nominated Jimmy to come with me in the kayak. The night was starless. The pond, between the retreating campfire and the slowly nearing lights of our neighbors' houses, was black. I could scarcely see his silhouette as it struggled for the rhythm of the stroke: left, a little turn with the wrists, right, the little turn reversed, left. Our paddles occasionally clashed, or snagged on the weeds that clog this pond. But the kayak sits lightly, and soon we put the confused conversation of the rowers, and their wildly careening flashlight beam, behind. Silence widened around us. Steering the rudder with the foot pedals, I let Jimmy paddle alone, and stared upward until I had produced, in the hazed sky overhead, a single, unsteady star. It winked out. I returned to paddling and received an astonishing impression of phosphorescence: every stroke, right and left, called into visibility a rich arc of sparks, animalcula hailing our passage with bright shouts. The pond was more populous than China. My son and I were afloat on a firmament warmer than the heavens.

"Hey, Dad."

His voice broke the silence carefully; my benevolence engulfed him, my fellow-wanderer, my leader, my gentle, secretive future. "What, Jimmy?"

"I think we're about to hit something."

We stopped paddling, and a mass, gray etched on gray, higher than a man, glided swiftly toward us and struck the prow of the kayak. With this bump, and my awakening laugh, the day of the dying rabbit ended. Exulting in homogenous glory, I had steered us into the bank. We pushed off, and by the lights of our neighbors' houses navigated to the dock, and waited some minutes for the rowboat with its tangle of voices and picnic equipment to arrive. The days since have been merely happy days. This day was singular in its, let's say, *tone*—its silver-bromide clarity. Between the cat's generous intentions and my son's lovingly calm warning, the dying rabbit sank like film in the developing pan, and preserved us all.

How to Love America and
Leave It at the Same Time

ARRIVE IN SOME TOWN around three, having been on the road since seven, and cruise the main street, which is also Route Whatever-It-Is, and vote on the motel you want. The wife favors a discreet back-from-the-highway look, but not bungalows; the kids go for a pool (essential), color TV (optional), and Magic Fingers (fun). Vote with the majority, pull in, and walk to the office. Your legs unbend weirdly, after all that sitting behind the wheel. A sticker on the door says the place is run by "The Plummers," so this is Mrs. Plummer behind the desk. Fifty-fivish, tight silver curls with traces of russet, face motherly but for the brightness of the lipstick and the sharpness of the sizing-up glance. In half a second she nails you: family man, no trouble. Sweet tough wise old scared Mrs. Plummer. Hand over your plastic credit card. Watch her give it the treatment: people used to roll their own cigarettes in machines with just that gesture. Accept the precious keys with their lozenge-shaped tags of plastic. Consider the career of motelkeeper, selling what shouldn't be buyable—rest to the weary, bliss to the illicit, space to the living. Providing television and telephones to keep us in touch with the unreal worlds behind, ahead. Shelter, a strange old commodity.

Untie the bags from the roof of the car. Your legs still feel weird, moving. The kids have the routine down pat: in three minutes in and out of their room and into the pool. Follow at a middle-aged pace, taking care not to disarray the suitcase in removing the bathing suits. The wife looks great, momentarily naked, but she claims she has a headache, after all those miles.

Wait until the kids get bored with yelling and splashing. Then, beside the pool, soak in the sun. Listen to the town. You have never heard of the town before: this is important. Otherwise, there are expectations, and a plan. This is not to say the town need be small. America conceals immense things. Here are thousands of busy souls as untangent to you as individual rocks on the moon. Say the town is in California, on the dry side of the Sierras; though it could as well be in Iowa, or Kentucky, or Connecticut. Out of nowhere, here it has arrived. Listen. The wavelets in the pool lap the tile gutter. The rush of traffic along Route Whatever-It-Is doesn't miss you; it sings, sighs, cruises, processes hurtling multitudes, passes like a river. Nearer by, car tires chew the gravel, creeping closer. Look. Two long-haired children in patched jeans, their clothes full of insignias, pale, scarcely older than your own children, emerge, with a reluctance somehow loving, from a crumpled green Volkswagen, and walk to the motel office. A far-off door slams. Retreating tires chew the gravel smaller and smaller. In the other direction, a laundry cart rattles. And beyond all this, enclosing it, like a transparent dome, an indecipherable murmur, like bees in the eaves or the continual excited liquid tremolo of newly hatched birds hidden in a tree trunk, waiting to be fed.

A siren sounds.

It sounds distant, then proximate, then distant again, and lower-pitched. This cry of emergency cuts through the afternoon like a crack in crystal. Disaster, here? An accident up the road, which might have been you, had you pressed on? A heart attack, high in the mountains? Relax. Let the lordly sun dry the drops of water on your chest. Imagine an old Californian, with parched white beard and a mountain goat's unfriendly stare, his whole life from birth soaked in this altitude, this view, this locality until an hour ago unknown to you and after tomorrow never to be known again—imagine him dead, his life in a blood-blind moment wrenched from his chest like a root from a tummock. The thought, curiously, is no more disturbing than the chuckling rush of traffic, than the animal ripple of the kids having returned their bodies to the pool, than the remote distinct voice that now and then, for reasons of its own, monotonously recites numbers into a kind of megaphone, an amplification system. "Fifteen . . . twenty . . ." Something to do with the disaster? An air alert? The voice drones on, part of the peace. Further sirens bleat, a black police car and a square white truck with blue flashers smoothly rip by, between the motel and the Mexican restaurant across Route Whatever-It-Is.

Beyond the restaurant's red tile roof lies a tawny valley; beyond it, a lesser range of mountains, gray, but gray multitudinously, with an infinity of shades—ash, graphite, cardboard, tomcat, lavender. Such beauty wants to make us weep. If we were crystal, we would shatter. The amplified voice goes on, "Twenty . . . thirty . . ." The kids begin to squabble. You have had enough sun. Time to reconnoitre.

The wife says her headache is better but she will stay in the motel room, to give herself a shampoo. Walk, family man, with the kids, out from the parking lot and down the main street. The heat from the sidewalk swims across your shins. The high mountain sun gives a tinny thin coating of glory to the orange Rexall signs, the red tongues of the parking meters, the pink shorts of girls whose brown backs are delicately trussed by the strings of minimal halters, the rags of Army-surplus green being worn alike by overmuscled youths and squinting, bent geezers. They drift, these natives, in their element. Love them because they are here. There is no better reason for love. They squint through you. To acquire substance, enter a store and buy something. Discover that the town offers postcards of itself; it is self-conscious, commercial. It contains many sporting-goods stores, veritable armories in the war against the wilderness—fishing rods, ski poles, hunting slingshots, collapsible rafts, folding tents, backpack racks, freeze-dried fruits in aluminum wrap, fanciful feathered fishing flies in plastic capsules, tennis rackets, tennis shirts, tennis balls the colors of candy. Your boys are enchanted, your girls are bored. Purchase five postcards, some freeze-dried pears for tomorrow's long drive through the desert, and exit. Out on the hot pavement, the little girl's sandals flop. She has been begging for new ones every day. Her hair is still wet from the motel pool. Take her into a shoe store. Solemnly the salesman seats her, measures her foot size. Marvel at the way in which his hand deigns to touch this unknown child's sticky bare foot. Alas, what he has in her size she does not like, and what she likes he does not have in her size. Express regret and leave. Crossing the dangerous thoroughfare, you take her hand, a touch more tender with her, having witnessed the tenderness of others. Across the street, in a little main square pared to insignificance by successive widenings of the highway, an old covered wagon instead of a statue stands. Think of those dead unknown—plodding flights of angels—who dared cross this land of inhuman grandeur without highways, without air conditioning, without even (a look underneath confirms) shock absorbers, jolting and rattling each inch, in order to arrive here and create this town, wherein this wagon has become a receptacle for (a look inside discovers) empty cans of Coors Beer, Diet Pepsi, and Mountain Dew.

America is a vast conspiracy to make you happy.

. . .

Or, alternatively, get into the car at the motel and drive around the back streets: a wooden church, a brick elementary school with basketball stanchions on a pond of asphalt, houses spaced and square-set and too clean-looking. There is something sterilizing about the high air here. The lawns look watered, like putting greens. They contrast vividly with spaces of unkempt parched hay. The houses out of their rectilinear, faintly glistening fronts strive to say something, a word you are anxious to hear, and would drive forever to hear finally. But the kids are bored, and beg to go "home." Home is the motel.

The wife's hair is springy and fragrant from her shampoo. The pool is deserted and looks chilly. Evening shadows have slid down from the mountain. The sun sets in the west, everywhere. The gray range to the east basks in light like an X-rayed bone. Where shall we eat? Discuss. The kids want a quick, clean, hamburgery place, with Formica tables and clear neutral windows giving on the stream of traffic that ties them securely to the future. You and the wife want something enclosed, with regional flavor and a liquor license. Perhaps the kids win, and you sit there looking out through the windows thinking, This is America, a hamburger kingdom, one cuisine, under God, indivisible, with pickles and potato chips for all. What you see through the clear windows looks blanched without sunglasses, which you have worn all day, assigning the landscape you were driving through an unnatural postcard brilliance: the blue sky dyed cobalt, the purple mesas and ochre rocks tinted as if by the pastel artist who timidly sells bad portraits at a country fair.

Or perhaps you talk the kids into the Mexican restaurant, and as they sit in candlelight struggling with their tacos and enchiladas you sip your salt-rimmed margarita and think, This is America, where we take everything in, tacos and chow mein and pizza and sauerkraut, because we are only what we eat, we are whatever we say we are. When a Japanese says "Japanese," he is trapped on a little definite racial fact, whereas when we say "American" it is not a fact, it is an act, of faith, a matter of lines on a map and words on paper, an outline it will take generations and centuries more to fill in. And, yes, the waitress bringing the sherbet and the check appears to illustrate these meditations, for she is lovely and young and deracinated, one of the no-name breed our coast-to-coast experiment has engendered, her bones grown straight on cheap food, her fertility encased in the chemical Saniwrap of the Pill, her accent pleasantly presupposing nothing, her skin tanned dark as an Indian's but her eyes blue and her hair sun-blond and loose down her back in Eve's timeless fall.

Be careful crossing the highway. In the motel parking lot, before you can reach the anonymity of your room, Mrs. Plummer, hustling from her car to the office clutching papers in her hand, has to cross your path, and smiles. This slightly spoils it. She knows you. You know her. When innocence ends, plans must be made. First, sleep. Then, early in the morning, when the traffic is spotty and the sun is feeble in the east, move on.

The Music School

My name is Alfred Schweigen and I exist in time. Last night I heard a young priest tell of a change in his Church's attitude toward the Eucharistic wafer. For generations nuns and priests, but especially (the young man said) nuns, have taught Catholic children that the wafer must be held in the mouth and allowed to melt; that to touch it with the teeth would be (and this was never doctrine, but merely a nuance of instruction) in some manner blasphemous. Now, amid the flowering of fresh and bold ideas with which the Church, like a tundra thawing, responded to that unexpected sun the late Pope John, there has sprung up the thought that Christ did not say *Take and melt this in your mouth* but *Take and eat*. The word is *eat*, and to dissolve the word is to dilute the transubstantiated metaphor of physical nourishment. This demiquaver of theology crystallizes with a beautiful simplicity in the material world; the bakeries supplying the Mass have been instructed to unlearn the science of a dough translucent to the tongue and to prepare a thicker, tougher wafer—a host, in fact, so substantial it *must* be chewed to be swallowed.

This morning I read in the newspaper that an acquaintance of mine had been murdered. The father of five children, he had been sitting at the dinner table with them, a week after Thanksgiving. A single bullet entered the window and pierced his temple; he fell to the floor and died there in minutes, at the feet of his children. My acquaintance with him was slight. He has become the only victim of murder I have known, and for such a role anyone seems drastically miscast, though in the end each life wears its events with a geological inevitability. It is impossible, today, to imagine him alive. He was a computer expert, a soft-voiced, broad-set man from Nebraska, whose intelligence, concerned as it was with matters so arcane to me, had a generous quality of reserve, and gave him, in my apprehension of him, the dignity of an iceberg, which floats so serenely on its hidden mass. We met (I think only twice) in the home of a mutual friend, a professional colleague of his who is my neighbor. We spoke, as people do whose fields of knowledge are miles apart, of matters where all men are ignorant—of politics, children, and, perhaps, religion. I have the impression, at any rate, that he, as is often the case with scientists and Midwesterners, had no use for religion, and I saw in him a typical specimen of the new human species that thrives around scientific centers, in an environment of discussion groups, outdoor exercise, and cheerful husbandry. Like those vanished gentlemen whose sexual energy was exclusively spent in brothels, these men confine their cleverness to their work, which, being in one way or another for the government, is usually secret. With their sufficient incomes, large families, Volkswagen buses, hi-fi phonographs, half-remodelled Victorian homes, and harassed, ironical wives, they seem to have solved, or dismissed, the paradox of being a thinking animal and, devoid of guilt, apparently participate not in this century but in the next. If I remember him with individual clarity, it is because once I intended to write a novel about a computer programmer, and I asked him questions, which he answered agreeably. More agreeably still, he offered to show me around his laboratories any time I cared to make the hour's trip to where they were. I never wrote the novel—the moment in my life it was meant to crystallize dissolved too quickly—and I never took the trip. Indeed, I don't believe I thought of my friend once in the year between our last encounter and this morning, when my wife at breakfast put the paper before me and asked, "Don't we know him?" His pleasant face with its eyes set wide like the eyes of a bear gazed from the front page. I read that he had been murdered.

I do not understand the connection between last night and this morning, though there seems to be one. I am trying to locate it this afternoon, while sitting in a music school, waiting for my daughter to finish her piano lesson. I perceive in the two incidents a common element of nourishment, of eating transfigured by a strange irruption, and there is a parallel movement, a flight immaculately direct and elegant, from an immaterial phenomenon (an exegetical nicety, a maniac hatred) to a material one (a bulky wafer, a bullet in the temple). About the murder I feel certain, from my knowledge of the victim, that his offense was blameless, something for which he could not have felt guilt or shame. When I try to picture it, I see only numbers and Greek letters, and conclude that from my distance I have witnessed an almost unprecedented crime, a crime of unalloyed scientific passion. And there is this to add: the young priest plays a twelve-string guitar, smokes mentholated cigarettes, and seemed unembarrassed to find himself sitting socially in a circle of Protestants and nonbelievers—like my late computer friend, a man of the future.

But let me describe the music school. I love it here. It is the basement of a huge Baptist church. Golden collection plates rest on the table beside me. Girls in their first blush of adolescence, carrying fawn-colored flute cases and pallid folders of music, shuffle by me; their awkwardness is lovely, like the stance of a bather testing the sea. Boys and mothers arrive and leave. From all directions sounds—of pianos, oboes, clarinets— arrive like hints of another world, a world where angels fumble, pause, and begin again. Listening, I remember what learning music is like, how impossibly difficult and complex seem the first fingerings, the first decipherings of that unique language which freights each note with a double meaning of position and duration, a language as finicking as Latin, as laconic as Hebrew, as surprising to the eye as Arabic or Chinese. How mysterious appears that calligraphy of parallel spaces, swirling clefs, superscribed ties, subscribed decrescendos, dots and sharps and flats! How great looms the gap between the first gropings of vision and the first stammerings of sound! Vision, timidly, becomes percussion, percussion becomes music, music becomes emotion, emotion becomes—vision. Few of us have the heart to follow this circle to its end. I took lessons for years, and never learned, and last night, watching the priest's fingers confidently prance on the neck of his guitar, I was envious and incredulous. My daughter is just beginning the piano. These are her first lessons, she is eight, she is eager and hopeful. Silently she sits beside me as we drive the nine miles to the town where the lessons are given; silently she sits beside me, in the dark, as we drive home. Unlike her, she does not beg for a reward of candy or a Coke, as if the lesson itself has been a meal. She only remarks—speaking dully, in a reflex of greed she has outgrown—that the store windows are decorated for Christmas already. I love taking her, I love waiting for her, I love driving her home through the mystery of darkness toward the certainty of supper. I do this taking and driving because today my wife visits her psychiatrist. She visits a psychiatrist because I am unfaithful to her. I do not understand the connection, but there seems to be one.

In the novel I never wrote, I wanted the hero to be a computer programmer because it was the most poetic and romantic occupation I could think of, and my hero had to be extremely romantic and delicate, for he was to die of adultery. Die, I mean, of knowing it was possible; the possibility crushed him. I conceived of him, whose professional life was spent in the sanctum of the night (when, I was told, the computers, too valuable to be unemployed by industry during the day, are free, as it were, to frolic), devising idioms whereby problems might be fed to the machines and emerge, under binary percussion, as the music of truth—I conceived of him as being too fine, translucent, and scrupulous to live in our coarse age. He was to be, if the metaphor is biological, an evolutionary abortion, a mammalian mutation crushed underfoot by dinosaurs, and, if the metaphor is mathematical, a hypothetical ultimate, one digit beyond the last real number. The title of the book was to be $N + 1$. Its first sentence went, *As Echo passed overhead, he stroked Maggy Johns' side through her big-flowered dress.* Echo is the artificial star, the first, a marvel; as the couples at a lawn party look upward at it, these two caress one another. She takes his free hand, lifts it to her lips, warmly breathes on, kisses, his knuckles. *His halted body seemed to catch up in itself the immense slow revolution of the earth, and the firm little white star, newly placed in space, calmly made its way through the older points of light, which looked shredded and faint in comparison.* From this hushed moment under the ominous sky of technological miracle, the plot was to develop more or less downhill, into a case of love, guilt, and nervous breakdown, with physiological complications (I had to do some research here) that would kill the hero as quietly as a mistake is erased from a blackboard. There was to be the hero, his wife, his love, and his doctor. In the end the wife married the doctor, and Maggy Johns would calmly continue her way through the comparatively faint . . . Stop me.

My psychiatrist wonders why I need to humiliate myself. It is the habit, I suppose, of confession. In my youth I attended a country church where, every two months, we would all confess; we kneeled on the uncarpeted floor and propped the books containing the service on the seats of the pews. It was a grave, long service, beginning, *Beloved in the Lord! Let us draw near with a true heart and confess our sins unto God, our Father. . . .* There was a kind of accompanying music in the noise of the awkward fat Germanic bodies fitting themselves, scraping and grunting, into the backwards-kneeling position. We read aloud, *But if we thus examine ourselves, we shall find nothing in us but sin and death, from which we can in no wise set ourselves free.* The confession complete, we would stand and be led, pew by pew, to the altar rail, where the young minister, a black-haired man with very small pale hands, would feed us, murmuring, *Take, eat; this is the true body of our Lord and Saviour Jesus Christ, given unto death for your sins.* The altar rail was of varnished wood and fenced off the chancel on three sides, so that, standing (oddly, we did not kneel here), one could see, one could not help seeing, the faces of one's fellow-communicants. We were a weathered, homely congregation, sheepish in our Sunday clothes, and the faces I saw while the wafer was held in my mouth were strained; above their closed lips their eyes held a watery look of pleading to be rescued from the depths of this mystery. And it distinctly seems, in the reaches of this memory so vivid it makes my saliva flow, that it was necessary, if not to chew, at least to touch, to embrace and tentatively shape, the wafer with the teeth.

We left refreshed. *We give thanks to thee, Almighty God, that Thou hast refreshed us through this salutary gift.* The church smelled like this school, glinting with strange whispers and varnished highlights. I am neither musical nor religious. Each moment I live, I must think where to place my fingers, and press them down with no confidence of hearing a chord. My friends are like me. We are all pilgrims, faltering toward divorce. Some get no further than mutual confession, which becomes an addiction, and exhausts them. Some move on, into violent quarrels and physical blows, and succumb to sexual excitement. A few make it to the psychiatrists. A very few get as far as the lawyers. Last evening, as the priest sat in the circle of my friends, a woman entered without knocking; she had come from the lawyers, and her eyes and hair were flung wide with suffering, as if she had come in out of a high wind. She saw our black-garbed guest, was amazed, ashamed perhaps, and took two backward steps. But then, in the hush, she regained her composure and sat down among us. And in this grace note, of the two backward steps and then again the forward movement, a coda seems to be urged.

The world is the host; it must be chewed. I am content here in this school. My daughter emerges from her lesson. Her face is fat and satisfied, refreshed, hopeful; her pleased smile, biting her lower lip, pierces my heart, and I die (I think I am dying) at her feet.

Man and Daughter in the Cold

"Look at that girl ski!" The exclamation arose at Ethan's side as if, in the disconnecting cold, a rib of his had cried out; but it was his friend, friend and fellow-teacher, an inferior teacher but superior skier, Matt Langley, admiring Becky, Ethan's own daughter. It took an effort, in this air like slices of transparent metal interposed everywhere, to make these connections and to relate the young girl, her round face red with windburn as she skimmed down the run-out slope, to himself. She was his daughter, age thirteen. Ethan had twin sons, two years younger, and his attention had always been focused on their skiing, on the irksome comedy of their double needs—the four boots to lace, the four mittens to find—and then their cute yet grim competition as now one and now the other gained the edge in the expertise of geländesprungs and slalom form. On their trips north into the White Mountains, Becky had come along for the ride. "Look how solid she is," Matt went on. "She doesn't cheat on it like your boys—those feet are absolutely together." The girl, grinning as if she could hear herself praised, wiggle-waggled to a flashy stop that sprayed snow over the men's ski tips.

"Where's Mommy?" she asked.

Ethan answered, "She went with the boys into the lodge. They couldn't take it." Their sinewy little male bodies had no insulation; weeping and shivering, they had begged to go in after a single T-bar run.

"What sissies," Becky said.

Matt said, "This wind is wicked. And it's picking up. You should have been here at nine; Lord, it was lovely. All that fresh powder, and not a stir of wind."

Becky told him, "Dumb Tommy couldn't find his mittens, we spent an *hour* looking, and then Daddy got the Jeep stuck." Ethan, alerted now for signs of the wonderful in his daughter, was struck by the strange fact that she was making conversation. Unafraid, she was talking to Matt without her father's intercession.

"Mr. Langley was saying how nicely you were skiing."

"You're Olympic material, Becky."

The girl perhaps blushed; but her cheeks could get no redder. Her eyes, which, were she a child, she would have instantly averted, remained a second on Matt's face, as if to estimate how much he meant it. "It's easy down here," Becky said. "It's babyish."

Ethan asked, "Do you want to go up to the top?" He was freezing standing still, and the gondola would give shelter from the wind.

Her eyes shifted to his, with another unconsciously thoughtful hesitation. "Sure. If you want to."

"Come along, Matt?"

"Thanks, no. It's too rough for me; I've had enough runs. This is the trouble with January—once it stops snowing, the wind comes up. I'll keep Elaine company in the lodge." Matt himself had no wife, no children. At thirty-eight, he was as free as his students, as light on his skis and as full of brave know-how. "In case of frostbite," he shouted after them, "rub snow on it."

Becky effortlessly skated ahead to the lift shed. The encumbered motion of walking on skis, not natural to Ethan, made him feel asthmatic: a fish out of water. He touched his parka pocket, to check that the inhalator was there. As a child he had imagined death as something attacking from outside, but now he knew that it was carried within; we nurse it for years, and it grows. The clock on the lodge wall said a quarter to noon. The giant thermometer read two degrees above zero. The racks outside were dense as hedges with idle skis. Crowds, any sensation of crowding or delay, quickened his asthma; as therapy he imagined the emptiness, the blue freedom, at the top of the mountain. The clatter of machinery inside the shed was comforting, and enough teen-age boys were boarding gondolas to make the ascent seem normal and safe. Ethan's breathing eased. Becky proficiently handed her poles to the loader with their points up; her father was always caught by surprise, and often as not fumbled the little maneuver of letting his skis be taken from him. Until, seven years ago, he had become an assistant professor at a New Hampshire college, he had never skied; he had lived in those Middle Atlantic cities where snow, its moment of virgin beauty by, is only an encumbering nuisance, a threat of suffocation. In those seven years, his children had grown up on skis.

Alone with his daughter in the rumbling isolation of the gondola, he wanted to explore her, and found her strange—strange in her uninquisitive child's silence, her accustomed poise in this ascending egg of metal. A dark figure with spreading legs veered out of control beneath them, fell forward, and vanished. Ethan cried out, astonished; he imagined that the man had buried himself alive. Becky was barely amused, and looked away before the dark spots struggling in the drift were lost from sight. As if she might know, Ethan asked, "Who was that?"

"Some kid." Kids, her tone suggested, were in plentiful supply; one could be spared.

He offered to dramatize the adventure ahead of them: "Are we going to freeze at the top?"

"Not exactly."

"What do you think it'll be like?"

"Miserable."

"Why are we doing this?"

"Because we paid the money for the all-day lift ticket."

"Becky, you think you're pretty smart, don't you?"

"Not really."

The gondola rumbled and lurched into the shed at the top; an attendant opened the door, and there was a howling mixed of wind and of boys whooping to keep warm. He was roughly handed two pairs of skis, and the handler, muffled to the eyes with a scarf, stared as if amazed that Ethan was so old. All the others struggling into skis in the lee of the shed were adolescent boys. Students: after fifteen years of teaching, Ethan tended to flinch from youth—its harsh noises, its cheerful rapacity, its cruel onward flow as one class replaced another, taking with it another year of his life.

Away from the shelter of the shed, the wind was a high monotonous pitch of pain. His cheeks instantly ached. His septum tingled and burned. He inhaled through his nose, and pushed off. Drifts ribbed the trail, obscuring Becky's ski tracks seconds after she made them; at each push through the heaped snow, his scope of breathing narrowed. By the time he reached the first steep section, the left half of his back hurt as it did only in the panic of a full asthmatic attack, and his skis, ignored, too heavy to manage, spread and swept him toward a snowbank at the side of the trail. He was bent far forward but kept his balance; the snow kissed his face lightly, instantly, all over; he straightened up, refreshed by the shock, thankful not to have lost a ski.

Down the slope, Becky had halted and was staring upward at him, worried. A huge blowing feather, a partition of snow, came between them. The cold, unprecedented in his experience, shone through his clothes like furious light, and as he rummaged through his parka for the inhalator he seemed to be searching glass shelves backed by a black wall. He found it, its icy plastic the touch of life, a clumsy key to his insides. Gasping, he exhaled, put it into his mouth, and inhaled; the isoproterenol spray, chilled into drops, opened his lungs enough for him to call to his daughter, "Keep moving! I'll catch up!"

Solid on her skis, as Matt had said, she swung down among the moguls and wind-bared ice, and became small, and again waited. The moderate slope seemed a cliff; if he fell and sprained anything, he would freeze. His entire body would become locked tight against air and light and thought. His legs trembled; his breath moved in and out of a narrow slot beneath the pain in his back. The cold and blowing snow all around him constituted an immense crowding, but there was no way out of this white cave except to slide downward toward the dark spot that was his daughter. He had forgotten all his skiing lessons. Leaning backward in an infant's tense snowplow, he floundered through alternating powder and ice.

"You O.K., Daddy?" Her stare was wide, its fright underlined by a pale patch on her cheek.

He used the inhalator again and gave himself breath to tell her, "I'm fine. Let's get down."

In this way, in steps of her leading and waiting, they worked down the mountain, out of the worst wind, into the lower trail that ran between birches and hemlocks. The cold had the quality not of absence but of force: an inverted burning. The last time Becky stopped and waited, the colorless crescent on her scarlet cheek disturbed him, reminded him of some injunction, but he could find in his brain, whittled to a dim determination to persist, only the advice to keep going, toward shelter and warmth. She told him, at a division of trails, "This is the easier way."

"Let's go the quicker way," he said, and in this last descent he recovered the rhythm—knees together, shoulders facing the valley, weight forward as if in the moment of release from a diving board—not a resistance but a joyous acceptance of falling. They reached the base lodge, and with unfeeling hands removed their skis. Pushing into the cafeteria, Ethan saw in the momentary mirror of the door window that his face was a spectre's; chin, nose, and eyebrows had retained the snow from that near-fall near the top. "Becky, look," he said, turning in the crowded warmth and clatter inside the door. "I'm a monster."

"I know, your face was absolutely white, I didn't know whether to tell you or not. I thought it might scare you."

He touched the pale patch on her cheek. "Feel anything?"

"No."

"Damn. I should have rubbed snow on it."

Matt and Elaine and the twins, flushed and stripped of their parkas, had eaten lunch; shouting and laughing with a strange guilty shrillness, they said that there had been repeated loudspeaker announcements not to go up to the top without face masks, because of frostbite. They had expected Ethan and Becky to come back down on the gondola, as others had, after tasting the top.

"It never occurred to us," Ethan said. He took the blame upon himself by adding, "I wanted to see the girl ski."

Their common adventure, and the guilt of his having given her frostbite, bound Becky and Ethan together in loose complicity for the rest of the day. They arrived home as sun was leaving even the tips of the hills; Elaine had invited Matt to supper, and while the windows of the house burned golden Ethan shovelled out the Jeep. The house was a typical New Hampshire farmhouse, less than two miles from the college, on the side of a hill, overlooking what had been a pasture, with the usual capacious porch running around three sides, cluttered with cordwood and last summer's lawn furniture. The woodsy, sheltered scent of these porches never failed to please Ethan, who had been raised in a Jersey City semi-detached, then a West Side apartment beseiged by other people's cooking smells and noises. The wind had been left behind in the mountains. The air was as still as the stars. Shovelling the light dry snow became a lazy dance. But when he bent suddenly, his knees creaked, and his breathing shortened so that he had to pause.

A sudden rectangle of light was flung from the shadows of the porch. Becky came out into the cold with him. She was carrying a lawn rake.

He asked her, "Should you be out again? How's your frostbite?" Though she was a distance away, there was no need, in the immaculate air, to raise his voice.

"It's O.K. It kind of tingles. And under my chin. Mommy made me put on a scarf."

"What's the lawn rake for?"

"It's a way you can make a path. It really works."

"O.K., you make a path to the garage, and after I get my breath I'll see if I can get the Jeep back in."

"Are you having asthma?"

"A little."

"We were reading about it in biology. Dad, see, it's kind of a tree inside you, and every branch has a little ring of muscle around it, and they tighten." From her gestures in the dark she was demonstrating, with mittens on.

What she described, of course, was classic unalloyed asthma, whereas his was shading into emphysema, which could only worsen. But he liked being lectured to—preferred it, indeed, to lecturing—and as the minutes of companionable silence with his daughter passed he took inward notes on the bright, quick impressions flowing over him like a continuous voice. The silent cold. The stars. Orion behind an elm. Minute scintillae in the snow at his feet. His daughter's strange black bulk against the white; the solid grace that had stolen upon her over time. He remembered his father shovelling their car free from a sudden unwelcome storm in the mid-Atlantic region. The undercurrent of desperation, his father a salesman and must get to Camden. Got to get to Camden, boy, get to Camden or bust. Dead of a heart attack at forty-seven.

Ethan tossed a shovelful into the air so the scintillae flashed in the steady golden chord from the house windows. He saw again Elaine and Matt sitting flushed at the lodge table, parkas off, in deshabille, as if sitting up in bed. Matt's enviable way of turning a half-circle on the top of a mogul, light as a diver, compared with the cancerous unwieldiness of Ethan's own skis. The callousness of students. The flawless cruelty of the stars, Orion intertwined with the silhouetted elm. A black tree inside him. His daughter, busily sweeping with the rake, childish yet lithe, so curiously demonstrating this preference for his company. It was female of her, he supposed, to forgive him her frostbite. A plow a half-mile away painstakingly scraped. He was missing the point of this silent lecture. The point was unstated: an absence. He was looking upon his daughter as a woman, but without lust. There was no need to possess her; she was already his. The music around him was being produced, in the zero air, like a finger on a glass rim, by this hollowness, this biological negation. *Sans* lust, *sans* jealousy. Space seemed love, bestowed to be free in, and coldness the price. He felt joined to the great dead whose words it was his duty to teach.

The Jeep came up unprotestingly from the fluffy snow. It looked happy to be penned in the garage with Elaine's station wagon, and the skis, and the oiled chain saw, and the power mower dreamlessly waiting for spring. Ethan was so full of happiness that, rather than his soul shatter, he uttered a sound: "Becky?"

"Yeah?"

"You want to know what else Mr. Langley said?"

"What?" They trudged toward the porch, up the path the gentle rake had cleared.

"He said you ski better than the boys."

"I bet," she said, and raced to the porch, and in the precipitate way, evasive and pleased, that she flung herself to the top step he glimpsed something generic and joyous, a pageant that would leave him behind.

The Rescue

HELPLESSLY Caroline Harris, her husband and son having seized the first chair, found herself paired with Alice Smith. Together they were struck in the backs of their knees and hurled upward. When Caroline had been a child, her father, conceited in his strength, would toss her toward the ceiling with the same brutal, swooping lurch.

Alice snapped the safety bar, and they were bracketed together. It was degrading for both of them. Up ahead, neither Norman nor Timmy deigned to glance back. From the rear, hooded and armed with spears, they were two of a kind, Timmy at twelve only slightly smaller than his father; and this, too, she felt as a desertion, a flight from her body. While she was dragged through the air, rudely joggled at each pier, the whiteness of the snow pressed on the underside of her consciousness with the gathering insistence of a headache. Her ski boots weighed; her feet felt captive. Rigid with irritation and a desire not to sway, she smoked her next-to-last cigarette, which was cheated of taste by the cold, and tried to decide if the woman beside her were sleeping with Norman or not.

This morning, as they drove north into New Hampshire, there had been in the automobile an excessive ease, as if the four of them knew each other better than Caroline remembered reason for. There had been, between Alice Smith and Norman, a lack of flirtation a shade too resolute, while on sleepy, innocent Timmy the woman had inflicted a curiously fervent playfulness, as if warm messages for the father were being forwarded through the son, or as if Alice were seeking to establish herself as a sexual nonentity, a brotherly sister. Caroline felt an ominous tug in this trip. Had she merely imagined, during their fumbling breakfast at Howard Johnson, a poignance in the pauses, and a stir of something, like toes touching, under the table? And was she paranoid to have suspected a deliberate design in the pattern of alternation that had her and her son floundering up the T-bar together as the other two expertly skimmed down the slope and waited, side by side, laughing vapor, at the end of the long and devious line? Caroline was not reassured, when they all rejoined at lunch, by Alice's smile, faintly flavored with a sweetness unspecified in the recipe.

Alice had been her friend first. She had moved to their neighborhood a year ago, a touching little divorcée with pre-school twins, utterly lost. Her only interest seemed to be sports, and her marital grief had given her an awkward hardness, as if from too much exercise. Norman had called her pathetic and sexless. Yet a winter later he had rescued his skis from a decade in the attic, enrolled Timmy in local lessons, and somehow guided his wife in the same dangerous direction, as irresistibly as this cable was pulling them skyward.

They were giddily lifted above the tops of the pines. Caroline, to brace her voice against her rising fear, spoke aloud: "This is ridiculous. At my age women in Tahiti are grandmothers."

Alice said seriously, "I think you do terribly well. You're a natural dancer, and it shows."

Caroline could not hate her. She was as helpless as herself, and there was some timid loyalty, perhaps, in Norman's betraying her with a woman she had befriended. She felt, indeed, less betrayed than diluted, and, turning with her cigarette cupped against the wind, she squinted at the other woman as if into an unkind mirror. Alice was small-boned yet coarse; muscularity, reaching upward through the prominent tendons of her throat, gave her face, even through the flush of windburn, a taut, sallow tinge. Her hair, secured by a scarlet ear warmer, was abundant but mousy, and her eyes were close-set, hazel, and vaguely, stubbornly inward. But between her insignificant nose and receding chin there lay, as if in ambush, a large, complicated, and (Caroline supposed) passionate mouth. This, she realized, as the chair swayed sickeningly, was exactly what Norman would want: a mouse with a mouth.

Disgust, disgust and anger, swung through her. How greedy men were! How conceited and brutish! The sky enlarged around her, as if to receive so immense a condemnation. With deft haste Alice undid the safety bar; Caroline involuntarily transposed the action into an undoing of Norman's clothes. Icy with contempt for her situation, she floated onto the unloading platform and discovered, slipping down the alarming little ramp, that her knees were trembling and had forgotten how to bend.

Of course, they were abandoned. The males had heedlessly gone ahead, and beckoned, tiny and black, from the end of a tunnel tigerishly striped with the shadows of birches. On whispering skis held effortlessly parallel, Alice led, while Caroline followed, struggling clumsily against the impulse to stem. They arrived where the men had been and found them gone again. In their place was a post with two signs. One pointed right to GREASED LIGHTNING (EXPERT). The other pointed left to THE LIGHTNING BUG (INTERMEDIATE–NOVICE).

"I see them," Alice said, and lightly poled off to the right.

"Wait," Caroline begged.

Alice christied to a stop. A long lavender shadow from a mass of pines covered her and for a painful instant, as her lithe body inquisitively straightened, she seemed beautiful.

"How expert is it?" The Harrises had never been to this mountain before; Alice had been several times.

"There's one mogully piece you can sideslip," Alice said. "The Bug will take you around the other side of the mountain. You'll never catch the men."

"Why don't you follow them and I'll go down the novice trail? I don't trust this mountain yet." It was a strange mountain, one of the lesser Presidentials, rather recently developed, with an unvarnished cafeteria and very young boys patrolling the trails in rawly bright jackets chevron-striped in yellow and green. At lunch, Norman said he twice had seen members of the ski patrol take spills. His harsh laugh, remembered at this bare altitude, frightened her. The trembling in her knees would not sub-side, and her fingertips were stinging in their mittens.

Alice crisply sidestepped back up to her. "Let's both go down the Bug," she said. "You shouldn't ski alone."

"I don't want to be a sissy," Caroline said, and these careless words apparently triggered some inward chain of reflection in the other woman, for Alice's face clouded, and it appeared certain that she was sleeping with Norman. Everything, every tilt of circumstance, every smothered swell and deliberate contraindication, confirmed it, even the girl's name, Smith—a nothing-name, a demimondaine's alias. Her hazel eyes, careful in the glare of the snow, flickeringly searched Caroline's and her expressive mouth froze on the verge of a crucial question.

"Track! Track!"

The voice was behind them, shrill and young. A teen-age girl, wearing a polka-dot purple parka, and her mother, a woman almost elderly, who seemed to have rouged the tip of her nose, turned beside them and casually plunged over the lip of Greased Lightning.

Caroline, shamed, said, "The hell with it. The worst I can do is get killed." Murderously stabbing the snow next to Alice's noncommital buckle-boots, she pushed off to the right, her weight flung wildly back, her uphill ski snagging, her whole body burning with the confirmation of her suspicions. She would leave Norman. Unsteady as a flame she flickered down the height, wavering in her own wind. Alice carefully passed her and, taking long traverses and diagrammatically deliberate turns, seemed to be inviting her not to destroy herself. Submitting to the sight, permitting her eyes to infect her body with Alice's rhythm, she found the snow yielding to her as if under the pressure of reason; and, swooping in complementary zigzags, the two women descended a long white waterfall linked as if by love.

Then there was a lazy flat run in the shadow of reddish rocks bearded with icicles, then another descent, through cataracts of moguls, into a wider, elbow-shaped slope overlooking, from the height of a mile, a toy lodge, a tessellated parking lot, and, vast and dim as a foreign nation, a frozen lake mottled with cloud shadows and islands of evergreen. Tensely sideslipping, Caroline saw, on the edge of this slope, at one side of the track, some trouble, a heap of dark cloth. In her haste to be with the men, Alice would have swept by, but Caroline snowplowed to a halt. With a dancing waggle Alice swerved and pulled even. The heap of cloth was the woman with the red-tipped nose, who lay on her back, her head downhill. Her daughter knelt beside her. The woman's throat was curved as if she were gargling, and her hood was submerged in snow, so that her face showed like a face in a casket.

Efficiently, Alice bent, released her bindings, and walked to the accident, making crisp boot prints. "Is she conscious?" she asked.

"It's the left," the casket face said, not altering its rapt relation with the sky. The dab of red was the only color not drained from it. Tears trickled from the corner of one eye into a fringe of sandy permed hair.

"Do you think it's broken?"

There was no answer, and the girl impatiently prompted, "Mother, does it feel broken?"

"I can't feel a thing. Take off the boot."

"I don't think we should take off the boot," Alice said. She surveyed the woman's legs with a physical forthrightness that struck Caroline as unpleasant. "We might disturb the alignment. It might be a spiral. Did you feel anything give?" The impact of the spill had popped both safety bindings, so the woman's skis were attached to her feet only by the break-away straps. Alice stooped and unclipped these, and stood the skis upright in the snow, as a signal. She said, "We should get help."

The daughter looked up hopefully. The face inside her polka-dot parka was round and young, its final form not quite declared. "If you're willing to stay," she said, "I'll go. I know some of the boys in the patrol."

"We'll be happy to stay," Caroline said firmly. She was conscious, as she said this, of frustrating Alice and of declaring, in the necessary war between them, her weapons to be compassion and patience. She wished she could remove her skis, for their presence on her feet held her a little aloof; but she was not sure she could put them back on at this slant, in the middle of nowhere. The snow here had the eerie unvisited air of grass beside a highway. The young daughter, without a backward glance, snapped herself into her skis and whipped away, down the hill. Seeing how easy it had been, Caroline dared unfasten hers and discovered her own boot-prints also to be crisp intaglios. Alice tugged back her parka sleeve and frowned at her wristwatch. The third woman moaned.

Caroline asked, "Are you warm enough? Would you like to be wrapped in something?" The lack of a denial left them no choice but to remove their parkas and wrap her in them. Her body felt like an over-sized doll sadly in need of stuffing. Caroline, bending close, satisfied herself that what looked like paint was a little pinnacle of sunburn.

The woman murmured her thanks. "My second day here, I've ruined it for everybody—my daughter, my son . . ."

Alice asked, "Where is your son?"

"Who knows? I bring him here and don't see him from morning to night. He says he's skiing, but I ski every trail and never see him."

"Where is your husband?" Caroline asked; her voice sounded lost in the acoustic depth of the freezing air.

The woman sighed. "Not here."

Silence followed, a silence in which wisps of wind began to decorate the snow-laden branches of pines with outflowing feathers of powder. The dense shadow thrown by the forest edging the trail was growing heavy, and cold pressed through the chinks of Caroline's sweater. Alice's thin neck strained as she gazed up at the vacant ridge for help. The woman in the snow began, tricklingly, to sob, and Caroline asked, "Would you like a cigarette?"

The response was prompt. "I'd adore a weed." The woman sat up, pulled off her mitten, and hungrily twiddled her fingers. Her nails were painted. She did not seem to notice, in taking the cigarette, that the pack became empty. Gesturing with stabbing exhalations of smoke, she waxed chatty. "I say to my son, 'What's the point of coming to these beautiful mountains if all you do is rush, rush, rush, up the tow and down, and never stop to enjoy the scenery?' I say to him, 'I'd rather be old-fashioned and come down the mountain in one piece than have my neck broken at the age of fourteen.' If he saw me now, he'd have a fit laughing. There's a patch of ice up there and my skis crossed. When I went over, I could feel my left side pull from my shoulders to my toes. It reminded me of having a baby."

"Where are you from?" Alice asked.

"Melrose." The name of her town seemed to make the woman morose. Her eyes focused on her inert boot.

To distract her, Caroline asked, "And your husband's working?"

"We're divorced. I know if I could loosen the laces it would be a world of relief. My ankle wants to swell and it can't."

"I wouldn't trust it," Alice said.

"Let me at least undo the knot," Caroline offered, and dropped to her knees, as if to weep. She did not as a rule like complaining women, but here in this one she seemed to confront a voluntary dramatization of her own possibilities. She freed the knots of both the outer and inner laces — the boot was a new Nordica, and stiff. "Does that feel better?"

"I honestly can't say. I have no feeling below my knees whatsoever."

"Shock," Alice said. "Nature's anesthetic."

"My brother will be furious. He'll have to hire a nurse for me."

"You'll have your daughter," Caroline said.

"At her age, it's all boys, boys on the brain."

This seemed to sum up their universe of misfortune. In silence, as dark as widows against the tilted acres of white, they waited for rescue. The trail here was so wide skiers could easily pass on the far side. A few swooped close, then veered away, as if sensing a curse. One man, a merry ogre wearing steel-framed spectacles and a raccoon coat, smoking a cigar, and plowing down the fall line with a shameless sprawling stem, shouted to them in what seemed a foreign language. But the pattern of the afternoon — the sun had shifted away from the trail — yielded few skiers. Empty minutes slid by. The bitter air had found every loose stitch in Caroline's sweater and now was concentrating on the metal bits of brassiere that touched her skin. "Could I bum another coffin nail?" the injured woman asked.

"I'm sorry, that was my last."

"Oh dear. Isn't that the limit?"

Alice, so sallow now she seemed Oriental, tucked her hands into her armpits and jiggled up and down. She asked, "Won't the men worry?"

Caroline took satisfaction in telling her, "I doubt it." Looking outward, she saw only white, a tilted rippled wealth of colorlessness, the forsaken penumbra of the world. Her private desolation she now felt in communion with the other two women; they were all three abandoned, cut off, wounded, unwarmed, too impotent even to whimper. A vein of haze in the sky passingly dimmed the sunlight. When it brightened again, a tiny upright figure, male, in green and yellow chevron stripes, stood at the top of the cataracts of moguls.

"That took eighteen minutes," Alice said, consulting her wristwatch again. Caroline suddenly doubted that Norman, whose pajama bottoms rarely matched his tops, could fall for anyone so finicking.

The woman in the snow asked, "Does my hair look awful?"

Down, down the tiny figure came, enlarging, dipping from crest to crest, dragging a sled, a bit clumsily, between its legs. Then, hitting perhaps the same unfortunate patch of ice, the figure tipped, tripped, and became a dark star, spread-eagled, a cloud of powder from which protruded, with electric rapidity, fragments of ski, sled, and arm. This explosive somersault continued to the base of the steep section, where the fragments reassembled and lay still.

The women had watched with held breaths. The woman from Melrose moaned, "Oh dear God." Caroline discovered herself yearning, yearning with her numb belly, for their rescuer to stand. He did. The boy (he was close enough to be a boy, with lanky legs in his tight racing pants) scissored his skis above his head (miraculously, they had not popped off), hopped to his feet, jerkily sidestepped a few yards uphill to retrieve his hat (an Alpine of green felt, with ornamental breast feathers), and skated toward them, drenched with snow, dragging the sled and grinning.

"That was a real eggbeater," Alice told him, like one boy to another.

"Who's hurt?" he asked. His red ears protruded and his face swirled with freckles; he was so plainly delighted to be himself, so clearly somebody's cherished son, that Caroline had to smile.

And as if this clown had introduced into vacuity a fertilizing principle, more members of the ski patrol sprang from the snow, bearing blankets and bandages and brandy, so that Caroline and Alice were pushed aside from the position of rescuers. They retrieved their parkas, refastened their skis, and tamely completed their run to the foot of the mountain. There, Timmy and Norman, looking worried and guilty, were waiting beside the lift shed. Her momentum failing, Caroline Harris actually skated—what she had never managed to do before, lifted her skis in the smooth alternation of skating—in her haste to assure her husband of his innocence.

Plumbing

THE OLD PLUMBER bends forward tenderly, in the dusk of the cellar of my newly acquired house, to show me a precious, antique joint. "They haven't done them like this for thirty years," he tells me. His thin voice is like a trickle squeezed through rust. "Thirty, forty years. When I began with my father, we did them like this. It's an old lead joint. You wiped it on. You poured it hot with a ladle and held a wet rag in the other hand. There were sixteen motions you had to make before it cooled. Sixteen distinct motions. Otherwise you lost it and ruined the joint. You had to chip it away and begin again. That's how we had to do it when I started out. A boy of maybe fifteen, sixteen. This joint here could be fifty years old."

He knows my plumbing; I merely own it. He has known it through many owners. We think we are what we think and see when in truth we are upright bags of tripe. We think we have bought living space and a view when in truth we have bought a maze, a history, an archaeology of pipes and cut-ins and traps and valves. The plumber shows me some stout dark pipe that follows a diagonal course into the foundation wall. "See that line along the bottom there?" A line of white, a whisper of frosting on the dark pipe's underside—pallid oxidation. "Don't touch it. It'll start to bleed. See, they cast this old soil pipe in two halves. They were supposed to mount them so the seams were on the sides. But sometimes they got careless and mounted them so the seam is on the bottom." He demonstrates with cupped hands; his hands part so the crack between them widens. I strain to see between his dark palms and become by his metaphor water seeking the light. "Eventually, see, it leaks."

With his flashlight beam he follows the telltale pale line backward. "Four, five new sections should do it." He sighs, wheezes; his eyes open wider than other men's, from a life spent in cellars. He is a poet. Where I see only a flaw, a vexing imperfection that will cost me money, he gazes fondly, musing upon the eternal presences of corrosion and flow. He sends me magnificent ironical bills, wherein catalogues of tiny parts—

1 1¼″ x 1″ galv bushing	58¢
1 ⅜″ brass pet cock	90¢
3 ½″ blk nipple	23¢

—itemized with an accountancy so painstaking as to seem mad, are in the end belittled and swallowed by a torrential round figure attributed merely to "Labor":

Labor	$550

I suppose that his tender meditations with me now, even the long pauses when his large eyes blink, are Labor.

The old house, the house we left, a mile away, seems relieved to be rid of our furniture. The rooms where we lived, where we staged our meals and ceremonies and self-dramatizations and where some of us went from infancy to adolescence—rooms and stairways so imbued with our daily motions that their irregularities were bred into our bones and could be traversed in the dark—do not seem to mourn, as I'd imagined they would. The house exults in its sudden size, in the reach of its empty corners. Floorboards long muffled by carpets shine as if freshly varnished. Sun pours unobstructed through the curtainless windows. The house is young again. It, too, had a self, a life, which for a time was eclipsed by our lives; now, before its new owners come to burden it, it is free. Now only moonlight makes the floor creak. When, some mornings, I return, to retrieve a few final oddments—andirons, picture frames—the space of the house greets me with virginal impudence. Opening the front door is like opening the door to the cat who comes in with the morning milk, who mews in passing on his way to the beds still warm with our night's sleep, his routine so tenuously attached to ours, by a single mew and a shared roof. Nature is tougher than ecologists admit. Our house forgot us in a day.

I feel guilty that we occupied it so thinly, that a trio of movers and a day's breezes could so completely clean us out. When we moved in, a dozen years ago, I was surprised that the house, though its beams and fireplaces were three hundred years old, was not haunted. I had thought, it being so old, it would be. But an amateur witch my wife had known at college tapped the bedroom walls, sniffed the attic, and assured us—like my plumber, come to think of it, she had unnaturally distended eyes—

that the place was clean. Puritan hay-farmers had built it. In the nineteenth century, it may have served as a tavern; the pike to Newburyport ran right by. In the nineteen-thirties, it had been a tenement, the rooms now so exultantly large then subdivided by plasterboard partitions that holes were poked through, so the tenants could trade sugar and flour. Rural days, poor days. Chickens had been kept upstairs for a time; my children at first said that when it rained they could smell feathers, but I took this to be the power of suggestion, of myth. Digging in the back yard, we did unearth some pewter spoons and chunks of glass bottles from a lost era of packaging. Of ourselves, a few plastic practice golf balls in the iris and a few dusty little Superballs beneath the radiators will be all for others to find. The ghosts we have left only we can see.

I see a man in a tuxedo and a woman in a long white dress stepping around the back yard, in a cold drizzle that makes them laugh, at two o'clock on Easter morning. They are hiding chocolate eggs in tinfoil and are drunk. In the morning, they will have headaches, and children will wake them with the shrieks and quarrels of the hunt, and come to their parents' bed with chocolate-smeared mouths and sickening-sweet breaths; but it is the apparition of early morning I see, from the perspective of a sober conscience standing in the kitchen, these two partygoers tiptoeing in the muddy yard, around the forsythia bush, up to the swing set and back. Easter bunnies.

A man bends above a child's bed; his voice and a child's voice murmur prayers in unison. They have trouble with "trespasses" versus "debts," having attended different Sunday schools. Weary, slightly asthmatic (the ghost of chicken feathers?), anxious to return downstairs to a book and a drink, he passes into the next room. The child there, a bigger child, when he offers to bow his head with her, cries softly, "Daddy, no, don't!" The round white face, dim in the dusk of the evening, seems to glow with tension, embarrassment, appeal. Embarrassed himself, too easily embarrassed, he gives her a kiss, backs off, closes her bedroom door, leaves her to the darkness.

In the largest room, its walls now bare but for phantasmal rectangles where bookcases stood and pictures hung, people are talking, gesturing dramatically. The woman, the wife, throws something—it had been about to be an ashtray, but even in her fury, which makes her face rose-red, she prudently switched to a book. She bursts into tears, perhaps at her puritan inability to throw the ashtray, and runs into another room, not forgetting to hop over the little raised threshold where strangers to the house often trip. Children sneak quietly up and down the stairs, pale, guilty, blaming themselves, in the vaults of their innocent hearts, for this disruption. Even the dog curls her tail under, ashamed. The man sits slumped on a sofa that is no longer there. His ankles are together, his head is bowed, as if shackles restrict him. He is dramatizing his conception of himself, as a prisoner. It seems to be summer, for a little cabbage butterfly irrelevantly alights on the window screen, where hollyhocks rub and tap. The woman returns, pink in the face instead of red, and states matters in a formal, deliberate way; the man stands and shouts. She hits him; he knocks her arm away and punches her side, startled by how pleasant, how spongy, the sensation is. A sack of guts. They flounce among the furniture, which gets in their way, releasing whiffs of dust. The children edge one step higher on the stairs. The dog, hunched as if being whipped, goes to the screen door and begs to be let out. The man embraces the woman and murmurs. She is pink and warm with tears. He discovers himself weeping; what a good feeling it is!—like vomiting, like sweat. What are they saying, what are these violent, frightened people discussing? They are discussing change, natural process, the passage of time, death.

Feeble ghosts. They fade like breath on glass. In contrast I remember the potent, powerful, numinous Easter eggs of my childhood, filled solid with moist coconut, heavy as ingots, or else capacious like theatres, populated by paper silhouettes—miniature worlds generating their own sunlight. These eggs arose, in their nest of purple excelsior, that certain Sunday morning, from the same impossible-to-plumb well of mystery where the stars swam, and old photographs predating my birth were snapped, and God listened. At night, praying, I lay like a needle on the surface of this abyss, in a house haunted to the shadowy corners by Disneyesque menaces with clutching fingernails, in a town that boasted a funeral parlor at its main intersection and that was ringed all around its outskirts by barns blazoned with hex signs. On the front-parlor rug was a continent-shaped stain where as a baby I had vomited. Myth upon myth: now I am three or four, a hungry soul, eating dirt from one of the large parlor pots that hold strange ferns—feathery, cloudy, tropical presences. One of my grandmother's superstitions is that a child must eat a pound of dirt a year to grow strong. And then, later, at nine or ten, I am lying on my belly, in the same spot, reading the newspaper to my blind grandfather— first the obituaries, then the rural news, and lastly the front-page headlines about Japs and Roosevelt. The paper has a deep smell, not dank like the smell of comic books but fresher, less sweet than doughnut bags but spicy, an exciting smell that has the future in it, a smell of things stacked and crisp and faintly warm, the smell of the *new*. Each day, I realize, this smell arrives and fades. And then I am thirteen and saying goodbye to the front parlor. We are moving. Beside the continent-shaped stain on the carpet are the round depressions left by the fern flowerpots. The uncurtained sunlight on these tidy dents is a revelation. They are stamped deep, like dinosaur footprints.

Did my children sense the frivolity of our Easter priesthoods? The youngest used to lie in her bed in the smallest of the upstairs rooms and suck her thumb and stare past me at something in the dark. Our house, in her, did surely possess the dimension of dread that imprints every surface on the memory, that makes each scar on the paint a clue to some terrible depth. She was the only child who would talk about death. Tomorrow was her birthday. "I don't want to have a birthday. I don't want to be nine."

"But you must grow. Everybody grows. The trees grow."

"I don't want to."

"Don't you want to be a big girl like Judith?"

"No."

"Then you can wear lipstick, and a bra, and ride your bicycle even on Central Street."

"I don't want to ride on Central Street."

"Why not?"

"Because then I will get to be an old old lady and die."

And her tears well up, and the man with her is dumb, as all the men ever with her will be on this point dumb, in this little room where nothing remains of us but scuffmarks and a half-scraped Snoopy decal on the window frame. If we still lived here, it would be time to put the screens in the windows.

Crocuses are up at the old house; daffodils bloom at the new. The children who had lived in the new house before us left Superballs under the radiators for us to find. In the days of appraisal and purchase, we used to glimpse these children skulking around their house, behind bushes and banisters, gazing at us, the usurpers of their future. In the days after they moved out but before our furniture moved in, we played hilarious games in the empty rooms—huge comic ricochets and bounces. Soon the balls became lost again. The rooms became crowded. We had moved in.

Tenderly, musingly, the plumber shows me a sawed-off section of the pipe that leads from the well to our pressure tank. The inside diameter of the pipe is reduced to the size of his finger by mineral accretions—a circle of stony layers thin as rolled-up paper. It suggests a book seen endwise, but one of those books not meant to be opened, that priests wisely kept locked. "See," he says, "this has built up over forty, fifty years. I remember my dad and me putting in the pump, but this pipe was here then. Nothing you can do about it, minerals in the water. Nothing you can do about it but dig it up and replace it with inch-and-a-quarter, inch-and-a-half new."

I imagine my lawn torn up, the great golden backhoe trampling my daffodils, my dollars flooding away. Ineffectually, I protest.

The plumber sighs, as poets do, with an eye on the audience. "See, keep on with it like this, you'll burn out your new pump. It has to work too hard to draw the water. Replace it now, you'll never have to worry with it again. It'll outlast your time here."

My time, his time. His eyes open wide in the unspeaking presences of corrosion and flow. We push out through the bulkhead; a blinding piece of sky slides into place above us, fitted with temporary, timeless clouds. All around us, we are outlasted.

The Orphaned Swimming Pool

MARRIAGES, like chemical unions, release upon dissolution packets of the energy locked up in their bonding. There is the piano no one wants, the cocker spaniel no one can take care of. Shelves of books suddenly stand revealed as burdensomely dated and unlikely to be reread; indeed, it is difficult to remember who read them in the first place. And what of those old skis in the attic? Or the doll house waiting to be repaired in the basement? The piano goes out of tune, the dog goes mad. The summer that the Turners got their divorce, their swimming pool had neither a master nor a mistress, though the sun beat down day after day, and a state of drought was declared in Connecticut.

It was a young pool, only two years old, of the fragile type fashioned by laying a plastic liner within a carefully carved hole in the ground. The Turners' side yard looked infernal while it was being done; one bulldozer sank into the mud and had to be pulled free by another. But by midsummer the new grass was sprouting, the encircling flagstones were in place, the blue plastic tinted the water a heavenly blue, and it had to be admitted that the Turners had scored again. They were always a little in advance of their friends. He was a tall, hairy-backed man with long arms, and a nose flattened by football, and a sullen look of too much blood; she was a fine-boned blonde with dry blue eyes and lips usually held parted and crinkled as if about to ask a worrisome, or whimsical, question. They never seemed happier, nor their marriage healthier, than those two summers. They grew brown and supple and smooth with swimming. Brad would begin his day with a swim, before dressing to catch the train, and Linda would hold court all day amid crowds of wet matrons and children, and Brad would return from work to find a poolside cocktail party in progress, and the couple would end their day at eleven, when their friends had finally left, by swimming nude, before bed. What ecstasy!

In darkness the water felt mild as milk and buoyant as helium, and the swimmers became giants, gliding from side to side in a single languorous stroke.

In May of the third summer, the pool was filled as usual, and the usual after-school gangs of mothers and children gathered, but Linda, unlike her, stayed indoors. She could be heard within the house, moving from room to room, but she no longer emerged, as in other years, with a cheerful tray of ice and a brace of bottles, and Triscuits and lemonade for the children. Their friends felt less comfortable about appearing, towels in hand, at the Turners' on weekends. Though Linda had lost some weight and looked elegant, and Brad was cumbersomely jovial, they gave off the faint, sleepless, awkward-making aroma of a couple in trouble. Then, the day after school was out, Linda fled with the children to her parents in Ohio. Brad stayed nights in the city, and the pool was deserted. Though the pump that ran the water through the filter continued to mutter in the lilacs, the cerulean pool grew cloudy. The bodies of dead horseflies and wasps dotted the still surface. A speckled plastic ball drifted into a corner beside the diving board and stayed there. The grass between the flagstones grew lank. On the glass-topped poolside table, a spray can of Off! had lost its pressure and a gin-and-tonic glass held a sere mint leaf. The pool looked desolate and haunted, like a stagnant jungle spring; it looked poisonous and ashamed. The postman, stuffing overdue notices and unanswered solicitations into the mailbox, averted his eyes from the side yard politely.

Some June weekends, Brad sneaked out from the city. Families driving to church glimpsed him dolefully sprinkling chemical substances into the pool. He looked pale and thin. He instructed Roscoe Chace, his neighbor on the left, how to switch on the pump and change the filter, and how much chlorine and Algitrol should be added weekly. He explained he would not be able to make it out every weekend—as if the distance that for years he had travelled twice each day, gliding in and out of New York, had become an impossibly steep climb back into the past. Linda, he confided vaguely, had left her parents in Akron and was visiting her sister in Minneapolis. As the shock of the Turners' joint disappearance wore off, their pool seemed less haunted and forbidding. The Murtaugh children— the Murtaughs, a rowdy, numerous family, were the Turners' right-hand neighbors—began to use it, without supervision. So Linda's old friends, with their children, began to show up, "to keep the Murtaughs from drowning each other." For, if anything were to happen to a Murtaugh, the poor Turners (the adjective had become automatic) would be sued for everything, right when they could least afford it. It became, then, a kind of duty, a test of loyalty, to use the pool.

July was the hottest in twenty-seven years. People brought their own lawn furniture over in station wagons and set it up. Teen-age offspring and Swiss *au-pair* girls were established as lifeguards. A nylon rope with flotation corks, meant to divide the wading end from the diving end of the pool, was found coiled in the garage and reinstalled. Agnes Kleefield contributed an old refrigerator, which was plugged into an outlet beside the garage door and used to store ice, quinine water, and soft drinks. An honor-system shoebox containing change appeared upon it; a little lost-and-found—an array of forgotten sunglasses, flippers, towels, lotions, paperbacks, shirts, even underwear—materialized on the Turners' side steps. When people, that July, said, "Meet you at the pool," they did not mean the public pool past the shopping center, or the country-club pool near the first tee. They meant the Turners'. Restrictions on admission were difficult to enforce tactfully. A visiting Methodist bishop, two Taiwanese economists, an entire girls' softball team from Darien, an eminent Canadian poet, the archery champion of Hartford, the six members of a black rock group called The Good Intentions, an ex-mistress of Aly Khan, the lavender-haired mother-in-law of a Nixon adviser not quite of Cabinet rank, an infant of six weeks, a man who was killed the next day on the Merritt Parkway, a Filipino who could stay on the pool bottom for eighty seconds, two Texans who kept cigars in their mouths and hats on their heads, three telephone linemen, four expatriate Czechs, a student Maoist from Wesleyan, and the postman all swam, as guests, in the Turners' pool, though not all at once. After the daytime crowd ebbed, and the shoebox was put back in the refrigerator, and the last *au-pair* girl took the last goosefleshed, wrinkled child shivering home to supper, there was a tide of evening activity, trysts (Mrs. Kleefield and the Nicholson boy, most notoriously) and what some called, overdramatically, orgies. True, late splashes and excited guffaws did often keep Mrs. Chace awake, and the Murtaugh children spent hours at their attic window with binoculars. And there was the evidence of the lost underwear.

One Saturday early in August, the morning arrivals found an unknown car with New York plates parked in the driveway. But cars of all sorts were so common—the parking tangle frequently extended into the road—that nothing much was thought of it, even when someone noticed that the bedroom windows upstairs were open. And nothing came of it, except that around suppertime, in the lull before the evening crowd began to arrive in force, Brad and an unknown woman, of the same physical type as Linda but brunette, swiftly exited from the kitchen door, got into her car, and drove back to New York. The few lingering baby-sitters and beaux thus unwittingly glimpsed the root of the divorce. The two lovers had been trapped inside the house all day; Brad was fearful of the legal consequences of their being seen by anyone who might write and tell Linda. The settlement was at a ticklish stage; nothing less than terror of Linda's lawyers would have led Brad to suppress his indignation at seeing, from behind the window screen, his private pool turned public carnival. For long thereafter, though in the end he did not marry the woman, he remembered that day when they lived together like fugitives in a cave, feeding on love and ice water, tiptoeing barefoot to the depleted cupboards, which they, arriving late last night, had hoped to stock in the morning, not foreseeing the onslaught of interlopers that would pin them in. Her hair, he remembered, had tickled his shoulders as she crouched behind him at the window, and through the angry pounding of his own blood he had felt her slim body breathless with the attempt not to giggle.

August drew in, with cloudy days. Children grew bored with swimming. Roscoe Chace went on vacation to Italy; the pump broke down, and no one repaired it. Dead dragonflies accumulated on the surface of the pool. Small deluded toads hopped in and swam around and around hopelessly. Linda at last returned. From Minneapolis she had gone on to Idaho for six weeks, to be divorced. She and the children had tan faces from riding and hiking; her lips looked drier and more quizzical than ever, still seeking to frame that troubling question. She stood at the window, in the house that already seemed to lack its furniture, at the same side window where the lovers had crouched, and gazed at the deserted pool. The grass around it was green from splashing, save where a long-lying towel had smothered a rectangle and left it brown. Aluminum furniture she didn't recognize lay strewn and broken. She counted a dozen bottles beneath the glass-topped table. The nylon divider had parted, and its two halves floated independently. The blue plastic beneath the colorless water tried to make a cheerful, otherworldly statement, but Linda saw that the pool in truth had no bottom, it held bottomless loss, it was one huge blue tear. Thank God no one had drowned in it. Except her. She saw that she could never live here again. In September the place was sold, to a family with toddling infants, who for safety's sake have not only drained the pool but sealed it over with iron pipes and a heavy mesh, and put warning signs around, as around a chained dog.

When Everyone Was Pregnant

I'M IN SECURITIES, but I read a lot, on the train. Read yesterday that the Fifties were coming back. All through the Sixties writers kept knocking them: Eisenhower, Lester Lanin, skirts below the knee, ho-hum. Well, turns out Eisenhower was a great antiwar President. Rock is dead. Skirts have dropped to the ankle. But *my* Fifties won't come back.

Kind years to me. Entered them poor and left them comfortable. Entered them chaste and left them a father. Of four and a miscarriage. Those the years when everyone was pregnant. Not only kind years but beautiful ones.

How they would float across the sand like billowed sails. My wife and the wives of our friends. Shakespeare, Titania to Oberon: "We have laughed to see the sails conceive, / And grow big-bellied with the wanton wind." In their sun-paled plaid maternity bathing suits, the pregnant young women. Tugging behind them the toddlers already born, like dinghies. We moved out of Boston to a town with a beach in '55: my first promotion, Nancy's second childbirth.

Coming along the water's edge, heads higher than the line of the sea. The horizon blue, sparkling, severe. Proust and the "little band" at Balbec. Yet more fully in flower than those, bellies swollen stately. Faces and limbs freckled in every hollow, burnished on the ball of the shoulder, the tip of the nose. Sunburned nostril-wings, peeling. The light in their eyes stealing sparkle from the far hard edge of the sea. Where a few sails showed, leaning, curling.

They would come up to us, joining us. Laughter, lightweight folding beach chairs, towels, infant sunhats, baby-food jars, thermoses chuckling in the straw hampers. Above me, edge of maternity skirt lifted by touch of wind, curl of pubic hair high inside thigh showed. Sickening sensation of love. Sand-warmed wind blowing cool out of the future.

They would settle with us, forming a ring. Their heads inward with gossip, their bare legs spokes of a wheel. On the rim, children with sand pails each digging by the feet of his own mother. The shades of sand darkening as they dug. The milk smell of sun lotion. The way our words drifted up and out: sandwich wrappers blowing.

Katharine, Sarah, Liz, Peggy, Angela, June. Notes of a scale, colors of a rainbow. Nancy the seventh. Now, in the Seventies, two have moved. To Denver, to Birmingham. Two are divorced. Two still among us with their husbands. But all are gone, receding. Can never be revisited, that time when everyone was pregnant. And proud of it.

Our fat Fifties cars, how we loved them, revved them: no thought of pollution. Exhaust smoke, cigarette smoke, factory smoke: part of life. Romance of consumption at its height. Shopping for baby food in the gaudy arrays of the supermarkets. Purchasing power: young, newly powerful, born to consume, to procreate. A smug conviction that the world was doomed. Beyond the sparkling horizon, an absolute enemy. Above us, bombs whose flash would fill the scene like a cup to overflowing. Who could blame us, living when we could?

Old slides. June's husband had a Kodak with a flash attachment (nobody owned Japanese cameras then). How young we were. The men scrawny as boys. Laughable military haircuts: the pea-brain look. The women with bangs and harshly lipsticked smiles. We look drunk. Sometimes we were.

Jobs, houses, spouses of our own. Permission to drink and change diapers and operate power mowers and stay up past midnight. At college Nancy had not been allowed to smoke upstairs, made herself do it in our home. Like a sexual practice personally distasteful but recommended by Van der Velde. Dreadful freedom: phrase fashionable then.

Had we expected to starve in the Depression? Be bayonetted by Japs when they invaded California? Korea seemed the best bargain we could strike: extremities of superpowers tactfully clashing in distant cold mud. The world's skin of fear shivered but held. Then came Eisenhower who gave us the *status quo ante* and a sluggishly rising market and a (revocable) license to have fun, to make babies. Viewed the world through two lenses since discarded: fear and gratitude. Young people now are many things, but they aren't afraid and aren't grateful.

Those summer parties. Should remember them better. Sunlight in the gin, the sprig of mint wilting. The smell of grass freshly mowed coming in through the evening screens. Children wandering in and out with complaints their mothers brushed away like cigarette smoke. What were we saying? The words we spoke were nonsense, except the breath we took to speak them was life—us alive, able.

Katharine's husband Jerry had only one eye, the other frosted by a childhood accident. No one felt sorry for him—too healthy, hearty. Born salesman. Jerry saying across to Sarah Harris, she pregnant in a big-flowered dress, sitting dreaming in a plush wing chair, "Sarah, sitting there you look just like a voluptuous big piece of wallpaper!" I thought, *has only one eye, everything looks flat to him.*

Years later I said to Sarah, "You voluptuous piece of wallpaper you," but she had forgotten and I had to explain.

Another night, my flat tire in the Connellys' newly gravelled driveway. Sharp bluestones. Two in the morning. Ed, a mass-going Catholic, came up out of his cellar holding high a cruciform lug wrench chanting "Veni Creator Spiritus." Shocked me. My own footsteps on the gravel, *unch, unch:* a monster coming closer. Most of us at least sent the kids to Sunday school.

Dancing. Hand squeezes. Moonlight songs, smoke getting in your eyes. All innocent enough. The bump, bump of pregnant bellies against me. Seeing each other's names in the Births column of the local paper a private joke. Hospital visits, wifeless nights. The time our fourth was born, night after the first storm of winter. Gynecologist swung by for her in his car on the way to the hospital. Just starting up practice, handsome man in ski hat. On the stark white empty street below our window looked like a lover tossing pebbles. Her contractions coming every three minutes, her little suitcase packed, hurrying from room to room kissing the children in their sleep. Gynecologist waiting, his face turned upward in the moonlight, in the silence. A lover howling.

Nervous of the creaking wind, I slept one or two of those nights with a golf club in the bed. I think a seven iron. Figured I could get it around on a burglar quicker than a wood.

The time Sarah was with me. Nancy off in the hospital with varicose veins. Diagnosis: no more babies. Our last baby cried. Sarah rose and mothered it. Child went silent, laughed, knew something was funny, maybe thought Sarah was Nancy making a face, pretending something. Same smell, woman smell. Panes of moonlight on Sarah's naked back, bent over crib. Baby gurgled and laughed. "Crazy kid you have here," she said, flipping her hair back in coming back to me. Too much love. Too many babies, breathing all over the dark house like searchlights that might switch on.

Sarah's lovely wide shoulders, big hips, breasts shallow and firm. First time I saw them it tore at me; I told her she had breasts like a Greek statue. She laughed and told me I read too much. But it had been torn out of me.

The ritual of taking out Nancy's hairpins one by one before making love. The sound they made on the bedside table, like rain on the roof. Fifties a house decade, we stayed off the streets. Cuba, Sputnik, Tibet: rain on the roof.

The brown line on her belly a woman brings back from the hospital, after being pregnant. Nobody had ever told me that line existed. Why hadn't they?

The babies got bigger. The parties got wilder. Time at the beach, after civil-rights dance, hot summer, must have been Sixties. We took off our clothes and swam. Scary tide, strong moon, could see the women had aged. Slack bellies, knees and faces full of shadow. Used their long formal dance dresses as towels. In the newspapers, riots. Assassinations, protests, a decade's overdue bills heaped like surf thunder on the sand bar. We were no longer young. Embarrassed, we groped for our underclothes and shoes. Yet still the warm kiss of wind off of the sand, even at night.

I make these notes on the train. My hand shakes. My town slides by, the other comfortable small towns, the pastures and glimpses of sea. A single horse galloping. A golf course with a dawn foursome frozen on the green, dew-white. And then the lesser cities, the little one-hotel disgruntled cities, black walls hurled like fists at our windows, broken factory windows, a rusted drawbridge halted forever at almost-down, a gravel yard with bluestones pyramided by size, a dump smoldering, trash in all the colors of jewels; then the metropolis, the tracks multiplying as swiftly as products in a calculator, the hazed skyscrapers changing relationship to one another like the steeples in Proust, the tunnels of billboards, the station, vast and derelict; the final stop. This evening, the same thing backward.

But never get bored with how the train slices straight, lightly rocking, through intersections of warning bells dinging, past playgrounds and back yards, warehouses built on a bias to fit the right-of-way. Like time: cuts through everything, keeps going.

Notes not come to anything. Lives not come to anything. Life a common stock that fluctuates in value. But you cannot sell, you must hold, hold till it dips to nothing. The big boys sell you out.

Edgar to blinded Gloucester: Ripeness is all. Have never exactly understood. Ripeness is all that is left? Or ripeness is all that matters? Encloses all, answers all, justifies all. Ripeness is God.

Now: our babies drive cars, push pot, shave, menstruate, riot for peace, eat macrobiotic. Wonderful in many ways, but not ours, never ours, we see now. Now: we go to a party and see only enemies. All the shared years have made us wary, survival-conscious. Sarah looks away. Spokes of the wheel are missing. Our babies accuse us. Treated them like bonuses, flourishes added to our happiness.

Did the Fifties exist? Voluptuous wallpaper. Crazy kid. Sickening sensation of love. The train slides forward. The decades slide seaward, taking us along. Still afraid. Still grateful.

Eros Rampant

THE MAPLES' HOUSE is full of love. Bean, the six-year-old baby, loves Hecuba, the dog. John, who is eight, an angel-faced mystic serenely unable to ride a bicycle or read a clock, is in love with his Creepy Crawlers, his monster cards, his dinosaurs, and his carved rhinoceros from Kenya. He spends hours in his room after school drifting among these things, rearranging, gloating, humming. He experiences pain only when his older brother, Richard Jr., sardonically enters his room and pierces his placenta of contentment. Richard is in love with life, with all outdoors, with Carl Yastrzemski, Babe Parelli, the Boston Bruins, the Beatles, and with that shifty apparition who, comb in hand, peeps back shiny-eyed at him out of the mirror in the mornings, wearing a mustache of toothpaste. He receives strange challenging notes from girls—*Dickie Maple you stop looking at me*—which he brings home from school carelessly crumpled along with his spelling papers and hectographed notices about eye, tooth, and lung inspection. His feelings about young Mrs. Brice, who confronts his section of the fifth grade with the enamelled poise and studio diction of an airline hostess, are so guarded as to be suspicious. He almost certainly loves, has always deeply loved, his older sister, Judith. Verging on thirteen, she has become difficult to contain, even within an incestuous passion. Large and bumptious, she eclipses his view of the television screen, loudly Frugs while he would listen to the Beatles, teases, thrashes, is bombarded and jogged by powerful rays from outer space. She hangs for hours by the corner where Mr. Lunt, her history teacher, lives; she pastes effigies of the Monkees on her walls, French-kisses her mother good night, experiences the panic of sleeplessness, engages in long languorous tussles on the sofa with the dog. Hecuba, a spayed golden retriever, races from room to room, tormented as if by fleas by the itch for adoration, ears flattened, tail thumping, until at last she runs up against the cats, who do not love her, and she drops exhausted, in grateful defeat, on the kitchen linoleum, and sleeps.

The cats, Esther and Esau, lick each other's fur and share a bowl. They had been two of a litter. Esther, the mother of more than thirty kittens mostly resembling her brother, but with a persistent black minority vindicating the howled appeal of a neighboring tom, has been "fixed"; Esau, sentimentally allowed to continue unfixed, now must venture from the house in quest of the bliss that had once been purely domestic. He returns scratched and battered. Esther licks his wounds while he leans dazed beside the refrigerator; even his purr is ragged. Nagging for their supper, they sit like bookends, their backs discreetly touching, an expert old married couple on the dole. One feels, unexpectedly, that Esau still loves Esther, while she merely accepts him. She seems scornful of his Platonic attentions. Is she puzzled by her abrupt surgical lack of what once drastically attracted him? But it is his big square tomcat's head that seems puzzled, rather than her triangular feminine feline one. The children feel a difference; both Bean and John cuddle Esau more, now that Esther is sterile. Perhaps, obscurely, they feel that she has deprived them of a miracle, of the semiannual miracle of her kittens, of drowned miniature piglets wriggling alive from a black orifice more mysterious than a cave. Richard Jr., as if to demonstrate his superior purchase on manhood and its righteous compassion, makes a point of petting the two cats equally, stroke for stroke. Judith claims she hates them both; it is her chore to feed them supper, and she hates the smell of horsemeat. She loves, at least in the abstract, horses.

Mr. Maple loves Mrs. Maple. He goes through troublesome periods, often on Saturday afternoons, of being unable to take his eyes from her, of being captive to the absurd persuasion that the curve of her solid haunch conceals, enwraps, a precarious treasure confided to his care. He cannot touch her enough. The sight of her body contorted by one of her yoga exercises, in her elastic black leotard riddled with runs, twists his heart so that he cannot breathe. Her gesture as she tips the dregs of white wine into a potted geranium seems infinite, like one of Vermeer's moments frozen in an eternal light from the left. At night he tries to press her into himself, to secure her drowsy body against his breast like a clasp, as if without it he will come undone. He cannot sleep in this position, yet maintains it long after her breathing has become steady and oblivious: can love be defined, simply, as the refusal to sleep? Also he loves Penelope Vogel, a quaint little secretary at his office who is recovering from a disastrous affair with an Antiguan; and he is in love with the memories of six or so other females, beginning with a seven-year-old playmate who used to steal his hunter's cap; and is half in love with death. He as well seems to love, perhaps alone in the nation, President Johnson, who is unaware of his existence. Along the same lines, Richard adores the moon; he studies avidly all the photographs beamed back from its uncongenial surface.

And Joan? Whom does she love? Her psychiatrist, certainly. Her father, inevitably. Her yoga instructor, probably. She has a part-time job in a museum and returns home flushed and quick-tongued, as if from sex. She must love the children, for they flock to her like sparrows to suet. They fight bitterly for a piece of her lap and turn their backs upon their father, as if he, the seed-bearing provider of their lives, were a grotesque intruder, a chimney sweep in a snow palace. None of his impersonations with the children—scoutmaster, playmate, confidant, financial bastion, factual wizard, watchman of the night—win them over; Bean still cries for Mommy when hurt, John approaches her for the money to finance yet more monster cards, Dickie demands that hers be the last good night, and even Judith, who should be his, kisses him timidly, and saves her open-mouthed passion for her mother. Joan swims through their love like a fish through water, ignorant of any other element. Love slows her footsteps, pours upon her from the radio, hangs about her, in the kitchen, in the form of tacked-up children's drawings of houses, families, cars, cats, dogs, and flowers. Her husband cannot reach her: she is solid but hidden, like the World Bank; presiding yet impartial, like the federal judiciary. Some cold uncoördinated thing pushes at his hand as it hangs impotent; it is Hecuba's nose. Obese spayed golden-eyed bitch, like him she abhors exclusion and strains to add her warmth to the tumble, in love with them all, in love with the smell of food, in love with the smell of love.

Penelope Vogel takes care to speak without sentimentality; six years younger than Richard, she has endured a decade of amorous ordeals and, still single at twenty-nine, preserves herself by speaking dryly, in the flip phrases of a still-younger generation.

"We had a good thing," she says of her Antiguan, "that became a bad scene."

She handles, verbally, her old affairs like dried flowers; sitting across the restaurant table from her, Richard is made jittery by her delicacy, as if he and a grandmother are together examining an array of brittle, enigmatic mementos. "A very undesirable scene," Penelope adds. "The big time was too much for him. He got in with the drugs crowd. I couldn't see it."

"He wanted to marry you?" Richard asks timidly; this much is office gossip.

She shrugs, admitting, "There was that pitch."

"You must miss him."

"There is that. He was the most beautiful man I ever saw. His shoulders. In Dickinson's Bay, he'd have me put my hand on his shoulder in the water and that way he'd pull me along for miles, swimming. He was a snorkel instructor."

"His name?" Jittery, fearful of jarring these reminiscences, which are also negotiations, he spills the last of his Gibson, and jerkily signals to order another.

"Hubert," Penelope says. She is patiently mopping with her napkin. "Like a girlfriend told me, Never take on a male beauty, you'll have to fight for the mirror." Her face is small and very white, and her nose very long, her pink nostrils inflamed by a perpetual cold. Only a Negro, Richard thinks, could find her beautiful; the thought gives her, in the restless shadowy restaurant light, beauty. The waiter, black, comes and changes their tablecloth. Penelope continues so softly Richard must strain to hear, "When Hubert was eighteen he had a woman divorce her husband and leave her children for him. She was one of the old planter families. He wouldn't marry her. He told me, If she'd do that to him, next thing she'd leave me. He was very moralistic, until he came up here. But imagine an eighteen-year-old boy having an effect like that on a mature married woman in her thirties."

"I better keep him away from my wife," Richard jokes.

"Yeah." She does not smile. "They *work* at it, you know. Those boys are *pros*."

Penelope has often been to the West Indies. In St. Croix, it delicately emerges, there was Andrew, with his goatee and his septic-tank business and his political ambitions; in Guadeloupe, there was Ramon, a customs inspector; in Trinidad, Castlereigh, who played the alto pans in a steel band and also did the limbo. He could go down to nine inches. But Hubert was the worst, or best. He was the only one who had followed her north. "I was supposed to come live with him in this hotel in Jamaica Plain but I was scared to go near the place, full of cop-out types and the smell of pot in the elevator; I got two offers from guys just standing there pushing the Up button. It was not a healthy scene." The waiter brings them rolls; in his shadow her profile seems wan and he yearns to pluck her, pale flower, from the tangle she has conjured. "It got so bad," she says, "I tried going back to an old boyfriend, an awfully nice guy with a mother and a nervous stomach. He's a computer systems analyst, very dedicated, but I don't know, he just never impressed me. All he can talk about is his gastritis and how she keeps telling him to move out and get a wife, but he doesn't know if she means it. His mother."

"He is . . . white?"

Penelope glances up; there is a glint off her halted butter knife. Her voice slows, goes drier. "No, as a matter of fact. He's what they call an Afro-American. You mind?"

"No, no, I was just wondering—his nervous stomach. He doesn't sound like the others."

"He's not. Like I say, he doesn't impress me. Don't you find, once you have something that works, it's hard to back up?" More seems meant than is stated; her level gaze, as she munches her thickly buttered bun, feels like one tangent in a complicated geometrical problem: find the point at which she had switched from white to black lovers.

The subject is changed for him; his heart jars, and he leans forward hastily to say, "See that woman who just came in? Leather suit, gypsy earrings, sitting down now? Her name is Eleanor Dennis. She lives down our street from us. She's divorced."

"Who's the man?"

"I have no idea. Eleanor's moved out of our circle. He looks like a real thug." Along the far wall, Eleanor adjusts the great loop of her earring; her sideways glance, in the shuffle of shadows, flicks past his table. He doubts that she saw him.

Penelope says, "From the look on your face, that was more than a circle she was in with you."

He pretends to be disarmed by her guess, but in truth considers it providential that one of his own old loves should appear, to countervail the dark torrent of hers. For the rest of the meal they talk about *him*, him and Eleanor and Marlene Brossman and Joan and the little girl who used to steal his hunter's cap. In the lobby of Penelope's apartment house, the elevator summoned, he offers to go up with her.

She says carefully, "I don't think you want to."

"But I *do*." The building is Back Bay modern; the lobby is garishly lit and furnished with plastic plants that need never be watered, Naugahyde chairs that were never sat upon, and tessellated plaques no one ever looks at. The light is an absolute presence, as even and clean as the light inside a freezer, as ubiquitous as ether or as the libido that, Freud says, permeates us all from infancy on.

"No," Penelope repeats. "I've developed a good ear for sincerity in these things, I think you're too wrapped up back home."

"The dog likes me," he confesses, and kisses her good night there, encased in brightness. Dry voice to the contrary, her lips are shockingly soft, wide, warm, and sorrowing.

"So," Joan says to him. "You slept with that little office mouse." It is Saturday; the formless erotic suspense of the afternoon—the tennis games, the cartoon matinees—has passed. The Maples are in their room dressing for a party, by the ashen light of dusk, and the watery blue of a distant streetlamp.

"I never have," he says, thereby admitting, however, that he knows who she means.

"Well, you took her to dinner."

"Who says?"

"Mack Dennis. Eleanor saw the two of you in a restaurant."

"When do the Dennises converse? I thought they were divorced."

"They talk all the time. He's still in love with her. Everybody knows that."

"O.K. When do he and *you* converse?"

Oddly, she has not prepared an answer. "Oh"—his heart falls through her silence—"maybe I saw him in the hardware store this afternoon."

"And maybe you didn't. Why would he blurt this out anyway? You and he must be on cozy terms."

He says this to trigger her denial; but she mutely considers and, sauntering toward her closet, admits, "We understand each other."

How unlike her, to bluff this way. "When was I supposedly seen?"

"You mean it happens often? Last Wednesday, around eight-thirty. You *must* have slept with her."

"I couldn't have. I was home by ten, you may remember. You had just gotten back yourself from the museum."

"What went wrong, darley? Did you offend her with your horrible pro-Vietnam stand?"

In the dim light he hardly knows this woman, her broken gestures, her hasty voice. Her silver slip glows and crackles as she wriggles into a black knit cocktail dress; with a kind of determined agitation she paces around the bed, to the bureau and back. As she moves, her body seems to be gathering bulk from the shadows, bulk and a dynamic elasticity. He tries to placate her with a token offering of truth. "No, it turns out Penelope only goes with Negroes. I'm too pale for her."

"You admit you tried?"

He nods.

"Well," Joan says, and takes a half-step toward him, so that he flinches in anticipation of being hit, "do you want to know who *I* was sleeping with Wednesday?"

He nods again, but the two nods feel different, as if a continent had hurtled by between them, at this terrific unfelt speed.

She names a man he knows only slightly, an assistant director in the museum, who wears a collar pin and has his gray hair cut long and tucked back in the foppish English style. "It was *fun*," Joan says, kicking at a shoe. "He thinks I'm *beau*tiful. He cares for me in a way you just *don't*." She kicks away the other shoe. "You look pale to me too, buster."

Stunned, he needs to laugh. "But we *all* think you're beautiful."

"Well, you don't make me *feel* it."

"*I* feel it," he says.

"You make me feel like an ugly drudge." As they grope to understand their new positions, they realize that she, like a chess player who has impulsively swept forward her queen, has nowhere to go but on the defensive. In a desperate attempt to keep the initiative, she says, "Divorce me. Beat me."

He is calm, factual, admirable. "How often have you been with him?"

"I don't know. Since April, off and on." Her hands appear to embarrass her; she places them at her sides, against her cheeks, together on the bedpost, off. "I've been trying to get out of it, I've felt horribly guilty, but he's never been at all pushy, so I could never really arrange a fight. He gets this hurt look."

"Do you want to keep him?"

"With you knowing? Don't be grotesque."

"But he cares for you in a way I just don't."

"Any lover does that."

"God help us. You're an expert."

"Hardly."

"What *about* you and Mack?"

She is frightened. "Years ago. Not for very long."

"And Freddy Vetter?"

"No, we agreed not. He knew about me and Mack."

Love, a cloudy heavy ink, inundates him from within, suffuses his palms with tingling pressure as he steps close to her, her murky face held tense against the expectation of a blow. "You whore," he breathes, enraptured. "My virgin bride." He kisses her hands; they are corrupt and cold. "Who else?" he begs, as if each name is a burden of treasure she lays upon his bowed shoulders. "Tell me all your men."

"I've told you. It's a pretty austere list. You know *why* I told you? So you wouldn't feel guilty about this Vogel person."

"But nothing happened. When you do it, it happens."

"Sweetie, I'm a woman," she explains, and they do seem, in this darkening room above the muted hubbub of television, to have reverted to the bases of their marriage, to the elemental constituents. Woman. Man. House.

"What does your psychiatrist say about all this?"

"Not much." The triumphant swell of her confession has passed; her ebbed manner prepares for days, weeks of his questions. She retrieves the shoes she kicked away. "That's one of the reasons I went to him, I kept having these affairs—"

"*Kept* having? You're killing me."

"Please don't interrupt. It was somehow very innocent. I'd go into his office, and lie down, and say, 'I've just been with Mack, or Otto—' "

"Otto. What's that joke? 'Otto' spelled backwards is 'Otto.' 'Otto' spelled inside out is 'toot.' "

"—and I'd say it was wonderful, or awful, or so-so, and then we'd talk about my childhood masturbation. It's not his business to scold me, it's his job to get me to stop scolding myself."

"The poor bastard, all the time I've been jealous of him, and he's been suffering with this for years; he had to listen every *day*. You'd go in there and plunk yourself still warm down on his couch—"

"It wasn't every day at all. Weeks would go by. I'm not Otto's only woman."

The artificial tumult of television below merges with a real commotion, a screaming and bumping that mounts the stairs and threatens the aquarium where the Maples are swimming, dark fish in ink, their outlines barely visible, known to each other only as eddies of warmth, as mysterious animate chasms in the surface of space. Fearing that for years he will not again be so close to Joan, or she be so open, he hurriedly asks, "And what about the yoga instructor?"

"Don't be silly," Joan says, clasping her pearls at the nape of her neck. "He's an elderly vegetarian."

The door crashes open; their bedroom explodes in shards of electric light. Richard Jr. is frantic, sobbing.

"Mommy, Judy keeps *teasing* me and getting in front of the *tele*vision!"

"I did not. I did not." Judith speaks very distinctly. "Mother and Father, he is a retarded liar."

"She can't help she's growing," Richard tells his son, picturing poor Judith trying to fit herself among the intent childish silhouettes in the little television room, pitying her for her size, much as he pities Johnson for his Presidency. Bean bursts into the bedroom, frightened by violence not on TV, and Hecuba leaps upon the bed with rolling golden eyes, and Judith gives Dickie an impudent and unrepentant sideways glance, and he, gagging on a surfeit of emotion, bolts from the room. Soon there arises from the other end of the upstairs an anguished squawk as Dickie invades John's room and punctures his communion with his dinosaurs. Downstairs, a woman, neglected and alone, locked in a box, sings about *amore*. Bean hugs Joan's legs so she cannot move.

Judith asks with parental sharpness, "What were you two talking about?"

"Nothing," Richard says. "We were getting dressed."

"Why were all the lights out?"

"We were saving electricity," her father tells her.

"Why is Mommy crying?" He looks, disbelieving, and discovers that, indeed, her cheeks coated with silver, she is.

At the party, amid clouds of friends and smoke, Richard resists being parted from his wife's side. She has dried her tears, and faintly swaggers, as when, on the beach, she dares wear a bikini. But her nakedness is only in his eyes. Her head beside his shoulder, her grave polite pleasantries, the plump unrepentant cleft between her breasts, all seem newly treasurable and intrinsic to his own identity. As a cuckold, he has grown taller, attenuated, more elegant and humane in his opinions, airier and more mobile. When the usual argument about Vietnam commences, he hears himself sounding like a dove. He concedes that Johnson is unlovable. He allows that Asia is infinitely complex, devious, ungrateful, feminine: but must we abandon her therefore? When Mack Dennis, grown burly in bachelorhood, comes and asks Joan to dance, Richard feels unmanned and sits on the sofa with such an air of weariness that Marlene Brossman sits down beside him and, for the first time in years, flirts. He tries to tell her with his voice, beneath the meaningless words he is speaking, that he loved her, and could love her again, but that at the moment he is terribly distracted and must be excused. He goes and asks Joan if it isn't time to go. She resists: "It's too rude." She is safe here among social proprieties and foresees that his exploitation of the territory she has surrendered will be thorough. Love is pitiless. They drive home at midnight under a slim moon nothing like its photographs—shadow-caped canyons, gimlet mountain ranges, gritty circular depressions around the metal feet of the mechanical intruder sent from the blue ball in the sky.

They do not rest until he has elicited from her a world of details: dates, sites, motel interiors, precisely mixed emotions. They make love, self-critically. He exacts the new wantonness she owes him, and in compensation tries to be, like a battered old roué, skillful. He satisfies himself that in some elemental way he has never been displaced; that for months she has been struggling in her lover's grasp, in the gauze net of love, her wings pinioned by tact. She assures him that she seized on the first opportunity for confession; she confides to him that Otto spray-sets his hair and uses a scent. She, weeping, vows that nowhere, never, has she encountered his, Richard's, passion, his pleasant bodily proportions and backwards-reeling grace, his invigorating sadism, his male richness. Then why . . . ? She is asleep. Her breathing has become oblivious. He clasps her limp body to his, wasting forgiveness upon her ghostly form. A receding truck pulls the night's silence taut. She has left him a hair short of satiety; her confession feels still a fraction unplumbed. The lunar face of the electric clock says three. He turns, flips his pillow, restlessly adjusts his arms, turns again, and seems to go downstairs for a glass of milk.

To his surprise, the kitchen is brightly lit, and Joan is on the linoleum floor, in her leotard. He stands amazed while she serenely twists her legs into the lotus position. He asks her again about the yoga instructor.

"Well, I didn't think it counted if it was part of the exercise. The whole point, darley, is to make mind and body one. This is pranayama—breath control." Stately, she pinches shut one nostril and slowly inhales, then pinches shut the other and exhales. Her hands return, palm up, to her knees. And she smiles. "This one is fun. It's called the Twist." She assumes a new position, her muscles elastic under the black cloth tormented into runs. "Oh, I forgot to tell you, I've slept with Harry Saxon."

"Joan, no. How often?"

"When we felt like it. We used to go out behind the Little League field. That heavenly smell of clover."

"But, sweetie, why?"

Smiling, she inwardly counts the seconds of this position. "You know why. He asked. It's hard, when men ask. You mustn't insult their male natures. There's a harmony in everything."

"And Freddy Vetter? You lied about Freddy, didn't you?"

"Now, *this* pose is wonderful for the throat muscles. It's called the Lion. You mustn't laugh." She kneels, her buttocks on her heels, and tilts back her head, and from gaping jaws thrusts out her tongue as if to touch the ceiling. Yet she continues speaking. "The whole theory is, we hold our heads too high, and blood can't get to the brain."

His chest hurts; he forces from it the cry, "Tell me everybody!"

She rolls toward him and stands upright on her shoulders, her face flushed with the effort of equilibrium and the downflow of blood. Her legs slowly scissor open and shut. "Some men you don't know," she goes on. "They come to the door to sell you septic tanks." Her voice is coming from her belly. Worse, there is a humming. Terrified, he awakes, and sits up. His chest is soaked.

He locates the humming as a noise from the transformer on the telephone pole near their windows. All night, while its residents sleep, the town murmurs to itself electrically. Richard's terror persists, generating mass as the reality of his dream sensations is confirmed. Joan's body asleep beside him seems small, scarcely bigger than Judith's, and narrower with age, yet infinitely deep, an abyss of secrecy, perfidy, and acceptingness; acrophobia launches sweat from his palms. He leaves the bed as if scrambling backwards from the lip of a vortex. He again goes downstairs; his wife's revelations have steepened the treads and left the walls slippery.

The kitchen is dark; he turns on the light. The floor is bare. The familiar objects of the kitchen seem discovered in a preservative state of staleness, wearing a look of tension, as if they are about to burst with the strain of being so faithfully themselves. Esther and Esau pad in from the living room, where they have been sleeping on the sofa, and beg to be fed, sitting like bookends, expectant and expert. The clock says four. Watchman of the night. But in searching for signs of criminal entry, for traces of his dream, Richard finds nothing but—clues mocking in their very abundance—the tacked-up drawings done by children's fingers ardently bunched around a crayon, of houses, cars, cats, and flowers.

Sublimating

THE MAPLES agreed that, since sex was the only sore point in their marriage, they should give it up: sex, not the marriage, which was eighteen years old and stretched back to a horizon where even their birth pangs, with a pang, seemed to merge. A week went by. On Saturday, Richard brought home in a little paper bag a large raw round cabbage. Joan asked, "What is *that?*"

"It's just a cabbage."

"What am I supposed to *do* with it?" Her irritability gratified him.

"You don't have to do *any*thing with it. I saw Mack Dennis go into the A & P and went in to talk to him about the new environment commission, whether they weren't muscling in on the conservation committee, and then I had to buy something to get out through the checkout counter, so I bought this cabbage. It was an impulse. You know what an impulse is." Rubbing it in. "When I was a kid," he went on, "we always used to have a head of cabbage around; you could cut a piece off to nibble instead of a candy. The hearts were best. They really burned your mouth."

"O.K., O.K." Joan turned her back and resumed washing dishes. "Well, I don't know where you're going to put it; since Judith turned vegetarian the refrigerator's already so full of vegetables I could cry."

Her turning her back aroused him; it usually did. He went closer and thrust the cabbage between her face and the sink. "*Look* at it, darley. Isn't it beautiful? It's so perfect." He was only partly teasing; he had found himself, in the A & P, ravished by the glory of the pyramided cabbages, the mute and glossy beauty that had waited ages for him to rediscover it. Not since preadolescence had his senses opened so innocently wide: the pure sphericity, the shy cellar odor, the cannonball heft. He chose, not the largest cabbage, but the roundest, the most ideal, and carried it naked in his hand to the checkout counter, where the girl, with a flicker of surprise, dressed it in a paper bag and charged him thirty-three cents. As he drove the mile home, the secret sphere beside him in the seat seemed a hole he had drilled back into reality. And now, cutting a slice from one pale cheek, he marvelled across the years at the miracle of the wound, at the tender compaction of the leaves, each tuned to its curve as tightly as a guitar string. The taste was blander than his childhood memory of it, but the texture was delicious in his mouth.

Bean, their baby, ten, came into the kitchen. "What is Daddy eating?" she asked, looking into the empty bag for cookies. She knew Daddy as a snack-sneaker.

"Daddy bought himself a cabbage," Joan told her.

The child looked at her father with eyes in which amusement had been prepared. There was a serious warmth that Mommy and animals, especially horses, gave off, and everything else had the coolness of comedy. "That was silly," she said.

"Nothing silly about it," Richard said. "Have a bite." He offered her the cabbage as if it were an apple. He envisioned inside her round head leaves and leaves of female psychology, packed so snugly the wrinkles dovetailed.

Bean made a spitting face and harshly laughed. "That's nasty," she said. Bolder, brighter-eyed, flirting: "*You're* nasty." Trying it out.

Hurt, Richard said to her, "I don't like you either. I just like my cabbage." And he kissed the cool pale dense vegetable once, twice, on the cheek; Bean gurgled in astonishment.

Her back still turned, Joan continued from the sink, "If you *had* to buy something, I wish you'd remembered Calgonite. I've been doing the dishes by hand for days."

"Remember it yourself," he said airily. "Where's the Saran Wrap for my cabbage?" But as the week wore on, the cabbage withered; the crisp planar wound of each slice by the next day had browned and loosened. Stubbornly loyal, Richard cut and nibbled his slow way to the heart, which burned on his tongue so sharply that his taste buds even in their adult dullness were not disappointed; he remembered how it had been, the oilcloth-covered table where his grandmother used to "snitz" cabbage into strings for sauerkraut and give him the leftover raw hearts for a snack. How they used to burn his tender mouth! His eyes would water with the delicious pain.

He did not buy another cabbage, once the first was eaten; analogously, he never returned to a mistress, once Joan had discovered and mocked her. Their eyes, that is, had married and merged to three, and in the middle, shared one, her dry female-to-female clarity would always oust his dripping romantic mists.

Her lovers, on the other hand, he never discovered while she had them. Months or even years later she would present an affair to him complete, self-packaged as nicely as a cabbage, the man remarried or moved to Seattle, her own wounds licked in secrecy and long healed. So he knew, coming home one evening and detecting a roseate afterglow in her face, that he would discover only some new layer of innocence. Nevertheless, he asked, "What have *you* been up to today?"

"Same old grind. After school I drove Judith to her dance lesson, Bean to the riding stable, Dickie to the driving range."

"Where was John?"

"He stayed home with me and said it was boring. I told him to go build something, so he's building a guillotine in the cellar; he says the sixth grade is studying revolution this term."

"What's he using for a blade?"

"He flattened an old snow shovel he says he can get sharp enough."

Richard could hear the child banging and whistling below him. "Jesus, he better not lose a finger." His thoughts flicked from the finger to himself to his wife's even white teeth to the fact that two weeks had passed since they gave up sex.

Casually she unfolded her secret. "One fun thing, though."

"You're taking up yoga again."

"Don't be silly; I was never anything to him. No. There's an automatic car wash opened up downtown, behind the pizza place. You put three quarters in and stay in the car and it just happens. It's hilarious."

"*What* happens?"

"Oh, you know. Soap, huge brushes that come whirling around. It really does quite a good job. Afterwards, there's a little hose you can put a dime in to vacuum the inside."

"I think this is very sinister. The people who are always washing their cars are the same people who are against abortion. Furthermore, it's bad for it. The dirt protects the paint."

"It needed it. We're living in the mud now."

Last fall, they had moved to an old farmhouse surrounded by vegetation that had been allowed to grow wild. This spring, they attacked the tangle of Nature around them with ominously different styles. Joan raked away dead twigs beneath bushes and pruned timidly, as if she were giving her boys a haircut. Richard scorned such pampering and attacked the problem at the root, or near the root. He wrestled vines from the barn roof, shingles popping and flying; he clipped the barberries down to yellow stubble; he began to prune some overweening yews by the front door and was unable to stop until each branch became a stump. The yews, a rare Japanese variety, had pink soft wood maddeningly like flesh. For days thereafter, the stumps bled amber.

The entire family was shocked, especially the two boys, who had improvised a fort in the cavity under the yews. Richard defended himself: "It was them or me. I couldn't get in my own front door."

"They'll never grow again, Dad," Dickie told him. "You didn't leave any green. There can't be any photosynthesis." The boy's own eyes were green; he kept brushing back his hair from them, with that nervous ladylike gesture of his long-haired generation.

"Good," Richard stated. He lifted his pruning clippers, which had an elbow hinge for extra strength, and asked, "How about a haircut?"

Dickie's eyes rounded with fright and he backed closer to his brother, who, though younger, had even longer hair. They looked like two chunky girls, blocking the front door. "Or why don't you both go down to the cellar and stick your heads in the guillotine?" Richard suggested. In a few powerful motions he mutilated a flowering trumpet vine. He had a vision, of right angles, clean clapboards, unclouded windows, level and transparent spaces from which the organic—the impudent, importunate, unceasingly encroaching organic—had been finally scoured.

"Daddy's upset about something else, not about your hair," Joan explained to Dickie and John at dinner. As the pact wore on, the family gathered more closely about her; even the cats, he noticed, hesitated to take scraps from his hand.

"What about, then?" Judith asked, looking up from her omelette. She was sixteen and Richard's only ally.

Joan answered, "Something grown-up." Her older daughter studied her for a moment, alertly, and Richard held his breath, thinking she might *see*. Female to female. The truth. The translucent vista of scoured space that was in Joan like a crystal tunnel.

But the girl was too young and, sensing an enemy, attacked her reliable old target, Dickie. "*You*," she said. "I don't ever see *you* trying to help Daddy, all you do is make Mommy drive you to golf courses and ski mountains."

"Yeah? What about *you*," he responded weakly, beaten before he started, "making Mommy cook two meals all the time because you're too *pure* to sully your lips with *an*imal matter."

"At least when I'm here I try to help; I don't just sit around reading books about dumb Billy Caster."

"Casper," Richard and Dickie said in unison.

Judith rose to her well-filled height; her bell-bottom hip-hugging Levi's dropped an inch lower and exposed a mingled strip of silken underpants and pearly belly. "I think it's *atro*cious for some people like us to have too many bushes and people in the ghetto don't even have a weed to look at, they have to go up on their rooftops to breathe. It's *true*, Dickie; don't make that face!"

Dickie was squinting in pain; he found his sister's body painful. "The young sociologist," he said, "flaunting her charms."

"You don't even know what a sociologist is," she told him, tossing her head. Waves of fleshly agitation rippled down toward her toes. "You are a very *spoiled* and *self*ish and *lim*ited person."

"Puh puh, big mature," was all he could say, poor little boy overwhelmed by this blind blooming.

Judith had become an optical illusion in which they all saw different things: Dickie saw a threat, Joan saw herself of twenty-five years ago, Bean saw another large warmth-source that, unlike horses, could read her a bedtime story. John, bless him, saw nothing, or, dimly, an old pal receding. Richard couldn't look. In the evening, when Joan was putting the others to bed, Judith would roll around on the sofa while he tried to read in the chair opposite. "Look, Dad. See my stretch exercises." He was reading *My Million-Dollar Shots*, by Billy Casper. The body must be coiled, tension should be felt in the back muscles and along the left leg at top of backswing. Illustrations, with arrows. The body on the sofa was twisting into lithe knots; Judith was double-jointed and her prowess at yoga may have been why Joan stopped doing it, outshone. Richard glanced up and saw his daughter arched like a staple, her hands gripping her ankles; a glossy bulge of supple belly held a navel at its acme. At the top of the backswing, forearm and back of the left hand should form a straight line. He tried it; it felt awkward. He was a born wrist-collapser. Judith watched him pondering his own wrist and giggled; then she kept giggling, insistently, flirting, trying it out. "Daddy's a narcissist." In the edge of his vision she seemed to be tickling herself and flicking her hair in circles.

"*Judith!*" He had not spoken to her so sharply since, as a toddler, she had spilled sugar all over the kitchen floor. In apology he added, "You are driving me crazy."

The fourth week, he went to New York, on business. When he returned, Joan told him during their kitchen drink, "This afternoon, everybody was being so cranky, you off, the weather lousy, I piled them all into the car, everybody except Judith; she's spending the night at Margaret Parillo's—"

"You *let* her? With that little tart and her druggy crowd? Are there going to be boys there?"

"I didn't ask. I hope so."

"Live vicariously, huh?"

He wondered if he could punch her in the face and at the same time grab the glass in her hand so it wouldn't break. It was from a honeymoon set of turquoise Mexican glass of which only three were left. With their shared eye she saw his calculations and her face went stony. He could break his fist on that face. "Are you going to let me finish my story?"

"Sure. *Dîtes-moi*, Scheherazade."

"—and we went to the car wash. The dog was hilarious, she kept barking and chasing the brushes around and around the car trying to defend us. It took her three rotations to figure out that if it went one way it would be coming back the other. Everybody absolutely howled; we had Danny Vetter in the car with us, and one of Bean's horsy friends; it was a real orgy." Her face was pink, recalling.

"That is a truly disgusting story. Speaking of disgusting, I did something strange in New York."

"You slept with a prostitute."

"Almost. I went to a blue movie."

"How scary for you, darley."

"Well, it was. Wednesday morning I woke up early and didn't have any appointment until eleven so I wandered over to Forty-second Street, you know, with this innocent morning light on everything, and these little narrow places were already open. So—can you stand this?"

"Sure. All I've heard all week are children's complaints."

"I paid three bucks and went in. It was totally dark. Like a fun house at a fairground. Except for this very bright-pink couple up on the screen. I could hear people breathing but not see anything. Every time I tried to slide into a row I kept sticking my thumb into somebody's eye. But nobody groaned or protested. It was like those bodies frozen in whatever circle it was of Hell. Finally I found a seat and sat down and after a while

I could see it was all men, asleep. At least most of them seemed to be asleep. And they were spaced so no two touched; but even at this hour, the place was half full. Of motionless men." He felt her disappointment; he hadn't conveyed the fairy-tale magic of the experience: the darkness absolute as lead, the undercurrent of snoring as from a single dragon, the tidy way the men had spaced themselves, like checkers on a board. And then how he had found a blank square, had jumped himself, as it were, into it, and joined humanity in stunned witness of its own process of perpetuation.

Joan asked, "How was the movie?"

"Awful. Exasperating. You begin to think entirely in technical terms: camera position, mike boom. And the poor cunts, God, how they work. Apparently to get a job in a blue movie a man has to be, A, blond, and, B, impotent."

"Yes," Joan said and turned her back, as if to conceal a train of thought. "We have to go to dinner tonight with the new Dennises." Mack Dennis had remarried, a woman much like Eleanor only slightly younger and, the Maples agreed, not nearly as nice. "They'll keep us up forever. But maybe tomorrow," Joan was going on, as if to herself, timidly, "after the kids go their separate ways, if you'd like to hang around . . ."

"No," he took pleasure in saying. "I'm determined to play golf. Thursday afternoon one of the accounts took me out to Long Island and even with borrowed clubs I was hitting the drives a mile. I think I'm on to something; it's all up here." He showed her the top of his backswing, the stiff left wrist. "I must have been getting twenty extra yards." He swung his empty arms down and through.

"See," Joan said, gamely sharing his triumph, "you're sublimating."

In the car to the Dennises', he asked her, "How is it?"

"It's quite wonderful, in a way. It's as if my senses are jammed permanently open. I feel all one with Nature. The jonquils are out behind the shed and I just looked at them and cried. They were so beautiful I couldn't stand it. I can't keep myself indoors, all I want to do is rake and prune and push little heaps of stones around."

"You know," he told her sternly, "the lawn isn't just some kind of carpet to keep sweeping, you have to make some decisions. Those lilacs, for instance, are full of dead wood."

"*Don't,*" Joan whimpered, and cried, as darkness streamed by, torn by headlights.

In bed after the Dennises (it was nearly two; they were numb on brandy; Mack had monologued about conservation and Mrs. Dennis about interior decoration, redoing "her" house, which the Maples still thought of as Eleanor's), Joan confessed to Richard, "I keep having this little vision—it comes to me anywhere, in the middle of sunshine—of me dead."

"Dead of what?"

"I don't know that, all I know is that I'm dead and it doesn't much matter."

"Not even to the children?"

"For a day or two. But everybody manages."

"Sweetie." He repressed his strong impulse to turn and touch her. He explained, "It's part of being one with Nature."

"I suppose."

"I have it very differently. I keep having this funeral fantasy. How full the church will be, what Spence will say about me in his sermon, who'll be there." Specifically, whether the women he has loved will come and weep with Joan; in the image of this, their combined grief at his eternal denial of himself to them, he glimpsed a satisfaction for which the transient satisfactions of the living flesh were a flawed and feeble prelude— merely the backswing. In death, he felt, as he floated on his back in bed, he would grow to his true size.

Joan with their third eye may have sensed his thoughts; where usually she would roll over and turn her sumptuous back, whether as provocation or withdrawal it was up to him to decide, now she lay paralyzed, parallel to him. "I suppose," she offered, "in a way, it's cleansing. I mean, you think of all that energy that went into the Crusades."

"Yes, I dare say," Richard agreed, unconvinced, "we may be on to something."

Nevada

Poor Culp. His wife, Sarah, wanted to marry her lover as soon as the divorce came through, she couldn't wait a day, the honeymoon suite in Honolulu had been booked six weeks in advance. So Culp, complaisant to the end, agreed to pick the girls up in Reno and drive them back to Denver. He arranged to be in San Francisco on business and rented a car. Over the phone, Sarah mocked his plan—why not fly? An expert in petroleum extraction, he hoped by driving to extract some scenic benefit from domestic ruin. Until they had moved to Denver and their marriage exploded in the thinner atmosphere, they had lived in New Jersey, and the girls had seen little of the West.

He arrived in Reno around five in the afternoon, having detoured south from Interstate 80. The city looked kinder than he had expected. He found the address Sarah had given him, a barn-red boardinghouse behind a motel distinguished by a giant flashing domino. He dreaded yet longed for the pain of seeing Sarah again—divorced, free of him, exultant, about to take wing into a new marriage. But she had taken wing before he arrived. His two daughters were sitting on a tired cowhide sofa, next to an empty desk, like patients in a dentist's anteroom.

Polly, who was eleven, leaped up to greet him. "Mommy's left," she said. "She thought you'd be here hours ago."

Laura, sixteen, rose with a self-conscious languor from the tired sofa, smoothing her skirt behind, and added, "Jim was with her. He got really mad when you didn't show."

Culp apologized. "I didn't know her schedule was so tight."

Laura perhaps misheard him, answering, "Yeah, she was really uptight."

"I took a little detour to see Lake Tahoe."

"Oh, Dad," Laura said. "You and your sightseeing."

"Were you worried?" he asked.

"Naa."

A little woman with a square jaw hopped from a side room behind the empty desk. "They was good as good, Mr. Culp. Just sat there, wouldn't even take a sandwich I offered to make for no charge. Laura here kept telling the little one, 'Don't you be childish, Daddy wouldn't let us down.' I'm Betsy Morgan, we've heard of each other but never met officially." Sarah had mentioned her in her letters: Morgan the pirate, her landlady and residency witness. Fred Culp saw himself through Mrs. Morgan's eyes: cuckold, defendant, discardee. Though her eye was merry, the hand she offered him was dry as a bird's foot.

He could only think to ask, "How did the proceedings go?"

The question seemed foolish to him, but not to Mrs. Morgan. "Seven minutes, smooth as silk. Some of these judges, they give a girl a hard time just to keep themselves from being bored. But your Sary stood right up to him. She has that way about her."

"Yes, she did. Does. More and more. Girls, got your bags?"

"Right behind the sofy here. I would have kept their room one night more, but then this lady from Connecticut showed up yesterday could take it for the six weeks."

"That's fine. I'll take them someplace with a pool."

"They'll be missed, I tell you truly," the landlady said, and she kissed the two girls on their cheeks. This had been a family of sorts, there were real tears in her eyes; but Polly couldn't wait for the hug to pass before blurting to her father, "We had pool privileges at the Domino, and one time all these Mexicans came and used it for a *bath*room!"

They drove to a motel not the Domino. Laura and he watched Polly swim. "Laura, don't you want to put on a suit?"

"Naa. Mom made us swim so much I got diver's ear."

Culp pictured Sarah lying on a poolside chaise longue, in the bikini with the orange and purple splashes. One smooth wet arm was flung up to shield her eyes. Other women noticeably had legs or breasts; Sarah's beauty had been most vivid in her arms, rounded and fine and firm, arms that never aged, without a trace of wobble above the elbow, though at her next birthday she would be forty. Indeed, that was how Sarah had put the need for divorce: she couldn't bear to turn forty with him. As if then you began a return journey that could not be broken.

Laura was continuing, "Also, Dad, if you *must* know, it's that time of the month."

With clumsy jubilance, Polly hurled her body from the rattling board

and surfaced grinning through the kelp of her own hair. She climbed
from the pool and slapfooted to his side, shivering. "Want to walk around
and play the slots?" Goose bumps had erected the white hairs on her
thighs into a ghostly halo. "Want to? It's fun."

Laura intervened maternally. "Don't *make* him, Polly. Daddy's tired
and depressed."

"Who says? Let's go. I may never see Reno again." The city, as they
walked, reminded him of New Jersey's little municipalities. The desert
clarity at evening had the even steel glint of industrial haze. Above drab
shop fronts, second-story windows proclaimed residence with curtains
and a flowerpot. There were churches, which he hadn't expected. And a
river, a trickling shadow of the Passaic, flowed through. The courthouse,
Mecca to so many, seemed too modest; it wore the dogged granite dignity
of justice the country over. Only the Reno downtown, garish as a carnival
midway, was different. Polly led him to doors she was forbidden to enter
and gave him nickels to play for her inside. She loved the slot machines,
loved them for their fruity colors and their sleepless glow and their sudden gush of release, jingling, lighting, as luck struck now here, now there,
across the dark casino. Feeling the silky heave of their guts as he fed the
slot and pulled the handle, rewarded a few times with the delicious spitting of coins into the troughs other hands had smoothed to his touch,
Culp came to love them, too; he and Polly made a gleeful, hopeful pair,
working their way from casino to casino, her round face pressed to the
window so she could see him play, and the plums jerk into being, and the
bells and cherries do their waltz of chance, 1-2-3. One place was wide
open to the sidewalk. A grotesquely large machine stood ready for silver
dollars.

Polly said, "Mommy won twenty dollars on that one once."

Culp asked Laura, who had trailed after them in disdainful silence,
"Was Jim with you the whole time?"

"No, he only came the last week." She searched her father's face for
what he wanted to know. "He stayed at the Domino."

Polly drew close to listen. Culp asked her, "Did you like Jim?"

Her eyes with difficulty shifted from visions of mechanical delight.
"He was too serious. He said the slots were a racket and they wouldn't get
a penny of his."

Laura said, "I thought he was an utter *pill*, Dad."

"You don't have to think that to please me."

"He *was*. I told her, too."

"You shouldn't have. Listen, it's her life, not yours." On the hospital-bright sidewalk, both his girls' faces looked unwell, stricken. Culp put a silver dollar into the great machine, imagining that something of Sarah had rubbed off here and that through this electric ardor she might speak to him. But the machine's size was unnatural; the guts felt sluggish, spinning. A plum, a bar, a star. No win. Turning, he resented that Polly and Laura, still staring, seemed stricken for *him*.

Laura said, "Better come eat, Dad. We'll show you a place where they have pastrami like back east."

As Route 40 poured east, Nevada opened into a strange no-color—a rusted gray, or the lavender that haunts the corners of overexposed color slides. The Humboldt River, which had sustained the pioneer caravans, shadowed the expressway, tinting its valley with a dull green that fed dottings of cattle. But for the cattle, and the cars that brushed by him as if he were doing thirty and not eighty miles an hour, and an occasional gas station and cabin café promising SLOTS, there was little sign of life in Nevada. This pleased Culp; it enabled him to run off in peace the home movies of Sarah stored in his head. Sarah pushing the lawn mower in the South Orange back yard. Sarah pushing a blue baby carriage, English, with little white wheels, around the fountain in Washington Square. Sarah, not yet his wife, waiting for him in a brown-and-green peasant skirt under the marquee of a movie house on Fifty-seventh Street. Sarah, a cool suburban hostess in chalk-pink sack dress, easing through their jammed living room with a platter of parsleyed egg halves. Sarah after a party, drunk in a black lace bra, doing the Twist at the foot of their bed. Sarah in blue jeans crying out that it was nobody's *fault*, that there was nothing he could *do*, just let her *alone*; and hurling a quarter-pound of butter across the kitchen, so the calendar fell off the wall. Sarah in miniskirt leaving their house in Denver for a date, just like a teen-ager, the sprinkler on their flat front lawn spinning in the evening cool. Sarah trim and sardonic at the marriage counsellor's, under the pressed-paper panelling where the man had hung not only his diplomas but his Aspen skiing medals. Sarah some Sunday long ago raising the shades to wake him, light flooding her translucent nightgown. Sarah lifting her sudden eyes to him at some table, some moment, somewhere, in conspiracy—he hadn't known he had taken so many reels, they just kept coming in his head. Nevada beautifully, emptily poured by. The map was full of ghost towns. Laura sat beside him, reading the map. "Dad, here's a town called Nixon."

"Let's go feel sorry for it."

"You passed it. It was off the road after Sparks. The next real town is Lovelock."

"What's real about it?"

"Should you be driving so fast?"

In the back seat, Polly struggled with her needs. "Can we stop in the next real town to eat?"

Culp said, "You should have eaten more breakfast."

"I hate hash browns."

"But you like bacon."

"The hash browns had touched it."

Laura said, "Polly, stop bugging Daddy, you're making him nervous."

Culp told her, "I am *not* nervous."

Polly told her, "I can't keep holding it."

"Baby. You just went less than an hour ago."

"I'm nervous."

Culp laughed. Laura said, "You're not funny. You're not a baby any more."

Polly said, "Yeah, and you're not a wife, either."

Silence.

"Nobody said I was."

Nevada spun by. Sarah stepped out of a car, their old Corvair convertible, wearing a one-piece bathing suit. Her hair was stiff and sunbleached and wild. She was eating a hot dog loaded with relish. Culp looked closer and there was sand in her ear, as in a delicate discovered shell.

Polly announced, "Dad, that sign said a place in three miles. 'Soft Drinks, Sandwiches, Beer, Ice, and Slots.' "

"Slots, slots," Laura spat, furious for a reason that eluded her father. "Slots and sluts, that's all there is in this dumb state."

Culp asked, "Didn't you enjoy Reno?"

"I hated it. What I hated especially was Mom acting on the make all the time."

"On the make," "sluts"—the language of women living together, it occurred to him, coarsens like that of men in the Army. He mildly corrected, "I'm sure she wasn't on the make, she was just happy to be rid of me."

"Don't kid yourself, Dad. She was on the make. Even with Jim about to show up she was."

"Yeah, well," Polly said, "you weren't that pure yourself, showing off for that Mexican boy."

"I wasn't showing off for any bunch of spics, I was practicing my diving, and I suggest you do the same, you toad. You look like a sick frog, the way you go off the board. A sick *fat* frog."

"Yeah, well. Mommy said you weren't so thin at my age yourself."

Culp intervened: "It's *nice* to be plump at your age. Otherwise, you won't have anything to shape up when you're Laura's age."

Polly giggled, scandalized. Laura said, "Don't flirt, Dad," and crossed her thighs; she was going to be one of those women, Culp vaguely saw, who have legs. She smoothed back the hair from her brow in a gesture that tripped the home-movie camera again: Sarah before the mirror. He could have driven forever this way; if he had known Nevada was so easy, he could have planned to reach the Utah line, or detoured north to some ghost towns. But they had made reservations in Elko, and stopped there.

The motel was more of a hotel, four stories high; on the ground floor, a cavernous dark casino glimmered with the faces of the slots and the shiny uniforms of the change girls. Though it was only three in the afternoon, Culp wanted to go in there, to get a drink at the bar, where the bottles glowed like a row of illumined stalagmites. But his daughters, after inspecting their rooms, dragged him out into the sunshine. Elko was a flat town, full of space, as airy with emptiness as an old honeycomb. The broad street in front of the hotel held railroad tracks in its center. To Polly's amazed delight, a real train—nightmarish in scale but docile in manner—materialized on these tracks, halted, ruminated, and then ponderously, thoughtfully dragged westward its chuckling infinity of freight cars. They walked down broad sunstruck sidewalks, past a drunken Indian dressed in clothes as black as his shadow, to a museum of mining. Polly coveted the glinting nuggets, Laura yawned before a case of old-fashioned barbed wire and sought her reflection in the glass. Culp came upon an exhibit, between Indian beads and pioneer hardware, incongruously devoted to Thomas Alva Edison. He and Sarah and the girls, driving home through the peppery stenches of carbon waste and butane from a Sunday on the beach at Point Pleasant, would pass a service island on the Jersey Turnpike named for Edison. They would stop for supper at another one, named for Joyce Kilmer. The hot tar on the parking lot would slightly yield beneath their rubber flip-flops. Sarah would go in for her hot dog wearing her dashiki beach wrapper—hip-length, with slits for her naked arms. These lovely arms would be burned pink in the crooks. The sun would have ignited a conflagration of clouds beyond the great retaining tanks. Here, in Elko, the sun rested gently on the overexposed purple of the ridges around them. On the highest ridge a large letter *E* had been somehow cut, or inset, in what seemed limestone. Polly asked why.

He answered, "I suppose for airplanes."

Laura amplified, "If they don't put initials up, the pilots can't tell the towns apart, they're all so boring."

"I like Elko," Polly said. "I wish we lived here."

"Yeah, what would Daddy do for a living?"

This was hard. In real life, he was a chemical engineer for a conglomerate that was planning to exploit Colorado shale. Polly said, "He could fix slot machines and then at night come back in disguise and play them so they'd pay him lots of money."

Both girls, it seemed to Culp, had forgotten that he would not be living with them in their future, that this peaceful dusty nowhere was an exception to the rule. He took Polly's hand, crossing the railroad tracks, though the tracks were arrow-straight and no train was materializing between here and the horizon.

Laura flustered him by taking his arm as they walked into the dining room, which was beyond the dark grotto of slots. The waitress slid an expectant glance at the child, after he had ordered a drink for himself. "No. She's only sixteen."

When the waitress had gone, Laura told him, "Everybody says I look older than sixteen; in Reno with Mom, I used to wander around in the places and nobody ever said anything. Except one old fart who told me they'd put him in jail if I didn't go away."

Polly asked, "Daddy, when're you going to play the slots?"

"I thought I'd wait till after dinner."

"That's too long."

"O.K., I'll play now. Just until the salad comes." He took a mouthful of his drink, pushed up from the table, and fed ten quarters into a machine that Polly could watch. Though he won nothing, being there, amid the machines' warm and fantastic colors, consoled him. Experimenting, he pressed the button marked CHANGE. A girl in a red uniform crinkling like embers came to his side inquisitively. Her face, though not old, had the Western dryness—eyes smothered in charcoal, mouth tightened as if about to say, *I thought so.* But something sturdy and hollow-backed in her stance touched Culp with an intuition. It was a little like oil extraction: you just sensed it, below the surface. Her uniform's devilish cut bared her white arms to the shoulder. He gave her a five-dollar bill to change into quarters. The waitress was bringing the salad. Heavy in one pocket, he returned to the table.

"Poor Dad," Laura volunteered. "That prostitute really turned him on."

"Laura, I'm not sure you know what a prostitute is."

"Mom said every woman is a prostitute, one way or another."

"You know your mother exaggerates."

"I know she's a bitch, you mean."

"Laura."

"She *is*, Dad. Look what she's done to you. Now she'll do it to Jim."

"You and I have different memories of your mother. You don't remember her when you were little."

"I don't want to live with her, either. When we all get back to Denver, I want to live with *you*. If she and I live together, it'll always be competing, that's how it was in Reno; who needs it? When *I* get to forty, I'm going to tell my lover to shoot me."

Polly cried out—an astonishing noise, like the crash of a jackpot. "*Stop it*," she told Laura. "Stop talking big. That's all you do, is talk big." The child, salad dressing gleaming on her chin, pushed her voice toward her sister through tears: "You want Mommy and Daddy to fight all the time instead of love each other even though they *are* divorced."

With an amused smile, Laura turned her back on Polly's outburst and patted Culp's arm. "Poor Dad," she said. "Poor old Dad."

Their steaks came, and Polly's tears dried. They walked out into Elko again and at the town's one movie theatre saw a Western. Burt Lancaster, a downtrodden Mexican, after many insults, including crucifixion, turned implacable avenger and killed nine hirelings of a racist rancher. Polly seemed to be sleeping through the bloodiest parts. They walked back through the dry night to the hotel. Their two adjoining rooms each held twin beds. Laura's suitcase had appeared on the bed beside his.

Culp said, "You better sleep with your sister."

"Why? We'll have the door between open, in case she has nightmares."

"I want to read."

"So do I."

"You go to sleep now. We're going to make Salt Lake tomorrow."

"Big thrill. Dad, she mumbles and kicks her covers all the time."

"Do as I say, love. I'll stay here reading until you're asleep."

"And then what?"

"I may go down and have another drink."

478 : FAMILY LIFE

Her expression reminded him of how, in the movie, the villain had
looked when Burt Lancaster showed that he, too, had a gun. Culp lay
on the bedspread reading a pamphlet they had bought at the museum,
about ghost towns; champagne and opera sets had been transported up
the valleys, where now not a mule survived. Train whistles at intervals
scooped long pockets from the world beyond his room. The breathing
from the other room had fallen level. He tiptoed in and saw them both
asleep, his daughters. Laura had been reading a book about the persecution of the Indians and now it lay beside her hand, with its childish short
fingernails. Relaxed, her face revealed its freckles, its plumpness, the sorrowing stretched smoothness of the closed lids. Polly's face wore a film of
night sweat on her brow; his kiss came away tasting salty. He did not kiss
Laura, in case she was faking. He switched off the light and stood considering what he must do. A train howled on the other side of the wall. The
beautiful emptiness of Nevada, where he might never be again, sucked at
the room like a pump.

Downstairs, his intuition was borne out. The change girl had noticed
him, and said now, "How's it going?"

"Fair. You ever go off duty?"

"What's duty?"

He waited at the bar, waiting for the bourbon to fill him; it couldn't,
the room inside him kept expanding, and when she joined him, after one
o'clock, sidling up on the stool (a cowboy moved over) in a taut cotton
dress that hid the tops of her arms, the blur on her face seemed a product
of her inner chemistry, not his. "You've a room?" As she asked him that,
her jaw went square: Mrs. Morgan in a younger version.

"I do," he said, "but it's full of little girls."

She reached for his bourbon and sipped and said, in a voice older than
her figure, "This place is lousy with rooms."

Culp arrived back in his own room after four. He must have been noisier
than he thought, for a person in a white nightgown appeared in the connecting doorway. Culp could not see her features, she was a good height,
she reminded him of nobody. Good. From the frozen pose of her, she was
scared—scared of him. Good.

"Dad?"

"Yep."

"You O.K.?"

"Sure." Though already he could feel the morning sun's grinding on
his temples. "You been awake, sweetie? I'm sorry."

"I was worried about you." But Laura did not cross the threshold into his room.

"Very worried?"

"Naa."

"Listen. It's not your job to take care of me. It's my job to take care of you."

The Gun Shop

BEN'S SON, Murray, looked forward to their annual Thanksgiving trip to Pennsylvania mostly because of the gun. A Remington .22, it leaned unused in the Trupp farmhouse all year, until little Murray came and swabbed it out and begged to shoot it. The gun had been Ben's. His parents had bought it for him the Christmas after they moved to the farm, when he was thirteen, his son's age now. No, Murray was all of fourteen, his birthday was in September. At the party, Ben had tapped the child on the back of the head to settle him down, and his son had pointed the cake knife at his father's chest and said, "Hit me again and I'll kill you."

Ben had been amazed. In bed that night, Sally told him, "It was his way of saying he's too big to be hit any more. He's right. He is."

But the boy, as he and Ben walked with the gun across the brown field to the dump in the woods, didn't seem big; solemn and beardless, he carried the freshly cleaned rifle under his arm, in imitation of hunters in magazine illustrations, and the barrel tip kept snagging on loops of matted orchard grass. Then, at the dump, with the targets of tin cans and bottles neatly aligned, the gun refused to fire, and Murray threw a childish tantrum. Tears filled his eyes as he tried to explain: "There was this little *pin*, Dad, that fell out when I cleaned it, but I put it back in, and now it's not *there!*"

Ben, looking down into this small freckled face so earnestly stricken, couldn't help smiling.

Murray, seeing his father's smile, said, *"Shit."* He hurled the gun toward an underbrush of saplings and threw himself onto the cold leaf mold of the forest floor. He writhed there and repeated the word as each fresh slant of injustice and of embarrassment struck him; but Ben couldn't quite erase his tense expression of kindly mockery. The boy's tantrums loomed impressively in the intimate scale of their Boston apartment, with his mother and two sisters and some fine-legged antiques as audience; but out here, among these mute oaks and hickories, his fury was rather comically dwarfed. Also, in retrieving and examining the .22, Ben had bent his face close into the dainty forgotten smell of gun oil and remembered the Christmas noon when his father had taken him out to the barn and shown him how to shoot the virgin gun; and this memory prolonged his smile.

That dainty scent. The dangerous slickness. The zigzag marks of burnishing on the bolt when it slid out, and the amazing whorl, a new kind of star, inside the barrel when it was pointed toward the sky. The snug, lethally smart clicks of reassembly. He had not known his father could handle a gun. He was forty-five when Ben was thirteen, and a schoolteacher; once he had been, briefly, a soldier. He had thrown an empty Pennzoil can into the snow of the barnyard and propped the .22 on the chicken-house windowsill and taken the first shot. The oil can had jumped. Ben remembered the way his father's mouth, seen from the side, sucked back a bit of saliva that in his concentration had escaped. Ben remembered the less-than-deafening slap of the shot and the acrid whiff that floated from the bolt as the spent shell spun away. Now, pulling the dead trigger and sliding out the bolt to see why the old gun was broken, he remembered his father's arms around him, guiding his hands on the newly varnished stock and pressing his head gently down to line up his eyes with the sights. "Squeeze, don't get excited and jerk," his father had said.

"*Get* up," Ben said to his son. "Shape up. Don't be such a baby. If it doesn't work, it doesn't work; I don't know why. It worked the last time we used it."

"Yeah, that was last Thanksgiving," Murray said, surprisingly conversational, though still stretched on the cold ground. "I bet one of these idiot yokels around here messed it up."

"Idiot yokels," Ben repeated, hearing himself in that phrase. "My, aren't we a young snob?"

Murray stood and brushed the sarcasm aside. "Can you fix it or not?"

Ben slipped a cartridge into the chamber, closed the bolt, and pulled the trigger. A limp click. "Not. I don't understand guns. You're the one who wants to use it all the time. Why don't we just point our fingers and say, '*bang*'?"

"Dad, you're quite the riot."

They walked back to the house. Ben lugged the disgraced gun while Murray ran ahead. Ben noticed in the dead grass the rusty serrate shapes of strawberry leaves, precise as fossils. When they had moved here, the land had been farmed out—"mined," in the local phrase—and the one undiscouraged crop consisted of the wild strawberries running from ditch to ridge on all the sunny slopes. At his son's age, Ben had no fondness for the strawberry leaves and the rural isolation they ornamented; it surprised him, gazing down, that their silhouettes fit so exactly a shape in his mind. The leaves were still here, and his parents were still in the square sandstone farmhouse. His mother looked up from her preparations for the feast and said, "I didn't hear the shots."

"There weren't any, that's why."

Something pleased or amused in Ben's voice tripped Murray's temper again; he went into the living room and kicked a chair leg and swore. "Goddamn thing *broke*."

"That's no reason to break a chair," Ben shouted after him. "That's not our furniture, you know."

Sally was helping in the kitchen, mashing the potatoes in an old striped bowl. "Hey," she said to her husband. "Gently."

"Well, hell," he said to her, "why are we letting the kid terrorize everybody?"

In a murderous mood, he followed the boy into the living room. The two girls, in company with their grandfather, were watching the Macy's parade on television. Murray, hearing his father approach, had hid behind the chair he had kicked. A sister glanced in his direction and pronounced, "Spoiled." The other sniffed in agreement. One girl was older than Murray, one younger; all of his life he would be pinched between them. Their grandfather was sitting in a rocker, wearing the knit wool cap that made him feel less cold. Obligingly he had taken the chair with the worst angle on the television screen, watching in fuzzy foreshortening a flicker of bloated animals, drum majorettes, and giant cakes bearing candles that were really girls waving.

"He's not spoiled," Ben's father told the girls. "He's like his daddy, a perfectionist."

Ben's father since that Christmas of the gun had become an old man, but a wonderfully strange old man, with a long yellow-white face, a blue nose, and the erect carriage of a child who is straining to see. His circulation was poor, he had been hospitalized, he lived from pill to pill, he had uncharacteristic quiet spells that Ben guessed were seizures of pain; yet his hopefulness still dominated any room he was in. He looked up at Ben in the doorway. "Can you figure it out?"

Ben said, "Murray says some pin fell out while he was cleaning it."

"It *did*, Dad," the child insisted.

Ben's father stood, prim and pale and tall. He was wearing a threadbare overcoat, in readiness for adventure. "I know just the man," he said. He called into the kitchen, "Mother, I'll give Dutch a ring. The kid's being frustrated."

"Aw, that's O.K., forget it," Murray mumbled. But his eyes shone, looking up at the promising apparition of his grandfather. Ben was hurt, remembering how his own knack, as father, was to tease and cloud those same eyes. There was something too finely tooled, too little yielding in the boy that Ben itched to correct.

The two women had crowded to the doorway to intervene. Sally said, "He doesn't *have* to shoot the gun. I hate guns. Ben, why do you always inflict the gun on this child?"

"I don't," he answered.

His mother called over Sally's shoulder, "Don't bother people on Thanksgiving, Murray. Let the man have a holiday."

Little Murray looked up, startled, at the sound of his name pronounced scoldingly. He had been named for his grandfather. Two Murrays: one small and young, one big and old. Yet alike, Ben saw, in a style of expectation, in a tireless craving for—he used to wonder for what, but people had a word for it now—"action."

"This man never takes a holiday," Ben's father called back. "He's out of this world. You'd love him. Everybody in this room would love him." And, irrepressibly, he was at the telephone, dialling with a touch of frenzy, the way he would scrub a friendly dog's belly with his knuckles. Hanging up, he announced with satisfaction, "Dutch says to bring the gun over this evening, when all the fuss has died down."

After a supper of leftover turkey, the males went out into the night. Ben drove his father's car. The dark road carried them off their hill into a valley where sandstone farmhouses had been joined by ranch houses, aluminum trailers, a wanly lit Mobil station, a Pentecostal church built of cinder blocks, with a neon JESUS LIVES. JESUS SAVES must have become too much of a joke.

"The next driveway on the left," his father said. The cold outdoor air had shortened his breath. No sign advertised a gun shop; the house was a ranch, but not a new one—one built in the early Fifties, when the commuters first began to come this far out from the city of Alton. In order of age, oldest to youngest, tallest to shortest, the Trupps marched up the flagstones to the unlit front door; Ben could feel his son's embarrassment at his back, deepening his own. They had offered to let little Murray carry the gun, but he had shied from it. Ben held the .22 behind him, so as not to terrify whoever answered his father's ring at the door. It was a fat woman in a pink wrapper. Ben saw that there had been a mistake: this was no gun shop, his father had blundered once again.

Not so. The woman said, "Why, hello, Mr. Trupp," giving the name that affectionate long German *u*; in Boston people rhymed it with "cup." "Come in this way, I guess; he's down there expecting everybody. Is this your son, now? And who's *this* big boy?" Her pleasantries eased their way across the front hall, with its braided rug and enamelled plaque of the Lord's Prayer, to the cellar stairs.

As they clattered down, Ben's father said, "I shouldn't have done that, that was a headache for his missus, letting us in, I wasn't thinking. We should have gone to the side, but then Dutch has to disconnect the burglar alarm. Everybody in this county's crazy to steal his guns. When you get to be my age, Ben, it hurts like Jesus just to *try* to think. Just to *try* not to annoy the hell out of people."

The cellar seemed bigger than the house. Cardboard cartons, old chairs and sofas, a refrigerator, stacked newspapers, shoot posters, and rifle racks lined an immense cement room. At the far end was a counter, and behind it a starkly lit workshop with a lathe. Little Murray's eyes widened; gun shops were new to him. In an alley of Ben's own boyhood there had been a mysterious made-over garage called "Repair & Ammo." Sounds of pounding and grinding came out of it, the fury of metals. On dark winter afternoons, racing home with his sled, Ben would see blue sparks shudder in the window. But he had never gone in; so this was an adventure for him as well. There was that about being his father's son: one had adventures, one blundered into places, one *went* places, met strangers, suffered rebuffs, experienced breakdowns, exposed oneself in a way that Ben, as soon as he was able, foreclosed, hedging his life with such order and propriety that no misstep could occur. He had become a lawyer, taking profit from the losses of others, reducing disorderly lives to legal folders. Even in his style of dress he had retained the caution of the Fifties, while his partners blossomed into striped shirts and bell-bottomed slacks. Seeing his son's habitual tautness relax under the spell of this potent, acrid cellar, Ben realized that he had been much less a father than his own had been, a father's duty being to impart the taste of the world. Golf lessons in Brookline, sailing in Maine, skiing in New Hampshire—what was this but bought amusement compared with the improvised shifts and hazards of poverty? In this cave the metallic smell of murder lurked, and behind the counter two men bent low over some-thing that gleamed like a jewel.

Ben's father went forward. "Dutch, this is my son, Ben, and my grand-son, Murray. The kid's just like you are, a perfectionist, and this cheap gun we got Ben a zillion years ago let him down this afternoon." To the other man in this lighted end of the cellar he said, "I know your face, mis-ter, but I've forgotten your name."

The other man blinked and said, "Reiner." He wore a Day-Glo hunt-ing cap and a dirty blue parka over a holiday-clean shirt and tie. He looked mild, perhaps because of his spectacles, which were rimless. He seemed to be a customer, and the piece of metal in the gunsmith's hand con-cerned him. It was a small slab with two holes bored in it; a shiny ring had been set into one of the holes, and Dutch's gray thumb moved back and forth across the infinitesimal edge where the ring was flush with the slab.

"About two-thousandths," the gunsmith slowly announced, growling the *ou*'s. It was hard to know whom he was speaking to. His eyelids looked swollen—leaden hoods set slantwise over the eyes, eclipsing them but for a glitter. His entire body appeared to have slumped away from its frame, from the restless ruminating jowl to the undershirted beer belly and bent knees. His shuffle seemed deliberately droll. His hands alone had firm shape—hands battered and nicked and so long in touch with greased machinery that they had blackened flatnesses like worn parts. The right middle finger had been shorn off at the first knuckle. "Two- or three-thousandths at the most."

Ben's father's voice had regained its strength in the warmth of this basement. He acted as interlocutor, to make the drama clear. "You mean you can just tell with your thumb if it's a thousandth of an inch off?"

"Yahh. More or less."

"That's incredible. That to me is a miracle." He explained to his son and grandson, "Dutch was head machinist at Hager Steel for thirty years. He had hundreds of men under him. Hundreds."

"A thousand," Dutch growled. "Twelve hunnert during Korea." His qualification slipped into place as if with much practice; Ben guessed his father came here often.

"Boy, I can't imagine it. I don't see how the hell you did it. I don't see how any man could do what you did; my imagination boggles. This kid here"—Murray, not Ben—"has what you have. Drive. Both of you have what it takes."

Ben thought he should assert himself. In a few crisp phrases he explained to Dutch how the gun had failed to fire.

His father said to the man in spectacles, "It would have taken me all night to say what he just said. He lives in New England, they all talk sense up there. One thing I'm grateful the kid never inherited from me, and I bet he is too, is his old man's gift for baloney. I was always embarrassing the kid."

Dutch slipped out the bolt of the .22 and, holding the screwdriver so the shortened finger lay along a groove of the handle, turned a tiny screw that Ben in all his years of owning the gun had never noticed. The bolt fell into several bright pieces, tinged with rust, on the counter. The gunsmith picked a bit of metal from within a little spring and held it up. "Firing pin. Sheared," he said. His mouth when he talked showed the extra flexibility of the toothless.

"Do you have another? Can you replace it?" Ben disliked, as emphasized by this acoustical cellar, the high, hungry pitch of his own voice. He was prosecuting.

Dutch declined to answer. He lowered his remarkable lids to gaze at the metal under his hands; one hand closed tight around the strange little slab, with its gleaming ring.

Ben's father interceded, saying, "He can make it, Ben. This man here can make an entire gun from scratch. Just give him a lump of slag is all he needs."

"Wonderful," Ben said, to fill the silence.

Reiner unexpectedly laughed. "How about," he said to the gunsmith, "that old Damascus double Jim Knauer loaded with triple FG and a smokeless powder? It's a wonder he has a face still."

Dutch unclenched his fist and, after a pause, chuckled.

Ben recognized in these pauses something of courtroom tactics; at his side he felt little Murray growing agitated at the delay. "Shall we come back tomorrow?" Ben asked.

He was ignored. Reiner was going on, "What was the make on that? A twelve-gauge Parker?"

"English gun," Dutch said. "A Westley Richards. He paid three hunnert for it, some dealer over in Royersford. Such foolishness, his first shot yet. Even split the stock." His eyelids lifted. "Who wants a beer?"

Ben's father said, "Jesus, I'm so full of turkey a beer might do me in."

Reiner looked amused. "They say liquor is good for bad circulation."

"I'd be happy to sip one but I can't take an oath to finish it. The first rule of hospitality is, Don't look a gift horse in the face." But an edge was going off his wit. After the effort of forming these sentences, the old man sat down, in an easy chair with exploded arms. Against the yellowish pallor of his face, his nose looked livid as a bruise.

"Sure," Ben said. "If they're being offered. Thank you."

"Son, how about you?" Dutch asked the boy. Murray's eyes widened, realizing nobody was going to answer for him.

"He's in training for his ski team," Ben said at last.

Dutch's eyes stayed on the boy. "Then you should have good legs. How about now going over and fetching four cans from that icebox over there?" He pointed with a loose fist.

"Refrigerator," Ben said to his son, acting as translator. As a child he had lived with a real icebox, zinc-lined oak, that digested a fresh block three times a week.

Dutch turned his back and fished through a shelf of grimy cigar boxes for a cylinder of metal that, when he held it beside the fragment of firing pin, satisfied him. He shuffled into the little room behind the counter, which brimmed with light and machinery.

As little Murray passed around the cold cans of Old Reading, his grandfather explained to the man in the Day-Glo hunting cap, "This boy is what you'd have to call an ardent athlete. He sails, he golfs, last winter he won blue medals at—what do they call 'em, Murray?"

"Slaloms. I flubbed the downhill, though."

"Hear that? He knows the language. If he was fortunate enough to live down here with you fine gentlemen, he'd learn gun language too. He'd be a crack shot in no time."

"Where we live in this city," the boy volunteered, "my mother won't even let me get a BB gun. She hates guns."

"The kid means the city of Boston. His father's on a first-name basis with the mayor." Ben heard the strained intake of breath between his father's sentences and tried not to hear the words. He and his son were tumbled together in a long, pained monologue. "Anything competitive, this kid loves. He doesn't get that from me. He doesn't get it from his old man, either. Ben always had this tactful way of keeping his thoughts to himself. You never knew what was going on inside his head. My biggest regret is I couldn't teach him the pleasure of working with your hands. He grew up watching me scrambling along by my wits and now he's doing the same damn thing. He should have had Dutch for a father. Dutch would have reached him."

To deafen himself Ben walked around the counter and into the workshop. Dutch was turning the little cylinder on a lathe. He wore no gog-

gles, and seemed to be taking no measurements. Into the mirror-smooth
blur of the spinning metal the man delicately pressed a tipped, hinged
cone. Curls of steel fell steadily to the scarred lathe table. Tan sparks flew
outward to the radius perhaps of a peony. The cylinder was becoming
two cylinders, a narrow one emerging from the shoulders of another. Ben
had once worked wood, in high-school shop, but this man could shape
metal: he could descend into the hard heart of things and exert his will.
Dutch switched off the lathe, with a sad grunt pushed himself away, and
shuffled splay-footed and swag-bellied, toward some other of his tools.
Ben, not wanting to seem to spy, returned to the larger room.

Reiner had undertaken a monologue of his own. ". . . you know your
average bullet comes out of the barrel rotating; that's why a rifle is called
that, for the rifling inside, that makes it spin. Now, what the North Viet-
namese discovered, if you put enough velocity into a bullet beyond a
critical factor, it tumbles, end over end like that. The Geneva Convention says you can't use a soft bullet that mushrooms inside the body like
the dumdum, but hit a man with a bullet tumbling like that, it'll tear his
arm right off."

The boy was listening warily, watching the bespectacled man's soft
white hands demonstrate tumbling. Ben's father sat in the exploded armchair, staring dully ahead, sucking back spittle, struggling silently for
breath.

"Of course, now," the lecture went on, "what they found was best over
there for the jungle was a plain shotgun. You take an ordinary twenty-
gauge, maybe mounted with a short barrel, you don't have visibility more
than fifty feet anyway, a man doesn't have a chance at that distance. The
spread of shot is maybe three feet around." With his arms Reiner placed
the circle on himself, centered on his heart. "It'll tear a man to pieces like
that. If he's not that close yet, then the shot pattern is wider and even a
miss is going to hurt him plenty."

"Death is part of life," Ben's father said, as if reciting a lesson learned
long ago.

Ben asked Reiner, "Were you in Vietnam?"

The man took off his hunting cap and displayed a bald head. "You got
me in the wrong rumpus. Navy gunner, World War Two. With those
forty-millimeter Bofors you could put a two-pound shell thirty thousand
feet straight up in the air."

Dutch emerged from his workshop holding a bit of metal in one hand
and a crumpled beer can in the other. He put the cylindrical bit down

amid the scattered parts of the bolt, fumbled at them, and they all came together.

"Does it fit?" Ben asked.

Dutch's clownish loose lips smiled. "You ask a lot of questions." He slipped the bolt back into the .22 and turned back to the workshop. The four others held silent, but for Ben's father's breathing. In time the flat spank of a rifle shot resounded, amplified by cement walls.

"That's miraculous to me," Ben's father said. "A mechanical skill like that."

"Thank you very much," Ben said, too quickly, when the gunsmith lay the mended and tested .22 on the counter. "How much do we owe you?"

Rather than answer, Dutch asked little Murray, "Didja ever see a machine like this before?" It was a device, operated by hand pressure, that assembled and crimped shotgun shells. He let the boy pull the handle. The shells marched in a circle, receiving each their allotment of powder and shot. "It can't explode," Dutch reassured Ben.

Reiner explained, "You see what this here is"—holding out the mysterious little slab with its bright ring—"is by putting in this bushing Dutch just made for me I can reduce the proportion of powder to shot, when I go into finer grains this deer season."

Murray backed off from the machine. "That's neat. Thanks a lot."

Dutch contemplated Ben. His verdict came: "I guess two dollars."

Ben protested, "That's not enough."

His father rescued him from the silence. "Pay the man what he asks; all the moola in the world won't buy God-given expertise like that."

Ben paid, and was in such a hurry to lead his party home he touched the side door before Dutch could switch off the burglar alarm. Bells shrilled, Ben jumped. Everybody laughed, even—though he had hated, from his schoolteaching days, what he called "cruel humor"—Ben's father.

In the dark of the car, the old man sighed. "He's what you'd have to call a genius and a gentleman. Did you see the way your dad looked at him? Pure adoration, man to man."

Ben asked him, "How do you feel?"

"Better. I didn't like Murray having to listen to all that blood and guts from Reiner."

"Boy," Murray said, "he sure is crazy about guns."

"He's lonely. He just likes getting out of the house and hanging around the shop. Must give Dutch a real pain in the old bazoo." Perhaps this sounded harsh, or applicable to himself, for he amended it. "Actually, he's harmless. He says he was in Navy artillery, but you know where he spent most of the war? Cruising around the Caribbean having a sunbath. He's like me. I was in the first one, and my big accomplishment was surviving the Spanish flu in camp. We were going to board in Hoboken the day of the Armistice."

"I never knew you were a soldier, Grandpa."

"Kill or be killed, that's my motto."

He sounded so faraway and fragile, saying this, Ben told him, "I hope we didn't wear you out."

"That's what I'm here for," Ben's father said, adding, as if reading a motto on the wall, "We aim to serve."

In bed, Ben tried to describe to Sally their adventure, the gun shop. "The whole place smelled of death. I think the kid was a little frightened."

Sally said, "Of course. He's only fourteen. You're awfully hard on him, you know."

"I know. My father was nice to me, and what did it get him? Chest pains. A pain in the old bazoo." Asleep, he dreamed he was a boy with a gun. A small bird, smaller than a dot in a puzzle, sat in the peach tree by the meadow fence. Ben aligned the sights and with a learned slowness squeezed. The dot fell like a stone. He went to it and found a wren's brown body, neatly deprived of a head. There was not much blood, just headless feathers. He awoke, and realized it was real. It had happened just that way, the first summer he had had the gun. He had been horrified.

After breakfast he and his son went out across the dead strawberry leaves to the dump again. There, the dream continued. Though Ben steadied his trembling, middle-aged hands against a hickory trunk and aimed so carefully his open eye burned, the cans and bottles ignored his shots. The bullets passed right through them. Whereas, when little Murray took the gun, the boy's freckled face gathered the muteness of the trees into his murderous concentration. The cans jumped, the bottles burst. "You're killing me!" Ben cried. In his relief and pride, he had to laugh.

Son

He is often upstairs, when he has to be home. He prefers to be elsewhere. He is almost sixteen, though beardless still, a man's mind indignantly captive in the frame of a child. I love touching him, but don't often dare. The other day, he had the flu, and a fever, and I gave him a back rub, marvelling at the symmetrical knit of muscle, the organic tension. He is high-strung. Yet his sleep is so solid he sweats like a stone in the wall of a well. He wishes for perfection. He would like to destroy us, for we are, variously, too fat, too jocular, too sloppy, too affectionate, too grotesque and heedless in our ways. His mother smokes too much. His younger brother chews with his mouth open. His older sister leaves unbuttoned the top button of her blouses. His younger sister tussles with the dogs, getting them overexcited, avoiding doing her homework. Everyone in the house talks nonsense. He would be a better father than his father. But time has tricked him, has made him a son. After a quarrel, if he cannot go outside and kick a ball, he retreats to a corner of the house and reclines on the beanbag chair in an attitude of strange—infantile or leonine—torpor. We exhaust him, without meaning to. He takes an interest in the newspaper now, the front page as well as the sports, in this tiring year of 1973.

He is upstairs, writing a musical comedy. It is a Sunday in 1949. He has volunteered to prepare a high-school assembly program; people will sing. Songs of the time go through his head, as he scribbles new words. *Up in de mornin', down at de school, work like a debil for my grades.* Below him, irksome voices grind on, like machines working their way through tunnels. His parents each want something from the other. "Marion, you don't understand that man like I do; he has a heart of gold." His father's charade is very complex: the world, which he fears, is used as a flail on his wife. But from his cringing attitude he would seem to an outsider the one being flailed. With burning-red face, the woman accepts the role of aggressor as penance for the fact, the incessant shameful fact, that *he* has to wrestle with the world while she hides here, in solitude, at home. This is normal, but does not seem to them to be so. Only by convolution have they arrived at the dominant/submissive relationship society has assigned them. For the man is maternally kind and with a smile hugs to himself his jewel, his certainty of being victimized; it is the mother whose tongue is sharp, who sometimes strikes. "Well, he gets you out of the house, and I guess that's gold to you." His answer is "Duty calls," pronounced mincingly. "The social contract is a balance of compromises." This will infuriate her, the son knows; as his heart thickens, the downstairs overflows with her hot voice. "*Don't* wear that smile at me! And *take* your hands off your hips; you look like a fairy!" Their son tries not to listen. When he does, visual details of the downstairs flood his mind: the two antagonists, circling with their coffee cups; the shabby mismatched furniture; the hopeful books; the framed photographs of the dead, docile and still like cowed students. This matrix of pain that bore him—he feels he is floating above it, sprawled on the bed as on a cloud, stealing songs as they come into his head (*Across the hallway from the guidance room / Lives a French instructor called Mrs. Blum*), contemplating the view from the upstairs window (last summer's burdock stalks like the beginnings of an alphabet, an apple tree holding three rotten apples as if pondering why they failed to fall), yearning for Monday, for the ride to school with his father, for the bell that calls him to homeroom, for the excitements of class, for Broadway, for fame, for the cloud that will carry him away, out of this, out.

He returns from his paper-delivery route and finds a few Christmas presents for him on the kitchen table. The year? 1911. Without opening them, he knocks them to the floor, puts his head on the table, and falls asleep. He must have been consciously dramatizing his plight: his father was sick, money was scarce, he had to work, to win food for the family when he was still a child. In his dismissal of Christmas, he expressed a fact: his love of anarchy, his distrust of the social contract. He treasured this moment of revolt; else why remember it, hoard a memory so bitter, and confide it to his son many Christmases later? He had a teaching instinct, though he claimed that life miscast him as a schoolteacher. His son suffered in his classes, feeling the noisy confusion as a persecution, but now wonders if his father's rebellious heart did not court confusion, not as Communists do, to impose their own order, but, more radical still, as an end pleasurable in itself, as truth's very body. Yet his handwriting (an old pink permission slip recently fluttered from a book where it had been marking a page for twenty years) was always considerately legible, and he was sitting up doing arithmetic the morning of the day he died.

And letters survive from that yet prior son, written in brown ink, in a tidy tame hand, home to his mother from the Missouri seminary where he was preparing for his vocation. The dates are 1887, 1888, 1889. Nothing much happened: he missed New Jersey, and was teased at a church social for escorting a widow. He wanted to do the right thing, but the little sheets of faded penscript exhale a dispirited calm, as if his heart already knew he would not make a successful minister, or live to be old. His son, my father, when old, drove hundreds of miles out of his way to visit the Missouri town from which those letters had been sent. Strangely, the town had not changed; it looked just as he had imagined, from his father's descriptions: tall wooden houses, rain-soaked, stacked on a bluff. The town was a sepia postcard mailed homesick home and preserved in an attic. My father cursed: his father's old sorrow bore him down into depression, into hatred of life. My mother claims his decline in health began at that moment.

He is wonderful to watch, playing soccer. Smaller than the others, my son leaps, heads, dribbles, feints, passes. When a big boy knocks him down, he tumbles on the mud, in his green-and-black school uniform, in an ecstasy of falling. I am envious. Never for me the jaunty pride of the school uniform, the solemn ritual of the coach's pep talk, the camaraderie of shook hands and slapped backsides, the shadow-striped hush of late afternoon and last quarter, the solemn vaulted universe of official combat, with its cheering mothers and referees striped like zebras and the bespectacled timekeeper alert with his claxon. When the boy scores a goal, he runs into the arms of his teammates with upraised arms and his face alight as if blinded by triumph. They lift him from the earth in a union of muddy hugs. What spirit! What valor! What skill! His father, watching from the sidelines, inwardly registers only one complaint: he feels the boy, with his talent, should be more aggressive.

They drove across the commonwealth of Pennsylvania to hear their son read in Pittsburgh. But when their presence was announced to the audience, they did not stand; the applause groped for them and died. My mother said afterwards she was afraid she might fall into the next row if she tried to stand in the dark. Next morning was sunny, and the three of us searched for the house where once they had lived. They had been happy there; it was said, indeed, that I had been conceived there, just before the temper of the Depression worsened and nipped my possible brothers and sisters in the bud. We found the library where she used to read Turgenev, and the little park where the bums slept close as paving stones in the summer night; but their old street kept eluding us, as we circled in the car. On foot, my mother found the tree. She claimed she recognized it, the sooty linden tree she would gaze into from their apartment windows. The branches, though thicker, had held their pattern. But the house itself, and the entire block, was gone. Stray bricks and rods of iron in the grass suggested that the demolition had been recent. We stood on the empty spot and laughed. They knew it was right, because the railroad tracks were the right distance away. In confirmation, a long freight train pulled itself east around the curve, its great weight gliding as if on a river current; then a silver passenger train came gliding as effortlessly in the other direction. The curve of the tracks tipped the cars slightly toward us. The Golden Triangle, gray and hazed, was off to our left, beyond a forest of bridges. We stood on the grassy rubble that morning, where something once had been, beside the tree still there, and were intensely happy. Why? Only we knew.

" 'No,' Dad said to me, 'the Christian ministry isn't a job you choose, it's a vocation for which you got to receive a call.' I could tell he wanted me to ask him. We never talked much, but we understood each other, we were both scared devils, not like you and the kid. I asked him, had he ever received the call? He said no. He said no, he never had. Received the call. That was a terrible thing, for him to admit. And I was the one he told. As far as I knew he never admitted it to anybody, but he admitted it to me. He felt like hell about it, I could tell. That was all we ever said about it. That was enough."

He has made his younger brother cry, and justice must be done. A father enforces justice. I corner the culprit in our bedroom; he is holding a cardboard mailing tube like a sword. The challenge flares white-hot; I roll my weight toward him like a rock down a mountain, and knock the weapon from his hand. He smiles. Smiles! Because my facial expression is silly? Because he is glad that he can still be overpowered, and hence is still protected? I do not hit him. We stand a second, father and son, and then as nimbly as on the soccer field he steps around me and out the door. He slams the door. He shouts obscenities in the hall, slams all the doors he can find on the way to his room. Our moment of smilingly shared silence was the moment of compression; now the explosion. The whole house rocks with it. Downstairs, his siblings and mother come to me and offer advice and psychological analysis. I was too aggressive. He is spoiled. What they can never know, mine alone to treasure, was that lucid many-sided second of his smiling and my relenting, before the world's inelastic balances of power resumed their rule.

As we huddle downstairs whispering, my son takes his revenge. In his room, he plays his guitar. He has greatly improved this winter; his hands getting bigger is the least of it. He has found in the guitar an escape. He plays the anonymous Romanza wherein repeated notes, with a sliding like the heart's valves, let themselves fall along the scale:

The notes fall, so gently he bombs us, drops feathery notes down upon us, our visitor, our prisoner.

Daughter, Last Glimpses of

JUST BEFORE SHE WENT AWAY to live with the red-bearded harpsichord-maker, our daughter asked us how to jitterbug. She had found these old Glenn Miller records in the closet. Eileen and I were embarrassed to tell her we didn't know how; though the jitterbug had been of our era, it was an era of the survival of the fittest, and for every Jack and Jill triumphantly trucking and twirling on the gymnasium floor to the local version of the Big Band sound there was a clutch of Eileens and Geoffreys slumping enviously against the padded wall, or huddling in the bleachers, wondering how it was done, wondering if anyone who knew how would ever invite them to dance. How much kinder, we urged upon our daughter, of your own generation to invent dances that require no skill, that indeed cannot be done wrong, and that therefore do not create hurtful distinctions between the ins and the outs, the adroit and the gauche, the beautiful and the un-.

Our daughter looked at us with wide eyes. Her face is mostly frontal, like a cat's. As she turned eighteen her eyes were exchanging that staring look of childhood for something softer and more inward, with a margin of distrust to it, to cushion amazement. But how, she seemed now to be asking, amazed, could two people unable even to jitterbug manage to get together and have *me?* She had been our first child. In our simplicity we had called her Joy.

There was dancing, in those last glimpses. My daughter had been taking ballet at school and would do backbends and cartwheels on the lawn, or slow, rolling splits and stretches in the front hall. For her birthday I had bought her an exercise barre, to use in her room, but she preferred the front hall, where the mailman sometimes showered letters in upon her. Her body, in black tights and leotard, was developing muscles and length; the front hall was too small, really, for these extensive exercises, which included resting her head—golden hair, platinum nape—between her knees, and then snapping it up, so that her eyes in her sudden face looked surprised at something discovered in *my* face. On her body the black cloth paled wherever it stretched around a bulge.

Though we failed to teach her to jitterbug (the motions she improvised to go with "In the Mood" and "I've Got a Gal in Kalamazoo" owed more to the African Dance Troupe than to the crisp, tart Forties), she taught her younger brother how to hold a girl and sway to James Taylor and Carole King. They did this in the study, where years ago the record-player had been mistakenly installed. Looking up from trying to read, I would see his face on her shoulder, chin high because she was taller, the angel face of my second son half lost in his sister's hair and engulfed by bliss, his eyelashes extensions of the sparkle of his slitted eyes as he and she swayed like seaweeds in the waves of amplified music—their feet, as far as I could see, doing no steps at all.

"Isn't Joy nice to Ethan?" I asked Eileen later, somewhat rhetorically.

"She's nice to all of us these days," she replied.

It was true. She set the dinner table for her mother and did the dishes. She read her little sister bedtime stories. I would see them, the two girls, framed by the doorway into Katharine's room, sitting on the bed beneath the tacked-up pictures of horses and dogs, Joy's face as solemn as a Sunday-school teacher's. The two profiles bent toward each other symmetrically, for all the six years between them, but that the younger girl's forehead had an apprehensive outward curve whereas Joy's brow was—is—flat and determined and square. Katharine at twelve was going through a troubled time. Joy would be talking to her about grades, or diets, or their grandmother. My mother was dying, that same spring, of cancer. The last time she came to the house (she knew it was the last time but disdained to admit it, as she disdained to admit she was dying; she had been a lifelong understater; her last words, to the attending nurse and me, were "Well, much obliged"), Joy did an adult thing: she hugged her at parting. A shy sideways hug, for the old lady had grown frail as sticks, her walk a precarious shuffle. "Hope you soon feel better," Joy said, hesitating and coming to a blush over the "feel better," knowing it would take a miracle. How big my daughter looked!—freckled, with sloping dancer's shoulders, standing at the height of health beside the shrunken stoic wraith from whom she was descended. And for me it was as if, in one of those thrilling swift crossovers the good jitterbuggers could do, they had switched positions from the distant moment when my toddling infant daughter had fallen against a hot woodstove in Vermont and her grandmother, so calm the cigarette never left her mouth, applied ice and butter and soothing words to the scorched arm that must have felt, to the astonished, shrieking child, seized by Death itself.

At the funeral, in our ancestral Unitarian church, Joy and Katharine not only prayed, they got up on their knees on the kneeling stool in upright Episcopalian style. And, their faces covered by their hands, they looked like twins, in dresses Joy had made for the ceremony, from the same dark, small-flowered cloth.

Her sewing worried me. "All she ever does is hang around the house and sit in her room and sew. She acts like some little spinster. Why doesn't she ever go out with boys? It isn't as if she's ugly. Is she?"

"Are you asking seriously?" my wife asked.

"I am. I can't tell. She's my daughter."

"You're shocking. She's gorgeous. Boys her own age just don't turn her on."

"The reason you're so complacent about it," I told Eileen, "is she does all your housework for you."

"She enjoys doing it. She's learning something."

"Yeah, how to be Cinderella."

"If that's your analogy, relax."

Left to rust in her room, the sewing machine is no trouble; but the rooster is. My daughter insisted, with all the determination in her solid brow (as a baby she used to beat it against the bars of the crib until we would lift her out), on getting chickens. Chickens? In our little yard? She said they would take up no room. They would turn our garbage into fresh eggs. They would in themselves constitute a natural cycle. Compared with an automobile, they consumed almost nothing. They would be aesthetic and amusing. Chickens.

Our bargain went that she would build the pen and little chicken house with me; but something about the hammering and sawing and the size of the nails and the roughness of my construction pained her, for she wandered away, and I built it alone. Mark, our older son, came out I thought to help, but he only intended to complain.

"God, Dad, it's homely."

"I'm making it the best I can."

"It's not you, it's the *idea*. Why should she have chickens? You won't even let me have a .22. Think of the noise pollution. Think of the feathers, Dad."

"I agree, I agree. Could you hold this two-by-four steady while I nail it down?"

"And another thing, I *hate* the way she drives the car. She's going to kill somebody, Dad, and you're going to have to pay for it."

Joy had consented to apply for her driver's license just that winter, after holding out, for ecology's sake, since the age of sixteen. It was true, when she drove the Ford the machine became loose-jointed and precarious in flight, like a flamingo. Beside her in the passenger's seat, I felt she was brushing things—mailboxes, hydrants—from the side of the road. Whereas, when Mark, freshly sixteen and instantly equipped with a learner's permit, drives, the automobile crouches low to the ground and noses rapidly along the highway like a tracking beagle, with nervous, sniffing jerks. "Not to mention the fact," he continued, "she's gotten Ethan all stirred up about sex."

"We learn by living," I told him, and drove a nail to end the conversation. When the chicken house was done, Joy came out of hiding and admired it—the little sliding door, the roost hinged to swing upward so that the poultrykeeper (ahem) could sweep and change the straw. In fact she did, at first, do a conscientious job, sweeping, scattering grain, gathering eggs in the morning dew like some thick-waisted lass out of Hardy. I remember how, as I sat down to breakfast, she would push open the back door with her shoulder, her eyes starry above the wonder of the eggs still warm in her hands. It was my paternal duty to eat one. The yolks were unpleasantly orange, thanks to the richness of our garbage. And my daughter danced around my eating, celebrating this miraculous completion, this cycle, this food for the breadwinner, this chicken and egg. She doted on those dowdy birds. She painted ivy on their house, watched them like a scientist, discovered that "pecking order" wasn't merely a phrase, papered the walls of her room with scratchy drawings of chickens, and even did poems; one line went, as I remember, *peck scrawk scrabble peck*. For all her mothering, the chickens gradually ceased to lay.

The idea of a rooster was hatched without consultation with me.

One Thursday after work I got out of the car and there he was, a little red-brown bird with absurdly long tail feathers and a dictatorial way of cocking his head. He was smaller than the hens, but already they followed him liquidly, bubbling in their throats and jostling for precedence, as he surveyed the pen and coop I had built, all unbeknownst for *him*. He had been brought in a psychedelic Volkswagen bus by a small bearded man with pink eyes and a mussed, unhappy air. Joy, Eileen, and Katharine were sitting with him at the kitchen table in the evening light. Strange thing, both Joy and Eileen had cigarettes in their hands. Eileen had quit when my mother's cancer was diagnosed, and as far as I knew Joy had never started. The rooster-bringer had heard of our need from a boyfriend of Joy's ecology instructor at school. Before I arrived, and though he mumbled, they had drawn a surprising mass of information from him: he was nearly thirty, his wife had left him a while ago, the "bunch of people" he was living with on this farm was breaking up, they were giving everything away—roosters, sheep, the Rototiller. Also, he had a cold, and couldn't find a satisfactory kind of industrial glue for his harpsichords. Soon after I arrived, he left.

"God, Dad, he was bogus," Mark said.

"I agree."

"I thought he was *cute*," Joy called from the other room. This was new; she never eavesdropped. What other people said or did, her stance had been these past years, did not touch her. She had lived in a world of her own making, with a serenity that floated dishes onto the table without a click.

Now, with a crash, her dependence on others, and ours on her, was declared. She begged or stole the Ford so often we have had to buy a second car, just as the gas shortage overtakes the world. Eileen is back to doing the dishes and smoking a pack a day. Katharine says that if Joy could have chickens she doesn't see why she can't have some sheep in the back yard. They would keep the grass short for me. Their wool would be worth money. They would look pretty. Mark has offered to shoot the chickens with his new .22. Ethan, his first partner fled, now goes to dances at the junior high, one of my neckties knotted loose, his hair combed without our nagging; he is so dolled up and beautiful we all have to laugh at him before he goes. As to Joy's departure, it was hurried and at the time not very real to the rest of us. I retain no glimpses. What coat was she wearing? What suitcase did she take? Did she slam the door? She may have said "Much obliged," but I didn't hear it.

The house seems bigger. The record-player, after its spell of Ralph Kirkpatrick, is back to Carole King, or silent. The front hall is clear to traffic. We come and go. Sometimes days pass before one of us remembers to bring in the eggs. Irregularly fed, the flock has pecked a gap beneath the chicken wire, and gets into the neighbor's lettuce. During one such outing, another neighbor's Labrador carried off the white hen with a toe missing—the lowest in the pecking order, uncannily. How did the dog know? He carried her in his mouth, white as fresh laundry in the dusk, up into the pines; the children heard her squawk and throbble until night fell.

If all is not well with his world, the rooster never admits it. Every morning, he gets up on those Ruberoid self-sealing Slate Green asphalt shingles I hammered down to make him a roof, a midair hop and skip from my bedroom window, and he crows. Lying awake, I can hear him practicing his crow in the small hours, inside his house: a rather gentle, even wheezy, half-unfurling of the magic scroll inside his chest. Maybe he is dreaming of the dawn, maybe the streetlight fools him. But there is no mistaking the real thing: as the windowpanes brighten from purple to mauve to white, he flaps up on his roof with a slap like a newspaper hitting the porch and gives a crow as if to hoist with his own pure lungs that sleepy fat sun to the zenith of the sky. He never moderates his joy, though I am gradually growing deafer to it. That must be the difference between soulless creatures and human beings: creatures find every dawn as remarkable as all the ones previous, whereas the soul grows calluses.

THE TWO ISEULTS

Solitaire

THE CHILDREN were asleep, and his wife had gone out to a meeting; she was like his father in caring about the community. He found the deck of cards in the back of a desk drawer and sat down at the low round table. He had reached a juncture in his life where there was nothing to do but play solitaire. It was the perfect, final retreat—beyond solitaire, he imagined, there was madness. Only solitaire utterly eased the mind; only solitaire created that blankness into which a saving decision might flow. Conviviality demanded other people, with their fretful emanations of desire; reading imposed the author's company; and one emerged from the anesthetic of drunkenness to find that the operation had not been performed. But in the rise and collapse of the alternately colored ranks of cards, in the grateful transpositions and orderly revelations and unexpected redemptions, the circuits of the mind found an occupation exactly congruent with their own secret structure. The mind was filled without being strained. The week after he graduated from college—already married, his brain worn to the point where a page of newspaper seemed a cruelly ramifying puzzle—he played solitaire night after night by the glow of a kerosene lamp on an old kitchen table in Vermont; and at the end of the week he had seen the way that his life must go in the appallingly wide world that had opened before him. He had drawn a straight line from that night to the night of his death, and began walking on it.

During that week he had remembered how in his childhood his mother would play solitaire by the light of the stained-glass chandelier in the dining room. His father would be out somewhere, doing good for the community, and he and his mother would be alone. He was an only child, and as such obscurely felt himself to be the center of the sadness that oppressed them. Frightened of her silence and of the slithering of the cards, he would beg her to stop. Tell me a story, come into the kitchen and make some toast, go to bed, anything; but stop playing solitaire.

"One more game," his mother would say, her faced pitted and dragged by the shadows cast by the overhead chandelier. And then she would slip into one of the impersonations whereby she filled their empty house with phantoms, as if to make up to him for the brothers and sisters she had not, somehow, been permitted to give him. "The weary gambler stakes his all," she said in a soft but heavy monotone. "The night is late. The crowds have left the gaming tables. One lonely figure remains, his house, his car, his yacht, his jewels, his very life hinging on the last turn of the cards."

"Don't, Mother; *don't!*" He burst into tears, and she looked up and smiled, as if greeting a fond forgotten sight upon her return from a long journey. He felt her wonder, *Who is this child?* It was as if the roof of the house were torn off, displaying the depth of night sky.

He knew now that her mind had been burdened in that period. Everything was being weighed in it. He remembered very faintly—for he had tried to erase it immediately—her asking him if he would like to go alone with her far away, to the sunny Southwest, and live a new life. *No,* must have been his answer, *Mother, don't!* For he had loved his father, loved him out of the silence and blindness that wait at the bottom of our brains as the final possibility, the second baptism; the removal of his father plunged him toward that black pool prematurely. And she, too, must have felt a lack of ripeness, for in the end she merely moved them all a little distance, to a farm where he grew up in solitude and which at the first opportunity he left, a farm where now his father and mother still performed, with an intimate expertness that almost justified them, the half-comic routines of their incompatibility. In the shrill strength of his childish fear he had forced this on them; he was, in this sense, their guardian, their father.

And now the father of others. Odd, he thought, setting a black nine below a red ten, how thoroughly our lives are devoted to doing the contrary of what our parents did. He had married early, to escape the farm, and had rapidly given his wife children, to make his escape irrevocable. Also, he had wished to spare his children the responsibility and terror of solitude. He wondered if they loved him as he had loved his father, wondered what depth of night sky would be displayed to them by his removal. To some extent he was already removed. They formed a club from which he was excluded. Their corporate commotion denied him access. The traces of his own face in their faces troubled him with the suspicion that he had squandered his identity. Slowly he had come to see that children are not our creations but our guests, people who enter the world by our invitation but with their smiles and dispositions already prepared in some mysterious other room. Their predictable woe and fright and the crippled shapes they might take had imperceptibly joined the finances and the legalities as considerations that were finite, manageable. Problems to which there is any solution at all, no matter how difficult and complex, are not really problems. *(Red four on black five.)* Night by night, lying awake, he had digested the embarrassments, the displacements, the disappointments, the reprimands and lectures and appeals that were certain; one by one he had made impossibilities possible. At last he had stripped the problem to its two white poles, the two women.

His wife was fair, with pale eyelashes and hair containing, when freshly shampooed, reddish lights. His mistress was as black-and-white as a drawing in ink: her breasts always shocked him with their electric silken pallor, and the contrast with the dark nipples and aureoles. In the summer, she tanned; his wife freckled. His wife had the more delicate mind, but his mistress, having suffered more, knew more that he didn't know. Their opposition was not simple. His wife's handwriting, developed out of the printing she had been taught at a progressive school, looked regular but was often illegible; the other's, with its hurried stenographic slant, was always clear, even when phrasing panic. His wife, carnally entered, opened under him as an intimidating moist void; his mistress in contrast felt dry and tight, so tight the first thrusts quite hurt. His wife, now that she saw herself on the edge of an abyss, clung to him with an ardor that his mistress would have found immodest. He had come to feel a furtive relief when a day passed without lovemaking being thrust upon him; pinned between whirlpools, he was sated with the sound and sight of women crying. His mistress cried big: with thrilling swiftness her face dissolved and, her mouth smeared out of all shape, she lurched against him with an awkward bump and soaked his throat in abusive sobs. Whereas his wife wept like a miraculous icon, her face immobile while the tears ran, and so silently that as they lay together in bed at night he would have to ask her, "Are you crying?" Back and forth, back and forth, like a sore fist his heart oscillated between them, and the oscillations grew in intensity as the two poles drew together and demanded that he choose one. He had allowed them to draw together, had allowed his wife to know, and allowed his mistress to know that she knew, in the hope that they would merge — would turn out to be, in fact, one woman, with no choice needed, or the decision settled between them. He had miscalculated. Though he had drawn them so close that one settling into his embrace could smell the other's perfume, each woman became more furiously herself.

(A king uncovered, but nowhere to put him.) How could he balance their claims and rights? The list was entirely one-sided. Prudence, decency, pity—not light things—all belonged to the guardian of his children and home; and these he would lose. He would lose the homely old neighborhood that he loved, the summer evenings spent scratching in his little garden of lettuce and tomatoes, the gritty adhesion of his elder daughter's hand to his as they walked to the Popsicle store, the decade of books and prints and records and furniture that had accumulated, the cellar full of carpentry tools, the attic full of old magazines. And he would as well lose his own conception of himself, for to abandon his children and a woman who with scarcely a complaint or a quarrel had given him her youth was simply not what he would do. He was the son of parents who had stayed together for his sake. That straight line, once snapped, could not be set straight again.

While on the other side there was nothing, or next to nothing— merely a cry, a cry for him that he had never heard before. No doubt it was momentary; but so was life. She had little to give him but bereavement and a doubtless perishable sense of his existing purely as a man. Her presence made him happy and her near presence made him very happy. Yet, even when they were so closely together their very skins felt wished away, strange glass obstacles came between them, transparent elbows and icy hard surfaces that constituted, he supposed, the structure of what is called morality.

The weary gambler stakes his all. This game was clearly headed nowhere. An ominous unanimity of red had pretty well blocked the seven ranks. The kings had been buried for lack of space, one of the aces was not yet up, and the cards left in his hand were few. He fanned them and found that in fact there were three. He turned the top one up. The eight of spades. He put it below a red nine, but this unblocked nothing. Two cards left. He decided upon a gamble. A card for his wife, a card for *her.* His heart began to tremble at this boldness. In the months past, he had learned to listen to his heart; he had never noticed before what a positive will this supposedly oblivious organ possessed. On his way to a tryst it would press in his throat like a large bird trying to escape a trap, and at night, when he lay down in the hope of sleeping, it would churn and rattle on his ribs like the blade of a Waring Blender chopping ice.

He turned the first card and looked down at it from what felt like a great height. The ten of diamonds, for his wife. It was a strong card. He felt frightened, and looked down at the spiderweb back of the last card with a sensation of his vision's being impaired by the roaring in his chest.

Instead of turning the last card over, he tore it across; the card was plastic-coated and tough, and crumpled before it tore. From a fragment he saw that it had been the missing ace. No matter. He was a modern man, not superstitious even alone with himself; his life must flow from within. He had made his decision, and sat inert, waiting for grief to be laid upon him.

Leaves

THE GRAPE LEAVES outside my window are curiously beautiful. "Curiously" because it comes upon me as strange, after the long darkness of self-absorption and fear and shame in which I have been living, that things are beautiful, that independent of our catastrophes they continue to maintain the casual precision, the effortless abundance of inventive "effect," which are the hallmark and specialty of Nature. Nature: this morning it seems to me very clear that Nature may be defined as that which exists without guilt. Our bodies are in Nature; our shoes, their laces, the little plastic tips of the laces—everything around us and about us is in Nature, and yet something holds us away from it, like the upward push of water that keeps us from touching the sandy bottom, ribbed and glimmering with crescental fragments of oyster shell, so clear to our eyes.

A blue jay lights on a twig outside my window. Momentarily sturdy, he stands astraddle, his dingy rump toward me, his head alertly frozen in silhouette, the predatory curve of his beak stamped on a sky almost white above the misting tawny marsh. See him? I do, and, snapping the chain of my thought, I have reached through glass and seized him and stamped him on this page. Now he is gone. And yet, there, a few lines above, he still is, "astraddle," his rump "dingy," his head "alertly frozen." A curious trick, possibly useless, but mine.

The grape leaves where they are not in each other's shadows are golden. Flat leaves, they take the sun flatly, and turn the absolute light, sum of the spectrum and source of all life, into the crayon yellow with which children render it. Here and there, wilt transmutes this lent radiance into a glowing orange, and the green of the still-tender leaves—for green persists long into autumn, if we look—strains from the sunlight a fine-veined chartreuse. The shadows these leaves cast upon each other, though vagrant and nervous in the wind that sends friendly scavenging rattles scurrying across the roof, are yet quite various and definite, containing innumerable barbaric suggestions of scimitars, flanged spears, prongs, and menacing helmets. The net effect, however, is innocent of menace. On the contrary, its intricate simultaneous suggestion of shelter and openness, warmth and breeze, invites me outward; my eyes venture into the leaves beyond. I am surrounded by leaves. The oak's are lobed paws of tenacious rust; the elm's, scant feathers of a feminine yellow; the sumac's, a savage, toothed blush. I am upheld in a serene and burning universe of leaves. Yet something plucks me back, returns me to that inner darkness where guilt is the sun.

The events need to be sorted out. I am told I behaved wantonly, and it will take time to integrate this unanimous impression with the unqualified righteousness with which our own acts, however admittedly miscalculated, invest themselves. And once the events are sorted out—the actions given motivations, the actors assigned psychologies, the miscalculations tabulated, the abnormalities named, the whole furious and careless growth pruned by explanation and rooted in history and returned, as it were, to Nature—what then? Is not such a return spurious? Can our spirits really enter Time's haven of mortality and sink composedly among the mulching leaves? No: we stand at the intersection of two kingdoms, and there is no advance and no retreat, only a sharpening of the edge where we stand.

I remember most sharply the black of my wife's dress as she left our house to get her divorce. The dress was a soft black sheath, with a scalloped neckline, and Helen always looked handsome in it; it flattered her pallor. This morning she looked especially handsome, her face utterly white with fatigue. Yet her body, that natural thing, ignored our catastrophe, and her shape and gestures were incongruously usual. She kissed me lightly in leaving, and we both felt the humor of this trip's being insufficiently unlike any other of her trips to Boston—to Symphony, to Bonwit's. The same search for the car keys, the same harassed instructions to the baby-sitter, the same little dip and thrust of her head as she settled behind the wheel of her car. And I, satisfied at last, divorced, studied my children with the eyes of one who had left them, examined my house as one does a set of snapshots from an irretrievable time, drove through the turning landscape as a man in asbestos cuts through a fire, met my wife-to-be—weeping yet smiling, stunned yet brave—and felt, unstoppably, to my horror, the inner darkness burst my skin and engulf us both and drown our love. The natural world, where our love had existed, ceased to exist. My heart shied back; it shies back still. I retreated. As I drove back, the leaves of the trees along the road stated their shapes to me. There is no more story to tell. By telephone I plucked my wife back; I clasped the black of her dress to me, and braced for the pain.

It does not stop coming. The pain does not stop coming. Almost every day, a new installment arrives by mail or face or phone. Every time the telephone rings, I expect it to uncoil some new convolution of consequence. I have come to hide in this cottage, but even here, there is a telephone, and the scraping sounds of wind and branch and unseen animals are charged with its electric silence. At any moment, it may explode, and the curious beauty of the leaves will be eclipsed again.

In nervousness, I rise, and walk across the floor. A spider like a white asterisk hangs in air in front of my face. I look at the ceiling and cannot see where its thread is attached. The ceiling is smooth plasterboard. The spider hesitates. It feels a huge alien presence. Its exquisite white legs spread warily, and of its own dead weight it twirls on its invisible thread. I catch myself in the quaint and antique pose of the fabulist seeking to draw a lesson from a spider, and become self-conscious. I dismiss self-consciousness and do earnestly attend to this minute articulated star hung so pointedly before my face; and am unable to read the lesson. The spider and I inhabit contiguous but incompatible cosmoses. Across the gulf we feel only fear. The telephone remains silent. The spider reconsiders its spinning. The wind continues to stir the sunlight. In walking in and out of this cottage, I have tracked the floor with a few dead leaves, pressed flat like scraps of dark paper.

And what are these pages but leaves? Why do I produce them but to thrust, by some subjective photosynthesis, my guilt into Nature, where there is no guilt? Now the marsh, level as a carpet, is streaked with faint green amid the shades of brown—russet, ochre, tan, *marron*—and on the far side, where the land lifts above tide level, evergreens stab upward sullenly. Beyond them, there is a low blue hill; in this coastal region, the hills are almost too modest to bear names. But I *see* it; for the first time in months I see it. I see it as a child, fingers gripping and neck straining, glimpses the roof of a house over a cruelly high wall. Under my window, the lawn is lank and green and mixed with leaves shed from a small elm, and I remember how, the first night I came to this cottage, thinking I was leaving my life behind me, I went to bed alone and read, in the way one reads stray books in a borrowed house, a few pages of an old edition of *Leaves of Grass*. And my sleep was a loop, so that in awaking I seemed still in the book, and the light-struck sky quivering through the stripped branches of the young elm seemed another page of Whitman, and I was entirely open, and lost, like a woman in passion, and free, and in love, without a shadow in any corner of my being. It was a beautiful awakening, but by the next night I had returned to my house.

The precise barbaric shadows on the grape leaves have shifted. The angle of illumination has altered. I imagine warmth leaning against the door, and open the door to let it in; sunlight falls flat at my feet like a penitent.

The Stare

THEN THERE IT WAS, in the corner of his eye. He turned, his heart frozen. The incredibility of her being here, now, at a table in this one restaurant on the one day when he was back in the city, did not check the anticipatory freezing of his heart, for when they had both lived in New York they had always been lucky at finding each other, time after time; and this would be one more time. Already, in the instant between recognition and turning, he had framed his first words; he would rise, with the diffidence she used to think graceful, and go to her and say, "Hey. It's you."

Her face would smile apologetically, lids lowered, and undergo one of its little shrugs. "It's me."

"I'm so glad. I'm so sorry about what happened." And everything would be understood, and the need of forgiveness once again magically put behind them, like a wall of paper flames they had passed through.

It was someone else, a not very young woman whose hair, not really the color of her hair at all, had, half seen, suggested the way her hair, centrally parted and pulled back into a glossy French roll, would cut with two dark wings into her forehead, making her brow seem low and intense and emphasizing her stare. He felt the eyes of his companions at lunch question him, and he returned his attention to them, his own eyes smarting from the effort of trying to press this unknown woman's appearance into the appearance of another. One of his companions at the table—a gentle gray banker whose affection for him, like a generous check, quietly withheld at the bottom a tiny deduction of tact, a modest minus paid as the fee for their mutual security—smiled in such a way as to balk his impulse to blurt, to confess. His other companion was an elderly female underwriter, an ex-associate, whose statistical insight was remorseless but who in personal manner was all feathers and feigned dismay. "I'm seeing ghosts," he explained to her, and she nodded, for they had, all three, with the gay, withering credulity of nonbelievers, been discussing ghosts. The curtain of conversation descended again, but his palms tingled, and, as if trapped between two mirrors, he seemed to face a diminishing multiplication of her stare.

The first time they met, in an apartment with huge slablike paintings and fragile furniture that seemed to be tiptoeing, she had come to the defense of something her husband had said, and he had irritably wondered how a woman of such evident spirit and will could debase herself to the support of statements so asinine, and she must have felt, across the room, his irritation, for she gave him her stare. It was, as a look, both blunt and elusive: somewhat cold, certainly hard, yet curiously wide, and even open—its essential ingredient shied away from being named. Her eyes were the only glamorous feature of a freckled, bony, tomboyish face, remarkable chiefly for its sharp willingness to express pleasure. When she laughed, her teeth were bared like a skull's, and when she stared, her great, grave, perfectly shaped eyes insisted on their shape as rigidly as a statue's.

Later, when their acquaintance had outlived the initial irritations, he had met her in the Museum of Modern Art, amid an exhibit of old movie stills, and, going forward with the innocent cheerfulness that her presence even then aroused in him, he had been unexpectedly met by her stare. "We missed you Friday night," she said.

"You did? What happened Friday night?"

"Oh, nothing. We just gave a little party and expected you to come."

"We weren't invited."

"But you *were*. I phoned your wife."

"She never said anything to me. She must have forgotten."

"Well, I don't suppose it matters."

"But it *does*. I'm so sorry. I would have loved to have come. It's very funny that she forgot it; she really just lives for parties."

"Yes." And her stare puzzled him, since it was no longer directed at him; the hostility between the two women existed before he had fulfilled its reason.

Later still, at a party they all did attend, he had, alone with her for a moment, kissed her, and the response of her mouth had been disconcerting; backing off, expecting to find in her face the moist, formless warmth that had taken his lips, he encountered her stare instead. In the months that unfolded from this, it had been his pleasure to see her stare relax. Her body gathered softness under his; late one night, after yet another

party, his wife, lying beside him in the pre-dawn darkness of her ignorance, had remarked, with the cool, fair appraisal of a rival woman, how
beautiful she—*she*, the other—had become, and he had felt, half dreaming in the warm bed he had betrayed, justified. Her laugh no longer
flashed out so hungrily, and her eyes, brimming with the secret he and
she had made, deepened and seemed to rejoin the girlishness that had lingered in the other features of her face. Seeing her across a room standing
swathed in the beauty he had given her, he felt a creator's, a father's,
pride. There existed, when they came together, a presence of tenderness
like a ghostly child who when they parted was taken away and set to
sleeping. Yet even in those months, in the depths of their secret, as they
lay together as if in a padded dungeon, discussing with a gathering urgency
what they would do when their secret crumbled and they were exposed,
there would now and then glint out at him, however qualified by tears
and languor, the unmistakable accusatory hardness. It was accusing, yet
that was not its essence; his conscience shied away from naming the pressure that had formed it and that, it imperceptibly became apparent, he
was helpless to relieve. Each time they parted, she would leave behind, in
the last instant before the door closed, a look that stayed with him, vibrating like a struck cymbal.

The last time he saw her, all the gentle months had been stripped away
and her stare, naked, had become furious. "Don't you love me?" Two
households were in turmoil and the rich instinct that had driven him to
her had been transformed to a thin need to hide and beg.

"Not enough." He meant it simply, as a fact, as something that already
had been made plain.

But she took it as a death blow, and in a face whitened and drawn by the
shocks of recent days, from beneath dark wings of tensely parted hair, her
stare revived into a life so coldly controlled and adamantly hostile that for
weeks he could not close his eyes without confronting it—much as a victim of torture must continue to see the burning iron with which he was
blinded.

Now, back in New York, walking alone, soothed by food and profitable
talk, he discovered himself so healed that his wound ached to be reopened.
The glittering city bristled with potential prongs. The pale disc of every
face, as it slipped from the edge of his vision, seemed to cup the possibility of being hers. He felt her searching for him. Where would she
look? It would be her style simply to walk the streets, smiling and striding, in the hope of their meeting. He had a premonition—and, yes,

there, waiting to cross Forty-third Street between two Puerto Rican messenger boys, it was she, with her back toward him; there was no mistaking the expectant tilt of her head, the girlish curve of her high, taut cheek, the massed roll of hair pulled so glossy he used to imagine that the hairpins gave her pain. He drew abreast, timid and prankish, to surprise her profile, and she became a wrinkled painted woman with a sagging lower lip. He glanced around incredulously, and her stare glimmered and disappeared in the wavering wall-window of a modernistic bank. Crossing the street, he looked into the bank, but there was no one, no one he knew—only some potted tropical plants that looked vaguely familiar.

He returned to work. His company had lent him for this visit the office of a man on vacation. He managed to concentrate only by imagining that each five minutes were the final segment of time he would have to himself before she arrived. When the phone on his desk rang, he expected the receptionist to announce that a distraught woman with striking eyes was asking for him. When he went into the halls, a secretary flickering out of sight battered his heart with a resemblance. He returned to his borrowed office, and was startled not to find her in it, wryly examining the yellowed children's drawings—another man's children—taped to the walls. The bored afternoon pasted shadows on these walls. Outside his window, the skyscrapers began to glow. He went down the elevator and into the cool, crowded dusk thankful for her consideration; it was like her to let him finish his day's work before she declared her presence. But now, now she could cease considerately hiding, and he could take her to dinner with a clear conscience. He checked his wallet to make sure he had enough money. He decided he would refuse to take her to a play, though undoubtedly she would suggest it. She loved the theatre's mock fuss. But they had too little time together to waste it in awareness of a third thing.

He had taken a room at what he still thought of as their hotel. To his surprise, she was not waiting for him in the lobby, which seemed filled with a party, a competition of laughter. Charles Boyer, one eyebrow arched, was waiting for the elevator. She would have liked that, that celebrity visitation, as she sat on the bench near the desk, waiting and watching, her long legs crossed and one black shoe jabbing the air with its heel and toe. He had even prepared his explanation to the clerk: This was his wife. They had had (voice lowered, the unavoidable blush not, after all, inappropriate) a fight, and impulsively she had followed him to New York, to make up. Irregular, but . . . women. So could his single reservation kindly be changed to a double? Thank you.

This little play was so firmly written in his head that he looked into the bar to make sure the leading actress was not somewhere in the wings. The bar was bluely lit and amply patronized by fairies. Their drawled, elaborately enunciating voices, discussing musical comedies in tones of peculiar passion, carried to him, and he remembered how she, when he had expressed distaste, had solemnly explained to him that homosexuals were people, too, and how she herself often felt attracted to them, and how it always saddened her that she had nothing, you know—her stare defensively sharpened—to give them. "That old bag, she's overexposed herself," one of the fairies stridently declared, of a famous actress.

He took the elevator up to his room. It was similar to ones they had shared, but nothing was exactly the same, except the plumbing fixtures, and even these were differently arranged. He changed his shirt and necktie. In the mirror, behind him, a slow curve of movement, like a woman's inquisitive step, chilled his spine; it was the closet door drifting shut.

He rushed from the suffocating vacant room into the streets, to inhale the invisible possibility of finding her. He ate at the restaurant he would have chosen for them both. The waiter seemed fussed, seating a solitary man. The woman of a couple at a nearby table adjusted an earring with a gesture that belonged to her; she had never had her ears pierced, and this naïveté of her flesh had charmed him. He abstained from coffee. Tonight he must court sleep assiduously.

He walked to tire himself. Broadway was garish with the clash of mating—sailors and sweethearts, touts and tarts. Spring infiltrates a city through the blood of its inhabitants. The side streets were hushed like the aisles of long Pullman sleepers being drawn forward by their diminishing perspective. She would look for him on Fifth Avenue; her window-shopper's instinct would send her there. He saw her silhouette at a distance, near Rockefeller Center, and up close he spotted a certain momentary plane of her face that flew away in a flash, leaving behind the rubble of a face he did not know, had never kissed or tranquilly studied as it lay averted on a pillow. Once or twice, he even glimpsed, shadowed in a doorway, huddled on a bench tipping down toward the Promethean fountain, the ghostly child of their tenderness, asleep; but never her, her in the fragrant solidity he had valued with such a strange gay lightness when it was upon him. Statistically, it began to seem wonderful that out of so many faces not one was hers. It seemed only reasonable that he could skim, like interest, her presence from a sufficient quantity of strangers—that he could refine her, like radium, out of enough pitchblende. She had never been reserved with him; this terrible tact of absence was unlike her.

The moon gratuitously added its stolen glow to the harsh illumination around the iceless skating rink. As if sensing his search, faces turned as he passed. Each successive instant shocked him by being empty of her; he knew so fully how this meeting would go. Her eyes would light on him, and her mouth would involuntarily break into the grin that greeted all her occasions, however grave and dangerous; her stare would pull her body forward, and the gathering nearness of his presence would dissolve away the hardness, the controlled coldness, the—what? What was that element that had been there from the beginning and that, in the end, despite every strenuous motion of his heart, he had intensified, like some wild vague prophecy given a tyrannical authority in its fulfillment? What was the thing he had never named, perhaps because his vanity refused to believe that it could both attach to him and exist before him?

He wondered if he were tired enough now. There was an ache in his legs that augured well. He walked back to the hotel. The air of celebration had left the lobby. No celebrity was in sight. A few well-dressed young women, of the style that bloom and wither by thousands in the city's public spaces, were standing waiting for an escort or an elevator. As he pressed, no doubt redundantly, the button, a face cut into the side of his vision at such an angle that his head snapped around and he almost said aloud, "Don't be frightened. Of course I love you."

Museums and Women

SET TOGETHER, the two words are seen to be mutually transparent; the *e*'s, the *m*'s blend—the *m*'s framing and squaring the structure lend resonance and a curious formal weight to the *m* central in the creature, which it dominates like a dark core winged with flitting syllables. Both words hum. Both suggest radiance, antiquity, mystery, and duty.

My first museum I would visit with my mother. It was a provincial museum, a stately pride to the third-class inland city it ornamented. It was approached through paradisiacal grounds of raked gravel walks, humus-fed plantings of exotic flora, and trees wearing tags, as if freshly named by Adam. The museum's contents were disturbingly various, its cases stocked with whatever scraps of foreign civilization had fallen to it from the imperious fortunes of the steel and textile barons of the province. A shredding kayak shared a room with a rack of Polynesian paddles. A mummy, its skull half masked in gold, lay in an antechamber like one more of the open-casket funerals common in my childhood. Miniature Mexican villages lit up when a switch was flicked, and a pyramid was being built by dogged brown dolls who never pulled their papier-mâché stone a fraction of an inch. An infinitely patient Chinaman, as remote from me as the resident of a star, had carved a yellow rhinoceros horn into an upright crescental city, pagoda-tipped, of balconies, vines, and thimble-sized people wearing microscopic expressions of pain.

This was downstairs. Upstairs, up a double flight of marble climaxed by a splashing green fountain, the works of art were displayed. Upstairs, every fall, the county amateur artists exhibited four hundred watercolors of peonies and stone barns. The rest of the year, somberly professional oils of rotting, tangled woodland had the walls to themselves, sharing the great cool rooms with cases of Philadelphia silver, chests decorated with hearts, tulips, and bleeding pelicans by Mennonite folk artists, thick aqua glassware left bubbled by the blowing process, quaint quilts, and strange small statues. Strange perhaps only in the impression they made on me. They were bronze statuettes, randomly burnished here and there as if by a caressing hand, of nudes or groups of nudes. The excuse for nudity varied; some of the figures were American Indians, some were mythical Greeks. One lady, wearing a refined, aloof expression, was having her clothes torn from her by a squat man with horns and hairy hooved legs hinged the wrong way. Another statue bodied forth two naked boys wrestling. Another was of an Indian, dressed in only a knife belt, sitting astride a horse bareback, his chin bowed to his chest in sorrow, his exquisitely toed feet hanging down both hard and limp, begging to be touched. I think it was the smallness of these figures that carried them so penetratingly into my mind. Each, if it could have been released into life, would have stood about twenty inches high and weighed in my arms perhaps as much as a cat. I itched to touch them, to interact with them, to insert myself into their mysterious silent world of strenuous contention — their muscles and tendons articulated, their violent poses detailed down to the fingernails. They were in their smallness like secret thoughts of mine projected into dimension and permanence, and they returned to me as a response that carried strangely into lower parts of my body. I felt myself a furtive animal stirring in the shadow of my mother.

My mother: like the museum, she filled her category. I knew no other, and accepted her as the index, inclusive and definitive, of women. Now I see that she, too, was a repository of treasure, containing much that was beautiful, but somewhat jumbled, and distorted by great gaps. She was an unsearchable mixture of knowledge and ignorance, openness and reserve; though she took me many Sundays to the museum, I do not remember our discussing anything in it except once when, noticing how the small statues fascinated me, she said, "Billy, they seem such unhappy little people." In her glancing way she had hit something true. The defeated Indian was not alone in melancholy; all the statuettes, as they engaged in the struggles or frolics that gave each group the metallic unity of a single casting, seemed fixed in a fate from which I yearned to rescue them. I wanted to touch them, yet I held my hand back, afraid of breaking the seal on their sullen, furious underworld.

My mood of dread in those high, cool galleries condensed upon the small statues but did not emanate from them; it seemed to originate above and behind me, as if from another living person in the room. Often my mother, wordlessly browsing by the wall on the paintings of woods and shaggy meadows, was the only other person in the room. Who she was was a mystery so deep it never formed into a question. She had descended to me from thin clouds of preëxistent time, enveloped me, and set me moving toward an unseen goal with a vague expectation that in the beginning was more hers than mine. She was not content. I felt that the motion which brought us again and again to the museum was an agitated one, that she was pointing me through these corridors toward a radiant place she had despaired of reaching. The fountain at the head of the stairs splashed unseen; my mother's footsteps rustled and she drew me into another room, where a case of silver stood aflame with reflections; it seemed the mouth of a dragon of beauty. She let me go forward to meet it alone. I was her son and the center of her expectations. I dutifully absorbed the light-struck terror of the hushed high chambers, and went through each doorway with a kind of timid rapacity.

This museum, my first, I associate with another, less ghostly hunt; for this was one of the places—others being the telephone company, the pretzel factory, and the county fair—where schoolchildren were taken on educational expeditions. I would usually be toward the end of the line, among the unpaired stragglers, and up front, in the loud nucleus of leaders, the freckled girl I had decided I loved. The decision, perhaps, was as much my mother's as mine. The girl lived in our neighborhood, one of a pack of sisters, and from the time she could walk past our front hedge my mother had taken one of her fancies to her. She spoke admiringly of her "spirit"; this admiration surprised me, for the girl was what was known locally as "bold," and as she grew older fell in with a crowd of children whose doings would certainly have struck my mother as "unhappy." My mother always invited her to my birthday parties, where she, misplaced but rapidly forgiving the situation, animated for a few dazzling hours my circle of shy, sheltered friends.

When I try to picture my school days, I seem to be embedded among boiling clouds straining to catch a glimpse of this girl, as if trapped in a movie theatre behind a row of huge heads while fragmented arcs of the screen confusingly flicker. The alphabet separated us; she sat near the front of the classroom and I, William Young, toward the rear. Where the alphabet no longer obtained, other systems intervened. In the museum, a ruthless law propelled her forward to gather with the other bold spirits, tittering, around the defenseless little naked statues, while I hung back, on the edge of the fountain, envious, angry, and brimming with things to say. I never said them.

.   .   .

The girl who was to become my wife was standing at the top of some stone museum steps that I was climbing. Though it was bitterly cold, with crusts of snow packed into the stone, she wore threadbare sneakers from which her little toes stuck out, and she was smoking. Awesome sheets of smoke and frozen vapor flew from her mouth and she seemed, posed against a fluted pilaster, a white-faced priestess immolating herself in the worship of tobacco. "Aren't your feet cold?" I asked her.

"A little. I don't mind it."

"A stoic."

"Maybe I'm a masochist."

"Already?"

She said nothing. Had I said something curious?

I lit a cigarette, though inhaling the raw air rasped my throat, and asked her, "Aren't you in Medieval Art? You sit near the front."

"Yes. Do you sit in the back?"

"I feel I should. I'm a history major."

"This is your first fine-arts course?"

"Yeah. It met at a good hour—late enough for a late breakfast and early enough for an early lunch. I'm trying to have a sophomore slump."

"Are you succeeding?"

"Not really. When the chips are down, I tend to grind."

"How do you like Medieval Art?"

"I love it. It's like going to a movie in the morning, which is my idea of sin."

"You have funny ideas."

"No. They're very conventional. It would never occur to me, for example, to stand outside in the snow in bare feet."

"They're not really bare."

Nevertheless, I yearned to touch them, to comfort them. There was in this girl, this pale creature of the college museum, a withdrawing that drew me forward. I felt in her an innocent sad blankness where I must stamp my name. I pursued her through the museum. It was, as museums go, rather intimate, built around a skylight-roofed replica of a sixteenth-century Italian courtyard. At the four corners of the flagstone courtyard floor, four great gray terra-cotta statues of the seasons stood. Bigger than life, they were French, and reduced the four epic passages of the year to four charming aristocrats, two male and two female, who had chosen to attend a costume ball amusingly attired in grapes and ribbons. Spring wore a floppy hat and carried a basket of rigid flowers. The stairways and galleries that enabled the museum to communicate with itself around the courtyard were distinctly medieval in feeling, and the vagaries of benefaction had left the museum's medieval and Oriental collections disproportionately strong, though a worthy attempt had been made to piece together the history of art since the Renaissance with a painting or at least a drawing by each master. But the rooms that contained these later works—including some Cézannes and Monets that, because they were rarely reproduced in art books, had the secret sweetness of flowers in a forest—were off the route of the course we were both taking. My courtship primarily led down stone corridors, past Romanesque capitals, through low archways giving on gilded altar panels.

I remember stalking her around a capital from Avignon; it illustrated Samson and his deeds. On one side he was bearing off the gates of Gaza, while around the corner his massive head was lying aswoon in Delilah's lap as she clumsily sawed his hair. The class had been assigned a paper on this capital, and as I rehearsed my interpretation, elaborately linear and accompanied by many agitated indications of my hands, the girl said thoughtfully, "You see awfully much in it, don't you?"

My hands froze and crept back, embarrassed; the terminology of fine-arts analysis was new to me, and in fact I did doubt that an illiterate carver of semi-barbaric Europe could have been as aesthetically ingenious as I was being. "What do *you* see in it?" I asked in self-defense.

"Not very much," she said. "I wonder why they assigned it. It's not that lovely. I think the Cluny ones are much nicer."

It thrilled me to hear her speak with such careless authority. She was a fine-arts major, and there was a sense in which she contained the museum, had mastered all the priceless and timeless things that would become, in my possessing her, mine as well. She had first appeared to me as someone guarding the gates.

Once I accompanied her into Boston, to the great museum there, to study, in connection with another course she was taking, an ancient Attic sphinx. This she liked, though it was just a headless winged body of white marble, very simple, sitting stiffly on its haunches, its broad breast glowing under the nicks of stylized feathers. She showed me the *S*-curve of its body, repeated in the tail and again, presumably, in the vanished head.

"It's a very *proud* little statue, isn't it?" I ventured, seeking to join her in her careless little heaven of appreciation. Again, I seemed to have said something curious, slightly "off."

"I love it" was all she replied, with a dent of stubbornness in her mouth and an inviting blankness in her eyes.

Outside, the weather was winter; the trees were medieval presences arching gray through gray. We walked and walked, and for a time the only shelter we shared was the museum. My courtship progressed; we talked solemnly; the childhood I had spent in such timid silence and foreboding had left me with much to say. She could listen; she was like a room of porcelain vases: you enter and find your sense of yourself abruptly clarified by a cool, shapely expectancy in the air. I see her sitting on the broad cold balustrade that at second-story height ran around the courtyard. Beyond her head, the flagstones shone as if wet, and Printemps in her wide hat was steeply foreshortened. An apprehension of height seized me; this girl seemed poised on the edge of a fall. I heard the volume of emptiness calling to her, calling her away from me, so full of talk. There was in her something mute and remote which spoke only once, when, after our lying side by side an entire evening, she told me calmly, "You know I don't love you yet."

I took this as a challenge, though it may have been meant as a release. I carried the chase through exams (we both got A-minuses) and into another course, a spring-term course called, simply, Prints. My mother, surprisingly, wrote warning me that I mustn't spread myself too thin—she thought now that that had been *her* mistake at college. I was offended, for I thought that without my telling her anything she would know I was in the process of capturing the very gatekeeper of the temple of learning that must be the radiant place she had pointed me toward so long ago. Yet she was withholding her blessing.

Here I must quickly insert, like a thin keystone, an imaginary woman I found in a faraway museum. It was another university museum, ancient and sprawling and resolutely masculine, full of battered weapons of war and unearthed agricultural tools and dull maps of diggings. All its contents seemed to need a dusting and a tasteful rearrangement by a female hand. But upstairs, in an out-of-the-way chamber, under a case of brilliantly polished glass, I one day discovered a smooth statuette of a nude asleep on a mattress. She was a dainty white dream, an eighteenth-century fancy; only that epicurean century would have so carefully rendered a mattress in marble. Not that every stitch and seam was given the dignity of stone; but the corners were rounded, the buttoned squares of plumpness shown, and the creases of "give" lovingly sculpted. In short, it was clear that the woman was comfortable, and not posed on an arbitrary slab, or slaughtered on an altar. She was asleep, not dead; the warm aroma of her slumber seemed to rise through the glass. She was the size

of the small straining figures that had fascinated my childhood, and, as
with them, smallness intensified sensual content. As I stood gazing into
the eternal privacy of her sleep—her one hand resting palm up beside
her averted head, one knee lifted in a light suggestion of restlessness—
I was disturbed by dread and a premonition of loss. Why? My wife was
also fair, and finely formed, and mute. Perhaps it was the mattress that
brought this ideal other woman so close; it was a raft on which she had
floated out of the inaccessible past and which had cast her, small and
intangible as a thought, ashore on the island of my bounded present. We
seemed about to release each other from twin enchantments. Was not my
huge face the oppressive dream that was making her stir? And was not
I, out of all the thousands who had visited this museum, the first to find
her here? What we seek in museums is the opposite of what we seek in
churches—the consoling sense of previous visitation. In museums, rather,
we seek the unvisited, the never-before-discovered.

Two more, two more of each, each nameless. None have names. Museums are in the end nameless and continuous; we turn a corner in the Louvre and meet the head of a sphinx whose body is displayed in Boston. So,
too, the women were broken arcs of one curve.

   She was the friend of a friend, and she and I, having had lunch with the
mutual friend, bade him goodbye and, both being loose in New York for
the afternoon, went to a museum together. It was a new one, recently
completed after the plan of a recently dead American wizard. It was
shaped like a truncated top and its floor was a continuous spiral around
an overweening core of empty vertical space. From the leaning, shining
walls immense rectangles of torn and spattered canvas projected on thin
arms of bent pipe. Menacing magnifications of textural accidents, they
needed to be viewed at a distance greater than the architecture afforded.
The floor width was limited by a rather slender and low concrete guard
wall that more invited than discouraged a plunge into the cathedralic
depths below. Too reverent to scoff and too dizzy to judge, my unexpected companion and I dutifully unwound our way down the exitless
ramp, locked in a wizard's spell. Suddenly, as she lurched backward from
one especially explosive painting, her high heels were tricked by the
slope, and she fell against me and squeezed my arm. Ferocious gumbos
splashed on one side of us; the siren chasm called on the other. She
righted herself but did not let go of my arm. Pointing my eyes ahead,
inhaling the presence of perfume, feeling like a cliff-climber whose companion has panicked on the sheerest part of the face, I accommodated my

arm to her grip, and, thus secured, we carefully descended the remainder of the museum. Not until our feet attained the safety of street level were we released. Our bodies then separated and did not touch again. Yet the spell was imperfectly broken, like the door of a chamber which, once unsealed, can never be closed quite tight.

Not far down the same avenue there is a museum which was once a mansion and still retains a homelike quality, if one can imagine people rich enough in self-esteem to inhabit walls so overripe with masterpieces, to dine from tureens by Cellini, and afterward to seat their bodies complacently on furniture invested with the blood of empires. There once were people so self-confident, and on the day of my visit I was one of them, for the woman I was with and I were perfectly in love. We had come from lovemaking, and were to return to it, and the museum, visited between the evaporation and the recondensation of desire, was like a bridge whose either end is dissolved in mist—its suspension miraculous, its purpose remembered only by the murmuring stream running in the invisible ravine below. Homeless, we had found a home worthy of us. We seemed hosts; surely we had walked these Persian rugs before, appraised this amphora with an eye to its purchase, debated the position of this marble-topped table whose veins foamed like gently surfing *aqua marina*. The woman's sensibility was more an interior decorator's than an art student's, and through her I felt furnishings unfold into a world of gilded scrolls, rubbed stuffs, lacquered surfaces, painstakingly inlaid veneers, varnished cadenzas of line and curve lovingly carved by men whose hands were haunted by the memory of women. Rustling beside me, her body, which I had seen asleep on a mattress, seemed to wear clothes as a needless luxuriance, an ultra-extravagance heaped upon what was already, like the museum, both priceless and free. Room after room we entered and owned. A lingering look, a shared smile was enough to secure our claim. Once she said, of a chest whose panels were painted with pubescent cherubs after Boucher, that she didn't find it terribly "attractive." The one word, pronounced with a worried twist of her eyebrows, delighted me like the first polysyllable pronounced by an infant daughter. In this museum I was more the guide; it was I who could name the modes and deliver the appreciations. Her muteness was not a reserve but an expectancy; she and the museum were perfectly open and mutually transparent. As we passed a dark-red tapestry, her bare-shouldered summer dress, of a similar red, blended with it, isolating her head and shoulders like a bust. The stuffs of every laden room conspired to flatter her, to elicit with tinted reflective shadows the shy structure of her face, to accent with sumptuous textures her matte skin. My knowledge of how she looked asleep gave a tender nap to the alert surface of her wakefulness now. My woman, fully searched, and my museum, fully possessed; for this translucent interval—like the instant of translucence that shows in a wave between its peaking and its curling under—I had come to a limit. From this beautiful boundary I could imagine no retreat.

The last time I saw this woman was in another museum, where she had taken a job. I found her in a small room lined with pale books and journals, and her face as it looked up in surprise was also pale. She took me into the corridors and showed me the furniture it was her job to catalogue. When we had reached the last room of her special province, and her cheerful, rather matter-of-fact lecture had ended, she asked me, "Why have you come? To upset me?"

"I don't mean to upset you. I wanted to see if you're all right."

"I'm all right. Please, William. If anything's left of what you felt for me, let me alone. Don't come teasing me."

"I'm sorry. It doesn't feel like teasing to me."

Her chin reddened and the rims of her eyes went pink as tears seized her eyes. Our bodies ached to comfort each other, but at any moment someone—a professor, a nun—might wander into the room. "You know," she said, "we really had it." A sob bowed her head and rebounded from the polished surfaces around us.

"I know. I know we did."

She looked up at me, the anger of her eyes blurred. "Then why—?"

I shrugged. "Cowardice. A sense of duty. I don't know. I can't do it to her. Not yet."

"Not yet," she said. "That's your little song, isn't it? That's the little song you've been singing me all along."

"Would you rather the song had been 'Not ever'? That would have been no song at all."

With two careful swipes of her fingers, as if she were sculpting her own face, she wiped the tears from below her eyes. "It's my fault. It's my fault for falling in love with you. In a funny way, it was unfair to you."

"Let's walk," I said.

Blind to all beauty, we walked through halls of paintings and statues and urns. A fountain splashed unseen off to our left. Through a doorway I glimpsed, still proud, its broad chest still glowing, the headless sphinx.

"No, it's my fault," I said. "I was in no position to love you. I guess I never have been." Her eyes went bold and her freckles leaped up child-ishly as she grinned, as if to console me.

Yet what she said was not consolatory. "Well, just don't do it to any-body else."

"Lady, there is nobody else. You're all of it. You have no idea, how beautiful you are."

"You made me believe it at the time. I'm grateful for that."

"And for nothing else?"

"Oh, for lots of things, really. You got me into the museum world. It's fun."

"You came here to please me?"

"Yes."

"God, it's terrible to love what you can't have. Maybe that's why you love it."

"No, I don't think so. I think that's the way you work. But not every-body works that way."

"Well, maybe one of those others will find you now."

"No. You were it. You saw something in me nobody else ever saw. I didn't know it was there myself. Now go away, unless you want to see me cry some more."

We parted and I descended marble stairs. Before pushing through the revolving doors, I looked back, and it came to me that nothing about museums is as splendid as their entrances—the sudden vault, the shapely cornices, the motionless uniformed guard like a wittily disguised arch-angel, the broad stairs leading upward into Heaven knows what mansions of expectantly hushed treasure. And it appeared to me that now I was condemned, in my search for the radiance that had faded behind me, to enter more and more museums, and to be a little less exalted by each new entrance, and a little more quickly disenchanted by the familiar contents beyond.

Avec la Bébé-Sitter

EVERYBODY, from their friends in Boston to the stewards on the boat, wondered why Mr. and Mrs. Kenneth Harris should suddenly uproot their family of three young children and take them to the South of France in the middle of November. They had no special affection or aptitude for the country. Janet Harris knew French as well as anyone who had taken six years of it in various respectable schools without ever speaking to a Frenchman, but Kenneth himself knew hardly any—indeed, he was not, despite a certain surface knowingness, an educated person at all. The magazine illustrations, poised somewhere between the ardently detailed earth of Norman Rockwell and the breezy blue clouds of Jon Whitcomb, with which Kenneth earned his considerable living were the outcome of a rather monomaniacal and cloistered apprenticeship. At his drawing board, in the spattered little room papered with graphic art, he was a kind of master, inventive and conscientious and mysteriously alert to the oscillations of chic that twitched the New York market; outside this room he was impulsive and innocent and unduly dependent upon improvisation. It was typical of him to disembark in Cannes with three exhausted, confused children (one still in diapers) and a harried, hurt-looking wife, without a villa, a car, or a single friendly face to greet them, at a time of year when the Mediterranean sunshine merely underlined the actual chill in the air. After a week spent in a deserted hotel whose solicitous Old World personnel, apparently all members of a single whispering family, were charging him ninety dollars a day, he blundered into an Antibes villa that, if it was not equal in conveniences or in floor space to their Marlborough Street brownstone, at least had enough beds and a postcard view of Fort Carré and the (on fair days) turquoise harbor beyond. It was two more weeks, while Janet wrestled alone with the housekeeping and shopping, before they acquired a badly needed baby-sitter. It was not only that Kenneth was incompetent; he was, like many people whose living comes to them with some agency of luck, a miser. The expense of this trip fairly paralyzed him, and, in truth, the even greater expense of the divorce to which it was the alternative was, among the decisive factors, not the least decisive.

The baby-sitter—their English-French dictionary gave no equivalent, and *bébé-sitter*, as a joke, was funnier than *une qui s'assied avec les bébés*—was named, easily enough, Marie, and was a short, healthy widow of about forty who each noon when she arrived would call *"Bonjour, monsieur!"* to Kenneth with a gay, hopeful ring that seemed to promise ripe new worlds of communication between them. She spoke patiently and distinctly, and in a few days had received from Janet an adequate image of their expectations and had communicated in turn such intricate pieces of information as that her husband had died suddenly of a heart attack (*"Cœur—bom!"*—her arm quickly striking from the horizontal into the vertical) and that the owners and summer residents of their villa were a pair of homosexuals (hands fluttering at her shoulders—*"Pas de femmes. Jamais de femmes!"*) who hired boys from Nice and Cannes for *"dix mille pour une nuit."* *"Nouveaux francs?"* Kenneth asked, and she laughed delightedly, saying, *"Oui, oui,"* though this couldn't be right; no boy was worth two thousand dollars a night. Marie was tantalizing, for he felt within her, as in a locked chest, inaccessible wealth, and he didn't feel that Janet, who was stiffly fearful, in conversing with her, of making a grammatical mistake, was gaining access either. As a result, the children remained hostile and frightened. They were accustomed, in Boston, to two types of baby-sitters: teen-age girls, upon whom his elder daughter, aged seven, inflicted a succession of giggling crushes, and elderly limping women, of whom the grandest was Mrs. Shea. She had a bosom like a bolster and a wispy saintly voice in which, apparently, as soon as the Harrises were gone, she would tell the children wonderful stories of disease, calamity, and anatomical malfunction. Marie was neither young nor old, and, hermetically sealed inside her language, she must have seemed to the children as grotesque as a fish mouthing behind glass. They clustered defiantly around their parents, routing Janet out of her nap, pursuing Kenneth into the field where he had gone to sketch, leaving Marie alone in the kitchen, whose floor she repeatedly mopped in an embarrassed effort to make herself useful. And whenever their parents left together, the children, led by the oldest, wailed shamelessly while poor Marie tried to rally them with energetic *"ooh"*s and *"ah"*s. It was a humiliating situation for everyone, and Kenneth was vexed by the belief that his wife, in an hour of undivided attention, could easily have built between the baby-sitter and the children a few word bridges that would have adequately carried all this stalled emotional traffic. But she, with the stubborn shyness that was alternately her most frustrating and most appealing trait, refused, or was unable, to do this. She was exhausted. One afternoon, after they had done a little shopping for the Christmas that in this country and climate seemed so wan a holiday, Kenneth had dropped her off at the Musée d'Antibes and drove back in their rented Renault to the villa alone.

Smoke filled the living room. The children and Marie were gathered in silence around a fire she had built in the fireplace. Her eyes looked inquisitively past him when he entered. "*Madame,*" he explained, "*est,* uh, *visitée?—la musée.*"

Comprehension dawned in her quick face. "*Ah, le Musée d'Antibes! Très joli.*"

"*Oui.* Uh"—he thought he should explain this, so she would not expect him to leave in the car again—"*madame est marchée.*" In case this was the wrong word, he made walking motions with his fingers, and, unable to locate any equivalent for "back," added, "*ici.*"

Marie nodded eagerly. "*À pied.*"

"I guess. Yes. *Oui.*"

Then came several rapid sentences that he did not understand at all. She repeated slowly, "*Monsieur,*" pointing at him, "*travaille,*" scribbling with her hands across an imaginary sketchbook.

"Oh. *Oui. Bon. Merci. Et les enfants?*"

From her flurry of words and gestures he gathered an assurance that she would take care of them. But when he did go outdoors with the pad and paintbox, all three, led by Vera, the two-year-old, irresistibly followed, deaf to Marie's shrill pleas. Flustered, embarrassed, she came onto the patio.

"*C'est rien,*" he told her, and wanted to tell her, "Don't worry." He tried to put this into his facial expression, and she laughed, shrugged, and went back into the house. Fort Carré was taking the sun on one chalk-yellow side in the cubistic way that happens only in French light, and the Mediterranean wore a curious double horizon of hazed blue, and Nice in the distance was like a long heap of pale flakes shed by the starkly brilliant Alps beyond. But Vera accidentally kicked the glass of water into the open paint tray, and as he bent to pick it up the freshly wet sketch fell face-down into the grass. He gathered up everything and returned to the house, the children following. Marie was in the kitchen mopping the floor. "I think we should have a French lesson," he announced firmly. To Marie he added, with an apologetic note of interrogation, *"Leçon français?"*

"Une leçon de français," she said, and they all went into the smoky living room. *"Fumée—foof!"* she exclaimed, waving her hands in front of her face and opening the side doors. Then she sat down on the bamboo sofa with orange cushions—the two homosexuals had a taste for highly colored, flimsy furniture—and crossed her hands expectantly in her lap.

"Now," Kenneth said. *"Maintenant. Comment dites-vous—?"* He held up a pencil.

"Le crayon," Marie said.

"Le crayon," Kenneth repeated proudly. How simple, really, it all was. "Nancy, say '*le crayon.*' "

The girl giggled and shuttled her eyes between the two adults, to make sure they were serious. "Luh crrayong," she said.

"Bon," Kenneth said. "Charlie. '*Le crayon.*' "

The boy was four, and his intelligence had a way of unpredictably sinking beneath waves of infantile willfulness. But, after a moment's hesitation, he brought out *"Le crayon"* with an expert twang.

"And Vera? '*Le crayon*'?"

The baby was just learning English, and he did not press her when she looked startled and said nothing. The lesson continued, through *le feu, le bois, la cheminée,* and *le canapé orange.* Having exhausted the objects immediately before them, Kenneth drew, and Marie identified, such basic components of the universe as *l'homme, la femme, le garçon, la jeune fille, le chien, le chat, la maison,* and *les oiseaux.* The two older children took to bringing things from other parts of the room—*un livre, une bouteille d'encre, un cendrier,* and an old *soulier* of Charlie's whose mate had mysteriously vanished out in the yard among the giant cactuses. Nancy fetched from her room three paper dolls of great men she had punched from a copy of *Réalités* left in the house. *"Ah,"* Marie said. *"Jules César, Napoléon, et Charles Baudelaire."*

Vera toddled into the kitchen and came back with a stale cupcake, which she held out hopefully, her little face radiant.

"Gâteau," Marie said.

"Coogie," Vera said.

"Gâteau."

"Coogie."

"Non, non. Gâteau."

"Coogie!"

"*Gâteau!*"

The baby burst into tears. Kenneth picked her up and said, "You're right, Vera. That's a cookie." To the other children he said, "O.K., kids. That's all for now. Tomorrow we'll have another lesson. Go outside and play." He set the baby down. With a frightened backward look at the baby-sitter, Vera followed her brother and sister outdoors. By way of patching things up, Kenneth felt he should stay with Marie and make conversation. Both remained sitting. He wondered how much longer it would be before Janet returned and rescued them. The unaccustomed sensation of yearning for his wife made him feel itchy and suffocated.

"*Le français*," Marie said, spacing her words clearly, "*est difficile pour vous.*"

"*Je suis très stupide,*" he said.

"*Mais non, non, monsieur est très doué, très*"—her hand scribbled over an imaginary sketch pad—"*adroit.*"

Kenneth winced modestly, unable to frame any disclaimer.

She directed at him an interrogative sentence which, though she repeated it slowly, with various indications of her hands, he could not understand. "Nyew Yurrk?" she said at last. "Weshing*ton?*"

"Oh. Where do I come from? Here. *Les États-Unis.*" He took up the pad again, turned a new leaf, and drew the Eastern Seaboard. "*Floride,*" he said as he outlined the peninsula and, growing reckless, indicated "*Le Golfe de Mexique.*" He suspected from her blank face that this was wrong. He put in a few dark dots: "Washington, New York, *et ici, une heure nord à* New York *par avion,* Boston! *Grande ville.*"

"*Ah,*" Marie said.

"We live," Kenneth went on, "uh, *nous vivons dans une maison comme ça.*" And he found himself drawing, in avidly remembered detail, the front of their house on Marlborough Street, the flight of brown steps with the extra-tall top step, the carpet-sized front lawn with its wrought-iron fence and its single prisoner of forsythia like a weeping princess, the coarse old English ivy that winter never quite killed, the tall bay windows with their transom lights of Tiffany glass; he even put the children's faces in the second-story windows. This was the window of Vera's room, these were the ones that Nancy and Charlie watched the traffic out of, this was the living-room window that at this time of year should show a brightly burdened Christmas tree, and up here, on the third story, were the little shuttered windows of the guest bedroom that was inhabited by a ghost with a slender throat, sleek hair, and naked moonlit shoulders. Emotion froze his hand.

Marie, looking up from the vivid drawing with very dark eyes, asked a long question in which he seemed to hear the words *"France"* and *"pourquoi."*

"Why did we come to France?" he asked her in English. She nodded. He said what he next said in part, no doubt, because it was the truth, but mainly, probably, because he happened to know the words. He put his hand over his heart and told the baby-sitter, *"J'aime une autre femme."*

Marie's shapely plucked eyebrows lifted, and he wondered if he had made sense. The sentence seemed foolproof; but he did not repeat it. Locked in linguistic darkness, he had thrown open the most tightly closed window of his life. He felt the relief, the loss of constriction, of a man who has let in air.

Marie spoke very carefully. *"Et madame? Vous ne l'aimez pas?"*

There was a phrase, Kenneth knew, something like *"Comme ci, comme ça,"* which might roughly outline the immense ambiguous mass of his guilty, impatient, fond, and forlorn feelings toward Janet. But he didn't dare it, and instead, determined to be precise, measured off about an inch and a half with his fingers and said, *"Un petit peu pas."*

"Ahhhh." And now Marie, as if the languages had been reversed, was speechless. Various American phrases traditional to his situation—"a chance to get over it," "for the sake of the kids"—revolved in Kenneth's head without encountering any equivalent French. *"Pour les enfants,"* he said at last, gesturing toward the outdoors and abruptly following the direction of his gesture, for Vera had begun to cry in the distance. About twice a day she speared herself on one of the cactuses.

Janet was walking up the driveway. As he saw her go in to the baby-sitter he felt only a slight alarm. It didn't seem possible that he could have been indiscreet in a language he didn't know. When he came indoors, Marie and his wife were talking at cheerful length about what he gathered to be the charm of Le Musée d'Antibes, and it occurred to him that the reserve that had existed between the two women had been as much the baby-sitter's as Janet's. Now, from this afternoon on, Marie became voluble and jolly, open and *intime*, with her mistress; the two held long kitchen conversations in which womanly intuition replaced whatever was lost in nuances of grammar. The children, feeling the new *rapprochement*, ceased yowling when their parents went away together, and under Marie's care developed a somewhat independent French, in which, if pencils were called crayons, crayons must be called pencils. Vera learned the word *gâteau* and the useful sentence *"Je voudrais un gâteau."* As to Kenneth, he was confident, without knowing what the women said to each other, that his strange confession was never mentioned. The *bébé-sitter* kept between herself and him a noticeable distance, whether as a sign of disapproval or of respect, he could not decide; at any rate, when she was in the house he was encouraged to paint by himself in the fields, and this isolation, wherein his wife's growing fluency spared him much further trouble of communication, suited his preoccupied heart. In short, they became a *ménage*.

Four Sides of One Story

Tristan

MY LOVE:

Forgive me, I seem to be on a boat. The shock of leaving you numbed me rather nicely to the usual humiliations of boarding—why is it that in a pier shed everyone, no matter how well-born and self-esteeming, looks like a rag-clad peasant, and is treated accordingly?—and even though we are now two days out to sea, and I can repose, technically, in your utter inaccessibility, I still am unable to focus on my fellow-passengers, though for a split second of, as it were, absent-minded sanity, I did prophetically perceive, through a chink in my obsession, that the waiter, having sized me up as one of the helpless solitaries of the world, would give me arrogant service and expect in exchange, at journey's end, an apologetically huge tip. No matter. The next instant, I unfolded the napkin, and your sigh, shaped exactly like a dove, the blue tint of its throat visibly clouding for a moment the flame of the candle on the table, escaped; and I was plunged back into the moist murmurs, the eclipsed whispers, the vows instantly hissingly retracted, the exchanged sweats, of our love.

The boat shakes. The vibration is incessant and ubiquitous; it has sniffed me out even here, in the writing room, a dark nook staffed by a dour young Turinese steward and stocked, to qualify as a library, with tattered copies of *Paris Match* and, behind glass, seventeen gorgeously bound and impeccably unread volumes of D'Annunzio, in of course Italian. So that the tremor in my handwriting is a purely motor affair, and the occasional splotches you may consider droplets of venturesome spray. As a matter of fact, there is a goodly roll, though we have headed into sunny latitudes. When they try to fill the swimming pool, the water thrashes and pitches so hysterically that I peek over the edge expecting to see a captured dolphin. In the bar, the bottles tinkle like some large but dainty Swiss gadget, and the daiquiris come to you aquiver, little circlets of agitation spinning back and forth between the center and the rim. The first day, having forgotten, in my landlocked days with you, the feel of an ocean voyage, I was standing in the cabin-class lobby, waiting to try to buy my way toward a higher deck and if possible a porthole, when, without any visible change in the disposition of furniture, lighting fixtures, potted palms, or polyglot bulletin board, the floor like a great flat magnet suddenly rendered my blood heavy—extraordinarily heavy. There were people around me, and their facial expressions did not alter by one millimeter. It was quite comic, for as the ship rolled back the other way my blood absolutely *swung* upward in my veins—do you remember how your arm feels in the first instant after a bruise?—and it seemed imminent that I, and, if I, all these deadpanned others too, would lift like helium balloons and be bumpingly pasted to the ceiling, from which the ship's staff would have to rescue us, irritably, with broom handles. The vision passed. The ship rolled again. My blood went heavy again. It seemed that you were near.

Iseult. I must write your name. Iseult. I am bleeding to death. Certainly I feel bloodless, or, more precisely, diluted, diluted by half, since everything around me—the white ropes, the ingenious little magnetic catches that keep the doors from swinging, the charmingly tessellated triangular shower stall in my cabin, the luxurious and pampered textures on every side—I seem to see, or touch, or smile over, with you, which means, since you are not here, that I only half see, only half exist. I keep thinking what a pity all this luxury is wasted on me, Tristan the Austere, the Perpetually Grieving, the Orphaned, the Homeless. The very pen I am writing this with is an old-fashioned dip, or nib, pen, whose flexibility irresistibly invites flourishes that sit up wet and bluely gleaming for minutes before finally deigning to dry. The holder is some sort of polished Asiatic wood. Teak? Ebony? You would know. It was enchanting for me, how you knew the names of surfaces, how you had the innocence to stroke a pelt and not flinch from the panicked little quick-eyed death beneath; for me, who have always been on the verge of becoming a vegetarian, which Mark, I know, would say was a form of death wish (I can't describe to you how stupid that man seems to me; unfairly enough, even what tiny truth there is in him seems backed by this immense capital— these armies, this downright empire—of stupidity, so that even when he says something intelligent it affects me like Gospel quoted in support of the separation of the races. This parenthesis has gotten out of all control. If it seems ugly to you, blame it on jealousy. I am not sure, however, if I hate your husband because he—if only legally—possesses you, or if, more subtly, because he senses my own fear of just such legal possession, which gives him, for all his grossness, his grotesque patronization and prattling, a curious moral hold over me which I cannot, writhe as I will, break. End parenthesis).

An especially, almost maliciously, prolonged roll of the boat just slid the ink bottle, unspilled, the width of my cubbyhole and gave me the choice of fixing my eyes on the horizon or beginning to be seasick.

Where was I?

For me it was wonderful to become a partner in your response to textures. Your shallowness, as my wife calls it—and, as with everything she says, there is something in it which, at the least, gives dismissal pause— broke a new dimension into my hitherto inadequately superficial world. Now, adrift in this luxurious island universe, where music plays like a constant headache, I see everything through your eyes, conduct circular conversations with you in my head, and rest my hand on the wiped mahogany of the bar as if the tremor beneath the surface is you, a mermaid rising. What are our conversations about? I make, my mind tediously sifting the rubble of the emotional landslide, small discoveries about us that I hasten to convey to you, who are never quite as impressed by them as I hoped you would be. Yesterday, for example, at about 3:30 p.m., when the sallow sun suddenly ceased to justify sitting in a deck chair, I discovered, in the act of folding the blanket, that I had never, in my heart, taken your sufferings as seriously as my own. That you were unhappy, I knew. I could diagram the mechanics of the bind you were in, could trace the vivacious contours and taste the bright, flat colors of your plight— indeed, I could picture your torment so clearly that I felt I was feeling it with you. But no, there was a final kind of credence that I denied your pain, which cheated it of dimension and weight. You were the object of my desire and as such *la belle dame sans merci*. And so, reciprocally, I showed you no mercy. For this I belatedly apologized. In my head you accepted the apology with a laugh, and then wished to go on and discuss the practical aspects of our elopement. Two hours later, pinning a quivering daiquiri to the bar with my fingers, I rather jerkily formulated this comforting thought: However else I failed you, I never pretended to feel other than love for you, I never in any way offered to restrict, or control, the love you felt for me. Whatever sacrifices you offered to make, whatever agony you volunteered to undergo for me, I permitted. In the limitless extent of my willingness to accept your love, I was the perfect lover. Another man, seeing you flail and lacerate yourself so cruelly, might have out of timid squeamishness (calling it pity) pretended to turn his back, and saved your skin at the price of your dignity. But I, whether merely hypnotized or actually suicidal, steadfastly kept my face turned toward the blaze between us, while my eyes watered, my nose peeled, and my eyebrows disappeared in twin whiffs of smoke. It took all the peculiar strength of my egotism not to flinch and flaw the purity of your generous fury. No? For several hours I discussed this with you, or, rather, vented exhaustive rewordings upon your silent phantom, whose comprehension effortlessly widened, in watery rings, to include every elaboration.

Then, at last weary, brushing my teeth while the shower curtains moved back and forth beside me like two sluggish, rustling pendulums, I received, as if it were a revelation absolutely gravitational in importance, the syllogism that (major premise), however much we have suffered because of each other, it is quite out of the question for me to blame you for my pain, though strictly speaking you were the cause; and, since (minor premise) you and I as lovers were mirrors and always felt the same, therefore (conclusion) this must also be the case with you. *Ergo*, my mind is at peace. That is, it is a paradoxical ethical situation to be repeatedly wounded by someone *because he or she is beloved*. Those small incidentals within my adoration, those crumbs of Mark's influence that I could never digest, those cinders from past flames unswept from your corners, the flecks of a callous queenliness, even moments when you seemed physically ordinary—it was never these that hurt me. It was your *perfection* that destroyed me, demented my logical workings, unmanned my healthy honor, bled me white. But I bear no grudge. And thus know that you bear none; and this knowledge, in the midst of my restless misery, gives me ease. As if what I wish to possess forever is not your presence but your good opinion.

I was rather disturbed to learn, from Brangien, just before I left, that you are seeing a psychiatrist. I cannot believe there is anything abnormal or curable about our predicament. We are in love. The only way out of it is marriage, or some sufficiently pungent piece of overexposure equivalent to marriage. I am prepared to devote my life to avoiding this death. As you were brave in creating our love, so I must be brave in preserving it. My body aches for the fatal surfeit of you. It creaks under the denial like a strained ship. A hundred times a day I consider casting myself loose from this implacable liner and giving myself to the waves on the implausible chance that I might again drift to you as once I drifted, pustular, harping, and all but lifeless, into Whitehaven. But I who slew the Morholt slay this Hydra of yearning again and again. My ship plows on, bleeding a straight wake of a paler, milky green, heading Heaven knows where, but away, away from the realms of compromise and muddle wherein our love, like a composted flower, would be returned to the stupid earth. Yes, had we met as innocents, we could have indulged our love and let it run its natural course of passion, consummation, satiety, contentment, boredom, betrayal. But, being guilty, we can seize instead a purity that will pass without interruption through death itself. Do you remember how, by the river, staking your life on a technicality, you seized the white-hot iron, took nine steps, and showed all Cornwall your cold, clean palms? It is from you that I take my example. Do you remember in the Isak Dinesen book I gave you the story in which God is described as He who says No? By saying No to our love we become, you and I, gods. I feel this is blasphemy and yet I write it.

The distance between us increases. Bells ring. The Turinese steward is locking up the bookcase. I miss you. I am true to you. Let us live, forever apart, as a shame to the world where everything is lost save what we ourselves deny.

T.

Iseult of the White Hands

Dear Kaherdin:

Sorry not to have written before. This way of life we've all been living doesn't conduce to much spare time. I haven't read a book or magazine in weeks. Now the brats are asleep (I think), the dishes are chugging away in the washer, and here I sit with my fifth glass of Noilly Prat for the day. You were the only one he ever confided in, so I tell you. He's left me again. On the other hand, he's also left her. What do you make of it? She is taking it, from appearances, fairly well. She was at a castle do Saturday night and seemed much the same, only thinner. Mark kept a heavy eye on her all evening. At least she has *him;* all I seem to have is a house, a brother, a bank account, and a ghost. The night before he sailed, he explained to me, with great tenderness, etc., that he married me as a kind of pun. That the thing that drew him to me was my having her name. It was all — seven years, three children — a kind of Freudian slip, and he was really charmingly boyish as he begged to be excused. He even made me laugh about it.

If I had any dignity I'd be dead or insane. I don't know if I love him or what love is or even if I want to find out. I tried to tell him that if he loved her and couldn't help it he should leave me and go to her, and not torment us both indefinitely. I've never much liked her, which oddly enough offends him, but I really do sympathize with what he must have put her through. He seems to think there's something so beautiful about hanging between us that he won't let go with either hand. He's rapidly going from the sublime to the ridiculous. Mark, who in his bullying way wants to be sensible and fair, had his lawyers on the move, and I was almost looking forward to six weeks on a ranch somewhere. But no. After his spending the whole summer climbing fences, faking appointments, etc., anything that looks like real action terrifies him and he gets on a boat. And through it all, making life a hell for everybody concerned, including the children, he wears this saintly pained look and insists he's trying to do the right thing. What was really annihilating wasn't his abuse of me, but what he called kindness.

I've mentally fiddled with your invitation to come back to Carhaix, but there seems no point. The children are in school, I have friends here, life goes on: I've explained his absence as a business trip, which everybody accepts and nobody believes. The local men are both a comfort and a menace—I guess it's their being a menace that makes them a comfort. My virtue is reasonably safe. It all comes back to me, this business of managing suitors, keeping each at the proper distance, not too close and not too far, trying to remember exactly what has been said to each. Mark's eye, for that matter, was heavy on *me* for a few moments at the party. It's essentially disgusting. But nothing else is keeping my ego afloat.

I could never get out of him what she had that I didn't. If you know, as a man, don't tell me, please. But I can't see that it was our looks, or brains, or even in bed. The better I was in bed, the worse it made him. He took it as a reproach, and used to tell me I was beautiful as if it were some cruel joke I had played on him. The harder I tried, the more I became a kind of distasteful parody. But of what? She is really too shallow and silly even for me to hate. Maybe that's it. I feel I'm dropped, *bump*, as one drops any solid object, but she, she is sought in her abandonment. His heart rebounds from shapeless surfaces—the sky, the forest roof, the sea—and gives him back a terror which is her form. The worst of it is, I sympathize. I'm even jealous of his misery. At least it's a kind of pointed misery. His version is that they drank from the same cup. It has nothing to do with our merits, but she loves him and I don't. I just think I do. But if I don't love him, I've never loved anything. Do you think this is so? You've known me since I was born, and I'm frightened of your answer. I'm frightened. At night I take one of the children into bed with me and hold him/her for hours. My eyelids won't close, it scalds when I shut them. I never knew what jealousy was. It's an endlessly hungry thing. It really just consumes and churns and I can't focus on anything. I remember how I used to read a newspaper and care and it seems like another person. In the day I can manage, and on the nights when I go out, but in the evenings when I'm alone, there is an hour, right now, when everything is so hollow there is no limit to how low I and my Noilly Prat can go. I didn't mean to put this into a letter. I wanted to be cheerful, and brave, and funny about it. You have your own life. My love to your family. The physical health here is oddly good. Please, *please* don't say anything to Mother and Daddy. They wouldn't understand and their worrying would just confuse me. I'm really all right, except right now. My fundamental impression I think is of the incredible wastefulness of being alive.

Love,
Iseult

Iseult the Fair
(Unsent)

Tristan:
  Tristan
  Tristan Tristan
  flowers—books—
  Your letter confused and dismayed me—I showed it to Mark—he is thinking of suing you again—pathetic—his attempts to make himself matter. Between words I listen for his knock on the door—if he knew what I was writing he would kick me out—and he's right.
  my king brought low
  forgive?????
  an easy word for you
  I wanted to grow fat in your arms and sleep—you ravished me with absences—enlarged our love at our expense—tore me every time we parted—I have lost 12 pounds and live on pills—I dismay myself.
  Your wife looks well.
  Trist
  Mr.
  Mrs.

the flowers are dead and the books hidden and a hard winter is here—
his knock on the door—

Kill You. I must kill you in my heart—shut you out—don't knock even
if I listen. Return to your wife—try—honestly try with her. She hates me
but I love her for the sorrow I have brought her—no—I hate her because
she would not admit what everybody could see—she had given you up. I
had earned you.

the pen in my hand

the whiteness of the paper

a draft on my ankles—the stone floor—the sounds of the castle—
your step?

Beware of Mark—he is strong—pathetic—my king brought low—he
protects me. I am teaching myself to love him.

I would have loved the boat.

Love is too painful.

If the narcissi you planted come up next spring I will dig them out.

What a funny thing to write—I can't tell if this is a letter to you or
not—I dismay myself—Mark thinks I should be committed—he is more
mature than you and I

do you remember the flowers and the books you gave me?

For my sake end it—your knock never comes—the winter here is
hard—children sledding—the mountains are sharp through the window—
I have a scratchy throat—Mark says psychosomatic—I hear you laugh.

Tr

Please return—nothing matters

King Mark

My Dear Denoalen:

Your advice has been followed with exemplary success. Confronted
with the actuality of marriage, the young man bolted even sooner than we
had anticipated. The Queen is accordingly disillusioned and satisfactorily
tractable.

Therefore I think that the several legal proceedings against them both
may be halted at this time. By no means, however, do I wish to waive all
possibility of further legal action. I am in possession of an interminable,
impudent, and incriminating letter written by the confessed lover subsequent to his defection. If you desire, I will forward it to you for photo-
static reproduction as a safeguard.

In the case that, through some event or events unforeseen, the matter were after all to come to court, I agree wholeheartedly that their plea of having accidentally partaken of a magic potion will not stand up. Yet your strong suggestion that execution should be the punishment for both does not seem to me to allow for what possible extenuating circumstances there are. It is indisputable, for example, that throughout the affair Tristan continued to manifest, in battle, perfect loyalty to me, and prowess quite in keeping with the standards he had set in the days prior to his supposed enchantment. Also, their twin protestations of affection for me, despite their brazen and neurotic pursuance of physical union, did not ring entirely falsely. It was, after all, Tristan's feat (i.e., slaying the dragon of Whitehaven) that brought her to Tintagel; and, while of course this is in no sense a legally defensible claim, I can appreciate that, in immature and excitable minds, it might serve as a shadow of a claim. It will do us both good, as fair-minded Englishmen, to remember that we are dealing here with a woman of Irish blood and a man whose upbringing was entirely Continental. In addition, there is the Queen herself as a political property to consider. Alive, she adorns my court. The populace is partial to her. Further, the long peace between Ireland and Cornwall which our marriage has assured should not be rashly jeopardized.

Weighing all these factors, then, and not excluding the private dispositions of my heart, I have settled on a course of action more moderate than that which you now advise. Tristan's banishment we may assume to be permanent. Return will result in recapture, trial, and death. The Queen will remain by my side. Her long sojourn in the Wood of Morois has without doubt heightened her appreciation of the material advantages she enjoys in my palace. My power and compassion have been manifested to her, and she is essentially too rational to resist their imperative appeal. As long as her present distracted state obtains, I am compelling her to submit to psychoanalysis. If her distraction persists without improvement, I will have her committed. I am confident this will not be necessary. On the remote chance that the "magic potion" is more than a fable, I have instructed my alchemists to develop an antidote. I am fully in control of matters at last.

All the best,
(Dictated but not signed)
MARK: REX

The Morning

He lived alone, in a room only she had ever made habitable. Each morning he awoke to the same walls and was always slightly surprised at the sameness of the cracks and nail holes and replastered patches, as if this pattern were a set of thoughts to which a night's solid meditation had not added the merest nick of a new idea. He awoke to the same ticking clock on the mock mantel, the same shivering half-height refrigerator, the same nagging sour smell that, behind the baseboard and around the sink, had come to live with him. He would dress, and boil an egg, and crack it on a piece of toast, and heat last evening's coffee, and rinse the plate and cup, and take up a book, and sit and wait. The chair would grow suffocating. The sense of the words would skid and circle senselessly under the print. He would rise, and walk around the room, pausing at every place where they had lain together, staring, as if terrified, at the bed that still bore two pillows. She was a nurse, and worked afternoons and evenings, and used to come to him in the mornings. He was a student, but of what, he had forgotten. As if to remember, he would look out the window.

Of the city outside, he could see several brick walls, and a small flat roof of pebbles her bare feet had consecrated in the summer past, and a rusty construct of metal, almost organically complex, that was a chimney or a vent or the mouth of a chute and that may or may not have been in use. In the broad gaps between brick walls he could see a skyline that had a gold dome in it, and delicate smokestacks which the morning sun whittled like church balusters, and parallel plumes of smoke quickly indistinguishable from natural clouds, and a kind of subdued twinkle, as upon a tranquil ocean, that testified to the world of activity the city concealed. At moments his dull attention caught, like a slack sail idly filling, a breath, from this multifaceted horizon, of the hope that set in motion and sus-

tained so many industrial efforts, so much commercial traffic, such ingenious cross-fertilization of profit, such energetic devotion to the metamorphosis of minerals, the transport of goods, the interplay of calculations, the
efficiency of machines. The skyline then spread itself before his eyes like
one of those laborious Asiatic pictorial conceits that compose an elephant
out of naked maidens, or depict a tree of gods whose faintest twig doubles
as a smile and whose smallest bud is also a fingernail. A sense of human
constructiveness would seize him and try to lift him again into the airy
realm of fresh ideas, eddying notes, scholarly ambition, and purpose. The
forgotten object of his studies would present itself to him like a long-
scorned wife who has taken a lover and again grown beautiful. He would
panic with jealousy. But the pang, like a flitting glimmer from something
reflective on the horizon, would pass; his eyes would shorten their focus
and he would leadenly observe how the rectangular windowpanes were
being rounded by the infringement of successive layers of paint carelessly
applied to the muntins. A kind of demon of disconnection would abruptly
occupy his body, and he felt his heart as an angrily pulsing intruder, his
hands as hanging presences weighted with blood sent from a great distance. He felt within himself the intricate scaffolding of mechanical connection and chemical coöperation that upheld his life, and experienced its
complexity as a terrible tenuousness. He would go to the sofa and lift one
of the cushions. There, in a dingy sanctum of upholstery, lay a few long
hairs, almost invisible on the black cloth. He would study them as if to
recreate the head from which they had strayed, and the face that had
masked this head with a soul, and the body that had given this soul exten-
sion. By picking up one hair and holding it to the light he could detect a
faint ghost of the red-gold color that used to spill, a careless gift, across
his bare shoulders. He would replace the hair, and restore the cushion, as
spinsters press a flower into a Bible.

The room was, if anything, bigger than it needed to be. When he sat
and tried to read, the unused space seemed to watch him with eyes of
knobs and nail holes and knotted configurations in the carpet. The space
cried for another person to occupy it. Two had just fitted in this room;
their voices had flattened the walls, pressed the furniture back into its
servile state of being wood and cloth, submerged the shuddering of the
refrigerator and the ticking of the clock. When he opened the door to her
(she always looked a little startled and wary, but why?—who could she
expect it to be but him?), his heart would fill his chest so tightly he had to
hold her against him, like a compress, for minutes while the threat of its
bursting subsided.

From the first, their embrace had seemed predetermined. His hands always went to the same places on her back, one at the nape of her neck, the other at the base of her spine. Always he rested his face on the same side of her head, so that for all he knew now she might have worn a different perfume behind the other ear. The perfume he inhaled was powdery, a hushed fragrance less of flowers than of spice, strangely far away in the wilds of her hair, and tinged, perhaps only in his imagination, with an ethereal sweetness left from the hospital corridors. She was clean, beautifully clean, and he had associated this also with her work in the hospital, work which, it seemed to him, in its daily experience of bodies enabled her to accept, so totally, so frontally, his own.

Usually she would be wearing a street dress when she came, blue or green or brown, and when she left, at noon, she would be wearing a nurse's white uniform. Between these two costumes there was a third, when she was clothed in her skin and its aura; so that the morning, which in the days before she first came had been so single in its purpose and so monotonous in its execution, became instead a triptych, whose two side panels, when her footsteps had receded down the stairs and the outer door of the building had closed behind her, folded in memory over the central panel, whose beauty could not be remembered but had to be, each time, revealed. The very hours took their tint from the pattern of her visits, the hour after nine being blue or green or brown, the hour after that tan and auburn and pink and pale, and the final hour, the most hurried, often reduced to a few quick minutes, sheer white, like the flash that engulfs the screen when the film has run out and clatters loosely in the projector. Perhaps because these minutes were closest to him, across the long gap that separated him from her last visit, he saw them most distinctly—the square folds of her starched blouse, the sudden bun she composed with the hairpins they could find, the flat white shoes and plain cotton stockings that, in innocently shaping her calves and starkly emphasizing her female solidity, revived the erotic fire that her natural body, in its pliant naturalness, had damped.

He loved her in her uniform, and on the occasions when he had ventured into the hospital for a glimpse of her he felt in the corridors of identically uniformed women as if he were raiding a harem, or a cloister of the lascivious nuns who populate French pornography. There was, in her rising from beside him to don white, something blasphemous and yet holy, a reassumption of virginity emblematic of the (to a man) mysterious inviolability of a woman. It was like nothing else in his experience. A book, once read, can only be reread; a machine, used, imperceptibly wears out.

But she, she came to him always beautifully clean and slightly startled, like a morning, and left, at noon, immaculate.

Dressed otherwise, she was in comparison disappointing. Often she left her heels and silk stockings and street dress behind in his room, as a pledge to return. Their presence was not as satisfying as it should have been; there was an unease surrounding them, a vague request to be explained and justified. And when, in the night, she returned, and passed from the uniform into them, it was a descent. Dressed as other women, she became one of them, a woman who sat in restaurants, and ate the food, and drank sometimes too much, and nervously crossed and recrossed the legs self-consciously lengthened by high spike heels, and talked a little awry. He impossibly expected of her conversation the same total frontal fit her body gave him. The woman separated from him by a restaurant table was a needless addition to the woman who was perfect; she wished to add to the love that needed nothing but endless continuance. It was this woman who hinted of marriage, and it was this woman who, in the dim restaurant light, misread his word "unable" to mean "unwilling," and took offense.

These evenings with her, which ended sharply and chastely at midnight, when the curfew fell in the supervised apartment where she lived, were less than entirely real and blended with the cramped dreams that dissolved under the triumphal advent of morning. Morning brought him onto another plane altogether, as when one looks up from a crowded printed page to a door upon which a knock has just sounded. Awake, he would gratefully drink the radiance that renewed every detail of his room, and rise, and shed his dreams, and make enough fresh coffee for them both, and begin to listen. The outer door downstairs would softly open; there was an alto squeak only she produced from the hinges. Her first steps on the flight of stairs would be inaudible. Her next, stealthily rising toward him, had the breathy lightness of expectation. Her feet would press the top treads firmly, evenly, like piano pedals; an abrasive slither would cross the linoleum hall; and her knock, three blurred beats with an inquisitive pause between the second and third, would sound.

He listened now. The downstairs door opened. In the little skip of silence following the squeak of the hinges, his heart found space to erect a towering certainty, which toppled as the first brutal, masculine steps assaulted the stairs. Still, perhaps she was wearing boots, perhaps in the empty months her manner of mounting had changed, perhaps she was angry, or rigid with determination, or heavy with fright. He noiselessly went to his door, his hand lifted to turn the knob. The footsteps slithered on the linoleum and passed by. He felt relieved. He had lived so long with the vain expectation of her coming that it, the expectation, had become a kind of companion he was afraid of losing. He stared at the wall, dumbstruck by its stupidity. He turned sick of himself, physically sick, so that his arms ached and his stomach fell and the nagging sour smell behind the baseboard seemed the odor of his own decaying body. He returned to the chair and tried to study.

The outer door opened again, delicately this time. His heartbeats timed the silence. He saw her, dressed in blue or green or brown, ascending the stairs toward him, her lips a little parted in the effort of stealth, and her hand, slightly reddened and bony from antiseptic scrubbings, lightly touching the wall for balance. The silence lengthened, lengthened beyond recall, and he forced himself to admit that there was no one on the stairs, that the wind or a child had idly opened the door from outside and let it fall shut. He rose from the chair in a rage; why didn't she *know*, know how he wanted her now, not in white, but in blue or green or brown? This was the woman he wanted, the woman much like other women, the woman who talked awry in restaurants, who wanted to marry him, the woman who came to him and not the woman, in white, who left. He had accepted her leaving because of the pledge to return she left behind, the clothes that at last he recognized as her essential clothes, the everyday clothes that contained her other costumes, as skin is beneath all cloth and white is the spin of all colors. He had dreaded in marriage the loss of their mornings, their transposition into the shadowy scale of evening. But she had not explained to him that the mornings were a gift, an extravagance on her part which could be curtailed. She had been neglectful not to explain this, and she was wrong now not to know that he, lagging behind her a distance of months, had followed in the steps of her love and now had reached the exact point she had reached when they had last parted, and that she had only to stop, and turn, and take one step up the stairs to meet him. Yes, she was stupid, hasty, and cruel not to know his heart, not to hear the great cry issuing from this room; and this blunt vision of her limitations failed to dull his love but instead dreadfully sharpened it, for love begins in earnest when we love what is limited.

"My nurse," he whispered aloud, at last putting forth, in conscious competition with the tiny notched sighing of the clock, the shuddering of the refrigerator, and the empty scratches of sound in the stairway and hallway, a sound of his own. This speaking, this invoking her aloud, was the only action he was capable of taking. To seek her out would be to risk the final refusal which the silence withheld. To leave the room would be to abandon the possibility of receiving her visit. Even to install a telephone would be to heap another silence upon the furious silence of the stairs and of the doors. He did nothing. He did nothing all morning but maintain, with the full strength of his scattered mind and attenuated body, an unanswered vigil.

At noon, the day's reprieve arrived. She could not come now. She would be at work. His strenuous wrestle with her absence could be suspended, and did not need to be resumed until tomorrow morning. Perhaps tomorrow he would be weaker and, therefore, less caring, stronger. He felt that these mornings were aging him; he looked in the mirror for traces of the strange painless pain that punished him, like a punctual masseur, for three hours each day. The mirror, too, was unanswering. If anything were to show, it would be in the eyes, and one's eyes, self-confronted, lose all expression. His frame slowly relaxed, and ceased to feel his heart as an intruder. Like someone dressing in clothes wildly scattered about on the night before, he could reassemble his presence and leave the room. He could enter the twinkling city, eat, keep appointments, confront people, confident that his outward appearance had not altered, that, just as his body had refused to burst in its fullness before, so now it failed to collapse in its emptiness. Resuming, in part, a student's interested demeanor, he heard himself talk, give answers, even laugh. He saw, with a double sense of being a fraud and defrauded both, that an existence could be patched together out of afternoons and nights. But his mornings had been destroyed, and the morning of his life taken from him.

My Lover Has Dirty Fingernails

THE MAN stood up when the woman entered the room, or, to be exact, was standing behind his desk when she opened the door. She closed the door behind her. The room was square and furnished in a strange cool manner, midway between a home (the pale-detailed Japanese prints on the wall, the thick carpet whose blue seemed a peculiarly intense shade of silence, the black slab sofa with its single prism-shaped pillow of Airfoam) and an office, which it was, though no instruments or books were on view. It would have been difficult to imagine the people who could appropriately inhabit this room, were they not already here. The man and woman both were impeccably groomed. The woman wore a gray linen suit, with white shoes and a white pocketbook, her silvery-blond hair done up tightly in a French roll. She never wore a hat. Today she wore no gloves. The man wore a summer suit of a gray slightly lighter than the woman's, though perhaps it was merely that he stood nearer the light of the window. In this window, like the square muzzle of a dragon pinched beneath the sash, an air conditioner purred, a little fiercely. Venetian blinds dimmed the light, which, since this side of the building faced away from the sun, was already refracted. The man had a full head of half-gray hair, rather wavy, and scrupulously brushed, a touch vainly, so that a lock overhung his forehead, as if he were a youth. The woman had guessed he was about ten years older than she. In addition to the possibility of vanity, she read into this casually overhanging forelock a suggestion of fatigue—it was afternoon; he had already listened to so much—and an itch to apologize, to excuse herself, scratched her throat and made her limbs bristle with girlish nervousness. He waited to sit down until she had done so; and even such a small concession to her sex opened a window in the wall of impersonality between them. She peeked through and was struck by the fact that he seemed neither handsome nor ugly. She did not know what to make of it, or what she was expected to make. His face, foreshortened downward, looked heavy and petulant. It lifted, and innocent expectation seemed to fill it. The customary flutter of panic seized her. Both bare hands squeezed the pocketbook. The purring of the air conditioner threatened to drown her first words. She felt the lack in the room of the smell of a flower; in her own home the sills were crowded with potted plants.

"I saw him only once this week," she said at last. Out of polite habit she waited for a reply, then remembered that there was no politeness here, and forced herself to go on alone. "At a party. We spoke a little; I began the conversation. It seemed so unnatural to me that we shouldn't even speak. When I did go up to him, he seemed very pleased, and talked to me about things like cars and children. He asked me what I was doing these days, and I told him, 'Nothing.' He would have talked to me longer, but I walked away. I couldn't take it. It wasn't his voice so much, it was his smile; when we were . . . seeing each other, I used to think that there was a smile only I could bring out in him, a big grin whenever he saw me that lit up his whole face and showed all his crooked teeth. There it was, when I walked up to him, that same happy smile, as if in all these months . . . nothing had changed."

She looked at the catch on her purse and decided she had begun badly. The man's disapproval was as real to her as the sound of the air conditioner. It flowed toward her, enveloped her in gray coolness, and she wondered if it was wrong of her to feel it, wrong of her to desire his approval. She tried to lift her face as if she were not flirting. In another room she would have known herself to be considered a good-looking woman. Here beauty ceased to exist, and she was disarmed, realizing how much she depended on it for protection and concealment. She wondered if she should try to express this. "He sees *through* me," she said. "It's what made him so wonderful then, and what makes him so terrible now. He *knows* me. I can't hide behind my face when he smiles, and he seems to be forgiving me, forgiving me for not coming to him even though . . . I can't."

The man readjusted himself in the chair with a quickness that she took for a sign of impatience. She believed she had an honest gift for saying what he did not want to hear. She tried to say something that, in its frankness and confusion, would please him. "I'm suppressing," she said. "He did say one thing that if he hadn't been my lover he wouldn't have said. He looked down at my dress and asked me, 'Did you put that on just to hurt me?' It was so un*fair*; it made me a little angry. I only have so many dresses, and I can't throw out all the ones that . . . that I wore when I was seeing him."

"Describe the dress."

When he did speak, the level of his interest often seemed to her disappointingly low. "Oh," she said, "an orangey-brown one, with stripes and a round neckline. A summer dress. He used to say I looked like a farm girl in it."

"Yes." He cut her short with a flipping gesture of his hand; his occasional rudeness startled her, since she could not imagine he had learned it from any book. She found herself, lately, afraid for him; he seemed too naïve and blunt. She felt him in constant danger of doing something incorrect. Once she had a piano teacher who, in performing scales with her side by side on the bench, made a mistake. She had never forgotten it, and never learned the piano. But as always she inspected his responses conscientiously, for a clue. She had reverted, in their conversations, again and again to this rural fantasy, as if, being so plainly a fantasy, it necessarily contained an explanation of her misery. Perhaps he was, with this appearance of merely male impatience, trying to lead her into acknowledging that she was too eager to dive to the depths. His own effort, insofar as she understood it, was, rather, to direct her attention to what was not obvious about the obvious. He asked, "Have you ever worn the dress here?"

How strange of him! "To see you?" She tried to remember, saw herself parking the car, Thursday after Thursday, locking the door, feeding the meter, walking down the sunny city street of bakeries and tailor shops and dentists' signs, entering the dour vestibule of his building, with its metal wall-sheathing painted over and over, seeing the shadow of her gloved hand reach to darken his bell. . . . "No. I don't think so."

"Do you have any thoughts as to why not?"

"There's nothing profound about it. It's a casual dress. It's young. It's not the identity a woman comes to Boston in. I don't come in just to see you; I buy things, I visit people, sometimes I meet Harold afterward for a drink and we have dinner and go to a movie. Do you want me to talk about how I feel in the city?" She was suddenly full of feelings about herself in the city, graceful, urgent feelings of sunlight and release that she was sure explained a great deal about her.

He insisted. "Yet you wore this quite informal dress to a dinner party last weekend?"

"It was a party of our *friends*. It's summer in the suburbs. The dress is simple. It's not *shabby*."

"When you picked it to wear to this party where you knew he would see you, did you remember his special fondness for it?"

She wondered if he wasn't overdirecting her. She was sure he shouldn't. "I don't remember," she said, realizing, with a flash of impatience, that he would make too much of this. "You think I did."

He smiled his guarded, gentle smile and shrugged. "Tell me about clothes."

"Just anything? You want me to free-associate about clothes in general?"

"Whatever comes to your mind."

The air conditioner flooded her silence with its constant zealous syllable. Time was pouring through her and she was wasting her session. "Well, he"—it was queer, how her mind, set free, flew like a magnet to this pronoun—"was quite funny about my clothes. He thought I overdressed, and used to kid me about what an expensive wife I'd make. It wasn't true, really; I sew quite well, and make a lot of my things, while Nancy wears these quiet clothes from R. H. Stearns that are really quite expensive. I suppose you could say my clothes were a fetish with him; he'd bury his face in them after I'd taken them off, and in making love sometimes he'd bring my underclothes back, so they'd get all tangled up between us." She stared at him defiantly, rather than blush. He was immobile, smiling the lightest of listening smiles, his brushed hair silvered by the window light. "Once, I remember, when we were both in the city together, I took him shopping with me, thinking he'd like it, but he didn't. The salesgirls didn't know quite who he was, a brother or a husband or what, and he acted just like a man—you know, restless and embarrassed. In a way, I liked his reacting that way, because one of my fears about him, when I was thinking of him as somebody I had a stake in, was that he might be effeminate. Not on the surface so much as down deep. I mean, he had this passive streak. He had a way of making me come to him without actually asking." She felt she was journeying in the listening mind opposite her and had come to a narrow place; she tried to retreat. What had she begun with? Clothes. "He was rather lazy about his own clothes. Do you want to hear about *his* clothes, or just *my* clothes? Next thing, I'll be talking about the children's clothes." She permitted herself to giggle.

He didn't respond, and to punish him she went ahead with the topic that she knew annoyed him. "He's sloppy. Even dressed up, the collars of his shirts look unbuttoned, and he wears things until they fall apart. I remember, toward the end, after we had tried to break it off and I hadn't seen him for several weeks, he came to the house to see how I was for a minute, and I ran my hand under his shirt and my fingers went through a hole in his T-shirt. It just killed me, I had to have him, and we went upstairs. I can't describe it very well, but something about the idea of this man, who had just as much money as the rest of us, with this big hole in his undershirt, it make me weak. I suppose there was something mothering about it, but it felt the opposite, as if his dressing so carelessly made him strong, strong in a way that I wasn't. I've always felt I had to pay great attention to my appearance. I suppose it's insecurity. And then in lovemaking, I'd sometimes notice — is this too terrible, shall I stop? — I'd notice that his fingernails were dirty."

"Did you like that?"

"I don't know. It was just something I'd notice."

"Did you like the idea of being caressed by dirty hands?"

"They were *his* hands."

She had sat bolt upright, and his silence, having the quality of a man's pain, hurt her. She tried to make it up to him. "You mean, did I like being — what's the word, I've suppressed it — debased? But isn't that a sort of womanly thing that everybody has, a little? Do you think I have it too much?"

The man reshifted his weight in the chair and his strikingly clean hands moved in the air diagrammatically; a restrained agitation possessed his presence, like a soft gust passing over a silver pond. "I think there are several things working here," he said. "On the one hand you have this aggressiveness toward the man — you go up to him at parties, you drag him on shopping expeditions that make him uncomfortable, you go to bed with him, you've just suggested, on your initiative rather than his."

She sat shocked. It hadn't been like that. Had it?

The man went on, running one hand through his hair so that the youthful lock, recoiling, fell farther over his forehead. "Even now, when the affair is supposedly buried, you continue to court him by wearing a dress that had a special meaning for him."

"I've explained about the dress."

"Then there is this dimension, which we keep touching on, of his crooked teeth, of his being effeminate, feeble, in tatters; of your being in comparison healthy and masterful. In the midst of an embrace you discover a hole in his undershirt. It confirms your suspicion that he is disintegrating, that you are destroying him. So that, by way of *repair* in a sense, you take him to bed."

"But he was *fine* in bed."

"At the same time you have these notions of 'womanliness.' You feel guilty at being the dynamic party; hence your rather doctrinaire slavishness, your need to observe that his fingernails are dirty—to go under, so to speak. Also in this there is something of earth, of your feelings about dirt, earth, the country versus the city, the natural versus the unnatural. The city, the artificial, represents life to you; earth is death. This man, this unbuttoned, unwashed man who comes to you in the country and is out of his element shopping with you in the city, is of the earth. By conquering him, by entangling him in your clothes, you subdue your own death; more exactly, you pass through it, and become a farm girl, an earth-girl, who has survived dying. It is along these lines, I think, that we need more work."

She felt sorry for him. There it was, he had made his little Thursday effort, and it was very pretty and clever, and used most of the strands, but it didn't hold her; she escaped. Shyly she glanced at the air conditioner and asked, "Could that be turned lower? I can hardly hear you."

He seemed surprised, rose awkwardly, and turned it off. He did not move well; like many men who sit for a living, he tended to waddle. She giggled again. "I'm proving your point, how bossy I am." He returned to his chair and glanced at his watch. Street noises—a bus shifting gears, a woman in heels walking rapidly—entered the room through the new silence at the window, and diluted its unreal air. "Can't earth," she asked, "mean life as much as death?"

He shrugged, displeased with himself. "In this sort of language, opposites can mean the same thing."

"If that's what I saw in him, what did he see in me?"

"I feel you fishing for a compliment."

"I'm not, I'm *not* fishing. I don't want compliments from you, I want the truth. I need help. I'm ridiculously unhappy, and I want to know why, and I don't feel you're telling me. I feel we're at cross-purposes."

"Can you elaborate on this?"

"Do you really want me to?"

He had become totally still in his chair, rigid—she brushed away the impression—as if with fright.

"Well"—she returned her eyes to the brass catch of her purse, where there was a mute focus that gave her leverage to lift herself—"when I came to you, I'd got the idea from somewhere that by this time something would have happened between us, that, in some sort of way, perfectly controlled and safe, I would have . . . fallen in love with you." She looked up for help, and saw none. She went on, in a voice that, since the silencing of the air conditioner, seemed harsh and blatant to her. "I don't feel that's happened. What's worse—I might as well say it, it's a waste of Harold's money if I keep anything back—I feel the opposite has happened. I keep getting the feeling that you've fallen in love with *me*." Now she hurried. "So I feel tender toward you, and want to protect you, and pretend not to reject you, and it gets in the way of everything. You put me into the position where a woman can't be honest, or weak, or herself. You make me be strategic, and ashamed of what I feel toward Paul, because it bothers you. There. That's the first time today either of us has dared mention his name. You're jealous. I pity you. At least, in a minute or two—I saw you look at your watch—I can go out into the street, and go buy a cheesecake or something at the bakery, and get into the car and drive through the traffic over the bridge; at least I loved somebody who loved me, no matter how silly you make the reasons for it seem. But you—I can't picture you ever getting out of this room, or getting drunk, or making love, or needing a bath, or anything. I'm sorry." She had expected, after this outburst, that she would have to cry, but she found herself staring wide-eyed at the man, whose own eyes—it must have been the watery light from the window—looked strained.

He shifted lazily in the chair and spread his hands on the glass top of his desk. "One of the arresting things about you," he said, "is your insistence on protecting men."

"But I wasn't *like* that with *him*. I mean, I knew I was giving him something he wanted and needed, but I *did* feel protected. I felt"—she glanced down, feeling herself blush—"that he was on top."

"Yes." He looked at his watch, and his nostrils dilated with the beginnings of a sigh. "Well." He stood and made worried eyebrows. A little off guard, she stood a fraction of a second later. "Next Thursday?" he asked.

"I'm sure you're right," she said, turning at the door to smile; it was a big countryish smile, regretful at the edges. The white of it matched, he noticed with an interior decorator's eye, her hair, her suit, and the white of her pocketbook and her shoes. "I *am* kind of crazy," she finished, and closed the door.

The sigh that he had begun while she was in the room seemed to have been suspended until she had left. He was winning, it was happening; but he was weary. Alone, in a soundless psychic motion like the brief hemispherical protest of a bubble, he subsided into the tranquil surface of the furniture.

Harv Is Plowing Now

Our lives submit to archaeology. For a period in my life which seems longer ago than it was, I lived in a farmhouse that lacked electricity and central heating. In the living room we had a fireplace and, as I remember, a kind of chocolate-colored rectangular stove whose top was a double row of slots and whose metal feet rested on a sheet of asbestos. I have not thought of this stove for years; its image seems to thrust one corner from the bottom of a trench. It was as high as a boy and heated a rectangular space of air around it; when I was sick, my parents would huddle me, in blankets, on a blue sofa next to the stove, and I would try to align myself with its margin of warmth while my fever rose and fell, transforming at its height my blanketed knees into weird, intimate mountains at whose base a bowl of broth seemed a circular lake seen from afar. The stove was fuelled with what we called coal oil. I wonder now, what must have been obvious then, if coal oil and kerosene are exactly the same thing. Yes, they must be, for I remember filling the stove and the kerosene lamps from the same can, a five-gallon can with a side spout and a central cap which had to be loosened when I poured—otherwise by some trick of air pressure the can would bob and buck in my hands like an awkwardly live thing, and the spurting liquid, transparent and pungent, would spill. What was kerosene in the lamps became coal oil in the stove: so there are essential distinctions as well as existential ones. What is bread in the oven becomes Christ in the mouth.

When spring came, our attention thawed and was free to run outdoors. From where we lived not a highway, not a tower, not even a telephone pole was visible. We lived on the side of a hill, surrounded by trees and grass and clouds. Across a shallow valley where a greening meadow lay idle, another farm faced ours from a mirroring rise of land. Though the disposition of the barns and sheds was different, the houses were virtually identical—sandstone farmhouses, set square to the compass and slightly tall for their breadth, as if the attic windows were straining to see over the trees. They must have been built at about the same time in the early nineteenth century, and had been similarly covered, at a later date, with sandy, warm-colored stucco now crumbling away in patches. On chill April and May mornings, thin blue smoke from the chimney of the far house would seem to answer the smoke from the chimney of ours and to translate into another dimension the hissing blaze of cherry logs I had watched my father build in our fireplace.

The neighboring farm was owned and run by a mother, Carrie, and a son, Harvey. Even in her prime Carrie could not have been much over five feet tall. Now she was so bent by sixty years of stooping labor that in conversation her face was roguishly uptwisted. She wore tight high-top shoes that put a kind of hop into all her motions, and an old-fashioned bonnet, so that in profile she frightened me with her resemblance to the first bogey of my childhood, the faceless woman on the Dutch Cleanser can, chasing herself around and around with a stick. Harvey—called, in the country way, Harv—was fat but silent-footed; his rap would rattle our door before we knew he was on the porch. There he would stand, surrounded by beagles, an uncocked shotgun drooping from his arm, while my parents vainly tried to invite him in. He preferred to talk outdoors, and his voice was faint and far, like wind caught in a bottle; when, at night, he hunted coons in our woods, which merged with his, the yapping of his beagles seemed to be escorting a silent spirit that travelled through the trees as resistlessly as the moon overhead travelled through the clouds.

In the spring, Harv hitched up their mule and in furrows parallel to the horizon plowed the gradual rise of land that mirrored the one where I stood in our front yard. The linked silhouettes of the man and the mule moved back and forth like a slow brush repainting the parched pallor of the winter-faded land with the wet dark color of loam. It seemed to be happening *in me;* and as I age with the twentieth century, I hold within myself this memory, this image unearthed from a pastoral epoch predating my birth, this deposit lower than which there is only the mineral void.

The English excavators of Ur, as they deepened their trench through the strata of rubbish deposited by successive epochs of the Sumerian civilization, suddenly encountered a bed of perfectly clean clay, which they at first took to be the primordial silt of the delta. But measurements were taken and the clay proved too high to be the original riverbed; digging deeper, they found that after eight feet the clay stopped, yielding to soil again pregnant with flints and potsherds. But whereas Sumerian pottery had been turned on a wheel and not painted, these fragments bore traces of color and had been entirely hand-formed. In fact, the remnants were of an entirely different civilization, called "al 'Ubaid," and the eight feet of clay were the physical record of the legendary Flood survived by Noah.

My existence seems similarly stratified. At the top there is a skin of rubbish, of minutes, hours, and days, and the events and objects that occupy these days. At the bottom there is the hidden space where Harv— who since his mother died has sold the farm and married and moved to Florida—eternally plows. Between them, as thick as the distance from the grass to the clouds and no more like clay than fire is like air, interposes the dense vacancy where like an inundation the woman came and went. Let us be quite clear. She is not there. But she *was* there: proof of this may be discerned in the curious hollowness of virtually every piece of debris examined in the course of scavenging the days. While of course great caution should attend assertions about evidence so tenuous and disjunct, each fragment seems hollow *in the same way;* and a kind of shape, or at least a tendency of motion which if we could imagine it continuing uninterrupted would produce a shape, might be hypothesized. But we will be on firmer ground simply describing the surface layer of days.

Abundantly present are small items of wearing apparel, particularly belts and shoelaces; china plates, patterned and plain; stainless-steel eating implements; small tables with one loose leg; glasses containing, like irregular jewels hurriedly stashed at the cataclysmic end of an antique queen's reign, ice cubes; children's faces, voices, and toys; newspapers; and isolated glimpses of weather, sky, towers, and vegetation. The order of occurrence is not random; generally, in the probing of each fresh stratum, a toothbrush is the first object encountered, often followed by an automobile gearshift and a ballpoint pen, or a fountain pen which is invariably dry. Contraceptive devices and vials apparently of medicine are not uncommon. Sometimes the page of a book is found involved with a bar of soap, and confusing snowstorms of cigarette filters and golf balls must be painstakingly worked through. Care is crucial; days, though in sum their supply of rubbish seems endless, are each an integument of ghostly thinness. At Ur, in the delicate excavations of the tomb of Queen Shub-ad, a clumsy foot might crush a hidden skull, or a pick driven an inch too deep might prematurely bring to light a bit of gold ribbon, or a diadem, or a golden beech leaf more fragile than a wafer.

So, too, the days of my life threaten, even where the crust appears to be most solid, to crumble and plunge my vision into a dreadful forsaken gold. At the touch of a memory, the wallpaper parts and reveals the lack of a wall. A lilac bush, and the woman's hair engulfs me. Guitar music drifts from a window, and I turn to see if she notices, and newly discover that she is not there: grief fills the cavern of my mouth with a taste like ancient metal, and loss like some sweeping hypothesis floods the transparent volume between the grass and the clouds. Broad streets open up, stream outward, under the revelation, and the entire world, cities and trees, seems a negative imprint of her absence, a kind of tinted hollowness from which her presence might be rebuilt, as wooden artifacts, long rotted to nothing, can be re-created from the impress they have left in clay, a shadow of paint and grain more easily erased by a finger than the dusty pattern on a butterfly's wing.

Imagine a beach. At night. The usual immutable web of stars overhead. Boats anchored off the sand, lightly swapping slaps with the water. Many people, a picnic; there is a large bonfire, lighting up faces. She is there. She, herself, is there, here. Cold with fear, under the mantle of darkness, I go up to her; restored beside my shoulder, her human smallness amazes and delights me. "How *are* you?" I ask.

"Fine, just fine."

"No. Really."

"Don't ask me. I'm all right. You're looking very well."

"Thank you."

The nervous glitter of her eyes, looking past my shoulder into the fire, translates into yet another dimension the fire my father had set to burning aeons ago. She looks at last at me. The fire goes out in her eyes. She asks, "Would you like some coffee?"

"I don't have a cup."

"I have a cup."

"Thank you. You're very kind." I add, touching the cup that she is touching (our fingertips don't touch), "Don't hate me."

"I don't hate you. I don't think I do."

The taste of metal follows the taste of coffee in my mouth. "I'm glad," I say. "For me, it's still bad."

"You like to think that. You enjoy suffering because you don't know what suffering is." And from the trapped quickness with which she moves her head from one side to the other, toward the fire and away, I realize that she is struggling not to cry; a towering exultation seizes me and for a moment I am again her master, riding the flood.

I protest, "I do know."

"No."

"I'm sorry you hate me," I say, to wrench a contradiction from her.

The contradiction does not come. "I don't think that's what it is," she says thoughtfully, and takes our cup from my hand, and sips as if to give her words precision. "I think it's just that I'm dead. I'm dead to you"— and with sweet firmness she pronounces my name. "Please try to understand. I expect nothing from you; it's a great relief. I'm very tired. All I want from you is to be left alone."

And I find myself saying, "Yes," as she walks away, her long hair bouncing on her back with the quick light step she has preserved, "yes," as if I am giving assent, aloof and scholarly, to the invincible facts around me: the rigid spatter of stars above, the sand that in passing accepts the print of my feet, the sea absent-mindedly tipping pale surf over the edge of darkness—ribbons of phosphorescent white that unravel again and again, always in the same direction, like a typewriter carriage.

Where am I? It has ceased to matter. I am infinitesimal, lost, invisible, nothing. I leave the fire, the company of the others, and wander beyond the farthest ring, the circumference where guitar music can still be heard. Something distant is attracting me. I look up, and the stars in their near clarity press upon my face, bear in upon my guilt and shame with the strange, liquidly strong certainty that, humanly considered, the universe is perfectly transparent: we exist as flaws in ancient glass. And in apprehending this transparence my mind enters a sudden freedom, like insanity; the stars seem to me a roof, the roof of days from which we fall each night and survive, a miracle. I await resurrection. Archaeology is the science of the incredible. Troy and Harappa were fables until the shovel struck home.

On the beach at night, it is never totally dark or totally silent. The sea soliloquizes, the moon broods, its glitter pattering in hyphens on the water. And something else is happening, something like the aftermath of a plucked string. What? Having fallen through the void where the woman was, I still live; I move, and pause, and listen, and know. Standing on the slope of sand, I know what is happening across the meadow, on the far side of the line where water and air maintain their elemental truce. Harv is plowing now.

I Will Not Let Thee Go,
Except Thou Bless Me

AT THE FAREWELL PARTY for the Bridesons, the Bridesons themselves were very tired. Lou (for Louise) had been sorting and packing and destroying for days, and her sleep was gouged by nightmares of trunks that would not close, of doors that opened to reveal forgotten secret rooms crammed with yet more debris from ten years' residence—with unmended furniture and outgrown toys and stacked *Life*s and *National Geographic*s and hundreds, thousands, of children's drawings, each one a moment, a memory, impossible to keep, impossible to discard. And there was another dream, recurrent, in which she and the children arrived in Texas. Brown horizon on all sides enclosed a houseless plain. They wheeled the airplane stairway away, and Tom was not there, he was not with them. Of course: he had left them. He had stayed behind, in green Connecticut. "Now, children"—she seemed to be shouting into a sandstorm—"we must keep together, together. . . ." Lou would awake, and the dark body beside hers in the bed was an alien presence, a visitor from another world.

And Tom, hurriedly tying up loose ends in the city, lunching one day with his old employers and the next day with representatives of his new, returning each evening to an emptier house and increasingly apprehensive children, slept badly also. The familiar lulling noises—car horn and dog bark, the late commuter train's slither and the main drag's murmur—had become irritants; the town had unravelled into tugging threads of love. Departure rehearses death. He lay staring with open sockets, a void where thoughts swirled until the spell was broken by the tinkle of the milkman, who also, it seemed, had loved him. Fatigue lent to everything the febrile import of an apparition. At the farewell party, his friends of over a decade seemed remote, yet garish. Linda Cotteral, that mouse, was wearing green eyeshadow. Bugs Leonard had gone Mod—turquoise

shirt, wide pink tie—and had come already drunk from cocktails somewhere else. Maggie Aldridge, as Tom was carrying the two coats to the
bedroom, swung down the hall in a white dress with astonishingly wide
sleeves. Taken unawares, Tom uttered the word "Lovely!" to hide his
loud heartbeat. She grinned, and then sniffed, as if to erase the grin. Her
grin, white above white, had been a momentary flash of old warmth, but
in the next moment, as she brushed by him, her eyes were cast ahead in
stony pretense of being just another woman. He recognized his impulse
to touch her, to seize her wrist, as that of a madman, deranged by lack of
sleep.

Drinks yielded to dinner, dinner to dancing. Gamely they tried to Frug
(or was it Monkey?) to the plangent anthems of a younger generation.
Then the rock music yielded, as their host dug deeper into his strata of
accumulated records, to the reeds and muted brass and foggy sighing
that had voiced the furtive allegiances of their own, strange, in-between
generation—too young to be warriors, too old to be rebels. Too tired to
talk, Tom danced. The men with whom he had shared hundreds of athletic Sunday afternoons had become hollow-voiced ghosts inhabiting an
infinite recession of weekends when he would not be here. His field was
computer software; theirs was advertising or securities or the law, and
though they all helped uphold the Manhattan tent pole of a nationwide
canopy of rockets and promises, they spoke different languages when
there was no score to shout. "If I was John Lindsay," a man began, and
rather than listen Tom seized a woman, who whirled him around. These
women: he had seen their beauty pass from the smooth bodily complacence of young motherhood to the angular self-possession, slightly gray
and wry, of veteran wives. To have witnessed this, to have seen in the
sides of his vision so many pregnancies and births and quarrels and near-
divorces and divorces and affairs and near-affairs and arrivals in vans and
departures in vans, loomed, in retrospect, as the one accomplishment of
his tenancy here—a heap of organic incident that in a village of old
would have moldered into wisdom. But he was not wise, merely older.
The thought of Texas frightened him: a desert of strangers; barbecues on
parched lawns, in the gaunt shade of oil rigs and radar dishes.

"We'll miss you," Linda Cotteral dutifully said. Mouselike, she nestled
when dancing; all men must look alike to her—a wall of damp shirt.

"I doubt it," he responded, stumbling. It surprised him that he didn't
dance very well. He had danced a lot in Connecticut, rather than make
conversation, yet his finesse had flattened along one of those hyperbolic
curves that computers delight in projecting. Men had been wrong ever to

imagine the universe as a set of circles; in reality, nothing closes, everything approaches, but never quite touches, its asymptote.

"Have you danced with Maggie?"

"Not for years. As you know."

"Don't you think you should?"

"She'd refuse."

"Ask her," Linda said, and left him for the arms of a man who would be
here next weekend, who was real.

Maggie liked living rooms; they flattered her sense of courtesy and display. She had spread herself with her sleeves on the big curved white sofa,
white on white. Lou's voice tinkled from the kitchen. Lou always gravitated, at parties, to the kitchen, just as others, along personal magnetic
lines, drifted outside to the screened porch, or sought safety in the bathroom. Picturing his wife perched on a kitchen stool, comfortably tapping
her cigarette ashes into the sink, Tom approached Maggie and, numb as a
moth, asked her to dance.

She looked up. Her eyes had been painted to look startled. "Really?"
she asked, and added, "I'm terribly tired."

"Me too."

She looked down to where her hands were folded in her white lap. Her
contemplative posture appeared to express the hope that he, like an un-
harmonious thought, would melt away.

Tom told her, "I'll never ask you again."

With a sigh, then sniffing as if to erase the sigh, Maggie rose and went
with him into the darkened playroom, where other adults were dancing,
folding each other into the old remembered music. She lifted her arms to
accept him; her wide sleeves made her difficult to grasp. Her body in his
arms, unexpectedly, felt wrong: something had unbalanced her—her
third drink, or time. Her hand in his felt overheated.

"You're taller," she said.

"I am?"

"I believe you've grown, Tom."

"No, it's just that your memory of me has shrunk."

"Please, let's not talk memories. You asked me to dance."

"I've discovered I don't dance very well."

"Do your best."

"I always have."

"No."

"Don't you believe it was my best?"

"Of course I don't believe that."

Her hot hand was limp, but her body, as he tried to contain and steer it, seemed faintly resistant, as perhaps any idea does when it is embodied. He did not feel that she was rigid deliberately, as a rebuke to him, but that they both, once again, were encountering certain basic factors of gravity and inertia. She did not resist when, trying to solve their bad fit—trying to devise, as it were, an interface—he hugged her closer to his chest. Nor, however, did he feel her infuse this submission with conscious willingness, as lovers do when they transmute their bodies into pure sensitivity and volition. She held mute. While he sought for words to fill their grappling silence, she sniffed.

He said, "You have a cold."

She nodded.

He asked, "A fever?"

Again she nodded, more tersely, with a touch of the automatic, a touch he remembered as intrinsic to her manner of consent.

Surer of himself, he glided them across waxed squares of vinyl and heard his voice emerge enriched by a paternal, protective echo. "You shouldn't have come if you're sick."

"I wanted to."

"Why?" He knew the answer: because of him. He feared he was holding her so close she had felt his heart thump; he might injure her with his heart. He relaxed his right arm, and she accepted the inch of freedom as she had surrendered it, without spirit—a merely metric adjustment. And her voice, when she used it, swooped at the start and scratched, like an old record.

"Oh, Tom," Maggie said, "you know me. I can't say no. If I'm invited to a party, I come." And she must have felt, as did he, that her shrug insufficiently broke the hold his silence would have clinched, for she snapped her head and said with angry emphasis, "Anyway, I *had* to come and say good*bye* to the Bridesons."

His silence had become a helpless holding on.

"Who have been so *kind*," Maggie finished. The music stopped. She tried to back out of his arms, but he held her until, in the little hi-fi cabinet with its sleepless incubatory glow, another record flopped from the stack. Softly fighting to be free, Maggie felt to him, with her great sleeves, like a sumptuous heavy bird that has evolved into innocence on an island, and can be seized by any passing sailor, and will shortly become extinct. Facing downward to avoid her beating wings, he saw her thighs, fat in net tights, and had to laugh, not so much at this befuddled struggle as at the comedy of the female body, that good kind clown, all greasepaint and bounce. To have seized her again, to feel her contending, was simply jolly.

"Tom, let go of me."

"I can't."

Music released them from struggle. An antique record carried them back to wartime radio they had listened to as children, children a thousand miles apart. Maggie smoothed her fluffed cloth and formally permitted herself to be danced with. Her voice had become, with its faint bronchial rasp, a weapon cutting across the involuntary tendency of her body to melt, to glide. She held her face averted and downcast, so that her shoulders were not quite square with his; if he could adjust this nagging misalignment, perhaps by bringing her feverish hand closer to his shoulder, the fit would be again perfect, after a gap of years. He timidly tugged her hand, and she said harshly, "What do you want me to say?"

"Nothing. Something inoffensive."

"There's nothing to say, Tommy."

"O.K."

"You said it all, five years ago."

"Was it five?"

"Five."

"It doesn't seem that long."

"It does if you live it, minute after minute."

"I lived it too."

"No."

"O.K. Listen—"

"No. You promised we'd just dance."

But only a few bars of music, blurred saxophones and a ruminating clarinet, passed before she said, in a dangerously small and dreaming voice, "I was thinking, how funny . . . five years ago you were my life and my death, and now . . ."

"Yes?"

"No, it wouldn't be fair. You're leaving."

"Come on, sweet Maggie, say it."

". . . you're just nothing."

He was paralyzed, but his body continued to move, and the music flowed on, out of some infinitely remote USO where doomed sailors swayed with their clinging girls.

She sniffed and repeated, "You're *nothing*, Tommy."

He heard himself laugh. "Thank you. I received the bit the first time."

Being nothing, he supposed, excused him from speech; his silence wrested an embarrassed giggle from her. She said, "Well, I suppose it proves I've grown."

"Yes," he agreed, trying to be inoffensive, "you are a beautifully growing girl."

"You were always full of compliments, Tommy."

Turquoise and pink flickered in the side of his vision; his shoulder was touched. Bugs Leonard asked to cut in. Tom backed off from Maggie, relieved to let go, yet hoping, as he yielded her, for a yielding glance. But her stare was stony, as it had been in the hall, except that there it had been directed past him, and here fell full upon him. He bowed.

The minutes after midnight, usually weightless, bent Tom's bones in a strained curve that pressed against the inside of his forehead. Too weary to leave, he stood in the darkened playroom watching the others dance, and observed that Bugs and Maggie danced close, in wide confident circles that lifted her sleeves like true wings. A man sidled up to him and said, "If I was John Lindsay, I'd build a ten-foot wall across Ninety-sixth Street and forget it," and lurched away. Tom had known this man once. He went into the living room and offered here and there to say goodbye, startling conspiracies of people deep in conversation. They had forgotten he was leaving. He went into the kitchen to collect Lou; she recognized him, and doused her cigarette in the sink, and stepped down from the stool, smoothing her skirt. On his way from the bedroom with their coats, he ducked into the bathroom to see if he had aged; he was one of those who gravitated, at parties, to the bathroom. Of these Connecticut homes he would remember best the bright caves of porcelain fixtures: the shower curtains patterned in antique automobiles, the pastel towelling, the shaggy toilet-seat coverlets, the inevitable cartoon anthology on the water closet. The lecherous gleam of hygiene. Goodbye, Crane. Goodbye, Kleenex. See you in Houston.

Lou was waiting in the foyer. A well-rehearsed team, they pecked the hostess farewell, apologized in unison for being party poops, and went into the green darkness. Their headlights ransacked the bushes along this driveway for the final time.

Safely on the road, Lou asked, "Did Maggie kiss you goodbye?"

"No. She was quite unfriendly."

"Why shouldn't she be?"

"No reason. She should be. She should be awful and she was." He was going to agree, agree, all the way to Texas.

"She kissed *me*," Lou said.

"When?"

"When you were in the bathroom."

"Where did she kiss you?"

"I was standing in the foyer waiting for you to get done admiring your-self or whatever you were doing. She swooped out of the living room."

"I mean where *on* you?"

"On the mouth."

"Warmly?"

"Very. I didn't know how to respond. I'd never been kissed like that, by another woman."

"*Did* you respond?"

"Well, a little. It happened so quickly."

He must not appear too interested, or seem to gloat. "Well," Tom said, "she may have been drunk."

"Or else very tired," said Lou, "like the rest of us."

TARBOX TALES

The Indian

THE TOWN, in New England, of Tarbox, restrained from embracing the sea by a margin of tawny salt marshes, locates its downtown four miles inland up the Musquenomenee River, which ceases to be tidal at the waterfall of the old hosiery mill, now given over to the manufacture of plastic toys. It was to the mouth of this river, in May of 1634, that the small party of seventeen men, led by the younger son of the governor of the Massachusetts Bay Colony—Jeremiah Tarbox being only his second in command—came in three rough skiffs with the purpose of establishing amid such an unpossessed abundance of salt hay a pastoral plantation. This, with God's forbearance, they did. They furled their sails and slowly rowed, each boat being equipped with four oarlocks, in search of firm land, through marshes that must appear, now that their grass is no longer harvested by men driving horses shod in great wooden discs, much the same today as they did then—though undoubtedly the natural abundance of ducks, cranes, otter, and deer has been somewhat diminished. Tarbox himself, in his invaluable diary, notes that the squealing of the livestock in the third skiff attracted a great cloud of "protestating sea-fowl." The first houses (not one of which still stands, the oldest in town dating, in at least its central timbers and fireplace, from 1642) were strung along the base of the rise of firm land called Near Hill, which, with its companion Far Hill, a mile away, in effect bounds the densely populated section of the present township. In winter the population of Tarbox numbers something less than seven thousand; in summer the figure may be closer to nine thousand.

The width of the river mouth and its sheltered advantage within Tarbox Bay seemed to promise the makings of a port to rival Boston; but in spite of repeated dredging operations the river has proved incorrigibly silty, and its shallow winding channels, rendered especially fickle where the fresh water of the river most powerfully clashes with the restless saline influx of the tide, frustrate all but pleasure craft. These Chris Craft and Kit-Kats, skimming seaward through the exhilarating avenues of wild hay, in the early morning may pass, as the fluttering rust-colored horizon abruptly yields to the steely-blue monotone of the open water, a few clammers in hip boots patiently harrowing the tidewater floor. The intent posture of their silhouettes distinguishes them from the few bathers who have drifted down from the dying campfires by whose side they have dozed and sung and drunk away a night on the beach—one of the finest and least spoiled, it should be said, on the North Atlantic coast. Picturesque as Millet's gleaners, their torsos doubled like playing cards in the rosy mirror of the dawn-stilled sea, these sparse representatives of the clamming industry, founded in the eighteen-eighties by an immigration of Greeks and continually harassed by the industrial pollution upriver, exploit the sole vein of profit left in the name of old Musquenomenee. This shadowy chief broke the bread of peace with the son of the governor, and within a year both were dead. The body of the one was returned to Boston to lie in the King's Chapel graveyard; the body of the other is supposedly buried, presumably upright, somewhere in the woods on the side of Far Hill where even now no houses have intruded, though the tract is rumored to have been sold to a developer. Until the post-war arrival of Boston commuters, still much of a minority, Tarbox lived (discounting the summer people, who came and went in the marshes each year like the wild ducks and red-winged blackbirds) as a town apart. A kind of curse has kept its peace. The handmade-lace industry, which reached its peak just before the American Revolution, was destroyed by the industrial revolution; the textile mills, never numerous, were finally emptied by the industrialization of the South. They have been succeeded by a scattering of small enterprises, electronic in the main, which have staved off decisive depression.

Viewed from the spur of Near Hill, where the fifth edifice, now called Congregationalist, of the religious society incorporated in 1635 on this identical spot thrusts its wooden spire into the sky and into a hundred colored postcards purchasable at all four local drugstores—viewed from this eminence, the business district makes a neat and prosperous impression. This is especially true at Christmastime, when colored lights are strung from pole to pole, and at the height of summer, when girls in shorts and bathing suits decorate the pavements. A one-hour parking limit is enforced during business hours, but the traffic is congested only during the evening homeward exodus. A stoplight has never been thought quite necessary. A new Woolworth's with a noble façade of corrugated laminated Fiberglas has been erected on the site of a burned-out tenement. If the building which it vacated across the street went begging nearly a year for a tenant, and if some other properties along the street nervously change hands and wares now and then, nevertheless there is not that staring stretch of blank shopwindows which desolates the larger mill towns to the north and west. Two hardware stores confront each other without apparent rancor; three banks vie in promoting solvency; several luncheonettes withstand waves of factory workers and high-school students; and a small proud army of petit-bourgeois knights— realtors and lawyers and jewellers—parades up and down in clothes that would not look quaint on Madison Avenue. The explosive thrust of superhighways through the land has sprinkled on the town a cosmopoli-tan garnish; one resourceful divorcée has made a good thing of selling unabashedly smart women's clothes and Scandinavian kitchen accessories, and, next door, a foolish young matron nostalgic for Vassar has opened a combination paperback bookstore and art gallery, so that now the Tarbox town derelict, in sneaking with his cherry-red face and tot of rye from the liquor store to his home above the shoe-repair nook, must walk a garish gauntlet of abstract paintings by a minister's wife from Gloucester. Indeed, the whole street is laid open to an accusatory chorus of brightly packaged titles by Freud, Camus, and those others through whose masterworks our civilization moves toward its doom. Strange to say, so virulent is the spread of modern culture, some of these same titles can be had, seventy-five cents cheaper, in the homely old magazine-and-newspaper store in the middle of the block. Here, sitting stoically on the spines of the radia-tor behind the large left-hand window, the Indian can often be seen.

He sits in this window for hours at a time, politely waving to any passerby who happens to glance his way. It is hard always to avoid his eye, his form is so unexpected, perched on the radiator above cards of pipes and pyra-mids of Prince Albert tins and fanned copies of *True* and *Male* and *Sport*. He looks, behind glass, somewhat shadowy and thin, but outdoors he is solid enough. During other hours he takes up a station by Bailey's Phar-maceuticals on the corner. There is a splintered telephone pole here that he leans against when he wearies of leaning against the brick wall. Occa-sionally he even sits upon the fire hydrant as if upon a campstool, arms folded, legs crossed, gazing across at the renovations on the face of Poirier's Liquor Mart. In cold or wet weather he may sit inside the drug-store, expertly prolonging a coffee at the counter, running his tobacco-dyed fingertip around and around the rim of the cup as he watches the steam fade. There are other spots—untenanted doorways, the benches halfway up the hill, idle chairs in the barbershops—where he loiters, and indeed there cannot be a square foot of the downtown pavement where he has not at some time or other paused; but these two spots, the window of the news store and the wall of the drugstore, are his essential habitat.

It is difficult to discover anything about him. He wears a plaid lumber-jack shirt with a gray turtleneck sweater underneath, and chino pants olive rather than khaki in color, and remarkably white tennis sneakers. He smokes and drinks coffee, so he must have some income, but he does not, apparently, work. Inquiry reveals that now and then he is employed—during the last Christmas rush he was seen carrying baskets of Hong Kong shirts and Italian crèche elements through the aisles of the five-and-ten—but he soon is fired or quits, and the word "lazy," given some-how more than its usual force of disapproval, sticks in the mind, as if this is the clue. Disconcertingly, he knows your name. Even though you are a young mutual-fund analyst newly bought into a neo-saltbox on the beach road and downtown on a Saturday morning to rent a wallpaper steamer, he smiles if he catches your eye, lifts his hand lightly, and says, "Good morning, Mr. ——," supplying your name. Yet his own name is impossi-ble to learn. The simplest fact about a person, identity's very seed, is in his case utterly hidden. It can be determined, by matching consistencies of hearsay, that he lives in that tall, speckle-shingled, disreputable hotel overlooking the atrophied railroad tracks, just down from the Amvets, where shuffling Polish widowers and one-night-in-town salesmen hang out, and in whose bar, evidently, money can be wagered and women may be approached. But his name, whether it is given to you as Tugwell or Frisbee or Wigglesworth, even if it were always the same name, would be in its almost parodic Yankeeness incredible. "But he's an Indian!"

The face of your informant—say, the chunky Irish dictator of the School Building Needs Committee, a dentist—undergoes a faint rapt transformation. His voice assumes its dental-chair coziness, an antiseptic murmur while your mouth is full. "Don't go around saying that. He doesn't like it. He prides himself on being a typical run-down Yankee."

But he *is* an Indian. This is, alone, certain. Who but a savage would have such an immense capacity for repose? His cheekbones, his never-faded skin, the delicate little jut of his scowl, the drooping triangularity of his eye sockets, the way his vertically lined face takes the light, the lus-treless black of his hair are all so profoundly Indian that the imagination, surprised by his silhouette as he sits on the hydrant gazing across at the changing face of the liquor store, effortlessly plants a feather at the back of his head. His air of waiting, of gazing; the softness of his motions; the proprietory ease and watchfulness with which he moves from spot to spot; the good humor that makes his vigil gently dreadful—all these are totally foreign to the shambling shy-eyes and moist lower lip of the failed Yankee. His age and status are too peculiar. He is surely older than forty and younger than sixty—but *is* this sure? And, though he greets everyone by name with a light wave of his hand, the conversation never passes beyond a greeting, and even in the news store, when the political contention and convivial obscenity literally drive housewives away from the door, he does not attempt to participate. He witnesses, and he now and then offers in a gravelly voice a debated piece of town history, but he does not participate.

It is caring that makes mysteries. As you grow indifferent, they lift. You live longer in the town, season follows season, the half-naked urban people arrive on the beach, multiply, and like leaves fall away again, and you have ceased to identify with them. The marshes turn green and withdraw through gold into brown, and their indolent, untouched, enduring existence penetrates your fibre. You find you must drive down toward the beach once a week or it is like a week without love. The ice cakes pile up along the banks of the tidal inlets like the rubble of ruined temples. You begin to meet, without seeking them out, the vestigial people: the unmarried daughters of the owners of closed mills, the retired high-school teachers, the senile deacons in their underheated seventeenth-century houses with attics full of old church records in spidery brown ink. You enter, by way of an elderly baby-sitter, a world where at least they speak of him as "the Indian." An appalling snicker materializes in the darkness on the front seat beside you as you drive your babysitter, dear Mrs. Knowlton, home to her shuttered house on a back road. "If you knew what they say, mister, if you knew what they say."

And at last, as when in a woods you break through miles of underbrush into a clearing, you stand up surprised, taking a deep breath of the obvious, agreeing with the trees that of course this is the case. Anybody who is anybody knew all along. The mystery lifts, with some impatience, here, in Miss Horne's low-ceilinged front parlor, which smells of warm fireplace ashes and of peppermint balls kept ready in red-tinted knobbed glass goblets for whatever open-mouthed children might dare to come visit such a very old lady, all bent double like a little gripping rose clump,

Miss Horne, a fable in her lifetime. Her father had been the fifth minister before the present one (whom she does *not* care for) at the First Church, and *his* father the next but one before him. There had been a Horne among those first seventeen men. Well—where was she?—yes, the Indian. The Indian had been loitering in the center of town when she was a tiny girl in gingham. And he is no older now than he was then.

The Hillies

Tarbox was founded, in 1634, as an agricultural outpost of the Boston colony, by men fearful of attack. They built their fortified meetinghouse on a rocky outcropping commanding a defensive view of the river valley, where a flotilla of canoes might materialize and where commerce and industry, when they peaceably came, settled of their own gravity. Just as the functions of the meetinghouse slowly split between a town hall and a Congregational church, the town itself evolved two centers: the hilltop green and the downtown. On the green stands the present church, the sixth successive religious edifice on this site, a marvel (or outrage, depending upon your architectural politics) of poured concrete, encircled by venerable clapboarded homes that include the tiny old tilting post office (built in 1741, decommissioned 1839) and its companion the onetime town jail, recently transformed into a kinetic-art gallery by a young couple from Colorado. Downtown, a block or more of false fronts and show windows straggles toward the factory—once productive of textiles, now of plastic "recreational products" such as inflatable rafts and seamless footballs. The street holds two hardware stores, three banks, a Woolworth's with a new façade of corrugated Fiberglas, an A & P, the granite post office (built in 1933) with its Japanese cherry trees outside and its Pilgrim murals inside, and a host of retail enterprises self-proclaimed by signs ranging in style from the heartily garish to the timidly tasteful, from 3-D neo-Superman to mimicry of the delicate lettering incised on colonial tombstones. This downtown is no uglier than most, and its denizens can alleviate their prospect by lifting their eyes to Near Hill, where the new church's parabolic peak gleams through the feathery foliage of the surviving elms. Between the green and the downtown lies an awkward steep area that has never been, until recently, settled at all. Solid ledge, this slope repelled buildings in the early days and by default became a half-hearted park, a waste tract diagonally skewered by several small streets, dotted with various memorial attempts—obelisks and urns—that have fallen short of impressiveness. There are a few park benches where, until recently, no one ever sat. For lately these leaden, eerily veined rocks and triangular patches of parched grass *have* been settled, by flocks of young people; they sit and lie here overlooking downtown Tarbox as if the spectacle is as fascinating as Dante's rose. Dawn finds them already in position, and midnight merely intensifies the murmur of their conversation, marred by screams and smashed bottles. The town, with the wit anonymously secreted within the most pedestrian of populations, has christened them "the hillies."

They are less exotic than hippies. Many are the offspring of prominent citizens; the son of the bank president is one, and the daughter of the meat-market man is another. But even children one recognizes from the sidewalk days when they peddled lemonade or pedalled a tricycle stare now from the rocks with the hostile strangeness of marauders. Their solidarity appears absolute. Their faces, whose pallor is accented by smears of dirt, repel scrutiny; returning their collective stare is as difficult as gazing into a furnace or the face of a grieving widow. In honesty, some of these effects—of intense embarrassment, of menace—may be "read into" the faces of the hillies; apart from lifting their voices in vague mockery, they make no threatening moves. They claim they want only to be left alone.

When did they arrive? Their advent merges with the occasional vagrant sleeping on a bench, and with the children who used to play here while their mothers shopped downtown. At first, they seemed to be sunning; the town is famous for its beach, and acquiring a tan falls within our code of comprehensible behavior. Then, as the hillies were seen to be sitting up and clothed in floppy costumes that covered all but their hands and faces, it was supposed that their congregation was sexual in motive; the rocks were a pickup point for the lovers' lanes among the ponds and pines and quarries on the dark edges of town. True, the toughs of neighboring villages swarmed in, racing their Hondas and Mustangs in a preening, suggestive fashion. But our flaxen beauties, if they succumbed, always returned to dream on the hill; and then it seemed that the real reason was drugs. Certainly their torpitude transcends normal physiology. And certainly the afternoon air is sweet with pot, and pushers of harder stuff come out from Boston at appointed times. None of our suppositions has proved entirely false, even the first, for on bright days some of the young men do shuck their shirts and lie spread-eagled under the sun, on the brown grass by the Civil War obelisk. Yet the sun burns best at the beach, and sex and dope can be enjoyed elsewhere, even—so anxious are we parents to please—in the hillies' own homes.

With the swift pragmatism that is triumphantly American, the town now tolerates drugs in its midst. Once a scandalous rumor on the rim of possibility, drugs moved inward, became a scandal that must be faced, and now loom as a commonplace reality. The local hospital proficiently treats fifteen-year-old girls deranged by barbiturates, and our family doctors matter-of-factly counsel their adolescent patients against the dangers, such as infectious hepatitis, of dirty needles. That surprising phrase woven into our flag, "the pursuit of happiness," waves above the shaggy, dazed heads on the hill; a local parson has suggested that the community sponsor a "turn-on" center for rainy days and cold weather. Yet the hillies respond with silence. They pointedly decline to sit on the green that holds the church, though they have been offered sanctuary from police harassment there. The town discovers itself scorned by a mystery beyond drugs, by an implacable "no" spoken here between its two traditional centers. And the numbers grow; as many as seventy were counted the other evening.

We have spies. The clergy mingle and bring back reports of intelligent, uplifting conversations; the only rudeness they encounter is the angry shouting ("Animals!" "Enlist!") from the passing carfuls of middle-aged bourgeoisie. The guidance director at the high school, wearing a three days' beard and blotched blue jeans, passes out questionnaires. Two daring young housewives have spent an entire night on the hill, with a tape recorder concealed in a picnic hamper. The police, those bone-chilled sentries on the boundaries of chaos, have developed their expertise by the intimate light of warfare. They sweep the rocks clean every second hour all night, which discourages cooking fires, and have instituted, via a few quisling hillies, a form of self-policing. Containment, briefly, is their present policy. The selectmen cling to the concept of the green as "common land," intended for public pasturage. By this interpretation, the hillies graze, rather than trespass. Nothing is simple. Apparently there are strata and class animosities within the hillies—the "grassies," for example, who smoke marijuana in the middle area of the slope, detest the "beeries," who inhabit the high rocks, where they smash their no-return bottles, fistfight, and bring the wrath of the town down upon them all. The grassies also dislike the "pillies," who loll beneath them, near the curb, and who take harder drugs, and who deal with the sinister salesmen from Boston. It is these pillies, stretched bemused between the Spanish-American War memorial urns, who could tell us, if we wished to know, how the trashy façades of Poirier's Liquor Mart and Bailey's Pharmaceuticals appear when deep-dyed by LSD and ballooned by the Eternal. In a sense, they see an America whose glory is hidden from the rest of us. The guidance director's questionnaires reveal some surprising statistics. Twelve percent of the hillies favor the Vietnam War. Thirty-four percent have not enjoyed sexual intercourse. Sixty-one percent own their own automobiles. Eighty-six percent hope to attend some sort of graduate school.

Each week, the *Tarbox Star* prints more of the vivacious correspondence occasioned by the hillies. One taxpayer writes to say that God has forsaken the country, that these young people are fungi on a fallen tree. Another, a veteran of the Second World War, replies that on the contrary they are harbingers of hope, super-Americans dedicated to saving a mad world from self-destruction; if he didn't have a family to support, he would go and join them. A housewife writes to complain of loud obscenities that wing outward from the hill. Another housewife promptly rebuts all such "credit-card hypocrites, installment-plan lechers, and Pharisees in pin curlers." A hillie writes to assert that he was driven from his own home by "the stench of ego" and "heartbreaking lasciviousness." The father of a hillie, in phrases broken and twisted by the force of his passion, describes circumstantially his child's upbringing in an atmosphere of love and plenty and in conclusion hopes that other parents will benefit from the hard lesson of his present disgrace—a punishment he "nightly embraces with grateful prayer." Various old men write in to reminisce about their youths. Some remember hard work, bitter winters, and penny-pinching; others depict a lyrically empty land where a boy's natural prankishness and tendency to idle had room to "run their course." One "old-timer" states that "there is nothing new under the sun"; another sharply retorts that *everything* is new under the sun, that these youngsters are "subconsciously seeking accommodation" with unprecedented overpopulation and "hypertechnology." The Colorado couple write from their gallery to agree, and to suggest that salvation lies in Hindu reposefulness, "free-form creativity," and wheat germ. A downtown businessman observes that the hillies have become something of a tourist attraction and should not be disbanded "without careful preliminary study." A minister cautions readers to "let him who is without sin cast the first stone." The editor editorializes to the effect that "our" generation has made a "mess" of the world and that the hillies are registering a "legitimate protest"; a letter signed by sixteen hillies responds that they protest nothing, they just want to sit and "dig." Dig? "Life as it just is," the letter (a document mimeographed and distributed by the local chapter of PAX) concludes, "truly grooves."

The printed correspondence reflects only a fraction of the opinions expressed orally. The local sociologist has told a luncheon meeting of the Rotary Club that the hillies are seeking "to reëmploy human-ness as a non-relative category." The local Negro, a crack golfer and horseman whose seat on his chestnut mare is the pride of the hunt club, cryptically told the Kiwanis that, "when you create a slave population, you must expect a slave mentality." The local Jesuit informed an evening meeting of the Lions that drugs are "the logical end product of the pernicious Protestant heresy of the 'inner light.' " The waitresses at the local restaurant tell customers that the sight of the hillies through the plate-glass windows gives them "the creeps." "Why don't they go to *work?*" they ask; their own legs are blue-veined from the strain of work, of waiting and hustling. The local Indian, who might be thought sympathetic, since some of the hillies affect Pocahontas bands and bead necklaces, is savage on the subject: "Clean the garbage out," he tells the seedy crowd that hangs around the news store. "Push 'em back where they came from." But this ancient formula, so often invoked in our history, no longer applies. They came from our own homes. And in honesty do we want them back? How much a rural myth is parental love? The Prodigal Son no doubt became a useful overseer; they needed his hands. We need our self-respect. That is what is eroding on the hill—the foundations of our lives, the identities our industry and acquisitiveness have heaped up beneath the flag's blessing. The local derelict is the only adult who wanders among them without self-consciousness and without fear.

For fear is the mood. People are bringing the shutters down from their attics and putting them back on their windows. Fences are appearing where children used to stray freely from back yard to back yard, through loose hedges of forsythia and box. Locksmiths are working overtime. Once we parked our cars with the keys dangling from the dashboard, and a dog could sleep undisturbed in the middle of the street. No more. Fear reigns, and impatience. The downtown seems to be tightening like a fist, a glistening clot of apoplectic signs and sunstruck, stalled automobiles. And the hillies are slowly withdrawing upward, and clustering around the beeries, and accepting them as leaders. They are getting ready for our attack.

The Tarbox Police

CAL.

Hal.

Sam.

Dan.

We have known them since they were boys in the high school. Good-natured boys, not among the troublemakers, going out for each sport as its season came along, though not usually among the stars.

Indeed, they are hard to tell apart, without a close look. Cal is an inch taller than Hal, and Dan has a slightly wistful set to his jaw that differentiates him from Sam, who until you see him smile looks mean. Downtown, they don't smile much; if they started, they would never stop, since they know almost everybody passing by. If you look them in the eye for a second they will nod, however. A bit bleakly, but nod. In the summer they wear sunglasses and their eyes are not there. In their short-sleeved shirts they would melt into the summer crowd of barefooted girls and bare-chested easy riders but for the knobby black armor of equipment, strapped and buckled to their bodies in even the hottest weather: the two-way radio in its perforated case, the billy club dangling overripe from their belts, the little buttoned-up satchel of Mace, and the implausible, unthinkable gun, its handle peeking from the holster like the metal-and-wood snout of an eyeless baby animal riding backward on its mother's forgetful hip.

They not only know everybody, they know everything. When dear Maddy Frothingham, divorced since she was twenty-two and not her fault, upped and married the charmer she met on some fancy island Down East, it was the Tarbox police who came around and told her her new husband was a forger wanted in four states, and took him away. When Janice Tugwell fell down the cellar stairs and miscarried, it was the police who knew what house down by the river Morris's car was parked in front of, and who were kind enough not to tell her how their knock brought him to the door fumbling with his buttons. It is the police who lock up Squire Wentworth Saturday nights so he won't disgrace himself; it is the police, when there's another fatal accident on that bad stretch of 87, who put the blanket over the body, so nobody else will have to see. Chief Chad's face, when the do-good lawyers come out from Boston to get our delinquents off, is a study in surprise, that the court should be asked to doubt things everybody *knows*. We ask them, the police, to know too much. It hardens them. Young as they are, their faces get cold, cold and prim. When in summer they put on their sunglasses, little is hidden that showed before.

They want to be invisible.

In an ideal state, they would wither away.

My wife and I had an eerie experience a year ago. Our male pup hadn't come back for his supper, and the more my wife thought about it the less she could sleep, so around midnight she got up in her nightie and we put on raincoats and went out in the convertible to search. It was a weekday night, the town looked dead. It looked like a fossil of itself, pressed pale into black stone. Except downtown—the blank shop fronts glazed under the blue arc lamps, the street wide as a prairie without parked cars—there was this cluster of shadows. I thought of a riot, except that it was quiet. I thought of witchcraft, except that it was 1971. Cal was there. His blue uniform looked purple under the lights. The rest were kids, the kids that hang around on the hill, the long hair and the Levi's making the girls hard to distinguish. Half in the street, half on the pavement, they were having a conversation, a party in the heart of our ghostly town.

My wife found her voice and asked Cal about the dog and he answered promptly that one had been hit but not badly by a car up near the new shopping center around four that afternoon, without a collar or a license, and we apologized about the license and explained how our little girl keeps dressing the dog in her old baby clothes and taking his collar off, and, sure enough, we found the animal in the dogcatcher's barn, shivering and limping and so relieved to see us he fainted in the driveway and didn't eat for two days; but the point is the strangeness of those kids and that policeman in the middle of nowhere, having what looked like a good time. What do they talk about? Does it happen every night? Is something brewing between them? Nobody can talk to these kids, except the police. Maybe, in the world that's in the making, they're the only real things to one another, kids and police, and the rest of us, me in my convertible and my wife in her nightie, are the shadows, the pale fossils. As we pulled away, we heard laughter.

But they have lives, too. The Sunday evening the man went crazy on Prudence Lane, Hal arrived in a suit as if fresh from church, and Dan wore a checked shirt and bowling shoes that sported a big number 9 on their backs. Dainty feet. Chief Chad had to feather his siren to press the cruiser through the crowd that had collected—sunburned young mothers pushing babies in strollers, a lot of old people from the nursing home up the street. All through the crowd people were telling one another stories. The man had moved here three weeks ago from Detroit. He was crazy on three days of gin. He was an acidhead. He went crazy because his wife had left him. He was a queer. He was a Vietnam veteran. His first shot from the upstairs window had hit a fire hydrant—ka-*zing!*—and the second kicked up dust under the nose of the fat beagle that sleeps by the curb there.

The crazy man was in the second story of the old Cushing place, which the new owners had fixed up for rental with that aluminum siding that looks just like clapboards until you study the corners. The Osborne house next door, without a front yard, juts out to the pavement, and most of the crowd stayed more or less behind the house, though the old folks kept pushing closer to see, and the mothers kept running into the line of fire to fetch back their toddlers, and the dogs raced around nervously wagging their tails the way they do at festivities.

It was strange, coming up the street, to see the cloud of gunsmoke drifting toward the junior high school, just like on television, only in better color. The police crouched down behind the cruiser, trading shots. Chief Chad was huddled behind the corner of the Osbornes', shouting into his radio. The siege lasted an hour. The crazy man, a skinny fellow in a tie-dyed undershirt, was in plain sight in the window above the porch roof, making a speech you couldn't understand and alternately reloading the two rifles he had. One of the old folks hobbled out across the asphalt to the police car and screamed, "*Kill* him! I paid good taxes all my life. What's the problem, he's right up there, *kill* him!" Even the crazy man went quiet to hear the old man carry on: the old guy was trembling; his face shone with tears; he kept yelling the word "taxes." Dan shielded him with his body and hustled him back to the crowd, where a nurse from the home wrestled him quiet.

The plan, it turned out, wasn't to kill anybody. The police were aiming around the window, making a sieve of that new siding, until the state police arrived with the tear gas. While the crazy man was being entertained out front, Chief Chad and a state cop sneaked into the back yard and plunked the canisters into the kitchen. The shooting died. The police went in the front door wearing masks and brought out on a stretcher a man swaddled like a newborn baby. A thin sort of baby with a sleeping green face. Though they say that at the hospital, when he got his crazy consciousness back, he broke all the straps and it took five men to hold him down for the injection.

"Go home!" Chief Chad shouted, shaking his rifle at the crowd. "The show's over! Damn you all, go home!"

Most people forgave him, he was overwrought.

Bits of the crowd clung to the neighborhood way past dark, telling one another what they saw or knew or guessed, giving it all a rerun. Experience is so vicarious these days, only recollecting it makes it actual. One theory was that the crazy man hadn't meant to hurt anybody, or he could have winged a dozen spectators. Yes, but on the corner of the Osbornes' you can still see where a bullet came through one side and out the other, right where Chief Chad's ear had been a second before. Out of all that unreality, the bullet holes remained to be mended. It took weeks for the aluminum-siding man to show up.

And then, this March, in a town meeting, the moderator got rattled and ejected a citizen. He was the new sort of citizen who has moved into the Marshview development, a young husband with a big honey-colored beard. They appear to feel the world owes them an explanation. We were on the sewer articles. We've been passing these sewer articles for years and the river never smells any better, but you pass them because the town engineer is president of the Odd Fellows and doing the best he can. Anyway, young Honeybeard had raised four or five objections, and had the selectmen up and down at the microphone like jack-in-the-boxes, and Bud Perley, moderator ever since he came back from Okinawa with his medals, got weary of recognizing him, and overlooked his waving hand. The boy—taxpayer, just like the old cuss at the shoot-out—had smuggled in a balloon and enough helium to float it up toward the gym ceiling.

LOVE, the balloon said.

"Eject that man," Perley said.

Who'll ever forget it? Seven hundred of us there, and we'd seen a lot of foolishness on the town-meeting floor, but we'd never seen a man ejected. Hal was over by the water bubbler, leaning against the wall, and Sam was on the opposite side joking with a bunch of high-school students up on the tumbling horses observing for their civics class. The two policemen moved at once, together. They sauntered, almost, across the front of the hall toward the center aisle.

And you saw they had billy clubs, and you saw they had guns, and nobody else did.

Actually, young Honeybeard was a friend of Sam's—they had gone smelt-fishing together that winter—and both smiled sheepishly as they touched, and the fellow went out making a big *V* with his arms, and people laughed and cheered and no doubt will vote him in for selectman if he runs.

But still. The two policemen had moved in unison, carefully, crabwise-cautious under their load of equipment, and you saw they were real; blundering old Perley had called them into existence, and not a mouth in that hall held more than held breath. This was it. This was power, our power hopefully to be sure, but this was *it*.

The Corner

THE TOWN is one of those that people pass through on the way to somewhere else; so its inhabitants have become expert in giving directions. Ray Blandy cannot be on his porch five minutes before a car, baffled by the lack of signs at the corner, will shout to him, "Is this the way to the wharf?" or "Am I on the right road to East Mather?" Using words and gestures that have become rote, Ray heads it on its way, with something of the satisfaction with which he mails a letter, or flushes a toilet, or puts in another week at Unitek Electronics. Catty-corner across the awkward intersection (Wharf Street swerves south and meets Reservoir Road and Prudence Lane at acute, half-blind angles), Mr. Latroy, a milkman who is home from noon on, and who is also an auxiliary policeman, directs automobiles uncertain if, to reach the famous old textile mill in Lacetown, they should bear left around the traffic island or go straight up the hill. There is nothing on the corner to hold cars here except the small variety store run by an old Dutch couple, the Van der Bijns. Its modest size and dim, rusted advertisements are geared to foot traffic. Children going to school stop here for candy, and townspeople after work stop for cigarettes and bread, but for long tracts of the day there is little for Mr. Van der Bijn to do but sit behind his display windows and grieve that the cars passing through take the corner too fast.

There have been accidents. Eight years ago, around eleven o'clock of a muggy July morning, when Susan Craven had been standing on her sidewalk wondering whether she should go to the playground or Linda Latroy's back yard, a clam truck speedily rounding the corner snapped a kingbolt, went right up over the banking, swung—while the driver wildly twisted the slack steering wheel—within a foot of unblinking, preoccupied Susan, bounced back down the banking, straight across Prudence Lane, and smack, in a shower of shingles, into the house then owned by Miss Beulah Cogswell. She has since died, after living for years on her telling of the accident: "*Well*, I was in the kitchen making my morning *tea* and naturally thought it was just *another* of those dreadful sonic booms. But, *when* I go with my cup and saucer into the front parlor, here *right* where my television set had been was this dirty windshield with a man's absolutely *white* face, mouthing like a fish, the carpet *drenched* with shingles and plaster and the corner cupboard three feet into the room and not one, would you be*lieve* it, not a single piece of bone china so much as *cracked!*"

Now her house is occupied by a young couple with a baby that cries all night. The Cravens have moved to Falmouth, selling their house to the Blandys. And the Latroy girls have heard that Susan is married, to a pilot from Otis Air Force Base; it's hard to believe. It seems just yesterday she was brushed by death, a rude little girl with fat legs.

Long before this, so long ago only the Van der Bijns and Mrs. Billy Hannaford witnessed the wreckage, a drunken driver took the corner too fast in the opposite direction from the truck and skidded up over the curb into the left-hand display window of the variety store. No one was hurt; the Van der Bijns were asleep upstairs and the drunk, well known locally, remained relaxed and amused. But the accident left a delicate scar on the corner, in the perceptible disparity between the two large plate-glass panes: the left one is less wavery and golden in tint than the right, and its frame is of newer molding, which does not perfectly match.

Somewhere between these two accidents there is an old man down from New Hampshire, lost, blinded, he said, by blazing headlights, who drove right over the traffic island, straddling it in his high 1939 Buick, shearing off the Stop sign and eviscerating his muffler on the stump. And lost in the snowy mists of time is the child who sledded down Reservoir Road and was crushed beneath a big black Peerless, in the days before cars could be counted on to be everywhere.

It is strange that more accidents do not occur. Everyone ignores the rusty Stop sign. Teen-agers begin drag races down by the wharf and use the traffic island as a finish post. Friday and Saturday nights, there is screeching and roaring until two and three in the morning. Trucks heave and shift gears, turning north. Summer weekends see a parade of motor-boats on trailers. The housing development, Marshview, on the east end of town, adds dozens of cars to the daily flow. The corner has already been widened—the Van der Bijns' house once had a front yard. Old photographs exist, on sepia cardboard, that show fewer wires on the poles, a great beech where none now stands, a front yard at the house that was not then a store, the dark house across from the Blandys' painted white, no porch at the Blandys', no traffic island, and a soft, trodden, lane-like look to the surface of the roadway. When the Van der Bijns move or die (the same thing to the town clerk), their house will be taken by eminent domain and the corner widened still further, enabling the cars to go still faster. Engineers' drawings are already on file at Town Hall.

Yet, though the inhabitants strain their ears at night waiting for the squeal of tires to mushroom into the crash of metal and the splintering of glass, nothing usually happens. The corner is one of those places where nothing much happens except traffic and weather. Even death, when it came for Miss Cogswell, came as a form of traffic, as an ambulance in the driveway, and a cluster of curious neighborhood children.

The weather happens mostly in the elm, a vast old elm not yet felled by the blight. Its branches overarch the corner. Its drooping twigs brush the roofs of the dark house, and the young couple's house, and the Latroys'. Shaped like a river system—meandering tributaries thickening and flowing into the trunk, but three-dimensional, a solid set of streets where pigeons strut, meet, and mate—the tree's pattern of limbs fills the Blandys' bedroom windows and their eyes on awaking in all weathers: glistening and sullen in November rain, so that you feel the awful weight the tree upholds, like a cast-iron cloud; airy tracery after a snow, or in the froth of bloom; in summer a curtain of green, with a lemon-yellow leaf, turned early, here and there like a random stitch. Lying bedridden in fever or in despair, each of the Blandys has concluded, separately, that, if there was nothing to life but lying here looking at the elm forever, it would suffice—it would be, though just barely, enough.

The elm's leaves in autumn blow by the bushel down Prudence Lane into the Van der Bijns' side yard, confirming the old man's contention that the weather is always outrageous. He came to this country before the war, foreseeing it, and still finds the intemperances of the American climate remarkable. The faithful gray damp of Holland is a benchmark in his bones. For months ahead of time, he foresees the troublesome wonder of snow, and gloats over his bizarre fate of having to shovel it. Though weak from his long days of sitting, he shovels compulsively, even during a blizzard trying to keep his forty feet of sidewalk as clean as swept tiles. Some ironical gallantry seems intended—a humorous grateful willingness to have the land that gave him refuge take his life with its barbaric weather. Our summer's extremes also astonish him. Four sunny days become a drought in his eyes, which are delft-blue and perpetually wide open, within deep, skeletal sockets. Each growing season, as he observes its effects on Mrs. Hannaford's bushes and lawn, seems in some way abnormal, unprecedented, weird. "Naaow, da forsydia last yaar wasn't aaout yet vor two weeks!" "Naaow, I'fe nefer once zeen da grass zo zoon brown!"

And Mrs. Hannaford, whose house of all the houses on the corner is most distant from the elm, regards this tree as a benign veil drawn across the tar-shingled roofs and ungainly dormers of the neighborhood. She sees it, too, as a sea fan superimposed on a cockleshell sunset, and as a living entity that has doubled its size since as a girl she studied it from the same windows she now sleeps behind. Once, when four or five, she thought she saw the robed shadow of Jesus moving in its branches, and prayed that the end of the world be not yet come.

The people on the corner do not know each other very well. It is the houses who know each other, whose windows watch. Mrs. Billy Hannaford goes to the Episcopal church whenever Communion is offered; she dresses in purple and walks with a cane, her cheeks painted salmon, her hair rinsed blue. Some weekend nights, cars belonging to the Blandys' friends are parked in front of their house until hours after midnight. The young couple's baby cries. The man who lives in the dark house is off in his car from seven to seven, and his wife is indistinguishable among the two or three ginger-haired women who come and go. The Latroys have beautiful blonde daughters, and much of the hot-rodding on the corner is for their benefit. This is what the houses know of each other's inner lives, what their windows can verify.

Rain made Ray Blandy romantic and he had hoped to romance his wife, but June Blandy had fallen asleep in the middle of an embrace, and he had risen from the bed in bad temper. It was Saturday midnight. He stood by the window, wanting to be loved by the rain. There was a nearing roar of motors and a braking slither, and he saw (this is what he thought he saw) a speeding VW bus pursued by a black sedan. The bus disappeared behind the edge of the dark house. The sedan skidded on the smooth patch where just that April some frost-heaves had been retarred; its weight swung from side to side, like an accelerated dance step. Out of control, the car went up with one pair of tires onto the sidewalk, and also disappeared. Then there was a thump, not deafening but definite, and deeply satisfying; and a silence. Then the high-pitched gear whine of a prolonged backing up. The VW bus appeared, backward, from behind the dark house. Shouting voices dropped to a mutter. Mr. Latroy, wearing his auxiliary-policeman's badge, appeared in front of his house. The Van der Bijns' lights went on.

June Blandy sat up in bed. "What was that?"

"You mean you weren't asleep, you were just faking?"

"I was sound asleep, but something thumped."

"Sonic boom," he told her. She missed the allusion. He told her, "A car lost control going around the corner and hit something up the street. I can't see what."

"Why are you just standing there? Let's *go*." Last year, when a dog had been hit on the corner and their neighbors from the curb idly watched it yelp and writhe, June had spontaneously run into the street and taken the broken animal into her arms. Now she put on her bathrobe and was past him, and down the stairs, and out of the door. He looked in two closets for a bathrobe or a raincoat to put over his pajamas and finally, afraid of missing everything, followed her into the drizzle in a short yellow slicker that barely covered his fly.

The corner had cracked open like a piñata, spilling absurdly dressed people. Mr. Van der Bijn wore a long nightcap, with a tassel—who would have imagined it? Mrs., her daytime braids undone, had gray hair down to her waist. The young mother, baby on hip, wore bell-bottom pants of crimson crushed velvet: her normal at-home costume? Why were so many people up and dressed after midnight? Mrs. Latroy wore a blue print dress, and her husband black trousers and his pin-striped Tarbox Dairy shirt, with a cream-colored logo. Did he never sleep? His milk route began at four. From the dark house emerged two middle-aged women, ginger-haired and flirtatious, in house slippers. "That's a cute costume," one of them said to Ray. A tense, slight man with a rash of pimples on his forehead, he looked down and adjusted his pajama fly.

June, who had reached the street earlier than he, told him, "About six people got out of the car into the bus and drove away. Shouldn't somebody have stopped them, or done *some*thing?" She had turned from him to address a larger audience, her voice lifted operatically.

The mother in red pants said, "One of them came into the house to call the police and another one came after her and said not to bother, they'd drive to the station, it'd be faster." She had a narrow, impoverished face but an exotic flat accent, Midwestern or Western. As she spoke, she kept bouncing the baby on her hip.

A ginger-haired lady said, "One of them said it was all right, she was the wife of a fireman."

"*Uh*-ohh," the other said. "He's been going to too many fires." There was general laughter.

The drizzle was lifting, but the neighbors drew snugly closer beneath the sheltering elm, as if to consolidate their sudden conquest of the distance the houses had always imposed between them. "Naaow, isn't dis wedder somezing," Mr. Van der Bijn said, and again they all laughed, having heard him say it so often before. The driver of the disabled car glanced toward them enviously. His sedan was up the street, sideways against a telephone pole; it had spun almost totally around. His gaze inhibited the carnival crowd on the corner. He smelled of recent danger, and was dangerous. The man who lived in the dark house emerged in pants and rumpled shirt and spectacles; his eyes looked rubbed, as after sleep or a long bout of television. His ladies grew animated; the more flirtatious one told Ray her version of the accident. The VW was coming down Prudence Lane, and didn't stop at the Stop sign, they never do, and the black sedan, to avoid hitting it, swerved to the left, into the pole. Ray told her, no, he had happened to be at his window, and the VW was being chased by the other—a drag race, obviously.

June asked, "Hasn't *any*body called the police?"

Mrs. Van der Bijn said, "Mr. Latroy has." But by this she meant, probably, that in a sense he *was* police; for he had not moved from the sidewalk. He stood there serenely, his face tilted upward, as if basking on a sunny day. The window above him lit up, and two of his beautiful daughters were framed in it, their blond hair incandescent. A carload of male teen-agers swung around the corner, abruptly braked, and eased by. The two daughters waved. Another car stopped, and asked the way to East Mather. Three voices at once—Ray, Mr. Latroy, and a ginger-haired lady—chorused the directions.

June was conferring with the girl in velvet pants. The girl agreed to go inside and call the police. Her husband was asleep. He was a very sound sleeper. "I can never get the lunk up, to take care of Emily. Every night, it's the same story."

"She has fear," Mrs. Van der Bijn announced. "You must sing her to sleep."

The girl studied Mrs. Van der Bijn and handed her the baby and went into her house. The baby began its feeble, well-practiced whimper, paced to last for hours. Mrs. Van der Bijn began to sing, in a distant lost language, its gutturals low in her throat.

The driver of the sedan came closer. He swaggered like a man with something to sell, his hands in his pockets. He was a stocky young man, with hair combed wet, so the tooth furrows showed. "It's all right," he told them. "I got everybody's number. Nothing to worry about," he said, and told them his story. There was a third car. A yellow convertible, a crazy man. Down by the wharf, it had cut right in front of him, and tried to run him off the road, into that metal rail there. He, the man telling the story, had braked just in time—he was lucky to have such fast reflexes— and then, seeing red, had given chase, lost control at the corner, and had this accident. There was a VW bus right behind him. It had stopped, and the people in it had said they knew the driver of the convertible, and would catch him and bring him back. As some kind of insurance, the sedan's passengers, a guy he knew and the guy's girlfriend, had crowded into the bus, and off they had all gone. They should be back any minute. At any rate, it didn't matter, because he had the license-plate numbers.

It was a strange story, but he pulled from a pocket the little pad upon which he had firmly written down two long numbers. Ray wondered how the man had focused his eyes on those speeding, shuttling vehicles, and why in Ray's own memory the bus had been ahead of the sedan, and why he had not seen the third car, the yellow convertible. The rest of the corner, too, distrusted the driver's story, and, amid polite comments and expressions of interest, slowly closed against him, isolating him again. Undiscouraged, like an encyclopedia salesman turned from the door, the driver walked briskly away, toward his crippled car and, farther down the street, an approaching blue twinkle.

The police car pulled up. They all knew the cops that emerged; one was a wife-beater, and the other had been a high-school quarterback. The baby's mother came out of her house and stood so close that Ray, looking down, saw cerise satin slippers, with bunny-tail pompoms, next to his own knobby bare feet. The erotic short-circuit nearly knocked him over.

It was as when bombs fall, baring swaths of wallpaper and plaster, unexpected bathroom tiles, dangling fixtures. The two policemen softly interviewed the driver, the people at the corner watched from a safe distance and kept their versions to themselves, the gentle event of the rain ceased, the law closed its notebook, the elm sighed, the little crowd reluctantly broke up and returned to their houses. Later, some heard, but only the streetlamp saw, the tow truck come and take the sedan away. Overhead, the clouds paled and pulled apart, revealing stars. The driver's story had been strange, but no stranger, to the people who live here, than the truth that the corner is one among many on the map of the town, and the town is a dot on the map of the state, and the state a mere patch on the globe, and the globe invisible from any of the stars overhead.

A & P

IN WALKS THESE THREE GIRLS in nothing but bathing suits. I'm in the second checkout slot, with my back to the door, so I don't see them until they're over by the bread. The one that caught my eye first was the one in the plaid green two-piece. She was a chunky kid, with a good tan and a sweet broad soft-looking can with those two crescents of white just under it, where the sun never seems to hit, at the top of the backs of her legs. I stood there with my hand on a box of Hi Ho crackers trying to remember if I rang it up or not. I ring it up again and the customer starts giving me hell. She's one of these cash-register-watchers, a witch about fifty with rouge on her cheekbones and no eyebrows, and I know it made her day to trip me up. She'd been watching cash registers for fifty years and probably never seen a mistake before.

By the time I got her feathers smoothed and her goodies into a bag—she gives me a little snort in passing, if she'd been born at the right time they would have hung her over in Salem—by the time I get her on her way the girls had circled around the bread and were coming back, without a pushcart, back my way along the counters, in the aisle between the checkouts and the Special bins. They didn't even have shoes on. There was this chunky one, with the two-piece—it was bright green and the seams on the bra were still sharp and her belly was still pretty pale so I guessed she just got it (the suit)—there was this one, with one of those chubby berry-faces, the lips all bunched together under her nose, this one, and a tall one, with black hair that hadn't quite frizzed right, and one of these sunburns right across under the eyes, and a chin that was too long—you know, the kind of girl that other girls think is very "striking" and "attractive" but never quite makes it, as they very well know, which is why they like her so much—and then the third one, who wasn't quite so tall. She was the queen. She kind of led them, the other two peeking around and hunching over a little. She didn't look around, not this queen, she just walked straight on slowly, on these long white prima-donna legs. She came down a little hard on her heels, as if she didn't walk in her bare feet that much, putting down her heels and then letting the weight move along to her toes as if she was testing the floor with every step, putting a little deliberate extra action into it. You never know for sure how girls' minds work (do you really think it's a mind in there or just a little buzz like a bee in a glass jar?) but you got the idea she had talked the other two into coming in here with her, and now she was showing them how to do it, walk slow and hold yourself straight.

She had on a kind of dirty-pink—beige maybe, I don't know—bathing suit with a little nubble all over it and, what got me, the straps were down. They were off her shoulders looped loose around the cool tops of her arms, and I guess as a result the suit had slipped a little on her, so all around the top of the cloth there was this shining rim. If it hadn't been there you wouldn't have known there could have been anything whiter than those shoulders. With the straps pushed off, there was nothing between the top of the suit and the top of her head except just *her*, this clean bare plane of the top of her chest down from the shoulder bones like a dented sheet of metal tilted in the light. I mean, it was more than pretty.

She had sort of oaky hair that the sun and salt had bleached, done up in a bun that was unravelling, and a kind of prim face. Walking into the A & P with your straps down, I suppose it's the only kind of face you *can* have. She held her head so high her neck, coming up out of those white shoulders, looked kind of stretched, but I didn't mind. The longer her neck was, the more of her there was.

She must have felt in the corner of her eye me and over my shoulder Stokesie in the first slot watching, but she didn't tip. Not this queen. She kept her eyes moving across the racks, and stopped, and turned so slow it made my stomach rub the inside of my apron, and buzzed to the other two, who kind of huddled against her for relief, and then they all three of them went up the cat-and-dog-food-breakfast-cereal-macaroni-rice-raisins-seasonings-spreads-spaghetti-soft-drinks-crackers-and-cookies aisle. From my slot I can look straight up this aisle to the meat counter, and I watched them all the way. The fat one with the tan sort of fumbled with the cookies, but on second thought she put the package back. The sheep pushing their carts down the aisle—the girls were walking against the usual traffic (not that we have one-way signs or anything)—were pretty hilarious. You could see them, when Queenie's white shoulders dawned on them, kind of jerk, or hop, or hiccup, but their eyes snapped back to their own baskets and on they pushed. I bet you could set off dynamite in an A & P and the people would by and large keep reaching and checking oatmeal off their lists and muttering, "Let me see, there was a third thing, began with *A*, asparagus, no, ah, yes, applesauce!" or whatever it is they do mutter. But there was no doubt, this jiggled them. A few houseslaves in pin curlers even looked around after pushing their carts past to make sure what they had seen was correct.

You know, it's one thing to have a girl in a bathing suit down on the beach, where what with the glare nobody can look at each other much anyway, and another thing in the cool of the A & P, under the fluorescent lights, against all those stacked packages, with her feet paddling along naked over our checkerboard green-and-cream rubber-tile floor.

"Oh, Daddy," Stokesie said beside me. "I feel so faint."

"Darling," I said. "Hold me tight." Stokesie's married, with two babies chalked up on his fuselage already, but as far as I can tell that's the only difference. He's twenty-two, and I was nineteen this April.

"Is it done?" he asks, the responsible married man finding his voice. I forgot to say he thinks he's going to be manager some sunny day, maybe in 1990 when it's called the Great Alexandrov and Petrooshki Tea Company or something.

What he meant was, our town is five miles from a beach, with a big summer colony out on the Point, but we're right in the middle of town, and the women generally put on a shirt or shorts or something before they get out of the car into the street. And anyway these are usually women with six children and varicose veins mapping their legs and nobody, including them, could care less. As I say, we're right in the middle of town, and if you stand at our front doors you can see two banks and the Congregational church and the newspaper store and three real-estate offices and about twenty-seven old freeloaders tearing up Central Street because the sewer broke again. It's not as if we're on the Cape; we're north of Boston and there's people in this town haven't seen the ocean for twenty years.

The girls had reached the meat counter and were asking McMahon something. He pointed, they pointed, and they shuffled out of sight behind a pyramid of Diet Delight peaches. All that was left for us to see was old McMahon patting his mouth and looking after them sizing up their joints. Poor kids, I began to feel sorry for them, they couldn't help it.

. . .

Now here comes the sad part of the story, at least my family says it's sad, but I don't think it's so sad myself. The store's pretty empty, it being Thursday afternoon, so there was nothing much to do except lean on the register and wait for the girls to show up again. The whole store was like a pinball machine and I didn't know which tunnel they'd come out of. After a while they come around out of the far aisle, around the lightbulbs, records at discount of the Caribbean Six or Tony Martin Sings or some such gunk you wonder they waste the wax on, six-packs of candy bars, and plastic toys done up in cellophane that fall apart when a kid looks at them anyway. Around they come, Queenie still leading the way, and holding a little gray jar in her hand. Slots Three through Seven are unmanned and I could see her wondering between Stokes and me, but Stokesie with his usual luck draws an old party in baggy gray pants who stumbles up with four giant cans of pineapple juice (what do these bums *do* with all that pineapple juice? I've often asked myself) so the girls come to me. Queenie puts down the jar and I take it into my fingers icy cold. Kingfish Fancy Herring Snacks in Pure Sour Cream: 49¢. Now her hands are empty, not a ring or a bracelet, bare as God made them, and I wonder where the money's coming from. Still with that prim look she lifts a folded dollar bill out of the hollow at the center of her nubbled pink top. The jar went heavy in my hand. Really, I thought that was so cute.

Then everybody's luck begins to run out. Lengel comes in from haggling with a truck full of cabbages on the lot and is about to scuttle into that door marked MANAGER behind which he hides all day when the girls touch his eye. Lengel's pretty dreary, teaches Sunday school and the rest, but he doesn't miss that much. He comes over and says, "Girls, this isn't the beach."

Queenie blushes, though maybe it's just a brush of sunburn I was noticing for the first time, now that she was so close. "My mother asked me to pick up a jar of herring snacks." Her voice kind of startled me, the way voices do when you see the people first, coming out so flat and dumb yet kind of tony, too, the way it ticked over "pick up" and "snacks." All of a sudden I slid right down her voice into her living room. Her father and the other men were standing around in ice-cream coats and bow ties and the women were in sandals picking up herring snacks on toothpicks off a big glass plate and they were all holding drinks the color of water with olives and sprigs of mint in them. When my parents have somebody over they get lemonade and if it's a real racy affair Schlitz in tall glasses with "They'll Do It Every Time" cartoons stencilled on.

"That's all right," Lengel said. "But this isn't the beach." His repeating this struck me as funny, as if it had just occurred to him, and he had been thinking all these years the A & P was a great big dune and he was the head lifeguard. He didn't like my smiling—as I say, he doesn't miss much—but he concentrates on giving the girls that sad Sunday-school-superintendent stare.

Queenie's blush is no sunburn now, and the plump one in plaid, that I liked better from the back—a really sweet can—pipes up. "We weren't doing any shopping. We just came in for the one thing."

"That makes no difference," Lengel tells her, and I could see from the way his eyes went that he hadn't noticed she was wearing a two-piece before. "We want you decently dressed when you come in here."

"We *are* decent," Queenie says suddenly, her lower lip pushing, getting sore now that she remembers her place, a place from which the crowd that runs the A & P must look pretty crummy. Fancy Herring Snacks flashed in her very blue eyes.

"Girls, I don't want to argue with you. After this come in here with your shoulders covered. It's our policy." He turns his back. That's policy for you. Policy is what the kingpins want. What the others want is juvenile delinquency.

All this while, the customers had been showing up with their carts but, you know, sheep, seeing a scene, they had all bunched up on Stokesie, who shook open a paper bag as gently as peeling a peach, not wanting to miss a word. I could feel in the silence everybody getting nervous, most of all Lengel, who asks me, "Sammy, have you rung up their purchase?"

I thought and said "No" but it wasn't about that I was thinking. I go through the punches, 4, 9, GROC, TOT—it's more complicated than you think, and after you do it often enough, it begins to make a little song, that you hear words to, in my case "Hello *(bing)* there, you *(gung)* hap-py *pee*-pul *(splat)*!"—the *splat* being the drawer flying out. I uncrease the bill, tenderly as you may imagine, it just having come from between the two smoothest scoops of vanilla I had ever known were there, and pass a half and a penny into her narrow pink palm, and nestle the herrings in a bag and twist its neck and hand it over, all the time thinking.

The girls, and who'd blame them, are in a hurry to get out, so I say "I quit" to Lengel quick enough for them to hear, hoping they'll stop and watch me, their unsuspected hero. They keep right on going, into the electric eye; the door flies open and they flicker across the lot to their car, Queenie and Plaid and Big Tall Goony-Goony (not that as raw material she was so bad), leaving me with Lengel and a kink in his eyebrow.

"Did you say something, Sammy?"

"I said I quit."

"I thought you did."

"You didn't have to embarrass them."

"It was they who were embarrassing us."

I started to say something that came out "Fiddle-de-doo." It's a saying of my grandmother's, and I know she would have been pleased.

"I don't think you know what you're saying," Lengel said.

"I know you don't," I said. "But I do." I pull the bow at the back of my apron and start shrugging it off my shoulders. A couple customers that had been heading for my slot begin to knock against each other, like scared pigs in a chute.

Lengel sighs and begins to look very patient and old and gray. He's been a friend of my parents for years. "Sammy, you don't want to do this to your mom and dad," he tells me. It's true, I don't. But it seems to me that once you begin a gesture it's fatal not to go through with it. I fold the apron, "Sammy" stitched in red on the pocket, and put it on the counter, and drop the bow tie on top of it. The bow tie is theirs, if you've ever wondered. "You'll feel this for the rest of your life," Lengel says, and I know that's true, too, but remembering how he made that pretty girl blush makes me so scrunchy inside I punch the No Sale tab and the machine whirs "*pee*-pul" and the drawer splats out. One advantage to this scene taking place in summer, I can follow it up with a clean exit, there's no fumbling around getting your coat and galoshes, I just saunter into the electric eye in my white shirt that my mother ironed the night before, and the door heaves itself open, and outside the sunshine is skating around on the asphalt.

I look around for my girls, but they're gone, of course. There wasn't anybody but some young married screaming with her children about some candy they didn't get by the door of a powder-blue Falcon station wagon. Looking back in the big windows, over the bags of peat moss and aluminum lawn furniture stacked on the pavement, I could see Lengel in my place in the second slot, checking the sheep through. His face was dark gray and his back stiff, as if he'd just had an injection of iron, and my stomach kind of fell as I felt how hard the world was going to be to me from here on in.

Lifeguard

BEYOND DOUBT, I am a splendid fellow. In the autumn, winter, and spring, I execute the duties of a student of divinity; in the summer, I disguise myself in my skin and become a lifeguard. My slightly narrow and gingerly hirsute but not necessarily unmanly chest becomes brown. My smooth back turns the color of caramel, which, in conjunction with the whipped cream of my white pith helmet, gives me, some of my teen-age satellites assure me, a delightfully edible appearance. My legs, which I myself can study, cocked as they are before me while I repose on my elevated wooden throne, are dyed a lustreless maple walnut that accentuates their articulate strength. Correspondingly, the hairs of my body are bleached blond, so that my legs have the pointed elegance of, within a flower, umber anthers dusted with pollen.

For nine months of the year, I pace my pale hands and burning eyes through immense pages of Biblical text barnacled with fudging commentary; through multivolumed apologetics couched in a falsely friendly Victorian voice and bound in subtly abrasive boards of finely ridged, prefaded red; through handbooks of liturgy and histories of dogma; through the bewildering duplicities of Tillich's divine politicking; through the suave table talk of Father D'Arcy, Étienne Gilson, Jacques Maritain, and other such moderns mistakenly put at their ease by the exquisite antique furniture and overstuffed larder of the hospitable St. Thomas; through the terrifying attempts of Kierkegaard, Berdyaev, and Barth to scourge God into being. I sway appalled on the ladder of minus signs by which theologians would escape the void. I tiptoe like a burglar into the house of naturalism to steal the silver. An acrobat, I swing from wisp to wisp. Newman's iridescent cobwebs crush in my hands. Pascal's blackboard mathematics are erased by a passing shoulder. The cave drawings, astoundingly vital by candlelight, of those aboriginal magicians, Paul and

Augustine, in daylight fade into mere anthropology. The diverting productions of literary flirts like Chesterton, Eliot, Auden, and Greene—whether they regard Christianity as a pastel forest designed for a fairyland romp or a deliciously miasmic pit from which chiaroscuro can be mined with mechanical buckets—in the end all infallibly strike, despite the comic variety of gongs and mallets, the note of the rich young man who on the coast of Judaea refused in dismay to sell all that he had.

Then, for the remaining quarter of the solar revolution, I rest my eyes on a sheet of brilliant sand printed with the runes of naked human bodies. That there is no discrepancy between my studies, that the texts of the flesh complement those of the mind, is the easy burden of my sermon.

On the back rest of my lifeguard's chair is painted a cross—true, a red cross, signifying bandages, splints, spirits of ammonia, and sunburn unguents. Nevertheless, it comforts me. Each morning, as I mount into my chair, my athletic and youthfully fuzzy toes expertly gripping the slats that form a ladder, it is as if I am climbing into an immense, rigid, loosely fitting vestment.

Again, in each of my roles I sit attentively perched on the edge of an immensity. That the sea, with its multiform and mysterious hosts, its savage and senseless rages, no longer comfortably serves as a divine metaphor indicates how severely humanism has corrupted our creed. We seek God now in flowers and good deeds, and the immensities of blue that surround the little scabs of land upon which we draw our lives to their unsatisfactory conclusions are suffused by science with vacuous horror. I myself can hardly bear the thought of stars, or begin to count the mortalities of coral. But from my chair the sea, slightly distended by my higher perspective, seems a misty old gentleman stretched at his ease in an immense armchair which has for arms the arms of this bay and for an antimacassar the freshly laundered sky. Sailboats float on his surface like idle and unrelated but benevolent thoughts. The sighing of the surf is the rhythmic lifting of his ripple-stitched vest as he breathes. Consider. We enter the sea with a shock; our skin and blood shout in protest. But, that instant, that leap, past, what do we find? Ecstasy and buoyance. Swimming offers a parable. We struggle and thrash, and drown; we succumb, even in despair, and float, and are saved.

With what timidity, with what a sense of trespass, do I set forward even this obliquely a thought so official! Forgive me. I am not yet ordained; I am too disordered to deal with the main text. My competence is marginal, and I will confine myself to the gloss of flesh with which this particular margin, this one beach, is annotated each day.

Here the cinema of life is run backwards. The old are the first to arrive. They are idle, and have lost the gift of sleep. Each of our bodies is a clock that loses time. Young as I am, I can hear in myself the protein acids ticking; I wake at odd hours and in the shuddering darkness and silence feel my death rushing toward me like an express train. The older we get, and the fewer the mornings left to us, the more deeply dawn stabs us awake. The old ladies wear wide straw hats and, in their hats' shadows, smiles as wide, which they bestow upon each other, upon salty shells they discover in the morning-smooth sand, and even upon me, downy-eyed from my night of dissipation. The gentlemen are often incongruous: withered white legs support brazen barrel chests, absurdly potent, bustling with white froth. How these old roosters preen on their "condition"! With what fatuous expertness they swim in the icy water—always, however, prudently parallel to the shore, at a depth no greater than their height.

Then come the middle-aged, burdened with children and aluminum chairs. The men are scarred with the marks of their vocation—the red forearms of the gasoline-station attendant, the pale X on the back of the overall-wearing mason or carpenter, the clammer's nicked ankles. The hair on their bodies has as many patterns as matted grass. The women are wrinkled but fertile, like the muddy, overworked Iraqi rivers that cradled the seeds of our civilization. Their children are odious. From their gaunt faces leer all the vices, the greeds, the grating urgencies of the adult, unsoftened by maturity's reticence and fatigue. Except that here and there a girl, the eldest daughter, wearing a knit suit striped horizontally with green, purple, and brown, walks slowly, carefully, puzzled by the dawn enveloping her thick smooth body, her waist not yet nipped but her throat elongated.

Finally come the young. The young matrons bring fat and fussing infants who gobble the sand like sugar, who toddle blissfully into the surf and bring me bolt upright on my throne. My whistle tweets. The mothers rouse. Many of these women are pregnant again, and sluggishly lie in their loose suits like cows tranced in a meadow. They gossip politics, and smoke against their doctors' advice, and lift their troubled eyes in wonder as a trio of flat-stomached nymphs parades past. These maidens take all our eyes. The vivacious redhead, freckled and white-footed, pushing against her boy and begging to be ducked; the solemn brunette, transporting the vase of herself with held breath; the dimpled blonde in the bib and diapers of her bikini, the lambent fuzz of her midriff shimmering like a cat's belly. Lust stuns me like the sun.

. . .

You are offended that a divinity student lusts? What prigs the unchurched are. Are not our assaults on the supernatural lascivious, a kind of indecency? If only you knew what de Sadian degradations, what frightful psychological spelunking, our gentle transcendentalist professors set us to, as preparation for our work, which is to shine in the darkness.

I feel that my lust makes me glow; I grow cold in my chair, like a torch of ice, as I study beauty. I have studied much of it, wearing all styles of bathing suit and facial expression, and have come to this conclusion: a woman's beauty lies, not in any exaggeration of the specialized zones, or in any general harmony that could be worked out by means of the *sectio aurea* or a similar aesthetic superstition; but in the arabesque of the spine. The curve by which the back modulates into the buttocks. It is here that Grace sits and rides a woman's body.

I watch from my white throne and pity women, deplore the demented judgment that drives them toward the braggart muscularity of the mesomorph and the prosperous complacence of the endomorph when it is we ectomorphs who pack in our scrawny sinews and exacerbated nerves the most intense gift, the most generous shelter, of love. To desire a woman is to desire to save her. Anyone who has endured intercourse that was neither predatory nor hurried knows how through it we descend, with a partner, into the grotesque and delicate shadows that until then have remained locked in the most guarded recess of our soul: into this harbor we bring her. A vague and twisted terrain becomes inhabited; each shadow, touched by the exploration, blooms into a flower of act. As if we are an island upon which a woman, tossed by her laboring vanity and blind self-seeking, is blown, and there finds security, until, an instant before the anticlimax, Nature with a smile thumps down her trump, and the island sinks beneath the sea.

There is great truth in those motion pictures which are slandered as true neither to the Bible nor to life. They are—written though they are by infidels and drunks—true to both. We are all Solomons lusting for Sheba's salvation. The God-filled man is filled with a wilderness that cries to be populated. The stony chambers need jewels, furs, tints of cloth and flesh, even though, as in Samson's case, the temple comes tumbling. Women are an alien race of pagans set down among us. Every seduction is a conversion.

Who has loved and not experienced that sense of rescue? It is not true that our biological impulses are tricked out with ribands of chivalry; rather, our chivalric impulses go clanking in encumbering biological armor. Eunuchs love. Children love. I would love.

My chief exercise, as I sit above the crowds, is to lift the whole mass into immortality. It is not a light task; the throng is so huge, and its members are so individually unworthy. No *memento mori* is as clinching as a photograph of a vanished crowd. Cheering Roosevelt, celebrating the Armistice, there it is, wearing its ten thousand straw hats and stiff collars, a fearless and wooden-faced bustle of life: it is gone. A crowd dies in the street like a derelict; it leaves no heir, no trace, no name. My own persistence beyond the last rim of time is easy to imagine; indeed, the effort of imagination lies the other way—to conceive of my ceasing. But when I study the vast tangle of humanity that blackens the beach as far as the sand stretches, absurdities crowd in on me. Is it as maiden, matron, or crone that the females will be eternalized? What will they do without children to watch and gossip to exchange? What of the thousand deaths of memory and bodily change we endure—can each be redeemed at a final Adjustments Counter? The sheer numbers involved make the mind scream. The race is no longer a tiny simian clan lording it over an ocean of grass; mankind is a plague racing like fire across the exhausted continents. This immense clot gathered on the beach, a fraction of a fraction—can we not say that this breeding swarm is its own immortality and end the suspense? The beehive in a sense survives; and is every body not proved to be a hive, a galaxy of cells each of whom is doubtless praying, from its pew in our thumbnail or esophagus, for personal resurrection? Indeed, to the cells themselves cancer may seem a revival of faith. No, in relation to other people oblivion is sensible and sanitary.

This sea of others exasperates and fatigues me most on Sunday mornings. I don't know why people no longer go to church—whether they have lost the ability to sing or the willingness to listen. From eight-thirty onward they crowd in from the parking lot, ants each carrying its crumb of baggage, until by noon, when the remote churches are releasing their gallant and gaily dressed minority, the sea itself is jammed with hollow heads and thrashing arms like a great bobbing backwash of rubbish. A transistor radio somewhere in the sand releases in a thin, apologetic gust the closing peal of a transcribed service. And right here, here at the very height of torpor and confusion, I slump, my eyes slit, and the blurred forms of Protestantism's errant herd seem gathered by the water's edge in impassioned poses of devotion. I seem to be lying dreaming in the infinite rock of space before Creation, and the actual scene I see is a vision of impossibility: a Paradise. For, had we existed before the gesture that split the firmament, could we have conceived of our most obvious possession, our most platitudinous blessing, the moment, the single ever-present moment that we perpetually bring to our lips brimful?

So: be joyful. *Be joyful* is my commandment. It is the message I read in your jiggle. Stretch your skins like pegged hides curing in the miracle of the sun's moment. Exult in your legs' scissoring, your waist's swivel. Romp; eat the froth; be children. I am here above you; I have given my youth that you may do this. I wait. The tides of time have treacherous undercurrents. You are borne continually toward the horizon. I have prepared myself; my muscles are instilled with everything that must be done. Some day my alertness will bear fruit; from near the horizon there will arise, delicious, translucent, like a green bell above the water, the call for help, the call, a call, it saddens me to confess, that I have yet to hear.

The Deacon

HE PASSES THE PLATE, and counts the money afterward—a large and dogged-looking man, wearing metal-framed glasses that seem tight across his face and that bite into the flesh around his eyes. He wears for Sunday morning a clean white shirt, but a glance downward, as you lay on your thin envelope and pass the golden plate back to him, discovers fallen socks and scuffed shoes. And as he with his fellow-deacons strides forward toward the altar, his suit is revealed as the pants of one suit (gray) and the coat of another (brown). He is too much at home here. During the sermon, he stares toward a corner of the nave ceiling, which needs repair, and slowly, reverently, yet unmistakably chews gum. He lingers in the vestibule, with his barking, possessive laugh, when the rest of the congregation has passed into the sunshine and the dry-mouthed minister is fidgeting to be out of his cassock and home to lunch. The deacon's car, a dusty Dodge, is parked outside the parish hall most evenings. He himself wonders why he is here so often, how he slipped into this ceaseless round of men's suppers, of Christian Education Committee meetings, choir rehearsals, emergency sessions of the Board of Finance where hours churn by in irrelevant argument and prayerful silences that produce nothing. "Nothing," he says to his wife on returning, waking her. "The old fool refuses to amortize the debt." He means the treasurer. "His Eminence tells us donations to foreign missions can't be applied to the oil bill even if we make it up in the summer at five-percent interest." He means the minister. "It was on the tip of my tongue to ask whence he derives all his business expertise."

"Why don't you resign?" she asks. "Let the young people get involved before they drop away."

"One more peace-in-Vietnam sermon, the old-timers will be pulling out anyway." He falls heavily into bed, smelling of chewing gum. As with men who spend nights away from home drinking in bars, he feels guilty, but the motion, the brightness and excitement of the place where he has been continues in him: the varnished old tables, the yellowing Sunday-school charts, the folding chairs and pocked linoleum, the cork bulletin board, the chatter of the children's choir leaving, the strange constant sense of dark sacred space surrounding their lit meeting room like Creation upholding a bright planet. "One more blessing on the damn Vietcong," he mumbles, and the young minister's face, white and worriedly sucking a pipestem, skids like a vision of the Devil across his plagued mind. He has a headache. The sides of his nose, the tops of his cheeks, the space above his ears—wherever the frames of his glasses dig—dully hurt. His wife snores, neglected. In less than seven hours, the alarm clock will ring. This must stop. He must turn over a new leaf.

His name is Miles. He is over fifty, an electrical engineer. Every seven years or so, he changes employers and locations. He has been a member of the council of a prosperous Methodist church in Iowa, a complex of dashing brick-and-glass buildings set in acres of parking lot carved from a cornfield; then of a Presbyterian church in San Francisco, gold-rush Gothic clinging to the back of Nob Hill, attended on Sundays by a handful of Chinese businessmen and prostitutes in sunglasses and whiskery, dazed dropout youths looking for a warm place in which to wind up their Saturday-night trips; then of another Presbyterian church, in New York State, a dour granite chapel in a suburb of Schenectady; and most recently, in southeastern Pennsylvania, of a cryptlike Reformed church sunk among clouds of foliage so dense that the lights were kept burning in midday and the cobwebbed balconies swarmed all summer with wasps. Though Miles has travelled far, he has never broken out of the loose net of Calvinist denominations that places millions of Americans within sight of a spire. He wonders why. He was raised in Ohio, in a village that had lost the tang of the frontier but kept its embattled narrowness, and was confirmed in the same colorless, bean-eating creed that millions in his generation have left behind. He was not, as he understood the term, religious. Ceremony bored him. Closing his eyes to pray made him dizzy. He distinctly heard in the devotional service the overamplified tone of voice that in business matters would signal either ignorance or dishonesty. His profession prepared him to believe that our minds, with their crackle of self-importance, are merely collections of electrical circuits. He saw nothing about his body worth resurrecting. God, concretely considered, had a way of merging with that corner of the church ceiling that showed signs of water leakage. That men should be good, he did not doubt, or that social order demands personal sacrifice; but the Heavenly hypothesis, as it had fallen upon his ears these forty years of Sundays, crushes us all to the same level of unworthiness, and redeems us all indiscriminately, elevating especially, these days, the irresponsible—the unemployable, the riotous, the outrageous, the one in one hundred that strays. More like the ninety-five in one hundred that stray. Neither God nor His ministers displayed love for deacons—indeed, Pharisees were the first objects of their wrath. Why persist, then, in work so thoroughly thankless, begging for pledges, pinching and scraping to save decaying old buildings, facing rings of Sunday-school faces baked to adamant cynicism by hours of television-watching, attending fruitless meetings where the senile and the frustrated dominate, arguing, yawning, missing sleep, the company of his wife, the small, certain joys of home? Why? He had wanted to offer his children the Christian option, to begin them as citizens as he had begun; but all have left home now, are in college or married, and, as far as he can tactfully gather, are unchurched. So be it. He has done his part.

A new job offer arrives, irresistible, inviting him to New England. In Pennsylvania the Fellowship Society gives him a farewell dinner; his squad of Sunday-school teachers presents him with a pen set; he hands in his laborious financial records, his neat minutes of vague proceedings. He bows his head for the last time in that dark sanctuary smelling of moldering plaster and buzzing with captive wasps. He is free. Their new house is smaller, their new town is wooden. He does not join a church; he stays home reading the Sunday paper. Wincing, he flicks past religious news. He drives his wife north to admire the turning foliage. His evenings are immense. He reads through Winston Churchill's history of the Second World War; he installs elaborate electrical gadgets around the house, which now and then give his wife a shock. They go to drive-in movies, and sit islanded in acres of fornication. They go bowling and square-dancing, and feel ridiculous, too ponderous and slow. His wife, these years of evenings alone, has developed a time-passing pattern—television shows spaced with spells of sewing and dozing—into which he fits awkwardly. She listens to him grunt and sigh and grope for words. But Sunday mornings are the worst, stirred up by the swish and roar of churchward traffic on the street outside. He stands by the window; the sight of three little girls, in white beribboned hats, bluebird coats, and dresses of starched organdy, scampering home from Sunday school, gives him a pang unholy in its keenness.

Behind him, his wife says, "Why don't you go to church?"

"No, I think I'll wash the Dodge."

"You washed it last Sunday."

"Maybe I should take up golf."

"You want to go to church. Go. It's no sin."

"Not the Methodists. Those bastards in Iowa nearly worked me to death."

"What's the pretty white one in the middle of town? Congregational. We've never been Congregationalists; they'd let you alone."

"Are you sure you wouldn't like to take a drive?"

"I get carsick with all this starting and stopping in New England. To tell the truth, Miles, it would be a relief to have you out of the house."

Already he is pulling off his sweater, to make way for a clean shirt. He puts on a coat that doesn't match his pants. "I'll go," he says, "but I'll be damned if I'll join."

He arrives late, and sits staring at the ceiling. It is a wooden church, and the beams and ceiling boards in drying out have pulled apart. Above every clear-glass window he sees the stains of leakage, the color of dried apples. At the door, the minister, a pale young man with a round moon face and a know-it-all pucker to his lips, clasps Miles's hand as if never to let it go. "We've been looking for you, Miles. We received a splendid letter about you from your Reformed pastor in Pennsylvania. As you know, since the UCC merger you don't even need to be reconfirmed. There's a men's supper this Thursday. We'll hope to see you there." Some minister's hands, Miles has noticed, grow fatty under the pressure of being so often shaken, and others dwindle to the bones; this one's, for all his fat face, is mostly bones.

The church as a whole is threadbare and scrawny; it makes no resistance to his gradual domination of the Men's Club, the Board of Finance, the Debt Liquidation and Building Maintenance Committee. He cannot help himself; he is a leader, a doer. He and a few shaggy Pilgrim Youth paint the Sunday-school chairs Chinese-red. He and one grimy codger and three bottles of beer clean the furnace room of forgotten furniture and pageant props, of warped hymnals and unused programs still tied in the printer's bundles, of the gilded remnants of a dozen abandoned projects. Once, he attends a committee meeting to which no one else comes. It is a gusty winter night, a night of cold rain from the sea, freezing on the roads. The minister has been up all night with the family of a suicide and cannot himself attend; he has dropped off the church keys with Miles.

. . .

The front-door key, no bigger than a car key, seems magically small for so large a building. Is it the only one? Miles makes a mental note: Have duplicates made. He turns on a light and waits for the other committee members—a retired banker and two maiden ladies. The furnace is running gamely, but with an audible limp in its stride. It is a coal burner converted to oil twenty years ago. The old cast-iron clinker grates are still heaped in a corner, too heavy to throw out. They should be sold for scrap. Every penny counts. Miles thinks, as upon a mystery, upon the prodigality of heating a huge vacant barn like this with such an inefficient burner. Hot air rises direct from the basement to the ceiling, drying and spreading the wood. The fuel needle keeps getting gummed up. Waste. Nothing but waste in this operation, salvage and waste. And weariness.

Miles removes his glasses and rubs the chafed spots at the bridge of his nose. He replaces them to look at his watch. His watch has stopped, its small face wet from the storm like an excited child's. The electric clock in the minister's study has been unplugged. There are books: concordances, daily helps, through the year verse by verse, great sermons, best sermons, sermon hints, all second-hand, no, third-hand, worse, hundredth-hand, thousandth-hand, a coin rubbed blank. The books are leaning on their sides and half the shelves are empty. Empty. The desk is clean. He tests the minister's fountain pen and it is dry. Dry as an old snakeskin, dry as a locust husk that still clings to a tree.

In search of the time, Miles goes into the sanctuary. The 1880 pendulum clock on the choir balustrade still ticks. He can hear it in the dark, overhead. He switches on the nave lights. A moment passes before they come on. Some shaky connection in the toggle, the wiring doubtless rotten throughout the walls, a wonder it hasn't burned down. Miles has never belonged to a wooden church before. Around and above him, like a stiff white forest, the hewn frame creaks and groans in conversation with the wind. The high black windows, lashed as if by handfuls of sand, seem to flinch, yet do not break, and Miles feels the timbers of this ark, with its ballast of box pews, give and sway in the fierce weather, yet hold; and this is why he has come, to share the pride of this ancient thing that will not quite die, to have it all to himself. Warm air from a floor grill breathes on his ankles. Miles can see upward past the clock and the organ to the corner of the unused gallery where souvenirs of the church's past—Puritan pew doors, tin footwarmers, velvet collection bags, Victorian commemorative albums, cracking portraits of wigged pastors, oval photographs of deceased deacons, and unlabelled ferrotypes of chubby cross children lined up under trees long since cut down—repose in dusty glass cases that are in themselves antiques. All this anonymous treasure Miles possesses by being here, like a pharaoh hidden with his life's rich furniture while the rain like a robber rattles to get in.

Yes, the deacon sees, it is indeed a preparation for death—an emptiness where many others have been, which is what death will be. It is good to be at home here. Nothing now exists but himself, this shell, and the storm. The windows clatter; the sand has turned to gravel, the rain has turned to sleet. The storm seizes the church by its steeple and shakes, but the walls were built, sawed and nailed, with devotion, and withstand. The others are very late, they will not be coming; Miles is not displeased, he is pleased. He has done his part. He has kept the faith. He turns off the lights. He locks the door.

The Carol Sing

SURELY one of the natural wonders of Tarbox was Mr. Burley at the Town Hall carol sing. How he would jubilate, how he would God-rest those merry gentlemen, how he would boom out when the male voices became Good King Wenceslas:

> Mark my footsteps, good my page;
> Tread thou in them boldly:
> Thou shalt find the winter's rage
> Freeze thy blood less co-*oh*-ldly.

When he hit a good "oh," standing beside him was like being inside a great transparent Christmas ball. He had what you'd have to call a God-given bass. This year, we other male voices just peck at the tunes: Wendell Huddlestone, whose hardware store has become the pizza place where the dropouts collect after dark; Squire Wentworth, who is still getting up petitions to protect the marsh birds from the atomic-power plant; Lionel Merson, lighter this year by about three pounds of gallstones; and that selectman whose freckled bald head looks like the belly of a trout; and that fireman whose face is bright brown all the year round from clamming; and the widow Covode's bearded son, who went into divinity school to avoid the draft; and the Bisbee boy, who no sooner was back from Vietnam than he grew a beard and painted his car every color of the rainbow; and the husband of the new couple that moved this September into the Whitman place on the beach road. He wears thick glasses above a little mumble of a mouth, but his wife appears perky enough.

> The-ey lo-okèd up and sa-haw a star,
> Shining in the east, beyond them far;
> And to the earth it ga-ave great light,
> And so it continued both da-hay and night.

She is wearing a flouncy little Christmassy number, red with white polka dots, one of those dresses so short that when she sits down on the old plush deacon's bench she has to help it with her hand to tuck under her behind, otherwise it wouldn't. A lively bit of a girl with long thighs as glossy as pond ice. She smiles nervously up over her cup of cinnamon-stick punch, wondering why she is here, in this dusty drafty public place. We must look monstrous to her, we Tarbox old-timers. And she has never heard Mr. Burley sing, but she knows something is missing this year; there is something failed, something hollow. Hester Hartner sweeps wrong notes into every chord: arthritis—arthritis and indifference.

> The first good joy that Mary had,
>   It was the joy of one;
> To see the blessèd Jesus Christ
> When he was first her son.

The old upright, a Pickering, for most of the year has its keyboard locked; it stands beneath the town zoning map, its top piled high with rolled-up plot plans being filed for variances. The Town Hall was built, strange to say, as a Unitarian church, around 1830, but it didn't take around here, Unitarianism; the sea air killed it. You need big trees for a shady mystic mood, or at least a lake to see yourself in like they have over to Concord. So the town bought up the shell and ran a second floor through the air of the sanctuary, between the balconies: offices and the courtroom below, more offices and this hall above. You can still see the Doric pilasters along the walls, the top halves. They used to use it more; there were the Tarbox Theatricals twice a year, and political rallies with placards and straw hats and tambourines, and get-togethers under this or that local auspices, and town meetings until we went representative. But now not even the holly the ladies of the Grange have hung around can cheer it up, can chase away the smell of dust and must, of cobwebs too high to reach and rats' nests in the hot-air ducts and, if you stand close to the piano, that faint sour tang of blueprints. And Hester lately has taken to chewing eucalyptus drops.

> And him to serve God give us grace,
> *O lux beata Trinitas.*

The little wife in polka dots is laughing now: maybe the punch is getting to her, maybe she's getting used to the look of us. Strange people look ugly only for a while, until you begin to fill in those tufty monkey features with a little history and stop seeing their faces and start seeing their lives.

Regardless, it does us good, to see her here, to see young people at the carol sing. We need new blood.

> This time of the year is spent in good cheer,
>   And neighbors together do meet,
> To sit by the fire, with friendly desire,
>   Each other in love to greet.
> Old grudges forgot are put in the pot,
>   All sorrows aside they lay;
> The old and the young doth carol this song,
>   To drive the cold winter away.

At bottom it's a woman's affair, a chance in the darkest of months to iron some man-fetching clothes and get out of the house. Those old holidays weren't scattered around the calendar by chance. Harvest and seedtime, seedtime and harvest, the elbows of the year. The women do enjoy it; they enjoy jostle of most any kind, in my limited experience. The widow Covode as full of rouge and purple as an old-time Scollay Square tart, when her best hope is burial on a sunny day, with no frost in the ground. Mrs. Hortense broad as a barn door, yet her hands putting on a duchess's airs. Mamie Nevins sporting a sprig of mistletoe in her neck brace. They miss Mr. Burley. He never married and was everybody's gallant for this occasion. He was the one to spike the punch, and this year they let young Covode do it, maybe that's why Little Polka Dots can't keep a straight face and giggles across the music like a pruning saw.

> *Adeste, fideles,*
> *Laeti triumphantes;*
> *Venite, venite*
> *In Bethlehem.*

Still that old tussle, *"v"* versus *"wenite,"* the *"th"* as hard or soft. Education is what divides us. People used to actually resent it, the way Burley, with his education, didn't go to some city, didn't get out. Exeter, Dartmouth, a year at the Sorbonne, then thirty years of Tarbox. By the time he hit fifty he was fat and fussy. Arrogant, too. Last sing, he two or three times told Hester to pick up her tempo. "Presto, Hester, not andante!" Never married, and never really worked. Burley Hosiery, that his grandfather had founded, was shut down and the machines sold south before Burley got his manhood. He built himself a laboratory instead and was always about to come up with something perfect: the perfect synthetic substitute for leather, the perfectly harmless insecticide, the beer can that turned itself into mulch. Some said at the end he was looking for a way to

turn lead into gold. That was just malice. Anything high attracts lightning, anybody with a name attracts malice. When it happened, the papers
in Boston gave him six inches and a photograph ten years old. "After a
long illness." It wasn't a long illness, it was cyanide, the Friday after
Thanksgiving.

> The holly bears a prickle,
>   As sharp as any thorn,
> And Mary bore sweet Jesus Christ
>   On Christmas day in the morn.

They said the cyanide ate out his throat worse than a blowtorch. Such a
detail is satisfying but doesn't clear up the mystery. Why? Health, money,
hobbies, that voice. Not having that voice makes a big hole here. Without his lead, no man dares take the lower parts; we just wheeze away at
the melody with the women. It's as if the floor they put in has been taken
away and we're standing in air, halfway up that old sanctuary. We peek
around guiltily, missing Burley's voice. The absent seem to outnumber
the present. We feel insulted, slighted. The dead turn their backs. The
older you get, the more of them snub you. He was rude enough last year,
Burley, correcting Hester's tempo. At one point, he even reached over,
his face black with impatience, and slapped her hands as they were still
trying to make sense of the keys.

> Rise, and bake your Christmas bread:
>   Christians, rise! The world is bare,
>   And blank, and dark with want and care,
> Yet Christmas comes in the morning.

Well, why anything? Why do *we*? Come every year sure as the solstice to
carol these antiquities that if you listened to the words would break your
heart. Silence, darkness, Jesus, angels. Better, I suppose, to sing than to
listen.

The Taste of Metal

METAL, strictly, has no taste; its presence in the mouth is felt as disciplinary, as a *No* spoken to other tastes. When Richard Maple, after many years of twinges, jagged edges, and occasional extractions, had all his remaining molars capped and bridges shaped across the gaps, the gold felt chilly to his cheeks and its regularity masked holes and roughnesses that had been a kind of mirror wherein his tongue had known itself. The Friday of the final cementing, he went to a small party. As he drank a variety of liquids that tasted much the same, he moved from feeling slightly less than himself (his native teeth had been ground to stumps of dentine) to feeling slightly more. The shift in tonality that permeated his skull whenever his jaws closed corresponded, perhaps, to the heightened clarity that fills the mind after a religious conversion. He saw his companions at the party with a new brilliance—a sharpness of vision that, like a camera's, was specific and restricted in focus. He could see only one person at a time, and found himself focusing less on his wife, Joan, than on Eleanor Dennis, the long-legged wife of a municipal-bond broker.

Eleanor's distinctness in part had to do with the legal fact that she and her husband were "separated." It had happened recently; his absence from the party was noticeable. Eleanor, in the course of a life that she described as a series of harrowing survivals, had developed the brassy social manner that converts private catastrophe into public humorousness; but tonight her agitation was imperfectly converted. She listened for an echo that wasn't there, and twitchily crossed and recrossed her legs. Her legs were handsome and vivid and so long that, after midnight, when parlor games began, she hitched up her brief shirt and kicked the lintel of a doorframe. The host balanced a glass of water on his forehead. Richard, demonstrating a headstand, mistakenly tumbled forward, delighted at his inebriated softness, which felt to be an ironical comment upon flesh that his new metal teeth were making. He was all mortality, all porous erosion save for these stars in his head, an impervious polar cluster at the zenith of his slow whirling.

His wife came to him with a face as unscarred and chastening as the face of a clock. It was time to go home. And Eleanor needed a ride. The three of them, plus the hostess in her bangle earrings and coffee-stained culottes, went to the door, and discovered a snowstorm. As far as the eye could probe, flakes were falling in a jostling crowd through the whispering lavender night. "God bless us, every one," Richard said.

The hostess suggested that Joan should drive.

Richard kissed her on the cheek and tasted the metal of her bitter earring and got in behind the wheel. His car was a brand-new Corvair; he wouldn't dream of trusting anyone else to drive it. Joan crawled into the back seat, grunting to emphasize the physical awkwardness, and Eleanor serenely arranged her coat and pocketbook and legs in the space beside him. The motor sprang alive. Richard felt resiliently cushioned: Eleanor was beside him, Joan behind him, God above him, the road beneath him. The fast-falling snow dipped brilliant—explosive, chrysanthemumesque— into the car headlights. On a small hill the tires spun—a loose, reassuring noise, like the slither of a raincoat.

In the knobbed darkness lit by the green speed gauge, Eleanor, showing a wealth of knee, talked at length of her separated husband. "You have no *idea*," she said, "you two are so sheltered you have no idea what men are capable of. I didn't know myself. I don't mean to sound ungracious, he gave me nine reasonable years and I wouldn't *dream* of punishing him with the children's visiting hours the way some women would, but that *man!* You know what he had the crust to tell me? He actually told me that when he was with another woman he'd sometimes close his eyes and pretend it was *me*."

"Sometimes," Richard said.

His wife behind him said, "Darley, are you aware that the road is slippery?"

"That's the shine of the headlights," he told her.

Eleanor crossed and recrossed her legs. Half the length of a thigh flared in the intimate green glow. She went on, "And his *trips*. I wondered why the same city was always putting out bond issues. I began to feel sorry for the mayor, I thought they were going bankrupt. Looking back at myself, I was so *good*, so wrapped up in the children and the house, always on the phone to the contractor or the plumber or the gas company trying to get the new kitchen done in time for Thanksgiving, when his silly, *silly* mother was coming to visit. About once a day I'd sharpen the carving knife. Thank God that phase of my life is over. I went to his mother—for sympathy, I suppose—and very indignantly she asked me, what had I done to her boy? The children and I had tunafish sandwiches by ourselves and it was the first Thanksgiving I've ever enjoyed, frankly."

"I always have trouble," Richard told her, "finding the second joint."

Joan said, "Darley, you know you're coming to that terrible curve?"

"You should see my father-in-law carve. Snick, snap, snap, snick. Your blood runs cold."

"On my birthday, my *birthday*," Eleanor said, accidentally kicking the heater, "the bastard was with his little dolly in a restaurant, and he told me, he solemnly told me—men are incredible—he told me he ordered cake for dessert. That was his tribute to me. The night he confessed all this, it was the end of the world, but I had to laugh. I asked him if he'd had the restaurant put a candle on the cake. He told me he'd thought of it but hadn't had the guts."

Richard's responsive laugh was held in suspense as the car skidded on the curve. A dark upright shape had appeared in the center of the windshield, and he tried to remove it, but the automobile proved impervious to the steering wheel and instead drew closer, as if magnetized, to a telephone pole that rigidly insisted on its position in the center of the windshield. The pole enlarged. The little splinters pricked by the linemen's cleats leaped forward in the headlights, and there was a flat whack surprisingly unambiguous, considering how casually it had happened. Richard felt the sudden refusal of motion, the *No*, and knew, though his mind was deeply cushioned in a cottony indifference, that an event had occurred which in another incarnation he would regret.

"You jerk," Joan said. Her voice was against his ear. "Your pretty new car." She asked, "Eleanor, are you all right?" With a rising inflection she repeated, "Are you all right?" It sounded like scolding.

Eleanor giggled softly, embarrassed. "I'm fine," she said, "except that I can't seem to move my legs." The windshield near her head had become a web of light, an exploded star.

Either the radio had been on or had turned itself on, for mellow, meditating music flowed from a realm behind time. Richard identified it as one of Handel's oboe sonatas. He noticed that his knees distantly hurt. Eleanor had slid forward and seemed unable to uncross her legs. Shockingly, she whimpered. Joan asked, "Sweetheart, didn't you know you were going too fast?"

"I am very stupid," he said. Music and snow poured down upon them, and he imagined that, if only the oboe sonata were played backwards, they would leap backwards from the telephone pole and be on their way home again. The little distances to their houses, once measured in minutes, had frozen and become immense, like those in galaxies.

Using her hands, Eleanor uncrossed her legs and brought herself upright in her seat. She lit a cigarette. Richard, his knees creaking, got out of the car and tried to push it free. He told Joan to come out of the back seat and get behind the wheel. Their motions were clumsy, wriggling in and out of darkness. The headlights still burned, but the beams were bent inward, toward each other. The Corvair had a hollow head, its engine being in the rear. Its face, an unimpassioned insect's face, was inextricably curved around the pole; the bumper had become locked mandibles. When Richard pushed and Joan fed gas, the wheels whined in a vacuum. The smooth encircling night extended around them, above and beyond the snow. No window light had acknowledged their accident.

Joan, who had a social conscience, asked, "Why doesn't anybody come out and help us?"

Eleanor, the voice of bitter experience, answered, "This pole is hit so often it's just a nuisance to the neighborhood."

Richard announced, "I'm too drunk to face the police." The remark hung with a neon clarity in the night.

A car came by, slowed, stopped. A window rolled down and revealed a frightened male voice. "Everything O.K.?"

"Not entirely," Richard said. He was pleased by his powers, under stress, of exact expression.

"I can take somebody to a telephone. I'm on my way back from a poker game."

A lie, Richard reasoned—otherwise, why advance it? The boy's face had the blurred pallor of the sexually drained. Taking care to give each word weight, Richard told him, "One of us can't move and I better stay with her. If you could take my wife to a phone, we'd all be most grateful."

"Who do I call?" Joan asked.

Richard hesitated between the party they had left, their baby-sitter at home, and Eleanor's husband, who was living in a motel on Route 128.

The boy answered for him: "The police."

Joan got into the stranger's car, a rusty red Mercury. The car faded through the snow, which was slackening. The storm had been just a flurry, an illusion conjured to administer this one rebuke. It wouldn't even make tomorrow's newspapers.

Richard's knees felt as if icicles were being pressed against the soft spot beneath the caps, where the doctor's hammer searches for a reflex. He got in behind the wheel again, and switched off the lights. He switched off the ignition. Eleanor's cigarette glowed. Though his system was still adrift in liquor, he could not quite forget the taste of metal in his teeth. That utterly flat *No:* through several dreamlike thicknesses something very hard had touched him. Once, swimming in surf, he had been sucked under by a large wave. Tons of sudden surge had enclosed him and, with an implacable downward shrug, thrust him deep into dense green bitterness and stripped him of weight; his struggling became nothing, he was nothing within the wave. There had been no hatred. The wave simply hadn't *cared*.

He tried to apologize to the woman beside him in the darkness.

She said, "Oh, please. I'm sure nothing's broken. At the worst I'll be on crutches for a few days." She laughed and added, "This just isn't my year."

"Does it hurt?"

"No, not at all."

"You're probably in shock. You'll be cold. I'll get the heat back." Richard was sobering, and an infinite drabness was dawning for him. Never again, never ever, would his car be new, would he chew on his own enamel, would she kick so high with her fine long legs. He turned the ignition back on and started up the motor, for warmth. The radio softly returned, still Handel.

Moving from the hips up with surprising strength, Eleanor turned and embraced him. Her cheeks were wet; her lipstick tasted manufactured. Searching for her waist, for the smallness of her breasts, he fumbled through thicknesses of cloth. They were still in each other's arms when the whirling blue light of the police car broke upon them.

Your Lover Just Called

THE TELEPHONE RANG, and Richard Maple, who had stayed home from work this Friday because of a cold, answered it: "Hello?" The person at the other end of the line hung up. Richard went into the bedroom, where Joan was making the bed, and said, "Your lover just called."

"What did he say?"

"Nothing. He hung up. He was amazed to find me home."

"Maybe it was *your* lover."

He knew, through the phlegm beclouding his head, that there was something wrong with this, and found it. "If it was *my* lover," he said, "why would she hang up, since I answered?"

Joan shook the sheet so it made a clapping noise. "Maybe she doesn't love you any more."

"This is a ridiculous conversation."

"You started it."

"Well, what would you think, if you answered the phone on a weekday and the person hung up? He clearly expected you to be home alone."

"Well, if you'll get under these covers I'll call him back and explain the situation."

"*You* think *I'll* think you're kidding but I know that's really what *would* happen."

"Oh, come on, Dick. Who would it be? Freddie Vetter?"

"Or Harry Saxon. Or somebody I don't know at all. Some old college friend who's moved to New England. Or maybe the milkman. I can hear you and him talking while I'm shaving sometimes."

"We're surrounded by hungry children. He's fifty years old and has hair coming out of his ears."

"Like your father. You're not averse to older men. There was that humanities section man when we first met. Anyway, you've been acting awfully happy lately. There's a little smile comes into your face when you're doing the housework. See, there it is!"

"I'm smiling," Joan said, "because you're so absurd. I have no lover. I have nowhere to put him. My days are consumed by devotion to the needs of my husband and his many children."

"Oh, so I'm the one who made you have all the children? While you were hankering after a career in fashion or in the exciting world of business. Aeronautics, perhaps. You could have been the first woman to design a nose cone. Or to crack the wheat-futures cycle. Joan Maple, girl agronomist. Joan Maple, lady geopolitician. But for that fornicating brute she mistakenly married, this clear-eyed female citizen of our everneedful republic—"

"Dick, have you taken your temperature? I haven't heard you rave like this for years."

"I haven't been betrayed like this for years. I hated that *click*. That nasty little I-know-your-wife-better-than-you-do *click*."

"It was some child. If we're going to have Mack for dinner tonight, you better convalesce now."

"It *is* Mack, isn't it? That son of a bitch. The divorce isn't even finalized and he's calling my wife on the phone. And then proposes to gorge himself at my groaning board."

"I'll be groaning myself. You're giving me a headache."

"Sure. First I foist off children on you in my mad desire for progeny, then I give you a menstrual headache."

"Get into bed and I'll bring you orange juice and toast cut into strips the way your mother used to make it."

"You're lovely."

As he was settling himself under the blankets, the phone rang again, and Joan answered it in the upstairs hall. "Yes . . . no . . . no . . . good," she said, and hung up.

"Who was it?" he called.

"Somebody wanting to sell us the *World Book Encyclopedia*," she called back.

"A very likely story," he said, with self-pleasing irony, leaning back onto the pillows confident that he was being unjust, that there was no lover.

Mack Dennis was a homely, agreeable, sheepish man their age, whose wife, Eleanor, was in Wyoming suing for divorce. He spoke of her with a cloying tenderness, as if of a favorite daughter away for the first time at camp, or as a departed angel nevertheless keeping in close touch with the abandoned earth. "She says they've had some wonderful thunderstorms. The children go horseback riding every morning, and they play Pounce at night and are in bed by ten. Everybody's health has never been better. Ellie's asthma has cleared up and she thinks now she must have been allergic to *me*."

"You should have cut all your hair off and dressed in cellophane," Richard told him.

Joan asked him, "And how's *your* health? Are you feeding yourself enough? Mack, you look thin."

"The nights I don't stay in Boston," Mack said, tapping himself all over for a pack of cigarettes, "I've taken to eating at the motel on Route 33. It's the best food in town now, and you can watch the kids in the swimming pool." He studied his empty upturned hands as if they had recently held a surprise. He missed his own kids, was perhaps the surprise.

"I'm out of cigarettes too," Joan said.

"I'll go get some," Richard said.

"And a thing of club soda if they have it."

"I'll make a pitcher of martinis," Mack said. "Doesn't it feel great, to have martini weather again?"

It was that season which is late summer in the days and early autumn at night. Evening descended on the downtown, lifting the neon tubing into brilliance, as Richard ran his errand. His sore throat felt folded within him like a secret; there was something reckless and gay in his being up and out at all after spending the afternoon in bed. Home, he parked by his back fence and walked down through a lawn rustling with fallen leaves, though the trees overhead were still massy. The lit windows of his house looked golden and idyllic; the children's rooms were above (the face of Judith, his bigger daughter, drifted preoccupied across a slice of her wallpaper, and her pink square hand reached to adjust a doll on a shelf) and the kitchen below. In the kitchen windows, whose tone was fluorescent, a silent tableau was being enacted. Mack was holding a martini shaker and pouring it into a vessel, eclipsed by an element of window sash, that Joan was offering with a long white arm. Head tilted winningly, she was talking with the slightly pushed-forward mouth that Richard recognized as peculiar to her while looking into mirrors, conversing with her elders, or otherwise seeking to display herself to advantage. Whatever she was saying made Mack laugh, so that his pouring (the silver shaker head glinted, a drop of greenish liquid spilled) was unsteady. He set the shaker down and displayed his hands—the same hands from which a little while ago a surprise had seemed to escape—at his sides, shoulder-high.

Joan moved toward him, still holding her glass, and the back of her head, done up taut and oval in a bun, with downy hairs trailing at the nape of her neck, eclipsed all of Mack's face but his eyes, which closed. They were kissing. Joan's head tilted one way and Mack's another to make their mouths meet tighter. The graceful line of her shoulders was carried outward by the line of the arm holding her glass safe in the air. The other arm was around his neck. Behind them an open cabinet door revealed a paralyzed row of erect paper boxes whose lettering Richard could not read but whose coloring advertised their contents—Cheerios, Wheat Honeys, Onion Thins. Joan backed off and ran her index finger down the length of Mack's necktie (a summer tartan), ending with a jab in the vicinity of his navel that might have expressed a rebuke or a regret. His face, pale and lumpy in the harsh vertical light, looked mildly humorous but intent, and moved forward, toward hers, an inch or two. The scene had the fascinating slow motion of action underwater, mixed with the insane silent suddenness of a television montage glimpsed from the street. Judith came to the window upstairs, not noticing her father standing in the shadow of the tree. Wearing a nightie of lemon gauze, she innocently scratched her armpit while studying a moth beating on her screen; and this too gave Richard a momentous sense, crowding his heart, of having been brought by the mute act of witnessing—like a child sitting alone at the movies—perilously close to the hidden machinations of things. In another kitchen window a neglected teakettle began to plume and to fog the panes with steam. Joan was talking again; her forward-thrust lips seemed to be throwing rapid little bridges across a narrowing gap. Mack paused, shrugged; his face puckered as if he were speaking French. Joan's head snapped back with laughter and triumphantly she threw her free arm wide and was in his embrace again. His hand, spread starlike on the small of her back, went lower to what, out of sight behind the edge of Formica counter, would be her bottom.

Richard scuffled loudly down the cement steps and kicked the kitchen door open, giving them time to break apart before he entered. From the far end of the kitchen, smaller than children, they looked at him with blurred, blank expressions. Joan turned off the steaming kettle and Mack shambled forward to pay for the cigarettes. After the third round of martinis, the constraints loosened and Richard said, taking pleasure in the plaintive huskiness of his voice, "Imagine my discomfort. Sick as I am, I go out into this bitter night to get my wife and my guest some cigarettes, so they can pollute the air and aggravate my already grievous bronchial condition, and, coming down through the back yard, what do I see? The two of them doing the Kama Sutra in my own kitchen. It was like seeing a blue movie and knowing the people in it."

"Where do you see blue movies nowadays?" Joan asked.

"Tush, Dick," Mack said sheepishly, rubbing his thighs with a brisk ironing motion. "A mere fraternal kiss. A brotherly hug. A disinterested tribute to your wife's charm."

"Really, Dick," Joan said. "I think it's shockingly sneaky of you to be standing around spying into your own windows."

"Standing around! I was transfixed with horror. It was a real trauma. My first primal scene." A profound happiness was stretching him from within; the reach of his tongue and wit felt immense, and the other two seemed dolls, homunculi, in his playful grasp.

"We were hardly doing anything," Joan said, lifting her head as if to rise above it all, the lovely line of her jaw defined by tension, her lips stung by a pout.

"Oh, I'm sure, by your standards, you had hardly begun. You'd hardly sampled the possible wealth of coital positions. Did you think I'd never return? Have you poisoned my drink and I'm too vigorous to die, like Rasputin?"

"Dick," Mack said, "Joan loves you. And if I love any man, it's you. Joan and I had this out years ago, and decided to be merely friends."

"Don't go Gaelic on me, Mack Dennis. 'If I love any mon, 'tis thee.' Don't give me a thought, laddie. Just think of poor Eleanor out there, sweating out your divorce, bouncing up and down on those horses day after day, playing Pounce till she's black and blue—"

"Let's eat," Joan said. "You've made me so nervous I've probably over-done the roast beef. Really, Dick, I don't think you can excuse yourself by trying to make it funny."

Next day, the Maples awoke soured and dazed by hangovers; Mack had stayed until two, to make sure there were no hard feelings. Joan usually played ladies' tennis Saturday mornings, while Richard amused the children; now, dressed in white shorts and sneakers, she delayed at home in order to quarrel. "It's desperate of you," she told Richard, "to try to make something of Mack and me. What are you trying to cover up?"

"My dear Mrs. Maple, I *saw*," he said, "I *saw* through my own windows you doing a very credible impersonation of a female spider having her abdomen tickled. Where did you learn to flirt your head like that? It was better than finger puppets."

"Mack always kisses me in the kitchen. It's a habit, it means nothing. You know for yourself how in love with Eleanor he is."

"So much he's divorcing her. His devotion verges on the quixotic."

"The divorce is her idea, obviously. He's a lost soul. I feel sorry for him."

"Yes, I saw that you do. You were like the Red Cross at Verdun."

"What I'd like to know is, why are you so pleased?"

"Pleased? I'm annihilated."

"You're delighted. Look at your smile in the mirror."

"You're so incredibly unapologetic, I guess I think you must be being ironical."

The telephone rang. Joan picked it up and said, "Hello," and Richard heard the click across the room. Joan replaced the receiver and said to him, "So. She thought I'd be playing tennis by now."

"Who's she?"

"You tell me. Your lover. Your loveress."

"It was clearly yours, and something in your voice warned him off."

"Go to her!" Joan suddenly cried, with a burst of the same defiant energy that made her, on other hungover mornings, rush through a mountain of housework. "Go to her like a man and stop trying to maneuver me into something I don't understand! I have no lover! I let Mack kiss me because he's lonely and drunk! Stop trying to make me more interesting than I am! All I am is a beat-up housewife who wants to go play tennis with some other exhausted ladies!"

Mutely Richard fetched from their sports closet her tennis racket, which had recently been restrung with gut. Carrying it in his mouth like a dog retrieving a stick, he got down on all fours and laid it at the toe of her sneaker. Richard Jr., their older son, a wiry nine-year-old presently obsessed by the accumulation of Batman cards, came into the living room, witnessed this pantomime, and laughed to hide his fright. "Dad, can I have my dime for emptying the wastebaskets?"

"Mommy's going to go out to play, Dickie," Richard said, licking from his lips the salty taste of the racket handle. "Let's all go to the five-and-ten and buy a Batmobile."

"Yippee," the small boy said limply, glancing wide-eyed from one of his parents to the other, as if the space between them had gone treacherous.

Richard took the children to the five-and-ten, to the playground, and to a hamburger stand for lunch. These blameless activities transmuted the residue of alcohol and phlegm into a woolly fatigue as pure as the sleep of infants. His sore throat was fading. Obligingly he nodded while his son described an endless plot: ". . . and then, see, Dad, the Penguin had an umbrella smoke came out of, it was neat, and there were these two other guys with funny masks in the bank vault, filling it with water, I don't know why, to make it bust or something, and Robin was climbing up these slippery stacks of like half-dollars to get away from the water, and then, see, Dad . . ."

Back home, the children dispersed into the neighborhood on the same mysterious tide that on other days packed their back yard with unfamiliar urchins. Joan returned from tennis glazed with sweat, her ankles coated with clay-court dust. Her body was swimming in the afterglow of exertion. He suggested they take a nap.

"Just a nap," she warned.

"Of course," he said. "I met my mistress at the playground and we satisfied each other on the jungle gym."

"Maureen and I beat Alice and Judy. It can't be any of those three, they were waiting for me half an hour."

In bed, the shades strangely drawn against the bright afternoon, and a glass of stale water standing bubbled with secret light, he asked her, "You think I want to make you more interesting than you are?"

"Of course. You're bored. You left me and Mack alone deliberately. It was very uncharacteristic of you, to go out with a cold."

"It's sad, to think of you without a lover."

"I'm sorry."

"You're pretty interesting anyway. Here, and here, and here."

"I said really a nap."

In the upstairs hall, on the other side of the closed bedroom door, the telephone rang. After four peals—icy spears hurled from afar—the ringing stopped, unanswered. There was a puzzled pause. Then a tentative, questioning *pring*, as if someone in passing had bumped the table, followed by a determined series, strides of sound, imperative and plaintive, that did not stop until twelve had been counted; then the lover hung up.

Commercial

IT COMES ON every night, somewhere in the eleven-o'clock news. A CHILD runs down a STAIRCASE. A rotund ELDERLY WOMAN stands at the foot, picks up the CHILD, gives him a shake (friendly), and sets him down. There is MUSIC, containing the words "laughing child," "fur-lined rug," etc.

The STAIRCASE looks unexpectedly authentic, oaken and knobby and steep in the style of houses where we have childhoods. We know this STAIRCASE. Some treads creak, and at the top there is a branching many-cornered darkness wherein we are supposed to locate security and to sleep. The wallpaper (baskets of flowers, at a guess, alternating with ivy-wreathed medallions) would feel warm, if touched.

The CHILD darts offscreen. We have had time to register that it is a BOY, with long hair cut straight across his forehead. The camera stays with the ELDERLY WOMAN, whom by now we identify as the GRANDMOTHER. She gazes after the (supposedly) receding BOY so fondly we can imagine "*(gazes fondly)*" in the commercial's script.

The second drags; her beaming threatens to become blank. But now, with an electrifying touch of uncertainty, so that we do not know if it was the director's idea or the actress's, GRANDMOTHER slowly wags her head, as if to say, *My, oh my, what an incorrigible little rascal, what a lovable little man-child!* Her heart, we feel, so brims with love that her plump body, if a whit less healthy and compact, if a whit less compressed and contained by the demands and accoutrements of GRANDMOTHERLINESS, would burst. GRANDMOTHERLINESS massages her from all sides, like the brushes of a car wash.

And now (there is so much to see!) she relaxes her arms in front of her, the fingers of one hand gently gripping the wrist of the other. This gesture tells us that her ethnic type is Anglo-Saxon. An Italian mama, say, would have folded her arms across her bosom; and, also, wouldn't the coquetry of Mediterranean women forbid their wearing an apron out of the kitchen, beside what is clearly a front STAIRCASE? So, while still suspended high on currents of anticipation, we deduce that this is not a commercial for spaghetti.

Nor for rejuvenating skin creams or hair rinses, for the camera cuts from GRANDMOTHER to the BOY. He is hopping through a room. Not quite hopping, or exactly skipping: a curious fey gait that bounces his cap of hair and evokes the tender dialectic of the child-director encounter. This CHILD, who, though a child actor acting the part of a child, is nevertheless also truly a child, has been told to move across the fictional room in a childish way. He has obeyed, moving hobbled by self-consciousness yet with the elastic bounce that Nature has bestowed upon him and that no amount of adult direction can utterly squelch. Only time can squelch it.

We do not know how many "takes" were sifted through to get this second of movement. Though no child in reality (though billions of children have crossed millions of rooms) ever moved across a room in quite this way, an impression of CHILDHOOD pierces us. We get the message: GRAND-MOTHER'S HOUSE (and the montage is so swift we cannot itemize the furniture, only concede that it appears fittingly fusty and congested) is cozy, safe—a place to be joyful in. Why? The question hangs.

We are in another room. A kitchen. A shining POT dominates the foreground. The BOY, out of focus, still bobbing in that unnatural, affecting way, enters at the background, comes forward into focus, becomes an alarmingly large face and a hand that lifts the lid of the POT. STEAM billows. The BOY blows the STEAM away, then stares at us with stagily popped eyes. Meaning? He has burned himself? There is a bad smell? The director, offscreen, has shouted at him? We do not know, and we are made additionally uncomfortable by the possibility that this is a spaghetti commercial after all.

Brief scene: GRANDMOTHER washing BOY's face. Bathroom fixtures behind. Theme of heat (cozy HOUSE, hot POT) subliminally emerges. Also: suppertime?

We do not witness supper. We are back at the STAIRCASE. New actors have arrived: a tall and vigorous YOUNG COUPLE, in stylish overcoats. Who? We scarcely have time to ask. The BOY leaps (flies, indeed; we do not see his feet launch him) upward into the arms of the MAN. These are his PARENTS. We ourselves, watching, welcome them; the depth of our welcome reveals to us a dread within ourselves, of something morbid and claustral in the old HOUSE, with its cunningly underlined snugness and its lonely household of benevolent crone and pampered, stagy brat. These other two radiate the brisk air of outdoors. To judge from their clothes, it is cold outside; this impression is not insignificant; our sense of subliminal coherence swells. We join in the BUSTLE OF WELCOME, rejoicing with the YOUNG COUPLE in their sexual energy and safe return and great good fortune to be American and modern and solvent and fertile and to have such a picture-book GRANDMOTHER to baby-sit for them whenever they partake of some innocent, infrequent SPREE.

But whose mother is GRANDMOTHER, the FATHER's or the MOTHER's?

All questions are answered. The actor playing the YOUNG FATHER ignores GRANDMOTHER with the insouciance of blood kinship, while the actress playing the YOUNG MOTHER hugs her, pulls back, reconsiders, then dips forward to bestow upon the beaming plump cheek a kiss GRAND-MOTHER does not, evidently, expect. Her beaming wavers momentarily, like a candle flame when a distant door is opened. The DAUGHTER-IN-LAW again pulls back, as if coolly to contemplate the product of her affectionate inspiration. Whether her tense string of hesitations was spun artfully by an actress fulfilling a role or was visited upon the actress as she searched her role for nuances (we can imagine how vague the script might be: *"Parents return. Greetings all around. Camera medium tight"*), a ticklish closeness of maneuver, amid towering outcroppings of good will, has been conveyed. The FAMILY is complete.

And now the underlying marvel is made manifest. The true HERO of these thirty seconds unmasks. The united FAMILY fades into a blue cartoon flame, and the MUSIC, no longer obscured by visual stimuli, sings with clarion brilliance, "NATURAL GAS is a Bee-uti-ful Thing!"

A MAN, discovered in BED, beside his WIFE, suffers the remainder of the NEWS, then rises and turns off the TELEVISION SET. The screen palely exudes its last quanta of daily radiation. The room by default fills with the dim light of the MOON. Risen, the MAN, shuffling around the BED with a wary gait suggestive of inelasticity and an insincerely willed silence, makes his way into the bathroom, where he urinates. He does this, we sense, not from any urgent physical need but conscientiously, even puritanically, from a basis of theory, to clear himself and his conscience for sleep.

His thoughts show, in vivid montage. As always when hovering above the dim oval of porcelain, he recalls the most intense vision of beauty his forty years have granted him. It was after a lunch in New York. The luncheon had been prolonged, overstimulating, vinous. Now he was in a taxi, heading up the West Side Highway. At the Fifty-seventh Street turn-off, the need to urinate was a feathery subliminal thought; by the Seventies (where Riverside Drive begins to rise), it was a real pressure; by the Nineties (Soldiers' and Sailors' Monument crumbling, Riverside Park a green cliff looming), it had become an agonizing imperative. Mastering shame, the MAN confessed his agony to the DRIVER, who, gradually suspending disbelief, swung off the highway at 158th Street and climbed a little cobblestone mountain and found there, evidently not for the first time, a dirty triangular GARAGE. Mechanics, black or blackened, stared with white eyes as the strange MAN stumbled past them, back through the oily and junk-lined triangle to the apex: here, pinched between obscene frescoes, sat the most beautiful thing he had ever seen. Or would ever see. It was a TOILET BOWL, a TOILET BOWL in its flawed whiteness, its partial wateriness, its total receptiveness: in the harmonious miracle of its infrangible *ens*, its lowly but absolute beauty. The beautiful, it came to him, is no more or less than what you need at the time.

Quick cameo mug shots of Plato, Aquinas, Santayana, and other theorists of beauty, *X*'ed in rough strokes to indicate refutation.

Brief scene: MAN brushing teeth, rinsing mouth, spitting.

Cut to MOON, impassive.

Return to MAN. He stands before the bathroom cabinet, puzzling. He opens the door, which is also a mirror. Zoom to tiny red BOX. What is in the BOX? Something, we sense, that he resists because it does not conform to his ideal of healthy normality. He closes the door.

He sniffs. As he has been standing puzzling, the odor of his own body has risen to him, a potato-ish, reproachful odor. When he was a child living, like the CHILD in the commercial, with adults, he imagined that adults emitted this odor on purpose, to chasten and discipline him. Now that it is his own odor, it does not seem chastening but merely nagging, like the pile of SLIT ENVELOPES that clutter the kitchen table every afternoon. Quick still of ENVELOPES. Replay of CHILD running down STAIRCASE to awaiting arms. We are, subliminally, affected.

Shuffling (in case he stubs his toe or steps on a pin), the MAN returns from the bathroom and proceeds around the BED. The TELEVISION SET is cold now. The MOON is cold, too. As if easing a read letter back into a slit envelope, he eases himself back into BED beside his WIFE. He sneaks his hand under her nightie and rubs her back; it is a ritual question. In ritual answer, the WIFE stirs in her sleep, awakens enough to realize that the room is cold, presses her body tight against that of the MAN, and falls again asleep. Asleep again. Again again. Asleep.

Now his half of the BED has been reduced to a third—a third, furthermore, crimped and indented by oblivious elbows and knees. The MAN's eyes close but his EARS open wider, terrible auditory eyes from which lids have been scissored, avid organs hungry for the whispers and crackles of the WORLD. He buries his EARS alternately in the pillow, but cannot stanch both at once. He thinks of masturbating, but decides there is not enough room. And there is the problem of the SPOT on the SHEET.

A radiator whistles: steam heat, oil-fired. Would natural gas be noiseless? A far car whirs. Surf, or wind, murmurs; or can it be a helicopter?

Now the CAT—a new actor!—mews a foot below the MAN's face. Svelte and insistent, the CAT wants to go out. The MAN, almost gratefully, rises. Better action than inaction, he thinks—in this a typical citizen of our unmeditative era. The CAT's whiskers, electric, twitching, tingle like frost on the MAN's bare ankles.

Together MAN and CAT go down a STAIRCASE. No oaken knobs here. The style is bare, modern. The MAN touches the wall: chill plaster.

The MAN opens the front door. GRASS, TREES, SKY, and STARS, abruptly framed, look colorless and flat, as if, thus surprised, they had barely had time to get their outlines together. The STARS, especially, appear perfunctory: bullet holes in a hangar roof. The CAT darts offscreen.

We are back in the BED. The MAN turns the pillow over, to explore with his cheek its dark side. Delicately, yet borrowing insistence from the CAT's example, he pushes his WIFE's body toward her side of the BED, inch by inert inch. Minutes of patient nudging are undone when, surfacing toward consciousness, she slumps more confidingly into him. Does she wake, or sleep? Is her reclamation of two-thirds of the BED an instinctive territorial assertion of her insensate body, or is it the product, cerebral enough, of some calculation scribbled on the shifting, tricky, flesh-heated marital ground between them? Here the MAN, our inadequate hero, seems to arrive at one of those fumbling points that usefully distract the brain with the motions of thinking while the body falls into thought-free bliss. Hopeful pits and bubbles and soft, stretching aches develop within him, forerunners of sleep's merciful dissolution of the tensions and desires of the day.

Abrupt cut: within a child's room—another new actor!—the HAMSTER, yielding to some sudden fantasy of speed and space, accelerates within his unoiled running wheel. The clatter is epic; the HAMSTER twirls the WORLD on a string.

We are back in the bathroom. The MAN decides he must urinate again. The shadowy TOILET BOWL again reminds him of absolute beauty. A forlorn sense of surrender suffuses the aroma of overripe potatoes. He is removing the little red BOX from the cabinet whose door is a mirror. He takes two small objects from this BOX. Zoom. They are little balls of WAX. Why? What in the WORLD?

Back in the bedroom. The MOON in the window has shrunk in size. In contracting, it has gained heat; its pallor looks white-hot, almost solar.

The MAN inserts himself back into the BED. He inserts the WAX EAR PLUGS into his ears. The sharp bright wires of noise etched on darkness dull down into gray threads, an indistinct blanket. He grows aware of the tangible wool blanket, as a source of goodness, a sheltering firmament tangent to him. His WIFE mysteriously, voluntarily shifts her weight away, toward the other side of the bed, toward the wide horizon where all pressures meet in a dull wedge. A subterranean whistling noise dawns upon the MAN as the sound of his own breathing. He is suppressing himself, his *ens*. The cave of his skull furs with nonsense. *(Pan, fade, dissolve.)*

That is how it happens most every night.

What is being advertised? Pick one:

(1) Ear plugs (2) Natural gas (3) Lucifer's fall (4) Nothing whatsoever.

Minutes of the Last Meeting

THE CHAIRMAN of the Committee again expressed his desire to resign.

The Secretary pointed out that the bylaws do not provide for resignation procedures, they provide however for a new slate of officers to be presented annually and a new slate of officers was being accordingly presented.

The Chairman responded that however on the new slate his name was again listed as Chairman. He said he had served since the founding of the Committee and sincerely felt that his chairmanship had become more of a hindrance than a help. He said that what the Committee needed at this point was new direction and a refined sense of purpose which he could not provide, being too elderly and confused and out of sympathy with things. That the time had come either for younger blood to take over the helm or possibly for the Committee to disband.

The Secretary pointed out that the bylaws do not provide for disbandment.

In answer to a query from the Chairman, Mrs. Hepple on behalf of the Nominating Sub-Committee explained that the Sub-Committee felt as a whole that the Chairman was invaluable in his present position, that support in the wider community would be drastically weakened by his resignation, and that the nomination of two vice-chairmen and the creation of appropriate sub-committees would effectively lighten his work load.

The Chairman asked how often the Nominating Sub-Committee had met. Mrs. Hepple responded that due to the holiday season they had convened once, by telephone. There was laughter. In the same humorous spirit the Chairman suggested that the only way he could effectively resign would be to shoot himself.

Mr. Langbehn, one of the newer members, said before presuming to participate in this discussion he would be grateful for having explained to him the original purposes and intents of the Committee.

The Chairman answered that he had never understood them and would be grateful himself.

Miss Beame then volunteered that though the youngest Founder present she would offer her impressions, which were that at the founding of the Committee their purpose was essentially the formal one of meeting to give approval to the activities of the Director. That without the magical personality and earnest commitment of the Director they would not have been gathered together at all. That beyond appointing him Director the bulk of the business at the first meeting had centered upon the name of the Committee, initially proposed as the Tarbox Betterment Committee, then expanded to the Committee for Betterment and Development of Human Resources. That the Director had felt that the phrase Equal Opportunity should also be included, and perhaps some special emphasis on youth as well, without appearing to exclude the senior citizens of the community. Therefore the title of Tarbox Committee for Equal Development and Betterment for Young and Old Alike was proposed and considered.

Dr. Costopoulos, a Founder, recalled that the Director did not however wish the Committee to appear to offer itself as a rival to already extant groups like the Golden Agers and the Teen Scene and had furthermore regretted in the official committee title any indication of a pervasive ecological concern. So a unanimous vote was taken to leave the name of the Committee temporarily open.

Mrs. Hepple added that even though the Director had been rather new in town it all had seemed a wonderful idea. He was the kind of young man who made things happen, she added.

Mrs. MacMillan, a new member, asked where the Director was.

Miss Beame explained that the Director had vanished after the founding meeting.

Leaving behind a cardboard suitcase and an unpaid phone bill, the Chairman volunteered. There was laughter.

The Secretary pointed out that the bylaws perfectly clearly specify the purpose of the Committee and read excerpts spelling out that "no political candidates or partisan causes should be publicly espoused," "no stocks or bonds were to be held with the objective of financial profit or gain," and "no gambling or licentious assignation would be permitted on any premises leased or owned entirely or in part by the said Committee."

Mr. Langbehn asked to see the bylaws.

The Secretary graciously complied.

Mr. Langbehn claimed after examination that this was a standard form purchasable in any office-supplies or stationery store.

Mrs. Hepple said she didn't see that it made any difference, that here we all are and that is the main point.

Mrs. MacMillan inquired as to why the Committee kept meeting in the absence of the Director.

The Treasurer interrupted to ask the evening's Hostess, Mrs. Landis, if it weren't time for refreshments to be served.

The Reverend Mr. Trussel asked if he might attempt to elucidate the question asked by the good Mrs. MacMillan. He said that at first the Committee had met in the expectation that the Director would reappear and then, in later sessions, as a board of inquiry into where the Director had gone. Finally, they had continued to meet because, in his opinion, they had come to love and need one another.

Miss Beame said she thought that was a touching and true description.

Mrs. Hepple said she didn't see where any of it mattered at this point because not only were most of the Founders in attendance but many new members as well. That the membership had grown instead of withering away as one would suppose if the Committee were entirely dependent upon the Director, who for that matter she had quite forgotten what he looked like.

Mr. de Muth volunteered that he had come onto the Committee in his capacity as a social-science teacher because he understood at that time there had been under consideration a program to arrange a lecture series or series of happenings on the theme of betterment of resources at the public schools.

Mr. Tjadel said he had come on in his capacity as a tree surgeon because of the "ecology angle."

Mrs. MacMillan said she had been given the impression her interest in oral contraception might be applied by the Committee to the town drinking water.

The Chairman stated that it was all a muddle and again offered his resignation.

The Secretary pointed out that all of these projects had been under consideration and as far as she was concerned still were.

Mr. Langbehn began to speak.

The Treasurer interrupted to compliment Mrs. Landis on the quality of her refreshments.

Mr. Langbehn thanked all present for bearing with him and filling him in so thoroughly. He said that though none of the projects described had apparently come to fruition he nevertheless did not feel that the members of the Committee including himself should entertain the fear that their efforts were in vain. That on the contrary they had created much talk and interest in the wider community, and that just the fact that they continued to attract to membership such distinguished and personable citizens as those present negated any idea of failure. [Several sentences missed here due to accident spilling glass. — SEC.] That what was needed was not any long-term narrowing of the horizons established by the Director but a momentary closer focus upon some doubtless limited but feasible short-term goal within the immediate community.

Mrs. Hepple suggested that a dance or rummage sale be held to raise funds so such a goal might be attacked.

Miss Beame thought that a square dance would be better than a black-tie dance so as to attract young people, who hate to dress up.

The Chairman moved that the bylaws be amended so as to permit the Committee to disband.

No one seconded.

Mr. Tjadel said he didn't see why there was all this worrying about human resources, in his opinion they had fine human resources right here in this room. If the trunk is solid, he said, the branches will flourish. There was laughter and applause.

The Treasurer volunteered that in his opinion this was the best meeting yet and that to make itself more effective the Committee should meet more often.

Miss Beame said her heart went out to the Chairman and she thought his wishes should be respected.

Reverend Mr. Trussel moved that the board of officers as presented by the Nominating Sub-Committee be accepted with the proviso that the Chairman be nominated as Chairman *pro tem* and that to assist his labors further a Sub-Committee on Goals and Purposes be created, with Mr. Langbehn and Miss Beame as co-chairpersons.

Mrs. Hepple and others seconded.

The affirmative vote was unanimous, the Chairman abstaining.

Believers

THE WOMAN next to him at the party is sipping ginger ale, though he knows her to be a devoted drinker of vodka martinis. He points at the sparkling beverage and says, "Lent?" She nods. Her eyes are calm as a statue's. He knows her to be a believer. So is he. Let us christen him Credo.

Credo is in the basement of a church. He is on the church Church Heritage Committee, along with four old ladies. Their problem is, they are going to move to a new church, of white plastic, and what shall they do with all this old religious furniture? It has been accumulating for centuries: box-pew doors and tin footwarmers from the edifice of 1736; carpeted kneeling stools and velvet collection bags from the edifice of 1812; a gargantuan Gothic deacon's bench, of pinnacled oak, from the edifice of 1885. It would sorely test and strain seventeen contemporary laymen to lift and move it; there must have been giants in those days, giants of faith.

One of the old ladies mounts up onto its padded arms. Puffs of dust sprout beneath her feet. She retrieves something—a kind of jewel—from the pinnacle of the ornate bench back. They pass it around. It is a little brown photograph embedded in cracked glass, of a Victorian child wearing a paper crown. "Maybe some church just starting up would like to buy it all," the first lady says.

"One of those new California sects," the second amplifies.

"Never," says Credo. "Nobody wants this junk."

"At least," the third lady begs, "let's get an antique dealer to appraise the picture frames." Behind an old spinet and cartons of warped hymnals they have uncovered perhaps forty picture frames, all empty. "People will pay a fortune for such things nowadays."

"What people?" Credo asks. He cannot believe it. The basement seems airless; he cannot breathe. The ancient furnace comes on. Its awakening shudder shakes loose flakes of asbestos wrapping from the pipes; like snow the flakes drift down onto old hymnals, picture frames, piano stools, broken little chairs from the Sunday-school, attendance charts with pasted-on gold stars coming unstuck, old men's-club bowling-league bowling shoes, kneeling stools worn like ox yokes, tin footwarmers perforated like cabbage graters. God, it is depressing. God.

The fourth old lady has brought a paper shopping bag. Out of it she pulls dust rags, a bottle of Windex, a rainbow of Magic Markers, some shipping tags in two colors—green for preserve, red for destroy. "Let's make some decisions," she says briskly. "Let's separate the sheep from the goats."

Credo is visiting with his minister. The minister is very well informed. He says, "The Dow Jones was off two-point-three today, that's one less soprano pipe on our new Fiberglas organ." The minister's wife brings them in tea and honey. The jar of honey glows in a shaft of dusty parsonage sunlight. The minister's wife's hair is up in a towering beehive; she is a voluptuous blonde. Credo's wife is a mousy brunette. *Buy now, pay later,* he thinks, piously sipping.

Credo surveys the new church. The glistening bubble-shaped shell of white plastic holds a multitude of pastel rooms. He served on the New Creation Committee, which worked with the team of architects; the endless meetings and countless blueprints have become reality. There are many petty disappointments. The altar spot has been rheostatted in sync with the pulpit spot. The pre-fab steeple weeps in a storm. The Sunday-school room dividers scrape and buckle when pulled into place. The organ sounds like Fiberglas. The duct blower blows down the wrong duct and keeps extinguishing the pilot light in the wall oven. The proportions of the boiler room do not uplift the heart. The foundation slab is already cracking. Credo follows the sinuous crack with his eyes. The earth, of course, slumps and shrugs; the continental plates are sliding. And yet, somehow one expects that it will hold firm beneath a church. And yet, by this pattern miracles would become everyday and a tyranny. And yet, it would have been nice had the Lisbon earthquake not occurred, and not given Voltaire a laughing-point.

. . .

He reads St. Augustine. It is too hot, too radiant, blinding, and wild. *Is there indeed, O Lord my God, aught in me that can contain Thee? do then heaven and earth, which Thou hast made, and wherein Thou hast made me, contain Thee? or, because nothing which exists could exist without Thee, doth therefore whatever exists contain Thee? Since, then, I too exist, why do I seek that Thou shouldest enter into me, who were not, wert Thou not in me? Why?* It is too serious, frightening, and exciting; Credo has to get up and dull himself with a drink so he can continue reading. Augustine scribbles on a dizzying verge: he nearly indicts God for his helplessly damned infancy, for his schoolboy whippings; then pulls back, blames himself, and exonerates the Lord. *Let not my soul faint under Thy discipline, nor let me faint in confessing unto Thee all Thy mercies, whereby Thou hast drawn me out of all my most evil ways, that Thou mightest become a delight to me above all the allurements which I once pursued.*

It is too terrific, there is no relenting; Credo makes another drink, stares out the window, lets in the cat, asks a child how his day went at school, anything for relief from this whirlwind. *Is not all this smoke and wind? and was there nothing else whereon to exercise my wit and tongue? Thy praises, Lord, Thy praises might have stayed the yet tender shoot of my heart by the prop of Thy Scriptures; so had it not trailed away amid these empty trifles, a defiled prey for the fowls of the air. For in more ways than one do men sacrifice to the rebellious angels.* Credo cannot go on, he has waited four decades to read this, his heart cannot withstand it. It is too strict and searing, fierce and judicious; nothing alloyed can survive within it. He reads the *New York Times Sunday Magazine* instead. "China: Old Hands and New." "The Black Bourgeoisie Flees the Ghetto." "I Was a Marigold Head." He flips through *Sports Illustrated, Art News, Rolling Stone.* He puts St. Augustine back on the shelf, between Marcus Aurelius and Boethius. The book is safe there. He will take it down again, when he is sixty-five, and ready. *These things Thou seest, Lord, and holdest Thy peace; long-suffering, and plenteous in mercy and truth. Wilt Thou hold Thy peace for ever?*

Credo is in a motel. He has brought a shaker of vodka and vermouth and ice, and a can of ginger ale, just in case. The woman with him cannot be tempted. It is still Lent. She sips from the can, and he from the shaker; they take off each other's clothes. Her body is radiant, blinding, strict, serious, exciting. They admire each other, they make of one another an occasion for joy. Because they are believers, their acts possess dimensions of glory and of risk; they are flirting with being damned, though they do not say this. They say only gracious things, commensurate with the gratitude and exaltation they feel. To arouse her again, he quotes St. Augustine: *If bodies please thee, praise God in occasion of them, and turn back thy love upon their Maker lest in these things which please thee, thou displease.*

Credo is in a hospital. He has had an accident, playing touch football, and then an operation, reattaching with a screw his tibial tuberosity. As the drugs in his blood ebb, pain rises beneath him like a poisonous squid rising beneath a bather floating gently in the ocean. It seizes his knee. It will not let go. By the luminescent watch on the night table it is two hours before he can ring the nurse and receive his next allotment of Demerol. A single window shows a dead town, lit by streetlights. Credo prays. Aloud. It is a long conversational prayer, neither apologetic nor dubious; his pain has won him a new status. He speaks aloud as if on television, giving the dead-of-the-night news. Abruptly, his chest breaks out in a sharp sweet copious sweat. He miraculously relaxes. The squid lets go, falls back, into unknowable depths. The nurse when she comes finds Credo asleep. It is morning. Up and down the hall, rosary beads click.

He is sitting on the Boston–Cambridge subway, jiggling and swaying opposite other men jiggling and swaying. Back to work, though he limps now. He will always limp. The body does not forgive; only God forgives. Between two stops, the subway surfaces over a bridge, into the light. Below, a river sparkles as if not polluted; sailboats tilt in the shining wind. Credo is reminded of that passage in the Venerable Bede when, arguing for conversion to Christianity, an ealdorman likens our life to the flight of a sparrow through the bright mead-hall. *Such appears to me, king, this present life of man on earth in comparison with the time which is unknown to us, as though you were sitting at the banquet with your leaders and thanes in winter and the fire was lighted and your hall warmed, and it rained and snowed and stormed outside; and there should come a sparrow and quickly fly through the house, come in through one door and go out through the other. . . . So this life of men appears save for but a little while; what goes before or what follows after we do not know.*

In this interval of brightness Credo notices a particular man opposite him, a commonplace, weary-looking man, of average height and weight, costumed unaggressively, yet with something profoundly uncongenial and *settled* about his mouth, and an overall look of perfect integration with the heartless machine of the world. Credo takes him for an atheist. He thinks, *Between this innocuous fellow and myself yawns an eternal abyss, because I am a believer.*

The subway, rattling, plunges back underground. Or, it may be, as some extreme saints have implied, that, crushed beneath the majesty of the Infinite, believers and non-believers are exactly alike.

Eclipse

I WENT OUT INTO THE BACK YARD and the usually roundish spots of dappled sunlight underneath the trees were all shaped like feathers, crescent in the same direction, from left to right. Though it was five o'clock on a summer afternoon, the birds were singing goodbye to the day, and their merged song seemed to soak the strange air in an additional strangeness. A kind of silence prevailed. Few cars were moving on the streets of the town. Of my children only the baby dared come into the yard with me. She wore just underpants, and as she stood beneath a tree, bulging her belly toward me in the mood of jolly flirtation she has grown into at the age of two, her bare skin was awash with pale crescents. It crossed my mind that she might be harmed, but I couldn't think how. *Cancer?*

The eclipse was to be over ninety percent in our latitude, and the newspapers and television for days had been warning us not to look at it. I looked up, a split-second Prometheus, and looked away. The bitten silhouette of the sun lingered redly on my retinas. The day was half cloudy, and my impression had been of the sun struggling, amid a furious knotted huddle of black-and-silver clouds, with an enemy too dreadful to be seen, with an eater as ghostly and hungry as time. Every blade of grass cast a long bluish-brown shadow, as at dawn.

My wife shouted from behind the kitchen screen door that as long as I was out there I might as well burn the wastepaper. She darted from the house, eyes downcast, with the wastebasket, and darted back again, leaving the naked baby and me to wander up through the strained sunlight to the wire trash barrel. After my forbidden peek at the sun, the flames dancing transparently from the blackening paper—yesterday's *Boston Globe*, a milk carton, a Hi Ho cracker box—seemed dimmer than shadows, and in the teeth of all the warnings I looked up again. The clouds seemed bunched and twirled as if to plug a hole in the sky, and the burning afterimage was the shape of a near-new moon, horns pointed down. It was gigantically unnatural, and I lingered in the yard under the vague apprehension that in some future life I might be called before a cosmic court to testify to this assault. I seemed to be the sole witness. The town around my yard was hushed, all but the singing of the birds, who were invisible. The feathers under the trees had changed direction, and curved from right to left.

Then I saw my neighbor sitting on her porch. My neighbor is a widow, with white hair and brown skin; she has in her yard an aluminum-and-nylon-net chaise longue on which she lies at every opportunity, head back, arms spread, prostrate under the sun. Now she hunched dismally on her porch steps in the shade, which was scarcely darker than the light. I walked toward her and hailed her as a visitor to the moon might salute a survivor of a previous expedition. "How do you like the eclipse?" I called over the fence that distinguished our holdings on this suddenly insubstantial and lunar earth.

"I don't like it," she answered, shading her face with a hand. "They say you shouldn't go out in it."

"I thought it was just you shouldn't look at it."

"There's something in the rays," she explained, in a voice far louder than it needed to be, for silence framed us. "I shut all the windows on that side of the house and had to come out for some air."

"I think it'll pass," I told her.

"Don't let the baby look up," she warned, and turned away from talking to me, as if the open use of her voice exposed her more fatally to the rays.

Superstition, I thought, walking back through my yard, clutching my child's hand as tightly as a good-luck token. There was no question in her touch. Day, night, twilight, noon were all wonders to her, unscheduled, free from all bondage of prediction. The sun was being restored to itself and soon would radiate influence as brazenly as ever—and in this sense my daughter's blind trust was vindicated. Nevertheless, I was glad that the eclipse had passed, as it were, over her head; for in my own life I felt a certain assurance evaporate forever under the reality of the sun's disgrace.

FAR OUT

Archangel

ONYX AND SPLIT CEDAR and bronze vessels lowered into still water: these things I offer. Porphyry, teakwood, jasmine, and myrrh: these gifts I bring. The sheen of my sandals is dulled by the dust of cloves. My wings are waxed with nectar. My eyes are diamonds in whose facets red gold is mirrored. My face is a mask of ivory: Love me. Listen to my promises:

Cold water will drip from the intricately chased designs of the bronze vessels. Thick-lipped urns will sweat in the fragrant cellars. The orchards never weary of bearing on my islands. The very leaves give nourishment. The banked branches never crowd the paths. The grape vines will grow unattended. The very seeds of the berries are sweet nuts. Why do you smile? Have you never been hungry?

The workmanship of the bowers will be immaculate. Where the elements are joined, a sword of the thinnest whisper will find its point excluded. Where the beams have been tapered, each swipe of the plane is continuous. Where the wood needed locking, pegs of a counter grain have been driven. The ceilings are high, for coolness, and the spaced shingles seal at the first breath of mist. Though the windows are open, the eaves of the roof are so wide that nothing of the rain comes into the rooms but its scent. Mats of perfect cleanness cover the floor. The fire is cupped in black rock and sustained on a smooth breast of ash. Have you never lacked shelter?

Where, then, has your life been touched? My pleasures are as specific as they are everlasting. The sliced edges of a fresh ream of laid paper, cream, stiff, rag-rich. The freckles on the closed eyelids of a woman attentive in the first white blush of morning. The ball rapidly diminishing down the broad green throat of the first at Cape Ann. The good catch, a candy sun slatting the bleachers. The fair at the vanished poorhouse. The white arms of girls dancing, taffeta, white arms violet in the hollows music its contours praise the white wrists of praise the white arms and the white paper trimmed the Euclidean proof of Pythagoras's theorem its tightening beauty and the thin viridian skin of an old copper found in the salt sand. The microscopic glitter in the ink of the letters of words that are your own. Certain moments, remembered or imagined, of childhood. The cave in the box hedge. The Hershey bar chilled to brittleness. Three-handed pinochle by the brown glow of the stained-glass lampshade, your parents out of their godliness silently wishing you to win. In New York, the Brancusi room, silent. *Pines and Rocks*, by Cézanne; and *The Lace-Maker* in the Louvre, hardly bigger than your spread hand.

Such glimmers I shall widen to rivers; nothing will be lost, not the least grain of remembered dust, and the multiplication shall be a thousand thousand fold; love me. Embrace me; come, touch my side, where honey flows. Do not be afraid. Why should my promises be vain? Jade and cinnamon: do you deny that such things exist? Why do you turn away? Is not my song a stream of balm? My arms are heaped with apples and ancient books; there is no harm in me; no. Stay. Praise me. Your praise of me is praise of yourself; wait. Listen. I will begin again.

The Dark

THE DARK, he discovered, was mottled; was a luminous collage of patches of almost-color that became, as his open eyes grew at home, almost ectoplasmically bright. Objects became lunar panels let into the air that darkness had given flat substance to. Walls dull in day glowed. Yet he was not comforted by the general pallor of the dark, its unexpected transparence; rather, he lay there waiting, godlessly praying, for those visitations of positive light that were hurled, unannounced, through the windows by the headlights of automobiles pausing and passing outside. Some were slits, erect as sentinels standing guard before beginning to slide, helplessly, across a corner, diagonally warping, up onto the ceiling, accelerating, and away. Others were yellowish rectangles, scored with panes, windows themselves, but watery, streaked, as if the apparition silently posed on a blank interior wall were being in some manner lashed from without by a golden hurricane.

He wondered if all these visitations were caused by automobiles; for some of them appeared and disappeared without any accompaniment of motor noises below, and others seemed projected from an angle much higher than that of the street. Perhaps the upstairs lamps in neighboring homes penetrated the atmosphere within his bedroom. But it was a quiet neighborhood, and he imagined himself to be, night after night, the last person awake. Yet it was a rare hour, even from two o'clock on, when the darkness in which he lay was untouched; sooner or later, with a stroking motion like a finger passing across velvet, there would occur one of those intrusions of light which his heart would greet with wild grateful beating, for he had come to see in them his only companions, guards, and redeemers.

Sounds served in a much paler way—the drone of an unseen car vanishing at a point his mind's eye located beyond the Baptist church; the snatched breath and renewed surge of a truck shifting gears on the hill; the pained squeak, chuffing shuffle, and comic toot of a late commuting train clumsily threading the same old rusty needle; the high vibration of an airplane like a piece of fuzz caught in the sky's throat. These evidences of a universe of activity and life extending beyond him did not bring the same liberating assurance as those glowing rectangles delivered like letters through the slots in his room. The stir, whimper, or cough coming from the bedroom of one or another of his children had a contrary effect, of his consciousness touching a boundary, an abrasive rim. And in the breathing of his wife beside him a tight limit seemed reached. The blind, moist motor of her oblivious breathing seemed to follow the track of a circular running of which he was the vortex, sinking lower and lower in the wrinkled bed until he was lifted to another plane by the appearance, long delayed, on his walls of an angel, linear and serene, of light stolen from another world.

While waiting, he discovered the dark to be green in color, a green so low-keyed that only eyes made supernaturally alert could have sensed it, a thoroughly dirtied green in which he managed to detect, under opaque integuments of ambiguity, a general pledge of hope. Hope for his specific case he had long given up. It seemed a childhood ago when he had moved, a grown man, through a life of large rooms, with white-painted moldings and blowing curtains, whose walls each gave abundantly, in the form of open doorways and flung-back French windows, into other rooms—a mansion without visible end. In one of the rooms he had been stricken with a pang of unease. Still king of space, he had moved to dismiss the unease and the door handle had rattled, stuck. The curtains had stopped blowing. Behind him, the sashes and archways sealed shut. Still, it was merely a question of holding one's breath and finding a key. If the door was accidentally locked—had locked itself—there was certainly a key. For a lock without a key is a monstrosity, and while he knew, in a remote way, that monstrosities exist, he also knew there were many more rooms; he had glimpsed them waiting with their white-painted and polished corners, their invisible breeze of light. Doctors airily agreed; but then their expressions fled one way—cherubic, smiling—while their words fled another, and became unutterable, leaving him facing the blankness where the division had occurred. He tapped his pockets. They were empty. He stooped to pick the lock with his fingernails, and it shrank from his touch, became a formless bump, a bubble, and sank into the wood. The door became a smooth and solid wall. There was nothing left for him but to hope that the impenetrability of walls was somehow an illusion. His nightly vigil investigated this possibility. His discoveries, of the varied texture of the dark, its relenting phosphorescence, above all its hospitality to vivid and benign incursions of light, seemed at moments to confirm his hope. At other moments, by other lights, his vigil seemed an absurd toy supplied by cowardice to entertain his last months.

He had months and not years to live. This was the fact. By measuring with his mind (which seemed to hover some distance from his brain) the intensity of certain sensations obliquely received, he could locate, via a sort of triangulation, his symptoms in space: a patch of strangeness beneath the left rib, an inflexible limitation in his lungs, a sickly-sweet languor in his ankles, which his mind's eye, as he lay stretched out in bed, located just this side of the town wharf. But space interested him only as the silver on the back of the mirror of time. It was in time, that utterly polished surface, that he searched for his reflection, which was black, but thin-lipped and otherwise familiar. He wondered why the difference between months and years should be qualitative when mere quantities were concerned, and his struggle to make "month" a variant of "year" reminded him of, from his deepest past, his efforts to remove a shoehorn from between his heel and shoe, where with childish clumsiness he had wedged it. How frighteningly tight the jam had seemed! How feeble and small he must have been!

He did not much revisit the past. His inner space, the space of his mind, seemed as alien as the space of his body. His father's hands, his mother's tears, his sister's voice shrilling across an itchy lawn, the rolls of dust beneath his bed that might, just might, be poisonous caterpillars—these glints only frightened him with the depth of the darkness in which they were all but smothered. He had forgotten almost everything. Everything in his life had been ordinary except its termination. His "life." Considered as a finite noun, his life seemed vastly unequal to the infinitude of death. The preposterous inequality almost made a ledge where his hope could grip; but the unconscious sighing of his wife's sagging mouth dragged it down. Faithlessly she lay beside him in the arms of her survival. Her unheeding sleep deserved only dull anger and was not dreadful like the sleep of his children, whose dream-sprung coughs and cries seemed to line the mouth of death with teeth. The sudden shortness of his life seemed to testify to the greed of those he had loved. He should have been shocked by his indifference to them; he should have grubbed the root of this coldness from his brain. But introspection, like memory, sickened him with its steep perspectives—afflicted him with the nausea of futile concentration, as if he were picking a melting lock. He was not interested in his brain but in his soul, his soul, that outward simplicity embodied in the shards and diagonal panes of light that wheeled around his room when a car smoothly passed in the street below.

From three o'clock on, the traffic was thin. As if his isolation had turned him into God, he blessed, with stately wordlessness, whatever errant teen-ager or returning carouser relieved the stillness of the town. Then, toward four, all such visits ceased. There was a quietness. Unwanted images began to impinge on the dark: a pulpy many-legged spider was offered wriggling to him on a fork. His teeth ached to think of biting, of chewing, its eyes, its tiny intermeshing fluid-bearing parts, its fur. . . .

It was time to imagine the hand.

He, who since infancy had slept best on his stomach, could now endure lying only on his back. He wished his lids, even if they were closed, to be pelted and bathed by whatever eddies of light animated the room. As these eddies died, and the erosion of sleeplessness began to carve his consciousness fantastically, he had taken to conceiving of himself as lying in a giant hand, his head on the fingertips and his legs in the crease of the palm. He did not picture the hand with total clarity, denied it nails and hair, and with idle rationality supposed it was an echo from Sunday school, some old-fashioned print; nevertheless, the hand was so real to him that he would stealthily double his pillow to lift his head higher and thereby fit himself better to the curve of the great fingers. The hand seemed to hold him at some height, but he had no fear of falling nor any sense of display, of being gazed at, as a mother gazes at the baby secure in her arms. Rather, this giant hand seemed something owed him, a basis upon which had been drawn the contract of his conception, and it had the same extensive, impersonal life as the pieces of light that had populated, before the town went utterly still, the walls of his room.

Now the phosphor of these walls took on a blueness, as if the yellowness of the green tinge of the darkness were being distilled from it. Still safe in the hand, he dared turn, with cunning gradualness, and lie on his side and touch with his knees the underside of his wife's thighs, which her bunched nightie had bared. Her intermittently restless sleep usually resolved into a fetal position facing away from him; and in a parallel position—ready at any nauseous influx of terror to return to his back—he delicately settled himself, keeping the soft touch of her flesh at his knees as a mooring. His eyes had closed. Experimentally he opened them, and a kind of gnashing, a blatancy, at the leafy window, which he now faced, led him to close them again. A rusty brown creaking, comfortable and antique, passed along his body, merging with the birdsong that had commenced beyond the window like the melodious friction of a machine of green and squeaking wood.

He smiled at himself, having for an instant imagined that he was adjusting his stiff arms around a massive thumb beside his face.

Comfort ebbed from the position; his wife irritably stirred and broke the mooring. Carefully, as gingerly as if his body were an assemblage of components any one of which might deflect his parabolic course, he moved to lie on his stomach, pressing himself on the darkness beneath him, as if in wrestling, upon some weary foe.

Panic jerked his dry lids open. He looked backward, past his shoulder, at the pattern of patches that had kept watch with him. A chair, with clothes tossed upon it, had begun to be a chair, distinctly forward from the wall. The air, he saw, was being visited by another invader, a light unlike the others, entering not obliquely but frontally, upright, methodically, less by stealth than like a hired presence, like a fine powder very slowly exploding, scouring the white walls of their moss of illusion, polishing objects into islands. He felt in this arrival relief from his vigil and knew, his chest loosening rapidly, that in a finite time he would trickle through the fingers of the hand; he would slip, blissfully, into oblivion, as a fold is smoothed from a width of black silk.

The Astronomer

I FEARED HIS VISIT. I was twenty-four, and the religious revival within myself was at its height. Earlier that summer, I had discovered Kierkegaard, and each week I brought back to the apartment one more of the Princeton University Press's elegant and expensive editions of his works. They were beautiful books, sometimes very thick, sometimes very thin, always typographically exhilarating, with their welter of title pages, subheads, epigraphs, emphatic italics, italicized catchwords taken from German philosophy and too subtle for translation, translator's prefaces and footnotes, and Kierkegaard's own endless footnotes, blanketing pages at a time as, crippled, agonized by distinctions, he scribbled on and on, heaping irony on irony, curse on curse, gnashing, sneering, praising Jehovah in the privacy of his empty home in Copenhagen. The demons with which he wrestled—Hegel and his avatars—were unknown to me, so Kierkegaard at his desk seemed to me to be writhing in the clutch of phantoms, slapping at silent mosquitoes, twisting furiously to confront presences that were not there. It was a spectacle unlike any I had ever seen in print before, and it brought me much comfort during those August and September evenings, while the traffic on the West Side Highway swished tirelessly and my wife tinkled the supper dishes in our tiny kitchen.

We lived at the time on the sixth floor of a building on Riverside Drive, and overlooked the Hudson. The river would become black before the sky, and the little New Jersey towns on the far bank would be pinched between two massive tongs of darkness until only a row of sparks remained. These embers were reflected in the black water, and when a boat went dragging its wake up the river the reflections would tremble, double, fragment, and not until long after the shadow of the boat passed reconstruct themselves.

The astronomer was a remnant of our college days. Two years had passed since we had seen him. When Harriet and I were both undergraduates, another couple, a married couple, had introduced him to us. The wife of this couple had gone to school with Harriet, and the husband was a teaching associate of the astronomer; so Bela and I were the opposite ends of a chain of acquaintance. He was a Hungarian. His parents had fled the terror of Kun's regime; they were well-to-do. From Vienna they had come to London; from there Bela had gone to Oxford, and from there come to this country, years ago. He was forty, a short, thickset man with a wealth of stiff black hair, combed straight back without a parting, like a bicyclist bent over the handlebars. Only a few individual hairs had turned white. He gave an impression of abnormal density; his anatomical parts seemed set one on top of another without any loose space between for leeway or accommodation of his innards. A motion in his foot instantly jerked his head. The Magyar cheekbones gave his face a blunt, aggressive breadth; he wore steel-rimmed glasses that seemed several sizes too small. He was now teaching at Columbia. Brilliant, he rarely deigned to publish papers, so that his brilliance was carried around with him as undiminished potency. He liked my wife. Like Kierkegaard, he was a bachelor, and in the old days his flirtatious compliments, rolled out with a rich, slow British accent and a broad-mouthed, thoughtful smile across a cafeteria table or after dinner in our friends' living room, made me feel foolish and incapable; she was not my wife then. "Ah, Harri-et, Harri-et," he would call, giving the last syllable of her name a full, French, roguish weight, "come and sit by me on this Hide-a-bed." And then he would pat the cushion beside him, which his own weight had caused to lift invitingly. Somewhat more than a joke, it was nevertheless not rude to me; I did not have enough presence in his eyes to receive rudeness.

He had an air of seeing beyond me, of seeing into the interstellar structure of things, of having transcended, except perhaps in the niggling matter of sexual attraction, the clouds of human subjectivity—vaporous hopes supported by immaterial rationalizations. It was his vigorous, clear vision that I feared.

When he came into our apartment, directing warmth into all its corners with brisk handshakes and abrupt pivotings of his whole frame, he spotted the paperback *Meno* that I had been reading, back and forth on the subway, two pages per stop. It is the dialogue in which Socrates, to demonstrate the existence of indwelling knowledge, elicits some geometrical truths from a small boy. "My Lord, Walter," Bela said, "why are you reading this? Is this the one where he proves two and two equals four?" And thus quickly, at a mere wink from this atheist, Platonism and all its attendant cathedrals came tumbling down.

We ate dinner by the window, from which the Hudson seemed a massive rent opened in a tenuous web of light. Though we talked trivially, about friends and events, I felt the structure I had painstakingly built up within myself wasting away; my faith (Christian existentialism padded out with Chesterton and Teilhard de Chardin), my prayers, my churchgoing (to a Methodist edifice where the spiritual void of the inner city reigned above the fragile hats of a dozen old ladies and the minister shook my hand at the door with a startled look on his face), all dwindled to the thinnest filaments of illusion, and in one flash, I knew, they would burn to nothing. I felt behind his eyes immensities of space and gas; I saw with him through my own evanescent body into gigantic systems of dead but furious matter—suns like match heads, planets like cinders, galaxies that were whirls of ash, and beyond them, more galaxies, and more, fleeing with sickening speed beyond the rim that our most powerful telescopes could reach. I had once heard him explain, in a cafeteria, how the dwarf star called the companion of Sirius is so dense that light radiating from it is tugged back by gravitation toward the red end of the spectrum.

My wife took our dessert dishes away; before she brought coffee, I emptied the last of the red wine into our glasses. Bela lit a cigar and, managing its fresh length and the wineglass with his electric certainty of touch, talked. Knowing that, since the principal business of my employment was to invent the plots of television commercials, I was to some extent a humorist, he told me of a parody he had seen of the BBC. Third Programme. It involved Bertrand Russell reading the first five hundred decimal places of π, followed by ten minutes of silent meditation led by Mr. T. S. Eliot, and then Bertrand Russell reading the *next* five hundred places of π.

If my laughter burst out excessively, it was because his acknowledgment, though minimal and oblique, that Bertrand Russell might by some conception be laughable and that meditation and the author of "Little Gidding" did at least *exist* momentarily relieved me of the strain of maintaining against the pressure of his latent opinions my own superstitious, faint-hearted self. This small remission of his field of force admitted worlds of white light, and my wife, returning to the room holding with bare arms at the level of our eyes a tray on which an old tin pot and three china demitasse cups stated their rectangular silhouettes, seemed a creature of intense beauty.

"Ah, Harri-et, Harri-et," Bela said, lowering his cigar, "married life has not dimmed thy lustre."

My wife blushed, rather too readily—her skin had always been discomfitingly quick to answer his praise—and set the tray on the table and took her chair and served us. Mixing wine and coffee in our mouths, we listened to Bela tell of when he first came to this country. He was an instructor in general science at a university in Michigan. The thermometer stayed at zero for months, the students carved elaborate snow sculptures on the campus, everyone wore earmuffs and unbuckled galoshes. At first, he couldn't believe in the earmuffs; they looked like something you would find among the most secluded peasantry of Central Europe. It had taken him months to muster the courage to go into a shop and ask for such childish things. But at last he had, and had been very happy in them. They were very sensible. He continued to wear them, though in the East they did not seem to be the fashion.

"I know," Harriet said. "In the winter here, you see all these poor Madison Avenue men—"

"Such as Walter," Bela smoothly interceded, shaping his cigar ash on the edge of his saucer.

"Well, yes, except it doesn't look so bad with him because he never cuts his hair. But all these other men with their tight little hats on the top of their haircuts right in the dead of this damp, windy winter—their ears are bright red in the subway."

"And the girls," Bela said, "the girls in the Midwest wear *immense puffs*, as big around as—" He cupped his hands, fingers spread, over his ears and, hunching his head down on his thick brief neck, darted glances at us to check that we were following his demonstration. He had retained, between two fingers, the cigar, so his head seemed to have sprouted, rather low, one smoking horn. His hands darted away; his chest expanded as he tried to conjure up those remote pompoms. "White, woolly," he said sharply, giving each adjective a lecturer's force; then the words glided as he suddenly exhaled: "They're like the snowballs that girls in your ice shows wear on their breasts." He pronounced the two *s*'s in "breasts" so distinctly it seemed the radiator had hissed.

It surprised us that he had ever seen an ice show. We had not thought of him as a sightseer. But it turned out that in those first years he had inspected the country thoroughly. He had bought an old Hudson one summer and driven all around the West by himself. With incongruous tourist piety, he had visited the Grand Canyon, Yosemite, a Sioux reservation. He described a long stretch of highway in New Mexico. "There are these black hills. Utterly without vegetation. Great, heavy, almost purplish folds, unimaginably ugly, mile after mile after mile. Not a gas station, not a sign of green. Nothing." And his face, turning rapidly from one to the other of us, underwent an expression I had never before seen him wear. His black eyebrows shot up in two arches stretching his eyelids smooth, and his upper lip tightened over his lower, which was sucked back and delicately pinched between his teeth. This expression, bestowed in silence and swiftly erased, confessed what he could not pronounce: he had been frightened.

On the table, below our faces, the cups and glasses broken into shards by shadows, the brown dregs of coffee and wine, the ashtrays and the ashes were hastily swept together into a little heap of warm dark tones distinct from the universal debris.

That is all I remember. The mingle on the table was only part of the greater confusion as in the heat of rapport our unrelated spirits and pasts scrambled together, bringing everything in the room with them, including the rubble of footnotes bound into Kierkegaard. In memory, perhaps because we lived on the sixth floor, this scene—this ghostly scene— seems to take place at a great height, as if we sat on a star suspended against the darkness of the city and the river. What is the past, after all, but a vast sheet of darkness in which a few moments, pricked apparently at random, shine?

The Witnesses

FRED PROUTY, I was told yesterday, is dead—dead, as I imagine it, of cigarettes, confusion, and conscience, though none of these was the *c* my informant named. He died on the West Coast, thousands of miles from both his ex-wives and all his sad expensive children. I pictured him lying in a highly clean hospital bed, smothering in debt, interlaced with tubular machinery, overlooking a sprawling colorless spireless landscape worlds removed from the green and pointed East that had formed him. Though we had come from the same town (New Haven) and the same schools (Hotchkiss, Yale) and the same background (our grandfathers had been ministers and our fathers lawyers), Fred and I never were very close. We belonged to a generation that expressed affection through shades of reserve. The war, perhaps, had made us conservative and cautious; our task had been to bring a society across a chasm and set it down safely on the other side, unchanged. That it changed later was not our affair. After the war Fred had gone into advertising, and I into securities. For a decade, we shared Manhattan and intermittent meals. The last time I had him in my home, there had been a strangeness and, worse, a tactlessness for which I suppose I never quite forgave him. It was the high noon of the Eisenhower era, just before Fred's first divorce. He called me at work and invited himself to our apartment for a drink, and asked, surprisingly, if he might bring a friend.

Jeanne and I had the West Thirteenth Street place then. Of our many apartments, I remember it most fondly. The front windows looked across the street into an elementary school, and the back windows, across some untended yards crammed with trees of heaven, into a mysterious factory. Whatever the factory made, the process entailed great shimmering ribbons and spinning reels of color being manipulated like giant harps by Negro men and Puerto Rican women. Rising in the morning, we could see them at work, and, eating breakfast in the front room, we looked into windows where children were snipping and pasting up, in season, Easter eggs and pumpkins, Christmas trees and hearts, hatchets and cherries. Almost always a breeze flowed through our two large rooms, now from bedroom to living room, from factory to school, and now the other way, bringing with it the sounds of street traffic, which included the drunks on the pavement outside the Original Mario's. Ours was the third floor—the lowest we have ever lived.

Fred came promptly at seven. As he climbed the stairs, I thought the woman behind him was his wife. Indeed, she resembled his wife—an inch taller, perhaps, and a bit more adventurously dressed, but the same physical type, heavy and rounded below the waist, slender above. The two women had the same kind of ears, cupped and protruding, which compelled the same cover-up hairdo and understated earrings. Fred introduced her to us as Priscilla Evans. Jeanne had not known Marjorie Prouty well, yet to ask her to meet and entertain this other woman on no basis beyond the flat implication of her being Fred's mistress was, as perhaps Fred in his infatuation imperfectly understood, a *gaffe*. Jeanne reached forward stiffly to take the girl's hand.

A "girl" more by status than by age. Priscilla was, though unmarried and a year or two younger, one of us—I never knew where Fred met her, but it could have been at work or a party or a crew race, if he still went to them. She had the social grace to be tense and quiet, and I wondered how Fred had persuaded her to come. He must have told her I was a very close friend, which perhaps, in his mind, I was. I was New Haven to him, distant and safe; touchingly, his heart had never left that middling town. I would like to reward the loyalty of a ghost by remembering that evening—hour, really, for we did not invite them for dinner—as other than dull. But, in part because Jeanne and I felt constrained from asking them any direct questions, in part because Priscilla put on a shy manner, and in part because Fred seemed sheepishly bewildered by this party he had arranged, our conversation was stilted. We discussed what was current in those departed days: McCarthy's fall, Kefauver's candidacy, Dulles's tactlessness. Dulles had recently called Goa a "Portuguese province," offending India, and given his "brinkmanship" interview, offending everyone. Priscilla said she thought Dulles deserved credit for at least his honesty, for saying out loud what everybody knew anyway. It is the one remark of hers that I remember, and it made me look at her again.

She was like Marjorie but with a difference. There was something twisted and wry about her face, some arresting trace of pain endured and wisdom reluctantly acquired. Her life, I felt, had been cracked and mended, and in this her form differed from that of Fred's wife or, for that matter, of my own. My attention, then, for an instant snagged on the irregularity where Fred's spirit had caught, taken root, and hastily flourished. I try to remember them sitting beside each other—he slumped in the canvas sling chair, she upright on the half of the Sheraton settee nearer him. He had reddish hair receding on a brow where the freckles advanced. His nose was thin and straight, his eyes pale blue and slightly bulged behind the silver-frame spectacles that, through some eccentricity of the nose pads, perched too far out from his face. Fred's mouth was one of those sharply cut sets of lips, virtually pretty, that frown down from portraits on bank walls. An atavistic farmerishness made his hands heavy; when he clasped his knee, the knuckles were squeezed white. In the awkward sling chair, he clasped his knee; his neck seemed red above the fresh white collar; he was anxious for her. He quickly, gently disagreed with her praise of Dulles, knowing we were liberals. She sat demure, yet with a certain gaudy and provocative tone to her clothes, and there was—I imagine or remember—a static energy imposed on the space between her body and Fred's, as in that visual fooler which now seems two black profiles and now a single white vase, so that the arm of the settee, the mahogany end table inlaid with satinwood, the unlit lamp with the base of beaten copper, the ceramic ashtray full of unfiltered butts shaped like commas, the very shadows and blurs of refraction were charged with a mysterious content, the "relationship" of these two nervous and unwelcome visitors.

I want to believe that Jeanne, however half-heartedly, invited them to dine with us; of course Fred refused, saying they must go, suddenly rising, apologetic, his big hands dangling, his lady looking up at him for leadership. They left before eight, and my embarrassed deafness lifts. I can hear Jeanne complaining distinctly, "Well, that was strange!"

"Very strange behavior, from Fred."

"Was he showing her that he has respectable friends, or what?"

"Surely that's a deduction she didn't need to have proved."

"She may have a mistrustful nature."

"What did you make of her?"

"I'm afraid I must say she struck me as very ordinary."

I said, "It's hilarious, how much of a copy she is of his wife."

"Yes, and not as finished as Marjorie. A poor copy."

"How far," I said, "people go out of their way to mess up their lives." I was trying to agree with some unstated assertion of hers.

"Yes," said Jeanne, straightening the bent cushions on the settee, "that was very dismal. Tell me. Are we going to have to see them again? Are we some sort of furniture so they can play house, or what?"

"No, I'm sure not. I'll tell Fred not, if I must."

"I don't care what people do, but I don't like being used."

I felt she expected me, though innocent, to apologize. I said, "I can't imagine what got into Fred. He's usually nothing if not correct."

For a moment, Jeanne may have considered letting me have the last word. Then she said firmly, "I found the whole thing extremely dreary."

The next day, or the day after, Fred called me at the office, and thanked me. He said, with an off-putting trace of the stammering earnestness his clients must have found endearing, that it had meant more to him than I could know, and some day he would tell me why. I may have been incurious and cool. He did not call again. Then I heard he was divorced, and had left Madison Avenue for a public relations outfit starting up in Chicago. His new wife, I was told, came originally from Indianapolis. I tried to remember if Priscilla Evans had had a Midwestern accent and could not.

Years later, but some time ago, when Kennedy Airport was still called Idlewild, Fred and I accidentally met in the main terminal—those acres of white floor where the islands of white waiting chairs cast no shadows. He was on his way back to Los Angeles. He was doing publicity work for one of the studios that can television series. Although he did not tell me, he was on the verge of his second divorce. He seemed heavier, and his hands were puffy. His hair was thinning now on the back of his skull; there were a few freckles in the bald spot. He was wearing horn-rimmed glasses, which did not make him look youthful. He kept taking them off, as if bothered by their fit, exposing, on the bridge of his nose, the red moccasin-shaped dents left by the pads of his old silver frames. He had somehow gone pasty, sheltered from the California sun, and I wondered if I looked equally tired and corrupt to him. Little in my life had changed. We had had one child, a daughter. We had moved uptown, to a bigger, higher, bleaker apartment. Kennedy's bear market had given me a dull spring.

Fred and I sought shelter in the curtained bar a world removed from the sun-stricken airfield and the glinting planes whose rows of rivets and portholes seemed to be spelling a message in punched code. He told me about his life without complaint and let me guess that it was not going well. He had switched to filtered cigarettes but there was a new recklessness in his drinking. I watched his hands and suddenly remembered how those same hands looked squeezed around the handle of a lacrosse stick. He apologized for the night he had brought the girl to our apartment.

I said that I had almost forgotten, but that at the time it had seemed out of character.

"How did we look?" he asked.

I didn't understand. "Worried," I said. "She seemed to us much like Marjorie."

He smiled and said, "That's how it turned out. Just like Marjorie." He had had three drinks and took off his glasses. His eyes were still a schoolboy's, but his mouth no longer would have looked well on a bank wall; the prim cut of it had been boozed and blurred away, and a dragging cynicism had done something ineradicable to the corners. His lips groped for precision. "I wanted you to see us," he said. "I wanted somebody to see us in love. I loved her so much," he said, "I loved her so much it makes me sick to remember it. Whenever I come back to the city, whenever I pass any place we went together when it was beginning, I fall, I kind of drop an inch or so inside my skin. Herbie, do you know what I'm talking about, have you ever had the feeling?"

I did not think that I was expected to answer such questions. Perhaps my silence was construed as a rebuke.

Fred rubbed his forehead and closed his watery blue eyes and said, "I knew it was wrong. I knew it was going to end in a mess, it had nowhere else to go." He opened his scared eyes and told me, "That's why I brought her over that time. She hated it, she didn't want to come. But I wanted it. I wanted somebody I knew to see us when it was good. No: I wanted somebody who knew me to see me happy. *Did* you see?"

I nodded, lying, but he was hurrying on: "I had never known I could be that happy. God. I wanted you and Jeanne to see us together before it went bad. So it wouldn't be totally lost."

A Constellation of Events

THE EVENTS felt spaced in a vast deep sky, its third dimension dizzying. Looking back, Betty could scarcely believe that the days had come so close together. But, no, there, flat on the calendar, they were, one after another—four bright February days.

Sunday, after church, Rob had taken her and the children cross-country skiing. They made a party of it. He called up Evan, because they had discussed the possibility at the office Friday, while the storm was raging around their green-glass office building in Hartford, and she, because Evan, a bachelor, was Lydia Smith's lover, called up the Smiths and invited them, too; it was the sort of festive, mischievous gesture Rob found excessive. But Lydia answered the phone and was delighted. As her voice twittered in Betty's ear, Betty stuck out her tongue at Rob's frown.

They all met at the Pattersons' field in their different-colored cars and soon made a line of dark silhouettes across the white pasture. Evan and Lydia glided obliviously into the lead; Rob and Billy, the son now almost the size of the father, and Fritzie Smith, who in imitation of her mother was quite the girl athlete, occupied the middle distance, the little Smith boy struggling to keep up with this group; and Betty and her baby—poor bitterly whining, miserably ill-equipped Jennifer—came last, along with Rafe Smith, who didn't ski as much as Lydia and whose bindings kept letting go. He was thinner than Rob, more of a clown, fuller of doubt, hatchet-faced and green-eyed: a sad, encouraging sort of man. He kept telling Jennifer, "Ups-a-daisy, Jenny, keep in the others' tracks, now you've got the rhythm, oops," as the child's skis scrambled and she toppled down again. Meanwhile, one of Rafe's feet would have come out of his binding and Betty would have to wait, the others dwindling in the distance into dots.

The fields were immense in their brilliance. Her eyes winced, taking them in. The tracks of their party, and the tracks of the Sno-Cats that had frolicked here in the wake of the storm, scarcely touched the marvellous blankness—slopes up and down, a lone oak on a knoll, rail fences like pencilled hatchings, weathered No Trespassing signs not meant for them. Rob had done business with one of the Patterson sons and would bluff a challenge through; the fields seemed held beneath a transparent dome of Rob's protection. A creek, thawed into audible life, ran where two slopes met. Betty was afraid to follow the tracks of the others here; it involved stepping, in skis, from snowbank to snowbank across a width of icy, confident, secretive water. She panicked and took the wooden bridge fifty yards out of their way. Rafe lifted Jennifer up and stepped across, his binding snapping on the other side but no harm done. The child laughed for the first time that afternoon.

The sun came off the snow hot; Betty thought her face would get its first touch of tan today, and then it would not be many weeks before cows grazed here again, bringing turds to the mayflowers. Pushing up the slope on the other side of the creek, toward the woods, she slipped backwards and fell sideways. The snow was moist, warm. "Shit," she said, and was pleasurably aware of the massy uplifted curve of her hip in jeans as she looked down over it at Rafe behind her, his green eyes sun-narrowed, alert.

"Want to get up?" he asked, and held out a hand, a damp black mitten. As she reached for it, he pulled off the mitten, offering her a bare hand, bony and pink and startling, so suddenly exposed to the air. "Ups-a-daisy," he said, and the effort of pulling her erect threw him off balance, and a binding popped loose again. Both she and Jenny laughed this time.

At the entrance of the path through the woods, Rob waited with evident patience. Before he could complain, she did: "Jennifer is going crazy on these awful borrowed skis. *Why* can't she have decent equipment like other children?"

"I'll stay with her," her husband said, both firm and evasive in his way, avoiding the question with an appearance of meeting it, and appearing selfless in order to shame her. But she felt the smile on her face persist as undeniably, as unerasably, as the sun on the field. Rob's face clouded, gathering itself to speak; Rafe interrupted, apologizing, blaming their slowness upon himself and his defective bindings. For a moment that somehow made her shiver inside—perhaps no more than the flush of exertion meeting the chill blue shade of the woods, here at the edge—the two men stood together, intent upon the mechanism, her presence for-gotten. Rob found the misadjustment, and Rafe's skis came off no more.

In the woods, Rob and Jennifer fell behind, and Rafe slithered ahead, hurrying to catch up to his children and, beyond them, to his wife and Evan. Betty tried to stay with her husband and child, but they were too maddening—one whining, the other frowning, and neither grateful for her company. She let herself ski ahead, and became alone in the woods, aware of distant voices, the whisper of her skis, the soft companionable heave of her own breathing. Pine trunks shifted about, one behind another and then another, aligned and not aligned, shadowy harmonies. Here and there the trees grew down into the path; a twig touched her eye, so lightly she was surprised to find pain lingering, and herself crying. She came to an open place where paths diverged. Here Rafe was waiting for her; thin, leaning on his poles, he seemed a shadow among others. "Which way do you think they went?" He sounded breathless and acted lost. His wife and her lover had escaped him.

"Left is the way to get back to the car," she said.

"I can't tell which are their tracks," he said.

"I'm so sorry," Betty said.

"Don't be." He relaxed on his poles, and made no sign of moving. "Where is Rob?" he asked.

"Coming. He took over dear Jennifer for me. I'll wait, you go on."

"I'll wait with you. It's too scary in here. Do you want that book?" The sentences followed one another evenly, as if consequentially.

The book was about Jane Austen, by an English professor Betty had studied under years ago, before Radcliffe called itself Harvard. She had noticed it lying on the front seat of the Smiths' car while they were all fussing with their skis, and had exclaimed with recognition, of a sort. In a strange suspended summer of her life, the summer when Billy was born, she had read through all six of the Austen novels, sitting on a sunporch waiting and waiting and then suddenly nursing. "If you're done with it."

"I am. It's tame, but dear, as you would say. Could I bring it by tomor-row morning?"

He had recently left a law firm in Hartford and opened an office here in town. He had few clients but seemed amused, being idle. There was something fragile and incapable about him. "Yes," she said, adding, "Jen-nifer comes back from school at noon."

And then Jennifer and Rob caught up to them, both needing to be pla-cated, and she forgot this shadowy man's promise, as if her mind had been possessed by the emptiness where the snowy paths diverged.

. . .

Monday was bright, and the peal at the door accented the musical dripping of the icicles ringing the house around with falling pearls. Rafe was hunched comically under the dripping from the front eaves, the book held dry against his parka. He offered just to hand it to her, but she invited him in for coffee, he seemed so sad, still lost. They sat with the coffee on the sofa, and soon his arms were around her and his lips, tasting of coffee, warm on her mouth and his hands cold on her skin beneath her sweater, and she could not move her mind from hovering, from floating in a golden consciousness of the sun on the floorboards, great slanting splashes of it, rhomboids broken by the feathery silhouettes of her houseplants on the windowsills. From her angle as he stretched her out on the sofa, the shadows of the drips leaped upward in the patches of sun, appearing to defy gravity as her head whirled. She sat up, pushed him off without rebuke, unpinned and repinned her hair. "What are we doing?" she asked.

"I don't know," Rafe said, and indeed he didn't seem to. His assault on her had felt clumsy, scared, insincere; he seemed grateful to be stopped. His face was pink, as his hand had been. In the light of the windows behind the sofa his eyes were very green. An asparagus fern hanging there cast a net of shadow that his features moved in and out of as he apologized, talked, joked. "Baby fat!" he had exclaimed of her belly, having tugged her sweater up, bending suddenly to kiss the crease there, his face thin as a blade, and hot. He was frightened, Betty realized, which banished her own fear.

Gently she maneuvered him away from her body, out of the door. It was not so hard; she remembered how to fend off boys from the college days that his book had brought back to her. In his gratitude he wouldn't stop smiling. She shut the front door. His body as he crossed the melting street fairly danced with relief. And for her, again alone in the empty house, it was as if along with her fear much of her soul had been banished; feeling neither remorse nor expectation, she floated above the patches of sun being stitched by falling drops, among the curved shining of glass and porcelain and aluminum kitchen equipment, in the house's strange warmth—strange as any event seems when only we are there to witness it. Betty lifted her sweater to look at her pale belly. Baby fat. Middle age had softened her middle. But, then, Lydia was an athlete, tomboyish and lean, swift on skis, with that something Roman and androgynous and enigmatic about her looks. It was what Rafe was used to; the contrast had startled him.

She picked up the book from the sofa. He was one of those men who could read a book gently, so it didn't look read. She surprised herself, in her great swimming calmness, by being unable to read a word.

Tuesday, as they had planned weeks ago, Rob took her to Philadelphia. She had been born there, and he had business there. Taking her along was his tribute, he had made it too plain, to her condition as a bored housewife. Yet she loved it, loved him, once the bumping, humming terror of the plane ride was past. The city in the winter sunlight looked glassier and cleaner than she remembered it, her rough and enormous dear drab City of Brotherly Love. Rob was here because his insurance company was helping finance a shopping mall in southern New Jersey; he disappeared into the strangely Egyptian old façade of the Penn Mutual Building—now doubly false, for it had been reconstructed as a historical front on a new skyscraper, a tall box of tinted glass. She wandered window-shopping along Walnut Street until her feet hurt, then took a cab from Rittenhouse Square to the Museum of Art. There was less snow in Philadelphia than in Connecticut; some of the grass beside the Parkway already looked green.

At the head of the stairs inside the museum, Saint-Gaudens's great verdigrised Diana—in Betty's girlhood imagination the statue had been somehow confused with the good witch of fairy stories (only naked, having shed the ball gown and petticoats good witches usually wear, the better to swing her long legs)—still posed, at her shadowy height, on one tiptoe foot. But elsewhere within the museum, there were many changes, much additional brightness. The three versions of *Nude Descending a Staircase* and the sadly cracked *Bride Stripped Bare by Her Bachelors, Even* no longer puzzled and offended her. The daring passes into the classic in our very lifetimes, while we age and die. Rob met her, just when he had promised, at three-thirty, amid the Impressionist paintings; her sudden love of him, here in this room of raw color and light, felt like a melting. She leaned on him, he moved away from her touch, and in her unaccustomed city heels Betty sidestepped to keep her balance.

They had tea in the cafeteria, out of place in their two dark suits among the students and beards and the studied rags that remained of the last decade's revolution. Here, too, the radical had become the comfortable. "How do you like being back?" Rob asked her.

"It's changed, I've changed. I like it where I am now. You were dear to bring me, though." She touched his hand, and he did not pull it away on the smooth tabletop, whose white reminded her of snow.

Happiness must have been on her face, glowing like a sunburn, for he looked at her and seemed for an instant to see her. The instant troubled him. Though too heavy to be handsome, he had beautiful eyes, tawny and indifferent like a lion's; they slitted and he frowned in the unaccustomed exercise of framing a compliment. "It's such a pity," he said, "you're my wife."

She laughed, astonished. "Is it? Why?"

"You'd make such a lovely mistress."

"You think? How do you know? Have you ever had a mistress?" She was so confident of the answer she went on before he could say no. "Then how do you know I'd make a lovely one? Maybe I'd make an awful one. Shrieking, possessive. Better just accept me as a wife," she advised complacently. The table was white and cluttered with dirty tea things between them; she could hardly wait until they were home, in bed. His lovemaking was like him, firm and tireless, and it always worked. She admired that. Once, she had adored it, until her adoration had seemed to depress him. And something in her now, at this glittering table, depressed him — perhaps the mistress he had glimpsed in her, the mistress that he of all the men in the world was barred from, could never have. She stroked his hand as if in acknowledgment of a shared sorrow. But happiness kept mounting in her, giddy and meaningless, inexplicable, unstoppable, though she saw that on its wings she was leaving Rob behind. And he had never seemed solider or kinder, or she more fittingly, as they rose and paid and left the museum together, his wife.

On the flight back, to calm her terror, she pulled the book from her handbag and read, *As Lionel Trilling was to say in 1957 (before women had risen in their might), "The extraordinary thing about Emma is that she has a moral life as a man has a moral life"; "A consciousness is always at work in her, a sense of what she ought to be and do."*

Rob looked over her shoulder and asked, "Isn't that Rafe's book?"

"One just like it," she answered promptly, deceit proving not such a difficult trick after all. "You must have seen it on the front seat of his car Sunday. So did I, and I found a copy at Wanamaker's this morning."

"It looks read."

"I was reading it. Waiting for you."

His silence she took to be a satisfied one. He rattled his newspaper, then asked, "Isn't it awfully dry?"

She feigned preoccupation. A precarious rumble changed pitch under her. "Mm. Dry but dear."

"He's a sad guy, isn't he?" Rob abruptly said. "Rafe."

"What's sad about him?"

"You know. Being cuckolded."

"Maybe Lydia loves him all the better for it," Betty said.

"Impossible," her husband decreed, and hid himself in the *Inquirer* as the 727, rumbling and shuddering, prepared to crash. She clutched at Rob's arm with that irrational fervor he disliked; deliberately he kept his eyes on the newspaper, shutting her out. Yet in grudging answer to her prayers he brought the plane down safely, with a corner of his inflexible mind.

In her dream she was teaching again, and among her students Rafe seemed lost. She had a question for him, and couldn't seem to get his attention, though he was not exactly misbehaving; his back was half turned as he talked to some arrogant skinny girl in the class. . . . It was so exasperating she awoke, feeling empty and slightly scared. Rob was out of the bed. She heard the door slam as he went to work. The children were downstairs quarrelling, a merciless sound as of something boiling over. Wednesday. When she stood, a residue of last night's lovemaking slid down the inside of her thigh.

The children off to school, she moved through the emptiness of the house exploring the realization that she was in love. Like the floorboards, the doorframes, the wallpaper, the fact seemed not so much arresting as necessary, not ornamental but functional in some way she must concentrate on perceiving. The snow on the roof had all melted; the dripping from the eaves had ceased, and a dry sunlight rested silently on the warm house, the bare street, the speckled rooftops of the town beyond the sunstruck, dirty windows. Valentines the children had brought home from school littered the kitchen counter. The calendar showed the shortest month, a rectangular candy box dotted with red holidays. Rafe's office number was newly listed in the telephone book. She dialled it, less to reach him than to test the extent of the day's emptiness. Alarmingly, the ringing stopped; he answered. "Rafe?" Her voice surprised her by coming out cracked.

"Hi, Betty," he said. "How was Philly?"

"How did you know I went?"

"Everybody knows. You have no secrets from us." He stopped joking, sensing that he was frightening her. "Lydia told me." Evan had told her; Rob had told him at work. There was a see-through world of love; her bright house felt transparent. "Was it nice?" Rafe was asking.

"Lovely." She felt she was defending herself. "The city seemed . . . tamer, somehow."

"What did you do?"

"Walked around feeling nostalgic. Went to the museum up on its hill. Rob met me there and we had tea."

"It does sound dear." His voice, by itself, was richer and more relaxed than his physical presence, with its helpless, humiliated clown's air. Her silence obliged him to say more. "Have you had time to look into the book?"

"I love it," she said. "It's so scholarly and calm. I'm reading it very slowly; I want it to last forever."

"Forever seems long."

"You want to see me?" Her voice, involuntarily, had thickened.

His answer was as simple and sharp as his green glance when she had exclaimed, "Shit." "Sure," he said.

"Where? This house feels so conspicuous."

"Come on down here. People go in and out of the building all day long. There's a hairdresser next to me."

"Don't you have any clients?"

"Not till this afternoon."

"Do I dare?"

"I don't know. Do you?" More gently, he added, "You don't have to *do* anything. You just want to *see* me, right? Unfinished business, more or less."

"Yes."

Downtown, an eerie silence pressed through the movement of cars and people. Betty realized she was missing a winter sound from childhood: the song of car chains. Snow tires had suppressed it. Time suppressed everything, if you waited. Rafe's building was a grim brick business "block" built a century ago, when this suburb of Hartford had appeared to have an independent future. An ambitious blazon of granite topped the façade, which might some day be considered historical. The stairs were linoleum and smelled like a rainy-day cloakroom. A whiff of singeing and shampoo came from the door next to his. He was waiting for her in his waiting room, and locked the door. On his sofa, a chill, narrow, and sticky couch of Naugahyde, beneath a wall of leatherbound laws, Rafe proved impotent. The sight of her naked seemed to stun him. Through his daze of embarrassment, he never stopped smiling. And she at him. He was beautiful, so lean and loosely knit, but needed to be nursed into knowing it. "What do you think the matter is?" he asked her.

"You're frightened," she told him. "I don't blame you. I'm a lot to take on."

He nodded, his eyes less green here in this locked, windowless anteroom. "We're going to be a lot of trouble, aren't we?"

"Yes."

"I guess my body is telling us there's still time to back out. Want to?"

On top of one set of bound statutes, their uniform spines forming horizontal streaks like train windows streaming by, lay a different sort of book, a little paperback. In the dim room, where their nakedness was the brightest thing, she made out the title: *Emma*. She answered, "No."

And, though there was much in the aftermath to regret, and a harm that would never cease, Betty remembered these days—the open fields, the dripping eaves, the paintings, the law books—as bright, as a single iridescent unit, not scattered as is a constellation but continuous, a rainbow, a U-turn.

Ethiopia

THE ADDIS ABABA HILTON has a lobby of cool and lustrous stone and a giant, heated, cruciform swimming pool. The cross-shape is plain from the balconies of the ninth-floor rooms, from which also one can see the long white façade of the Emperor's palace. In the other direction, there are acres of tin shacks, and a church on a hill like the nipple on a breast of dust. Emerging from the pool, which feels like layers of rapidly tearing silk, one shivers uncontrollably until dry, though the sun is brilliant, and the sky diamond-pure. The land is high, and the air not humid. One dries quickly. The elevators are swift and silent. From the high floors the white umbrellas on the restaurant tables beside the pool make a rosary of perfect circles. All this is true. What is not true is that Prester John doubles as the desk clerk, and the Queen of Sheba manages the glass-walled gift shop, wherein one can buy tight-woven baskets of multicolored straw, metal mirrors, and Coptic crosses of carved wood costing thousands of Ethiopian dollars, which relate to the American dollar as seven to three.

The young American couple arrived at the hotel very tired, having been ten days in Kenya, where they had seen and photographed lions, leopards, cheetahs, hyraxes, oryxes, dik-diks, steinboks, klipspringers, oribis, topis, kudus, impalas, elands, Thomson's gazelles, Grant's gazelles, hartebeests, wildebeests, waterbucks, bushbucks, zebras, giraffes, flamingos, marabou storks, Masai warriors, baboons, elephants, warthogs, and rhinoceroses—everything hoped for, indeed, except hippos. There had been one asleep in a pool in the Ngorongoro Crater, but it had looked too much like a rock to photograph, and the young man of the American couple had passed it by, confident there would be more. There never were. It had been his only chance to get a hippopotamus on film. Prester John, cool behind his desk of lustrous green marble, divined this, and efficiently, gratuitously arranged that they spend the night away from

Addis Ababa, in the Ethiopian countryside. The countryside was light brown. Distant figures swathed in white trod the tan landscape with the floating step of men trying to steady themselves on a trampoline. But these were women, all beautiful. The beauty of their black faces, glimpsed, lashed the windows of the car like fistfuls of thrown sand. Some carried yellow parasols. Some led white donkeys. A few rode in rubber-wheeled carts, rickety and polychrome, their mouths and nostrils veiled against the dust. He tried to photograph these women, but they turned their heads, and the results would come out blurred.

The hotel was cushioned in bougainvillea and stuffed with Germans. At six o'clock a bus took all the Germans away and the young Americans became the only guests. They walked the blossoming grounds, and looked from their balcony to the brown lake distilled from the tan landscape by a cement dam, and in their room read magazines taken from the hotel lobby—*Ce Soir*, *Il Tempo*, *Sturm und Drang*, the English edition of the official monthly publication of the Polish Chamber of Commerce, the annual handbook of Yugoslavian soccer, the quarterly journal of the Australian Dermatology Association (incorporating *Tasmanian Hides*). "God, I love this country," he announced aloud, letting his magazine sink beside him to the bed.

"Quiet," she said. "I'm reading." The Brazilian edition of *Newsweek*.

"If you ever get tired of reading," he began.

"It's too hot," she said.

"Really? Actually, as evening comes on, in these high, dry countries—"

"Have it your way, then," she said, noisily turning a tissue-thin page. "It's too cold."

There was a knock on the door. It was their driver, asking in his excellent English if they wanted to see the hippopotami before dinner. Yes, they did. Their limousine wound through low, menacing foliage to a sluggish brown river. It seemed empty and scarcely flowing. They walked along a dim path beside the riverbank and met Prester John, barefoot, in rags, and carrying a staff. Though he seemed a shade darker than in his hotel uniform, he was recognizably the same man—small, clever, with beautiful feminine hands and a hurt, monkish, liverish look beneath his eyes. He looked, she thought, like Sammy Davis, Jr.; but, then, so many men in Ethiopia look like Sammy Davis, Jr. Prester John led them to a shaggy point above the river and made a noise of sonorous chuckling deep in his throat—deeper than his throat; his entire body and belly thrummed and resonated with the noise. And then in the dusk little snags appeared in the river current: hippopotamus eyes. As the Americans grew accustomed to the dusk, and the dusk to them, to the eyes were added ears, and the tops of heads appeared above the water, and the bulbous immensity of a back arched upward into a dive. It was a family, a clan, with two babies among them, all calling to one another; their deep soft snorting continued underwater as an unheard, vibrating jubilance. The air became as full of it as the river, one brown world flooded with familial snorting, until the hippopotami had tugged themselves around the bend and into night. Prester John accepted his tip with a bow and the shadow of a genuflexion. The driver was relieved to find his car unharmed in the bushes. Back at the hotel, the young American couple were served dinner in solitary splendor. Unseen hands had prepared a banquet; for all its eerie isolation, the meal was delicious. He wondered how the hotel turned a profit. He thought of sharing the question with his bride, but kept silent. Oh, if only he knew how to talk to her! The silence between them grated the plates and made the silver clash with the fury of swords. His thoughts moved on, to the hippos. If only there had been a notch or two more light! Oh, if only he had brought a longer lens!

Back in Addis, Prester John perceived that they were bored, and arranged to have a party thrown for them. He himself was the host; the Queen of Sheba was the hostess. Her hair was up in the halo of an Afro, and as she moved in her robe of all possible colors her body tapped now here, now there. The rings on her fingers formed a hoard and the little gold circles of her granny glasses gave her eyes a monkish humor. Her blackness was the shade in which God had designed Adam and Eve, a color from which the young American couple felt their own whiteness as a catastrophic falling off, caused helter-skelter by the Northern clime, snow, wolves, camouflage, and the survival of the fittest. The Queen of Sheba introduced them to beautiful, static people whose titles of courtesy were Ato, Woizero, and Woizerit. A Woizerits was unmarried. It seemed an elaborate way to say it. Also elaborately, the Emperor was never referred to but as His Imperial Majesty, which became HIM.

"... until we are rid of HIM ..."

"... the latest story about HIM ..."

"I understand," the young American said to a stately Woizerit who had studied three years at the University of Iowa, "you're in television."

Prester John gracefully interceded. "This lovely lady," he said, "*is* Ethiopian television." His magical feminine hand turned a dial, and there she was, giving news about the latest Palestinian hijacking.

"Hitler," a swarthy but handsome gentleman was telling the young

American wife, "had the correct idea but was not permitted to complete it. A vivid proof of God's non-existence."

"Suppose I told you," she said, "I was Jewish?"

He surveyed her face, and then her blond body, lovingly. "It would not lessen," he told her, "my reverence for Hitler." But reverence for her was what he expressed, for he clung pinchingly to her arm as if she had consented to join him in some superb indecency.

Her husband had found a fellow-American, a pale-brown Black woman from Detroit, in the pay of the American Embassy. They huddled close together, sharing remembrance of that remote exotic land of Lincoln Continentals and Drake's Cakes. "You happy here?" he asked at last.

"It'll do," she said, shrugging and, obliged to elaborate on the shrug, adding, "I can't get servants. They're very polite, and I offer top dollar, but the Ethiopians will not work for me."

"But why not?"

Seeing that he truly didn't know, very graciously she made a little gesture as if parting curtains, disclosing—herself. Seeing that he still didn't know, she elaborated, "They have this racial hang-up. They keep telling you how Semitic they are."

The Queen of Sheba clapped her hands imperiously. No Westerner could have produced that sound, as if with blocks of wood: worlds of body language are being lost. The guests sat to eat around great multicolored baskets lined with a delicious rubbery bread. One ate by tearing off pieces and seizing food as if picking up coals with a pot holder. The young Americans were delighted to be engaging in a custom. Prester John admired their pragmatism. His voice was high, reedy, and not accidentally unpleasant. "I would not want to say," he said, "the many negative things I could say about America. But you have done this one thing of genius. The credit card. Money without money. That is a thing truly revolutionary. The world is thus transformed, while the political philosophers amuse one another."

"Is that what you do? I mean, are you a political scientist? A teacher?" The American was not sure this was still Prester John—he seemed frailer, edgier.

"What do I do? I read Proust, over and over. And I write."

"Could I read your books?" the American wife chimed in, from across the basket, at whose rim the admirer of Hitler was showing her how to eat raw meat, an Ethiopian delicacy.

"No," was the response, said caressingly. "In Ethiopia, there is no publishing."

"You understand," the television Woizerit murmured on the American's other side. "HIM."

"I write and I write," the frail clever host elaborated, "and then I read it all aloud to one special friend. And then I destroy it. All."

"How terrible. Is that friend here?"

"No." He smiled, forming a little prayer tent with his hands. He was certainly Prester John. A medieval face twitched in his midnight skin. "Do not eat raw meat. The uninitiated vomit for days." He relaxed, slumped in his gaudy robes. "Yes." His voice went high again, reedy, mockingly informative. "In this ancient kingdom, misplaced to Africa, we have been compelled to raise the art of living to the point of the tenuous."

Though the party was gathering strength, the young Americans were tired. The Queen of Sheba and Prester John insisted on accompanying them back to the hotel, since marauders roam the slums with impunity; the poverty is acute despite massive infusions of American aid, corruption and reaction reign here as everywhere save China, not even one's driver of twenty years' service can be trusted, terrorists on behalf of Eritrean independence are ubiquitous. A curious optical effect: in the darkness within the car, the two legendary Ethiopians disappeared but for their clothes, which rustled with utmost courtesy, and but for their words, paraphrased above. Nevertheless, a disturbing and flattering possibility, indecent yet not impractical, communicated itself to the minds of their guests, as through layers of fluttering, tearing silk. In the cool lobby their shouted farewells echoed of disappointment. Oh, what *was* the custom?

In his twin bed on the ninth floor, the man of the young couple thought, The Queen of Sheba, black yet not Black, boyoboyoboy. Mine, she could be mine, as the darkness inside me is mine, as the spangled night sky is mine. God, I love this country. The jewels. The arid height. The Hilton corridors of greenish stone. The tiny dried-up Emperor. The bracing sense of never having been colonized by any European power. How long and lustrous her ebony limbs would feel in the darkness. But I might disappoint her. I might feel lost in her. She might mock me. My sickly pallor. My Free World hang-ups. Better simply snap her picture when she undresses. But the flash batteries died in the Serengeti, that night by the water hole. Darn it! Her breasts. Armpits. Belly. Down, down he is led from one dusky thought to the next. Travel is so sexy. Would the granny glasses come off first, or last?

And beside him his fair wife on her twin bed thinks of airplanes. She dreads flying, especially in Ethiopia, with its high escarpments, small national budget, daredevil pilots trained by Alitalia. Perhaps, if she slept with Prester John, by one of his miracles he could prevent her plane from crashing. Sleeping with men, especially black men, more fancy than fact, if they gave women decent educations they could think about something else. But still . . . His wicked ascetic smile and look of monkish sorrow did cut into her. In the car, his touch, or a fold of his silken robe, accidentally? If he could guarantee on a stack of Bibles the plane wouldn't crash . . . The dedicated hijackers with stockings over their faces, the sudden revolver shots from the security guards disguised as Lebanese businessmen, the rush of air, the lurch above the clouds, the inane patter of the brave stewardesses, the lurid burst of flame from the port engine, the long slow nightmare fall, the mile-wide splash of char on the earth, the scattered suitcases . . . Oh God yes, I'll do anything you want, consider me your slave, your toy. For without life how can there be virtue?

Because of security checks, one must appear at the airport two and a half hours before scheduled departure time. The young American is in the glass-walled hotel shop, dickering with the Queen of Sheba for a Coptic cross. He has reduced her price to fourteen hundred Ethiopian dollars, which is no longer divisible by seven in his head, because of the most recent American dollar devaluation. Fourteen hundred divided by two and one-third minus a little . . . She is bored. The Queen of Sheba thrusts a retractable ballpoint into her towering teased coiffure, and her ebony fingers drum with surprising percussive effect on a glass case. Her nose is straight, her nostrils are narrow. She sighs. These Americans, rendered insubstantial by rising gold, like drops of water running from the back of an aroused crocodile. He asks, will she accept a credit card?

Prester John appears, in shabby livery, with the young American wife in tow. She is flushed, pink, sleepy. Though the lobby is cool, blond ringlets cling to her brow. Hurry, the clever little black man says, you must see the monastery, there is just time before the airplane, it has been arranged.

Trailing protests like dust, the young American is led through the lobby, away from his luggage. It is not the usual limousine this time but a little red Fiat. Prester John does not seem to understand the gears. As he grapples with them, he looks comically like Sammy Davis, Jr. They head out of the city, uphill; the paved road becomes dirt. Prester John gossips nervously about the Queen of Sheba. "She is a magnificent woman, but thoroughly Oriental. I enjoy her loyalty, yet am vexed by, how shall I say, the lack of *stereo* in her sensibility. She cannot lift her thoughts above jewelry, lechery, and airbases. My intention was to irradiate her with Christian faith, fresh, even raw, from the desert Fathers—to make, here, upon this plateau, a dream to solace the tormented sleep of Europe. Instead, she has made of it something impossibly heavy, a mere fact, like the Catholicism of Ireland, or the Communism of Albania." He cannot move the gearshift above second gear, so thus roaring they proceed up a dirt road transected by ridges of rock like the backs of sleeping hippopotami. At first, clouds of people in white had rimmed the roadway; now they meet, and swerve to avoid, intermittent donkeys and women staggering beneath wide bundles of little trees. One of these women, bent double like a scorpion, in rags, her feet bare, with long, dark heels and pale, cracked soles, looks familiar; the American turns in his seat. Dust obscures his view. He is certain only that she was not wearing her granny glasses.

Prester John sweats, embarrassed. The road is all rocks now, tan, with a white dusting. "I am growing worried," he confesses, "about your airplane. It is possible I underestimated the difficulty." He stops the car where the view falls away on one side. The Hilton pool twinkles like a dim star far below them. On the other side, stony sere pastures mount to a copse of viridian trees. Between the trees peep ruddy hints of a long wall. That is the monastery. "Perhaps," Prester John offers nervously, "a photograph? I am profoundly sorry; the road, and these recalcitrant gears . . ."

What the young American sees through his finder looks exactly like the sepia illustrations in his Sunday-school Bible. He sets the lens at infinity and snaps the shutter. But his inward attention is upon his wife, for her calmness, as their next airplane flight draws nearer, puzzles him. Prester John grindingly backs the Fiat around and hurtles downward along the cruel road of rocks; she lightly smiles and with dusty fingertips brushes back the hair from her drying brow. She feels she is already on the airplane—all of Ethiopia is an airplane, thousands of feet above sea level; and it cannot crash. This is true.

Transaction

IN DECEMBER of the year 197–, in the city of N——, a man of forty was walking toward his hotel close to the hour of midnight. The conference that had kept him in town had dispersed; he was more than a touch drunk; in his arms he carried Christmas presents for his loved ones— wife, children. At the edge of the pavement, beneath his eyes, bloomed painted young women, standing against the darkened shop fronts in attitudes that mingled expectancy and insouciance, vulnerability and guardedness, solitude and solidarity. A scattered army, was his impression, mustering half-heartedly in retreat. Neon syllables glowed behind them; an unlit sign, MASSAGE PARLOR, hung at second-story level, and his face, uptilted, received an impression of steam, though the night was as cold as the spaces between the stars.

A large Negress in a white fur coat drew abreast of him at a red light, humming. His eyes slid toward her; her humming increased in volume, was swelled from underneath, by a taunting suggestion of *la-di-da*, into almost a song. Fear fingered his heart. He shifted his paper Christmas bags to make a shield between him and this sudden, fur-coated, white-booted, melodious big body. The light broke; under the permission of green he crossed the avenue known as T—— and walked up the hard, faintly tugging slant of sidewalk that would lead him to the voluminous anonymity of his hotel, the rank of silver elevator doors, the expectant emptiness of his room.

A glass office building floated above his shoulder, silent as an ice floe. Amid this deathly gray of winter and stone, a glistening confusion of contrary possibility was born in him, an incipient nest of color. In the unlit grated window of a corner drugstore, cardboard Magi were bringing their gifts. He turned left and circled the block, though his arms ached with his packages and his feet with the cold.

The routed but raffish army of females still occupied their corner and dim doorways beyond. Our passerby hesitated on the corner diagonally opposite, where in daytime a bank reigned amid a busy traffic of supplicants and emissaries, only to become at nightfall its own sealed mausoleum. He saw the prettiest of the girls, her white face a luminous child's beneath its clownish dabs of rouge and green, approached by an evidently self-esteeming young man, a rising insurance agent or racketeer, whose flared trouser-legs protruded beneath a camel-colored topcoat, correctly short. He talked to the girl earnestly; she listened; she looked diagonally upward as if to estimate something in the aspiring architecture above her; she shook her head. He repeated his proposition, bending forward engagingly; she backed away; he smartly turned and walked off.

Had it been a pack of schoolchildren, the others would have crowded around her, eager for details. But the other women ignored her, maintaining each her own vigil.

Seeing an approach having been made emboldened our onlooker to cross to their side of the avenue and to walk through the cloud of them again. His packages perhaps betrayed him; he was a comet returning. They recognized him. He felt caught up, for all the seasonal good will in his heart, in a warfare of caution and invisibility. His breath held taut against some fantastic hazard, he passed through the prime concentration, centered upon the luminous face of the child beauty. Only when the cloud thinned did he dare glance sideways, at an apparition in a doorway, who, the glance told him, was far from pretty—bony, her narrow face schoolteacherishly beaked—but who, even as he reproached himself, did accept his signal.

"Hi," she said. A toothy white smile suddenly slashed the doorway shadows. With triggered quickness she came forward from her niche and at the same mechanical speed inserted her hand in the crevice between his body and his arm, among the rustling bags decorated with bells, conifers, snowmen.

He answered, "Hi." He felt his voice dip deep into a treasure of composure, warmth, even power. Her touch was an immense relief.

"Thirty O.K.?" she asked in a rapid whisper.

"Sure." The back of his throat itched with silliness, which rose to counter the humorless, slithering urgency of her question.

She posed another: "You got a place?"

He named the hotel, the R——, fearing it told too much about him— solid, square, past its prime.

Indeed, the name did seem to amuse her, for she repeated it, skipping with the same breath to put herself in step with him and tightening her grip on his arm. His clothes, layer upon layer, felt transparent. He plaintively accused, "You don't like my hotel."

"Why wouldn't I?" she asked, with that intimidating, soft-voiced rapidity. He saw that the stratagems, the coaxing ironies useful and instinctive in his usual life, would have small application in this encounter. I produce, you produce. Provocation had zero value.

He wanted to do the right thing. Would she expect to be taken to a bar? He had already drunk, he estimated, more than enough. And wouldn't it be to her profit to go to his room promptly and be done? She was a treasure so clumsily wrapped as to be of indeterminate size. Experimentally, he turned left, as on his prior circuit; she did not resist; together they crossed the avenue and climbed the hard little slant of pavement he had climbed before. Her grip tightened on his arm; he felt a smile break the mask of cold on his face. He was her prize; she, his. She asked, "What's your name?"

Amid his sensations of cold and alcohol and pleasure at this body warm and strange and tugging against his, he imagined his real name would break the spell. He lied, "Ed."

She repeated it, as she had the name of the hotel, testing it in her mouth. Many names had passed through her mouth. Her voice, it seemed to him, had an East Coast edge without being indigenous to N——. She volunteered, "Mine's Ann."

He was touched to sense that she was not lying. He said, "Hello, Ann."

"Hello." She squeezed his arm, so his mind's eye saw his bones. "What do you do, travel for some company?" Her question and answer were one.

"Sure," he said, and changed the subject. "Am I walking too fast for you?" Something chalklike was coating his words. He mustn't, he told himself, be frightened of this woman; his fright would not serve either of them. Yet her presence nearly submerged his spirit in wonder. She loomed without perspective, like an abutment frozen in the headlights the moment after a car goes out of control. He glanced at her obliquely. City light had soaked into her face. Her long nose looked waxen. She was taller than the average woman, though still shorter than he. In his elementary school there had been a once-a-week penmanship teacher who had seemed ageless to him then but whose bony ranginess when she was young would have resembled Ann's.

She answered carefully. "No. You're walking fine. Who are the presents for?"

His own question, he felt, had been subtly mocked. He answered hers mockingly: "People."

They did not talk again for some minutes.

The little paved rise crested. His hotel filled the block before them. In its grid of windows some burned; most were dark. Midnight had passed. The great building blazed erratically, like a ship going down. He said, "There's a side entrance up this way." She may have known this, but didn't indicate so. Had she been here before? Often? He could have asked, but did not; he did not ask, in retrospect, so many questions she might have willingly answered. For women, it turns out, always in retrospect, were waiting to be asked.

The side entrance was locked. The revolving door was chained.

Against them? Not only was Ed a stranger to the etiquette of prostitution, but hotels puzzled him. Was a hotel merely a store that sells rooms, or is it our watchdog and judge, with private detectives eyeing every corridor through dummy fire extinguishers, and lawyers ready to spring from the linen closets barking definitions of legal occupancy? They had to walk, Ann and Ed, another half-block in the interstellar cold and to brave the front entrance. The maroon-capped doorman, blowing on his hands, let them pass as if by a deliberate oversight. Mounting the stairs to the lobby, Ed was aware of the brass rods, slimmer than jet trails, more polished than presentation pens, that held the red carpet to the marble. He was aware of the warmth flowing down from the lobby and of, visible beneath her black maxicoat as she preceded him by a step, tall laced boots of purple suede. The lobby was calm. The cigar stand was shrouded for the night. Behind the main desk, men murmured into telephones and transposed coded numerals with the muffled authority of Houston manipulating a spacecraft. A few men in square gray suits, travelling men, rumpled but reluctant to be launched toward bed, stood about beneath the chandeliers. With his crackling packages and his bought woman packaged in black maxi and laced boots, Ed felt disadvantageously encumbered. His eyes rigidly ahead, he crossed to the elevator doors of quilted colorless metal. He pushed the Up button. The wait built tall in his throat before an arriving car flung back a door. It was theirs. No one at the control desk looked up. At the last second, as the doors sighed to close, two men in gray pushed in with them, and stared at Ann, and smiled. One man began to hum, like the Negress on the street.

Didn't Ann look like a wife? Didn't all young women dress like whores these days? She was plain, plainly dressed, severe, and pale. He could not quite look at her, or venture a remark, even as he inched closer to protect her from the strangers' gazing. The elevator grew suffocating with the exhalations of masculinity, masculinity inflated by booze. The humming grew louder, and plainly humorous. Perhaps an apparent age-difference had betrayed them, though Ed had always been told, by those who loved him, that he looked young for his years. One man shifted his weight. The other cleared his throat. Ed lifted his eyes to the indicator glow, as it progressed through the numbers 4, 5, and 6 and, after a yawning interval in which assault and murder might have been committed, halted at 7, his floor. As the two of them stepped out, she halted, not knowing whether to turn right or left. One of the men behind them called musically, "Good night."

Bastard. Buy your own whore.

"To the left," he told her, when the elevator door had sucked shut. In a mirror set diagonally where the corridor turned, he imagined a spectator, a paid moral agent of some sort, watching them approach the turning. Then, after they turned, the agent—with his fat cigar and tinfoil badge—was transposed in a magical knight's move to where they had been, now watching them recede, Ed's back eclipsing his packages. Ann's maxi swung stiffly, a cloth bell tolling the corridor's guilty silence.

The key balked at fitting. He could not open the door to his room, which he had paid for. Struggling, blushing, he dropped a package, which his companion stooped to retrieve. That was good of her. This service free of charge. The key turned. The door opened into a dark still space as tidy and kind as a servant waiting up.

He held open the door for Ann to precede him, and in this gesture discovered his mood: mock courtesy. The hotel corridor, with its walls of no certain color and its carpet cut from an endless artificial tundra of maroon, somehow came with her, past his nose, into the room. The pallor of her face, momentarily huge, bounced his gaze to the window, its rectangle of diffuse city light flayed by venetian blinds. As his eyes adjusted, the walls glowed. The package she had retrieved she set down on the gleam of a glass bureau top. He set the other packages down beside it; his arm ached in relief. He found the wall switch, but the overhead light was too bright. He could not look at her in such bright light. He brushed the switch off and groped at the base of the large ceramic lamp standing on the bureau top. This light, softer, showed her a distance away, standing by the bed, her hand on the second button of her long dark coat, undoing it; by this gesture of undoing she transposed his sense of her as packaged from the coat to the room itself, to the opaque plaster walls that contained her, to the fussy ceiling fixture like the bow at the top of a box. She was his, something he had bought. Yet she was alive, a person, unpredictable, scarcely approachable indeed. For his impulse to kiss her was balked by unstated barriers, a professional prohibition she radiated even as she smiled again that unexpected slash of a toothy smile and, after hesitating, as she had when stepping from the elevator door, handed him her coat—heavy, chill, black—to hang in the closet, which he did happily, his courtesy not altogether mock.

He turned. Who are you? he asked her, within himself. His apprehensions ricocheted confusedly, in the room's small space, off this other, who, standing in its center, simultaneously rendered it larger and many-sided and yet more shallow, as if she were a column faced with little mirrors. He stood motionless, perhaps also a column faced with mirrors—as in ballrooms, theatre lobbies, roller-skating rinks. Absurd, of course, to place two such glittering pillars so close together in so modest a room; but, then, perhaps in just such disproportion does sex loom amid the standardized furniture of our lives.

She moved a step. Something spilling from one of the packages attracted her: a book. She pulled it forth; it was Blake's *Auguries of Innocence*, illustrated by Leonard Baskin woodcuts—a present for his wife, who in the early years of their marriage used to carve a woodcut as their annual Christmas card. Ann opened the pages, and the look of poetry on the page surprised her. "What's it about?" she asked.

"Oh," he said. "It's about everything, in a way. About seeing a world in a grain of sand, and Heaven in a wild flower." He heard a curious, invariable delay in the answers they made each other: tennis with sponge rackets. It might have been his thicknesses of alcohol. The brandy had been the worst mistake.

She let a page turn itself under her fingers, idle. "I used to work in a library."

"Where?" Under cover of her apparent interest in the book, he moved two steps to be behind her, and touched the zipper at the back of her sweater. It was magenta, wool, a turtleneck, somehow collegiate in quality, perhaps borrowing this quality from their bookish conversation. He thought of pulling the zipper and gingerly didn't dare; he thought of how, with any unbought woman, in such a sealed-off midnight room, hands and lips would have rushed into the vacuum of each other's flesh, sliding through clothes, ravenous for skin.

She answered his question reluctantly, not lifting her attention from the book. "In Rhode Island."

"What town?"

Her attention lifted. "You know Rhode Island?"

"A little. We used to have some friends we'd visit in Warwick."

"The library was in Pawtucket."

"What's Pawtucket like?"

She said, "Not bad. It's not all as ugly as what you see from Route One."

He pulled down her zipper, a little pink zipper, enough to let her head slip through. Her cervical vertebrae and some down at her neck's nape were bared. "Did you like it," he asked, "working in the library?" Under his fingertips her nape down tingled; he felt her expecting him to ask how she had got from the library into this profession. He refused to ask, discovering a second mood, after mock courtesy, of refusal. For hadn't she, silently, by some barrier in her manner, refused him a kiss?

She moved away from his touch. "Yeah, I did." She was young and lean, he saw, a brunette, her hair crimpy and careless and long. Not only her nose but her teeth were too big, so that her lips, in fitting over them, took on an earnest, purposeful expression; she appeared to him, again, as a schoolteacher, with a teacher's power of rebuke. He laughed, rebelling— laughed at her moving away from him so pensively. As the outdoor cold melted out of his body, the alcohol blossomed into silliness, foaming out of him like popcorn from a popper. Acting the bad boy, he pulled off his overcoat, suit coat, and tie; ashamed of his silliness and the fear it confessed, he went toward her as if for an embrace but instead tugged the hem of her sweater out of her skirt and pulled it upward. Understanding, surrendering, she shook her head to loosen her hair and raised her arms; the sweater came free. Lifting it from her hands, he saw she had long oval nails, painted with clear polish. Her bra was severely white, hospital-plain. This surprised him, in an era when even the primmest of suburban women wore coquettish, lace-trimmed underwear. And he was additionally surprised that, though his whore's shoulders were bony and bore the same glazed pallor as her face, her breasts were a good size, and firm. Amid the interlock of these small revelations an element clicked apart and permitted him to place his arms around her hard shoulders and tighten them so that the winter chill and stony scent of her hair flowed from the top of her head into his nostrils. His voice leaped from the cliff of her tingling hair; he asked, "You want your thirty now or after?"

"Whichever," she said, then—a concession, her first, possibly squeezed from her by alarm, for his extreme reasonableness did, he perceived, resemble insanity—"after."

"So you're a librarian," he sighed.

His relief must have been too huge, too warm; she pushed his chest away with iron fingertips. "Why don't you go into the bathroom," she suggested, using a disciplinarian's deceptive softness of tone, "and"—she lightly tapped his fly with the back of her hand—"wash them up."

Them! The idea of designating his genitals a population, a little gabbling conclave of three, made his silliness soar and his complementary mood of refusal deepen, darken toward cruelty. With the deliberateness of an insult or of a routine of marriage he sat in the hotel armchair and took off his shoes and socks, tucking the socks in the shoes. Then he stood and, insolent but for the trembling of his fingers and the wave of alcohol tipping him forward, unbuttoned his shirt, pulled off his undershirt, managed the high-wire two-step of trouser removal. He was aware of her motionless by the bed, but could not look directly at her, to gauge the image she was reflecting, or to catch a glimmer of himself. She was a pillar of black facets. A wave of alcohol must then have broken over him, for he lost her entirely, and found himself standing naked before the bathroom basin, on tiptoe, soaping his genitals above the lunar radiance of its porcelain and still smiling at the idea of calling them *them.*

As he washed, the concepts her directive had planted—dirt, germs, disease, spoilage—infiltrated the lathery pleasure, underminingly. His tumescence, he observed, was slight. He rinsed, splashing cold water with a cupped hand, dried himself with a towel, tucked the towel modestly about his waist, and walked out into the other room.

Ann was naked but for her boots. Purple suede, they were laced up to her knees. Were they too tedious to unlace? Was this a conventional turn-on? A put-down? An immense obscure etiquette whose principles hulked out of the city night to crowd them into this narrow space of possible behavior blocked him from asking why she had kept them on or whether she might take them off. As if another woman in undressing had revealed a constellation of moles or a long belly scar, he was silent, and accepted the boots along with the slim waxen whiteness of the rest of her, a milk snake with one black triangular marking.

He had worn the towel as provocation, hoping she might untuck it for him. His current mistress, most graciously, unlaced his shoes, and stayed on her knees. But Ann's sole move was to tuck back her hair as if to keep it clear of the impending spatter of dirty business. He let his towel drop and held her, with no more pressure than causes a stamp to adhere to an envelope. He in bare feet, she still in boots, they came closer in height than on the street, and his prick touched her belly just above the black triangle. She backed off sharply: "You're icy!"

"I washed like you told me to."

"You could have used warm water."

"I did, I thought."

She bent down, but to pick up the towel. She handed it to him. "Dry yourself, can't you?"

"Jesus, you're fussy." He must counterattack. "How about you?" he asked. "Don't you want to use the bathroom?"

"No."

"Don't you need to go wee-wee or anything, standing around on the street for hours?"

"No, thank you."

"It's a perfectly good bathroom."

Just when he had figured her as mechanically one-track, she changed her mind. "O.K. I will." She went into the bathroom. She closed the door! So he couldn't watch. No free pleasures, he saw, was one of the rules. Naked, he sat on the bed, picked the Blake from the bureau top, and read,

> The Lamb misus'd breeds Public strife
> And yet forgives the Butcher's Knife.
> The Bat that flits at close of Eve
> Has left the Brain that won't Believe.

The toilet flushed; the faucets purred. She emerged still wearing those bothersome, unlovely boots, and gave his limp penis a glance he thought scornful. Only the alcohol helped him ask, "Want to lie down?"

Without voicing assent, she sat on the bed stiffly and let herself be pulled horizontal. Her skin felt too young, too firm and smooth. Passing his hands down the mathematically perfect curves of her sides and buttocks, he calculated that the journey of happiness from these hands into his head and from there down his spine to his prick was, rendered tenuous and errant by his drunkenness, too long. He stroked her breasts, so firmly and finely tipped as to feel conical. His sense of breasts had been shaped by his overflowing wife. Once when she was nursing one of their babies he had sucked a mouthful of milk from her and, not swallowing, filled her own mouth with it, so she, too, could know the taste. By comparison this kid's tits were so firm as to feel unkind. Her belly was flat, with the sheen of a tabletop beneath his fingers, and the hair of her pussy was thick, stiff, brushlike. The first time he had slept with a woman not his wife, she had been a mutual friend, a shy and guilty woman who had undressed out of sight and come back to him wearing her slip over nothing; touched, her pussy beneath the nylon had been so startlingly soft he had exclaimed, "Oh," and she with him—"*Oh!*"—as if together on a walk they had simultaneously sighted a rare flower, or a sun-splashed bed of moss.

Ann, stroked, took this as the signal to set her own hand, cool and unfeeling, on his prick. Too rapidly she twitched the loose skin back and forth; he huddled inside his drunkenness and giggled.

"What's so funny?" she asked.

"You're so nice," he lied. It came to him that the part-time penmanship teacher would sometimes touch him, reaching over his shoulder to roughly grab his wrist and push and pull his hand back and forth to give him the idea of not writing with his wrist and fingers but with his forearm.

Ann sat up to continue with better leverage her attack on his prick. It tickled, twittered, and stung; his consciousness drew back, higher, as a man climbs higher into the bleachers for a more analytical view of the game. Either this girl had no aptitude for her profession, or love cannot be aped. She flicked her head haughtily, stopped her futile agitation of his penis, put her mouth to his ear, and whispered with that slithering urgency she affected, "Do you like me?"

"Sure."

"Well, *look* at it." She flipped it. He looked. It lay sideways, enviably asleep. She asked, "How long do you expect me to keep at it?"

"Not long," he said pleasantly; her fingers, inert, felt pleasant. "You can go now. I'll get you your thirty dollars. Sorry I'm such a flop."

Her face, softer in shadow, pondered. "Ed, look. I'll stay, but it'll take a little more."

"How much more, for how long?" The prompt specificity of his question took her aback. He helped her, though he was new at this and she wasn't. "How about one hour," he proposed, "for thirty more? In an hour the drinks should wear off enough so I can get it up. I'm sorry, I'd like to fuck you, I really would."

Displeasingly, her whisper hoarsened, becoming theatrical, seductive. "How about being Frenched? Like that? For twenty more I'll French you. Would you like that, Ed?"

Naked and lazy, he shifted position on the bed. Impotent or not, he was the boss. In daylight transactions he hated haggling; but this was different. She was so young she could be teased. Her youth furthermore made her an enemy. For this was the era of student revolts, of contempt for the old virtues, of energy-worship. "Twenty more!" he protested. "That makes eighty all told. You'll bankrupt me. Why would a nice girl like you want to come in off the street and bankrupt some poor john?"

She ignored his irony, asking with her closest approximation to true excitement, "How much cash you got?"

"Want me to count it?"

"Don't you *know?*"

"Like I said, I was Christmas shopping. Jesus. Hold on. Don't go away mad."

He hoisted himself from the bed, located his pants draped on the back of the plush-covered armchair, found the wallet within them, and counted the bills. One hundred ten, one twenty, twenty-two, three. "O.K.," he told her. "Eighty-four dollars total. I can just spare eighty. That's for one hour, starting now, not when you came in, and including you Frenching me. Agreed?"

"O.K."

He considered asking that she remove her boots in the bargain; but he feared she would put a price on that, and, though he could inflict upon her the suspense of haggling, he would always end, he knew, by meeting her price. Also, there was a mystery about the boots that made him squeamish. To watch him count his money, Ann had lifted herself on the bed, up on her knees like a little girl playing jacks. Ed touched her cold shoulder, silently bidding her to hold the position, and then fit himself into her pose so a nipple met his mouth. He lapped, sucked, rubbed. She said, "Ow."

He removed his mouth an inch. "What do you mean, 'Ow'?"

"Didn't you shave today?"

"Not since this morning. Can you notice?"

"*Feel* it," she said.

He rubbed his own chin and upper lip. "That can't hurt," he told her. "It does."

He looked up, and her face and torso held a stillness that for the first time, it seemed to his sheepish sense, admitted a glimmer of erotic heat into the frozen space between them. Since he could not impress her by anger, not being angry, nor by being himself, since he had sold himself short by applying to her at all, he would act out compliance. He would overwhelm her with docility. "I'll go shave, then."

She did not object.

He asked, before moving, "Will the shaving time come out of my hour?"

She said, not even audibly bored, her voice was so flat, "If you're going to do it, Ed, do it."

Standing again above the basin's bright moon, he felt his genitals stir, sweeten, with the idea of it: the idea of shaving, so domestically, to oblige this ungrateful stringy whore in the next room, street-cold still clinging to her skin. When he returned, his cheeks gleaming, his loins bobbling, she observed his excitement and in an act of swift capture produced from somewhere (her boot?) a prophylactic and snapped it into place around his semi-erect prick and lay on her back with legs spread. Though he held stiff enough to enter her and momentarily think, *I'm fucking this woman*, the scent and pinch of rubber, and an inelasticity within her, and something unready and resentful in himself—*and she couldn't care less*, was the successor thought—combined to dwindle him. His few dud thrusts were like blank explosions by whose flash he exposed the full extent of their interlocked abasement. Apologetically, he withdrew, and tugged off the condom and, not knowing upon what hotel surface he could place it without offending her stern standards of hygiene, held the limp little second skin dangling in his hand as he stretched out sorrowfully beside her defeated female form. "Those things cost, you know," she said.

What shall we do? Ann lay in a sulk, but he imagined a rift in the surface of her impatience, a ledge to which he might cling. With his free hand (the other arm tucked back under his head so the condom hung cleanly over the edge of the bed) he stroked the long cold curve of her side, illumined by the window with Venetian blinds. He told her, "You're gorgeous."

As if equivalently, she asked him, "You married?"

"Sure." She might have thought this was the door, at last, to the confident intimacy between them that he, she must now realize, needed. But it opened instead on a cul-de-sac, the marriage that had put them here; they lay inside his wife's sexual nature as in a padded, bolted dungeon. Ed could have attempted to share this vision with Ann, but attempted more simply to return the friendliness she seemed now willing, if only out of fear of being trapped with him forever, to concede. He asked her, "How old are you?"

"Twenty-two." A new tone, bitter. Did she feel so soon blighted, hopelessly fallen? Her beakish, colorless profile lifted above him, into the square cloud of light leaking from the circumambient city. "You?"

"Fortyish."

"The prime of life."

"Depends." He rubbed his mouth across her nipples, then his cheek, asking, "That smooth enough?"

"It's better."

"You like it? I mean, normally, does it leave you cold, turn you off, or what?"

She didn't answer; he had trespassed, he realized, into another dark clause of their contract: her pleasure was not at issue. Able to do no right, and therefore no wrong, he slid his face from her breast to her belly and, as she lay back, past her wiry pubic bush to her thigh. He rested his head there. He laid the condom on the sheet beside her waist and with his hands parted her thighs; she complied guardedly. An edge of one boot scraped his ear as he moved his head back, as when reading a telephone book, to see better. Between her legs lay darkness. He stroked her mons veneris, and the tendoned furred hollows on either side; he ran his thumb the length of her labia, parted them, softly sank his thumb in the cleft in which, against all tides of propriety and reasonableness, a little moisture was welling. He withdrew his thumb and inserted his middle finger, his thumb finding socket on her anus.

The diffuse light was gathering to his eyes now, and he saw the silver plane of the inner thigh turned to the window, and the same light sliding on his tapering forearm and moving wrist, and the two bright round corners of her buttocks beneath, and the pale meadow of her foreshortened belly, the taut hills of her breasts, the far underside of her chin. From the angle of her chin she was gazing out the window, at the strange night sky of N——, like the sky of no other city, brown and golden, starless, permeated with the aureole of its own swamp-fire static. Through the warp and blur of alcohol the inner configurations of her cunt, the granular walls, the elusive slippery hooded central hardness, began to cut an image in his mind, and to give him a jeweller's intent, steady joy.

She spoke. Her voice floated hoarse across the silver terrain of her body. Her words were most surprising. "Do you ever," she asked, hesitating before finishing, "use your tongue?"

"Sure," he said.

Bending his face to her aperture, he felt blow through his skull the wind of all those who had passed this way before him. Yet, though no doubt men had flooded this space with their spunk and Heaven knew what perversities had been visited upon her by strangers struggling to feel alive, her cunt did not taste of anything; it was clean of any scent, even that of deodorant, and its surround of brushlike hair had the prickly innocence of a child's haircut or of the pelt of a young nocturnal omnivore such as a raccoon. He regretted that in the politics of their positioning his mouth did not come at it upside down but more awkwardly, frontally, with his body trailing between and beyond her legs like an unusably heavy kite tail, and with his neck bent back to the point of aching. Seeking to penetrate, his tongue tensed behind it the entire length of his spine. Opening his eyes, he saw a confused wealth of light-struck filaments that might be vegetation on Mars, or mildew under the microscope.

A miracle, she seemed to be moving. In response. She was. She was heaving her hips to help his tongue go deeper. He suspected a put-on. He was willing to believe that he could arouse his shy, plump mistress: he was a popularizer of astronomy and she his research assistant, and when she would swing her crotch around to his face its spread wet halves would swamp his consciousness like a star map of both hemispheres, not only the stars one saw but the Southern constellations—Lupus, Phoenix, Fornax. But this waxen street-lily surely was beyond him, another galaxy, far out. Yet the girl lifted her pelvis and rotated it and forcefully sighed. She had been so unemphatic and forbidding in all else, he doubted she would fake this. The thought that he was giving her pleasure invited cruelty, as a clean sheet invites mussing. His prick was becoming a weapon; in the air beyond the foot of the bed he felt it enlarging, presenting more surface to the air. He pulled himself up, still drunker than he should be, his shaved chin wet with her, and asked, "Didn't you say you'd French me?"

As if abruptly awakened, Ann seemed to find her body heavy. She pushed her weight up onto her arms as he relaxed his length into the trough of warmth she had left on the narrow, single bed. She tucked back her hair from her temples. She straightened his stiffened prick with her fingers and bent her lips to the glans. Her lips made a silent *O* as he pushed up. Her head bobbed in and out of the cloud of light. She moved her mouth up and down as rapidly and ruthlessly as she had her hand; he watched with drowsy amazement, wondering what book of instructions she had read. This fanciful impression, that she had learned to perform this service from a manual and was performing it mechanically, an application of purely exterior knowledge, with none of the empathy for the other sex that Eros in blindness bestows, excited him, so he did not lose his erection to his schoolmarm's rote blowing. How many times a night did she do this? He saw, dismally but indulgently, his prick as a product, mass-produced and mass-consumed in a few monotonous ways. Poor dear child. With a distant affection he let his fingertips drift to one nipple and followed its sympathetic rise and fall; so Galileo followed the rhythmic radiance of Jupiter's revolving satellites. Hard and small and perfect and glossy and cool, her nipple. Hers, an outpost of her nervous system. He was growing accustomed to her, her temperature, texture, manner, pulse, and saliva. His hard prick glittered when her profile did not eclipse it.

Time slipped by for him, but a meter in her head told her she had Frenched twenty dollars' worth. Swiftly, as a fisherman transfers the kicking fish to the net, she lifted the circle of her lips from his phallus, retrieved the condom from the bedsheet, deftly rerolled it, slipped it down upon his cock, and set herself astride, handsome and voracious in silhouette. She told him, with a trace of her old slithering, too-practiced urgency—modified in tone, however, by something unpracticed, young, experimental, and actually interested—"We'll try it with me on top." She lowered herself carefully, and he was inside her. Magnetically his fingertips had never left her nipple.

"That's a good way," he told her, just to say something, so she wouldn't feel utterly alone.

She moved her cunt and her body with it up and down with the same unfeeling presto that must be, he deduced, the tempo most men like; how had he been misled into languorous full pulls and voyeuristic lingering? Too many prefatory years, he supposed, of fantasy and masturbation. *Mr. Push-pull lives in here*, he remembered his penmanship teacher shouting to the class, "in here" being the circle she had had them pen, in wet ink on blue-lined paper, with rigid wrists and forearms.

Though Ann's fucking felt like an attack, his prick held its own, and his hypnotic touch on her nipple also held. They were a strange serene boat, its engine pumping, gliding it could be forever through the glowing tan fog of the city night. With his other hand, again to let her know she was not wholly alone with the mechanical problem she was being paid to solve, he patted, then pushed her bottom. He thought, *I haven't fucked a woman this young for years*, and knew he was home. The canal lock had lifted, scenic point in the mountain pass had been attained, it was all downhill, he would have to come. The girl was virtually jumping now, out of a squat and back into it. Her boots were rough on his sides, her hair swung like a mop, her skin felt cool as a snake's: never mind, he would come, he would give it to her, the gift we are made to give, the seething scum the universe exists to float.

She squatted deep. His sleepy prick released a little shivery dream. Not a thumping come, but distinct and, for such a drunk, triumphant. Her shoulders and face were above him, dark, as the madonna in the icon is dark in that Russian movie where the damned hero attempts to pray.

But her darkness held a smile. She was above him like a mother nursing, darkness satisfied and proud, having been challenged and found not wanting.

"Oh, thank you," he said. "*Thank* you. Sorry to have made you work so hard. *Sorry* to be so much trouble. Usually I come like a flash. My wife bitches about it."

She did not bother to doubt this. There was no way he could win promotion from her classroom of the sexually defective. Indeed, had he not shown that only the most patient manipulation could enroll him among fornicators? Ann lifted her loins from his, with a delicate shrug of disentanglement—a giantess wading through muck on her knees. A novel sensation told him that she was not carrying his seed away with her, as his wife or mistress would. Rather, she had sealed it in at its source: sticky consequences. He disdained to remove the condom. She had enlisted him in a certain hostility toward the third member of their party, the pivotal presence in the room, though silent—his willful, erratic prick. Stew in your own juice.

Ann, too, acted lazy. Instead of wading on, out of his narrow bed, she lay down beside him in her boots. He felt why: it was warm here, and enclosed, and now she knew him, and was not frightened of him. He asked her, "Aren't you anxious to get back out on the street?" He giggled, as if the joke were still on himself. "And get away," he continued, "from these awful out-of-town husbands who are too drunk to fuck decently?"

She mistook him, still viewing him as a conquest. Absurd in her booted nakedness, she cuddled against him and said in the slithering breathy voice of her propositions, "If you paid me enough I could stay all night. I bet you don't have enough money for me to stay all night."

"I bet too I don't," he told her soberly.

"For another thirty you might talk me into it." Had she seen into his wallet? Or did she just know that all men are cheats?

He calculated: if the alcohol wore off, and he got a few hours' sleep, he could manage one more piece of ass; but then getting her out of here in the morning light, through the bustle of breakfast trays and suitcases, loomed as a perilous campaign. The men in the elevator had told him that she somehow looked like a whore. With her in this narrow bed with him he'd sleep badly and drag through the rest of the day. Not worth it.

He told her, "Honest, Ann, I don't have thirty more. I don't have *any* more."

He stared down into her face for the seconds it took her to realize she was being spurned. His fear now was that she would offer to stay free. She sat up. He sat up on the edge of the bed with her. She waved her hand, as if to touch (but she did not touch) his penis, shrunken, wearing the trailing white prophylactic like an old-fashioned nightcap. *And Ma in her kerchief, and I in my cap . . .*

She asked, "You gonna keep that as a souvenir?"

He asked, "You want it back?"

"No, Ed. You can keep it."

"Thanks. I keep saying 'Thanks' to you, you notice?"

"I hadn't noticed." She stood, her buttocks fair as Parian marble. "Mind if I use your john before I go?"

"No, please do. Please."

"Don't want to keep you from your beauty sleep." But even this mild revelation of injury must have tasted unprofessional, passing her lips, for she relented and, gesturing again at the sheath on his prick, offered, "Want me to flush that for you?"

"No. It's mine. I want it."

She gathered some clothes, and he regretted afterwards that he had not pressed into his memory these last poses of her naked body. But a wave of blankness was emitted by the still-operant alcohol and ended by the soft slam of the bathroom door. Delicately he pulled off the condom and held it, pendulous, laden, while debating where to set it. At home he was hyperconscious of wineglass and water stains on furniture; but here, looking for a coaster, he saw only an ashtray. Removing the matches, he laid the sheath in it. She was taking her time in the bathroom. He picked up the Blake and tried to resume where he had left off. He couldn't find the place; instead his eye was taken by the typographical clasps of

> Every Morn & every Night
> Some are Born to sweet delight.
> Some are Born to sweet delight,
> Some are Born to Endless Night.

What was she doing in the bathroom? Did he hear her gargle and spit? He read on, more lines that also seemed too simple:

> We are led to Believe a Lie
> When we see not Thro' the Eye
> Which was Born in a Night to perish in a Night
> When the Soul Slept in Beams of Light.

He didn't understand this, nor why Blake hadn't bothered to make the lines scan.

Ann emerged from the bathroom wearing the purple boots, her antiseptically white bra, and the maxiskirt whose shade he had not observed before (charcoal). She glanced around for her sweater; he spotted its magenta spilled at the foot of the bed and held it out to her with a courtesy mocked by his total nakedness. She took it without a smile and pulled it over her head. She needed more fun in her life; in a better world his function might have been to brighten her gray classroom with a joke or two. She awkwardly reached behind her; he darted to her back and pulled up the zipper, covering her three cervical vertebrae and the faint dark down. In a serious voice he asked, "Want me to get dressed and escort you out of the hotel?"

"No, Ed. I can find my way. I'll be all right."

"All alone?"

She did not accept his invitation to say that she was always alone.

"I hate to think of you going back to stand around on that cold corner where it says Massage Parlor."

To this, too, any reply would have been playing his game.

He chose to understand that she was eager to return, to the street of others grosser and more potent than he. You whore. You poor homely whore. You don't love me, I don't love you. "What do you do in the day?" he asked.

That she answered surprised him, as did her answer. "Take care of my kid."

"You have a kid?" His sense of her underwent a revolution. Those small hard nipples had given milk; that brisk cunt had lent passage to a baby's head.

She nodded. The climate around her was exactly that as when she had answered, "Twenty-two." A central fact had been taken from her. Of the many possible questions, the one he asked, with stupid solicitude, was, "Who's taking care of it now?"

"A baby-sitter," Ann said.

What color was the baby-sitter? What color was the child? What about its future schooling? When are you going back to the library? How do you get out of this? How do I? He said, "Your money. We got to get you your money."

He went to his pants and picked the wallet from them too swiftly; the thin wedge of a hangover headache was inserted with the motion. "Thirty," he said, counting off tens to steady himself, "and then thirty more for staying the hour, and twenty for the Frenching. Right? And then let's add ten for the baby-sitter. Ninety. O.K.?" Handing her the bills, he inspected her smile; it was not as wide as the smile she had brought forward from the doorway. An extra ten might have widened it, but he held it back, and instead said, to win her denial, "Sorry I was such a difficult customer."

She considered her answer deliberately; she was not an easy grader. "You weren't a difficult customer, Ed. I've had lots worse, believe me. Lots worse." Her lingering on this thought felt irritatingly like a request for sympathy.

"Pass with push, huh?" he said.

The joke didn't seem to register; perhaps by the time she had gone to high school the phrase had disappeared. She lifted her skirt and tucked the folded bills into one of her boots. Her boots were her bank, no wonder she wouldn't remove them. Still, by keeping them on, she had held off a potential beauty in him—in him and her together, naked, with the bare feet of animals made in the image of Blake's angels. "I hate thinking," he said, "of you walking down that long corridor all by yourself."

"I'll be all right, Ed." Her saying his false name had become a nagging. As she put on her heavy all-concealing coat, he felt her movements were slowed by the clinging belief that he would relent and ask her to spend the night.

Naked, he dodged past her to the door. Her coat as he passed breathed the chill of outdoors onto his skin. "O.K., Ann. Here we go. Thank you very much. You're great."

She said nothing, merely tensed—her long nose wax-white, her eyelids the color of crème de menthe—in expectation of his opening the door. As he reached for the knob, his hand appeared to him a miracle, an intricate marvel of bone and muscle and animating spirit. An abyss of loss seemed disclosed in the wonder of such anatomy. Her body, breathless and proximate, participated in the wonder; yet, anxious to sleep and seal himself in, he could not think of anything to do but dismiss this body, this wild flower.

The turn and click of the knob came like the snap of a bone breaking. He opened the door enough to test the emptiness of the corridor, but while he was still testing she pushed around him and into the hall. "Hey," he said. "Goodbye." Forgive me, help me, adore me, screw me, forget me, carry me with you into the street.

Ann turned in surprise, recalled to duty. She whispered, from afar, " 'Bye," and gave him half of her slash of a smile, the half not turned to the future. With that triggered quickness of hers she turned the corner and was gone. Her steps made no retreating sound on the hotel carpet.

Ed closed the door. He put across the safety chain. He took the prophylactic from the ashtray into the bathroom, where he filled it full of water, to see if it leaked. The rubber held, though it swelled to a transparent balloon in which water wobbled like life eager within a placenta. Good girl. A fair dealer. He had not given her a baby, she had not given him venereal disease.

What she had given him, delicately, was death. She had made sex finite. Always, until now, it had been too much, bigger than all systems, an empyrean as absolute as those first boyish orgasms, when his hand would make his soul pass through a bliss as dense as an ingot of gold. Now, at last, in the prime of life, he saw through it, into the spaces between the stars. He emptied the condom of water and brought it with him out of the bathroom and in the morning found it, dry as a husk, where he had set it, on the glass bureau top among the other Christmas presents.

Augustine's Concubine

To CARTHAGE *I came, where there sang all around me in my ears a cauldron of unholy loves. I loved not yet, yet I loved to love, and out of a deep-seated want, I hated myself for wanting not. I sought that I might love, in love with loving, and safety I hated, and a way without snares.*

She was, in that cauldron of the dark and slim, fair enough to mock, with a Scythian roundness to her face, and in her curious stiff stolidity vulnerable, as the deaf and blind are vulnerable, standing expectant in an agitated room. "Why do you hate me, Aurelius?" she asked him at a party preceding a circus.

"I don't," he answered, through the smoke, through the noise, through the numbness that her presence even then worked upon his heart. "Rather the contrary, as a matter of fact." He was certain she heard this last; she frowned, but it may have been an elbow in her side, a guffaw too close to her ear. She was dressed compactly, in black, intensifying her husband's suit of dark gray, suiting her female smallness, which was not yet slimness, her waist and arms and throat being, though not heavy, rounded, of substance, firm, pale, frontal. She had, he felt, no profile; she seemed always to face him, or to have her back turned, both positions expressive not of hostility (he felt) but of a resolution priorly taken, either to ignore him, or to confront him, he was undecided which. She was, he sensed, *new*, new, that is, to life, in a way not true of himself, youth though he was (*aet.* eighteen), or true of the Carthaginians boiling about them.

"Love your dress," he said, seeing she would make no reply to his confession of the contrary of hatred.

"It's just a dress," she said, with that strange dismissive manner she had, yet staring at him as if a commitment, a dangerous declaration, had been made. They were to proceed by contradiction. Her eyes were of a blue pale to the whiteness of marble, compared with the dark Mediterranean glances that upheld them like the net of a conspiracy, beneath the smoke and laughter and giddying expectation of a murderous circus.

"Absolute black," he said. "Very austere." Again meeting silence from her, he asked, a touch bored and *ergo* reckless, "*Are* you austere?"

She appeared to give the question unnecessarily hard thought, the hand accustomed to holding the cigarette (she had recently given up smoking) jerking impatiently. Her manner, contravening her calm body, was all stabs, discontinuous. "Not austere," she said. "Selective."

"Like me," he said, instantly, with too little thought, automatically teasing his precocious reputation as a rake, her manner having somehow saddened him, sharpened within him his hollow of famine, his hunger for God.

"No," she replied, seeming for the first time pleased to be talking with him, as pleased as an infant who has seized, out of the blur of the world, a solid toy, "not like you. The opposite, in fact."

For this space of nine years (from my nineteenth year to my eight-and-twentieth) we lived seduced and seducing, deceived and deceiving, in divers lusts; openly, by sciences which they call liberal; secretly, with a false-named religion; here proud, there superstitious, every where vain!

At their first trysts, the pressure of time, which with his other conquests had excited him to demonstrations of virile dispatch, unaccountably defeated him; her calm pale body, cool and not as supple as the dark warm bodies he had known, felt to exist in a slower time, and to drag him into it, as a playful swimmer immerses another. What was this numbness? Her simplicity, it crossed his mind, missed some point. She remained complacent through his failures, her infant's smile of seizure undimmed. Her waist was less voluptuously indented than he had expected, her breasts were smaller than they appeared when dressed. She offered herself unembarrassed. There was some nuance, of shame perhaps, of sin, that he missed and that afflicted him, in the smiling face of her willingness, with what amounted to loss of leverage. Yet her faith proved justified. She led him to love her with a fury that scourged his young body.

Strangely, he did not frighten her. She met his lust frontally, amused and aroused, yet also holding within her, companion to her wanton delight, the calm and distance of the condemned.

In those years I had one,—not in that which is called lawful marriage, but whom I had found out in a wayward passion, void of understanding; yet but

one, remaining faithful even to her; in whom I in my own case experienced
what difference there is betwixt the self-restraint of the marriage-covenant,
for the sake of issue, and the bargain of a lustful love, where children are born
against their parents' will, although, once born, they constrain love.

Her husband, dark-gray shadow, she did not forsake; nor did she, under questioning, reveal that love between them had been abandoned. Rather, she clave to this man, in her placid and factual manner, and gave him what a man might ask; that her lover found this monstrous, she accepted as another incursion, more amusing than not, into this her existence, which she so unambiguously perceived as having been created for love.

"You love him?" However often posed, the question carried its accents of astonishment.

Her hand, small and rounded as a child's, though cleaner, made its impatient stab in air, and an unintended circlet of smoke spun away. She had resumed the habit, her one concession to the stresses of her harlot's life. "We make love."

"And how is it?"

She thought. "Nice."

"Perhaps you were right. I do hate you."

"But he's my husband!"

The word, religious and gray, frightened him. "Is it as it is," he asked, "with me?"

"No. Not at all." Her white eyes stared. Was she sincere?

How often do you do it? In what positions? Are you silent, or do the two of you speak throughout? What do you say? The litany, attempting to banish the mystery of her rounded limbs so simply laid open for another, won from her more tears than answers; it appeared, to this amorous youth whose precocious and epochal intuition it already was to seek truth and truth's Lord not in mathematics nor the consensus of the *polis* but in one's own unique and uniquely configured self, that the details eluded her; she had forgotten; they didn't matter. Incredible! His jealousy would not rest, kept gnawing at this substantial shadow, her husband. He permitted the scandal to become open, and her husband faded a little, out of pride. The man's attentions, sensed through the veil of her, became indifferent, ironical; still her husband lived with her, shared her nights, could touch her at whim, shared the rearing of their children, a sacred sharing. This could not be borne. Aurelius made her pregnant.

And the husband did vanish, with their common goods. The lover and his concubine travelled to Rome, and then to Milan. Their child they called Adeodatus. The name, surprisingly, came from her; it subtly displeased him, that she fancied herself religious.

. . . time passed on, but I delayed to turn to the Lord; and from day to day deferred to live in Thee, and deferred not daily to die in myself. Loving a happy life, I feared it in its own abode, and sought it, by fleeing from it. I thought I should be too miserable, unless folded in female arms. . . .

Her compliance disturbed him. Her love seemed of the darkness, demonic in its exemption from fatigue. Years after she should have wearied of his body, he would wake and find that in their sleep she had crowded him to the edge of the bed, her indistinct profile at rest in the curve of his armpit. Milan's night traffic gleamed and glittered below; travelling torchlight shuddered on the walls. A cry arose, close to them. She would rise and smother the child with her breasts, that the father might sleep. Lying nevertheless awake, he felt her merge with the darkened room, in which there was this unseen horizon, of smallness and limit, of the coolness with which she assumed any position, placated any need, however sordid. Her spirit was too bare, like her face when, each morning, for coolness in the humid submontane heat, she pulled back her hair with both hands to knot it; her face gleamed taut and broad, perspiring, a Scythian moon of a face. She had grown plump in her years of happiness. He remembered how she smoked, and wished she would begin again. He wished she would die. The blanched eyes, the blunt nose, the busy plump self-forgetful hands. Her lips, pouting in concentration, were startled to a smile by sudden awareness of his studying her; she would come forward and smother him as if he, too, had been crying. *Concupiscentia.* Its innocence disturbed him, the simplicity of her invitation to descend with her into her nature, into Nature, and to be immersed. Surely such wallowing within Creation was a deflection of higher purposes. Like bubbles, his empty spaces wanted to rise, break into air, and vanish. Their bodies would become one, but his soul was pulled back taut, like the hair at the back of her skull.

Meanwhile my sins were being multiplied, and, my concubine being torn from my side as a hindrance to my marriage, my heart which clave unto her was torn and wounded and bleeding. And she returned to Afric, vowing unto Thee never to know any other man, leaving with me my son by her.

She had been, the mother of Adeodatus, strangely calm in receiving the news, anxious foremost to understand, to avoid misunderstanding; her quest for clarity, which had made her appear rigid, frontal, iconic, brusque at the pre-circus party more than a decade ago, had tunnelled through all their intervening ecstasies. She was in his arms, her face tear-blurred but held back from his, contemplating his naked shoulder as if the truth might rest upon it like a butterfly. "Monica has found you a wife?"

"My mother deems it crucial to my salvation that I marry."

"And the betrothed—?"

"Is two years under the fit age."

"Not fit, but beautiful?" she asked. *De pulchro et apto* had been the title of his first dissertation, composed in Carthage and read aloud to her there. She was illiterate. Since, he had ceased to share his compositions— *De vita beata, De immortalitate animae*. He had felt these subjects as betrayals of her, prefatory to this great betrayal.

"Not beautiful, but sufficiently pleasing," he factually answered, unprepared for the sirocco of her grief. "But not you, not like you," were all the words he could call into her weeping, repeating, "Not like you at all," recognizing, at last, her firmness and smallness so close yet remote in his arms as that of an unformed person. The recognition hardened his heart. His cruelty as he held her heightened him. He saw over her head, where gray hairs had come, scarcely distinguishable, to mingle with the fair, back to the fact that she had had a husband and had accepted that husband and her lover as if they were kindred manifestations of the same force, as if he himself were not incomparable, unique, with truth's sole Lord within him. For this she was rightly punished. Punished, nay, obliterated, as a heresy is obliterated, while love for the heretic burns in the heart of the condemner. Aurelius grew immortally tall against her grieving; he felt in her, who had so often sobbed in love's convulsion against his body, the benign enemy he was later to find in Pelagius, who held that Adam's sin touched only Adam, that men were born incorrupt, that unbaptized infants did not go to Hell. Such liberal plausibilities poisoned the water of eternal life as it sprang from the stricken rock. So with her softness, her stolid waist and child's small eager hands, the austerity of her dress, the brazen circlets she wore as earrings, the halo of fine white hairs her skin bore everywhere: the sum was ease, and ease was deception, and deception evil. So with her love for him. There was more. There must be more. *Verus philosophus est amator Dei.*

Nor was that my wound cured, which had been made by the cutting away of the former, but after inflammation and most acute pain, it mortified, and my pains became less acute, but more desperate.

To Thee be praise, glory to Thee, Fountain of Mercies. I was becoming more miserable, and Thou nearer.

In Africa, the sky almost never shows a cloud. The heat the desert bestows upon its green shore is severe but not oppressive, unlike that heavy Milanese heat wherein she had pulled back her hair from damp temples. She, too, could taste the dry joy of lightness, of renunciation. She cut off her hair. She forgot her son. Nor would she ever make love again; there was no moderation in what mattered.

Among the women of the cenobium she entered, she moved not as one with a great grief behind her but as one who, like a child, had yet to live. Blue was the color of the order, her color, between Hellenic white and medieval black. *The Beautiful and the Fitting:* this, the first of Augustine's dissertations, and the only one of which she was the substance, stayed in her memory and conspired, among these whispering gowned women and these sun-dazed walls of clay, to refine that aesthetic of rite and symbol with which half-formed Christianity, amid its renunciations, was to enrich the vocabulary of beauty. Though illiterate, she drew to herself, from these her sisters—the maimed and fanatic and avoidant—authority. Her complacence, which had never doubted the body's prerogatives, seemed here, in these corridors cloistered from the sun, to manifest purity. Her shamelessness became a higher form of self-surrender. Her placid carriage suggested triumph. It was as if her dynamic and egocentric lover, whom she had never failed to satisfy, in his rejection of her had himself failed, and been himself rejected, even as his verbal storms swept the Mediterranean and transformed orthodoxy.

She was a saint, whose name we do not know. For a thousand years, men would endeavor to hate the flesh, because of her.

During the Jurassic

WAITING FOR THE FIRST GUESTS, the iguanodon gazed along the path and beyond, toward the monotonous cycad forests and the low volcanic hills. The landscape was everywhere interpenetrated by the sea, a kind of metallic-blue rottenness that daily breathed in and out. Behind him, his wife was assembling the hors d'oeuvres. As he watched her, something unintended, something grossly solemn, in his expression made her laugh, displaying the leaf-shaped teeth lining her cheeks. Like him, she was an ornithischian, but much smaller—a compsognathus. He wondered, watching her race bipedally back and forth among the scraps of food (dragonflies wrapped in ferns, cephalopods on toast), how he had ever found her beautiful. His eyes hungered for size; he experienced a rage for sheer blind size.

The stegosauri, of course, were the first to appear. Among their many stupid friends these were the most stupid, and the most punctual. Their front legs bent outward and their tiny, beak-tipped, filmy-eyed faces virtually skimmed the ground; the upward sweep of their backs was mountainous, and the double rows of giant bone plates along the spine clicked together in the sway of their cumbersome gait. With hardly a greeting, they dragged their tails, quadruply spiked, across the threshold and maneuvered themselves toward the bar, which was tended by a minute and shapeless mammal hired for the evening.

Next came the allosaurus, a carnivorous bachelor whose dangerous aura and needled grin excited the female herbivores; then the rhamphorhynchus, a pterosaur whose much-admired "flight" was in reality a clumsy brittle glide ending in an embarrassed bump and trot. The iguanodon despised these gangly pterosaurs' pretensions; he thought grotesque the precarious elongation of the single finger from which their levitating membranes were stretched, and privately believed that the less hand-somely underwritten archaeopteryx, though sneered at as unstable and feathered, had more of a future. The hypsilophodon, with her grace-ful hands and branch-gripping feet, arrived escorted by the timeless crocodile—an incongruous pair, but both were recently divorced. Still the iguanodon gazed down the path.

Behind him, the conversation gnashed on a thousand things—houses, mortgages, lawns, fertilizers, erosion, boats, winds, annuities, capital gains, recipes, education, the day's tennis, last night's party. Each party was consumed by discussion of the previous one. Their lives were subject to constant cross-check. When did you leave? When did *you* leave? We'd been out every night this week. We had an amphibious baby-sitter who had to be back in the water by one. Gregor had to meet a client in town, and now they've reduced the Saturday schedule, it means the 7:43 or nothing. Trains? I thought they were totally extinct. Not at all. They're coming back, it's just a matter of time until the government . . . In the long range of evolution, they are still the most efficient . . . Taking into account the heat-loss/weight ratio and assuming there's no more glacia-tion . . . Did you know—I think this is fascinating—did you know that in the financing of those great ornate stations of the eighteen-eighties and nineties, those real monsters, there was no provision for amortization? They weren't amortized at all, they were financed on the basis of eternity! The railroad was conceived of as the end of Progress! *I* think—though not an expert—that the key word in this overall industrio-socio-what-have-you-oh nexus or syndrome or bag or whatever is "overextended." Any competitorless object *bloats*. Personally, I miss the trolley cars. Now, don't tell me I'm the only creature in the room old enough to remember the trolley cars!

The iguanodon's high pulpy heart jerked and seemed to split; the brontosaurus was coming up the path.

Her husband, the diplodocus, was with her. They moved together, rhythmic twins, buoyed by the hollow assurance of the huge. She paused to tear with her lips a clump of feathery leaves from an overhanging paleo-cycas. From her deliberate grace the iguanodon received the impression that she knew he was watching her. Indeed, she had long guessed his love, as had her husband; the two saurischians entered his party with the lan-guid confidence of the specially cherished. Even as the iguanodon gritted his teeth in assumption of an ironical stance, her bulk, her gorgeous size, enraptured him, swelling to fill the massive ache he carried when she was not there. She rolled outward across his senses—the dawn-pale under-parts, the reticulate skin, the vast bluish muscles whose management required a second brain at the base of her spine.

Her husband, though even longer, was more slenderly built, and per-haps weighed less than twenty-five tons. His very manner was attenuated and tabescent. He had recently abandoned a conventional career in finance to enter an Episcopalian seminary. This regression—as the iguanodon felt it—seemed to make his wife more prominent, less sup-ported, more accessible.

How splendid she was! For all the lavish solidity of her hips and legs, the modelling of her little flat diapsid skull was exquisite. Her facial essence appeared to narrow, along the diagrammatic points of her auri-cles and eyes and nostrils, toward a single point, located in the air, of impermutable refinement and calm. This irreducible point was, he real-ized, in some sense her mind: the focus of the minimal interest she brought to play upon the inchoate and edible green world flowing all about her, buoying her, bathing her. The iguanodon felt himself as an upright speckled stain in this world. He felt himself, under her distant dim smile, to be impossibly ugly: his mouth a sardonic chasm, his throat a pulsing curtain of scaly folds, his body a blotched bulb. His feet were heavy and horny and three-toed and his thumbs—strange adaptation!—were erect rigidities of pointed bone. Wounded by her presence, he sav-agely turned on her husband.

"Comment va le bon Dieu?"

"Ah?" The diplodocus was maddeningly good-humored. Seconds elapsed as stimuli and reactions travelled back and forth across his length.

The iguanodon insisted. "How are things in the supernatural?"

"The supernatural? I don't think that category exists in the new theology."

"N'est-ce pas? What *does* exist in the new theology?"

"Love. Immanence as opposed to transcendence. Works as opposed to faith."

"Work? I had thought you had quit work."

"That's an unkind way of putting it. I prefer to think that I've changed employers."

The iguanodon felt in the other's politeness a detestable aristocracy, the unappealable oppression of superior size. He said gnashingly, "The Void pays wages?"

"Ah?"

"You mean there's a living in nonsense? I said nonsense. Dead, fetid nonsense."

"Call it that if it makes it easier for you. Myself, I'm not a fast learner. Intellectual humility came rather natural to me. In the seminary, for the first time in my life, I feel on the verge of finding myself."

"Yourself? That little thing? *Cette petite chose?* That's all you're looking for? Have you tried pain? Myself, I have found pain to be a great illuminator. *Permettez-moi.*" The iguanodon essayed to bite the veined base of the serpentine throat lazily upheld before him; but his teeth were too specialized and could not tear flesh. He abraded his lips and tasted his own salt blood. Disoriented, crazed, he thrust one thumb deep into a yielding gray flank that hove through the smoke and chatter of the party like a dull wave. But the nerves of his victim lagged in reporting the pain, and by the time the distant head of the diplodocus was notified, the wound was already healing.

The drinks were flowing freely. The mammal crept up to the iguanodon and murmured that the dry vermouth was running out. He was told to use the sweet, or else substitute white wine. Behind the sofa the stegosauri were Indian-wrestling; each time one went over, his spinal plates raked the recently papered wall. The hypsilophodon, tipsy, perched on a banister; the allosaurus darted forward suddenly and ceremoniously nibbled her tail. On the far side of the room, by the great slack-stringed harp, the compsognathus and the brontosaurus were talking. The iguanodon was drawn to the pair, surprised that his wife would presume to engage the much larger creature—would presume to insert herself, with her scrabbling nervous motions and chattering leaf-shaped teeth, into the crevices of that queenly presence. As he drew closer to them, music began. His wife confided to him, "The salad is running out."

"Amid all this greenery?" he responded, incredulous, and turned to the brontosaurus. "*Chère madame, voulez-vous danser avec moi?*"

Her dancing was awkward, but even in this awkwardness, this ponderous stiffness, he felt the charm of her abundance. "I've been talking to your husband about religion," he told her, as they settled into the steps they could do.

"I've given up," she said. "It's such a deprivation for me and the children."

"He says he's looking for himself."

"It's so selfish," she blurted. "The children are teased at school."

"Come live with me."

"Can you support me?"

"No, but I would gladly sink under you."

"You're sweet."

"*Je t'aime.*"

"Don't. Not here."

"Somewhere, then?"

"No. Nowhere. Never." With what delightful precision did her miniature mouth encompass these infinitesimal concepts!

"But I," he said, "but I lo—"

"Stop it. You embarrass me. Deliberately."

"You know what I wish? I wish all these beasts would disappear. What do we see in each other? Why do we keep getting together?"

She shrugged. "If they disappear, we will too."

"I'm not so sure. There's something about us that would survive. It's not in you and not in me but between us, where we almost meet. Some vibration, some enduring cosmic factor. Don't you feel it?"

"Let's stop. It's too painful."

"Stop dancing?"

"Stop being."

"That is a beautiful idea. *Une belle idée.* I will if you will."

"In time," she said, and her fine little face precisely fitted this laconic promise; and as the summer night yielded warmth to the multiplying stars—fresher, closer, bigger then—he felt his blood sympathetically cool, and grow thunderously, fruitfully slow.

Under the Microscope

IT WAS NOT HIS KIND OF POND; the water tasted slightly acid. He was a cyclops, the commonest of copepods, and this crowd seemed exotically cladoceran—stylish water-fleas with transparent carapaces, all shimmer and bubbles and twitch. His hostess, a magnificent daphnia fully an eighth of an inch tall, her heart and cephalic ganglion visibly pulsing, welcomed him with a lavish gesture of her ciliate, branching antennae; for a moment he feared she would eat him. Instead she offered him a platter of living desmids. They were bright green in color and shaped like crescents, hourglasses, omens. "Who do you know here?" Her voice was a distinct constant above the din. "Everybody knows *you*, of course. They've read your books." His books, taken all together, with generous margins, would easily have fitted on the period that ends this sentence.

The cyclops modestly grimaced, answered "No one," and turned to a young specimen of water mite, probably *Hydrachna geographica*, still bearing ruddy traces of the larval stage. "Have you been here long?" he asked, meaning less the party than the pond.

"Long enough." Her answer came as swiftly as a reflex. "I go back to the surface now and then; we breathe air, you know."

"Oh, I know. I envy you." He noticed she had only six legs. She was newly hatched, then. Between her eyes, arranged in two pairs, he counted a fifth, in the middle, and wondered if in her he might find his own central single optic amplified and confirmed. His antennules yearned to touch her red spots; he wanted to ask her, *What do you see?* Young as she was, partially formed, she appeared, alerted by his abrupt confession of envy, ready to respond to any question, however presuming.

But at that moment a monstrous fairy shrimp, nearly an inch in length and extravagantly tinted blue, green, and bronze, swam by on its back, and the water shuddered. Furious, the cyclops asked the water mite, "Who invites *them?* They're not even in our scale."

She shrugged permissively, showing that indeed she had been here, in this tainted pond, long enough. "They're entomostracans," she said, "just like Daphnia. They amuse her."

"They're going to eat her up," the cyclops predicted.

Though she laughed, her fifth eye gazed steadily into his wide lone one. "But isn't that what we all want? Subconsciously, of course."

"Of course."

An elegant, melancholy flatworm was passing hors d'oeuvres. The cyclops took some diatoms, cracked their delicate shells of silica, and ate them. They tasted golden brown. Growing hungrier, he pushed through to the serving table and had a volvox in algae dip. A shrill little rotifer, his head cilia whirling, his three-toothed mastax chattering, leaped up before him, saying, with the mixture of put-on and pleading characteristic of this environment, "I wead all your wunnaful books, and I have a wittle bag of pomes I wote myself, and I would wove it, *wove* it if you would wead them and wecommend them to a big bad pubwisher!" At a loss for a civil answer, the cyclops considered the rotifer silently, then ate him. He tasted slightly acid.

The party was thickening. A host of protozoans drifted in on a raft of sphagnum moss: a trumpet-shaped stentor, apparently famous and interlocked with a lanky, bleached spirostomum; a claque of paramecia, swishing back and forth, tickling the crustacea on the backs of their knees; an old vorticella, a plantlike animalcule as dreary, the cyclops thought, as the batch of puffs rooted to the flap of last year's *succès d'estime*. The kitchen was crammed with ostracods and flagellates engaged in mutually consuming conversation, and over in a corner, beneath an African mask, a great brown hydra, the real thing, attached by its sticky foot to the hissing steam radiator, rhythmically swung its tentacles here and there until one of them touched, in the circle of admirers, something appetizing; then the poison sacs exploded, the other tentacles contracted, and the prey was stuffed into the hydra's swollen coelenteron, which gluttony had stretched to a transparency that veiled the preceding meals like polyethylene film protecting a rack of dry-cleaned suits. Hairy with bacteria, a simocephalus was munching a rapt nematode. The fairy shrimps, having multiplied, their crimson tails glowing with hemoglobin, came cruising in from the empty bedrooms. The party was thinning.

Suddenly fearful, fearing he had lost her forever, the cyclops searched for the water mite, and found her miserably crouching in a corner, quite drunk, her seventh and eighth legs almost sprouted. "What do you see?" he now dared ask.

"Too much," she answered swiftly. "Everything. Oh, it's horrible, horrible."

Out of mercy as much as appetite, he ate her. She felt prickly inside him. Hurriedly—the rooms were almost depleted, it was late—he sought his hostess. She was by the doorway, her antennae frazzled from waving goodbye, but still magnificent, Daphnia, her carapace a liquid shimmer of psychedelic pastel. "Don't go," she commanded, expanding. "I have a *minus*cule favor to ask. Now that my children, all thirteen million of them, thank God, are off at school, I've taken a part-time editing job, and my first real break is this manuscript I'd be *so* grateful to have you read and comment on, whatever comes into your head; I admit it's a little long, maybe you can skim the part where Napoleon invades Russia, but it's the first *effort* by a perfectly delightful midge larva I know you'd enjoy meeting—"

"I'd adore to, but I can't," he said, explaining, "my eye. I can't afford to strain it, I have only this one. . . ." He trailed off, he felt, feebly. He was beginning to feel permeable.

"You poor dear," Daphnia solemnly pronounced, and ate him.

And the next instant, a fairy shrimp, oaring by inverted, casually gathered her into the trough between his eleven pairs of undulating gill-feet and passed her toward his brazen mouth. Her scream, tinier than even the dot on this *i*, went unobserved.

The Baluchitherium

IN 1911, C. Forster-Cooper of the British Museum unearthed in Baluchistan some extraordinary foot bones and a single provocative neck vertebra. Thus the baluchitherium first intruded upon modern consciousness. Eleven years later, in Mongolia, an almost complete skull of the creature was uncovered, and in 1925 the four legs and feet of another individual, evidently trapped and preserved in quicksand, came to light. From these unhappy fragments an image of the living baluchitherium was assembled. His skull was five feet long, his body twenty-seven. He stood eighteen feet high at the shoulders (where the North American titanothere measured a mere eight feet, the bull African elephant eleven). Though of the family Rhinocerotidae, the baluchitherium's face was innocent of any horn; his neck was long and his upper lip prehensile, for seizing leaves twenty-five feet above the ground. He was the largest mammal that ever lived on land.

Recently, I had the pleasure of an interview with the baluchitherium. The technical process would be tedious to describe; in brief, it involved feeding my body into a computer (each cell translates into approximately 120,000,000 electronic "bits") and then transecting the tape with digitized data on the object and the coördinates of the moment in time-space to be "met." The process proved painless; a sustained, rather dental humming tingled in every nerve, and a strange, unpopulous vista opened up around me. I knew I was in Asia, since the baluchitheres in the millions of years of their thriving never left this most amorphous of continents. The landscape was typical Oligocene: a glossy green mush of subtropical vegetation—palms, fig trees, ferns—yielded, on the distant pink hillsides of aeolian shale, to a scattering of conifers and deciduous hardwoods. Underfoot, the spread of the grasses was beginning.

Venturing forward, I found the baluchitherium embowered in a grove of giant extinct gymnosperms. He was reading a document or missive printed on a huge sheet of what appeared to be rough-textured cardboard. When I expressed surprise at this, the baluchitherium laughed genially and explained, "We pulp it by mastication and then stamp it flat with our feet." He held up for my admiration one of his extraordinary feet—columnar, ungulate, odd-toed. What I had also not been led by the fossil record to expect, his foot, leg, and entire body as far as my eye could reach were covered by a lovely fur, bristly yet lustrous, of an elusive color I can only call reddish-blue, with tips of white in the underparts. Such are the soft surprises with which reality pads the skeleton of hard facts.

"How curious it is," the baluchitherium said, "that you primates should blunder upon my five-foot skull without deducing my hundred-kilogram brain. True, our technology, foreseeing the horrors of industrialism, abjured the cruel minerals and concerned itself purely with vegetable artifacts—and these solely for our amusement and comfort." He benignly indicated the immense chaise longue, carved from a single ginkgo trunk, that he reposed upon; the rug beside it, artfully braided of wisteria vines; the hardwood sculptures about him, most of them glorifying, more or less abstractly, the form of the female baluchitherium. "All, of course," he said, "by your time sense, fallen into dust aeons ago."

By now, I had adjusted my tape recorder to the immense volume and curious woofing timbre of his voice, so his remaining statements are not at the mercy of my memory. His accent, I should say, was Oxonian, though his specialized upper lip and modified incisors played havoc with some of our labials and fricatives, and he quaintly pronounced all silent consonants and even the terminal *e* of words. To my natural query as to his own time sense, he replied, with a blithe wave, "If you are able from a few crusty chips of calcium to posit an entire phylum of creature, why should not I, with a brain so much greater, be able, by a glance at my surroundings, to reconstruct, as it were, the future? The formation of your pelvis, the manner of your speech, even the moment of your visit are transparent in the anatomy of yon single scuttling insectivore." He gestured toward what my lower perspective would have missed—a tiny gray plesiadipid miserably cowering high in a primitive magnolia.

The baluchitherium brandished the printed sheet in his hand; it rattled like thunder. "In here, for instance," he said, "one may read of numerous future events—the mammoth's epic circumambulation of the globe, the drastic shrinkage of the Tethys Sea, the impudent and hapless attempt of the bird kingdom, in the person of the running giant diatryma, to forsake the air and compete on land. Hah! One may even find"—he turned the sheet, to what seemed to be its lesser side—"news of *Homo sapiens*. I see here, for example, that your wheat-growing cultures will make war upon your rice-growers, having earlier defeated the maize-growers. And one also finds," he continued, "horoscopes and comic strips and a lively correspondence discussing whether God is, as I firmly believe, odd-toed or, as the artiodactyls vainly hold, even-toed."

"B-but," I said, stammering in my anxiety to utter this, the crucial question, "given, then, such a height of prescience and civilized feeling, why did you make the evolutionary error—the gross, if I may so put it, miscalculation—of brute size? That is, with the catastrophic example of the dinosaurs still echoing down the silted corridors of geologic time—"

Imperiously he cut me short. "The past," he said, "is bunk. The future"— and he trumpeted—"is our element."

"But," I protested, "the very grasses under my feet spell doom for large leaf-browsers, presaging an epoch of mobile plains-grazers." As if to illustrate my point, a rabbit darted from the underbrush, chased by a dainty eohippus. "As you must know," I said, "the artiodactyls, in the form of swine, camels, deer, cattle, sheep, goats, and hippopotami, will flourish, whereas the perissodactyls, dwindled to a few tapirs and myopic rhinoceri in my own era, will meet extinct—"

"Size," he bellowed, pronouncing it "siz-eh," "is not a matter of choice but of destiny. Largeness was thrust upon us. We bear it—bore it, bear it, will bear it—as our share of the universal heaviness. We bear it gratefully, and gratefully will restore it to the heaviness of the earth." And he fixed me with a squint so rhinoceroid I involuntarily backed a step, tripping the computer's reverse mechanism. All my nerves began humming. The baluchitherium, as he faded, stretched himself toward the leaf-clouded sky; the reddish-blue fur on his throat shimmered white. Ravenously he resumed what I saw to be, under one form or another, an endless, unthinkable meal.

The Invention of the Horse Collar

In the darkest Dark Ages, the horse collar appeared. A Frankish manuscript of the tenth century first depicts it, along with the concomitantly epochal shafts and traces *attached to the middle of the collar*. In antiquity, from primitive Egypt to decadent Rome, horse harness consisted of a yoke *attached at the withers* by a double girth passing under the chest and around the throat of the animal. When the horse pulled at his load, the throat girth rode up, cutting into his windpipe, compressing his vein walls, and slowing his heartbeat. The loss of tractive power was three- or fourfold. Yet antiquity, which sentimental humanism so much encourages us to admire, did little to remedy this strangling, but for ineffectual measures like passing a strap between the forelegs to keep the throat band low (observable on a Greek vase *c.* 500 B.C.) or tying the two bands at the horse's sides, as illustrated in a bone carving of a war chariot on the side of a Byzantine casket.

No, it fell to some obscure fellow in the Dark Ages, a *villein* no doubt, to invent the horse collar. His name, I imagine, was Canus—an odd name, meaning "gray," though our hero is young; but name-giving, like everything else in this ill-lit and anarchic period, is in a muddled, transitive condition. Canus sits in his thatched hut pondering. Beside him, on a bench of hewn planks and dowels, lies a sheaf of sketches, an array of crude tools both blunt and sharp, an ox yoke for purposes of comparison, and a whitened fragment of equine scapula with the stress lines marked in charcoal. Outside, darkness reigns unrelieved; even noon, in this year of (say) 906, has about it something murky, something slanting and askew. Roman ruins dot the landscape. Blind eyes gaze from the gargantuan heads of marble emperors half buried in the earth. Aqueducts begin and halt in midair. Forested valleys seclude mazelike monasteries where quill-wielding clerics copy Vergil over and over, having mistaken him for a magician. Slit-windowed castles perch fantastically on unscalable out-croppings and lift villages upward toward themselves like ladies gathering their skirts while crossing a stretch of mud. In the spaces between these tentative islands of order, guttural chieftains, thugs not yet knights, thunder back and forth, bellowing in a corrupt Latin not yet French, trampling underfoot the delicate stripwork of a creeping agriculture. Canus is one of those who work these precarious fields, urging forward the gagging, staggering plow-horse. He has been troubled, piqued. There must be . . . something better. . . . Now, under his hands, the mock-up of the first horse collar, executed in straw and flour paste, has taken shape!

The door of the hut wrenches open. Enter Ablatus, Canus's brother. Though they are twins, born in the last year of the nonexistent reign of Charles the Fat, they are not identical. Canus in his eyes and hair shows the scaly brilliance of burnished metal and of the hardened peat called coal; Ablatus, the more elusive lambency of clouds, of water running over quartz, of fire sinking in the hearth. Canus tends toward the swarthy, Ablatus toward the fair. Both are clad in the era's style of shapelessness, between toga and cloak, bunches of colorless cloth such as a poor child would use to wrap a doll of sticks. On his head Ablatus wears a hat like a beanbag. He takes it off. He stares at the bright hoop of straw. "What is that?" he asks, in a language whose archaic music is forever lost to human ears.

Triumphantly Canus explains his invention. He describes new worlds: the fourfold tractive increase, the improved deep plowing, the more rapid transportation, the ever more tightly knit and well-fed Christendom. Cathedrals shall arise; the Viking and the Mohammedan will be repulsed. Crusades can be financed. Out of prosperity will arise city-states, usury, and a middle class—all these blessings pouring from this coarse circlet of glued straw. He concludes, "The real collars, of course, will be leather, padded, with increasing ingenuity, to eliminate chafing and to render the horse's pulling all the more pleasurable."

Toward the end of his twin's long recital, Ablatus betrays agitation. He flings down his scythe, scarcely changed in design since the Egyptians first lopped maize. His pallid eyes throw sparks. "My own brother," he utters at last, "a devil!"

"Nay," says Canus, rising from his bench in surprise, "an angel, rather, to relieve both beasts and men by the means of an insensate and efficient"—and here, groping for the Latin *"mechina,"* he slurs into creation a new word—"machine. I have created"—and again he must coin the word—"horsepower."

"You would bind up the anarchy that has set us free," Ablatus pursues, pacing the rectangle of dirt floor in his visionary distress. "You would bring back the ponderous order of Rome, that crazed even emperors, ere the sea of slaves dried up and like a galleon of millstones the Empire sank. Oh, Canus, *frater meus*, reflect! With the great flail of bishops and barbarians God broke Rome into a thousand fragments so that men might breathe. In the subsequent darkness, in this our confusion, men have found their souls, have fallen into right relation with one another—the lords protecting the vassals, the vassals supporting the lord, on all sides love and enlightened self-interest. True, there is brutality and waste, but they stem from our natures; they are true to our image, which is God's. The seal of the divine sits upon the organic. Out of Eden, Adam groaned at toil and Eve screamed in the travail of birth so that men might know their sin. Wisely the ancients took up the first poor tools and disdained to improve them. You would presume to forge a second Nature—better the hellish blackness of midnight than a blasphemous Paradise! Better impede the windpipes of beasts than strangle the souls of men! From this impudent seed of invention, what iron vines will flourish! With interconnection comes restriction; with organization, oppression. This device of yours, so beneficent in its apparent effects, is Satan's stalking horse, wherewith to conquer again the kingdom so dearly redeemed by Christ's blood! You call it a blessing, I call it a curse! I call it a—*pollution!*" And, inspired, fair Ablatus seizes one of the candles that in this dark age burn even at midday, and hurls it upon the artifact of straw, and it becomes a hoop of flame.

Canus, inspired in his swarthier fashion, takes up one of the blunt tools from his bench and strikes his brother a firm blow.

"Devil!" exclaims Ablatus, sinking.

"Fool," replies Canus, and, with one of the sharp tools from the same set, deftly finishes his brother off.

Ablatus abolitus est. It does not arouse remorse in us when we slay a twin; it is too much like suppressing an aspect of ourselves. Serenely Canus carries off the body *(Ablatus ablatus est)* and digs the grave. The earth is heavy, Northern soil—more resistant and more rewarding than the earth the ancients scratched. In the distance, a scrimmage of nobility reverberates. A monastery bell—a silver thread thrown across a chasm— sounds from a muffling valley. The Dark Ages begin to fade. As Canus leans on the shovel, a breeze of evening caresses his face, and he idly reflects that here is power too, to be harnessed. He imagines sails, gears, driveshafts. Inside the hut, he composes himself for sleep. His muscles agreeably ache from useful labor performed. The prototypical horse collar lies consumed beside the bench, but the ashes preserve the design. Tomorrow he will reconstruct it. The slippery little half-dreams that augur sleep begin to visit him. And tomorrow, he thinks, he will invent the horizontal-shafted windmill . . . and the next day, *Deus volens*, the wheelbarrow. . . .

Jesus on Honshu

Japanese Legend Says
Jesus Escaped to Orient
—Headline, and passages in italics below, from the New York Times.

TOKYO—*A Japanese legend has excited some curiosity here, that Jesus did not die on the cross outside Jerusalem, but lived in a remote village on the northern part of the Japanese island of Honshu until his death at 106 years of age.*

The distances within His blue eyes used to frighten the children. Though toward the end, when His age had passed eighty, His stoop and careful movements within the kimono approximated the manner of an elderly Japanese, His face, up close, never conformed—the olive skin, the tilted nostrils sprouting hair, the lips excessive in flesh and snarling humor, the eyelids very strange, purplish and wrinkled like the armpits of a salamander. There was never much doubt in the village that He was some sort of god. Even had His eyes given on less immensity, had their celestial blue been flawed by one fleck of amber or rust, He would have been revered and abhorred by the children. His skin was abnormally porous. His voice came from too deep in His body.

Jesus, so the legend runs, first arrived in Japan at the age of 21 during the reign of the emperor Suinin in what would have been the year 27 B.C. He remained for 11 years under the tutorship of a sage of Etchu Province, the modern Toyama prefecture, from whom he learned much about the country and its customs.

Strangely, the distances had melted within Him, leaving little more trace than the ice cakes along the northern shore leave in spring. What a man does when young becomes a legend to himself when he is old. The straight roads through drifting deserts, the goat paths winding through mauve mountains, the silver rivers whose surfaces He discovered He could walk, the distant herds like wandering lakes, the clouds of birds darkening the sun, the delegations of brown people, of yellow people, the green forests where sunlight fell in tiger stripes, the purple forests (tree trunks shaggy as bears, star-blue butterflies fluttering in glades no man had entered before), emerald meadows sparkling with springs and freshets, sheets of snow a month of walking did not dismiss, and in the distance always more mountains, more deserts, the whole world then tasting of vastness as of nectar, glistening, men huddling in mud nests like wasps, the spaces innocent. He had walked because, obscurely, His Father had told Him to. His Father was an imperious restlessness within Him. At last He came to the land of Wa, beyond which extended only an enamelled sea without a nether edge. The sage of Etchu took Him in and taught Him many things. He taught the young Jesus that dual consciousness was not to be avoided but desired: only duality reflected the universe. That the eight hundred myriads of daemons (*yao-yorodzu-no-kami*) are false save in that they stand guard against an even more false monism. That the huntsman must bend his thought upon the prey and not upon the bow. That a faith containing fear is an imperfect faith. That the mountains wait to be moved by the touch of a child. That the motions of the mind are full of *kami* (holy force). That the ways of the gods (*shintō*) are the ways of plants. That a seed must die to live. That the weak are the strong, the supple outlast the stiff, the child speaks truer than the man. And many more such things He later preached, and forgot, as the ice cake deposits pebbles and straw in melting. After eleven years, the restlessness seized Him again, and He returned. The trip returning, strangely, was the more difficult of the two; He kept searching for familiar landmarks, and there were none.

Jesus returned to Jerusalem, passing through Monaco on the way, to tell his own people of his experiences in the Orient, it is said. It was his younger brother, known in Japanese as Isukiri, who was later crucified, according to the legend.

No one ever got it quite right, and He Himself ceased trying to understand. Judas (Isukiri) had not been His brother; he had been the troublesomely sensitive disciple, the cloying adorer. Selecting the twelve, Jesus had chosen solid men, to whom a miracle was a way of affecting matter, a species of work. Judas, with his adoration and high hopes and theoretical demands on the Absolute, had attached himself hysterically. The kiss in the garden was typical—all showmanship. Then, the priesthood proving obdurate (and why not? any Messiah at all would put them out of a job), Judas had offered to be crucified instead, as if we were dealing with some

Moloch that had a simple body quota to meet. The poor Romans were out of their depth; eventually they hanged Judas, as they generally hanged informers—a straightforward policy of prudence. For Him, there had been nails in the palms, and a crying out, and then dark coolness, a scuffle in which He overheard women's voices, and a scarlet dawn near the borders of Palestine. For the first days eastward, until the wounds in His feet healed, He was carried in a litter and had a mounted escort, He dimly remembered. Gruff men, officials of some sort.

Jesus is said to have escaped and come back to Japan after wandering through the wastes of Siberia. The legend has it that he landed at Hachinoe in Aomori, and settled in Herai, whose name, it has been suggested, derives from the Japanese for Hebrew (Heburai). He married and became the father of three daughters, according to the legend.

Asagao was the oldest, Oigimi the youngest; both married before the age of fifteen, and in them and their children He saw no trace of Himself, only of His wife and the smooth race that had taken Him in, as a pond swallows a stone. Ukifune, the middle daughter, called Dragonfly, was tall like Him, with His wrinkled lids and big-knuckled hands and surges of restlessness and mockery. She never married; her scandals affronted the village until she was found dead in her hut, black-lipped, cold. He would have called her back to life, but her face had been monstrously slashed. Poisoned and disfigured by a lover or the wife of a lover. She left a fatherless male infant, Kaoru. Shared between the households of his aunts, the infant grew to be a man, living always in the village, as a mender of nets and thatching. Conscious of himself only as Japanese, Kaoru grew old, with white hair and warts, and Jesus, now over a hundred, would suddenly, senselessly, weep to see in this venerable grandson—hook-nosed profile bent above a chisel, his forearms as gnarled as grapevines—the very image of old Joseph of Bethlehem, seen upward through the eyes of a child. Things return, form in circles, unravel and reravel, the sage had insisted, crouching with the young traveller on a ledge in the mauve mountains of Etchu, in view of the enamelled sea. Jesus had argued, insisting that there was also a vertical principle in the world, something thrusting, which did not repeat. Now, Himself ancient, He had come to exemplify the sage's scorned truth. He lived in the village as a healer, and the healed kept coming back to Him, their health unravelled, and again He would lay on His hands, and the devils would flee, and the healed would depart upright and rejoicing; only to unravel again, and at last to die, even as He must. A soft heaviness sweetened His veins; His naps lengthened. As death neared, His birth and travail far ago, in that clamorous desert place, among Rome's centurions, seemed more and more miraculous: a seed He had left behind, and that had died, engendering a growth perhaps as great as a mustard tree. Or perhaps His incarnation there, those youthful events, were lost in the scuffle of history, dust amid dust. Whatever the case, He never doubted that He was unique, the only son of God. In this, at least, He resembled all men.

One family in the village says it is descended from Jesus. Many of the children have the star of David sewn on their clothes, and parents sometimes mark the sign of the cross in ink on the foreheads of children to exorcise evil spirits. . . . An annual "Christ festival," held on June 10, attracts many visitors.

The Slump

THEY SAY REFLEXES, the coach says reflexes, even the papers now are saying reflexes, but I don't think it's the reflexes so much—last night, as a gag to cheer me up, the wife walks into the bedroom wearing one of the kids' rubber gorilla masks and I was under the bed in six-tenths of a second, she had the stopwatch on me. It's that I can't see the ball the way I used to. It used to come floating up with all seven continents showing, and the pitcher's thumbprint, and a grass smooch or two, and the Spalding guarantee in ten-point sans-serif, and—*whop!*—I could feel the sweet wood with the bat still cocked. Now, I don't know, there's like a cloud around it, a sort of spiral vagueness, maybe the Van Allen belt, or maybe I lift my eye in the last second, planning how I'll round second base, or worrying which I do first, tip my cap or slap the third-base coach's hand. You can't see a blind spot, Kierkegaard says, but in there now, between when the ball leaves the bleacher background—all those colored shirts—and when I hear it smack safe and sound into the catcher's mitt, there's somehow just nothing, where there used to be a lot, everything in fact, because they're not keeping me around for my fielding, and already I see the afternoon tabloid has me down as trade bait.

The flutters don't come when they used to. It used to be, I'd back the convertible out of the garage and watch the electric eye put the door down again and head out to the stadium, and at about the bridge turnoff I'd ease off grooving with the radio rock, and then on the lot there'd be the kids waiting to get a look and that would start the big butterflies, and when the attendant would take my car I'd want to shout *Stop, thief!* and, walking down that long cement corridor, I'd fantasize like I was going to the electric chair and the locker room was some dream after death, and I'd wonder why the suit fit, and how these really immortal guys, that I recognized from the bubble-gum cards I used to collect, knew my name.

They knew *me*. And I'd go out and the stadium mumble would scoop at me and the grass seemed too precious to walk on, like emeralds, and by the time I got into the cage I couldn't remember if I batted left or right.

Now, hell, I move over the bridge singing along with the radio, and brush through the kids at just the right speed, not so fast I knock any of them down, and the attendant knows his Labor Day tip is coming, and we wink, and in the batting cage I own the place, and take my cuts, and pop five or six into the bullpen as easy as dropping dimes down a sewer grate. But when the scoreboard lights up, and I take those two steps up from the dugout, the biggest two steps in a ballplayer's life, and kneel in the circle, giving the crowd the old hawk profile, where once the flutters would ease off, now they dig down and begin.

They say I'm not hungry, but I still feel hungry, only now it's a kind of panic hungry, and that's not the right kind. Ever watch one of your little kids try to catch a ball? He gets so excited with the idea he's going to catch it he shuts his eyes. That's me now. I walk up to the plate, having come all this way—a lot of hotels, a lot of shagging—and my eyes feel shut. And I stand up there trying to push my eyeballs through my eyelids, and my retinas register maybe a little green, and the black patch of some nuns in far left field. That's panic hungry.

Kierkegaard called it dread. It queers the works. My wife comes at me without the gorilla mask and when in the old days *whop!*, now she slides by with a hurt expression and a flicker of gray above her temple. I go out and ride the power mower and I've already done it so often the lawn is brown. The kids get me out of bed for a little fungo and it scares me to see them trying, busting their lungs, all that shagging ahead of them. In Florida—we used to love it in Florida, the smell of citrus and marlin, the flat pink sections where the old people drift around smiling with transistor-radio plugs in their ears—we lie on the beach after a workout and the sun seems a high fly I'm going to lose and the waves keep coming like they've been doing for a billion years, up to the plate, up to the plate. Kierkegaard probably has the clue, somewhere in there, but I picked up *Concluding Unscientific Postscript* the other day and I couldn't see the print, that is, I could see the lines, but there wasn't anything on them, like the rows of deep seats in the shade of the second deck on a Thursday afternoon, just a single ice-cream vendor sitting there, nobody around to sell to, a speck of white in all that shade, old Søren Sock himself, keeping his goods cool.

I think maybe if I got beaned. That's probably what the wife is hinting at with the gorilla mask. A change of pace, like the time DiMaggio broke his slump by Topping's telling him to go to a nightclub and get plastered. I've stopped ducking, but the trouble is, if you're not hitting, they don't brush you back. On me, they've stopped trying for even the corners; they put it right down the pike. I can see it in the pitcher's evil eye as he takes the sign and rears back, I can hear the catcher snicker, and for a second of reflex there I can see it like it used to be, the continents and trade routes and state boundaries distinct as stitches, and the hickory sweetens in my hands, and I feel the good old sure hunger. Then something happens. It all blurs, the pitch sinks, the light changes, I don't know. It's not caring enough, is what it probably is; it's knowing that none of it—the stadium, the averages—is really there, just *you* are there, and it's not enough.

The Sea's Green Sameness

I WRITE THIS on the beach. Let us say, then, that I am a writer on the beach. It was once considered bad manners to admit anything of the sort, just as people walking to and from the bathroom were supposed to be invisible; but this is a rude age. Nothing is hidden. Yet everything is. In a sense a person *observed* walking to a closed door is *less* "there" than someone being forcibly imagined to be invisible.

I sit opposite the sea.[1] Its receding green surface is marked everywhere by millions of depressions, or nicks, of an uncertain color: much as this page is marked. But this page yields a meaning, however slowly, whereas the marks on the sea are everywhere the same. That is the difference between Art and Nature.

But the marks on the sea move, which is somehow portentous. And large distinctions in tone are perceptible: the purple shadows of clouds from above, of coral reefs from below. The horizon is darker than the middle distance—almost black—and the water near me is tinted with the white of the sand underneath, so that its clear deep-throated green is made delicate, acidulous, artificial. And I seem to see, now and then, running vertically with no regard for perspective, veins of a metallic color; filaments of silver or gold—it is hard to be certain which—waver elusively, but valuably, at an indeterminate distance below the skin of the massive, flat, monotonous volume.

Enough, surely. It is a chronic question, whether to say simply "the sea" and trust to people's imaginations, or whether to put in the adjectives. I have had only fair luck with people's imaginations; hence tend to trust adjectives. But are they to be trusted? Are they—words—anything substantial upon which we can rest our weight? The best writers say so.

---

1. The Caribbean—hence its idyllic aspect.

Sometimes I believe it. But the illogic of the belief bothers me: From whence did words gather this intrinsic potency? The source of language, the spring from which all these shadows (tinted, alliterative, shapely, but still shadows) flow, is itself in shadow.

But what, then, am I to do? Here am I, a writer, and there is the sea, a subject. For mathematical purity, let us exclude everything else—the sky, the clouds, the sand on my elbows, the threat of my children coming down the beach to join me. Let us posit a world of two halves: the ego and the external object. I think it is a fair representation of the world, a kind of biform Parliament, where two members sit, and speak for all parties. Tell me what I must do. Or, rather, give me my excuse; for my vote is foreordained, it must be in opposition, and our Parliament will be stale-mated until one of us dies.

The incantor of tales about the cave fire was excused by the hungry glitter[2] of eyes. Homer swung his tides on this attention. Aeschylus felt excused; Sophocles heroically bluffed out any doubt; with Euripides we definitely arrive at the sudden blankness, the embarrassed slapping of the pockets, the stammer, the flustered prolixity. But then a splendid excuse appeared, it seemed eternally. Dante had it. Milton. Tolstoy, Dickens, Balzac picked its bones. It was a huge creature and still gives some nour-ishment. Shakespeare and Dr. Johnson wrote for money; it kept them scribbling, but is presently considered a weak excuse. Beauty, said Keats. A trick of optics. Self, said Wordsworth and Goethe. A tautology. Reality, said the Realists, and the Opposition swamped them with pamphlets. I bore you. Even this raises an issue. Is it my duty not to bore you; my excuse, that I do not? This would bring me safely into the cozy hotel of pornographers, dinner guests, and television personalities. But you would be truly amazed, how indignantly I, the peer of the immense sea, reject such shelter. Forgive me; I know you made the offer with warm hearts. To continue my story—Conrad and James offer Groping as an End in Itself, and Proust and Joyce round out the tale with a magnificent display of superb, if somewhat static, effects. I may, in this summation, have left out a few names, which you yourself can supply. The remaining question of interest: Were Proust and Joyce an ending or a beginning? They seemed, from their newness, a beginning, but as time passes does not their continued newness make it clear that they are the opposite, that everything since forms a vacuum in which the surfaces of these

---

2. Why were they hungry? Is there a narrative appetite as instinctive as the sexual? Why would Nature put it there? But, then, why does Nature do half the things she does?

old works, that should be cracked and sunken, are preserved like fresh pigment?

How tired I am! All my intricate maneuvers, my loudly applauded and widely reprinted perorations, my passionate lobbying—all my stratagems are exhausted. I am near death. And the Opposition seems as young as ever. You see, he never exerts himself. The clerks—all the quick clerks have gone over to his side; I am left with but a few ancient men, hanging on for the pension, the prizes—elicit his answers to prepared questionnaires, which he gives very reluctantly, with much coaxing. He never gets up on his feet and says a word the gallery can hear. Yet more and more his influence spreads among them. Oh, they still muster a few handclaps for my most gallant efforts, bent and breathless as I am; but it is his power they respect. Out with this metaphor—take away these congressional trappings! There. I still have some power of my own. His silence can still be twisted to my advantage.

I am writing this in the sun, which is difficult; perhaps here is a clue. You cannot write in the sun, or in perfect health. I must make myself sick with cigarettes before I can perform. Some writers use alcohol. Some read copiously. Some are gifted with infirmities. Health, sanity, and sunshine have deserted us. Even the clergy, as we labor to save them, despise us. Sitting on this beach, I wonder if I am one of those large, sluggish crabs whom the operator of the Time Machine discovers at the extreme limit of the earth's senility scraping across a beach, stiffly waving their tentacles at a red and distended sun. Perhaps I am the last writer in the world. Perhaps, coming from a backward region of the country, to which news travels slowly, I arrived in the capital a moment before the gates were locked forever. Perhaps all of us latter-day writers are like the priests that the peasantry continued to supply to the Church long after the aristocracy acknowledged that the jig was up.

For I look at the sea, my topic, and it seems null. No longer am I permitted to conceive charming legends about how it came to be salt, for this is known. Its chemistry, its weight, its depth, its age, its myriad creatures so disturbingly evocative of our own mortality—what is not known of these things, will be known. The veins of silver (or gold) in it are all mapped and will be mined tomorrow. This leaves, you say, its essence, its *ens*. Yes, but what, really, can we hope for in this line, after Plato, after Aquinas, after Einstein? Have not their brave fancies already gone the way of Poseidon?

Yet, surprisingly, I do have something new to contribute to human knowledge of the sea. It has just come to me. A revelation. If you lie down, put your head in the sand, and close one eye, the sea loses its third dimension and becomes a wall. The black rim of the perfectly smooth top seems as close to me as the pale, foaming bottom. A curious sideways tugging in the center of the wall, a freedom of motion inexplicable in a wall whose outlines are so inflexibly fixed, makes the vision strange. But it does not lead me to imagine that the wall is a fragile cloth that an assault by me would pierce. No, my fists and forehead are too sore for me to entertain such an illusion. However, I do feel—and feel, as it were, from the outside, as if I were being beckoned—that if I were to run quickly to it, and press my naked chest against its vibrating perpendicular surface, and strain my body against it from my head to my toes, I should feel upon my beating heart the answer of another heart beating. I sit up, excited, foul with sand, and open both eyes, and the ocean withdraws again into its distance. Yet I hear in the sigh of its surf encouragement from the other side of the apparent wall—sullen, muffled encouragement, the best it can do, trapped as it is also—encouragement for me to repeat the attempt, to rush forward in my mind again and again.

I have reverted, in my art (which I gaily admit I have not mastered[3]), to the first enchanters, who expected their nets of words to capture the weather, to induce the trees to bear and the clouds to weep, and to drag down advice from the stars. I expect less. I do not expect the waves to obey my wand or support my weight. My modesty, perhaps, damns me. All I hope for is that once into my carefully spun web of words the thing itself, *das Ding an sich*, will break: make an entry and an account of itself. Not cast its vote with mine, and issue a unanimous decree: I have no hope of this. Not declare its intentions; these are no mystery. I can observe. It intends to do away with me. The session already lasts into the late afternoon. I wish the opposition to yield only on the point of its identity. What is it? Its breadth, its glitter, its greenness and sameness balk me. *What is it?* If I knew, I could say.

---

3. As who has? Is not the Muse a mermaid whose slippery-scaled body pops from our arms the moment we try to tighten our embrace?

THE SINGLE LIFE

The Bulgarian Poetess

"YOUR POEMS. Are they difficult?"

She smiled and, unaccustomed to speaking English, answered carefully, drawing a line in the air with two delicately pinched fingers holding an imaginary pen. "They are difficult—to write."

He laughed, startled and charmed. "But not to read?"

She seemed puzzled by his laugh, but did not withdraw her smile, though its corners deepened in a defensive, feminine way. "I think," she said, "not so very."

"Good." Brainlessly he repeated "Good," disarmed by her unexpected quality of truth. He was, himself, a writer, this fortyish young man, Henry Bech, with his thinning curly hair and melancholy Jewish nose, the author of one good book and three others, the good one having come first. By a kind of oversight, he had never married. His reputation had grown while his powers declined. As he felt himself sink, in his fiction, deeper and deeper into eclectic sexuality and bravura narcissism, as his search for plain truth carried him farther and farther into treacherous realms of fantasy and, lately, of silence, he was more and more thickly hounded by homage, by flat-footed exegetes, by arrogantly worshipful undergraduates who had hitchhiked a thousand miles to touch his hand, by querulous translators, by election to honorary societies, by invitations to lecture, to "speak," to "read," to participate in symposia trumped up by ambitious girlie magazines in shameless conjunction with venerable universities. His very government, in airily unstamped envelopes from Washington, invited him to travel, as an ambassador of the arts, to the other half of the world, the hostile, mysterious half. Rather automatically, but with some faint hope of shaking himself loose from the burden of himself, he consented, and found himself floating, with a passport so stapled with visas it fluttered when pulled from his pocket, down into the dim airports of Communist cities.

He arrived in Sofia the day after a mixture of Bulgarian and African students had smashed the windows of the American legation and ignited an overturned Chevrolet. The cultural officer, pale from a sleepless night of guard duty, tamping his pipe with trembling fingers, advised Bech to stay out of crowds and escorted him to his hotel. The lobby was swarming with Negroes in black wool fezzes and pointed European shoes. Insecurely disguised, he felt, by an astrakhan hat purchased in Moscow, Bech passed through to the elevator, whose operator addressed him in German. *"Ja, vier,"* Bech answered, *"danke,"* and telephoned, in his bad French, for dinner to be brought up to his room. He remained there all night, behind a locked door, reading Hawthorne. He had lifted a paperback collection of short stories from a legation windowsill littered with broken glass. A few curved bright crumbs fell from between the pages onto his blanket. The image of Roger Malvin lying alone, dying, in the forest— "Death would come like the slow approach of a corpse, stealing gradually towards him through the forest, and showing its ghastly and motionless features from behind a nearer and yet a nearer tree"—frightened him. Bech fell asleep early and suffered from swollen, homesick dreams. It had been the first day of Hanukkah.

In the morning, venturing downstairs for breakfast, he was surprised to find the restaurant open, the waiters affable, the eggs actual, the coffee hot, though syrupy. Outside, Sofia was sunny and (except for a few dark glances at his big American shoes) amenable to his passage along the streets. Lozenge-patterns of pansies, looking flat and brittle as pressed flowers, had been set in the public beds. Women with a touch of Western chic walked hatless in the park behind the mausoleum of Georgi Dimitrov. There was a mosque, and an assortment of trolley cars salvaged from the remotest corner of Bech's childhood, and a tree that talked— that is, it was so full of birds that it swayed under their weight and emitted volumes of chirping sound like a great leafy loudspeaker. It was the inverse of his hotel, whose silent walls presumably contained listening microphones. Electricity was somewhat enchanted in the Socialist world. Lights flickered off untouched and radios turned themselves on. Telephones rang in the dead of the night and breathed wordlessly in his ear. Six weeks ago, flying from New York City, Bech had expected Moscow to be a blazing counterpart and instead saw, through the plane window, a skein of hoarded lights no brighter, on that vast black plain, than a girl's body in a dark room.

Past the talking tree stood the American legation. The sidewalk, heaped with broken glass, was roped off, so that pedestrians had to detour into the gutter. Bech detached himself from the stream, crossed the little barren of pavement, smiled at the Bulgarian militiamen who were sullenly guarding the jewel-bright heaps of shards, and pulled open the bronze door. The cultural officer was crisper after a normal night's sleep. He clenched his pipe in his teeth and handed Bech a small list. "You're to meet with the Writers' Union at eleven. These are writers you might ask to see. As far as we can tell, they're among the more progressive."

Words like "progressive" and "liberal" had a somewhat reversed sense in this world. At times, indeed, Bech felt he had passed through a mirror, a dingy flecked mirror that reflected feebly the capitalist world; in its dim depths everything was similar but left-handed. One of the names ended in "-ova." Bech said, "A woman."

"A poetess," the cultural officer said, sucking and tamping in a fury of bogus efficiency. "Very popular, apparently. Her books are impossible to buy."

"Have you read anything by these people?"

"I'll be frank with you. I can just about make my way through a newspaper."

"But you always know what a newspaper will say anyway."

"I'm sorry, I don't get your meaning."

"There isn't any." Bech didn't quite know why the Americans he met here behind the mirror irritated him—whether because they garishly refused to blend into this shadow-world or because they were always so solemnly sending him on ridiculous errands.

At the Writers' Union, he handed the secretary the list as it had been handed to him, on U.S. legation stationery. The secretary, a large stooped man with the hands of a stonemason, grimaced and shook his head but obligingly reached for the telephone. Bech's meeting was already waiting in another room. It was the usual one, the one that, with small differences, he had already attended in Moscow and Kiev, Yerevan and Alma-Ata, Bucharest and Prague: the polished oval table, the bowl of fruit, the morning light, the gleaming glasses of brandy and mineral water, the lurking portrait of Lenin, the six or eight patiently sitting men who would leap to their feet with quick blank smiles. These men would include a few literary officials, termed "critics," high in the Party, loquacious and witty and destined to propose a toast to international understanding; a few selected novelists and poets, mustachioed, smoking, sulking at this invasion of their time; a university professor, the head of the Anglo-American Literature department, speaking in a beautiful withered English of Mark Twain and Sinclair Lewis; a young interpreter with a moist handshake; a shaggy old journalist obsequiously scribbling notes; and, on the rim of the group, in chairs placed to suggest that they had invited themselves, one or two gentlemen of ill-defined status, fidgety and tieless, maverick translators who would turn out to be the only ones present who had ever read a word by Henry Bech.

Here this type was represented by a stout man in a tweed coat leather-patched at the elbows in the British style. The whites of his eyes were distinctly red. He shook Bech's hand eagerly, made of it almost an embrace of reunion, bending his face so close that Bech could distinguish the smells of tobacco, garlic, cheese, and alcohol. Even as they were seating themselves around the table, and the Writers' Union chairman, a man elegantly bald, with very pale eyelashes, was touching his brandy glass as if to lift it, this anxious red-eyed interloper blurted at Bech, "Your *Travel Light* was so marvellous a book. The motels, the highways, the young girls with their lovers who were motorcyclists, so marvellous, so American, the youth, the adoration for space and speed, the barbarity of the advertisements in neon lighting, the very poetry. It takes us truly into another dimension."

Travel Light was the first novel, the famous one. Bech disliked discussing it. "At home," he said, "it was criticized as despairing."

The man's hands, stained orange with tobacco, lifted in amazement and plopped noisily to his knees. "No, no a thousand times. Truth, wonder, terror even, vulgarity, yes. But despair, no, not at all, not one iota. Your critics are dead wrong."

"Thank you."

The chairman softly cleared his throat and lifted his glass an inch from the table, so that it formed with its reflection a kind of playing card.

Bech's admirer excitedly persisted. "You are not a *wet* writer, no. You are a dry writer, yes? You have the expressions, am I wrong in English, dry, hard?"

"More or less."

"I want to translate you!"

It was the agonized cry of a condemned man, for the chairman coldly lifted his glass to the height of his eyes, and like a firing squad the others followed suit. Blinking his white lashes, the chairman gazed mistily in the direction of the sudden silence, and spoke in Bulgarian.

The young interpreter murmured in Bech's ear. "I wish to propose now, ah, a very brief toast. I know it will seem doubly brief to our honored American guest, who has so recently enjoyed the, ah, hospitality of our Soviet comrades." There must have been a joke here, for the rest of the table laughed. "But in seriousness permit me to say that in our country we have seen in years past too few Americans, ah, of Mr. Bech's progressive and sympathetic stripe. We hope in the next hour to learn from him much that is interesting and, ah, socially useful about the literature of his large country, and perhaps we may in turn inform him of our own proud literature, of which perhaps he knows regrettably little. Ah, so let me finally, then, since there is a saying that too long a courtship spoils the marriage, offer to drink, in our native plum brandy *slivovica*, ah, firstly to the success of his visit and, in the second place, to the mutual increase of international understanding."

"Thank you," Bech said and, as a courtesy, drained his glass. It was wrong; the others, having merely sipped, stared. The purple burning revolved in Bech's stomach, and a severe distaste—for himself, for his role, for this entire artificial and futile process—lighted upon a small brown spot on a pear in the bowl so shiningly posed before his eyes.

The red-eyed fool smelling of cheese was ornamenting the toast. "It is a personal honor for me to meet the man who, in *Travel Light*, truly added a new dimension to American prose."

"The book was written," Bech said, "ten years ago."

"And since?" A slumping, mustached man sat up and sprang into English. "Since, you have written what?"

Bech had been asked that question often in these weeks and his answer had grown curt. "A second novel called *Brother Pig*, which is St. Bernard's expression for the body."

"Good. Yes, and?"

"A collection of essays and sketches called *When the Saints*."

"I like the title less well."

"It's the beginning of a famous Negro song."

"We know the song," another man said, a smaller man, with the tense, dented mouth of a hare. He lightly sang, "Lordy, I just want to be in that number."

"And the last book," Bech said, "was a long novel called *The Chosen* that took five years to write and that nobody liked."

"I have read reviews," the red-eyed man said. "I have not read the book. Copies are difficult here."

"I'll give you one," Bech said.

The promise seemed, somehow, to make the recipient unfortunately conspicuous; wringing his stained hands, he appeared to swell in size, to intrude grotesquely upon the inner ring, so that the interpreter took it upon himself to whisper, with the haste of an apology, into Bech's ear, "This gentleman is well known as the translator into our language of *Alice in Wonderland*."

"A marvellous book," the translator said, deflating in relief, pulling at his pockets for a cigarette. "It truly takes us into another dimension. Something that must be done. We live in a new cosmos."

The chairman spoke in Bulgarian, musically, at length. There was polite laughter. Nobody translated for Bech. The professorial type, his black hair as rigid as a toupee, jerked forward. "Tell me, is it true, as I have read"—his phrases whistled slightly, like rusty machinery—"that the stock of Sinclair Lewis has plummeted under the Salinger wave?"

And so it went, here as in Kiev, Prague, and Alma-Ata, the same questions, more or less predictable, and his own answers, terribly familiar to him by now, mechanical, stale, irrelevant, untrue, claustrophobic. Then the door opened. In came, with the rosy air of a woman fresh from a bath, a little breathless, having hurried, hatless, a woman in a blond coat, her hair also blond. The secretary, entering behind her, seemed to make a cherishing space around her with his large curved hands. He introduced her to Bech as Vera Something-ova, the poetess he had asked to meet. None of the others on the list, he explained, answered their telephones.

"Aren't you kind to come?" As Bech asked it, it was a genuine question, to which he expected some sort of an answer.

She spoke to the interpreter in Bulgarian. "She says," the interpreter told Bech, "she is sorry she is so late."

"But she was just called!" In the warmth of his confusion and pleasure Bech turned to speak directly to her, forgetting he would not be understood. "I'm terribly sorry to have interrupted your morning."

"I am pleased," she said, "to meet you. I heard of you spoken in France."

"You speak English!"

"No. Very little amount."

"But you *do*."

A chair was brought for her from a corner of the room. She yielded her coat, revealing herself in a suit also blond, as if her clothes were an aspect of a total consistency. She sat down opposite Bech, crossing her legs. Her legs were visibly good; her face was perceptibly broad. Lowering her lids, she tugged her skirt to the curve of her knee. It was his sense of her having hurried, hurried to him, and of being, still, graciously flustered, that most touched him.

He spoke to her very clearly, across the fruit, fearful of abusing and breaking the fragile bridge of her English. "You are a poetess. When I was young, I also wrote poems."

She was silent so long he thought she would never answer; but then she smiled and pronounced, "You are not old now."

"Your poems. Are they difficult?"

"They are difficult—to write."

"But not to read?"

"I think—not so very."

"Good. Good."

Despite the decay of his career, Bech had retained an absolute faith in his instincts; he never doubted that somewhere an ideal course was open to him and that his intuitions were pre-dealt clues to his destiny. He had loved, briefly or long, with or without consummation, perhaps a dozen women; yet all of them, he now saw, shared the trait of approximation, of narrowly missing an undisclosed prototype. The surprise he felt did not have to do with the appearance, at last, of this central woman; he had always expected her to appear. What he had not expected was her appearance here, in this remote and bullied nation, in this room of morning light, where he discovered a small knife in his fingers and on the table before him, golden and moist, a precisely divided pear.

Men travelling alone develop a romantic vertigo. Bech had already fallen in love with a freckled embassy wife in Prague, a buck-toothed chanteuse in Romania, a stolid Mongolian sculptress in Kazakhstan. In the Tretyakov Gallery he had fallen in love with a recumbent statue, and at the Moscow Ballet School with an entire roomful of girls. Entering the room, he had been struck by the aroma, tenderly acrid, of young female sweat. Sixteen and seventeen, wearing patchy practice suits, the girls were twirling so strenuously their slippers were unravelling. Demure student faces crowned the unconscious insolence of their bodies. The room was doubled in depth by a floor-to-ceiling mirror. Bech was seated on a bench at its base. Staring above his head, each girl watched herself with frowning eyes frozen, for an instant in the turn, by the imperious delay and snap of her head. Bech tried to remember the lines of Rilke that expressed it, this snap and delay: *did not the drawing remain / that the dark stroke of your eyebrow / swiftly wrote on the wall of its own turning?* At one point the teacher, a shapeless old Ukrainian lady with gold canines, a *prima* of the Thirties, had arisen and cried something translated to Bech as, "No, no, the arms free, *free!*" And in demonstration she had executed a rapid series of pirouettes with such proud effortlessness that all the girls, standing this way and that like deer along the wall, had applauded. Bech had loved them for that. In all his loves, there was an urge to rescue—to rescue the girls from the slavery of their exertions, the statue from the cold grip of its own marble, the embassy wife from her boring and unctuous husband, the chanteuse from her nightly humiliation (she could not sing), the Mongolian from her stolid race. But the Bulgarian poetess presented herself to him as needing nothing, as being complete, poised, satisfied, achieved. He was aroused and curious and, the next day, inquired about her of the man with the vaguely contemptuous mouth of a hare—a novelist turned playwright and scenarist, who accompanied him to the Rila Monastery. "She lives to write," the playwright said. "I do not think it is healthy."

Bech said, "But she seems so healthy." They stood beside a small church with whitewashed walls. From the outside it looked like a hovel, a shelter for pigs or chickens. For five centuries the Turks had ruled Bulgaria, and the Christian churches, however richly adorned within, had humble exteriors. A peasant woman with wildly snarled hair unlocked the door for them. Though the church could hardly ever have held more than fifty worshippers, it was divided into three parts, and every inch of wall was covered with eighteenth-century frescoes. Those in the narthex depicted a Hell where the devils wielded scimitars. Passing through the tiny nave, Bech peeked through the iconostasis into the screened area that, in the symbolism of Orthodox architecture, represented the next, the hidden world—Paradise. He glimpsed a row of books, an easy chair, a pair of ancient oval spectacles. Outdoors again, he felt released from the unpleasantly tight atmosphere of a children's book. They were on the side of a hill. Above them was a stand of pines whose trunks wore shells of ice. Below them sprawled the monastery, a citadel of Bulgarian national feeling during the years of the Turkish Yoke. The last monks had been moved out in 1961. An aimless soft rain was falling in these mountains, and there were not many German tourists today. Across the valley, whose little silver river still turned a water wheel, a motionless white horse stood silhouetted against a green meadow, pinned there like a brooch.

"I am an old friend of hers," the playwright said. "I worry about her."

"Are the poems good?"

"It is difficult for me to judge. They are very feminine. Perhaps shallow."

"Shallowness can be a kind of honesty."

"Yes. She is very honest in her work."

"And in her life?"

"As well."

"What does her husband do?"

The other man looked at him with parted lips and touched his arm, a strange Slavic gesture, communicating an underlying racial urgency, that Bech no longer shied from. "But she has no husband. As I say, she is too much for poetry to have married."

"But her name ends in '-ova.'"

"I see. You are mistaken. It is not a matter of marriage; I am Petrov, my unmarried sister is Petrova. All females."

"How stupid of me. But I think it's such a pity, she's so charming."

"In America, only the uncharming fail to marry?"

"Yes, you must be very uncharming not to marry."

"It is not so here. The government indeed is alarmed; our birthrate is one of the lowest in Europe. It is a problem for economists."

Bech gestured at the monastery. "Too many monks?"

"Not enough, perhaps. With too few of monks, something of the monk enters everybody."

The peasant woman, who seemed old to Bech but who was probably younger than he, saw them to the edge of her domain. She huskily chattered in what Petrov said was very amusing rural slang. Behind her, now hiding in her skirts and now darting away, was her child, a boy not more than three. He was faithfully chased, back and forth, by a small white pig, who moved, as pigs do, on tiptoe, with remarkably abrupt changes of direction. Something in the scene, in the open glee of the woman's parting smile and the untamed way her hair thrust out from her head, something in the mountain mist and spongy rutted turf into which frost had begun to break at night, evoked for Bech a nameless absence to which was attached, like a horse to a meadow, the image of the poetess, with her broad face, her good legs, her Parisian clothes, and her sleekly brushed hair. Petrov, in whom he was beginning to sense, through the wraps of foreignness, a clever and kindred mind, seemed to have overheard his thoughts, for he said, "If you would like, we could have dinner. It would be easy for me to arrange."

"With her?"

"Yes, she is my friend, she would be glad."

"But I have nothing to say to her. I'm just curious about such an intense conjunction of good looks and brains. I mean, what does a soul do with it all?"

"You may ask her. Tomorrow night?"

"I'm sorry, I can't. I'm scheduled to go to the ballet, and the next night the legation is giving a cocktail party for me, and then I fly home."

"Home? So soon?"

"It does not feel soon to me. I must try to work again."

"A drink, then. Tomorrow evening before the ballet? It is possible? It is not possible."

Petrov looked puzzled, and Bech realized that it was his fault, for he was nodding to say Yes, but in Bulgaria nodding meant No, and a shake of the head meant Yes. "Yes," he said. "Gladly."

The ballet was entitled *Silver Slippers*. As Bech watched it, the word "ethnic" kept coming to his mind. He had grown accustomed, during his trip, to this sort of artistic evasion, the retreat from the difficult and disappointing present into folk dance, folk tale, folk song, with always the implication that, beneath the embroidered peasant costume, the folk was really one's heart's own darling, the proletariat.

"Do you like fairy tales?" It was the moist-palmed interpreter who accompanied him to the theatre.

"I *love* them," Bech said, with a fervor and gaiety lingering from the previous hour. The interpreter looked at him anxiously, as when Bech had swallowed the brandy in one swig, and throughout the ballet kept murmuring explanations of self-evident events on the stage. Each night, a princess would put on silver slippers and dance through her mirror to tryst with a wizard, who possessed a magic stick that she coveted, for with it the world could be ruled. The wizard, as a dancer, was inept, and once almost dropped her, so that anger flashed from her eyes. She was, the princess, a little redhead with a high round bottom and a frozen pout and beautiful free arm motions, and Bech found it oddly ecstatic when, preparatory to her leap, she could dance toward the mirror, an empty oval, and another girl, identically dressed in pink, would emerge from the wings and perform as her reflection. And when the princess, haughtily adjusting her cape of invisibility, leaped through the oval of gold wire, Bech's heart leaped backward into the enchanted hour he had spent with the poetess.

Though the appointment had been established, she came into the restaurant as if, again, she had been suddenly summoned and had hurried. She sat down between Bech and Petrov slightly breathless and fussed, but exuding, again, that impalpable warmth of intelligence and virtue.

"Vera, Vera," Petrov said.

"You hurry too much," Bech told her.

"Not so very much," she said.

Petrov ordered her a cognac and continued with Bech their discussion of the newer French novelists. "It is tricks," Petrov said. "Good tricks, but tricks. It does not have enough to do with life, it is too much verbal nervousness. Is that sense?"

"It's an epigram," Bech said.

"There are just two of their number with whom I do not feel this: Claude Simon and Samuel Beckett. You have no relation, Bech, Beckett?"

"None."

Vera said, "Nathalie Sarraute is a very modest woman. She felt motherly to me."

"You have met her?"

"In Paris I heard her speak. Afterward there was the coffee. I liked her theories, of the, oh, *what?* Of the *little* movements within the heart." She delicately measured a pinch of space and smiled, through Bech, back at herself.

"Tricks," Petrov said. "I do not feel this with Beckett; there, in a low form, believe it or not, one has human content."

Bech felt duty-bound to pursue this, to ask about the theatre of the absurd in Bulgaria, about abstract painting. These were the touchstones of American-style progressiveness; Russia had none, Romania some, Czechoslovakia plenty. Instead, he asked the poetess, "Motherly?"

Vera explained, her hands delicately modelling the air, rounding into nuance, as it were, the square corners of her words. "After her talk, we— talked."

"In French?"

"And in Russian."

"She knows Russian?"

"She was born Russian."

"How is her Russian?"

"Very pure but—old-fashioned. Like a book. As she talked, I felt in a book, safe."

"You do not always feel safe?"

"Not always."

"Do you find it difficult to be a woman poet?"

"We have a tradition of woman poets. We have Elisaveta Bagriyana, who is very great."

Petrov leaned toward Bech as if to nibble him. "Your own works? Are they influenced by the *nouvelle vague?* Do you consider yourself to write anti-*romans?*"

Bech kept himself turned toward the woman. "Do you want to hear about how I write? You don't, do you?"

"Very much yes," she said.

He told them, told them shamelessly, in a voice that surprised him with its steadiness, its limpid urgency, how once he had written, how in *Travel Light* he had sought to show people skimming the surface of things with their lives, taking tints from things the way that objects in a still life color one another, and how later he had attempted to place beneath the melody of plot a countermelody of imagery, interlocking images which had risen to the top and drowned his story, and how in *The Chosen* he had sought to make of this confusion the theme itself, an epic theme, by showing a population of characters whose actions were all determined, at the deepest level, by nostalgia, by a desire to get back, to dive, each, into the springs of their private imagery. The book probably failed; at least, it was badly received. Bech apologized for telling all this. His voice tasted flat in his mouth; he felt a secret intoxication and a secret guilt, for he had contrived to give a grand air, as of an impossibly noble and quixotically complex experiment, to his failure, when at bottom, he suspected, a certain simple laziness was the cause.

Petrov said, "Fiction so formally sentimental could not be composed in Bulgaria. We do not have a happy history."

It was the first time Petrov had sounded like a Communist. If there was one thing that irked Bech about these people behind the mirror, it was their assumption that, however second-rate elsewhere, in suffering they were supreme. He said, "Believe it or not, neither do we."

Vera calmly intruded. "Your personae are not moved by love?"

"Yes, very much. But as a form of nostalgia. We fall in love, I tried to say in the book, with women who remind us of our first landscape. A silly idea. I used to be interested in love. I once wrote an essay on the orgasm—you know the word?—"

She shook her head. He remembered that it meant Yes.

"—on the orgasm as perfect memory. The one mystery is, what are we remembering?"

She shook her head again, and he noticed that her eyes were gray, and that in their depths his image (which he could not see) was searching for the thing remembered. She composed her fingertips around the brandy glass and said, "There is a French poet, a young one, who has written of this. He says that never else do we, do we so gather up, collect into ourselves, oh—" Vexed, she spoke to Petrov in rapid Bulgarian.

He shrugged and said, "Concentrate our attention."

"—concentrate our attention," she repeated to Bech, as if the words, to be believed, had to come from her. "I say it foolish—foolishly—but in French it is very well put and—*correct.*"

Petrov smiled neatly and said, "This is an enjoyable subject for discussion, love."

"It remains," Bech said, picking his words as if the language were not native even to him, "one of the few things that still warrant meditation."

"I think it is good," she said.

"Love?" he asked, startled.

She shook her head and tapped the stem of her glass with a fingernail, so that Bech had an inaudible sense of ringing, and she bent as if to study the liquor, so that her entire body borrowed a rosiness from the brandy and burned itself into Bech's memory—the silver gloss of her nail, the sheen of her hair, the symmetry of her arms relaxed on the white tablecloth, everything except the expression on her face.

Petrov asked aloud Bech's opinion of Dürrenmatt.

Actuality is a running impoverishment of possibility. Though he had looked forward to seeing her again at the legation cocktail party and had made sure that she was invited, when it occurred, though she came, he could not get to her. He saw her enter, with Petrov, but he was fenced in by an attaché of the Yugoslav Embassy and his burnished Tunisian wife; and, later, when he was worming his way toward her diagonally, a steely hand closed on his arm and a rasping American female told him that her fifteen-year-old nephew had decided to be a writer and desperately needed advice. Not the standard crap, but real brass-knuckles advice. Bech found himself balked. He was surrounded by America: the voices, the narrow suits, the watery drinks, the clatter, the glitter. The mirror had gone opaque and gave him back only himself. He managed, in the end, as the officials were thinning out, to break through and confront her in a corner. Her coat, blond, with a rabbit collar, was already on; from its side pocket she pulled a pale volume of poems in the Cyrillic alphabet. "Please," she said. On the flyleaf she had written, "to H. Beck, sincerelly, with bad spellings but much"—the last word looked like "leave" but must have been "love."

"Wait," he begged, and went back to where his ravaged pile of presentation books had been and, unable to find the one he wanted, stole the legation library's jacketless copy of *The Chosen*. Placing it in her expectant hands, he told her, "Don't look," for inside he had written, with a drunk's stylistic confidence,

Dear Vera Glavanakova—

It is a matter of earnest regret for me that you and I must live on opposite sides of the world.

The Hermit

HE HAD HAD BROTHERS—two older than he, and one younger. He remembered his childhood as a tussle, a noisy competition for food, for clothes that fit, for attention. Now, in the woods, there was no noise. There was sound, but not noise. In the beginning, during the first nights, the scrabbling and travelling of animals—the house apparently adjoined a confluence of paths—felt loud and harsh to him, a crackling and rustling that overflowed his consciousness, which was held cupped for sleep. Now he no longer heard these sounds, as a mechanic is deaf to a machine that is working smoothly. As he settled in, as March yielded to April and April to May, everything in his sudden environment sank into invisibility, into the utter transparency of perfect order.

And yet never in his life had he seen so well, seen so much. He had never excelled at school or in the competition within the family; something he could not quite believe was as simple as stupidity clouded his apprehension. Something numbed his grip at the moment of grasping, unfocused his wits at the demand for concentration, scattered his purpose when it needed to be single. It was as if his mind, or that set of switches and levers that translated his mind into the motions of the outer world, was too finely adjusted to bear the jostle of others, to function in the heavy damp climate human activity bred. The climate of humanity, he saw now, had never been congenial to him.

He had found the house while hunting, deep in the tract of second- or third-growth forest owned by a steel company. The steel company was at the other end of the state, in Pittsburgh. Fifteen years ago it had bought local land wholesale, on the speculation that it contained low-grade iron ore. The company had not yet mined it and perhaps never would. In the meantime, these hundreds of acres grew wild, submerging their interior demarcations—old boundary stones and tumbling dry walls and rusting barbed-wire fences like strands of a forgotten debate.

The house frightened him when he first saw it. A roofless sandstone shell with some cedar shingles still clinging to a lean-to, it had no business being there. Its ghostly presence turned the wilderness menacing. How old was it? The trees around it were tall but not thick, and a vestigial farmyard remained, earth too packed to encourage roots. Perhaps the land had been cleared a century ago, perhaps it had been farmed as recently as before the war. He saw no sign of a fire in the ruin. Not only the roof but the floor had been carried away by weather; the cellar hole, brimming with tumbled rocks and matted brambles, gaped between the floor beams, which were still solid enough to support his weight. They were spaced a stride apart, and when he looked up, the blue sky showing between the naked rafters exhilarated him, as if, a little dizzily, he had taken flight in a skeletal basket attached to a great blue balloon. With necessarily rhythmic motions he stepped from beam to beam, remembering an uncle of his who played the organ in the Lutheran church, and how precisely this uncle's feet would dance on the pedal keyboard.

Part of the house was still sheltered. What must have been the kitchen, the lean-to, still held its roof and its floor. There was even part of an interior wall—papered pine boarding rather than plaster-and-lath—and a doorframe from which the door had long vanished. Another doorless rectangle straddled a sandstone threshold bearing two damp depressions— puddles smaller than saucers—and a patch of parallel grooves left by the mason's serrated chisel. The stone was intact, and the timbering that boxed in the shattered windows seemed, though pitted and warped, sound enough. With doors, fresh sashes, some reboarding and shingling, the room could be made weathertight. He wondered why no one else had thought of it. The site seemed ignored even by vandals. The initials gouged here and there were as gray as the wood. The cola cans scattered in the cellar hole had rotted with rust, and the empty shotgun shells below one sill seemed older than last hunting season. Perhaps, he thought, the steel company had discouraged trespassers and then lost interest, in the lordly way of giants. Certainly the house seemed to be waiting for no one but him, not even for lovers.

His younger brother, the schoolteacher, was the first to visit him. He had not been here a week and was still engaged in carpentry. A factory-puttied window sash, each pane labelled with the purple emblem of the glass company, was leaning against a birch, giving the bits of moss and grass around the roots the refracted, pampered look of greenhouse shoots. It was March, and the undergrowth was still simple and precious. Each mottled spear of skunk cabbage nosing its way up through the leaf mold had an air of arrival. A smothered spring made the ground on this side of the house very damp.

"It's not your land, Stanley," his brother told him. "It's not even government land."

"Well, they can kick me off, then. All I can lose is the lumber and nails."

"How much do you want to use it?"

"I don't know yet."

"Is there a woman you're going to bring up?" Morris's delicate skin registered a blush; Stanley had to laugh. Morris was younger even than his years. He was now in his late twenties, and had grown a mustache; it was as if a child had painted a male doll with the delicate pink of a girl and then, realizing its mistake, had solemnly dabbed black beneath the nose.

Stanley said, "Couldn't I use my room for a woman?" It was an unkind joke, for Morris had complained about such use. Their rooms were side by side on the third floor of the parental house. There all of the brothers lived except Tom, who had moved to California. Their parents were dead. Bernard, the oldest brother, a contractor, with his wife and two sons occupied most of the house, though by the terms of the will they all owned it equally. Stanley's right to live there had never been questioned.

Morris winced, and spoke rapidly. "I guess," he said. "You have before. Anyway, none of your whores could hike this far." To emphasize his sharpness and coldness of voice he kicked a clump of skunk cabbage, smashing it, so that its scent of carrion flooded the air. "You'll make a fool of the family," he added, and Stanley was struck by how loud, for all of Morris's rosy delicacy, how loud his presence was—how he seemed to fill, with the speed of a spreading odor, so much of the bowl-shaped greening space around the house.

Stanley felt pressed, defensive. "Nobody need know."

"Will you work?"

Stanley could not quite grasp the essence of this question. He had two jobs: he was a custodian—a janitor—at the school where Morris taught, and in the summer he worked for Bernard, as a common laborer, digging trenches, mixing cement, knocking together forms, since he had some skill as a carpenter. Though he had always seemed to himself on the verge of a decisive inner graduation, Stanley had not finished the eleventh grade; there was a light above him he could not rise to out of the surrounding confusion, a din that infected his head.

"Well, why not?" he answered, and Morris grunted, satisfied.

But it had been a good question, for in fact the trek through the mile of woods to the town seemed to lengthen rather than, as do most distances, shorten with use. Each piece of furniture fetched from his room to the old kitchen added weight to each departure. It was especially unnatural to set out at dawn, in the moist brown muddle before the slanting light had sorted out the tree trunks, when the twigs were heavy with clouded drops that seemed congelations of the starry night; Stanley felt, pushing out from his clearing, as if he were tearing a skin, forcing a ripeness. His house had grown tight around him. He liked especially the contrast between the weathered lumber, seeming to seek through wind and rain its original twisted, branching state, and his patches of fresh pine, trim and young-smelling. Patchwork, with its sensation of thrift, had always pleased him. He had preferred, once past the stylishness of adolescence, to wear old clothes skillfully held back from the rag pile, in this way frus-trating time—though the presence of these mended rents and barely visible patches had given him, for all their skill, a forlorn and crazy aura. And this same instinctive hatred of waste, a conservative desire for post-ponement, led him to prolong the periods between haircuts and to shave only on alternate days, doubling the life of the blades. So that his pas-sionate inward neatness was expressed in outward dishevelment—an inversion typical of his telescopic relations with society. He found himself increasingly unwilling to enter this society, even by way of the subter-ranean passages of the high-school basement. The students, he knew, mocked his stoop, his considerate slowness. Tentatively, expecting, as in his early experiments with sex, to be rebuked and instead emptying his sin into a strange indifference, he stayed away from work an odd day now and then, and then an entire week. He let himself grow a beard. To his surprise it came out red, though the rest of his hair was black. His oldest brother came to see him.

Bernard's presence, though less anxious than Morris's, was bigger; his voice, to ears accustomed to nothing more declamatory than birdsong and nocturnal animals' rustle, seemed huge, a massive rupture in the web of life. Bernard was wearing a dark suit in the green glade; it was Sunday. He was sweating, angry. "I had Hell's own time finding you."

"There's a stone wall you must keep on your left. I used to get lost myself." Stanley's voice sounded strange to him, a dry crackling; he had not used it for days except, in a vague way, to sing.

"Tell me one thing. Are you as crazy as you look?"

"I can shave when I go to town."

"I didn't mean just the beard—but, speaking of that, do you know it's come out orange?"

"I know. I have a mirror."

"My boys ask, 'Where's Uncle Stan?' "

"Bring them out. They can spend the night if they'd like. But just them, not their friends. I couldn't put up too many."

"Then in your mind this is camping out?"

Stanley wanted to understand; so much importance seemed attached to his understanding. "Camping out?"

"You know what they're saying in town?"

"About me?"

"They say you've become a hermit."

An odd joy, the tepid blow of morning light, touched Stanley. Dignity and certainty were assigned to the vague thing he had been doing. He had been becoming a hermit. One brother was a contractor, another taught school, another lived in California, and he was a hermit. It was better than a diploma; but he hadn't earned it. He said cautiously, "I hadn't thought of it that way."

Bernard in turn seemed pleased. He shifted his feet as if he had at last found sockets solid enough for their intense weight. "How had you thought of it exactly? Does this have to do with Loretta, or Leinbach, or who?"

Stanley remembered these names. Leinbach was the head custodian and Loretta was a woman who lived alone in a trailer. Leinbach was slender and fussy, with sunken temples and bright broken veins in his nose. Each day he wore a freshly laundered gray shirt to work, carrying his wife on his back in the sheen of her ironing. He demonstrated such jealous concern for the school's three great boilers that it seemed their heat kept his own blood warm. Loretta was pink and white and smooth, and loved her beer, and laughed when she thought of how life had unhitched her trailer and stranded her on the edge of a cornfield. Morning glories twined up the cinder-block supports that had replaced the trailer's wheels. Stanley was always delighted by how thriftily the bathroom and kitchen fixtures, unfolding on nickel-coated hinges, were fitted into their envelopes of space. But at times Loretta was frantic and bitter; a coarse grief and sourceless storm of outrage would cancel out her smoothness and shake the trailer's dainty compartments. He gathered that somehow even he, Stanley, was wronging her. Once, on the last day before Christmas vacation, he had accidentally smothered the fire in the third boiler with too great a draught of pea coal. Leinbach, his face grim, his veins livid, had rushed to revive the flames with such fierce haste and spat such vile language that Stanley wondered if it had been a quadrant of Leinbach's own heart he had mistakenly allowed to flicker and choke. This possible confusion cooled, strangely, his feelings for Loretta. There was a passion loose in the world that might burn him. He told Bernard, "No, it's nobody in particular."

"Then what? What's this about? You'll rot here."

"Have you seen Leinbach?"

"He told me to tell you to stay away. The school can't keep a queer on the staff, they must think of the kids."

This ugly word "queer" (he could see Leinbach's mouth twist, pronouncing it) made Stanley stubborn. "Because of where I live?"

"And he hasn't even seen the beard. When are you going to shave?"

"Not when Leinbach tells me."

Bernard laughed; the noise broke like a shot. "Stay, then. You can start work for me early. I've commenced a row of foundations out toward the cemetery hill."

"If you don't need me yet, I'd just as soon wait a while."

Bernard took off his coat and appeared to enter, combatively, into the spirit of the woods. "*I* don't need *you*, Stan," he said. "It's the other way around." When Stanley neither admitted this nor argued, Bernard said, louder, "Go crazy, then."

"It's the other way, like you say. I'm trying to clear my head."

"Sit and stink out here. Squat on your own shit. You'll be crawling down soon enough. Here. I'll leave you my cigarettes."

"Bernie, thanks, but I don't smoke that much out here."

Stanley was left, after the thrashing footsteps receded from his ears, with the ringing sense—heartening, on the whole—of having struggled with his brother and having achieved the usual postponement of total defeat.

With tendrils of habit the hermit rooted himself in the woods. Solitude is a two-dimensional condition whose problems can be neatly plotted. Pure water ran in a nearby rivulet. Stanley cooked, on a double kerosene burner, canned foods bought once a week at the dying corner store on the near edge of town, a store grateful for his business. Though he had his gun, he shot nothing, for fear of poaching and offending the invisible authorities who left him undisturbed. The cooking conveniently partitioned the days, and, rewarming and combining leftovers, he was able to indulge his fondness for patchwork. The problem of elimination he solved with a succession of deeply dug and gradually refilled holes that he imagined would always exist, as wells of special fertility in the woods. For exercise, he cut fallen wood, and for warmth burned it in the ancient kitchen fireplace that he had cleared in the old manner, by pulling a small pine tree down the chimney. He read very little. Kerosene, lugged through the woods in a five-gallon can, was too precious to be used for light. On one of his scavenging trips to his old home he went into the dark attic and took two books at random from the dusty stacks his mother had accumulated. She had been a tireless reader—a hermit in her way. Downstairs he found in his hands a dun-colored novel of English society dated 1913 and the moss-green memoirs of an actress who had toured the American West after the Civil War. He read a few pages from one or the other each twilight, in the magical spirit in which people used to read the Bible, expecting not continuous sense but abrupt, fragmentary illumination. And, indeed, he was rarely disappointed, for whether the scene was the ballroom of a Sussex manor house or an improvised arena in Dodge City, the events (the daughter of an impoverished nobleman declines to dance with the son of a powerful industrialist; a Mexican bandit is assassinated during the mad scene of *King Lear*) had the same brilliant surprisingness, quick high tints suggestive of a supernatural world.

> The gallant old Duchess, her hopes so insolently dashed, indicated her desire to be carried from the room, toward a sanctum where their scintillating fragments could be considered with a loving eye, perhaps, to their reassembly.

It was a rare page that did not contain some sentence striking in its oblique pertinence, curving from the page upward into Stanley's eyes, his mind, his life.

> I felt the presence of dread Panic in the audience. I maintained my prattling song uninterruptedly but the menacing murmur swelled. Inspired by desperation, I stood, tore off my cap and bells, and allowed my long hair to cascade around my motley. Better than I had dared dream, the revelation that the Fool was a Woman shocked the crowd into silence and composure. The ovation which I received at the end of the act from these rough men left me weak and weeping.

In such passages Stanley seemed to encounter some angel within himself, a woman sexlessly garbed, demanding he continue his climb up the stairs of his days toward a plateau of final clarification.

Though the days submitted to a design, the nights proved slippery; an uncontrollable intruder appeared—insomnia—to ravage and mock the order of his existence. Several nights, sleep evaded him entirely; often he awoke under a cold moon and, trying to hurry with closed eyes back through the dark door that had blown ajar, found it locked until dawn, with a breath of light, blew it open again. It was as if in lightening himself of so much of the world he had made himself too buoyant to sink—as if in purging himself of so much dross he had violated an animal necessity that took its revenge on his stripped nerves, like teeth that hurt after a cleaning. To relax himself, he would remember women, but his emissions into these ghosts merely amplified his hollowness. Lying awake, he dreamed he was a stone drained of weight, a body without personality, and wondered if his personal existence had ever been actual or was merely an illusion that these women had given him.

First there had been his mother, gloating over him as one of her four growing boys even though in some respects he looked to be the slow one, and then the straggling succession of kind encouragers ending with Loretta, who in intimacy had praised this and that about his body, so that the memory of her, or even the vision of her two-toned trailer sitting with its hitch ensnarled in vines, physically broadened his chest, tightened his skin. Why, indeed, did he keep a mirror but as a kind of woman, in whom he sought—cocking his head to catch the best light, smoothing his beard, smiling secretively—the angles previously made vivid by admiration? Even when under his mother's care he had sensed that the very quality which made him laggard in some respects gave his outward form the leisure to fill itself out with a fullness skimped in his less passive brothers. He was glad when Loretta came to see him. It happened late in April. Her incongruous body, in a blue dress and gray sweater, approached through the trees and waded across the treeless farmyard. The farmyard was now filled with ferns that swallowed her ankles. Her ankles were fine for so fat a woman.

"Well, Jesus," she said, halting. "Look at you."

"Look at *you*," he said. "I didn't know you could walk so far."

Unlike the others, she had come toward evening. She asked, "Aren't you going to have me in?"

"Sure," he said. Her advance was smooth, unstoppable. "It's not as tidy as your trailer." He felt fussed and pleased, invaded to his bones, as she stepped across the grooved and pitted threshold and examined the efficient interior he had formed, and found nothing to laugh at.

"You've done all right," she said seriously, awed. Then she laughed.

"What are you laughing at?"

"It reminded me of something, and now I know what. I once knew a Chinese bachelor who lived like this, in the middle of Philly. It smelled like this. Maybe it's the kerosene. Let me smell you." She unbuttoned the two top buttons of his shirt, tugged down the neck of his undershirt, put her snub nose against his skin, and sniffed. "You don't smell Chinese yet, you still smell like Stanley. Your heart's thumping."

"It's been a time."

"I didn't think you wanted me to come."

"I don't think I did want you to come."

"But I'm here now, huh?"

"You're here."

"How cold does it get at night?"

"Not so bad now. We'll be O.K. Are you hungry?"

"Thirsty."

He looked down into her face to see in what sense she meant thirst, but the sun was low and his own body blocked her from the window light, so all he felt of her face was its shadowy warmth and a gingery perfume that perhaps dwelled in her hair. He gave her the cot and put a blanket on the floor beside it, so that each time he awoke that night he saw her above him, her bare bent arm luminous, her heavy body floating cloudlike on the spindly crossed legs of the cot and bellying the underside of the canvas. As if it had become possible to tamper with the sky and move the moon, he reached and touched, and then became confused, for, as her body encircled his and slipped across his fingertips, she seemed now vast and now terribly thin, thin with a child's expectant thinness as her frame yearned toward some sought position in relation to the fixed stars of his own system.

He slept late, awaking to the sound of her working on his stove. The metallic rummaging annoyed him; she seemed to be tinkering inside his head. From the back, in faded blue, she looked swollen, having feasted on him. She cursed his kerosene burners, which were reluctant to light. He turned her from his stove and, naked, used his body as a wedge to separate her from the instruments, the stove and pans, of his private life. She yielded complacently at first, but by the time he was through her eyes were strained by anger. Dabs of sunlight shuffled on the coarse floor like coins perpetually being counted. He lay upon an adversary who in a single space of breathing might swell enough to overthrow him. They rose, and her storm came—the tears, the scorn, the stony-voiced repetitions, the pitiable reversals toward tenderness. Looking past her head, his chin burning in the halo of her uncombed hair, he saw the window giving on the morning woods as an aquarium from whose magic jagged world of green leaves stricken with sunshine this weeping would keep him forever sealed. He gave her breakfast and walked her to the edge of the land, where the steel company's No Trespassing signs were posted.

"I won't come again," she said.

"It's too hard for you," he told her.

"You know what you're doing?" she asked, and then answered, "You're pouring yourself down the drain."

"I'm just like you in the trailer," he said, smiling and watching her face for the reflection of his smile. "Independent."

"No," she said, in the tone of dry calm that followed her storms, "it's been forced on me. But you're choosing."

How grateful he was, after all, to his visitors!—for each of them left him something to clarify his situation. He was choosing, yes, and, treading back through the woods, welcomed by the calls of unseen birds and the gestures of unnamed plants, he sought for some further choice, some additional dismissal with which he could atone for the night's parasitic pleasure. He smashed the mirror. He held it squarely above the hearthstone, so the last thing it reflected was a slice of blue zenith, and let it drop. The fragments he swept up and buried in a place far from the house, covering the earth with leaves so he could not find the spot again. But from that sector of woods, for a while, he felt watched, by buried eyes. The sensation passed in daylight but persisted at night, when it gave his sleep depth, as had knowing when he was a child that his mother, moving around downstairs, would on her way to bed come into his room and touch his forehead and tuck the kicked covers around him. Insomnia ceased to visit him. After Loretta's visit, he grew drowsy at twilight, was often unable to read a word, and rose with the sun.

He never saw so well, saw so much. Chill April yielded to frilly May. Buds of a hundred designs had broken unbidden. He became aware, intensely, of tiny distinctions—shades of brown and gray in the twigs, differences in the shapes of leaves, the styles of growing, a cadence expressed in the angle at which a hooved branchlet thrust from the parent branch. That he could not articulate these distinctions or could hardly name a dozen trees and flowers bathed the populations of growth in a glistening transparency like that left by mist; as his mind slowly sorted the sea of green into types, he greeted each recognized specimen not with its name but with its very image, as one remembers a sister whose name, through marriage, has ceased to apply. His mind became a beautiful foreign book whose illustrations were enhanced, in precision and wonder, by the unintelligibility of the text. First venturing onto the spaced beams of the floorless house, he had thought of a church organ's pedals, and now the finely tuned strata of distinctions, fixed yet pliant, seemed a greater instrument, either waiting to be struck or else played so continually that an instant of silence would have boomed in his ears. The patient intricacy of moss and grass fascinated him. There was no realm so small that it repelled distinctions. Stanley felt the green and reticulate mass around him as so infinitely divisible that the thickness of a veil was coarse in comparison. Nature, that sturdy net of interlocking rapacity, dissolved for him in its own unsayable exactness, and ceased to exist, or existed merely as the description of something else.

Some boys came to see him: his two nephews and a friend. The friend was thin, new in the town, with a close-cropped skull and brown eyes so dark they seemed round. Stanley felt, awkwardly entertaining his guests, that he was addressing mostly this stranger, for the familiar leeringness and the competitive jostling of his brother's boys were things which he had determinedly ignored even when he shared a house with their noise. His visitors seemed chastened by his strangeness. He could not think what to show them; these boys had expected, perhaps, some piece of work, some monument to testify to the accumulation of his days. But there was nothing, nothing except the shelter on which he had ceased to make improvements—that, and Stanley's delicately altered sense of actuality. He walked them through the woods, showed them the overgrown rectangle of rubble where a barn must have stood, pointed out the tidy deposits of pellets with which the smaller mammals of the woods declared their presence, bid the boys bend with him to examine a bank where a combination of exposed roots, rocks, moss, and erosion had created a castle, or chain of castles, inhabited by ants. The boys began to crush the ants; Stanley shouted, and they backed from him, and he glimpsed his gauntness, his bristling red beard, in their eyes. They explored, taking him farther in the woods than he had ever thought to go alone, to a point from which the smoking chimney of a house and a glinting strip of highway could be seen. On the way they made themselves clubs and smashed them against dead branches and pitched their entire weight against dead young trees whose skeletons had hung vertical, undisturbed, for years, upheld by the arms of the trees that had stifled them. Wherever they circled, the boys flushed death, finding the cough balls of owls wadded with mouse bones, the bloated elongated corpse of a groundhog mangled by dogs, the mysteriously severed forefoot of a deer. The matrix of abundant life held for them only these few nodes of slaughter. Stanley gave each boy an apple to provision their trek home, and sent them off with no invitation to return. In parting he sensed a susceptibility in the third child, a curiosity in those round eyes not quite satisfied, a willingness to be taught that offered itself to Stanley, in the midst of his slow learning, as a new temptation—to be a teacher. But the boy disappeared with the two others.

Stanley, who when he had lived among men had infrequently bathed, because the drawing and pollution of water seemed a waste, now bathed often, because in the nearby rivulet the water ran pure night and day and not to have used it would have been a waste. The stream was only inches deep and a man's width wide; to wet himself Stanley had to lie on the bed of red sand and smoothed sandstones and make of himself a larger stone that the little stream, fumbling at first, consented to lave. To wet his back he would roll over and lie staring up at the explosive blue rents in the canopy of leaves and feel the icy stream divide at his scalp. Then he would rise, dripping, a silver man, and walk naked back, slightly uphill, through the warm ragged mulch of last autumn's leaves. He had thought of building a dam, but the thought offended him. Still water would attract mosquitoes. More obscurely, the gap of water while the stream pooled would carry through the woods toward the sea as a kind of outcry betraying his existence here. Yet, though there was no natural pool where he could so much as squat, it was important in this bathing that every inch of him, even his eyelids, know the water. Otherwise he could not walk through the woods married to the surrounding purity.

One day, thus returning, he was conscious of being watched, but blamed the buried mirror until he saw, standing startled in the lake of ferns in front of the house, the third boy, alone. The boy was the first to speak. "I'm sorry," he said, and turned to run, and Stanley, seized by an abrupt fear of loss, of being misunderstood, ran after him—a terrifying figure, probably, gaunt and wet and wordlessly openmouthed among the serene verticals of the trees, his penis bobbing. The boy ran faster, and Stanley soon stopped. His pounding heart seemed to run a few paces farther and then return to the protection of his shaking rib cage. He was amazed at himself, ashamed. His spurt of pursuit had reversed months of patient waiting, waiting—he saw now—for himself to be overtaken. He saw how narrowly he had escaped a ruinous distraction, a disciple who would have diluted his vulnerable solitude and siphoned goodness from him faster than it could be secreted.

Now, each morning, he awoke with a sense of having been called. At first, it was the slightest of sensations, imparting a shadowy, guilty restlessness to his waking motions. Gradually, as the sensation was repeated on the following three mornings, the unheard voice gathered to itself clear impressions of masculinity, of infinite gentleness and urgency. It was distinct from any dream; he knew what dreams were, and this call cut through them. The call took place, as near as he could judge, in the instant between his dreams' stopping and his eyelids' opening. But also it seemed to underlie the dreams, like a telephone ringing in another room; the dream phantoms derived from his memories of humanity were mocked and made doubly phantasmal, performing in patterns constantly twisted and interrupted by an underlying pressure. In his desire to hear the voice, so to speak, face to face, to grasp its masculinity and taste its urgency direct, Stanley fell asleep as if diving toward a rendezvous. For two nights, in reprimand, the voice was silent. A humble learner, he concluded that the voice had been unreal, that he was drawing close, as Bernard had predicted, to going crazy. The next morning, the seventh since the sensation had first touched him, it touched him strongly, just as the dark was softening. He sat up in answer to a command spoken in the room and perceived that the call was a condensation, like the dawn dew, of a reality that existed continually, that persisted through daylight. The minute truth of bark textures, the many-layered translucence of leaves, the stately gliding intervals between tree trunks all bespoke something that wanted to be answered, a silence unsure of itself. But it was so shy, so tactful, that to hear it distinctly would be like—as Stanley had once read of counterfeiters doing—dividing a dollar bill edgewise with a razor blade.

Though he turned aside to cook, to eat, to swing his ax into a fallen birch, the sensation remained, singing in the spaces between ax strokes, permeating the day. It was within reach, the graduation he sought, the final clarity, a tissue width removed from apprehension; it was waiting for him to be totally still. Then, he knew, this vaporous presence would condense into words and pour itself generously into his mind. He bathed, dried himself, dressed in fresh clothes he had himself washed in the brook and to whose clean faded fibres adhered a few reddish granules of sand, like sacred salt. He composed himself on the broad flat threshold, and listened. A single twig lay half in, half out of an oval of moisture that the shape of the stone had collected. A breeze transparently touched the tree-tops, and in a flickering of green the high leaves sharpened themselves against the whetstone of light. A silence embraced all phenomena; the sound beneath the silence approached. Stanley leaned his back against the door frame, wondered vaguely what the wood itself felt, and relaxed into a joy not very different from fear.

The forest shattered; Morris broke from the trees and ran panting toward him, shook him, cursed him. "You've ruined us! You've made fools of all of us!"

Stanley could not speak, he was so deeply locked in the fibrous grasp of what had almost overtaken him. He looked up at his brother and saw a walking fever, a flushed pink skin that seared his green mind painfully.

"What got into you? The kid was so scared he went for days without telling. Bernie's been fighting to keep you out of jail. They're right behind me. I ran ahead to get you to put your clothes on."

But he had them on. Though tempted to protest, and aware that Morris wanted a response, Stanley chose not to desecrate his portion of the silence. He turned his head and saw the erect shadows that had appeared on the far edge of the field of ferns. Bernard, his two boys eager like hounds, the third boy, quailing, transfixed in the cataract of misunderstanding. There were two other men. One wore wine-colored slacks, a zebra shirt, and sunglasses, which he removed. It was Tom, come from California, clothed more strangely than a hermit. And a man in a gray business suit: with his new clarity of vision Stanley saw that he was a medical officer, or an agent of the steel company. He saw them all as standing upon a sea of more than crystalline fragility, achieved cell by cell in silence. Then they came rapidly toward him, and there was a thumping, a bumbling, a clumsy crushing clamor.

I Am Dying, Egypt, Dying

CLEM CAME FROM BUFFALO and spoke in the neutral American accent that sends dictionary makers there. His pronunciation was clear and colorless, his manners were impeccable, his clothes freshly laundered and appropriate no matter where he was, however far from home. Rich and unmarried, he travelled a lot; he had been to Athens and Rio, Las Vegas and Hong Kong, Leningrad and Sydney, and now Cairo. His posture was perfect, but he walked without swing; people at first liked him, because his apparent perfection reflected flatteringly upon them, and then distrusted him, because his perfection disclosed no flaw. As he travelled, he studied the guidebooks conscientiously, picked up words of the local language, collected prints and artifacts. He was serious but not humorless; indeed, his smile, a creeping but finally complete revelation of utterly even and white front teeth, with a bit of tongue flirtatiously pinched between them, was one of the things that led people on, that led them to hope for the flaw, the entering crack. There were hopeful signs. At the bar he took one drink too many, the hurried last drink that robs the dinner wine of taste. Though he enjoyed human society, he couldn't dance, politely refusing always.

He had a fine fair square-shouldered body, surely masculine and yet somehow neutral, which he solicitously covered with oil against the sun that, as they moved up the Nile, grew sharper and more tropical. He fell asleep in deck chairs, uncannily immobile, glistening, as the two riverbanks at their safe distance glided by—date palms, taut green fields irrigated by rotating donkeys, pyramids of white round pots, trapezoidal houses of elephant-colored mud, mud-colored children silently waving, and the roseate desert cliffs beyond, massive parentheses. Glistening like a mirror, he slept in this gliding parenthesis with a godlike calm that possessed the landscape, transformed it into a steady dreaming. Clem said of himself, awaking, apologizing, smiling with that bit of pinched tongue, that he slept badly at night, suffered from insomnia. This also was a hopeful sign. People wanted to love him.

There were not many on the boat. The Six-Day War had discouraged tourists. Indeed, at Nag Hammadi they did pass under a bridge in which Israeli commandos had blasted three neat but not very conclusive holes; some wooden planks had been laid on top and the traffic of carts and rickety lorries continued. And at Aswan they saw anti-aircraft batteries defending the High Dam. For the cruise, the war figured as a luxurious amount of space on deck and a pleasant disproportion between the seventy crewmen and the twenty paying passengers. These twenty were:

Three English couples, middle-aged but for one miniskirted wife, who was thought for days to be a daughter.

Two German boys; they wore bathing trunks to all the temples, yet seemed to know the gods by name and perhaps were future archaeologists.

A French couple, in their sixties. The man had been tortured in World War II; his legs were unsteady, and his spine had fused in a curve. He moved over the desert rubble and uneven stairways with tiny shuffling steps and studied the murals by means of a mirror hung around his neck. Yet he, too, knew the gods and would murmur worshipfully.

Three Egyptians, a man and two women, in their thirties, of a professional class, teachers or museum curators, cosmopolitan and handsome, given to laughter among themselves, even while the guide, a cherubic old Bedouin called Poppa Omar, was lecturing.

A fluffy and sweet, ample and perfumed American widow and her escort, a short bald native of New Jersey who for fifteen years had run tours in Africa, armed with a fancy fly whisk and an impenetrable rudeness toward natives of the continent.

A small-time travelogue-maker from Green Bay working his way south to Cape Town with a hundred pounds of photographic equipment.

A stocky blond couple, fortyish, who kept to themselves, hired their own guides, and were presumed to be Russian.

A young Scandinavian woman, beautiful, alone.

Clem.

Clem had joined the cruise at the last minute; he had been in Amsterdam and become oppressed by the low sky and tight-packed houses, the cold canal touring boats and the bad Indonesian food and the prostitutes illuminated in their windows like garish great candy. He had flown to Cairo and not liked it better. A cheeseburger in the Hilton offended him by being gamy: a goatburger. In the plaza outside, a man rustled up to him and asked if he had had any love last night. The city, with its incessant twinkle of car horns and furtive-eyed men in pajamas, seemed unusable, remote. The museum was full of sandbags. The heart of King Tut's treasure had been hidden in case of invasion; but his gold sarcophagus, feathered in lapis lazuli and carnelian, did touch Clem, with its hint of death, of flight, of floating. A pamphlet in the Hilton advertised a six-day trip on the Nile, Luxor north to Abydos, back to Luxor, and on south to Aswan, in a luxurious boat. It sounded passive and educational, which appealed to Clem; he had gone to college at the University of Rochester and felt a need to keep rounding off his education, to bring it up to Ivy League standards. Also, the tan would look great back in Buffalo.

Stepping from the old DC-3 at the Luxor airport, he was smitten by the beauty of the desert, rose-colored and motionless around him. His element, perhaps. What was his travelling, his bachelorhood, but a search for his element? He was thirty-four and still seemed to be merely visiting the world. Even in Buffalo, walking the straight shaded streets where he had played as a small boy, entering the homes and restaurants where he was greeted by name, sitting in the two-room office where he put in the hour or two of telephoning that managed the parcel of securities and property fallen to him from his father's death, he felt somehow light— limited to forty-four pounds of luggage, dressed with the unnatural rigor people assume at the outset of a trip. A puff of air off Lake Erie and he would be gone, and the city, with its savage blustery winters, its deep-set granite mansions, its factories, its iron bison in the railroad terminal, would not have noticed. He would leave only his name in gilt paint on a list of singles tennis champions above the bar of his country club. But he knew he had been a methodical, joyless player to watch, a back-courter too full of lessons to lose.

He knew a lot about himself: he knew that this lightness, the brittle unmarred something he carried, was his treasure, which his demon willed him to preserve. Stepping from the airplane at Luxor, he had greeted his demon in the air—air ideally clean, dry as a mirror. From the window of his cabin he sensed again, in the glittering width of the Nile—much bluer than he had expected—and in the unflecked alkaline sky and in the tapestry strip of anciently worked green between them, that he would be happy for this trip. He liked sunning on the deck that first afternoon. Only the Scandinavian girl, in an orange bikini, kept him company. Both were silent. The boat was still tied up at the Luxor dock, a flight of stone steps; a few yards away, across a gulf of water and paved banking, a traffic of peddlers and cart drivers stared across. Clem liked that gulf and liked it when the boat cast loose and began gliding between the fields, the villages, the desert. He liked the first temples: gargantuan Karnak, its pillars upholding the bright blank sky; gentler Luxor, with its built-in mosque and its little naked queen touching her king's giant calf; Hollywoodish Dendera—its restored roofs had brought in darkness and dampness and bats that moved on the walls like intelligent black gloves.

Clem even, at first, liked the peddlers. Tourist-starved, they touched him in their hunger, thrusting scarabs and old coins and clay mummy dolls at him, moaning and grunting English: "How much? How much you give me? Very fine. Fifty. Both. Take both. Both for thirty-five." Clem peeked down, caught his eye on a turquoise glint, and wavered; his mother liked keepsakes and he had friends in Buffalo who would be amused. Into this flaw, this tentative crack of interest, they stuffed more things, strange sullied objects salvaged from the desert, alabaster vases, necklaces of mummy heads. Their brown hands probed and rubbed; their faces looked stunned, unblinking, as if, under the glaring sun, they were conducting business in the dark. Indeed, some did have eyes whitened by trachoma. Hoping to placate them with a purchase, Clem bargained for the smallest thing he could see, a lapis-lazuli bug the size of a fingernail. "Ten, then," the old peddler said, irritably making the "give me" gesture with his palm. Holding his wallet high, away from their hands, Clem leafed through the big notes for the absurdly small five-piaster bills, tattered and fragile with use. The purchase, amounting to little more than a dime, excited the peddlers; ignoring the other tourists, they multiplied and crowded against him. Something warm and hard was inserted into his hand, his other sleeve was plucked, his pockets were patted, and he wheeled, his tongue pinched between his teeth flirtatiously. It was a nightmare; the dream thought crossed his mind that he might be scratched, marred.

He broke away and rejoined the other tourists in the sanctum of a temple courtyard. One of the Egyptian women came up to him and said, "I do not mean to remonstrate, but you are torturing them by letting them see all those fifties and hundreds in your wallet."

"I'm sorry." He blushed like a scolded schoolboy. "I just didn't want to be rude."

"You must be. There is no question of hurt feelings. You are the man in the moon to them. They have no comprehension of your charm."

The strange phrasing of her last sentence, expressing not quite what she meant, restored his edge and dulled her rebuke. She was the shorter and the older of the two Egyptian women; her eyes were green and there was an earnest mischief, a slight pressure, in her upward glance. Clem relaxed, almost slouching. "The sad part is, some of their things, I'd rather like to buy."

"Then do," she said, and walked away, her hips swinging. So a move had been made. He had expected it to come from the Scandinavian girl.

That evening the Egyptian trio invited him to their table in the bar. The green-eyed woman said, "I hope I was not scolding. I did not mean to remonstrate, merely to inform."

"Of course," Clem said. "Listen. I was being plucked to death. I needed rescuing."

"Those men," the Egyptian man said, "are in a bad way. They say that around the hotels the shoeshine boys are starving." His face was triangular, pock-marked, saturnine. A heavy, weary courtesy slowed his speech.

"What did you buy?" the second woman asked. She was sallower than the other, and softer. Her English was the most British-accented.

Clem showed them. "Ah," the man said, "a scarab."

"The incarnation of Khepri," the green-eyed woman said. "The symbol of immortality. You will live forever." She smiled at everything she said; he remembered her smiling with the word "remonstrate."

"They're jolly things," the other woman pronounced, in her stately way. "Dung beetles. They roll a ball of dung along ahead of them, which appealed to the ancient Egyptians. Reminded them of themselves, I suppose."

"Life is that," the man said. "A ball of dung we push along."

The waiter came and Clem said, "Another whiskey sour. And another round of whatever they're having." Beer for the man, Scotch for the taller lady, lemonade for his first friend.

Having bought, he felt, the right to some education, Clem asked, "Seriously. Has the"—he couldn't bring himself to call it a war, and he had noticed that in Egypt the words "Israel" and "Israeli" were never pronounced—"trouble cut down on tourism?"

"Oh, immensely," the taller lady said. "Before the war, one had to book for this boat months ahead. Now my husband was granted two weeks and we were able to come at the last moment. It is pathetic."

"What do you do?" Clem asked.

The man made a self-deprecatory and evasive gesture, as a deity might have, asked for employment papers.

"My brother," the green-eyed woman stated, smiling, "works for the government. In, what do you call it, planning?"

As if in apology for having been reticent, her brother abruptly said,

"The shoeshine boys and the dragomen suffer for us all. In everyone in my country, you have now a deep distress of humiliation."

"I noticed," Clem said, very carefully, "those holes in the bridge we passed under."

"They brought *Jeeps* in, Jeeps. By helicopter. The papers said bombs from a plane, but it was Jeeps by helicopters from the Red Sea. They drove onto the bridge, set the charges, and drove away. We are not warriors. We are farmers. For thousands of years now, we have had others do our fighting for us—Sudanese, Libyans, Arabs. We are not Arabs. We are Egyptians. The Syrians and Jordanians, they are Arabs—crazy men. But we, we don't know who we are, except we are very old. The man who seeks to make warriors of us creates distress."

His wife put her hand on his to silence him while the waiter brought the drinks. His sister said to Clem, "Are you enjoying our temples?"

"Quite." But the temples within him, giant slices of limestone and sun, lay mute. "I also quite like," he went on, "our guide. I admire the way he says everything in English to some of us and then in French to the rest."

"Most Egyptians are trilingual," the wife stated. "Arabic, English, French."

"Which do you think in?" Clem was concerned, for he was conscious in himself of an absence of verbal thoughts; instead, there were merely glints and reflections.

The sister smiled. "In English, the thoughts are clearest. French is better for passion."

"And Arabic?"

"Also for passion. Is it not so, Amina?"

"What so, Leila?" She had been murmuring with her husband.

The question was restated in French.

"Oh, *c'est vrai, vrai.*"

"How strange," Clem said. "English doesn't seem precise to me; quite the contrary. It's a mess of synonyms and lazy grammar."

"No," the wife said firmly—she never, he suddenly noticed, smiled— "English is clear and cold, but not *nuancé* in the emotions, as is French."

"And is Arabic *nuancé* in the same way?"

The green-eyed sister considered. "More *angoisse.*"

Her brother said, "We have ninety-nine words for 'camel dung.' All different states of camel dung. Camel dung, we understand."

"Of course," Leila said to Clem, "Arabic here is nothing compared with the pure Arabic you would hear among the Saudis. The language of the Koran is so much more—can I say it?—gutsy. So guttural, nasal:

strange, wonderful sounds. Amina, does it still affect you inwardly, to hear it chanted? The Koran."

Amina solemnly agreed, "It is terrible. It tears me all apart. It is too much passion."

Italian rock music had entered the bar via an unseen radio, and one of the middle-aged English couples was trying to waltz to it. Noticing how intently Clem watched, the sister asked him, "Do you like to dance?"

He took it as an invitation; he blushed. "No, thanks, the fact is I can't."

"Can't dance? Not at all?"

"I've never been able to learn. My mother says I have Methodist feet."

"Your mother says that?" She laughed: a short shocking noise, the bark of a fox. She called to Amina, *"Sa mère dit que l'américain a les pieds méthodistes!"*

"Les pieds méthodiques?"

"Non, non, aucune méthode, la secte chrétienne—méthodisme!"

Both barked, and the man grunted. Clem sat there rigidly, immaculate in his embarrassment. Leila's green eyes, curious, pressed on him like gems scratching glass. The three Egyptians became overanimated, beginning sentences in one language and ending in another, and Clem understood that he was being laughed at. Yet the sensation, like the blurred plucking of the scarab salesmen, was better than untouched emptiness. He had another drink before dinner, the drink that was one too many, and when he went in to his single table, everything—the tablecloths, the little red lamps, the waiting droves of waiters in blue, the black windows beyond which the Nile glided—looked triumphant and glazed.

He slept badly. There were bumps and scraping above him, footsteps in the hall, the rumble of the motors, and, at four o'clock, the sounds of docking at another temple site. Once, he had found peace in hotel rooms, strange virgin corners where his mind could curl into itself, cut off from all nagging familiarities, and painlessly wink out. But he had known too many hotel rooms, so they had become themselves familiar, with their excessively crisp sheets and gleaming plumbing and easy chairs one never sat in but used as clothes racks. Only the pillows varied—neck-cracking fat bolsters in Leningrad, in Amsterdam hard little wads the size of a lady's purse, and as lumpy. Here on the floating hotel *Osiris*, two bulky pillows were provided and, toward morning, Clem discovered it relaxed him to put his head on one and his arms around the other. Some other weight in the bed seemed to be the balance that his agitated body, oscillating with hieroglyphs and sharp remonstrative glances, was craving. In his dream, the Egyptian women promised him something marvellous and showed him two tall limestone columns with blue sky between them. He awoke unrefreshed but conscious of having dreamed. On his ceiling there was a dance of light, puzzling in its telegraphic rapidity, more like electronic art than anything natural. He analyzed it as sunlight bouncing off the tremulous Nile through the slats of his venetian blinds. He pulled the blinds and there it was again, stunning in its clarity: the blue river, the green strip, the pink cliffs, the unflecked sky. Only the village had changed. The other tourists—the Frenchman being slowly steered, like a fragile cart, by an Arab boy—were already heading up a flight of wooden stairs toward a bus. Clem ran after them, into the broad day, without shaving.

Their guide, Poppa Omar, sat them down in the sun in a temple courtyard and told them the story of Queen Hatshepsut. "Remember it like this," he said, touching his head and rubbing his chest. "Hat—cheap—suit. She was wonderful woman here. Always building the temples, always winning the war and getting the nigger to be slaves. She marry her brother Tuthmosis and he grow tired here of jealous and insultation. He say to her, 'O.K., you done a lot for Egypt, take it more easy now.' She say to him, 'No, I think I just keep rolling along.' What happen? Tuthmosis die. The new king also Tuthmosis, her niece. He is a little boy. Hatshepsut show herself in all big statues wearing false beard and all flatness here." He rubbed his chest. "Tuthmosis get bigger and go say to her now, 'Too much jealous and insultation. Take it easy for Egypt now.' She say, 'No.' Then she die, and all over Egypt here, he take all her statue and smash, hit, hit, so not one face of Hatshepsut left and everywhere her name in all the walls here become Tuthmosis!" Clem looked around, and the statues had, indeed, been mutilated, thousands of years ago. He touched his own face and the whiskers scratched.

On the way back in the bus, the Green Bay travelogue-maker asked them to stop so he could photograph a water wheel with his movie camera. A tiny child met them, weeping, on the path, holding one arm as if crippled. "*Baksheesh, baksheesh*," he said. "*Musha, musha.*" One of the British men flicked at him with a whisk. The bald American announced aloud that the child was faking. Clem reached into his pocket for a piaster coin, but then remembered himself as torturer. Seeing his gesture, the child, and six others, chased after him. First they shouted, then they tossed pebbles at his heels. From within the haven of the bus, the tourists could all see the child's arm unbend. But the weeping continued and was evidently real. The travelogist was still doing the water wheel, and the peddlers began to pry open the windows and thrust in scarabs, dolls, alabaster vases not without beauty. The window beside Clem's face slid back and a brown hand insinuated an irregular parcel about six inches long, wrapped in brown cloth. "Feesh mummy," a disembodied voice said, and to Clem it seemed hysterically funny. He couldn't stop laughing; the tip of his tongue began to hurt from being bitten. The Scandinavian girl, across the aisle, glanced at him hopefully. Perhaps the crack in his surface was appearing.

Back on the *Osiris,* they basked in deck chairs. The white boat had detached itself from the brown land, and men in blue brought them lemonade, daiquiris, salty peanuts called *soudani.* Though Clem, luminous with suntan oil, appeared to be asleep, his lips moved in answer to Ingrid beside him. Her bikini was chartreuse today. "In my country," she said, "the summers are so short, naturally we take off our clothes. But it is absurd, this myth other countries have of our paganism, our happy sex. We are a harsh people. My father, he was like a man in the Bergman films. I was forbidden everything growing up—to play cards, lipstick, to dance."

"I never did learn to dance," Clem said, slightly shifting.

"Yes," she said, "I saw in you, too, a stern childhood. In a place of harsh winters."

"We had two yards of snow the other year," Clem told her. "In one storm. Two *meters.*"

"And yet," Ingrid said, "I think the thaw, when at last it comes in such places, is so dramatic, so intense." She glanced toward him hopefully.

Clem appeared oblivious within his gleaming placenta of suntan oil.

The German boy who spoke a little English was on the other side of him. By now, the third day, the sunbathers had declared themselves: Clem, Ingrid, the two young Germans, the bald-headed American, the young English wife, whose skirted bathing suits were less immodest than her ordinary dresses. The rest of the British sat on the deck in the shade of the canopy and drank; the three Egyptians sat in the lounge and talked; the supposed Russians kept out of sight altogether. The travelogist was talking to the purser about the immense chain of tickets and reservations that would get him to Cape Town; the widow was in her cabin with Egyptian stomach and a burning passion to play bridge; the French couple sat by the rail, in the sun but fully dressed, reading guidebooks, his chair tipped back precariously, so he could see the gliding landscape.

The German boy asked Clem, "Haff you bot a caftan?"

He had been nearly asleep, beneath a light, transparent headache. He said, "*Bitte?*"

"*Ein* caftan. You shoot. In Luxor; vee go back tonight. He vill measure you and haff it by morning, ven vee go. Sey are good—wery cheap."

Hatcheapsuit, Clem thought, but grunted that he might do it. His frozen poise contended within him with a promiscuous and American quality that must go forth and test, and purchase. He felt, having spurned so many scarabs and alabaster vases, that he owed Egypt some of the large-leafed money that fattened his wallet uncomfortably.

"It vood be wery handsome on you."

"Ravishing," the young English wife said behind them. She had been listening. Clem sometimes felt like a mirror that everyone glanced into before moving on.

"You're all kidding me," he announced. "But I confess, I'm a sucker for costumes."

"Again," Ingrid said, "like a Bergman film." And languorously she shifted her long arms and legs; the impression of flesh in the side of his vision disturbingly merged, in his sleepless state, with a floating sensation of hollowness, of being in parentheses.

That afternoon they toured the necropolis in the Valley of the Kings. King Tut's small two-chambered tomb—how had they crammed so much treasure in? The immense tunnels of Ramses III; or was it Ramses IV? Passageways hollowed from the limestone chip by chip, lit by systems of tilted mirrors, painted with festive stiff figures banqueting, fishing, carrying offerings of fruit forward, which was always slightly down, down past pits dug to entrap grave-robbers, past vast false chambers, toward the real and final one, a square room that would have made a nice nightclub. Its murals had been left unfinished, sketched in gray ink but uncolored. The tremors of the artist's hand, his nervous strokes, were still there, over three millennia later.

Abdul, the Egyptian planner, murmured to him, "Always they left something unfinished; it is a part of their religion that no one understands. It is thought perhaps they dreaded finishing, as closing in the dead, limiting the life beyond." They climbed up the long slanting passageway, threaded with electric lights, past hundreds of immaculate bodies carried without swing. "The dead, you see, are not dead. In their language, the word for 'death' and the word for 'life' are the same. The death they feared was the second one, the one that would come if the tomb lacked provisions for life. In the tombs of the nobles, more than here, the scenes of life are all about, like a musical—you say 'score'?—that only the dead have the instrument to play. These hieroglyphs are all instructions to the dead man, how to behave, how to make the safe journey."

"Good planning," Clem said, short of breath.

Abdul was slow to see the joke, since it was on himself.

"I mean the dead are much better planned for than the living."

"No," Abdul said flatly, perhaps misunderstanding. "It is the same."

Back in Luxor, Clem left the safe boat and walked toward the clothing shop, following the German boy's directions. He seemed to walk a long way. The narrowing streets grew shadowy. Pedestrians drifted by him in a steady procession, carrying offerings forward. No peddlers approached him; perhaps they all kept businessmen's hours, went home and totalled up the sold scarabs and fish mummies in double-entry ledgers. Radio Cairo blared and twanged from wooden balconies. Dusty intersections flooded with propaganda (or was it prayer?) faded behind him. The air was dark by the time he reached the shop. Within its little cavern of brightness, a young woman was helping a small child with homework, and a young man, the husband and father, lounged against some stacked bolts of cloth. All three persons were petite; Egyptian children, Clem had observed before, are proportioned like miniature adults, with somber staring dolls' heads. He felt oversized in this shop, whose reduced scale was here and there betrayed by a coarse object from the real world—a steam press, a color print of Nasser on the wall. Clem's voice, asking if they could make a caftan for him by morning, seemed to boom; when he tuned it down, it cracked and trembled. Measuring him, the small man touched him all over; and touches that at first had been excused as accidental declared themselves as purposeful, determined.

"Hey," Clem said, blushing.

Shielded from his wife by the rectangular bulk of Clem's body, the young man, undoing his own fly with a swift light tailor's gesture, exhibited himself. "I can make you very happy," he muttered.

"I'm leaving," Clem said.

He was at the doorway instantly, but the tailor had time to call, "Sir, when will you come back tomorrow?" Clem turned; the little man was zipped, the woman and child had their heads bent together over the homework. Nasser, a lurid ochre, scowled toward the future. Clem had intended to abandon the caftan but pictured himself back in Buffalo, wearing it to New Year's Eve at the country club, with sunglasses and sandals. The tailor looked frightened. His little mustache twitched uncertainly and his brown eyes had been worn soft by needlework.

Clem said he would be back no later than nine. The boat sailed south after breakfast. Outside, the dry air had chilled. From the tingling at the tip of his tongue, he realized he had been smiling hard.

Ingrid was sitting at the bar in a backwards silver dress, high in the front and buckled at the back. She invited herself to sit at his table during dinner; her white arms, pinched pink by the sun, shared in the triumphant glaze of the tablecloth, the glowing red lamp. They discussed religion. Clem had been raised as a Methodist, she as a Lutheran. In her father's house, north of Stockholm, there had been a guest room held ready against the arrival of Jesus Christ. Not quite seriously, it had been a custom, and yet . . . She supposed religion had bred into her a certain *expectancy*. Into him, he responded, groping, peering with difficulty into that glittering blank area which in other people, he imagined, was the warm cave of self—into him the Methodist religion had bred a certain compulsive neatness, a *dislike of litter*. It was a disappointing answer, even after he had explained the word "litter." Reckless on his third pre-dinner drink, he advanced the theory that he was a royal tomb, once crammed with treasure, that had been robbed. Her white hand moved an inch toward him on the tablecloth, intelligent as a bat, and he began to cry. The tears felt genuine to him, but she said, "Stop acting."

He told her that a distressing thing had just happened to him.

She said, "That is your flaw; you are too self-conscious. You are always in costume, acting. You must always be beautiful." She was so intent on delivering this sermon that only as an afterthought did she ask him what had been the distressing thing.

He found he couldn't tell her; it was too intimate, and his own part in provoking it had been, he felt, unspeakably shameful. The tailor's homosexual advance had been, like the child's feigning a crippled arm, evoked by his money, his torturing innocence. He said, "Nothing. I've been sleeping badly and don't make sense. Ingrid: have some more wine." His palms were sweating from the effort of pronouncing her name.

After dinner, though fatigue was making his entire body shudder and itch, she asked him to take her into the lounge, where a three-piece band from Alexandria was playing dance music. The English couples waltzed. Gwenn, the young wife, Frugged with one of the German boys. The green-eyed Egyptian woman danced with the purser. Egon, the German boy who knew some English, came and, with a curt bow and a curious hard stare at Clem, invited Ingrid. She danced, Clem observed, very close, in the manner of one who, puritanically raised, thinks of it only as a substitute for intercourse. After many numbers, she was returned to him unmarred, still silver, cool, and faintly admonitory. Downstairs, in the corridor where their cabin doors were a few steps apart, she asked him, her expression watchful and stern, if he would sleep better tonight. Compared with her large eyes and long nose, her mouth was small; she pursed her lips in a thoughtful pout, holding as if in readiness a small dark space between them.

He realized that her face was stern because he was a mirror in which she was gauging her beauty, her power. His smile sought to reassure her. "Yes," he said, "I'm sure I will. I'm dead beat, frankly."

And he did fall asleep quickly, but woke in the dark, to escape a dream in which the hieroglyphs and pharaonic cartouches had left the incised walls and inverted and become stamps, sharp-edged stamps trying to indent themselves upon him. Awake, he identified the dream blows with the thumping of feet and furniture overhead. He could not sink back into sleep; there was a scuttling, an occasional whispering in the corridor that he felt was coming toward him, toward his door. But once, when he opened his door, there was nothing in the corridor but bright light and several pairs of shoes. The problem of the morning prevented him from sinking back. If he went to pick up his caftan, it would seem to the tailor a submission. He would be misunderstood and vulnerable. Also, there was the danger of missing the boat. Yet the caftan would be lovely to have, a shimmering striped polished cotton, with a cartouche containing Clem's monogram in silver thread. In his agitation, his desire not to make a mistake, he could not achieve peace with his pillows; and then the telegraphic staccato of sunlight appeared on his ceiling and Egypt, that green thread through the desert, was taut and bright beyond his blinds. Leaving breakfast, light-headed, he impulsively approached the bald American on the stairs. "I beg your pardon; this is rather silly, but could you do me an immense favor?"

"Like what?"

"Just walk with me up to this shop where something I ordered should be waiting. Uh . . . it's embarrassing to explain."

"The boat's pulling out in half an hour."

"I know."

The man sized Clem up—his clean shirt, his square shoulders, his open hopeful face—and grunted, "O.K. I left my whisk in the cabin, I'll see you outside."

"Gee, I'm very grateful, uh—"

"Walt's the name."

Ingrid, coming up the stairs late to breakfast, had overheard. "May I come, too, on this expedition that is so dangerous?"

"No, it's stupid," Clem told her. "Please eat your breakfast. I'll see you on the deck afterward."

Her face attempted last night's sternness, but she was puffy beneath her eyes from sleep, and he revised upward his estimate of her age. Like him, she was over thirty. How many men had she passed through to get here, alone; how many self-forgetful nights, traumatic mornings of separation, hungover heartbroken afternoons? It was epic to imagine, her history of love; she loomed immense in his mind, a monumental statue, forbidding and foreign, even while under his nose she blinked and puckered her lips, rejected. She went into breakfast alone.

On the walk to the shop, Clem tried to explain what had happened the evening before. Walt impatiently interrupted. "They're scum," he said. "They'll sell their mother for twenty piasters." His accent still had Newark gravel in it. A boy ran shyly beside them, offering them *soudani* from a bowl. "Amscray," Walt said, brandishing his whisk.

"Is very good," the boy said.

"You make me puke," Walt told him.

The woman and the boy doing homework were gone from the shop. Unlit, it looked dingy; Nasser's glass was cracked. The tailor sprang up when they entered, pleased and relieved. "I work all night," he said.

"Like hell you did," Walt said.

"Try on?" the tailor asked Clem.

In the flecked dim mirror, Clem saw himself gowned; a shock, because the effect was not incongruous. He looked like a husky woman, a big-boned square-faced woman, quick to blush and giggle, the kind of naïve healthy woman, with money and without many secrets, that he tended to be attracted to. He had once loved such a girl, and she had snubbed him to marry a Harvard man. "It feels tight under the armpits," he said.

The tailor rapidly caressed and patted his sides. "That is its cut," he said.

"And the cartouche was supposed to be in silver thread."

"You said gold."

"I said silver."

"Don't take it," Walt advised.

"I work all night," the tailor said.

"And here," Clem said. "This isn't a pocket, it's just a slit."

"No, no, no pocket. Supposed to let the hand through. Here, I show." He put his hand in the slit and touched Clem until Clem protested, "Hey."

"I can make you very happy," the tailor murmured.

"Throw it back in his face," Walt said. "Tell him it's a god-awful mess."

"No," Clem said. "I'll take it. The fabric is lovely. If it turns out to be too tight, I can give it to my mother." He was sweating so hard that the garment became stuck as he tried to pull it over his head, and the tailor, assisting him, was an enveloping blur of caresses.

From within the darkness of cloth, Clem heard a slap and Walt's voice snarl, "Hands off, sonny." The subdued tailor swiftly wrapped the caftan in brown paper. As Clem paid, Walt said, "I wouldn't buy that rag. Throw it back in his face." Outside, as they hurried back toward the boat, through crowded streets where women clad all in black stepped sharply aside, guarding their faces against the evil eye, Walt said, "The little queer."

"I don't think it meant anything, it was just a nervous habit. But it scared me. Thanks a lot for coming along."

Walt asked him, "Ever try it with a man?"

"No. Good heavens."

Walt said, "It's not bad." He nudged Clem in walking and Clem shifted his parcel to that side, as a shield. All the way to the boat, Walt's conversation was anecdotal and obscene, describing a night he had had in Alexandria and another in Khartoum. Twice Clem had to halt and shift to Walt's other side, to keep from being nudged off the sidewalk. "It's not bad," Walt insisted. "It'd pleasantly surprise you, I guarantee it. Don't have a closed mind."

Back on the *Osiris*, Clem locked the cabin door while changing into his bathing suit. The engines shivered; the boat glided away from the Luxor quay. On deck, Ingrid asked him if his dangerous expedition had been successful. She had reverted to the orange bikini.

"I got the silly thing, yes. I don't know if I'll ever wear it."

"You must model it tonight; we are having Egyptian Night."

Her intonation saying this was firm with reserve. Her air of pique cruelly pressed upon him in his sleepless, sensitive, brittle state. Ingrid's lower lip jutted in profile; her pale eyes bulged beneath the spears of her lashes. He tried to placate her by describing the tailor shop—its enchanted smallness, the woman and child bent over schoolwork.

"It is a farce," Ingrid said, with a bruising positiveness, "their school-ing. They teach the poor children the language of the Koran, which is difficult and useless. The literacy statistics are nonsense."

Swirls of Arabic, dipping like bird flight from knot to knot, wound through Clem's brain and gently tugged him downward into a softness where Ingrid's tan body stretching beside him merged with the tawny strip of desert gliding beyond the ship's railing. Lemonade was being served to kings around him. On the ceiling of a temple chamber that he had seen, the goddess Nut was swallowing the sun in one corner and giving birth to it in another, all out of the same body. A body was above him and words were crashing into him like stones. He opened his eyes; it was the Ameri-can widow, a broad cloud of cloth eclipsing the sun, a perfumed mass of sweet-voiced anxiety resurrected from her cabin, crying out to him, "Young man, you *look* like a bridge player. We're *des*perate for a fourth!"

The caftan pinched him under the arms; and then, later in Egyptian Night, after the meal, Ingrid danced with Egon and disappeared. To these discomforts the American widow and Walt added that of their company. Though Clem had declined her bridge invitation, his protective film had been broken and they had plunked themselves down around the little table where Clem and Ingrid were eating the buffet of *foule* and pilaf and *qualeema* and falafel and *maamoule*. To Clem's surprise, the food was to his taste—nutty, bland, dry. Then Ingrid was invited to dance and failed to return to the table, and the English couples, who had befriended the widow, descended in a cloud of conversation.

"This place was a hell of a lot more fun under Farouk," said the old man with a scoured red face.

"At least the poor *fellah*," a woman perhaps his wife agreed, "had a lit-tle glamour and excitement to look up to."

"Now what does the poor devil have? A war he can't fight and Soviet slogans."

"They *hate* the Russians, of course. The average Egyptian, he loves a show of style, and the Russians don't have any. Not a crumb."

"The poor dears."

And they passed on to ponder the inability, mysterious but proven a thousand times over, of Asiatics and Africans—excepting, of course, the Israelis and the Japanese—to govern themselves or, for that matter, to conduct the simplest business operation efficiently. Clem was too tired to talk and too preoccupied with the pressure chafing his armpits, but they all glanced into his face and found their opinions reflected there. In a sense, they deferred to him, for he was prosperous and young and as an American the inheritor of their colonial wisdom.

All had made attempts at native costume. Walt wore his pajamas, and the widow, in bedsheet and sunglasses and *kaffiyeh*, did suggest a fat sheik, and Gwenn's husband had blacked his face with an ingenious paste of Bain de Soleil and instant coffee. Gwenn asked Clem to dance. Blushing, he declined, but she insisted. "There's nothing to it—you simply bash yourself about a bit," she said, and demonstrated.

She was dressed as a harem girl. For her top, she had torn the sleeves off one of her husband's shirts and left it unbuttoned, so that a strip of skin from the base of her throat to her navel was bare; she was not wearing a bra. Her pantaloons were less successful: yellow St.-Tropez slacks pinned in loosely below the knees. A blue gauze scarf across her nose— setting her hectic English cheeks and heavily lashed Twiggy eyes eerily afloat—and gold chains around her ankles completed the costume. The band played "Delilah." As Clem watched Gwenn's bare feet, their shuffle, and the glitter of gold, and the ten silver toenails seemed to be rapidly writing something indecipherable. There was a quick half-step she seemed unaware of, in counterpoint with her swaying head and snaking arms. "Why—oh—whyyy, De-liii-lah," the young Egyptian sang in a Liverpool whine. Clem braced his body, hoping the pumping music would possess it. His feet felt sculpturally one with the floor; it was like what stuttering must be for the tongue. The sweat of incapacity fanned outward from the pain under his arms, but Gwenn obliviously rolled on, her pantaloons coming unpinned, her shirt loosening so that, as she swung from side to side, one shadowy breast, and now the other, was entirely revealed. She had shut her eyes, and in the shelter of her blindness Clem did manage to dance a little, to shift his weight and jerk his arms, though he was able to do it only by forgetting the music. The band changed songs and rhythms without his noticing; he was conscious mostly of the skirt of his caftan swinging around him, of Gwenn's English cheeks burning and turning below sealed slashes of mascara, and of her husband's stained face. He had come onto the dance floor with the American widow; as the Bain de Soleil had sunk into his skin, the instant coffee had powdered his galabia. At last the band took a break. Gwenn's husband claimed her, and Leila, the green-eyed Egyptian woman, as Clem passed her table, said remonstratingly, "You *can* dance."

"He is a dervish," Amina stated.

"All Americans are dervishes," Abdul sighed. "Their energy menaces the world."

"I am the world's worst dancer; I'm hopeless," Clem said.

"Then you should sit," Leila said. All three Egyptians were dressed, disdainfully, in Western dress. Clem ordered a renewal of their drinks and a brandy for himself.

"Tell me," he begged Abdul. "Do you think the Russians have no style?"

"It is true," Abdul said. "They are a very ugly people. Their clothes are very baggy. They are like us, Asiatic. They are not yet convinced that this world absolutely matters."

"Mon mari veut créer une grande théorie politique," Amina said to Clem.

Clem persisted. Fatigue made him desperate and dogged. "But," he said, "I was surprised, in Cairo, even now, with our ambassador kicked out, and all these demonstrations, how many Americans were standing around the lobby of the Hilton. And all the American movies."

"For a time," Amina said, "they tried films only from the Soviet Union and China, about farming progressively. The theatre managers handed their keys in to the government and said, 'Here, you run them.' No one would come. So the Westerns came back."

"And this music," Clem said, "and your clothes."

"Oh, we love you," Abdul said, "but with our brains. You are like the stars, like the language of the Koran. We know we cannot be like that. There is a sullen place"—he moved his hand from his head to his stomach—"where the Russians make themselves at home."

The waiter brought the drinks and Amina said "Shh" to her husband.

Leila said to Clem, "You have changed girlfriends tonight. You have many girlfriends."

He blushed. "None."

Leila said, "The big Swede, she danced very close with the German boy. Now they have both gone off."

"Into the Nile?" Amina asked. "Into the desert? How jolly romantic."

Abdul said slowly, as if bestowing comfort, "They are both Nordic. They are at home within each other. Like us and the Russians."

Leila seemed angry. Her green eyes flashed and Clem feared they would seek to scratch his face. Instead, her ankle touched Clem's beneath the table; he flinched. "They are both," she said, "ice—ize—? They hang down in winter."

"Icicles?" Clem offered.

She curtly nodded, annoyed at needing rescue. "I have never seen one," she said in self-defense.

"Your friends the British," Abdul said, indicating the noisy table where they were finger-painting on Gwenn's husband's face, "understood us in their fashion. They had read Shakespeare. It is very good, that play. How we turned our sails and ran. Our cleverness and courage are all female."

"I'm sure that's not so," Clem protested.

Leila snapped, "Why should it not be so? All countries are women, except horrid Uncle Sam." And though he sat at their table another hour, her ankle did not touch his again.

Floating on three brandies, Clem at last left the lounge, his robe of polished cotton swinging around him. The Frenchman was tipped back precariously in a corner, watching the dancers. He lifted his mirror in salute as Clem passed. Though even the Frenchman's wife was dancing, Ingrid had not returned, and this added to Clem's lightness, his freedom from litter. Surely he would sleep. But when he lay down on his bed, it was trembling and jerking. His cabin adjoined that of the unsociable plump couple thought to be Russian. Clem's bed and one of theirs were separated by a thin partition. His shuddered as theirs heaved with a playful, erratic violence; there was a bump, a giggle, a hoarse male sibilance. Then the agitation settled toward silence and a distinct rhythm, a steady, mounting beat that put a pulsing into the bed taut under Clem. Two or three minutes of this. Then: "Oh." The woman's exclamation was at a middle pitch, gender-neutral; a man's guttural grunt came right on top of it. Clem's bed, in its abrupt stillness, seemed to float and spin under him. Then, from beyond the partition, some murmurs, a sprinkling of laughter, the word *"Khorosho,"* and a resonant heave as one body left the bed. Soon, twin snoring. Clem had been robbed of the gift of sleep.

After shapeless hours of pillow wrestling, he went to the window and viewed the Nile gliding by, the constellations of village lights, and the desert stars, icy in their clarity. He wanted to open the window to smell the river and the desert, but it was sealed shut, in deference to the air conditioning. Clem remembered Ingrid and a cold silver rage, dense as an ingot, upright as an obelisk, filled his body. "You bitch," he said aloud and, by repeating those two words, over and over, leaving his mind no space to entertain any other images, he managed to wedge himself into a few hours' sleep, despite the tempting, problematical scuttle of presences in the hall, who now and then brushed his door with their fingernails. *You bitch, you bitch, you* . . . He remembered nothing about his dreams, except that they all took place back in Buffalo, amid aunts and uncles he had thought he had forgotten.

. . .

Temples. Dour, dirty, heavy Isna sunk in its great pit beside a city market where Clem, pestered by flies and peddlers, nearly vomited at the sight of ox palates, complete with arcs of teeth, hung up for sale. Vast sunstruck Idfu, an endless square spiral climb up steps worn into troughs toward a dizzying view, the amateur travelogist calmly grinding away on the unparapeted edge. Cheery little Kom Ombo, right by the Nile, whiter and later than the others. In one of them, dead Osiris was resurrected by a hawk alighting on his phallus; in another, Nut the sky goddess flowed above them nude, swimming amid gilt stars. A god was having a baby, baby Horus. Poppa Omar bent over and tenderly patted the limestone relief pitted and defaced by Coptic Christians. "See now here," he said, "the lady squat, and the other ladies hold her by the arms so, here, and the baby Horus, out he comes here. In villages all over Egypt now, the ladies there still have the babies in such manner, so we have too many the babies here." He looked up at them and smiled with unflecked benevolence. His eyes, surprisingly, were pale blue.

The travelogist from Wisconsin was grinding away, Walt from New Jersey was switching his whisk, the widow was fainting in the shade, beside a sphinx. Clem helped the Frenchman inch his feet across some age-worn steps; he was like one of those toys that walk down an inclined ramp but easily topple. The English and Egyptians were bored: too many temples, too much Ramses. Ingrid detached herself from the German boys and came to Clem. "How did you sleep?"

"Horribly. And you?"

"Well. Very well. I thought," she added, "you would be soothed by my no longer trying to rape you."

At noon, in the sun, as the *Osiris* glided toward Aswan, she took her accustomed chair beside Clem. When Egon left the chair on the other side of him and clamorously swam in the pool, Clem asked her, "How is he?"

"He is very nice," she said, holding her bronze face immobile in the sun. "Very earnest, very naïve. He is a revolutionary."

"I'm glad," he said, "you've found someone congenial."

"Have I? He is very young. Perhaps I went with him to make another jealous." She added, expressionless, "Did it?"

"Yes."

"I am pleased to hear it."

In the evening, she was at the bar when he went up from an unsuccessful attempt at a nap. They had docked for the last time; the boat had ceased trembling. She had reverted to the silver dress that looked put on backwards. He asked, "Where are the Germans?"

"They are with the Egyptians in the lounge. Shall we join them?"

"No," Clem said. Instead, they talked with the lanky man from Green Bay, who had ten months of advance tickets and reservations to Cape Town and back, including a homeward cabin on the *Queen Elizabeth II*. He spoke mostly to women's groups and high schools, and he detested the Packers. He said to Clem, "I take pride in being an eccentric, don't you?" and Clem was frightened to think that he appeared eccentric, he who had always been praised, even teased, by his mother as typically American, as even *too* normal and dependable. She sometimes implied that he had disappointed her by not defying her, by always dutifully returning from his trips alone.

After dinner, he and Ingrid walked in Aswan: a receding quay of benches, open shops burning a single lightbulb, a swish of vehicles, mostly military. A true city, where the appetites are served. He had bought some postcards and let a boy shine his dusty shoes. He paid the boy ten piasters, shielding his potent wallet with his body. They returned to the *Osiris* and sat in the lounge watching the others dance. A chaste circle around them forbade intrusion; or perhaps the others, having tried to enter Clem and failed, had turned away. Clem imagined them in the eyes of the others, both so composed and now so tan, two stately cool children of harsh winters. Apologizing, smiling, after three iced arracks, he bit his tongue and rose. "Forgive me, I'm dead. I must hit the hay. You stay and dance."

She shook her head, with a preoccupied stern gesture, gathered her dress tight about her hips, and went with him. In the hall before his door, she stood and asked, "Don't you want me?"

A sudden numbness lifted from his stomach and made him feel giddily tall. "Yes," he said.

"Then why not take me?"

Clem looked within himself for the answer, saw only glints refracted and distorted by a deep fatigue. "I'm frightened to," he told her. "I have no faith in my right to take things."

Ingrid listened intently, as if his words were continuing, clarifying themselves; she looked at his face and nodded. Now that they had come so far together and were here, her gaze seemed soft, as soft and weary as the tailor's. "Go to your room," she said. "If you like, then, I will come to you."

"Please do." It was as simple, then, as dancing—you simply bash yourself about a bit.

"Would you like me to?" She was stern now, could afford to be guarded.

"Yes. *Please* do."

He left the latch off, undressed, washed, brushed his teeth, shaved the second time that day, left the bathroom light on. The bed seemed immensely clean and taut, like a sail. Strange stripes, nonsense patterns, crossed his mind. The sail held taut, permitting a gliding, but with a tipping. The light in the cabin changed. The door had been opened and shut. She was still wearing the silver dress; Clem had imagined she would change. She sat on his bed; her weight was the counterweight he had been missing. He curled tighter, as if around a pillow, and an irresistible peace descended, distinctly, from the four corners of space, along forty-five-degree angles marked in charcoal. He opened his eyes, discovering thereby that they had been shut, and the sight of her back—the belling solidity of her bottom, the buckle of the backwards belt, the scoop of cloth exposing the nape of blond neck and the strong crescent of shoulder waiting to be touched—covered his eyes with silver scales. On one of the temple walls, one of the earlier ones, Poppa Omar had read off the hieroglyphs that spelled *Woman is Paradise*. The moored ship and its fittings were still. Confident she would not move, he postponed the beginning for one more second.

He awoke feeling rich, full of sleep. At breakfast, he met Ingrid by the glass dining-room doors and apologetically smiled, blushing and biting his tongue. "God, I'm sorry," he said. He added in self-defense, "I told you I was dead."

"It was charming," she said. "You gave yourself to me that way."

"How long did you sit there?"

"Perhaps an hour. I tried to insert myself into your dreams. Did you dream of me?" She was a shade shy, asking.

He remembered no dreams but did not say so. Her eyes were permanently soft now toward him; they had become windows through which he could admire himself. It did not occur to him that he might admire her in the same fashion: in the morning light, he saw clearly the traces of age on her face and throat, the little scars left by time and a presumed promiscuity, for which he, though not heavily, did blame her. His defect was that, though accustomed to reflect love, he could not originate light within himself; he was as blind as the silvered side of a mirror to the possibility that he, too, might impose a disproportionate glory upon the form of another. The world was his but slid through him.

In the morning, they went by felucca to Lord Kitchener's gardens, and the Aga Khan's tomb, where a single rose was fresh in a vase. The afternoon expedition, and their last, was to the Aswan High Dam. Cameras were forbidden. They saw the anti-aircraft batteries and the worried brown soldiers in their little wooden cartoon guardhouses. The desert became very ugly: no longer the rose shimmer that had surrounded him at the airport in Luxor, it was a merciless gray that had never entertained a hope of life, not even fine in texture but littered to the horizon with black flint. And the makeshift pitted roads were ugly, and the graceless Russian machinery clanking and sitting stalled, and the styleless, already squalid propaganda pavilion containing a model of the dam. The dam itself, after the straight, elegantly arched dam the British had built downriver, seemed a mere mountain of heaped rubble, hardly distinguishable from the inchoate desert itself. Yet at its heart, where the turbines had been set, a plume like a cloud of horses leaped upward in an inverted Niagara that dissolved, horse after horse, into mist before becoming the Nile again and flowing on. Startled greenery flourished on the gray cliffs that contained the giant plume. The stocky couple who had been impassive and furtive for six days beamed and crowed aloud; the man roughly nudged Clem to wake him to the wonder of what they were seeing. Clem agreed: "*Khorosho.*" He waited but was not nudged again. Gazing into the abyss of the trip that was over, he saw that he had been happy.

Separating

THE DAY was fair. Brilliant. All that June the weather had mocked the Maples' internal misery with solid sunlight—golden shafts and cascades of green in which their conversations had wormed unseeing, their sad murmuring selves the only stain in Nature. Usually by this time of the year they had acquired tans; but when they met their elder daughter's plane on her return from a year in England they were almost as pale as she, though Judith was too dazzled by the sunny opulent jumble of her native land to notice. They did not spoil her homecoming by telling her immediately. Wait a few days, let her recover from jet lag, had been one of their formulations, in that string of gray dialogues—over coffee, over cocktails, over Cointreau—that had shaped the strategy of their dissolution, while the earth performed its annual stunt of renewal unnoticed beyond their closed windows. Richard had thought to leave at Easter; Joan had insisted they wait until the four children were at last assembled, with all exams passed and ceremonies attended, and the bauble of summer to console them. So he had drudged away, in love, in dread, repairing screens, getting the mowers sharpened, rolling and patching their new tennis court.

The court, clay, had come through its first winter pitted and windswept bare of redcoat. Years ago the Maples had observed how often, among their friends, divorce followed a dramatic home improvement, as if the marriage were making one last effort to live; their own previous worst crisis had come amid the plaster dust and exposed plumbing of a kitchen renovation. Yet, a summer ago, as canary-yellow bulldozers churned a grassy, daisy-dotted knoll into a muddy plateau, and a crew of pigtailed young men raked and tamped clay into a plane, this transformation did not strike them as ominous, but festive in its impudence; their marriage could rend the earth for fun. The next spring, waking each day at dawn to a sliding sensation as if the bed were being tipped, Richard found the barren tennis court—its net and tapes still rolled in the barn—an environment congruous with his mood of purposeful desolation, and the crumbling of handfuls of clay into cracks and holes (dogs had frolicked on the court in a thaw; rivulets had eroded trenches) an activity suitably elemental and interminable. In his sealed heart he hoped the day would never come.

Now it was here. A Friday. Judith was reacclimated; all four children were assembled, before jobs and camps and visits again scattered them. Joan thought they should be told one by one. Richard was for making an announcement at the table. She said, "I think just making an announcement is a cop-out. They'll start quarrelling and playing to each other instead of focusing. They're each individuals, you know, not just some corporate obstacle to your freedom."

"O.K., O.K. I agree." Joan's plan was exact. That evening, they were giving Judith a belated welcome-home dinner, of lobster and champagne. Then, the party over, they, the two of them, who nineteen years before would push her in a baby carriage along Fifth Avenue to Washington Square, were to walk her out of the house, to the bridge across the salt creek, and tell her, swearing her to secrecy. Then Richard Jr., who was going directly from work to a rock concert in Boston, would be told, either late, when he had returned on the train, or early Saturday morning, before he went off to his job; he was seventeen and employed as one of a golf-course maintenance crew. Then the two younger children, John and Margaret, could, as the morning wore on, be informed.

"Mopped up, as it were," Richard said.

"Do you have any better plan? That leaves you the rest of Saturday to answer any questions, pack, and make your wonderful departure."

"No," he said, meaning he had no better plan, and agreed to hers, though to him it showed an edge of false order, a hidden plea for control, like Joan's long chore-lists and financial accountings and, in the days when he first knew her, her overly-copious lecture notes. Her plan turned one hurdle for him into four—four knife-sharp walls, each with a sheer blind drop on the other side.

All spring he had moved through a world of insides and outsides, of barriers and partitions. He and Joan stood as a thin barrier between the children and the truth. Each moment was a partition, with the past on one side and the future on the other, a future containing this unthinkable *now*. Beyond four knifelike walls a new life for him waited vaguely. His skull cupped a secret, a white face, a face both frightened and soothing, both strange and known, that he wanted to shield from tears, which he felt all about him, solid as the sunlight. So haunted, he had become obsessed with battening down the house against his absence, replacing screens and sash cords, hinges and latches—a Houdini making things snug before his escape.

The lock. He had still to replace a lock on one of the doors of the screened porch. The task, like most such, proved more difficult than he had imagined. The old lock, aluminum frozen by corrosion, had been deliberately rendered obsolete by manufacturers. Three hardware stores had nothing that even approximately matched the mortised hole that its removal (surprisingly easy) left. Another hole had to be gouged, with bits too small and saws too big, and the old hole fitted with a block of wood— the chisels dull, the saw rusty, his fingers thick with lack of sleep. The sun poured down, beyond the porch, on a world of neglect. The bushes already needed pruning, the windward side of the house was shedding flakes of paint, rain would get in when he was gone. Insects, rot, death. His family, the family he was about to lose, filtered through the edges of his awareness as he struggled with screw holes, splinters, opaque instructions, minutiae of metal.

Judith sat on the porch, a princess returned from exile. She regaled them with stories of fuel shortages, of bomb scares in the Underground, of Pakistani workmen loudly lusting after her as she walked past on her way to dance school. Joan came and went, in and out of the house, calmer than she should have been, praising his struggles with the lock as if this were one more and not the last of their long succession of shared chores. The younger of his sons, John, now at fifteen suddenly, unwittingly handsome, for a few minutes held the rickety screen door while his father clumsily hammered and chiselled, each blow a kind of sob in Richard's ears. His younger daughter, having been at a slumber party the night before, slept on the porch hammock through all the noise—heavy and pink, trusting and forsaken. Time, like the sunlight, continued relentlessly; the sunlight slowly slanted. Today was one of the longest days, but not long enough. The lock clicked, worked. He was through. He had a drink; he drank it on the porch, listening to his daughter. "It was so sweet," she was saying, "during the worst of it, how all the butchers and bakery shops kept open by candlelight. They're all so plucky and cute. From the papers, things sounded so much worse here—people shooting people in gas lines, and everybody freezing."

Richard asked her, "Do you still want to live in England forever?" *For-*

ever: the concept, now a reality upon him, pressed and scratched at the back of his throat.

"No," Judith confessed, turning her oval face to him, its eyes still childishly far apart, but the lips set as over something succulent and satisfactory. "I was anxious to come home. I'm an American." She was a woman. They had raised her; he and Joan had endured together to raise her, alone of the four. The others had still some raising left in them. Yet it was the thought of telling Judith—the image of her, their first baby, walking between them arm in arm to the bridge—that broke him.

The partition between his face and tears broke. Richard sat down to the celebratory meal with the back of his throat aching; the champagne, the lobster seemed phases of sunshine; he saw them and tasted them through tears. He blinked, swallowed, croakily joked about hay fever. The tears would not stop leaking through; they came not through a hole that could be plugged but through a permeable spot in a membrane, steadily, purely, endlessly, fruitfully. They became, his tears, a shield for himself against these others—their faces, the fact of their assembly, a last time as innocents, at a table where he sat the last time as head. Tears dropped from his nose as he broke his lobster's back; salt flavored his champagne as he sipped it; the raw clench at the back of his throat was delicious. He could not help himself.

His children tried to ignore his tears. Judith, on his right, lit a cigarette, gazed upward in the direction of her too-energetic, too-sophisticated exhalation; on her other side, John earnestly bent his face to the extraction of the last morsels—legs, tail segments—from the scarlet corpse. Joan, at the opposite end of the table, glanced at him surprised, her reproach displaced by a quick grimace, of forgiveness, or of salute to his superior gift of strategy. Between them, Margaret, no longer called Bean, thirteen and large for her age, gazed from the other side of his pane of tears as if into a shopwindow at something she coveted—at her father, a crystalline heap of splinters and memories. It was not she, however, but John who, in the kitchen, as they cleared the plates and carapaces away, asked Joan the question: *"Why is Daddy crying?"*

Richard heard the question but not the murmured answer. Then he heard Bean cry, "Oh, no-oh!"—the faintly dramatized exclamation of one who had long expected it.

John returned to the table carrying a bowl of salad. He nodded tersely at his father and his lips shaped the conspiratorial words "She told."

"Told what?" Richard asked aloud, insanely.

The boy sat down as if to rebuke his father's distraction with the example of his own good manners. He said quietly, "The separation."

Joan and Margaret returned; the child, in Richard's twisted vision, seemed diminished in size, and relieved, relieved to have had the bogeyman at last proved real. He called out to her—the distances at the table had grown immense—"You knew, you always knew," but the clenching at the back of his throat prevented him from making sense of it. From afar he heard Joan talking, levelly, sensibly, reciting what they had prepared: it was a separation for the summer, an experiment. She and Daddy both agreed it would be good for them; they needed space and time to think; they liked each other but did not make each other happy enough, somehow.

Judith, imitating her mother's factual tone, but in her youth off-key, too cool, said, "I think it's silly. You should either live together or get divorced."

Richard's crying, like a wave that has crested and crashed, had become tumultuous; but it was overtopped by another tumult, for John, who had been so reserved, now grew larger and larger at the table. Perhaps his younger sister's being credited with knowing set him off. "Why didn't you *tell* us?" he asked, in a large round voice quite unlike his own. "You should have *told* us you weren't getting along."

Richard was startled into attempting to force words through his tears. "We *do* get along, that's the trouble, so it doesn't show even to us—" *That we do not love each other* was the rest of the sentence; he couldn't finish it.

Joan finished for him, in her style. "And we've always, *especially*, loved our children."

John was not mollified. "What do you care about *us?*" he boomed. "We're just little things you *had*." His sisters' laughing forced a laugh from him, which he turned hard and parodistic: "Ha ha *ha*." Richard and Joan realized simultaneously that the child was drunk, on Judith's homecoming champagne. Feeling bound to keep the center of the stage, John took a cigarette from Judith's pack, poked it into his mouth, let it hang from his lower lip, and squinted like a gangster.

"You're not little things we had," Richard called to him. "You're the whole point. But you're grown. Or almost."

The boy was lighting matches. Instead of holding them to his cigarette (for they had never seen him smoke; being "good" had been his way of setting himself apart), he held them to his mother's face, closer and closer, for her to blow out. He lit the whole folder—a hiss and then a torch, held against his mother's face. The flame, prismed by tears, filled

Richard's vision; he didn't know how it was extinguished. He heard Margaret say, "Oh, stop showing off," and saw John, in response, break the cigarette in two and put the halves entirely into his mouth and chew, sticking out his tongue to display the shreds to his sister.

Joan talked to him, reasoning—a fountain of reason, unintelligible. "Talked about it for years . . . our children must help us . . . Daddy and I both want . . ." As the boy listened, he wadded a paper napkin into the leaves of his salad, fashioned a ball of paper and lettuce, and popped it into his mouth, looking around the table for the expected laughter. None came. Judith said, "Be mature," and dismissed a plume of smoke.

Richard got up from this stifling table and led the boy outside. Though the house was in twilight, the outdoors still brimmed with light, the lovely waste light of high summer. Both laughing, he supervised John's spitting out the lettuce and paper and tobacco into the pachysandra. He took him by the hand—a square gritty hand, despite its softness a man's. Yet it held on. They ran together up into the field, past the tennis court. The raw banking left by the bulldozers was dotted with daisies. Past the court and a flat stretch where they used to play family baseball stood a soft green rise glorious in the sun, each weed and species of grass as distinct as illumination on parchment. "I'm sorry, so sorry," Richard cried. "You were the only one who ever tried to help me with all the goddamn jobs around this place."

Sobbing, safe within his tears and the champagne, John explained, "It's not just the separation, it's the whole crummy year, I *hate* that school, you can't make any friends, the history teacher's a scud."

They sat on the crest of the rise, shaking and warm from their tears but easier in their voices, and Richard tried to focus on the child's sad year— the weekdays long with homework, the weekends spent in his room with model airplanes, while his parents murmured down below, nursing their separation. How selfish, how blind, Richard thought; his eyes felt scoured. He told his son, "We'll think about getting you transferred. Life's too short to be miserable."

They had said what they could, but did not want the moment to heal shut, and talked on, about the school, about the tennis court, whether it would ever again be as good as it had been that first summer. They walked to inspect it and pressed a few more tapes more firmly down. A little stiltedly, perhaps trying now to make too much of the moment, Richard led the boy to the spot in the field where the view was best, of the metallic blue river, the emerald marsh, the scattered islands velvety with shadow in the low light, the white bits of beach far away. "See," he said. "It goes on being beautiful. It'll be here tomorrow."

"I know," John answered, impatiently. The moment had closed.

Back in the house, the others had opened some white wine, the champagne being drunk, and still sat at the table, the three females, gossiping. Where Joan sat had become the head. She turned, showing him a tearless face, and asked, "All right?"

"We're fine," he said, resenting it, though relieved, that the party went on without him.

In bed she explained, "I couldn't cry I guess because I cried so much all spring. It really wasn't fair. It's your idea, and you made it look as though I was kicking you out."

"I'm sorry," he said. "I couldn't stop. I wanted to but couldn't."

"You *didn't* want to. You loved it. You were having your way, making a general announcement."

"I love having it over," he admitted. "God, those kids were great. So brave and funny." John, returned to the house, had settled to a model airplane in his room, and kept shouting down to them, "I'm O.K. No sweat."

"And the way," Richard went on, cozy in his relief, "they never questioned the reasons we gave. No thought of a third person. Not even Judith."

"That *was* touching," Joan said.

He gave her a hug. "You were great too. Very reassuring to everybody. Thank you." Guiltily, he realized he did not feel separated.

"You still have Dickie to do," she told him. These words set before him a black mountain in the darkness; its cold breath, its near weight affected his chest. Of the four children, his elder son was closest to his conscience. Joan did not need to add, "That's one piece of your dirty work I won't do for you."

"I know. I'll do it. You go to sleep."

Within minutes, her breathing slowed, became oblivious and deep. It was quarter to midnight. Dickie's train from the concert would come in at one-fourteen. Richard set the alarm for one. He had slept atrociously for weeks. But whenever he closed his lids some glimpse of the last hours scorched them—Judith exhaling toward the ceiling in a kind of aversion, Bean's mute staring, the sunstruck growth in the field where he and John had rested. The mountain before him moved closer, moved within him;

he was huge, momentous. The ache at the back of his throat felt stale. His wife slept as if slain beside him. When, exasperated by his hot lids, his crowded heart, he rose from bed and dressed, she awoke enough to turn over. He told her then, "Joan, if I could undo it all, I would."

"Where would you begin?" she asked. There was no place. Giving him courage, she was always giving him courage. He put on shoes without socks in the dark. The children were breathing in their rooms, the downstairs was hollow. In their confusion they had left lights burning. He turned off all but one, the kitchen overhead. The car started. He had hoped it wouldn't. He met only moonlight on the road; it seemed a diaphanous companion, flickering in the leaves along the roadside, haunting his rearview mirror like a pursuer, melting under his headlights. The center of town, not quite deserted, was eerie at this hour. A young cop in uniform kept company with a gang of T-shirted kids on the steps of the bank. Across from the railroad station, several bars kept open. Customers, mostly young, passed in and out of the warm night, savoring summer's novelty. Voices shouted from cars as they passed; an immense conversation seemed in progress. Richard parked and in his weariness put his head on the passenger seat, out of the commotion and wheeling lights. It was as when, in the movies, an assassin grimly carries his mission through the jostle of a carnival—except the movies cannot show the precipitous, palpable slope you cling to within. You cannot climb back down; you can only fall. The synthetic fabric of the car seat, warmed by his cheek, confided to him an ancient, distant scent of vanilla.

A train whistle caused him to lift his head. It was on time; he had hoped it would be late. The slender drawgates descended. The bell of approach tingled happily. The great metal body, horizontally fluted, rocked to a stop, and sleepy teen-agers disembarked, his son among them. Dickie did not show surprise that his father was meeting him at this terrible hour. He sauntered to the car with two friends, both taller than he. He said "Hi" to his father and took the passenger's seat with an exhausted promptness that expressed gratitude. The friends got in the back, and Richard was grateful; a few more minutes' postponement would be won by driving them home.

He asked, "How was the concert?"

"Groovy," one boy said from the back seat.

"It bit," the other said.

"It was O.K.," Dickie said, moderate by nature, so reasonable that in his childhood the unreason of the world had given him headaches, stom-

796 : THE SINGLE LIFE

ach aches, nausea. When the second friend had been dropped off at his dark house, the boy blurted, "Dad, my eyes are killing me with hay fever! I'm out there cutting that mothering grass all day!"

"Do we still have those drops?"

"They didn't do any good last summer."

"They might this." Richard swung a U-turn on the empty street. The drive home took a few minutes. The mountain was here, in his throat. "Richard," he said, and felt the boy, slumped and rubbing his eyes, go tense at his tone, "I didn't come to meet you just to make your life easier. I came because your mother and I have some news for you, and you're a hard man to get a hold of these days. It's sad news."

"That's O.K." The reassurance came out soft, but quick, as if released from the tip of a spring.

Richard had feared that his tears would return and choke him, but the boy's manliness set an example, and his voice issued forth steady and dry. "It's sad news, but it needn't be tragic news, at least for you. It should have no practical effect on your life, though it's bound to have an emotional effect. You'll work at your job, and go back to school in September. Your mother and I are really proud of what you're making of your life; we don't want that to change at all."

"Yeah," the boy said lightly, on the intake of his breath, holding himself up. They turned the corner; the church they erratically attended loomed like a gutted fort. The home of the woman Richard hoped to marry stood across the green. Her bedroom light burned.

"Your mother and I," he said, "have decided to separate. For the summer. Nothing legal, no divorce yet. We want to see how it feels. For some years now, we haven't been doing enough for each other, making each other as happy as we should be. Have you sensed that?"

"No," the boy said. It was an honest, unemotional answer: true or false in a quiz.

Glad for the factual basis, Richard pursued, even garrulously, the details. His apartment across town, his utter accessibility, the split vacation arrangements, the advantages to the children, the added mobility and variety of the summer. Dickie listened, absorbing. "Do the others know?"

"Yes."

"How did they take it?"

"The girls pretty calmly. John flipped out; he shouted and ate a cigarette and made a salad out of his napkin and told us how much he hated school."

His brother chuckled. "He did?"

"Yeah. The school issue was more upsetting for him than Mom and me. He seemed to feel better for having exploded."

"He did?" The repetition was the first sign that he was stunned.

"Yes. Dickie, I want to tell you something. This last hour, waiting for your train to get in, has been about the worst of my life. I hate this. *Hate* it. My father would have died before doing it to me." He felt immensely lighter, saying this. He had dumped the mountain on the boy. They were home. Moving swiftly as a shadow, Dickie was out of the car, through the bright kitchen. Richard called after him, "Want a glass of milk or anything?"

"No thanks."

"Want us to call the course tomorrow and say you're too sick to work?"

"No, that's all right." The answer was faint, delivered at the door to his room; Richard listened for the slam that went with a tantrum. The door closed normally, gently. The sound was sickening.

Joan had sunk into that first deep trough of sleep and was slow to awake. Richard had to repeat, "I told him."

"What did he say?"

"Nothing much. Could you go say good night to him? Please."

She left their room, without putting on a bathrobe. He sluggishly changed back into his pajamas and walked down the hall. Dickie was already in bed, Joan was sitting beside him, and the boy's bedside clock radio was murmuring music. When she stood to go, an inexplicable light—the moon?—outlined her body through the nightie. Richard sat on the warm place she had indented on the boy's narrow mattress. He asked him, "Do you want the radio on like that?"

"It always is."

"Doesn't it keep you awake? It would me."

"No."

"Are you sleepy?"

"Yeah."

"Good. Sure you want to get up and go to work? You've had a big night."

"I want to. They expect me."

Away at school this winter he had learned for the first time that you can go short of sleep and live. As an infant he had slept with an immobile, sweating intensity that had alarmed his baby-sitters. In adolescence he had often been the first of the four children to go to bed. Even now, he would go slack in the middle of a television show, his sprawled legs hairy and brown. "O.K. Good boy. Dickie, listen. I love you so much, I never knew how much until now. No matter how this works out, I'll always be with you. Really."

Richard bent to kiss an averted face but his son, sinewy, turned and with wet cheeks embraced him and gave him a kiss, on the lips, passionate as a woman's. In his father's ear he moaned one word, the crucial, intelligent word: *"Why?"*

Why. It was a whistle of wind in a crack, a knife thrust, a window thrown open on emptiness. The white face was gone, the darkness was featureless. Richard had forgotten why.

Gesturing

SHE TOLD HIM with a little gesture he had never seen her use before. Joan had called from the station, having lunched with her lover, Richard guessed. He had been spending the Saturday babysitting for his own children, in the house the Maples had once shared. Her new Volvo was handier in the driveway, but for several minutes it refused to go into first gear for him. By the time he had reached the center of town, she had walked down the main street and up the hill to the green. It was September, leafy and warm, yet with a crystal chill on things, an uncanny clarity. Even from a distance they smiled to see one another. She opened the door and seated herself, fastening the safety belt to silence its chastening buzz. Her face was rosy from her walk; her city clothes looked like a costume; she carried a small package or two, token of her "shopping." Richard tried to pull a U-turn on the narrow street, and in the long moment of his halting and groping for reverse gear she told him. "Darley," she said, and, oddly, tentatively, soundlessly, tapped the fingers of one hand into the palm of the other, a gesture between a child's clap of glee and an adult's signal for attention, "I've decided to kick you out. I'm going to ask you to leave town."

Abruptly full, his heart thumped; it was what he wanted. "O.K.," he said carefully. "If you think you can manage." He glaced sideways at her face to see if she meant it; he could not believe she did. A red, white, and blue mail truck that had braked to a stop behind them tapped its horn, more reminder than rebuke; the Maples were known in the town. They had lived here most of their married life.

Richard found reverse, backed up, and completed the turn. The car, so new and stiff, in motion felt high and light, as if it too had just been vaporized in her little playful clap. "Things are stagnant," she explained, "stuck; we're not going anywhere."

"I will not give her up," he interposed.

"Don't tell me, you've told me."

"Nor do I see you giving him up."

"I would if you asked. Are you asking?"

"No. Horrors. He's all I've got."

"Well, then. Go where you want; I think Boston would be most fun for the kids to visit. And the least boring for you."

"I agree. When do you see this happening?" Her profile, in the side of her vision, felt brittle, about to break if he said a wrong word, too rough a word. He was holding his breath, trying to stay up, high and light, like the car. They went over the bump this side of the old stone bridge; cigarette smoke jarred loose from Joan's face.

"As soon as you can find a place," she said. "Next week. Is that too soon?"

"Probably."

"Is this too sad? Do I seem brutal to you?"

"No, you seem wonderful, very gentle and just, as always. It's right. It's just something I couldn't do myself. How can you possibly live without me in town?"

In the edge of his vision her face turned; he turned to see, and her expression was mischievous, brave, flushed. They must have had wine at lunch. "Easy," Joan said. He knew it was a bluff, a brave gesture; she was begging for reprieve. But he held silent, he refused to argue. This way, he had her pride on his side.

The curves of the road poured by, mailboxes, trees some of which were already scorched by the turn of the year. He asked, "Is this your idea, or his?"

"Mine. It came to me on the train. All Andy said was, I seemed to be feeding you all the time." In the weeks since their summer of separated vacations, Richard had been sleeping in a borrowed seaside shack two miles from their home; he tried to cook there, but each evening, as the nights grew shorter, it seemed easier, and kinder to the children, to eat the dinner Joan had cooked. He was used to her cooking; indeed, his body, every cell, was composed of her cooking. Dinner would lead to a post-dinner drink, while the children (two were off at school, two were still homebound) plodded through their homework or stared at television, and drinking would lead to talking, confidences, harsh words, maudlin tears, and an occasional uxorious collapse upward, into bed. She was right; it was not healthy, or progressive. The twenty years were by, when it would have been convenient to love one another.

. . .

He found the apartment in Boston on the second day of hunting. The real-estate agent had red hair, a round bottom, and a mask of makeup worn as if to conceal her youth. Richard felt happy and scared, going up and down stairs behind her. Wearier of him than he was of her, she fidgeted the key into this lock, bucked the door open with her shoulder, and made her little open-handed gesture of helpless display.

The floor was not the usual wall-to-wall shag or splintered wood, but black and white tile, like the floor in a Vermeer; he glanced to the window, saw the skyscraper, and knew that this would do. The skyscraper, for years suspended in a famous state of incompletion, was a beautiful disaster, famous because it was a disaster (glass kept falling from it) and disastrous because it was beautiful: the architect had had a vision. He had dreamed of an invisible building, though immense; the glass was meant to reflect the sky and the old low brick skyline of Boston, and to melt into the sky. Instead, the windows of mirroring glass kept falling to the street, and were replaced by ugly opacities of black plywood. Yet enough reflecting surface remained to give an impression, through the wavery old window of this sudden apartment, of huge blueness, a vertical cousin to the horizontal huge blueness of the sea that Richard awoke to each morning, in the now bone-deep morning chill of his unheated shack. He said to the redhead, "Fine," and her charcoal eyebrows lifted. His hands trembled as he signed the lease, having written "Sep" in the space for marital status. From a drugstore he phoned the news, not to his wife, whom it would sadden, but to his mistress, equally far away. "Well," he told her in an accusing voice, "I found one. I signed the lease. Incredible. In the middle of all this fine print there was the one simple sentence, 'There shall be no waterbeds.' "

"You sound so shaky."

"I feel I've given birth to a black hole."

"Don't do it, if you don't want to." From the way Ruth's voice paused and faded he imagined she was reaching for a cigarette, or an ashtray, settling herself to a session of lover-babying.

"I do want to. She wants me to. We all want me to. Even the children are turned on. Or pretend to be."

She ignored the "pretend." "Describe it to me."

All he could remember was the floor, and the view of the blue disaster with reflected clouds drifting across its face. And the redhead. She had told him where to shop for food, where to do his laundry. He would have laundry?

"It sounds nice," was Ruth's remote response, when he had finished saying what he could. Two people, one of them a sweating black mailman, were waiting to use the phone booth. He hated the city already, its crowding, its hunger.

"What sounds nice about it?" he snapped.

"Are you so upset? Don't do it if you don't want to."

"Stop *saying* that." It was a tedious formality both observed, the pretense that they were free, within each of their collapsing marriages, to do as they pleased; guilt avoidance was the game, and Ruth had grown expert at it. Her words often seemed not real words but blank counters, phrases of a prescribed etiquette. Whereas his wife's words always opened inward, transparent with meaning.

"What else can I say," Ruth asked, "except that I love you?" And at its far end the phone sharply sighed. He could picture the gesture: she had turned her face away from the mouthpiece and forcefully exhaled, in that way she had, expressive of exasperation even when she felt none, of exhaling and simultaneously stubbing out a cigarette smoked not halfway down its length, so it crumpled under her impatient fingers like an angry sentence thought better of. Her conspicuous unthriftiness pained him. All waste pained him. He wanted abruptly to hang up, but saw that, too, as a wasteful gesture, and hung on.

Alone in his apartment, he discovered himself to be a neat and thrifty housekeeper. When a woman left, he would promptly set about restoring his bachelor order, emptying the ashtrays which, if the visitor had been Ruth, brimmed with long pale bodies prematurely extinguished and, if Joan, with butts so short as to be scarcely more than filters. Neither woman, it somehow pleased him to observe, ever made more than a gesture toward cleaning up—the bed a wreck, the dishes dirty, each of his three ashtrays (one glass, one pottery, and one a tin cookie-jar lid) systematically touched, like the bases in baseball. Emptying them, he would smile at Ruth's messy morgue, or at Joan's nest of filters, discreet as white pebbles in a bowl of narcissi. When he chastised Ruth for stubbing out cigarettes still so long, she pointed out, of course, with her beautiful, unblinking assumption of her own primary worth, how much better it was for *her*, for her lungs, to kill the cigarette early; and of course she was right, better other-destructive than self-destructive. Ruth was love, she was life, that was why he loved her. Yet Joan's compulsive economy, her discreet death wish, was as dearly familiar to him as her tiny repressed handwriting and the tight curls of her dark pubic hair, so Richard smiled emptying her ashtrays also. His smile was a gesture without an audience. He, who had originated his act among parents and grandparents, siblings and pets, and who had developed it for a public of schoolmates and teachers, and who had carried it to new refinements before an initially rapt audience of his own children, could not in solitude stop performing. He had engendered a companion of sorts, an admirer from afar—the blue skyscraper. He felt it with him all the time.

Blue, it showed greener than the sky. For a time Richard was puzzled, why the clouds reflected in it drifted in the same direction as the clouds behind it. With an effort of spatial imagination he perceived that a mirror does not reverse our motion, though it does transpose our ears, and gives our mouths a tweak, so that the face even of a loved one looks unfamiliar and ugly when seen in a mirror, the way she—queer thought!—always sees it. He saw that a mirror posed in its midst would not affect the motion of an army; and often half a reflected cloud matched the half of another beyond the building's edge, moving as one, pierced by a jet trail as though by Cupid's arrow. The disaster sat light on the city's heart. At night, it showed as a dim row of little lights, as if a slender ship were sailing the sky, and during a rain or fog it vanished entirely, while the brick chimney pots and ironstone steeples in Richard's foreground swarthily intensified their substance. Even unseen, it was there; so Richard himself, his soul, was always there. He tried to analyze the logic of window replacement, as revealed in the patterns of gap and glass. He detected no logic, just the slow-motion labor of invisible workers, emptying and filling cells of glass with the brainlessness of bees. If he watched for many minutes, he might see, like the condensation of a dewdrop, a blank space go glassy, and reflective, and greenish-blue. Days passed before he realized that, on the old glass near his nose, the wavery panes of his own window, ghostly previous tenants armed with diamonds had scratched initials, names, dates, and, cut deepest and whitest of all, the touching, comical vow, incised in two trisyllabic lines,

With this ring
I thee wed

What a transparent wealth of previous lives overlay a city's present joy! As he walked the streets his own happiness surprised him. He had expected to be sad, guilty, bored. Instead, his days were snugly filled with his lists, his quests for food and hardware, his encounters with such problematical wife-substitutes as the Laundromat, where students pored over Hesse and picked at their chins while their clothes tumbled in circular fall, and where young black housewives hummed as they folded white linen. What an unexpected pleasure, walking home in the dark hugging to himself clean clothes hot as fresh bread, past the bow windows of Back Bay glowing like display cases. He felt sober and exhilarated and justified at the hour when in the suburbs, rumpled from the commute, he would be into his hurried second pre-dinner drink. He liked the bringing home of food, the tautological satisfaction of cooking a meal and then eating it all, as the radio fed Bach or Bechet into his ears and a book gazed open-faced from the reading stand he had bought; he liked the odd orderly game of consuming before food spoiled and drinking before milk soured. He liked the way airplanes roamed the brown night sky, a second, thinner city laid upon this one, and the way police sirens sang, scooping up some disaster not his. It could not last, such happiness. It was an interim, a holiday. But an oddly clean and just one, rectilinear, dignified, though marred by gaps of sudden fear and disorientation. Each hour had to be scheduled lest he fall through. He moved like a waterbug, like a skipping stone, upon the glassy tense surface of his new life. He walked every-where. Once he walked to the base of the blue skyscraper, his companion and witness. It was hideous. Heavily planked and chicken-wired tunnels, guarded by barking policemen, protected pedestrians from falling glass, and the owners of the building, already millions in the hole, from more lawsuits. Trestles and trucks jammed the cacophonous area. The lower floors were solid plywood, of a Stygian black; the building, so lovely in air, had tangled mucky roots. Richard avoided walking that way again.

When Ruth visited, they played a game, of washing—scouring, with a Brillo Pad—one white square of the Vermeer floor, so eventually it would all appear clean. The black squares they ignored. Naked, scrub-bing, Ruth seemed on her knees a plump little steed, long hair swinging, soft breasts swaying in rhythm to her energetic circular strokes. Behind, her pubic hair, uncurly and fair, made a kind of nether mane. So lovably strange, she rarely was allowed to clean more than one square. Time, carefully regulated when he was alone, sped for them, and vanished. There seemed time to talk only at the end, her hand on the door. She asked, "Isn't that building amazing, with the sunset in it?"

"I love that building. And it loves me."

"No. It's me who loves you."

"Can't you share?"

"No."

She felt possessive about the apartment; when he told her Joan had been there, too, and, just for "fun," had slept with him, her husband, Ruth wailed into the telephone. "In *our* bed?"

"In *my* bed," he said, with uncharacteristic firmness.

"In your bed," she conceded, her voice husky as a sleepy child's. When the conversation finally ended, his mistress sufficiently soothed, he had to go lean his vision against his inanimate, giant friend, dimming to mauve on one side, still cerulean on the other, faintly streaked with reflections of high cirrus. It spoke to him, as the gaze of a dumb beast speaks, of beauty and suffering, of a simplicity that must perish, of time. Evening would soften its shade to slate; night would envelop its sides. Richard's focus shortened, and he read, with irritation, for the hundredth time, that impudent, pious marring, that bit of litany, etched bright by the sun's fading fire.

> With this ring
> I thee wed

Ruth, months ago, had removed her wedding ring. Coming here to embark with him upon an overnight trip, she wore on that naked finger, as a reluctant concession to imposture, an inherited diamond ring. When she held her hand in the sunlight by the window, a planetary system of rainbows wheeled about the room and signalled, he imagined, to the skyscraper. In the hotel in New York, she confided again her indignation at losing her name in the false assumption of his.

"It's just a convenience," he told her. "A gesture."

"But I *like* who I am now," she protested. That was, indeed, her central jewel, infrangible and bright: she liked who she was.

In Manhattan they had gone separate ways and, returning before him, she had asked at the hotel desk for the room key by number. The clerk asked her her name. It was a policy. He would not give the key to a number.

"And what did you tell him your name was?" Richard asked, in this pause of her story.

In her pause and opaque blue stare, he saw re-created her hesitation when challenged by the clerk. Also, she had been, before her marriage, a second-grade teacher, and Richard saw now the manner—prim, wide-eyed, and commanding—with which she must have stood before the blackboard and confronted those roomfuls of children. "I told him Maple."

Richard had smiled. "That sounds right."

. . .

Taking Joan out to dinner felt illicit. She suggested it, for "fun," at the end of one of the children's Sundays. He had been two months in Boston, new habits had replaced old, and it was tempting to leave their children, who were bored and found it easier to be bored by television than by this bossy visitor. "Stop telling me you're bored," he had scolded John, the most docile of his children, and the one he felt guiltiest about. "Fourteen is *supposed* to be a boring age. When I was fourteen, I lay around reading science fiction. You lie around looking at *Kung Fu*. At least I was learning to read."

"It's good," John protested, his adolescent voice cracking in fear of being distracted from an especially vivid piece of slow-motion *tai chi*. Richard, when living here, had watched the program with him often enough to know that it was, in a sense, good; the hero's Oriental passivity, relieved by spurts of mystical violence, was insinuating into the child a system of ethics, just as Richard had taken ideals of behavior from dime movies and comic books—coolness from Bogart, debonair recklessness from Errol Flynn, duality and deceit from Superman.

He dropped to one knee beside the sofa where the boy, his upper lip fuzzy and his eyebrows manly dark, stoically gazed into the transcendent flickering; Richard's own voice nearly cracked, asking, "Would it be less boring if Dad still lived here?"

"No-*oh*": the answer was instantaneous and impatient, as if the question had been anticipated. Did the boy mean it? His eyes did not for an instant glance sideways, perhaps out of fear of betraying himself, perhaps out of genuine boredom with grownups and their gestures. On television, satisfyingly, gestures killed. Richard rose from his supplicant position, relieved to hear Joan coming down the stairs. She was dressed to go out, in the snug black dress with the scalloped neckline, and a collar of Mexican silver. He was wary. He must be wary. They had had it. They must have had it.

Yet the cocktails, and the seafood, and the wine displaced his wariness; he heard himself saying, to the so familiar and so strange face across the table, "She's lovely, and loves me, you know"—he felt embarrassed, like a son suddenly aware that his mother, though politely attentive, is indifferent to the urgency of an athletic contest being described—"but she does spell everything out, and wants everything spelled out to her. It's like being back in the second grade. And the worst thing is, for all this explaining, for all this glorious fucking, she's still not real to me, the way—you are." His voice did break; he had gone too far.

Joan put her left hand, still bearing their wedding ring, flat on the tablecloth in a sensible, level gesture. "She will be," she promised. "It's a matter of time."

The old pattern was still the one visible to the world. The waitress, who had taught their children in Sunday school, greeted them as if their marriage were unbroken; they ate in this restaurant three or four times a year, and were on schedule. They had known the ginger-haired contractor who had built it, this mock-antique wing, a dozen years ago, and then left town, bankrupt but oddly cheerful. His memory hovered between the beams. Another couple, older than the Maples—the husband had once worked with Richard on a town committee—came up to their booth beaming, jollying, in that obligatory American way. Did they know? It didn't much matter, in this nation of temporary arrangements. The Maples jollied back as one, and tumbled loose only when the older couple moved away. Joan gazed after their backs. "I wonder what they have," she asked, "that we didn't."

"Maybe they had less," Richard said, "so they didn't expect more."

"That's too easy." She was a shade resistant to his veiled compliments; he was grateful. Please resist.

He asked, "How do you think the kids are doing? John seemed withdrawn."

"That's how he is. Stop picking at him."

"I just don't want him to think he has to be your little husband. That house feels huge now."

"You're telling me."

"I'm sorry." He was; he put his hands palms up on the table.

"Isn't it amazing," Joan said, "how a full bottle of wine isn't enough for two people any more?"

"Should I order another bottle?" He was dismayed, secretly: the waste. She saw this, and said, "No. Just give me half of what's in your glass."

"You can have it all." He poured.

She said, "So your fucking is really glorious?"

He was embarrassed by the remark now, and feared it set a distasteful trend. As with Ruth there was an etiquette of independent adultery, so with Joan some code of separation must be maintained. "It usually is," he told her, "between people who aren't married."

"Is dat right, white man?" A swallow of his wine inside her, Joan began to swell with impending hilarity. She leaned as close as the table would permit. "You must *promise*"—a gesture went with "promise," a protesting little splaying of her hands—"never to tell this to anybody, not even Ruth."

"Maybe you shouldn't tell me. In fact, don't." He understood why she had been laconic up to now; she had been wanting to talk about her lover, holding him warm within her like a baby. She was going to betray him. "Please don't," Richard said.

"Don't be such a prig. You're the only person I can talk to, it doesn't mean a thing."

"That's what you said about our going to bed in my apartment."

"Did she mind?"

"Incredibly."

Joan laughed, and Richard was struck, for the thousandth time, by the perfection of her teeth, even and rounded and white, bared by her lips as if in proof of a perfect skull, an immaculate soul. Her glee whirled her to a kind of heaven as she confided stories about herself and Andy—how he and a motel manageress had quarrelled over the lack of towels in a room taken for the afternoon, how he fell asleep for exactly seven minutes each time after making love. Richard had known Andy for years, a slender swarthy specialist in corporation law, himself divorced, though professionally engaged in the finicking arrangement of giant mergers. A fussy dresser, a churchman, he brought to many occasions an undue dignity and perhaps had been more attracted to Joan's surface glaze, her New England cool, than the mischievous imps underneath. "My psychiatrist thinks Andy was symbiotic with you, and now that you're gone, I can see him as absurd."

"He's not absurd. He's good, loyal, handsome, prosperous. He tithes. He has a twelve handicap. He loves you."

"He protects you from me, you mean. His buttons!—we have to allow a half-hour afterwards for him to do up all his buttons. If they made four-piece suits, he'd wear them. And he washes—he washes *everything*, every time."

"Stop," Richard begged. "Stop telling me all this."

But she was giddy amid the spinning mirrors of her betrayals, her face so flushed and aquiver the waitress sympathetically giggled, pouring the Maples their coffee. Joan's face was pink as a peony, her eyes a blue pale as ice, almost transparent. He saw through her words to what she was saying—that these lovers, however we love them, are not us, are not sacred as reality is sacred. We are reality. We have made children. We gave each other our young bodies. We promised to grow old together.

Joan described an incident in her house, once theirs, when the plumber unexpectedly arrived. Richard had to laugh with her; that house's plumbing problems were an old joke, an ongoing saga. "The back-door bell rang, Mr. Kelly stomped right in, you know how the kitchen echoes in the bedroom, we had *had* it." She looked, to see if her meaning was clear. He nodded. Her eyes sparkled. She emphasized, of the knock, "Just at the *ve*ry moment," and, with a gesture akin to the gentle clap in the car a world ago, drew with one fingertip a *v* in the air, as if beginning to write "very." The motion was eager, shy, exquisite, diffident, trusting: he saw all its meanings and knew that she would never stop gesturing within him, never; though a decree come between them, even death, her gestures would endure, cut into glass.

Killing

LYNNE'S FATHER'S HAND felt warm and even strong, though he lay unconscious, dying. In this expensive pastel room of the nursing home, he was starving, he was dying of thirst, as surely as if he had been abandoned in a desert. His breath stank. The smell from the parched hole that had been his mouth was like nothing else bodily she had ever smelled—foul but in no way fertile, an acid ultimate of carnality. Yet the presence was still his; in his unconscious struggle for breath, his gray face flitted, soundlessly muttering, into expressions she knew—the helpless raised eyebrows that preceded an attempt at the dinner table to be droll, or a sudden stiffening of the upper lip that warned of one of his rare, pained, carefully phrased reprimands. A lawyer, lost to his family in the machinations of cities and corporations, he had been a distant father, reluctant to chastise, the dinnertime joke his most comfortable approach to affection. He had spent his free time out of the house, puttering at tasks he lacked a son to share. In New Hampshire, over many summers, he had built a quarter-mile of stone wall with his own hands; in Boston, there had been the brick terrace to level and weed; in the suburb of his retirement, compost heaps to tend and broken fences to repair and redesign. In the year past, his hand had lost its workman's roughness. There was no task his failing brain could direct his hand to seize. Unthinkingly, Lynne had asked him, this past summer, to help one of the children to build a birdhouse; manfully, chuckling with energy, he had assembled the tools, the wood, the nails. His pipe clenched in his teeth as jauntily as ever, he had gone through the familiar motions while his grandson gazed in gathering disbelief at the hammered-together jumble of wood. The old man stood back at last, gazed with the child, saw clearly for a moment, and abandoned such jobs forever. Dry and uncallused, his hand rested warm in his daughter's.

Sometimes it returned her squeeze, or the agitation that passed across his face caused his shallow pulse to race. "Just relax," she would chant to him then, bending close, into his caustic breath. "Re-lax. It's all right. I'm right here, Daddy. I won't go away."

Lynne was reminded, in these hours of holding and waiting, of a childhood episode scarcely remembered for thirty years. It had been so strange, so out of both their characters. She had been a cheerful child—what they called in those years "well adjusted." At the age of thirteen or so, the first of three daughters to be entering womanhood, she was visited by insomnia, an inexplicable wakefulness that made sleep a magic kingdom impossible to reach and that turned the silhouetted furniture of her room into presences that might, if left unwatched, come horribly to life. Her mother dismissed the terror with the same lightness with which she had explained menstruation, as an untidiness connected with "the aging process"; it was her father, surprisingly, who took the development seriously. As Lynne remembered it, he would come home pale from one of his innumerable meetings—the cold of the Common on his face, the weight of City Hall on his shoulders—and, if he found her awake, would sit by her bed for hours, holding her hand and talking enough to be "company." Perhaps what had seemed hours to her had been a few minutes, perhaps her recollection had expanded a few incidents into a lengthy episode. In her memory, his voice had been not merely paternal but amused, leisurely, enjoying itself, as if this visiting were less a duty than an occasion to be relished, in the manner of the country world where he had been a boy, where sitting and talking had been a principal recreation. He had not begrudged her his time, and she wanted not to begrudge him her company now. She would put him to sleep.

Yet she hated the nursing home, hated and fled it—its cloaked odors, its incessant television, its expensive false order and hypocrisy of false cheer, its stifling vulgarity. These common dying and their coarse nurses were the very people her father had raised her to avoid, to rise above. "Well, aren't you the handsome boy!" the supervisor had exclaimed to him upon admittance, and tapped him on the arm like a brash girlfriend.

His body, tempered by the chores he had always assigned himself, had stubbornly outlasted his judicious brain; then, suddenly, it began to surrender. A succession of little strokes had brought him, who a week earlier could shuffle down the hall between Lynne and a male nurse, to the point where he could not swallow. A decision arose. "The decision is yours," the doctor said. His face was heavy, kindly, self-protective, formal. The decision was whether or not to move her father to a hospital, where he could be fed intravenously and his life could be prolonged. She had decided not. The fear that the ambulance ride would compromise her father's dignity had been uppermost in her mind. But from the way the doctor seized her hand and pronounced with a solemn, artificial clarity, "You have made a wise decision," Lynne realized that her decision had been to kill her father. He could not swallow. He could not drink. Abandoned, he must die.

Her voice took flight over the telephone, seeking escape from this responsibility. Why had the doctors given it to her? Couldn't they do it themselves? What would her mother have done? Lynne called her sisters, one in Chicago, one in Texas. Of course, they agreed, she had made the right decision. The only decision. Their common inheritance, their mother's common sense, spoke through them so firmly that she almost forgave her sisters the safe distance from which they spoke. Yet their assurances evaporated within an hour. She called her minister; he came and had tea and told her that her decision was right, even holy. He seemed hard-boiled and unctuous both. After he left, she sat and held in her palms, votively, a teacup that had been her mother's. Her mother had died two years ago, leaving her daughters her china, her common sense, and a stately old man disintegrating from the head down. The cup, with its rim of gold and its band of cinnamon-red arabesques, had become sacred in this extremity; Lynne closed her eyes and waited for her mother to speak through the fragile cool shape in her hands. Sensing nothing but a widening abyss, she opened her eyes and telephoned her husband, who was estranged from her and living in Boston. He had lodged himself in the grid of Back Bay, a few blocks from where she had grown up.

"Of course, dear," Martin said, his voice grave and paternal, as it had become. "You've made the only possible decision."

"Oh, you can say that, you can all say that," Lynne cried into the hard receiver, heavier than the cup had been. "But I'm the one who had to do it. I'm killing him, and I'm the one who has to go watch it happen. It's incredible. His mouth *wants water.* He's drying *up!*"

"Why visit him?" Martin asked. "Isn't he unconscious?"

"He might wake up and be frightened," she said, and the image sprang a sobbing so great she had to hang up.

Martin called back a judicious while later. Lynne was touched, thinking that he had telepathically given her time to cry herself out, go to the bathroom, and heat some coffee. But it seemed he had spent the time discussing her with his mistress. "Harriet says," he said, authoritatively, "the other decision would be downright neurotic, to cart him to the hospital and torture him with a lot of tubes. Not to mention the money."

"Tell Harriet I certainly don't want to do anything that would seem neurotic to her. She can relax about the money, though; she is not one of his heirs."

Martin sounded hurt. "She was very sympathetic with you. She started to cry herself."

"Tell her thanks a lot for her sympathy. Why doesn't she show it by letting you come back?"

"I don't want to come back," Martin said, in his new, grave, paternal voice.

"Oh, *shit* to you." Hanging up, Lynne wondered at her sensation of joy, of release; then realized that, in her anger with this man and his presumptuous mistress, she had for the first time in days thought of something other than the nursing home, and her father's dying, and her guilt.

She could not make herself stay. She would hold his hand for minutes that seemed hours, having announced her presence in his deaf ear, having settled herself to wait by his side. His face as it dried was sinking in upon itself, with that startled expression mummies have; the distance between his raised eyebrows and lowered eyelashes seemed enormous. His hand would twitch, or her hand, wandering, would come upon his pulse, and the sign of life would horrify her, like the sight of roaches scuttling in the sink when, in the middle of the night, the kitchen light is suddenly turned on. "Daddy, I must leave for a minute," she would say, and flee.

Her step seemed miraculously elastic to herself as she strode down the hall. The heads of the dying bobbed about her amid white sheets. There was a little gauzy-haired, red-faced lady who, locked into a geriatric chair, kept crying "Help" and clapping her hands. She paused as Lynne passed, then resumed. "Help." Clap clap. "*Help.*" The barred door. Air. Life. Barberry and pachysandra had been planted in square beds around the entrance. The parking lot was newly paved. This mundane earth and asphalt amazed Lynne. The sun burned like a silver sore place low in the gray November sky. She slid into her car; its engine came alive.

The neighborhood of the nursing home was unfamiliar. She bought dinner for herself and the children in the innocent carnival of a super-market where she had never shopped before. She let herself be fed a sandwich and a Coke in a diner full of strange men. She inhaled the fragrances of a gasoline station where a chunky attendant in green coveralls filled her tank so matter-of-factly that it seemed impossible the life of another man, whose sperm had become her life, was draining away, by her decision, beneath this chalky cold sky in a city of utter strangers.

Dying, her father had become sexual. Her mother no longer intervening, his manhood was revealed. For a time, after she died, Lynne and Martin had thought to have him live with them. But, the first night of his trial visit, he had woken them, clearing his throat in the hall outside their bedroom. When Lynne had opened the door, he told her, his face pale with fury, the top and bottom of his pajamas mismatched, that no one had ever hurt him as she had this night. At first she didn't understand. Then she blushed. "But, Daddy, he's my husband. You're my father. I'm not Mother, I'm Lynne." She added, desperate to clarify, "Mother died, don't you remember?"

The anger was slow to leave his face, though the point seemed taken. His eyes narrowed with a legal canniness. "Allegedly," he said.

Martin had laughed at that, and the two of them led him back to his bed. But they were as little able to get back to sleep as if they had, indeed, been lovers and the man thrashing in the adjacent bedroom was the wronged husband. She perceived only later an irony of that night: the man who was with her didn't want to be. Martin's affair with Harriet had begun, and his willingness to try living with her father was his last husbandly kindness. She remembered later his great relief when she announced it wouldn't work. While her father, back in his own house, grew more puzzled and rebellious, passing from a succession of housekeepers to a live-in couple to a burly male nurse, her husband confessed more and more, and asked to separate. Once the old man was safely placed in a nursing home, Martin left. Then, abandoned, Lynne perceived the gallantry of her father's refusal to submit to dying. As his reason fell away, he who had been so mild and legal had become violent and lawless; his life-long habit of commanding respect was now twisted into a tyrannical rage, a defiant incontinence, a hitting of nurses with his fists, a struggle against a locked geriatric chair until both toppled. In his pugnacity and ferocity Lynne saw the force, now naked, that had carved from the hard world a shelter for his four dependent females. With Martin's leaving, she, too, was naked. Herself helpless, she at last loved her father in his helplessness. Her love made all the more shameful her inability to stay with him, to lull his panic at the passage facing him as he had once lulled her panic at entering womanhood.

For three days after her commended decision, Lynne came and went, marvelling at the fury of her father's will to live. His face, parched and unfed, grew rigid. His mouth made an *O* like a baby's at the breast. His breathing poured forth a stench like a stream of inexpressible scorn. His hand lived in hers. He could not die, she could not stay; as with the participants of a great and wicked love, there was none to forgive them save each other.

He died unobserved. Shortly a nurse noticed and drew the sheet up over his face and called his nearest relative. Lynne had been raking leaves from her frostbitten lawn, thinking she should be with him. The world, which had made a space of privacy and isolation around them, then gathered and descended in a fluttering of letters and visits, of regards and reminiscences; her father's long, successful life was rebuilt in words before her. The funeral was a success, a rally of the surviving, a salute to the useful and presentable man who had passed away some time ago, while his body had still lived. Her sisters descended from airplanes and cried more than she could. Elderly faces that had floated above her childhood, her father's old friends, materialized. Lynne was kissed, hugged, caressed, complimented. Yet she had been his executioner. There was no paradox, she saw. They were grateful. The world needed death. It needed death exactly as much as it needed life.

After the burial service, Martin came home with her and the children. "I'm surprised," Lynne said to him as soon as they were alone, "Harriet wasn't there."

"Did you want her to be? We assumed you didn't."

"That was correct."

"She would have liked to be, of course. She admired what you did."

Lynne saw that for him the funeral had been an opportunity for Harriet's advancement. In his mind he had leaped beyond their separation, beyond the divorce, to some day when she, his first wife, would be gracious to his second, repaying this supposed admiration. How small, Lynne thought, he had grown: a promoter, a liaison man. "I did nothing," she said.

"You did everything," he responded, and this, too, was part of his game: to sell her herself as well as Harriet, to sell her on the idea that she was competent and independent; she could manage without him.

Could she? Not for the first time since the nurse had given her, over the telephone, the awaited gift of her father's death did Lynne feel in her new freedom an abysmal purposelessness; she glimpsed the possibility that her father had needed her as none of the living did, that her next service to everyone, having killed him, was herself to die. Martin was lethal in his new manner, all efficient vitality, hugging the children ardently, talking to each with a self-conscious and compressed attentiveness unknown in the years when he had absent-mindedly shared their home. He even presumed to tap Lynne on the bottom as she stood at the stove, as if she were one more child to be touched. In the hour before dinner, he raced around the house changing lightbulbs, bleeding the furnace, replacing window shades that had fallen from the temperamental little sockets up high. His virtuoso show of dutifulness—his rapid survey of the photographs the boys had developed in their darkroom, the brisk lesson in factoring he administered to his younger daughter—to Lynne felt intended to put her to shame. His removal, rather than bringing her and the children closer together, had put distance between them. They blamed her for losing him. They blamed themselves. Night after night they sat wordless around the dinner table, chewing their failure. Now he was here, pulling the wine cork, celebrating her father's death. "Lynne, dear"—a locution of Harriet's he had acquired—"tell us all why you can't seem to replace the burned-out light bulbs. Is it the unscrewing or the screwing in that frightens you?" Lethal, but attractive; Harriet had made of him something smaller but more positive, less timorous and diffuse. Before, he had been in the house like the air they unthinkingly breathed; now he manifested himself among them as a power, his show of energy and duty vindictive—the display of a treasure they had wasted.

Lynne told him, "I've been so busy getting my father to die I didn't notice which bulbs were on and which were off. I haven't even read a newspaper for days."

Martin ignored her defense. "Poor Grandpa," he said, gazing about at the children as if one more parental duty fallen to him was to remind them to mourn.

Hate, pure tonic hatred of this man, filled her and seemed to lift her free; he sensed it, from his end of the table, through the candlelit mist of children, and smiled. He wanted her hate. But it flickered off, like a bad lightbulb. She was not free.

He helped her do the dishes. Living alone, Martin had learned some habits of housework: another new trick. As he moved around her, avoiding touching her, drying each dish with a comical bachelor care, she felt him grow weary; he, too, was mortal. In his weariness, he had slipped from Harriet's orbit back into hers. "Want me to go?" he asked, shyly.

"Sure. Why not? You always do."

"I thought, Grandpa dead and everything, you might get too depressed alone."

"Don't you want to go tell Harriet all about the marvellous funeral she missed?"

"No. She doesn't expect it. She said to be nice to you."

So his offer came from Harriet, not him. He was being given a night out, like the vulgarest of lower-class husbands. And Lynne was herself too weary to fight the gift, to scorn it.

"The children are all here," she told him. "There's no extra bed. You'll have to sleep with me."

"It won't kill us," he said.

"Who's us?" Lynne asked.

Months had passed since she had felt his body next to hers in bed. He had grown thinner, harder, more precisely knit, as if exercised by the distance he strained to keep between them. Perhaps only at first had it been a strain for him. When with a caress she offered to make love, he said, "No. That would be too much." In her fatigue, she was relieved. Sleep came to her swiftly, even though his presence barred her from the center of the bed, to which she had grown accustomed. In a dream, she was holding her father's hand, and he horrified her by sitting up energetically and beginning to scold, in that sardonic way Lynne felt he had always reserved for her, the oldest; he showed her younger sisters only his softer side. She awoke and found her husband twisting next to her. It did not surprise her that he was there. Surprise came the other nights, when the bed was empty. Martin was up on one elbow, trying to plump his pillow. *"Why,"* he asked, as if they had been talking all along, "have you given the kids all the airfoam pillows and left yourself with these awful old feather things? It's like trying to sleep with your head on a pancake."

"Can't you go to sleep?"

"Of course not."

"Have I been asleep?"

"As usual."

"What do you think's the matter?"

"I don't know. Guilt, I suppose. I feel guilty about Harriet. Sleeping with you."

"Don't tell me about it. This was your idea, not mine."

"Also, I feel rotten about Grandpa. He was so *good.* He knew something was wrong, but he couldn't put his finger on it. The way he said 'allegedly' that time. And that day we took him to the nursing home — the way he accepted me as the boss. So brave and quiet, like a child going off to camp. This big Boston lawyer, who had always looked at me as sort of a chump, really. I had become the boss. Remember how he kept advising me to watch out for the other cars? He had become—what's the word?—deferential."

"I know. It was pathetic."

"He didn't want me to hit another car, though. He wanted good care of himself taken."

"I know. I loved his will to live. It put me to shame. It puts us all to shame."

"Why?"

His blunt question startled her: the new Martin. The old one and she had understood each other without trying. She understood him now: he was saying, *Put yourself to shame, put yourself to death, but don't include me: I'm alive. At last.* She tried to explain, "I feel very disconnected these days."

"Well, I guess you are."

"Not just from you. Disconnected from everybody. The sermon today, I couldn't cry. It had nothing to do with Daddy, with anybody real. I couldn't keep my eyes off you and the boys. The way the backs of your heads were all the same."

He twisted noisily, and looped his arm around her waist. Her heart flipped, waiting for his hand to enclose her breast, his old way. It didn't happen. It was as if his arm had been sliced off at the wrist. He said, in a soft, well-meant voice, "I'm sorry. Of course I feel guiltiest about you. Lying here is very conflicting. I felt conflicted all week, you calling me every hour on the hour to say your dear father hadn't kicked the bucket yet."

"Don't exaggerate. And don't say 'dear.' "

"You called a lot, I thought. And it went on and on, he just wouldn't die. What a tough old farmer he turned out to be."

"Yes."

"You were in agony. And there I sat in Back Bay, no use at all. I hated myself. I still do."

His confession, Lynne saw, was an opportunity another woman—Harriet, certainly—would seize. His taut body wanted to make love. But, as had happened so many nights when they were married, by the same mechanism whereby the television news had lulled her, commercials and disasters and weather and sports tumbling on with the world's rotation, so her awareness of Martin's wishing to make love—of male energy alive in the world and sustaining it—put her to sleep, as her father's once sitting by her bedside had.

. . .

When Lynne awoke again, he was still fighting with the pillow. By the quality of the moonlight, time had passed, but whether two minutes or an hour she couldn't tell. She knew she had failed once more, but the quality of this, too, was different. It was not so grievous, because everything was steeped and flattened in the moonlight of grief. She asked, "How can you be still awake?"

"This is a very unsuccessful experiment," he said, with satisfaction, of their sleeping together. "You do something to the bed that makes me nervous. You always did. With Harriet I have no problem. I sleep like a baby."

"Don't tell me about it."

"I'm just reporting it as a curious physiological fact."

"Just relax. Re-lax."

"I can't. Evidently you can. Your poor father's being dead must be a great relief."

"Not especially. Lie on your back."

He obeyed. She put her hand on his penis. It was warm and silky-small and like nothing else, softer than a breast, more fragile than a thumb, yet heavy. Together, after a minute, they realized it was not rising, and would not rise. For Martin, it was a triumph, a proof. "Come on," he taunted. "Do your worst."

For Lynne it had been, in his word, an experiment. Among her regrets was one that, having held her dying father's hand so continuously, she had not been holding it at the moment in which he passed from life to death; she had wanted, childishly, to know what it would have felt like. It would have felt like this. "Go to sleep," someone was pleading, far away. "Let's go to sleep."

Problems

1. During the night, *A*, though sleeping with *B*, dreams of *C*. *C* stands at the farthest extremity or (if the image is considered two-dimensionally) the apogee of a curved driveway, perhaps a dream-refraction of the driveway of the house that had once been their shared home. Her figure, though small in the perspective, is vivid, clad in a tomato-red summer dress; her head is thrown back, her hands are on her hips, and her legs have taken a wide, confident stance. She is flaunting herself, perhaps laughing; his impression is of intense female vitality, his emotion is of longing. He awakes troubled. The sleep of *B* beside him is not disturbed; she rests in the certainty that *A* loves her. Indeed, he has left *C* for her, to prove it.

PROBLEM: Which has he more profoundly betrayed, *B* or *C*?

2. *A* lives 7 blocks from the Laundromat he favors. He lives 3.8 miles from his psychiatrist, the average time of transit to whom, in thick afternoon traffic, is 22 minutes. The normal session, with allowances for pre- and post-therapy small talk, lasts 55 minutes. The normal wash cycle in the type of top-loader the Laundromat favors runs for 33 minutes. The psychiatrist and the Laundromat are in the same outbound direction.

PROBLEM: Can *A* put his laundry in a washer on the way to his psychiatrist and return without finding his wet clothes stolen?

PROBLEMS FOR EXTRA CREDIT: If the time of the psychiatric appointment is 3 p.m., and a city block is considered to be one-eighth (⅛) of a mile, and if *A* arranges the 2 purgative operations serially, placing the laundry second, and if, further, the drying cycle purchasable for a quarter (25¢) lasts a quarter of an hour (15 minutes) and the average load requires 2 such cycles or else is too damp to be carried home without osmotically moistening the chest of the carrier, at what time will A be able to pour himself a drink? Round to the nearest minute.

Calculate the time for 2 drinks.

Calculate the time for 3, with a wet chest.

3. A has 4 children. Two are in college, 2 attend private school. Annual college expenses amount to $6,300 each, those of private school to $4,700. A's annual income is n. Three-sevenths ($^3/_7$) of n are taken by taxes, federal and state. One-third ($^1/_3$) goes to C, who is having the driveway improved. Total educational expenses are equivalent to five–twenty-firsts ($^5/_{21}$) of n. The cost each week of a psychiatric session is $45, of a Laundromat session $1.10. For purposes of computation, consider these A's only expenses.

PROBLEM: How long can A go on like this? Round to the nearest week.

4. The price of pea stone is $13 a cubic yard. A truckload consists of $3\frac{1}{4}$ cubic yards. C's driveway is 8' 6" wide and describes an ellipse of which the foci are 2 old croquet stakes 31 yards apart. A line perpendicular to a line drawn between the stakes and intersecting this line at midpoint strikes the edge of the driveway in just 9 paces, as paced off by the driveway contractor. He is a big man and wears size 12 shoes. The average desirable depth, he says, of pea stone in a suburban driveway is one and one-half inches ($1\frac{1}{2}$"). Any more, you get troughing; any less, you don't get that delicious crunching sound, like marbles being swished in a coffee can.

In addition to the ellipse there is a straight spur connecting it to Pleasant Avenue. The length of the spur is to the radius of the ellipse as $\sqrt{2}$ is to π.

In addition to the base cost per truckload there is $10.50 an hour for the driver, plus an occasional gratuitous, graciously offered beer, @ $1.80 per six-pack.

PROBLEM: Why is C doing all this?

5. A's psychiatrist thinks he is experiencing growth, measurable in psychic distance attained from C. However, by Tristan's Law appealingness is inversely proportional to attainability. Attainability is somewhat proportional to psychic distance. As a psychic mass M is reduced in apparent size by the perspectives of recession, its gravitational attraction proportionally increases. There exists a curve whereby gravitational attraction overpowers reason, though the apparent source of attraction may be, like the apparent position of all but the nearest stars, an illusion.

PROBLEM: Plot this curve. Find the starlike point where *A*'s brain begins to bend.

HELPFUL HINTS: The "somewhat" above translates to $3/7$.

Midas's Law: Possession diminishes perception of value, immediately.

6. *B* is beautiful. Clear blue eyes, blue denim miniskirt, dear little blue veins behind her silken knees. *C* is receding rapidly, a tomato-red speck in an untroubled azure. *A*'s 4 children have all been awarded scholarships. His psychiatrist has moved his couch to walnut-panelled, shag-carpeted quarters above the Laundromat, up just one quick flight of 22 steps. The price of pea stone has dropped dramatically, because of the recession. It is a beautiful day, a bright-blue Monday.

PROBLEM: Something feels wrong. What is it?

The Man Who Loved Extinct Mammals

SAPERS lived rather shapelessly in a city that shall be nameless. It was at a juncture of his life when he had many ties, none of them binding. Accordingly, he had much loose time, and nothing, somehow, better filled it than the perusal of extinct mammals. Living species gave him asthma, and the dinosaurs had been overdone; but in between lay a marvellous middle world of lumpy, clumping, hairy, milk-giving creatures passed from the face of the earth. They tended to be large: "During these early periods," writes Harvey C. Markman in his pamphlet *Fossil Mammals* (published by the Denver Museum of Natural History), "many of the mammals went in for large size and absurdity." For example, *Barylambda*. It was nearly eight feet long and half as high. It had a short face, broad feet, muscular legs, and a very stout tail. "It combined"—to quote Markman again—"many anatomical peculiarities which together had little survival value. One might say of this race, and other aberrant groups, that they tried to specialize in too many ways and made very little progress in the more essential directions." It was extinct by the end of the Paleocene. "Who could not love such a creature?" Sapers asked himself.

And who is to say what is an "essential direction"?

Barylambda was an amblypod, meaning "blunt foot," an order (or suborder) of ungulates that had, Webster's Dictionary told Sapers, "very small smooth brains." The "small" was to be expected, the "smooth" was surprising. It was nice. The man who loved extinct mammals resented the way Markman kept chaffing the amblypods; nothing about them, especially their feet and their teeth, was specialized enough to suit him. One could hear Markman sigh, like the sardonic instructor of a class of dullards, as he wrote, "At least one more family of amblypods must be mentioned: the uintatheres. By late Eocene time some of these grotesque creatures had attained the size of circus elephants. Arranged along the face and forehead they had three pairs of bony protuberances resembling horns. . . ." In the accompanying photograph of a *Uintacolotherium* skull, the bony protuberances looked artful, Arp-like. Sapers didn't think them necessarily grotesque, if you tried to view them from the standpoint of the Life Force instead of from ours, the standpoint of Man, with his huge, rough brain. Sapers shut his eyes and tried to imagine the selective process whereby a little bud of a bony protuberance achieved a tiny advantage, an edge, in battle, food-gathering, or mating, which would favor an exaggeration from generation to generation. He almost had it in focus—some kind of Platonic ideal pressing upon the uintathere fetuses, tincturing uintathere milk—when the telephone shrilled near his ear.

It was Mrs. Sapers. Her voice—alive, vulnerable, plaintive, his—arose from some deep past. She told him, not uninterestingly, of her day, her depressions, her difficulties. Their daughter had flunked a math exam. The furnace was acting funny. Men were asking her to go out on dates. One man had held her hand in a movie and her stomach had flipped over. What should she do?

"Be yourself," he advised. "Do what feels natural. Call the furnace man. Tell Dorothy I'll help her with her math when I visit Saturday."

"If I had a gun, some nights I'd shoot myself."

"That's why they have firearms-control laws," he told her reassuringly, wondering then why she wasn't reassured.

For she began to cry into the telephone. He tried to follow her reasoning but gathered only the shadowy impression that she loved him, which he felt to be a false impression, from previous fieldwork as her husband. Anyway, what could he do about it now? "Nothing," Mrs. Sapers snapped, adding, "You're grotesque." Then, with that stoic elegance she still possessed, and he still admired, she hung up.

Mammae, he read, are specialized sweat glands. A hair is a specialized scale. When a mammal's body gets too hot, each hair lifts up so the air can reach the skin. The bizarre *Arsinoitherium*, superficially like a rhinoceros but anatomically in a class by itself, may be distantly related to the tiny, furry hyrax found in nooks of Asia and Africa. The saber-toothed tiger was probably less intelligent than a house cat. Its "knife tooth" was developed to prey on other oversized mammals, and couldn't have pinned a rabbit. Rabbits have been around a long time—though nothing as long, of course, as the crocodile and the horseshoe crab. Sapers thought of those saber teeth, and of the mastodon's low-crowned molars, with the enamel in a single layer on top, which were superseded by the mammoth's high-crowned molars, which never wore out, the enamel distributed in vertical plates, and he tried to picture the halfway tooth, or the evolutionary steps to baleen; his thoughts wandered pleasantly to the truth that the whale and the bear and Man are late, late models, *arrivistes* in the fossil record. What is there about a bear, that we love him? His flat, archaic feet. The amblypods are coming back! There was a delicate message Sapers could almost make out, a graffito scratched on the crumbling wall of time. His mistress called, shattering the wall.

She loved him. She told him so. He told her vice versa, picturing her young anatomy, her elongate thighs, her small smooth head, its mane, her spine, her swaying walk, and wondering, mightn't his middle-aged body break, attempting to cater to such a miracle? She told him of her day, her boredom, her boring job, her fear that he would go back to his wife.

"Why would I do that?" he asked.

"You think I'm too crass. I get so frightened."

"You're not especially crass," he reassured her. "But you *are* young. I'm old, relatively. In fact, I'm ancient. Wouldn't you like to get a nice youngish lover, with a single gristly horn, like a modern-day rhinoceros, one of the few surviving perissodactyls?"

He was offering to divert her, but she kept insisting on her love, his bones crunching at every declaration. Rhinoceroses, he learned when at last she had feasted enough and hung up, had been backed with unguarded enthusiasm by the investment councils of the Life Force. Some species had attained the bulk of several elephants. There had been running rhinoceroses—"long-legged, rather slender-bodied"—and amphibious rhinoceroses, neither of them the ancestor of the "true" rhinoceros; that honor belonged to hornless *Trigonia*, with his moderate size, "stocky body," fourteen toes, and "very conservative" (Sapers could hear Markman impatiently sighing) dentition.

What *is* this prejudice in favor of progress? The trouble with his mistress, Saper decided, was that she had too successfully specialized, was too purely a mistress, perfect but fragile, like a horse's leg, which is really half foot, extended and whittled and tipped with one amazing toenail. The little *Eohippus*, in its forest of juicy soft leaves, scuttled like a raccoon; and even *Mesohippus*, though as big as a collie, kept three toes of each foot on the ground. *Eohippus*, it seemed to Sapers, was like a furtive little desire that evolves from the shadows of the heart into a great, clattering, unmanageable actuality.

· · ·

His wife called back. Over the aeons of their living together she had evolved psychic protuberances that penetrated and embraced his mind. "I'm sorry to keep spoiling your wonderful privacy," she said, in such a way that he believed in her solicitude for his privacy even as she sarcastically invaded it, "but I'm at my wits' end." And he believed this, too, though also knowing that she could induce desperation in herself as a weapon, a hooked claw, a tusk. Perhaps she shouldn't have added, "I tried to call twice before but the line was busy"; yet this hectoring, too, he took into himself as pathos, her jealousy legitimate and part of her helplessness, all organs evolving in synchrony. She explained that their old pet dog was dying; it couldn't eat and kept tottering off into the woods, and she and their daughter spent hours calling and searching and luring the poor creature back to the house. Should they put the dog into the car and take her to the vet's, to be "put to sleep"?

Sapers asked his wife what their daughter thought.

"I don't know. I'll put her on."

The child was fourteen.

"Hi, Daddy."

"Hi, sweet. Is Josie in much pain?"

"No, she's just like drunk. She stands in the puddle in the driveway and looks at the sky."

"She sounds happy, in a way. Whose idea is it to take her to the vet's?"

"Mommy's."

"And what's your idea?"

"To let Josie do what she wants to do."

"That sounds like my idea, too. Why don't you let her just stay in the woods?"

"It's beginning to rain here and she'll get all wet." And the child's voice, so sensible and direct up to this point, generated a catch, tears, premonitions of eternal loss; the gaudy parade of eternal loss was about to turn the corner, cymbals clanging, trombones triumphant, and enter her mind. Keep calm, Sapers told himself. One thing at a time.

He said, "Then put her in the back room with some newspapers and a bowl of water. Talk to her so she doesn't feel lonely. Don't take her to the vet's unless she seems to be in pain. She always gets scared at the vet's."

"O.K. You want to talk any more to Mom?"

"No. Sweetie? I'm sorry I'm not there to help you all."

"That's O.K." Her voice grew indifferent, small and smooth. She was about to hang up.

"Oh, and, baby?" Sapers called across the distance.

"Yeah?"

"Don't flub up any more math exams. It drives Mommy wild."

Giant and bizarre mammalian forms persisted well after the advent of Man. The splendid skeleton of an imperial mammoth, *Archidiskodon imperator*, exhibited in the Denver Museum of Natural History, was found associated with a spear point. Neanderthal men neatly stacked, with an obscure religious purpose, skulls of *Ursus spelaeus*, the great cave bear. Even the incredible *Glyptodon*, a hard-shelled mammal the size and shape of a Volkswagen, chugged about the South American pampas a mere ten thousand years ago, plenty late enough to be seen by the wary, brown-faced forebears of the effete Inca kings. Who knows who witnessed the fleeting life of *Stockoceros*, the four-pronged antelope? Of *Syndyoceras*, the deerlike ruminant with two pairs of horns, one pair arising from the middle of its face? Of *Oxydactylus*, the giraffe-camel? Of *Daphoenodon*, the bear-dog? Of *Diceratherium*, the small rhinoceros, or *Dinohyus*, the enormous pig? Again and again, in the annals of these creatures, Sapers found mysterious disappearances, unexplained departures. "By the end of the Pliocene period all American rhinos had become extinct or wandered away to other parts of the world." "After the horse family had been so successful in North America . . . its disappearance from this hemisphere has no ready explanation."

Sapers looked about his apartment. He observed with satisfaction that there was no other living thing in it. No pets, no plants. Such cockroaches as he saw he killed. But for himself, the place had a Proterozoic purity. He breathed easy.

The telephone rang. It was his mother. He asked, "How are you?" and received a detailed answer—chest pains, neuralgia, shortness of breath, numbness in the extremities. "What can I do about it?" he asked.

"You can stop being a mental burden to me," she answered swiftly, with a spryness unseemly, he thought, in one so dilapidated. "You can go back to your loved ones. You can be a good boy."

"I *am* a good boy," he argued. "All I do is sit in my room and read." Such behavior had pleased her once; it failed to do so now. She sighed, like Markman over a uintathere, and slightly changed the subject.

"If I go suddenly," she said, "you must get right down here and guard the antiques. Terrible things happen in the neighborhood now. When Ginny Peterson went, they backed a truck right up to the door, so the daughter flew in from Omaha to find an empty house. All that Spode, and the corner cupboard with it."

"You won't go suddenly," he heard himself telling her; it sounded like a rebuke, though he had meant it reassuringly.

After a pause, she asked, "Do you ever go to church?"

"Not as often as I should." . . . *no ready explanation.*

"Everybody down here is praying for you," she said.

"Everybody?" *The herds had just wandered away.*

"I slept scarcely an hour last night," his mother said, "thinking about you."

"Please stop," Sapers begged. When the conversation ended, he sat still, thinking, We are all, all of us living, contemporary with the vanishing whale, the Florida manatee, the Bengal tiger, the whooping crane.

He felt asthmatic. The pages about extinct mammals suffocated him with their myriad irrelevant, deplorable facts. *Amebelodon,* a "shovel-tusker" found in Nebraska, had a lower jaw six feet long, with two flat teeth sticking straight out. Whereas *Stenomylus* was a dainty little camel. Why is a horse's face long? Because its eyes are making room for the roots of its high-crowned upper grinders. But even *Eohippus,* interestingly, had a diastema. Creodonts, the most primitive of mammalian carnivores, moved on flat, wide-spreading feet; indeed, the whole animal, Sapers had to admit, looked indifferently engineered, compared with cats and dogs. "The insectivores, however, have made very little progress in any direction." With a sudden light surge of cathexis that shifted his weight in the chair, Sapers loved insectivores; he hugged their shapeless, conservative archetype to his heart. "Feet and teeth provide us with most of our information about an extinct mammal's mode of existence. . . ." Of course, Sapers thought. They are what hurt.

Love Song, for a Moog Synthesizer

SHE WAS GOOD IN BED. She went to church. Her IQ was 150. She repeated herself. Nothing fit; it frightened him. Yet Tod wanted to hang on, to hang on to the bits and pieces, which perhaps were not truly pieces but islands, which a little lowering of sea level would reveal to be rises on a sunken continent, peaks of a subaqueous range, secretly one, a world.

He called her Pumpkin, or Princess. She had been a parody of a respectable housewife—active in all causes, tireless in all aspects of housekeeping from fumigation to floor-waxing, an ardent practitioner of the minor arts of the Halloween costumer and the Cub Scout den mother, a beaming, posing, conveniently shaped ornament to her husband at cocktail parties, beach parties, dinner parties, fund-raising parties. Always prim, groomed, proper, perfect.

But there was a clue, which he picked up: she never listened. Her eyebrows arched politely, her upper lip lifted alertly; nevertheless she brushed her gaze past the faces of her conversational partners in a terrible icy hurry, and repeated herself so much that he wondered if she were sane.

Her heart wasn't in this.

She took to jabbing him at parties, jabbing so hard it hurt. This piece of herself, transferred to his ribs, his kidneys, as pain, lingered there, asked to be recognized as love.

His brain—that impatient organ, which deals, with the speed of light, in essences and abstractions—opted to love her perhaps too early, before his heart—that plodder, that problem-learner—had had time to collect quirks and spiritual snapshots, to survey those faults and ledges of the not-quite-expected where affection can silt and accumulate. He needed a body. Instead there was something skeletal, spacy.

But, then, the shivering. That was lovable. As they left a fine restaurant in an elegant, shadowy district of the city, Princess complained (her talk was unexpectedly direct) that her underpants kept riding up. Drunk, his drunkenness glazing the bricks of the recently restored pavement beneath them, the marquee of the cunningly renovated restaurant behind them, the other pedestrians scattered around them as sketchily as figures in an architectural drawing, and the artificially antique streetlamp above them, its wan light laced by the twigs of a newly planted tree that had also something of an architect's stylization about it, Tod knelt down and reached up into her skirt with both hands and pulled down her underpants, so adroitly she shivered. She shivered, involuntarily, expressing— what? Something that came upon her like a breeze. Then, recovering poise, with an adroitness the equal of his, she stepped out of her underpants. Her black high heels, shiny as Shirley Temple dancing pumps, stepped from the two silken circles on the bricks—one, two, primly, quickly, as she glanced over her shoulder, to see if they had been seen. She was wearing a black dress, severe, with long sleeves, that he had last seen her wear to a mutual friend's funeral. Tod stood and crumpled his handful of warm gossamer into his coat pocket. They walked on, her arm in his. He seemed taller, she softer. The stagy light webbed them, made her appear all circles. She said she could feel the wind on her cunt.

He had loved that shiver, that spasm she could not control; for love must attach to what we cannot help—the involuntary, the telltale, the fatal. Otherwise, the reasonableness and the mercy that would make our lives decent and orderly would overpower love, crush it, root it out, tumble it away like a striped tent pegged in sand.

Time passed. By sunlight, by a window, he suddenly saw a web, a radiating system, of wrinkles spread out from the corners of her eyes when she smiled. From her lips another set of creases, so delicate only the sun could trace them, spread upward; the two systems commingled on her cheeks. Time was interconnecting her features, which had been isolated in the spaces of her face by a certain glossy, infantile perfection. She was growing old within their love, within their suffering. He examined a snapshot he had taken a year ago. A smooth, staring, unlistening face. Baby fat.

Tod liked her aging, felt warmed by it, for it too was involuntary. It had happened to her with him, yet was not his fault. He wanted nothing to be his fault. This made her load double.

. . .

As mistress, she adapted well to the harrowing hours, the phone conversations that never end, the posing for indecent photographs, the heavy restaurant meals. She mainly missed of her former, decent, orderly life the minor blessings, such as shopping in the A & P without fear of being snubbed by a fellow-parishioner, or of encountering Tod's outraged wife across a pyramid of dog food.

Their spouses' fixed fury seemed rooted in a kind of professional incredulity; it was as if they had each been specialists (a repairer of Cyrillic typewriters, or a gerbil currier) whose specialty was so narrow there had been no need to do it very well.

But how he loved dancing with Pumpkin! She was so solid on her feet, her weight never on him, however close he held her. She tried to teach him to waltz—her husband having been a dashing, long-legged waltzer. But Tod could not learn: the wrong foot, the foot that had just received his weight, would dart out again, as if permanently appointed Chief Foot, at the start of the new trio of steps; he was a binary computer trying to learn left-handedness from a mirror.

So Tod too had his gaps, his spaces. He could not learn to repeat himself. He could do everything only once.

On a hotel bed, for variety, he sat astride her chest and masturbated her, idly at first, then urgingly, the four fingers of his right hand vying in massage of her electric fur, until her hips began to rock and she came, shivering. He understood that shivering better now. He was the conduit, the open window, by which, on rare occasions, she felt the *ventus Dei*. In the center of her sensuality, she was God's plaything.

And then, in another sort of wind, she would rage, lifted above reason; she would rage in spirals of indignation and frenzy fed from within, her voice high, a hurled stone frozen at the zenith of its arc, a mask of petulance clamped so hard upon her face that the skin around the lips went quite white. Strange little obstructions set her off, details in her arrangements with her husband; it was a fault, a failure, Tod felt, in himself, that he did not afford her an excuse for such passion. She would stare beyond him, exhausted in the end as if biologically, by the satisfaction of a cycle. It fairly frightened him, such a whirlwind; it blew, and blew itself out, in a region of her where he had never lived. An island, but in a desert. Her lips and eye-whites would look parched afterwards.

At times it occurred to him that not everyone could love this woman. This did not frighten him. It made him feel like a child still young enough to be proud that he has been given a special assignment.

And yet he felt great rest with her. Her body beside his, he would fall in the spaces of her, sink, relax, one of her cool hands held at his chest, and the other, by a physical miracle he never troubled to analyze, lightly clasped above his head, by the hand of his of which the arm was crooked beneath his head as a pillow. How her arm put her hand there, he never could see, for his back was turned, his buttocks nestled in her lap. Sleep would sweep them away simultaneously, like mingled heaps of detritus.

Though in college a soc.-sci. major, and in adult life a do-gooder, she ceased to read a newspaper. When her husband left, the subscription lapsed. Whereas Tod, sleeping with her, his consciousness diffused among the wide spaces of their shared self-forgetfulness, dreamed of statesmen, of Gerald Ford and Giscard d'Estaing, of the great: John Lennon had a comradely arm about him, and Richard Burton, murmuring with his resonant actor's accent, was seeking marital advice.

Sometimes her storms of anger and her repetitions threatened to drive him away, as the blows in his ribs had offered to do. (Was that why he held her hands, sleeping—a protective clinch?) And he thought of organizing a retreat from sexuality, a concession of indefensible territory: Kutuzov after Borodino, Thieu before Danang. A strategic simplification.

But then the awful emptiness. "O Pumpkin," he would moan in the dark, "never leave me. Never: promise." And the child within him would cringe with a terror for which, when daylight dawned bleak on the scattered realities of their situation, he would silently blame her, and hope to make her pay.

They became superb at being tired with one another. They competed in exhaustion. "Oh, God, Princess, how long can this go on?" Their conversations were so boring. Them. Us. Us and them others. The neighbors, the children, the children's teachers, the lawyers' wives' investment brokers' children's piano teachers. "It's killing me," she cheerfully admitted. Away from her, he would phone when she was asleep. She would phone in turn when he was napping. Together at last, they would run to the bed, hardened invalids fighting for the fat pillow, for the side by the window, with its light and air. They lay on their rumpled white plinth, surrounded by ashtrays and books, subjects of a cosmic quarantine.

. . .

First thing in the morning, Pumpkin would light a cigarette. Next thing, Tod would scold. She wanted to kill herself, to die. He took this as a personal insult. She was killing herself to make him look bad. She told him not to be silly, and inhaled. She had her habits, her limits. She had her abilities and her disabilities. She could not pronounce the word "realtor." She could spread her toes to make a tense little monkey's foot, a foot trying to become a star. He would ask her to do this. Grimacing pridefully, she would oblige, first the right foot, then the left, holding them high off the sheets, the toe tendons white with the effort, her toenails as round and bridal as confetti bits. He would laugh, and love, and laugh again. He would ask her to say the word "realtor."

She would refuse. This tiny refusal stunned him. A blow to the heart. They must be perfect with each other, they must. He would beg. He had wagered his whole life, his happiness and the happiness of the world around him, on this, this little monkey's stunt she would not do. Just one word. "Realtor."

Still she refused, primly, princesslike; her eyes brushed by his in a terrible icy hurry. He could pronounce "realtor" if he wanted, she chose not to.

She had her severe limitations.

And yet, and yet. One forenoon, unforeseen, he felt her beside him and she was of a piece, his. They were standing somewhere, in a run-down section of the city, themselves tired, looking at nothing, and her presence beside him was like the earth's beneath his feet, continuous, extensive, and dry, there by its own rights, unthinkingly assumed to be there. She had become his wife.

Index of Titles

Each title is followed by its date of composition—that is, the date on which a completed draft was sent off in the mails, irrespective of later revisions—and the book in which it later appeared. These are abbreviated as follows:

> *AP = Assorted Prose* (Knopf, 1965)
> *HS = Hugging the Shore* (Knopf, 1983)
> *M&W = Museums and Women* (Knopf, 1972)
> *MS = The Music School* (Knopf, 1966)
> *P = Problems* (Knopf, 1979)
> *PF = Pigeon Feathers* (Knopf, 1962)
> *SD = The Same Door* (Knopf, 1959)
> *TFTG = Too Far to Go* (Fawcett, 1979)
> *TM = Trust Me* (Knopf, 1987)

A Note About the Author

John Updike was born in 1932, in Shillington, Pennsylvania. He graduated from Harvard College in 1954, and spent a year in Oxford, England, at the Ruskin School of Drawing and Fine Art. From 1955 to 1957 he was a member of the staff of *The New Yorker*; since 1957 has lived in Massachusetts. He is the author of twenty novels as well as a number of collections of short stories, poems, and criticism. His novels have won the Pulitzer Prize, the National Book Award, the American Book Award, the National Book Critics Circle Award, the Rosenthal Award, and the Howells Medal.

A Note on the Type

The text of this book was set in a digitized version of Janson, a typeface long thought to have been made by the Dutchman Anton Janson, who was a practicing type founder in Leipzig during the years 1668–1687. However, it has been conclusively demonstrated that these types are actually the work of Nicholas Kis (1650–1702), a Hungarian, who most probably learned his trade from the master Dutch type founder Dirk Voskens. The type is an excellent example of the influential and sturdy Dutch types that prevailed in England up to the time William Caslon developed his own incomparable designs from them.

Composed by Creative Graphics,
Allentown, Pennsylvania
Printed and Bound by R. R. Donnelley,
Crawfordsville, Indiana